WHERE BUTTERFLIES DREAM

Also by Cindy Brandner

Exit Unicorns Series

Exit Unicorns
Mermaid in a Bowl of Tears
Flights of Angels
In the Country of Shadows

Short Stories

Spindrift
Bare Knuckle

WHERE BUTTERFLIES DREAM

CINDY BRANDNER

Starry Night Press

Published in Canada by
Starry Night Press

First Edition

For Tracy Bhoola, who has walked this journey with me and put so much work into each and every page.

And for Noelle—I will see you on the other side, girl.

Acknowledgments

The author's gratitude to:

Everyone who had a hand in editing this big old book of mine: Tracy Bhoola, Diane Russo Karpowicz, Heather Horsch, Emily Bukauskas, Mary Foley Hurst. A special thank you to Denise Ferrari for coming in at the last minute and giving the manuscript a very swift and thorough going over—you're a lifesaver!

The beta-readers: Janine Percival Corbets, Lisa Chester, Jackie Helus, Amy Ehmann, Nancy Albano Burley, Karen Barth, Dianne Skaggs, Elaine Godsey Freim, Laura Molina and Stephanie McCartha Williams. If I've forgotten anyone please forgive me, and know that if you contributed in any way, shape or form to help me tidy this manuscript up, you have my immense gratitude.

My daughter Devon for the beautiful butterfly which became the centrepiece of the cover design.

Stevie Blaue for always managing to take my rather vague descriptions of what I want for the cover and turning them into something beautiful.

Arlene Gillen for always answering all my nitpicky questions about Belfast and the North of Ireland.

Rob Siders of 52 Novels because he always does a fabulous job of making the text of my books look great.

Gary Furlong, narrator extraordinaire, who has brought the first three books of this series to life on a whole other level and will, I know, one day do the same for this book.

My kindred spirit Jamie Rigsby for always managing to remind me that art and beauty have always mattered, and always will.

And for my Paddy, who is both heart and soul.

And many an ante-natal tomb
Where butterflies dream of the life to come.

PERCY BYSSHE SHELLEY

Prologue

EACH OF US *carries within a map of memory. The map is worn at the folds—sometimes right through—and so place names are missing first letters or last or have a hole through the middle. We carry those maps with us always, and this map is mine—an island on the edge of the world and beyond it a place of dragons and sunken cities with bells that still ring a thousand years on. Look more closely now, for maps of memory are very personal things, and contain small details that others might never notice, but which for us are crossroads where all of life changed.*

Fields of the loveliest green in the world—forty shades they say, though I always thought there were a thousand and more. Cliffs and woods, lakes gleaming silver-blue and dark ponds tucked away in old forests of oak and beech where long ago a swan woman drowned. That corner was mine, there where a swan woman went to her death, with lily pads for her pillow, and dark water for her blanket. I knew all the dips and hollows of that bit of land, I knew the scent of the dirt, and the sound of the grass growing in the spring.

And so, this corner of a small country, of no importance to any other, but for me a place of enchantment and belonging. See it with me, look and find a moon on a string, full of wild honey, setting all the countryside around to a lambent gold. This half-light rests upon a cottage with a roof of reeds and walls of old and crumbling stone. Around the cottage, fields are overgrown, but there are traces of care and tillage in the not-too-distant past. Old fields once filled with barley and potatoes, with rye and—if you breathe deep into memory—the sweet scent of early hay.

Can you see it then—the land? Land is gold, land is the worth of a man. Land roots us and gives us wings, for that particular spot on the map which is yours, is a place to return when flight becomes wearisome.

Wars are fought over land, even plots so small as this one—a potato field, a bit of hay, a house of stone and reed. Blood has been shed for less.

Look deeply and you can see history rise even in one old field, long abandoned. Go back far enough, and you'll see where it began, the rains and burning sun which helped to mold it, the shifts in the earth's mantle, showing her face in a new light with each eon that passed. You can see the animals which crossed it, in their long and endless migrations, and you can see the first man who came with his small tribe and set up a home here—one of skin, one of wood and finally one of stone and reed.

The ancients believed that land could be sanctified through sacrifice, and of course the bigger the sacrifice the greater the sanctification. And so, there were men who went willingly and gave their blood and there were those who kicked and screamed, but still were sacrificed. As it was, so it is, for the sacrificial wheel keeps turning.

Unfold the map a little further and see there a woman standing in the garden near to the cottage. The garden is long grown over with ivy and brambles, but the woman's gaze is upon that honeyed moon. There is a great yearning in her, so great that it is tangible even to such as me, and I feel that if I were to reach out, I might actually touch it—that longing, that need. But I know such thoughts are merely wishful thinking, for it has been long and long since I touched anything on the earthly plane. I know her need though, for it is mine as well. I turn away—unquenched yearning is a fool's game, even for a ghost.

I rise a little and look again to the land, the narrow twisting roads, the streams, the imaginary boundaries of borders, and I feel the love of this country rise in me like a dark well filling. Oh yes, I love this land, loved it enough to place myself upon the blood wheel that—in this country—never stops grinding.

The only thing the Irish love more than land is story. Land and story, inextricably linked. So come with me to this land, and hear her tale, let me tell it to you; I know the words, for her story is also mine.

Part One

Awake and Dreaming

Chapter One

Return from the Dead
December 1978

PATRICK RIORDAN STEPPED out into the street with a quiver of foreboding in his bones. He'd had an uneasy feeling all day, as though someone was watching him—someone who hovered about the edges of his peripheral vision, like a wraith which could be seen from the corner of a man's eye but disappeared if viewed head-on. He had found himself turning about sharply more than once, the hair on the back of his neck rising in primitive warning.

The day had been a dark one with low scudding clouds and a bitter wind coming in from the west. The atmosphere, combined with the feeling of eyes watching him from the shadows, had called to mind his Grandmother Murphy's old tales of the *sluagh sidhe*—the dark host of fairies who lingered waiting to snatch the souls of those too ill or despairing to fight them. He was neither ill nor despairing, even if his brother had been a great deal on his mind today. Mind you, Grandma Murphy had said that a healthy soul could draw the *sluagh* as well, simply by the mere utterance of their name, but that was a thing he was not fool enough to do, not on a thin winter day like this one. Still, the odd prickling sensation lingered all day and was still with him when the sun, slurking along the horizon had set, blood-red and brooding below curdled clouds of dark grey. He'd fastened the locks on the west-facing windows and cursed himself for a superstitious fool. It was what his grandmother had said—that the *sluagh sidhe* flew in from the west, disguised as a flock of blackbirds, though when they descended to snatch your soul the only warning would be a whirlwind of shadows and then you'd be gone.

"*There are ones to whom the sluagh are partial, an' such ones have been carried off an' away by them more than the once.*"

It was how he thought of his missing brother at times, that he'd been stolen away to another land, somewhere kinder maybe, somewhere that his end hadn't been bloody and filled with pain and terror, as Pat feared was only too likely.

Considering all that had happened in the last month it was surprising that he hadn't taken to carrying a gun and a large cross about with him. Between his sister-in-law having been kidnapped and almost killed, his wife's brother dying, and his wee niece Kathleen being born to her estranged parents, he'd had enough stress to last him a good long while.

Now with the early night long fallen, sleet coming down in sheets, and the night as dark as fifty black cats hiding under a nun's habit, he wished he'd left while there was still light in the sky. He locked the door to the law firm, though *firm* seemed a bit of a grand word for himself, his irascible partner Tomas, their energetic clerk, Bob, and the woman who ruled them all without so much as disturbing a hair in her steel-plated bun, Miss Dervla Mundy. He was the last man standing tonight, as he'd been working on his opening statements for a case involving a young man wrongfully accused of a shooting death. He didn't like leaving quite so late; the streets were far too empty this time of night. Just last week a fellow lawyer had narrowly escaped death when it was discovered a bomb had been taped to the under-carriage of her car. Complacency was not a luxury a person had in Belfast.

Empty streets, his grandmother had said, were another place the *sluagh sidhe* liked to hang about, waiting for their unsuspecting victims. He gave his head a shake. "Get a grip, man," he said sternly. It was then he heard a noise, soft, so that it might have been distant, though he knew it wasn't. He turned abruptly, and his car keys flew from his hand. He heard them land with a small splash somewhere near to the building.

"Christ on a piece of toast," he said in utter frustration, kneeling down in the wet and hoping to catch a stray gleam from his keys so he didn't have to crawl around looking for them. He had just located them, filthy and wet, when the prickle along his spine suddenly became a red-hot wire. He held his breath, adrenaline surging through his blood like a tidal wave. He was not alone, and it wasn't some mythical shape-shifting fairy he need worry about, but a flesh and blood human who was likely armed with a gun. He peered into the night in the general direction of the threatening presence. He stood up slowly—if he was going to die, he would meet it standing and not on his knees in the muck. Good Catholic boy that he was, prayer came to him—for Kate and their unborn child, for Pamela and his nieces and nephew. He stood so for a minute, the prayer in his mind repeating over and over but whatever entity stood in the shadows clearly didn't believe in delivering him a quick death. He clutched his keys tightly and took a breath.

"Can I help ye with somethin'?" he asked, keeping his voice firm, though he felt like running off into the night at top speed.

"Patrick," the man stepped forward—for it was a man, no woman could possibly be that size—water dripping from the brim of his hat. Pat stepped back automatically. While most of the death threats he and Tomas received on a weekly basis came to nothing, it didn't do to take any of them less than deathly seriously. This man was big; Patrick doubted he could outrun him, nor would he stand much chance in a hand-to-hand grapple. A man couldn't outrun or out-grapple a bullet anyway and the odds were better than even that he was armed.

"Aye," he said cautiously.

"Patrick," the voice choked a little, as though something was wrong with the man's throat. But Pat was frozen, and it wasn't in terror, though his heart was going like a triphammer. "It's me."

Pat wanted to move, but he feared he was dreaming and to move would cause him to wake. The world 'round about seemed to have slowed to a thick dream-like movement and feel. He wanted to say the man's name, but he couldn't for fear that everything would shatter if he did, and the world would crumble down around him the way dreams did when you missed someone with your whole heart and soul.

The man stepped into the light that hung above the office door. "Will ye speak, brother? Ye'd think ye'd seen a ghost."

Pat put a hand up against the wall. The brick was dirty and slick with sleet. It felt real enough to be sure, as did the tightness in his chest.

"H-how," he managed to gasp out while one part of his mind—the primitive part—wondered if he'd summoned up his own brother, conjured him out of the strange day—a spirit come over from the other side. However, he seemed solid enough, and not in the least vapourous or phantom-like.

"It's a very long story, an' I'd as soon not tell it to ye out here in the sleet," his brother said in answer to his stuttering. His brother. Casey. His brother. He was going to faint, right here in the street. Kate would be wondering where the hell he was. If he was five minutes late she started to worry and with no small cause. He felt like his mind was a derailed train car, having flown off track and now wildly careening around extremely rough terrain.

"Come inside," he said, and turned to unlock the office door. His voice seemed to echo in the black night, despite the sleet and wind, despite the sound and presence of the man following him into the dark office building.

Miss Mundy always left her desk lamp on overnight, so the lobby was lit with a soft glow; the small light gave Pat some reassurance. He turned as Casey shut the door behind him, thinking he was having a bizarre fever dream, which felt real but could not possibly be.

Casey stood in front of him, all six feet four inches of him, with wet patches on his coat. He took off the cap which had hidden part of his face outside and then gave Pat a tense smile.

"Well then, brother."

"Well then," Pat echoed faintly, certain he was about to have the vapors like a character in a Victorian novel. "Oh God, Casey," he said and then his brother had his arms around him, holding him up so he wouldn't go to his knees on the floor. And it *was* Casey, despite the dark, forbidding stranger who had looked out from his face. He knew this man, knew this grip and knew the gentle manner in which he led him to a chair and sat him in it as though he was no more substantial than a wee child.

Pat looked at the man who then settled in the chair across from him. He was the same, and yet utterly changed, though his features were as familiar to Pat as the ones he saw each morning in the mirror.

"Does Pamela know?" Pat asked, thinking of his sister-in-law's shock and ultimate joy.

Casey shook his head and looked away for the first time. "No, I wanted to see ye first, get a sense of how she is an' how things stand with her."

"She's all right at present," Pat said, a sneaking suspicion tickling at the back of his mind. "Ye know about the baby?" he asked. It was a brutal moment of truth, and if Casey didn't already know, it was inexcusable; but he could tell by the sudden lines around the man's mouth and the way he kept his eyes hidden from him that he did indeed know.

"Aye, I know about the baby," he said, voice bland—bland enough to tell Pat it was going to be a barbed topic at best.

"So ye know who the daddy is?"

"Aye, I know who the daddy is. Is he part of the picture, does he plan to marry Pamela?"

"Their situation is a little complex," Pat said uneasily. "Besides, it's moot now, isn't it? She's married to you after all."

"Is she? That's only a matter of legalities, no?"

"No, it's not, an' if ye remember even the slightest bit of what ye had with her then ye know that's in no way true."

"Could we maybe set the topic of Pamela aside for just a moment, Patrick?" Casey asked, though there was an edge to his tone that told Pat the man had some definite issues around what had taken place in his absence regarding his wife.

Pat shifted in his chair. "I'm goin' to make some tea, an' I need to call Kate, she'll be half-mad with worry over me bein' this late home. An' then, my brother, you are goin' to explain where the hell ye've been an' just how much ye know of what took place in yer very long absence."

In the small office kitchen, Pat put the kettle on the tiny burner and then called Kate. He didn't dare tell her why he was staying here over the phone and so he used their code, which was simply that he was working on a blue file and would be late home. She replied, telling him to be careful and be certain to be home before midnight. After telling her he loved her in a rather fervent tone, he let her go. Blue file meant something more serious was going on, and he would be delayed indefinitely but could not talk about it over the telephone.

He took down the whiskey he kept in the cupboard for clients who needed a wee bit of lubrication to be able to speak comfortably. He added a good dollop to the pot and put it on the tray. His knees still felt like badly-set jelly and he was having a hard time catching his breath. He wanted to call Pamela right now and tell her to put her babies in the car and come meet him.

Casey was up wandering around the office, peering out into the sleet and wind, every cell of him as restless and cagey as a panther shut up in a small space. Pat took a moment to truly look at him. He was still the same big, powerful dark man who had a presence that was like few others. But there were changes too, small things, the stiff knee which had changed his gait, the look on his face that would cause most strangers to back away or walk swiftly to the opposite side of the street should their paths cross with his. Mind, he'd always had the ability to do that, only it was far more pronounced now.

"Will ye sit?" he asked, and put the tray with whiskey and tea down on his desk.

"Aye," Casey said and smiled at him, as if to reassure him in the way that he once had as a big brother. He sat, though Pat could tell it was hard for the man to settle even for a moment. Something struck him suddenly and he blurted it out.

"It was you, wasn't it—it was you who saved Pamela last month, in that old workhouse?"

Casey looked at him sharply. "What makes ye think that?"

"Because it's the one thing that makes sense."

"It was me that shot those bastards who had her captive if that's what ye mean."

"That means ye've been back at least two weeks. Two weeks, an' ye've not seen fit to tell yer wife ye're alive nor been to see yer children?"

Casey took a long breath through his nose and looked down at the carpet at his feet. It was an answer in itself.

"Oh, I see," Pat said slowly, "ye've been back far more than two weeks. Just how long has it been, my brother?"

"I've been back for months, but before ye hit me," Casey said wryly, "ye need to know it was a long while before my memory came back to me, an' even what I have now is in patches. I had little notion of who I was or who my family was when I came back. I found myself standin' on my own land one day, with no notion of why the place felt so familiar."

Casey placed his hands on his knees and Pat saw the knuckles were white with tension. He also noted that Casey still wore the plain silver band which was his wedding ring. "How is she now? Since—since the workhouse?"

"She's fine physically speakin'. The baby was born healthy an' whole, an' Pamela survived what had to be a livin' nightmare more or less intact. She's not talked about it just yet—at least not to me. Yer appearance certainly makes sense of one question both she an' I had, though, about avengin' angels an' their ability to shoot with such deadly accuracy. The baby is a wee girl, in case ye were wonderin'."

"No," Casey said quietly, "that much I know. Father Jim told me."

"Father Jim knows ye're alive?"

"Aye, a priest seemed the best place to go to begin. I still don't know, Patrick, what exactly happened to me an' who might be ill pleased to see me return from the dead, as it were. The good Father, bein' bound by the confessional, can't tell anyone. I hesitated even to come here, but in the end, I simply had to see ye."

"I'm grateful for that, man," he said, softly. "It's a miracle to just be sittin' here lookin' at ye. That mug of yers is not somethin' I ever thought to see again in my life. Can ye—will ye tell me what happened an' why ye were gone so long?"

"Aye, I can tell ye, though it's a bit of a mad tale an' it will take a little time in the tellin'."

"I've time," Pat said stoutly.

Casey smiled, though there was a sadness in the smile that hurt Pat's heart to see.

"All right, here it is then," Casey said and then began to relay the story of his long disappearance—about where he had been and what he had done for these last three years. About the beating and the bullet that had been extracted from his skull on a ship, about his loss of memory and the loss of much more than that. He told him of his time in San Francisco, and how he'd made his money fighting in pits and barns and pubs. And of a man named Edward Two Feet Walking who had helped him back to life and what little memory he had. Then he told him just how long he'd been back in Ireland, and how he'd been drawn here by a memory which was no more than instinct, like that of a homing pigeon for its own roost.

"I knew the land as soon as I lit upon the shore. It was in my cells, an' it restored somethin' in me, even if it didn't give me back myself whole. Comin' back here put solid ground beneath my feet an' the courage to know who I was, though it was an old Traveller woman who restored our last name to me. It was Finn Egan who put the last piece of the puzzle in place."

"Tomas' cousin? The wee odd man from down Wicklow way?"

"Aye, that would be the one. He came to visit Tomas on a fact findin' mission on my behalf. He meant to ask Tomas to find out if a man with my name was missin'. Ye walked in for dinner that night though, before he could ask. He said he knew ye had to be my brother the minute he saw ye. I worked in his pub for a bit," Casey said, by way of explanation. Pat shook his head thinking this was no explanation at all, and that he would have to sort through the threads of all Casey had told him before he could make of it a whole cloth. That would take time, but time they now had. He felt a rush of giddy joy as the fact of Casey's survival and return began to sink in.

"So, Casey, what of Pamela?" he asked. "She's been mournin' ye for the last three years. I thought at times she might not survive her own anguish. An' yet no one believed more that ye might still be alive, might still be out there, as mad as it seemed to the rest of us. She was literally sick with grief."

"Still, she managed to have a child with Jamie." The words were uttered lightly, but Pat saw the look on Casey's face.

"Ye were gone three years, Casey. *Three years*. Jamie was there for her, as he always has been. He was her friend, an' then he was more. Surely ye can't be overly surprised by that. An' forgive me if I'm mistaken but I believe ye asked the man to look after her an' yer children should somethin' happen to ye."

"Aye, I did, but I thought I'd be dead in that case. Are ye mad at me, Patrick?" Casey asked, dark eyes fixed to his brother's face.

Pat laughed, but it wasn't humour that prompted him to do so. "Aye, I'm mad at ye. I'm furious with ye. I mourned ye too, ye know. Ye're my brother, an' I thought ye'd done some damn stupid thing an' got yerself killed an' we would never know how or why. I'd lie awake at night picturin' ye in some anonymous grave or tossed into the sea after havin' been tortured. It near to drove me mad. So maybe ye can imagine what it did to Pamela."

"Aye, I can imagine. If ye think I don't have regrets an' pain over that, think again."

"Ye have to go see her, Casey. Regardless of what's happened to ye or to her, ye owe her that much."

"I'm a stranger to her now, Patrick. Christ, I'm a stranger to myself most days. I never know how my moods will change from moment to moment, it's part of trauma to the head, or so the doctors told me. I can hardly just walk back into her life an' expect that we'll pick up where we left off. We aren't those people anymore."

"I would ask ye one thing—do ye love her?"

Casey ran a hand over his face, as if he could scrub his mind clean and begin again.

"Aye, I do. Even when I didn't know who I was, or where I'd come from, or who she was for that matter, I loved her."

"There is no choosing for her, Casey, not from the day she first met you."

"How do ye know that, Patrick?"

"Because I know her, an' I know she has loved ye every day since she met ye, an' she loves ye still."

"She loves the man I was, not this man."

"Maybe ye need to give her the choice of gettin' to know who ye are now an' let her decide if she can love this man too."

"Aye, well we'll see," Casey said, and there was a finality to his tone that told Pat it was time to cease and desist, at least for now.

"Where are ye stayin'?"

"Don't worry about me, little brother, I have a place to lay my head."

Pat cocked a brow at Casey. "And where would that be?"

Casey hesitated a second, no more than the space of a heartbeat and Pat was surprised to find the hesitation on his brother's part hurt like a lash across his soul.

"Don't tell me then, if ye feel ye can't trust me," he said stiffly.

"It's not that, Patrick," Casey said with a mild look of reproof. "Where I live is well hidden away in the mountains, but I think I'll not head back there just yet. I need to decide what to do about Pamela. I think it's best if I stay in or near the city until I figure that out. But yer place isn't safe, is it? What with yer mad career an' every Loyalist in the country gunnin' for ye."

"The hut—our old hut in the Wicklow Mountains? It *was* you livin' there then. I made a trip up there a couple of months past. Conor found yer drawin' in the fairy house."

"Aye, I lived there for a bit. 'Twas as if some part of me—instinct maybe—remembered the place, an' I felt safe there."

"Clearly ye remembered yer own house too at some point."

"I found myself there one day, wanderin' the property with no idea that it was my own." Casey shrugged. He seemed uncomfortable. "It felt familiar an' not at the same time. I went back later when I knew but I never found the courage to knock at the door."

Pat felt it suddenly—the abyss of time and absence his brother was currently staring into and how frightening that might be to a man.

"Ye better not even be considerin' *not* goin' to see the woman. I will tell her if ye don't, but I think it will go a deal easier on ye, man, if ye go see her yerself. Maybe ye don't remember her personality quite so well?"

"Ah no, I remember well enough to know I've likely cooked my own goose with waitin' here, but I have to be certain I'm doin' what's right for her and the wee ones."

"Is it wee Kathleen? Is that why ye're stallin'?"

Casey took a sharp breath in through his nose and let it out all at once.

"I think ye'd know me for a liar did I say it makes no difference to me. In truth though, I'd hesitate anyway. It could be that Jamie is far better for the lot of them these days than I could possibly be. The children will love him too, no?"

The words were spoken casually but Pat heard the pain behind them. Casey had been gone three years, not so much time on the calendar, but when it came to life and how much changed in such a short space, it was an eternity. Casey had always been a pragmatic man; he would understand that he might not be welcomed with open arms by a woman whose life had moved on in many ways, even if her heart had not. He knew his sister-in-law as well as anyone other than Jamie, but he couldn't quite say how she might react to the ghost of her husband rising, very solid, from the grave.

"Jamie is married, Casey. That's part of the complexity I mentioned."

"He's *married*—Pamela has had a child with a married man?" Casey's eyebrows rose toward his hairline.

"Aye," Pat said drily, "apparently there's a thing or two Father Jim didn't inform ye about."

"I suppose the man thought I could only manage so many shocks all at once."

"To be fair he wasn't married when Pamela got pregnant—or rather he was, but they thought the wife gone for good." He thought to explain any further just now was both unwise and unnecessary. Casey was right, a man could only absorb so many shocks at one go.

"I will go see her. I can't be this close an' stay away. I need to see my children too. But can ye give me a few days at least? I need to sort my thoughts out around the fact of this new baby."

"All right," he agreed with some reluctance, "but don't wait too long, Casey. She's had a helluva road these last few years, don't make her walk it too much longer. An' make no mistake, if ye do take too long, I *will* tell her."

"Yer threat is duly noted, man. I'm a wee bit scared to go see her. I was terrified just to come see you, truth be told. I'm glad I did though." He smiled. "It's so good to see ye, Patrick. It's like I was missin' somethin' an' didn't know what it was until I saw ye come out the door."

"Ye remembered enough to come home. That tells me ye've always known where ye belong. Time an' healin' will do the rest." Pat prayed that it was so. He had not lied when he said things were complicated, only he hoped that complications wouldn't run amok with consequences the way they so often did.

Casey smiled again, but it was a wary expression.

"I remember feelins' more than actual events. It's as though there's this series of puzzles an' I have some of the pieces, even some that fill in a corner of the picture but there are still blank spaces. But sittin' here now, lookin' at you—I feel like I would have known ye even if I'd passed ye on the street in San Francisco. Ye're my little brother an' my blood knows it." His voice faltered a little and Pat stood and walked over to him. He knelt down on the threadbare carpet and put his arms around Casey.

"An' ye're my big brother. Always have been an' always will be. Welcome home, *mo dheartháir*."

Chapter Two

Secrets

THE HOUSE IN THE HOLLOW was filled with familiar faces when Pat arrived the following afternoon.

His niece and nephew were outside playing in the fading light of a December day, their cheeks rosy and glowing with the cold. They were watched over by the indomitable Pru, whose services as nanny had been transferred from Kolya to Kathleen for the time being. It was a mark of Jamie's formidable will and, he thought, Pamela's exhaustion that she'd allowed it. Pru was a known quantity to her though, as she'd looked after the children in Maine two summers before and all of them were clearly fond of her. He was glad Pamela had the help and the company. Vanya still lived with her too, but he worked full time at a pub in the village and was away from the house a fair bit.

Pru looked up from where she was re-buttoning Isabelle's coat and smiled. She might have a Puritan name and the no-nonsense personality one might expect from a New Englander, but she had an Irish face, round and freckled, it had—as his father might have said—the map of Ireland laid right over it.

"Uncle Pat!" Conor ran across the yard and hugged him around his legs, almost upending him onto the frosty ground. He lifted his nephew and returned the hug, finding a warm steadiness in Conor which never failed to remind him of his father, Brian. It took everything he had within him not to tell the lad he was going to see his father very soon—this wee boy who remembered his daddy well enough to still miss him. Isabelle scampered across the yard with her arms up, and he swept her up to receive a smacking and slightly gritty kiss. He went inside, a child on each arm, with Pru following behind.

Inside, the house smelled wonderfully of butter, sugar and ginger with an under-note of baby—talcum powder, milk and the scent of freshly laundered nappies drying by the fire. Kate was by the stove pulling out a batch of biscuits and she looked up, smiling as he entered on a waft of chilly air. He walked over and kissed her, his heart lifting merely at the sight of her. She was seven months pregnant with their first child and in the stage where she was glowing with good health and hormones. Isabelle traded his arms for her auntie's and Conor, always restless, got down on the floor, going over to his mother to check on his baby sister.

Pamela had told him how vigilant Conor had been since her return from the workhouse and hospital with the baby. He couldn't blame the boy, he felt hyper-protective himself. Tears stung the back of his eyes, as he watched his nephew place a careful kiss on Kathleen's wee face. Since Pamela's near-death experience in the workhouse he'd been terribly emotional over all his loved ones, and now that his brother was back, he felt slightly out of control.

Pamela looked up at him and smiled. She was sitting in the rocking chair, a cup of tea and a plate of fresh biscuits on the table next to her. Kathleen was slumbering blissfully in her arms. The biscuits were untouched however, and he noted that her teacup was more than half-filled. He was worried about her. She was recovering from her ordeal, but not quickly, despite all the care Jamie was taking with her and the baby. She was pale and looked as though a stiff wind would knock her down. He wondered, rather worriedly, what a huge shock might do.

He bent over her and gave her a gentle squeeze, worried that even that much might hurt her.

"Can I take the baby?" he asked. He sat down on the chair beside her and held out his arms.

"Of course you can," she said, and handed his tiny redheaded niece to him. Despite the fact that Kathleen was not blood in the way that Conor and Isabelle were, Pat still felt strongly connected to her. She was family, regardless of who had fathered her. Besides, he was fond of Jamie, very fond, and had come to consider the man both dear friend and family over these last few years. None of which served to make him less nervous about this current situation.

He snugged the baby tight to his chest and looked down at her. Just the sight of the tiny face calmed him a little. The transfer from her mother's arms to his hadn't disturbed her in the least and she still slept, pearly eyelids sealed shut and red-gold lashes fanned against the milky skin.

Oh, little one, if you only knew the complications that are about to arise in this household, he thought. He looked up to find Pamela watching him with a slightly suspicious look on her face. He smiled in an effort to alleviate any worry on her part.

"How are ye?" It was a weak question considering all that had happened to her in the last while, but with the children present it was the most he dared ask.

"I'm tired, that's all." Her tone was flat and conveyed far more than her four simple words.

"Ye just seem a wee bit transparent," Pat said, for lack of a better way to describe the exhaustion and strange distance that hung around her like an aura. It was invisible, but it was there, nevertheless.

"I'm all right, Pat," she said softly, and put her hand to his arm giving him a reassuring squeeze. She then touched the baby's face, Kathleen's red hair a soft glow against her hand. "I came so close to losing her. I feel like it's all hitting me now—everything that's happened. Noah, the baby, Jamie offering his life in exchange for ours. It's a lot to take in," she finished, looking down into the baby's face so that he could not see her expression.

Light from the nearby window sparked on her hand, and he saw that she was wearing her wedding ring again. Just a simple silver band, and yet the small piece of metal held a weight of meaning. She'd removed the ring when she started wearing Noah's big sapphire on her hand, and he'd understood why but it had hurt to see it even if he'd known full well she had not put Casey behind her.

He felt a spurt of anger at his brother both for putting him in this situation and for not coming back to this woman right away. He understood why on a practical level, but on an emotional one he was simply mad and afraid.

"You, on the other hand," she said quietly, "look like you've something weighing on your mind."

"Oh, work ye know, we just have a case that's keepin' me preoccupied. Nothin'," he added hastily, lest Pamela ask for details, "that I am allowed to discuss though."

"Ye've a glass face an' a prickly conscience, laddie, a good liar ye'll never be."

"Aye, Daddy, I know," he said under his breath, though Pamela crooked an eyebrow at him.

He looked down at the baby again, hoping Pamela wouldn't ask him to repeat what he'd said. "Make sure ye let everyone help ye. I know ye can manage a lot, Pamela, but ye don't have to do it alone."

"I know that, Patrick. I promise you I'll ask for help when I need it. I will be fine," she said, and he saw something deep in her eyes which was more than equal to the resolve of her words. "I owe it to my children and to your brother."

He forgot sometimes that there was a ruthlessness to this woman, something indomitable which allowed her to survive loss and heartbreak and to even pit herself against evil and come out whole.

He almost blurted it out then, the promise he'd made Casey seeming ridiculous suddenly. Just then though the door opened and Jamie came in with his arms laden with parcels; and so he didn't speak.

Lord James Kirkpatrick was the sort of man who made an entrance merely by walking through the door. For as long as Pat had been friends with Jamie, he could still find himself a touch overawed by the man. Right now, he felt like a master interrogator had entered the room and he was the hapless prisoner about to be questioned.

Jamie said hello to Kate and hugged both Conor and Isabelle, who rushed up to him in the same manner that they'd done with Pat. Jamie was family to both of his brother's children. He crossed the room to where they sat, and Pat handed Kathleen to her father. Jamie smiled as he took the baby, his face lit up in a way Patrick had never witnessed before. His heart clenched to see it, for Pamela's face had flooded with a soft pink as she looked up at the man holding their child. He didn't quite know the geography of their relationship, but that the two of them loved each other was something he was in no doubt about. Mind, it had been something his brother had known as well. Still, things were a great deal more complicated now, what with this wee girl cooing in Jamie's arms.

"She is daddy's girl," Pamela said, "much like Isabelle was with Casey."

He started a little and Pamela gave him a sharp look. "What in heaven's name is the matter, Pat? You're as jumpy as a frog on a piece of hot tin."

"Too much tea today, no doubt," he said, realizing he sounded ridiculous and that now he wasn't going to be able to have a cup which would have at least had the tonic effect of steadying his nerves a wee bit.

His father had been right—an accomplished liar he never would be—though practicing law had certainly taught him the art of keeping his thoughts well hidden, only he didn't seem able to manage it today.

A stay of execution came in the form of Kate asking him to fetch some neeps for the dinner. Pat gratefully beat a hasty retreat into the small cold room. Standing there amidst the burlap bags of potatoes, turnips and carrots, he drew in an earthy—if shaky—breath and attempted to calm his hammering heart. There he stood, a fine beading of sweat crowning his brow, cursing his brother ten ways from Sunday for putting him in this position. There was still a small part of him that wondered if he'd dreamed it—that meeting with Casey. Was it possible that overwork and worry had finally driven him to hallucinations?

He was just taking the ties off the burlap sack which held the turnips when Jamie entered the cold room. The cold room wasn't big and neither of them were particularly small, so Pat backed up causing the cream cans to knock together loudly.

"What is it?" Pat asked, going on the offense in the hopes of throwing Jamie off. Jamie crossed his arms over his chest and leaned back against the cold room door, treating Pat to a narrowed green eye.

"You just look rather like the cat who found a mouse in its cream but drank it anyway."

"I—what? I'm just preoccupied with work things—a tricky sort of case that I'm working on."

"You're always working on a tricky case, Patrick, it's what you specialize in."

He smiled weakly. Pamela, he thought he could fool; she was tired and still in that post-baby haze which, she said, left her feeling about as keen as a cow which had awakened in the wrong field. Jamie on the other hand was, despite his own recent trauma, always as sharp as a needle picking its way through a person's brain. A hot needle. Pat swallowed, aware that Jamie was perusing his every expression. The man was not a comfortable man when he had suspicions resting upon you.

"If you're upset over something that might in any way touch Pamela or the children, then you need to tell me."

"I would," Pat said, though in truth his brother's return from the presumed grave was going to touch Pamela and the children in a way very little else could. He had promised Casey though, and Casey was his blood. The thought shored up his spine a little.

"Would you?" Jamie said, and cocked a dubious golden brow at him. "She can't afford any more upset in her life, Pat—you know that."

"I do know that. I would never do anything to harm her or the children."

"Why on earth are you two hissing over the potatoes?" Pamela asked, poking her head around the door. "Kate wants to know if you're growing the turnips yourselves? Do you think one of you could bring some out when you're done with your tête-à-tête?"

"Aye," Pat said, striving to keep the one word nonchalant. He wondered how much she'd heard. Jamie, cool bastard that he was, merely smiled at Pamela and dug four turnips out of their burlap sacking and handed them over to her. Jamie exited the cold room then and Pat followed behind him, knowing if Jamie had suspicions the conversation was far from over.

Pamela was lifting a steaming pot of potatoes off the stove, and Pat went over to take it from her, earning himself an eye roll from the woman.

"Go sit, I can help Kate finish up here," he said. He busied himself with mashing the potatoes and avoiding Jamie's speculative gaze.

Tomas arrived just as dinner was set upon the table, smelling of chilled earth and air and the pine needles that had come in on his coat. Pat suspected he'd stopped for a wee nip under the trees outside, for there was a faint tang of whiskey along with all the other scents.

"Ah, there she is, the wee angel," he said and bent over Kathleen, who was in her cradle. He had a bushel of flowers under his arm and he handed a posy of anemones to Pamela and planted a kiss on her pale cheek. For Kate there was a lovely cluster of violets and a kiss as well. There was also a small stuffed dog for Isabelle, some building blocks for Conor and a velveteen giraffe for Kathleen.

"Tomas, you have to stop bringing them gifts," Pamela protested.

"Ah, let me spoil them a little. I've never had wee ones to dote over," he said, taking his overcoat off and throwing it over the umbrella tree by the front door. It made an audible clank causing Pamela to raise a disapproving eyebrow at him. Pat knew Tomas always carried a flask of whiskey in the inside pocket of his coat. Pamela had been trying to persuade him to cut down his alcohol consumption ever since she'd met him.

There was the bustle then of getting everyone seated at the table. Made from a long slab of bog oak, the table was big, sturdy and beautiful. Casey had built it so that it would last for generations. It was near to black in colour from its long time in the bog, and in the well-lit kitchen, it glowed like a length of polished onyx. Casey's spot still sat empty, for everyone knew no one had sat in his chair from the day he'd disappeared. The sight of it had made Pat sad for the last three years; now looking at it caused his nerves to flare up again.

He loaded his plate up with food, hungry despite the disquiet in his body. There was wine on the table, and he poured himself a glass hoping it would take the edge off his nerves. He would prefer the whiskey hidden in Tomas' coat, but as that wasn't on offer, he'd have to settle for the wine.

They spoke of many things, carefully skirting anything too serious—the political goings on in the outside world, and most particularly in their own country the unending violence and how it had recently touched so deeply upon their own lives. And the biggest no man's land topic of all—Noah. It was as if some silent pact had been made amongst all of them, not to speak of him. Even Kate who was the man's sister and had loved him more than anyone else, hadn't said much, not even in the privacy of their home though he knew she mourned her brother deeply. He knew Pamela mourned him as well, but the doctors had told Jamie not to push her on the subject of what had happened in the workhouse, feeling that she would speak if, and when, she was ready. Until then, they were to keep as much stress away from her as possible. Looking at her now, he wondered if she would ever be ready.

There was laughter and chatter about an adventure Pru had had in the city centre last week, if one could call anything that included armed and nervy soldiers an adventure. Conor told them about his week at school and showed them a diorama he was building about winter. He had his father's talent with wood and stone, and it was an impressive undertaking for a five-year-old, Pat thought, admiring the woodland scene built from moss and bark and bits of stone. There was even a tiny squirrel and a dusting of icing sugar over the trees depicting snow. The scene had depth and invited the imagination in. Casey could always build things in just the same manner; even when they were small boys he'd been able to do so.

"It's the wood where ye took me walkin', Uncle Pat. Ye know the one ye go to when ye're mad about somethin'?"

Kate stifled a laugh on his other side and Conor continued to point out the small details of the project to his uncle. It felt wonderfully normal and a bit of calm descended over him as he listened to his nephew.

He realized suddenly that Jamie was talking about him and though the words were spoken casually, he knew they were anything but.

"Patrick said the two of you were working on a tricky case," Jamie was saying, and Tomas flashed Pat a questioning look. Pat merely looked back with a neutral expression, hoping Tomas would understand.

"Aye," Tomas said, leaning back in his chair, wine glass in hand, "we are, but aren't they all tricky? And on that point, James, there's a matter I need to speak to ye about, a bit later."

Jamie merely nodded, and Pat wondered if it was about his custodial rights regarding Kolya. Jamie was the boy's father in all but biology, and Pat thought it would be a tragedy if Kolya was taken away from the only parent he'd ever known. He also knew it would break Jamie's heart.

The conversation became general after that, much to Pat's relief. Tomas delighted in Jamie's company and their talks were always highly entertaining as the two men rarely agreed on anything, though Pat suspected that Tomas played devil's advocate more often than not simply to watch Jamie's mind at work. Jamie enjoyed the old buzzard every bit as much and was always good-natured about the baiting.

The dark of the winter evening had closed in during dinner, and the light was reflected in the few windows where the curtains had yet to be drawn. Pat knew Pamela would draw them soon though, as she'd felt exposed here since the events at the workhouse. Still, despite that, there was a cozy feeling to the gathering, something insular and safe, and he knew that right now Casey stood outside of that.

Kate squeezed his hand and he looked over at her, grateful for her silent understanding. Even when she didn't know the particulars, she always understood the generalities.

"I thought ye should know," she said in a low tone, "yer mam is plannin' a visit in the next week or two."

"What?" A frisson of alarm darted through him just at the thought. Casey returning to find their mother *in situ*—a mother with whom he'd barely begun to be cordial when he'd disappeared—while trying to come to terms with a small redheaded cuckoo in his nest wasn't likely to make for a calm re-entry to his old life.

Kate's brow furrowed slightly. "Aye, she wants to meet wee Kathleen. She'll come again when this one is born, so ye'd best reconcile yerself to her presence." She rubbed the side of her belly, where the contents had shifted. Pat put his own hand there.

"Foot or hand?" he asked, as the small pokes thumped softly against his fingers.

"Foot—that's the heel ye're feelin'," Kate said, as the occupant of her belly kicked once more, dislodging its father's hand. He leaned over and kissed Kate, feeling a rush of gratitude that the universe had seen fit to place this woman in his life. She was the steady core at the heart of his world.

He turned back to Conor, but the boy was down on the floor now, adjusting one of the trees in his diorama. Conor looked up at him and smiled, one cheek dimpling. It startled Pat for he hadn't noticed it before. It was in the exact same spot as Casey's had been, or rather was, he thought.

Isabelle had crawled into Jamie's lap partway through dinner, proceeded to eat his food instead of her own and then promptly fell asleep, madly curly head lolling against his chest with Jamie's right arm keeping her from slipping off his lap altogether. Kathleen was tucked neatly in the crook of his left arm. It was, Pat thought, a beautiful slice of domesticity. This man was family to Pamela and the children. It didn't fail to occur to him that as far as the children were concerned—particularly Isabelle—Jamie was more family than Casey. It made his heart hurt to know it.

Despite this, he realized he felt a bit defensive on wee Kathleen's behalf. After all, she hadn't asked to be born into this rather mad situation. As if sensing her uncle's thoughts, a tiny hand rose from the bundle in Jamie's arm, one finger uncurling slowly and then the next and the next, like pink petals emerging from an ivory petiole. Jamie kissed the tiny hand, and it retracted like a flower folding up at the touch of a breeze.

"Is she stirring?" Pamela asked. Pat noticed she had a tendency to hover and there was always an undernote of anxiety in even the simplest question to do with Kathleen. He could hardly blame her though, considering all she had been through, and her fear only short weeks ago that the baby would be born and die in the waking nightmare of the workhouse.

"She's fine," Jamie said. Over the head of their blissfully slumbering daughter, Jamie's eyes met Pamela's and a look of such understanding and affinity passed between them that Pat felt slightly sick. This here—this moment between two people who had long loved one another and now had come to a place where that bond had been cemented by a child—this was what his brother was afraid of and, he thought with a sinking feeling in his stomach, rightly so.

"All right, I'm going to go do the evening feed then," she said, pushing her chair back from the table.

"Let me," Pat said, standing up so quickly that he nearly upended his chair. "I remember how to do it, an' I could use a breath of air."

Kate was looking up at him with a question in her face, and both Pamela and Jamie had crooked an eyebrow in his direction. Even Tomas was eyeing him up with suspicion. He could feel a fine beading of sweat break out on his forehead again. *Daddy, ye were right, a good liar I'll never be.*

Outside, in the chilly night, he paused to take a deep lungful of cold air and then released it with a gust of relief as he walked across the yard.

The byre was warm, packed with fresh straw both on the floor and in the loft above and with the heat that healthy animals exuded. Still, he could see a soft exhalation of breath from Khamsin's stall, and heard Paudeen's bleat of protest at the cold air he'd let in.

Khamsin was like a ghost in the faint light, a negative image where the dark blended into the greater darkness of the night, the reflection from the yard light shining in his eye and rendering it into a crystal orb.

Pat found the paraffin lantern and lit it. There was electricity running out to the byre, but he preferred the softer light of the lantern. Khamsin tossed his head a little and Pat clucked his tongue at him to soothe him. He was a beautiful horse, with shimmering blue-green notes in the midnight tones of his coat. He had been a gift from Noah to Pamela when she had agreed to marry him.

Pamela preferred to mix her own feed for her horse, so he simply followed the recipe which was pinned to the wall. Oats, corn, barley, beet pulp and a vitamin mixture she got from a horse farm down in Wexford. He added a touch of molasses as well, and the strong scent of it, combined with the dustiness of the oats and earthy smell of the beet pulp, filled his nostrils. Khamsin stamped one imperious hoof impatiently. He gave the horse his meal and then grabbed an armful of hay for Paudeen. The ram looked up at him with a baleful glare but set to chewing happily, nevertheless.

The homely task of feeding the animals had given him back his equilibrium though he was in no rush to go back into the house. He stood in the doorway, with the sounds of Khamsin snorting in his feed and Paudeen rustling in his nest of straw, behind him. There was a light above the byre doors haloed against the dark sky beyond. A few snowflakes drifted through the halo, visible for only a second and then gone. It would be Christmas in two weeks. Even if the ghost of Christmas future was to alight before him now and demand that he state his desires, he doubted he would know what to wish for. All those people inside that house where the windows glowed with light, were people he loved and worried over but none more so than Pamela right now.

An old pair of gloves wedged in the junction of two beams caught his eye. They were Casey's and were still in the exact place he'd put them three years ago. Pamela had simply left them there, as if to move them would be to admit her man wasn't coming back. But now he had. Pat pulled the gloves down from their spot and put them on. They were a bit loose, as Casey's hands were just that bit bigger than his. It gave him a feeling of reassurance though, for despite all the complications which were going to arise, there was no gift more miraculous than having his big brother back, alive and relatively whole. He could only pray Pamela felt the same.

He took the gloves off and put them back in their spot, wedged in so they wouldn't fall and waiting for the hands which had once worn them to return. Sighing, he walked back out into the night, securing the byre door behind him. The last time he'd been here in this building with his brother they'd had a very serious conversation, one that came back to him now, fraught with meaning.

He had been helping Casey with the evening work on his and Pamela's property, the air chill and frosted, so that their words were festooned with small clouds of sparkling fog. Kate was inside with Pamela and the children, and occasionally the two men could hear a high-pitched cry from the house.

"Aye," Casey said ruefully, noting Pat's wince at an especially piercing cry, "the wee girl has a set of lungs on her an opera singer would envy. My ear drums go numb some nights." He heaved a fresh bale of hay over the gate of Phouka's stall, and dug his pocket knife out to cut the baling string. The scent of clover and summer sun wafted up into their noses and set Pat to sneezing. "'Tis her fussy time, from now until around ten, can't do a blessed thing to make her happy for those few hours. It will pass, Pamela assures me. I think Conor spoiled us, he was peaceful even as a tiny babe."

"Ye can't fool me, brother, ye're absolutely besotted with that wee girl."

"Oh aye," Casey smiled, "I am, she's goin' to have her daddy right where she wants him her whole life."

"Will ye have more of the wee squeakers, do ye think?"

"Well, that will be up to Pamela ultimately, but aye, I'd like one or two more if the woman is willin'. An' speakin' of babbies, when are ye goin' to make an honest woman of that one in there?"

"One day, when the woman says yes, we'll make it all legal an' bindin'. She won't let me ask just yet though, says it's not the right time because she still feels the shadow of Sylvie upon me now an' again." Pat shrugged. "I'm not entirely certain I know what she means, but I'll wait until she's ready."

They walked outside, not wanting to go in just yet. Casey dug a cigarette out of a battered packet he kept in his coat pocket and lit it, the coal a small lamp in the night. He draped his elbows over the gate and took a long drag off the cigarette. Pat joined him there, propping his own arms up on the top of the paddock fence. The night was rich with the scents of late autumn and the moon lit the frosted rails with a gilt glow.

Casey blew out his first lungful of smoke in soft rippling rings. "Sweet mother of Christ, but that's fine."

"I thought ye were quittin'," Pat said, "ye know, for the hundredth time this year."

Casey gave him a dark look over the top of his next mouthful of smoke.

"I'm down to one every other day. Aye, ye can look as doubtful as ye like, it's the truth. Pamela said she won't have it anymore, that she wants me around for the long haul, an' cigarettes are not likely to further that cause."

"Well, the woman has a point. Ye've children to raise after all."

Casey cleared his throat and Pat glanced over at him, for the air around them had suddenly taken on that aura of hesitant expectancy that it tended to when a person was about to say something the other person did not particularly want to hear.

"There's somethin' I would say, Patrick."

"Aye?" Pat said, noting the sudden tension in his brother, how he no longer relaxed over the gate, but stood tall and still. He shivered a little, for he had seen his father stand just so with that subtle electric current to him when he was about to say something that had always felt to Pat like a thing that was more prophecy than ordinary words.

"Should somethin' happen to me, ye'd see that in time, a goodly amount mind ye, that she turned toward Jamie."

"Is somethin' likely to happen to ye?" Pat asked, feeling abruptly angry with the turn of this conversation.

"Jaysus, man, I'm just sayin' should it happen. I could get hit by a fockin' bus, like any other man, that's all. Only with the babies now, I want to be certain she's looked after, that if somethin' were to happen an' I weren't here to see to her needs, that another man, one day, would. Ye know as well as I do that the obvious answer to that is Jamie."

"What's a goodly amount of time?" Pat asked, the sarcasm thick in his voice.

Casey looked at him with a strange patience in his face, dark eyes utterly serious. "I suppose that would be for Pamela to decide, but I don't think she will take to it easily. The woman is bloody stubborn, an' I don't want that stubbornness to make a mess of her life. She won't let me speak of it with her, she gets angry as a bee trapped in a jar if I so much as hint at it. I'm only sayin' that should ye see her turn to him, should the time come..." Casey trailed off as though he had an obstruction in his throat which the words would have to be forced past.

"Aye, I understand what ye're sayin' man, only it would kill her should somethin' happen to ye, so short of a bus hittin' ye, could ye take precautions an' try to stay breathin'? For my sake too, ye're a bastard but ye're the only brother I have an' that's no small thing."

"It's no small thing to me either, Pat. But ye'll think of what I've asked ye, should the time ever, God an' his saints forbid, come."

"Oh aye, ye daft bastard, I did think about it an' look where it's got us all now," he said venting his frustration to the night sky. Here he stood three years later wondering if he'd played a part in what his brother had suggested and what had come to pass in that time. Had he pushed her toward Jamie or even suggested it as a possibility? Was he guilty to any degree in what had happened? Aye, he supposed he was. He'd mentioned Jamie when he'd found out she was engaged to Noah and if he were honest with himself, he had seen what was happening between them last Christmas at Jamie's house. He'd understood that Pamela had begun to move on from his brother in some respects and while it had hurt his heart to witness it, he had also been glad of it because he wanted her to be happy and he knew her chances for that state were best with Jamie.

If only life were as simple as putting on an old pair of gloves, if only a man could just slip into his old skin and wear his life once more. Life, of course, was not so simple. If a man left his life behind, whether through purpose or accident, another man was likely to pick it up, and fill the void.

The night before had been the full moon, and he could just catch a glimpse of it now over the house, slipping in and out between the clouds and lighting the frost on the thatch of the house, silver. It was a Christmas moon, the sort to make wishes upon.

"Casey, my brother," he said, "ye'd best get yerself home soon."

Jamie had built up the fire and then come to sit for one last cuddle with his daughter. It had become routine for them—this nightly time of quiet with their baby. She knew it likely cost him at home, but also knew these moments with Kathleen were something he would pay any price to have.

Pru had taken Conor and Isabelle upstairs right after dinner where she saw to their nightly routine of teeth brushing, face washing and then read them each a bed time story. After, she had retired to her room, which was technically Vanya's, though he often stayed away at night, claiming that he slept in the rooms over the Emerald Pub where he worked. Pamela thought it was possible he was staying elsewhere, but also acknowledged it was none of her business. He was a grown man and deserved his privacy. If he had found love somewhere in the wilds of County Down, then she was happy for him.

Wafting mint steam, Pamela came to sit beside Jamie with a cup of cat-mint tea for each of them. The firelight touched his hair, sparking the gold to life. Kathleen was looking up at him with the solemn gravity of a three-week-old who still hoarded universal secrets within her tiny body. Pamela sighed, feeling an exhaustion from the roots of her hair to the bottoms of her feet.

Jamie waited until she was settled in and sipping her tea before asking, "How are you?"

"Tired and sore, but that's just part of a new baby. Pru has been brilliant, things are done before I can even remember they need doing."

"That's good, you don't need extra on your plate right now."

"I can't simply lie about, changing the occasional nappy and feeding Kathleen. I'm starting to feel a little decadent, and not in a good way," she said.

"Pamela, you know you need time to recover and not just from having a baby."

They hadn't spoken of the workhouse, and all that had taken place there, more than once since their narrow escape. It didn't mean they weren't both thinking about it, though. She saw it in her dreams still; the dank peeling walls, the long drifting ivy, the scent of blood and pain and fear. It would, she knew, always form a part of her now, always be there somewhere in memory, something she could not clutch close enough to avoid looking at it.

She looked over at Jamie, his presence steadying her and banishing the vision of the workhouse back to that nightmare plane on which it lived. The fire left half his face in shadow and the other half touched with flickers of gold and red, painting him light-dark against the rough plaster wall behind him. She wished she could sketch him—could capture this moment with him and Kathleen, as if drawing the two of them would distill the moment and hold it, golden as honey, somewhere in time's bottle.

"Mostly," she said, quietly, "I've been trying not to think about it. I don't think I have room for more grief right now. The last few years have been hard enough, I can't add anything onto that pile just now. Not when I've just had a baby. She is likely my last, and I want to enjoy her. I don't want any of this to touch her."

The truth was she couldn't talk about Noah. His death was still too close and thinking about it could send her into a state of glassy anxiety. There was something oddly intimate about those last hours with him, though she supposed there was little that was more intimate than sharing someone's death with them.

"Nor do I," Jamie said lightly, though she saw the look of worry in his eyes. Wisely, he changed the subject to one they both delighted in. "Look at the wee ears on her, would you? They're so fine you can see the light through them."

"Your grandmother says she's got fairy blood in her," Pamela said. "I figure if anyone would recognize such a thing, it's Finola."

It was true, Kathleen did look as though she had strayed across the borders of fairyland and been left under a cabbage leaf for a human to find. There was little doubting her paternity though, for even in these tender weeks,

Kathleen already bore the unmistakable stamp of her father in her features. That she was Jamie's daughter there could be no doubt.

"Vanya not coming back for the night?" Jamie asked, echoing her thoughts from before.

"No, he's staying over at the pub, though I suspect that's not entirely true. I think it's possible he's found someone, though I've no idea who."

"I do," Jamie said. "Do you remember Darin, the vet that David was involved with before his death?"

"Of course I do. I had him here to look at Khamsin's hoof last month when he stepped on a nail—oh, do you think so?" she asked, twigging to his meaning.

"I know so," Jamie said. "Vanya was with me when I went to visit Darin a few months back. They hit it off immediately."

She was quiet for a moment, mentally crossing herself as she always did when David was mentioned. He had been her friend and he had also been a British soldier and spy; his life had been complicated in all sorts of ways and the private side had been no less problematic than the professional.

"That's lovely. I'm glad. I know Darin has been alone since David's death."

"I just hope they are wise about it. This isn't exactly Paris or London. If people find out, it could go badly for both of them."

Kathleen stretched just then, both small fists rising up above her head, the tiny rosebud mouth pursing into a perfect 'O' and one eye opening a tiny bit to squint at her father, before settling back again with a soft coo like that of a contented dove.

"Is it just me, or is she utterly perfect?" Pamela said, with the certainty of a mother.

"She *is* utterly perfect," Jamie said, and there was a small catch in his voice which she did not miss. He looked up at her then, his eyes soft and searching in their expression. "I hope," he said, "there aren't any regrets for you. I was irresponsible that morning in Paris, and I feel I owe you an apology for that."

"I knew what I was risking that morning, Jamie. But it felt right and I'm so glad that we did risk it."

"So am I." His eyes held hers for another moment and she smiled. Since Kathleen's birth there had been a healing of the breach which had grown between them during her pregnancy and engagement to Noah. In these last three weeks a lovely sort of peace had settled around them. She just wanted to enjoy their baby and have him do the same. Thus far, it was working. She wasn't naïve enough to believe it always would stay the same.

She yawned widely, eyes watering. She was exhausted but knew once she went to bed she would likely lie there, wide-eyed, mind churning over the events and images from a few weeks ago. Despite the presence of Vanya most nights and Pru every night and the fact that she knew Jamie had hired a couple of men to keep watch over the house, she still found herself checking on the children several times a night and hovering over Kathleen even when the baby was fast asleep.

"Why don't you go up to bed?" Jamie said. "I'll sit up with her until the first feed."

"Jamie, you don't have to stay. I worry that your evenings here are causing tension for you at home."

"Do you think I care about that? Compared to having time with our daughter it doesn't signify, Pamela."

She didn't bother to protest further for she knew he meant what he said; it did not, for him, signify. It did worry her that Kolya had not accompanied him yet on any of his visits. Kolya was family to her and the children, and Kathleen was, for all intents and purposes, his sister.

She stood and picked up the detritus that always came with a baby—blankets, diaper pins, bottles of lotion, a soother and the velveteen giraffe Tomas had brought for Kathleen.

"Both you and Pat seemed rather preoccupied today," she said, suspecting Jamie wasn't going to tell her anything he'd felt the need to hide in the cold room to discuss.

"Just legal business, nothing you need worry over," Jamie said lightly, taking in her dubious expression.

She was too tired and frankly too absorbed in the baby to worry about it right now, but she still had the sense something larger was afoot than either man was admitting to.

"I think I will go up and try to get some sleep, as long as you're happy to stay."

"More than happy," he said, "go and get some rest."

She kissed Kathleen before she went and rested her hand for a moment on Jamie's and gave it a light squeeze. He squeezed back and smiled at her.

In the bed, she closed her eyes and hoped that sleep would come readily. Despite exhaustion and the demands of a newborn in the house, she had found sleep rather elusive since she'd come home from the hospital. A psychiatrist had visited her a few times while she was still in in the maternity ward and warned her about the fallout which might occur from her experience in the workhouse. Depression, anxiety, panic, and worry over the slightest things. She might, he'd said, have trouble sleeping, a loss of appetite, or just feel a great grey blankness at times. He hadn't been wrong, though Kathleen, Conor and Isabelle were helping to keep the worst of it at bay. Still, in moments like these when she was alone in the quiet, she could feel it hovering just out beyond the edges of the light. She needed to sleep before Jamie had to leave, because once he was gone her rest would be patchy at best. Every little movement and creak of the house jolted her awake and set her adrenaline into full flood.

Rusty had followed her up the stairs and was tucking his madly purring warmth in next to her. She stroked his ragged ears, grateful for his small furry presence.

A few minutes later, she rolled over on her back, giving the ceiling an owlish look. Then she looked over at the empty pillow beside her.

"It's been three years," she said to no one in particular. Three years—both a lifetime and hardly any time at all. When Casey had been here with her she used to roll over into his spot after he got up in the morning, not even waking, simply moving into the warmth he'd left behind. Now she kept to her own side of the bed, as though at night a phantom lay down beside her and she must leave room for it. The actual anniversary had come and gone while she was in the hospital and though she had acknowledged the date, the presence of medical staff and the general busyness of the maternity ward had somehow made it easier. Now that she was back home though, it was a different matter.

For a long time after Casey's disappearance, she thought she felt his hand holding hers during the night. When she woke the feeling would slowly fade, the memory of his touch dissipating into the night. Eventually even that had stopped, and she had realized that in some way her psyche was forcing her to move on. Yet, strangely the other day, she'd been outside with the children, watching them play while she held Kathleen, and she'd felt him for a moment. As if he stood right there, just out of sight and reach, and she'd thought that perhaps it was the anniversary which had made him feel close. Mind you, she often thought she felt someone watching. Her logical mind knew it was the residue of all the events with the Reverend and Elspeth, and the knowledge that Elspeth had been in her house, had walked her property, gone through her things and violated the sanctity of her home. She had washed clothes that were clean and folded in both closet and bureau, scrubbed walls and pulled out all the dishes and washed them in scalding hot water. The thought that Elspeth may have touched any of these things made her skin crawl in revulsion.

Jamie had caught her at it one day and ordered her to go lie down while he finished washing all the cutlery and fine china for her. He understood the need but reminded her gently that the doctors had said she needed rest and peace above all else.

With everything that had been going on at the time it had been easy to avoid the usual feelings that besieged her on that date, avoid acknowledging that yet another year had fallen away and off the calendar since Casey had walked out the door one morning and simply disappeared.

Disappeared. It was a weak word for what it actually meant, and how it actually felt. You counted time differently when someone you loved had disappeared. It was counted in missed events, and sleepless nights and inches added to the growing bodies of children. It was counted in false hopes which were then dashed like a vase dropped from a great height. It was counted in despair and breath, taking one after another even when you didn't feel you could, and many times did not want to. Disappeared. It almost sounded innocuous.

"Dead, Pamela just bloody say it," she said angrily, "he's dead. He's been dead for three years and you know it."

It hurt to say it out loud, and yet it was a bit of a relief as well. As if by simply admitting it she had at least approached a hurdle, even if she wasn't quite ready to go over it.

She realized suddenly that her fingers were fisted in the blankets, as though she was trying to hang onto something which was slipping from her grasp. She unclenched her hands, the bones aching with tension, and put one to the pillow beside her, the linen cool to her touch. She sighed and closed her eyes. Casey might never again visit in her dreams and she might never again feel that fleeting touch in the night, for even a phantom had the right to move on to wherever it was phantoms went when the living opened their hands and let them go.

Chapter Three

Courage — In Spades

THE NIGHT HAD its own sound. It was, Casey Riordan thought, the sound of the earth breathing. He was walking the edge of a field out beyond Finn Egan's pub, trying to sort through his feelings. He'd come back here to Wicklow because he needed a little time to catch his breath and to think about what he was going to do. Not that, he thought, recalling his meeting with his brother, he'd much choice about it. He knew Pat would make good on his threat to tell Pamela, so he understood his time for gathering his wits and making decisions was limited in the extreme. Still, there was no regret in him for the meeting. It had been like manna to his soul to see his brother and witness the joy in Pat's face at his return. It had shored up some of his uncertainties and filled his heart with gratitude that someone was so happy to see him home.

On the edge of the wood he could hear the dry whisper of the aspens as the few leaves that remained in the winter winds trembled. The Celts had considered aspens to be trees that straddled the divide between this world and that. Long ago, his father had told him that trees had their feet in the ground but their head in the heavens and so were beings in two separate planes.

Right now, he wished there was some sort of direct conduit through those trees—that he could whisper into the leaves and they could relay his words to his father.

His father. Brian Riordan. A man who was no more than memory, and yet he *was* memory and for that Casey was intensely grateful. It was like the light one saw through fog, diffused and scattered, but beautiful. With memory though had come other things. It had been strange for he hadn't expected the grief. But when the memory of Brian had come back to him, it had been as though his father had died the day before, not the many years which it had actually been. His grief had been reborn, and it had driven him to his knees. He missed the man with that raw sort of pain which followed a death, the disbelief that clutched fast around a person in those first weeks when it seemed impossible that the loved one could be gone. It was the same feeling he'd had when his da had actually died—a feeling of abandonment, of becoming an orphan all at once, despite the fact that his mother was still living.

The image of his father rose up in his mind, and he grasped at it the way he was still grasping at all these memories as they came—like a man grabbing onto a life preserver, afraid the memory would go as quickly as it had come. He had been a big man, Brian Riordan, standing only an inch shorter than Casey himself. But for most of his growing years his father had seemed a giant in his eyes, and he remained so for who he had been as a man, even when Casey had grown taller than him. There was a space in his chest that ached for his da—as much as he could ever remember needing his father, he needed him now.

"So Da, d'ye have any advice for me? I could use some fatherly wisdom right about now."

The only reply was that of the wind in the trees, a soft rustling whisper which spoke of things unknown to man. He walked over to the stone wall which girded the property and hopped up on it, seating himself comfortably on a patch of moss. The cold of the stone seeped through his pants, but he didn't mind. He'd long been used to discomfort and pain, such a small thing as cold hardly dented the surface of his consciousness. Emotional discomfort, however, was a whole other issue.

He had been a contrary mix of feelings ever since that horrible night in the workhouse—sad, angry, jealous, elated—he had run through the entire gamut more than once. He wanted to go home, and yet he was afraid, more afraid than he could ever remember being of anything in his life. He longed to hold his children. Two nights ago, he had stood on the edge of the wood, hidden, and for a painful and wonderful few minutes watched his son and his daughter play in the yard, while their mother sat on a bench by the house watching over them with another man's child in her arms.

He'd understood what he was doing—trying to sate a hunger he'd carried for three years, trying to imprint every sound and expression onto his patchy memory so he could pull it out later like a letter much loved and worn in which the writing only grew more precious with the repeated reading. Conor was no longer a small boy, he was growing tall already and losing the soft outlines of the small child. His son, who had left letters to him asking him to come home, his son who'd had faith that he *would* come home—that in itself seemed a miracle to Casey. And Isabelle—his wee baby girl, a baby no longer, and not really even a toddler any more.

At the last, just before he turned away, he allowed himself to look at Pamela, really look at her as he hadn't all those long moments of standing in a wood beside a house he had once called home. She was wrapped in a crimson shawl—thick and luxuriant, it set off the delicate porcelain of her skin and the dark lustre of her hair. She looked exhausted and fragile and yet with the curious soft glow of new motherhood upon her. He had seen her so before, with their children. If he'd had doubts about his feelings for her, looking at her now would have banished them. His heart ached just at the sight of her, in part because of all she'd been through, and in part for the time they'd lost.

What did he owe her? What could he offer her? And was he—broken in both body and mind the right man to provide those things for her? Oh and yet, he wanted to. He wanted to walk across the space which divided them—that of time, regret and grief—and simply gather her up in his arms and make promises it wasn't even possible to keep.

Now here he was, sitting in this field looking for answers to questions he couldn't even ask himself. And so, what remained was this—what was it that he was so terrified of? He had lived without her for three years, and had survived. He understood who she was well enough to know that she would never deny him the right to see his children and to be part of their lives. But what if she no longer wanted him as part of hers? What if she had found something with Jamie which rendered him unnecessary to her?

Patrick said she loved him still, and he did not doubt that. He remembered enough of what they'd had together to understand that it had been something altogether rare. It had been the one thing more than any other which had drawn him home across the sea. And he knew then what it was—he was afraid that having come this far, he would return home a stranger and she would look in his eyes and see him for one.

Around him night was sifting in, the air turning a chilly blue and the landscape—trees, field, stones—began to lose its delineation. The delicate and golden round of the moon rose slowly behind the trees, snatches of the smoky luminosity that came with winter peeking through the branches. He was getting cold and he knew Finn had one of his hearty stews on the simmer for supper. The pub would be busy tonight and Finn would need his help. It would be good to be distracted for a bit. The people here knew him and had accepted him some time ago as part of their community and so there was an ease to his interactions with them which he found comforting.

He braced his hands on the wall to ease his way down; his knee was paining him and he couldn't risk landing on it wrong. It was just then that one of those scattershot memories came, a glimpse in his head of the life before, another piece fastening into the incomplete puzzle.

"Jaysus Murphy an' the little green men, Casey Riordan, are ye determined to be the death of me, boy?"

His father's voice was so prescient in his head that he almost fell off the wall. He knew quite suddenly that this particular question was one his father had asked him on multiple occasions, and that he'd never had an answer for the man other than 'no'. It had been moot anyway, being that the query was one of those fond but exasperated rhetorical questions a parent threw out when at their wit's end. It was one particular episode he was remembering though; a time when he'd faced down a known IRA member for his persecution of a local boy who was slow-witted and prone to take things which didn't belong to him if they caught his fancy. Casey had been, if he recalled correctly, about fifteen at the time. His father had been justifiably upset, understanding the dangers in a way a fifteen-year-old reckless boy, could not.

In retrospect he had come to see the foolhardiness of his actions, and his father had been instrumental in driving that point home, calling him a 'mad eejit' and a 'suicidal jackass.'

"D'ye not have the smallest grain of sense, boyo? That man might have killed ye right there in the street."

"No," he said bravely. *"It's you after all that's always tellin' me I don't have the sense God gave me. I don't regret it. I'm sorry if I've upset ye, Da, but someone had to step in an' stop him."*

"Aye, but does it always have to be you? Ye're goin' to get yerself killed one of these days."

"It's yer own fault, Da. 'Twas you who taught us to always stick up for anyone smaller or weaker. Ye told us ye could tell the measure of a man by how kind he was to anyone who needed help. That boy needed my help today, an' so I had to give it."

Brian sighed and looked up at his stubborn eldest son. "I can tell ye this much, boyo, I did not raise a coward when I raised you."

Casey sighed and stood, brushing the leaves and needles from his pants. That one statement there, he supposed, was all the paternal advice he was getting tonight. As advice went though, it was to the point and the message was unmistakable. Well, if he remembered one thing clearly about his daddy it was that the man never pulled his punches. Casey knew what he needed to do, and he understood what was required. Courage—in spades.

Chapter Four

The Stranger's Face

SLEEP BEING, AT present, a more precious commodity than gold in the Riordan household, Pamela found herself feeling rather homicidal toward the person who had the temerity to knock on her door early one morning three and a half weeks after Kathleen's birth. Both she and the baby were blissfully asleep, curled up together in the bed. The knocking, sharp and staccato, had the effect of wrenching her from sleep, her heart pounding and her senses scattering like leaves in a brisk wind. Had she barred the door last night? Yes, she'd bolted it behind Jamie when he'd left. He always waited on the doorstep until he heard the bolt slide home.

Kathleen stirred, arching her back and making the small noises which meant she was soon going to be up and aware of her empty tummy. Pamela peered at the clock—it wasn't yet eight A.M. Whoever was at the door really was, she thought grimly, taking their life into their own hands.

The knocking increased in both fervour and decibel, and she stumbled from the bed, wrapping her dressing gown around her body and peering in the small, murky mirror which hung over the wash basin. Her hair bore a rather pointed resemblance to a hedgehog which had been pulled backwards through a hedge, and her face was creased from the pillow, eyes puffy with sleep. The all too familiar feeling of panic, which had been her almost constant companion since her abduction and Noah's death, started to pool in her stomach, sending darts of adrenaline out into her blood. She scooped up Kathleen, and made her way down the stairs into the cacophony of Finbar barking, with

Conor—hair sticking out around his head and only wearing his rumpled py-jama bottoms—thumping his way down the stairs ahead of her.

A jolt of worry halted her on the landing. She didn't want Conor down-stairs right now, not until she determined who was outside that door. Since her return home, he'd hovered around her at all times, and it scared her, won-dering how much damage had been done to her steady wee son because he was too small to save her from the bad things which had happened.

He had been terrified when she was abducted and rightly so. She knew it was folly to expect that what had happened to her hadn't affected her chil-dren quite badly, but she wouldn't risk him overhearing something he was too young to understand. The fallout from her relationship with Noah could cause trouble in their lives for quite some time to come. She needed Conor to understand there was a line behind which he would need to stay, for the sake of her nerves if nothing else.

"Go back upstairs, Conor, lock your door and keep your sister occupied. I'll call you when it's safe to come down," she said, meeting his eyes with a stern look. Protest began to form on his face, but she shook her head at him. He took a short breath which told her he was upset, but he went, for which small mercy she was grateful.

She went down the remaining stairs, to find Pru coming out of her room, rose-gilt hair tousled with sleep, and a look of annoyance on her face.

The knocking on the door had ceased and had been replaced by the sound of a scuffle, a decided thump and then an indignant exclamation, which didn't sound, Pamela thought, like a mad killer bent on mayhem. Still, she needed to exercise caution.

"Take her upstairs, please," she said, handing Kathleen off to Pru, who nodded and took the baby from her arms and went hastily up the stairs. Kath-leen, having been taken from her anticipated morning meal, began to shriek like a tiny and very irate tea kettle.

She opened the door slowly, foot braced on the kick plate and her free hand holding Conor's baseball bat, left handily by the door.

Outside stood two men, both of whom she recognized. One was being held by his collar and was slightly rumpled, and more than slightly annoyed judging by the look on his face. The other was a man who Jamie had hired to keep an eye on the house until such time as he felt it was safe to pull him off—which might be the twelfth of never, to quote an old song, considering how hard her heart was hammering. The first man was a detective who had briefly interviewed her in the hospital before Tomas had abruptly ejected him from the room. Neither her heart nor her blood pressure was reassured by the sight of him here now.

"It's all right," she nodded at Jamie's man. "He can come in, I know who he is. Detective Holroyd," she said, addressing the policeman, and with the utterance of his name, letting him know she remembered who he was.

The detective stepped in through the door, looking slightly relieved to be free of his erstwhile captor, and removed his shoes. He wore a pair of boldly chequered socks, which lent his dark suit a bit of flash.

"Please take a seat," she said, polite but making it clear he was in no way welcome.

As detectives went he was young, which was always a bit worrisome because it meant he was also very ambitious and likely keen to make a name for himself.

He sat at the table, a neutral expression on his face, his suit slightly rumpled from the contretemps outside, and his hair a gleaming model of what a civil servant's hair should be—not a strand out of place, even if the comb marks were still visible in it. She remembered him from the hospital as a rather pointed questioner—not partisan, rather just someone who wanted to get at the truth—which made him entirely dangerous to her right now.

"I believe my lawyer told you he would need to be present from here on out."

He raised his eyebrows. "Yes, I do remember him saying as much. However this is about another matter entirely, though I guess in a roundabout way it is connected."

"What other matter might that be?" she asked, though she feared she knew. She sat opposite the detective; her knees were shaking and she felt suddenly weak.

"I'm looking into the disappearance of Constable Blackwood. You knew him, I believe?"

Dear God, it *was* what she'd feared. And now that horrible soft rabbity panic was beating in her chest—the same panic she'd felt almost every day since she'd been rescued from that house of horrors. She felt about as brave as a cornered rabbit too, frozen here in her kitchen, still in her dressing gown, with her hair unkempt and milk leaking from her breasts to soak the front of her nightgown.

Pru came into the kitchen just then, holding a freshly clothed Kathleen. She pulled out a chair and sat down right beside Pamela, her sea-blue eyes fixed on the policeman with a polite hostility. Pamela wanted to grab the girl's hand in utter gratitude, for Pru's steady and unflinching presence had the effect of shoring her up immensely.

"I've called Mr. Egan; he'll be here directly. Mrs. Riordan, perhaps you'd like to go upstairs and change. Surely the detective has the manners to wait while you do that, being that he's arrived without notice. I'll make him tea while you're gone." The New England ice in her voice conveyed a fine frost over the entire room, and Pamela thought the detective would be lucky if his tea was served without a side of arsenic.

Upstairs, she took a breath and changed into clean panties and bra, put the soft flannel pads, which she used to guard against leaks, into the cups of the bra, and then washed her face, and brushed out her hair, tying it back in a no-nonsense ponytail. She took a moment before going back down the stairs, to try to calm the storm in her chest. The blood of panic was thumping through her entire body though, and she knew there was little she could do to calm it. She would just have to bluff her way through until Tomas arrived.

Downstairs, the detective was thumbing through his notepad as though he was gathering his thoughts, but she thought it was merely a ruse and that he knew exactly what he wanted to ask without needing to refer back to non-existent notes.

She flicked a glance at Pru, and then settled at the table beside the girl. A hot mug of tea had been set at her place, small wisps of steam escaping from it into the morning light.

The detective cleared his throat and then launched into the first of his questions.

"I believe you had dealings with Constable Blackwood?"

The panic was swooshing through her veins so hard now that it felt like her pulse was a fast drumbeat in her ears. Small black spots were dancing in her vision, and she wondered if a person could actually faint from panic.

"Yes, I was," she said, remembering Tomas' strict admonition to answer with as few words as possible. 'Give the bastards as little as possible while ye're waitin' on the cavalry to arrive.'

"Are you aware that the constable disappeared in June of '77?" The detective had schooled the Belfast out of his voice, but she could hear it in the undernotes, that hard accent with its clipped consonants.

"Yes, I believe I remember reading about it in the papers," she said, careful not to let fear into her voice.

"It's our understanding that the night before he disappeared he was witnessed in a car, following a woman who was on foot, through certain streets in Belfast."

"Oh?" Pamela said, trying to sound faintly disinterested.

"The witness went on to say that they saw the woman slip out of an alleyway some time later, after the car with the constable and his friends left. They felt she must have hidden somewhere in that alleyway and then, when the men didn't find her, managed to make her escape."

"I'm not sure I understand what this has to do with me," Pamela said, her chest so tight suddenly that she was amazed she could actually get the words out in such a calm fashion.

"I've done a little digging and it appears you were in Belfast that evening." He made a show of checking his notepad again. "You attended a wedding where you were the photographer, I believe."

"I'd have to check my appointment book. I'd have to know which wedding you're referring to. If I was though, I would have taken the pictures and then driven home. I certainly wasn't hiding from a gang of men, in an alleyway. Had I been, I'm certain I would remember it."

Even as she spoke the words, she was suddenly there in that alley, desperately searching for a place to hide, certain with every fibre of her being that she was about to die. Die in a horrific fashion—tortured, raped and then disposed of like all the other victims to whom the constable and his gang had dealt death. Flashes of the workhouse mingled in with the stench of the pipe she'd crawled into, and the feeling of the rat she'd shared the space with, breathing its small fetid breath on her neck. The workhouse—Noah's screams, his blood drenching her clothes, his hand slipping from hers as he left her there alone, so horribly alone. She could still hear his final words echoing in her ears—*I'm just counting the stars.* The words had come with long gaps, where his breath stuttered and his grip on life slowly slid away. Her fingers curled under in her lap, as though she were trying to grasp him again, keep him safe and present, even as she felt the blood between her fingers, causing their hands to slip apart. It was as though the cozy homeliness of her kitchen had melted away, and there was only blood, pain and terror. She fumbled in the pocket of her pants for the hair pin she'd put there. She kept one on her person at all times. It was a tactic one of the doctors had suggested to her—to focus her mind during panic by the simple trick of inflicting a little bit of pain on herself. She jammed the pin into her thigh, hoping it would stop the sensation of falling into a pit from which she might never emerge.

"Isn't that so, Pamela?" Pru said, and touched her lightly on her knee. It was enough to jolt her into the here and now, where she realized her breathing was ragged and that a fine dew of sweat had broken out on her forehead. She felt sick, and was afraid for one brief moment that she might throw up in front of the detective. Which would certainly not look like the action of an innocent woman.

"I'm sorry," she said, realizing she had missed whatever it was Pru had said.

"I was just saying to the detective that you've come over funny a few times since the birth—and no wonder all things considered. The doctors said she's not to have any stress, so I'm afraid you'll have to leave, Mr.—" Pru let the word hang, to indicate that she couldn't recall his name. Being that Prudence had a memory like a steel trap, Pamela knew it was meant as a slight. The detective merely narrowed his eyes at the girl, but he didn't press further on that particular topic. However, he did have another matter he wished to discuss.

"It's my understanding that you were also acquainted with a Special Branch agent—one Andrew Davison?"

"If by acquainted you mean he broke into my house, stole money and attempted to blackmail me more than once, then yes I was acquainted with him."

The last night she'd seen the agent, he'd begged her to kill him, but that too, was information the detective didn't need. Davison had tried to goad her into the act, to spare himself what he knew was coming at the hands of Noah and his men. He had thought a woman would have more mercy; he had been wrong.

"He too disappeared. I did wonder if you ever saw him with Mr. Murray?"

"No, I didn't. My encounters with Mr. Davison consisted of the things I've already mentioned."

He then spent some time jotting things down on his notepad, though Pamela suspected he might be merely writing out his grocery list. The act was meant to unnerve her because there was no detail she had given him which he didn't already know. He finished with a flourish and then snapped the notebook shut, though not before she saw the words, *'pick up dry cleaning, tuna for cat, get hair trimmed.'* Somehow this worried her more than if he'd taken her words down verbatim. He wanted to scare her, but to what end?

"That's all for now, Mrs. Riordan, but I may have more questions as my investigation advances."

She nodded, not being capable of more than that at present. Her throat had gone dry, and she knew if she tried to speak it would come out as little more than a croak. Pru being indefatigable even at the most stressful of times, spoke for her.

"I think from here on out you should call Mr. Egan first if you have any more questions for Mrs. Riordan."

He stood, every hair still in place, though he appeared slightly frustrated with her lack of answers.

He turned back at the door and gave Pamela a level look. "Surely, you can understand why we would want to question you? He wasn't kind to you, was he, the constable? In fact, I can see why it's possible that you would have wanted him dead, why you may have wished Agent Davison gone too. Noah Murray was certainly a man who could easily make those things happen for you."

"I'm not in the habit of asking men to kill people for me," she said, having found her voice. Strictly speaking this was true, as she had never outright asked Noah to have either man killed, though she'd wanted it, and he'd understood that. And then he'd simply had it done.

"No? All right then, I'd best be on my way," he said, with a sudden false friendliness, though the effort came across a little like a bunny that smiles only to reveal it has fangs.

She stood at the window watching him, until he got in his car and pulled out of the drive. Pru came and stood beside her, taking Pamela's hand in hers and giving it a squeeze of reassurance.

"Thank you, Pru. Did you really call for Tomas?"

"I did, but he wasn't in the office. I didn't think the detective needed to know that, however. Now, I'm going to get you and the children some breakfast. You go sit down, I think this one," she kissed Kathleen's forehead, "wants feeding."

Pamela took the baby in her arms and sat in the rocking chair to feed her. In the kitchen, Pru started making breakfast for the children and Pamela watched the girl as she moved about the room, cutting bread and cheese and putting the kettle on the hob to boil. For someone who'd only been on the earth for not quite nineteen years, she had a self-possession that was a little awe-inspiring. The weak morning sunlight touched the girl, setting her hair alight and gilding her face, which was smooth and flushed with the heat from the Aga. Jamie had chosen well when he'd hired her as a nanny for Kolya, and now for Kathleen. Just her presence was steadying, like an even-keeled boat that the most ferocious of storms couldn't move from its path. Pamela was utterly grateful for the girl's presence, for she had the sense that the entire interview could have become something much worse without Pru.

She took a few deep breaths, attempting to still her rapidly beating heart. She didn't want the baby to feel her agitation and get upset. Nothing of this, none of the darkness, none of the fear and worry was going to touch her children anymore if there was any way for her to prevent it. Conor had already been through too much. Isabelle, fortunately, was of an age where she was mostly blissfully unaware.

She bared one breast and got Kathleen situated to feed, and then leaned back into the chair, feeling the prickling of nerves all along her skin. It wasn't even nine o'clock yet and she was already exhausted. The panic attacks did that—left her feeling flattened, as though she'd been run down by an enormous rock. The doctors had assured her such feelings were normal, and perhaps they were. But the shape of her life had changed so much over these last few years, that sometimes she barely recognized it as hers. There had been so many days since Casey had disappeared when she had felt that she willed herself through each hour, each day, each month and now each year. It felt like trying to breathe in a strange medium, something thick like tar, meant for some slow-moving ancient monster, and not a woman who felt exceedingly fragile most days.

At times it felt that her life was no longer known—like looking into the face of someone who'd once been beloved, and finding that she did not recognize him. And so she had made the conscious choice to love that which was no longer familiar. One had to choose to love the stranger's face each and every day, and this she would do, because quite simply, there was no other choice to be had.

Chapter Five

Make a Wish

EVENINGS WITH JAMIE had become a ritual for them since Kathleen's birth, one which they all looked forward to. Tonight it was a scene of some chaos, with all the children present: Conor, Isabelle, and a rare but very welcome visit from Kolya. Kolya, whom none of them had seen since Violet's return that fateful morning in Paris.

Isabelle had yelled *"Koly!"* in pure joy at seeing her vanquished playmate once again upon the field. Kolya had responded in kind, promptly dropping the things he'd brought with him—toys, his blue wool coat, and a stuffed mermaid which Pamela suspected he'd brought as a gift for his new sister. He ran to where Isabelle stood and treated her to one of his uncompromising Russian hugs.

"Nikolai, your shoes," Jamie said, and then laughed as Kolya simply took them off where he stood and kept moving. Jamie picked up the shoes and put them by the door, then retrieved the mermaid, which was, indeed, for Kathleen. Composed of scraps of azure and turquoise silks, the doll had knots of fine red woolen hair, netted with tiny pearls.

"He picked it out himself, because of the red hair," Jamie said, glancing over at his son, who was already on the floor with Conor, building blocks littering the floor all around the two of them.

"It's lovely. I'll be sure to thank him later, when he's less distracted."

"That could be hours," Jamie said. "He's missed Conor and Isabelle terribly."

"They've missed him too, but I think Isabelle made that very clear."

She looked at the children, making sure they were well occupied before she spoke her next words.

"A detective was here yesterday," she said, keeping her voice light so as not to alert Conor that they were discussing something serious.

Jamie gave her a considering look. "Was Tomas here?"

"No, but I called him after and filled him in."

"Did it seem," Jamie asked quietly, "as though the detective was trying to catch you off guard?"

"A little, yes. He wanted to talk about Constable Blackwood," she said, glancing over at Conor, relieved to see that he was blissfully absorbed in building an airplane with Kolya. "They asked if I thought Noah was involved in his disappearance."

"And was he?" Jamie asked, his voice so low she could barely hear him, but knew what he'd asked all the same. Jamie had long been trained to keep his voice below the level which a recording device would pick up.

She merely looked at him, over the head of their child. She knew he'd always suspected, and found that now she could no longer keep the truth from him. The green eyes with which she was so familiar in all their variety of moods—freezing scorn, fury, laughter and most often these last few years, love—were at present, alight with understanding. He knew—he had always known—he had merely asked her to confirm, which she had just done with her silence. The original lie she had told him was because she didn't want the constable's death touching him. Now it was far too late for such measures, and indeed, she had been foolhardy in thinking that she was sparing this man anything.

"Before he died, Noah told me he'd been working for Special Branch," she said, joggling Kathleen a little as Jamie started the water running for her bath. The sound of the sink filling would cover over anything they said.

This time the eyes betrayed shock. "What?" he said, rolling up one sleeve and sticking his elbow in the water to check the temperature.

"He said they'd fixed a lot of things for him, looked the other way with the gun-running and smuggling. He said he was certain that Casey's disappearance and death was at least partly on his hands because he thought they may have thrown Casey to the wolves in order to keep Noah's cover."

"Did he know what had happened to Casey?" Jamie asked.

"No, he didn't. He was really just assuming."

Jamie shook his head. "David would never have sacrificed Casey, and he was the only person who knew that he was feeding Casey the names of targets. He wouldn't have told his higher-ups, I'd bet my life on that. He kept Casey and Pat out of all his reports, that much I know for fact."

She didn't ask *how* he knew that for fact, for if Jamie wanted to get his hands on something, classified or otherwise, he was usually able to do so. He looked slightly troubled by the news she'd just delivered. She'd debated on whether or not to tell him, as the information had come to her by way of No-ah's deathbed confession.

"But what if…" she began and then hesitated.

"No, Pamela, I'm certain what he told you about is the extent of what he was doing. I don't believe Casey was in any deeper than he said he was."

"But there was the money I found in the cupboard. I still don't know where that came from, or why he had it."

"That I can't answer, but I looked into every angle when he went missing, he wasn't involved with British forces beyond David. If he was, I couldn't find even the smallest hint of it. What he did, he did to save lives, don't let doubt tarnish your memory of him."

"I just think that—" she began, but was interrupted by Isabelle.

"Mama, look—bubbles!" Isabelle said, and Pamela turned to find her daughter clutching a bubble hoop, with Kathleen's baby soap—which she'd just made this morning—dripping from her hands.

"Here, Isa-bit, let's put this up and make a few bubbles," Jamie said, taking in the look on Pamela's face. She sighed gratefully and set to readying Kathleen for her bath.

A few minutes later the kitchen was filled with floating iridescent orbs, glittering dizzily as they caught every draft of air. The soap had been put away discreetly while Isabelle chased about the kitchen clapping at bubbles and laughing as they popped. Jamie then joined Pamela at the sink, taking Kathleen from her and gently placing her in the bath. He cupped the baby's head in his right hand, and took a soft cloth, drizzled with a little soap, in his left.

It was a cozy scene—the children playing at the far end of the kitchen now, Finbar stretched out by the hearth emitting a low rumbling snore, and Jamie speaking lovely nonsense to his daughter while Kathleen cooed up at him. To see Jamie so filled her with happiness. What it might mean to him to be able to love a child of his without trepidation or fear, she thought she knew. These evenings consisted of moments carefully carved out, like the most delicate calligraphy inside an oyster shell, and she knew to treasure each one as it passed. Jamie looked over just then and smiled at her, as though sensing her thoughts.

A bubble floated down between them, like sugar blown fine and thin, drifting through the gold of the firelight. She reached up a hand and it settled, feather-light, on the tips of her fingers.

"Make a wish," she said, before she could think about the wisdom of such light words.

He blew the bubble off her hand and it floated across the room, a rainbow of colours caught inside of it. It continued, soundless and luminous, to the ceiling of the room, where it landed, shimmering, on a beam, before disappearing with a soundless *pop*.

"What did you wish for?" she asked.

Jamie laughed and flicked a few suds at her. "You're not meant to ask that."

"When has that ever stopped me?" She dipped her fingers in the bathwater and flicked a few suds back at him.

"Never," he said, but smiled as if he didn't mind this trait of hers in the least.

They simply stood quiet for a moment then—Jamie's hand still cupping the back of the baby's head, while her tiny feet, each joint like a miniature pearl, kicked at the milk-warm water—drinking in the sight of their daughter with the absorption of smitten parents.

Moments like these were wonderfully soothing and Pamela could feel the warmth and peace of it purling through her blood, healing the invisible fractures and cuts of the last few years. She watched Jamie as he caught the baby's feet and kissed them, and felt his joy in this beautiful child. There was, despite the worries about Kathleen's health, no hesitancy in his emotion. He had given himself over to this child with a whole heart, and it gave her a sense of profound gratitude to see it.

Kathleen, despite maternal bias, Pamela thought, *was* a beautiful baby: hair like wisps of saffron silk, curling up around the small face, still with its silver trace of down touching the brow; and the green eyes—green as the matting of a merrow's cave—outlined with astonishingly thick lashes, the colour of red-gold embers. Small fronded fingers paddled the water, spiking it into tiny crystalline wavelets. A sudden smile creased one corner of her mouth, and while someone other than a mother might claim it was trapped air, Pamela knew better, and saw the sweet curve, made topsy-turvy by a sucking blister, for what it was—pure, undiluted baby joy.

Jamie laughed in response to the smile, and Kathleen kicked her feet harder, splashing both parents with warm lavender-scented water. He spoke then, and though he still looked down at the baby, his words were for her.

"You asked what I wished for," he said.

"I did. You don't have to oblige my curiosity, though."

"I wished for this—just this exact moment—that, regardless of what may or may not come to pass, we will be able to hold this moment, and all the others like it, forever."

"It seems almost impossible," she said in response. "All the sorrow of the last few years, and then to have something wonderful come from it."

"The liquid drops of tears that you have shed shall come again, transform'd to orient pearl," Jamie quoted softly.

"Well, *you* can take the pearl out of the water," Pamela said. "She howls like a banshee when I do it."

Kathleen loved to be in the water, even when it started to turn cold, and would protest violently when Pamela tried to remove her. When her father took her out though, she was as passive as a lamb in a field of clover.

"There's something I'd like to discuss with you," Jamie said, putting Kathleen over his shoulder, now wrapped snugly in a warm towel.

"Yes?" She turned, alerted by his tone that the matter was something serious.

"I'd like to have her christened."

"Yes, I had assumed we'd be doing that," she said, slightly puzzled.

"I'd like to go to the monastery. I think, all things considered Pamela, it might be best for us to have a small private christening. Just us and our daughter, and our few nearest and dearest. If we invite everyone, we have to include Violet, and I don't see that being a comfortable situation for anyone. In fact, I think it might be rather miserable for all concerned. We can have a gathering later, where everyone is invited. This part though is sacred, and I'd like to keep it that way. Nor do I want to cause anyone pain around the simple act of having Kathleen christened."

"Will you tell her?" she asked. Jamie never spoke of Violet unless she asked him a direct question about her.

"Yes, I'll tell her, I think it's only fair, but as she dropped back into my life like a bomb she will have to give me some leeway in how I choose to deal with her."

There were times she thought she might actually explode from curiosity over what Jamie's home life was like currently. Somehow though she knew he didn't want to talk about Violet at all. His time here, with Kathleen was something sacred to him, and she wanted her home to be as inviolate for him as possible during this short stretch while Kathleen was still so new.

The rest of the evening passed in a lovely haze of laughter and talk with the children. Pamela sat down to give Kathleen her last feed before bed, and Jamie got the children into their pyjamas and then read to them on the kitchen sofa. Both Isabelle and Kolya fell to sleep there, and Conor stayed awake awhile longer, his curly head turned up toward Jamie as the two of them had a long talk about something. She wondered what it was. Conor had been worrying over her since her return home. She feared that he felt he needed to protect her, and that he was upset over not having done so the night she was taken by the mad Elspeth. Jamie was very good at listening and reassuring Conor though, so she left them to it.

After, Jamie stayed and they had a cup of tea together. She scrambled up some eggs, made toast and fried up yesterday's ham for him as well, for she knew he often forgot to eat. She put the food in front of him, and then sat down with a sigh. It gave her a deep pleasure to see a man eat when he was hungry, and so she merely watched Jamie until he put the last bite in his mouth, and washed it down with what was left of his tea.

When he was done, he fixed her with a worried look. "If the police come back again, Pamela, I think it's best if you don't speak to them at all until Tomas is with you. Tell them they can talk to you in an official setting, but not in your home any more. I don't like the idea of them being here when you're alone. If they are talking to you about Blackwood, then there's a larger agenda here."

She shivered a little, for Jamie's words echoed what she'd felt herself—that the police visit wasn't just about one of their colleagues disappearing, but about something bigger—something that might end with her in a great deal of trouble from which it would be difficult to extricate herself. There was little more to say on the matter though, and so she switched gears to another topic, so that she might say something she'd needed to for some time now.

"I want to thank you for everything, Jamie. For these last three years, and all the searching you've done on my behalf trying to find out what happened to Casey. I want you to know how much I appreciate it because I know you asked even when it became clear the effort was fruitless."

"Not entirely fruitless if it gave you any peace of mind. I will continue, Pamela, but only if you want me to. Just know that not every file is open for my perusal, and not everyone is willing to talk to me. I have to tread lightly, because I'm not going in heavy-handed when the blowback could hit you and the children. You know what a spiderweb this country is. If I touch the wrong thread and set it thrumming, it could alert all sorts of predators and bring them out to bite. If it was just me, I'd take that risk, but I will not risk you and the children."

She reached across and took his hand. "I know that, Jamie. I wasn't meaning that you needed to look into this further. What Noah told me is just weighing on me. I'm beginning to understand that I likely won't ever have an answer to what happened to Casey, but it's never going to sit well with me."

"I know that, Pamela, and I would do anything to make that go away for you, but I have dug deep on this to no avail."

"We need you to be safe too, Jamie. All of us, so let it be," she said. "It's time for me to come to a certain acceptance of the things I cannot control."

"Sometimes I think that's life in a nutshell—finding acceptance for the things we can't control."

After that they spoke of less weighty things: Conor's rebellion against homework, the household prohibition on chewing gum until Isabelle saw fit to quit storing gobs of it under her pillow, the shed roof which had blown half off during the last storm, and whether Kathleen was gaining weight quickly enough to satisfy her doctors.

After he left she readied herself for bed, going through the small rituals that comprised a mother's bed time: making certain all the windows and doors were locked, that the dog had fresh water, that Conor's lunch was ready for the mad rush of getting out to the bus on time, and that everything was tidied away so that the morning didn't have any extra obstacles to it beyond that of taking care of three young children. As she did all these things she found herself thinking about what Jamie had said about the acceptance of things they could not control. She thought the phrase meant much more to Jamie than just a statement of fact about his search for Casey's fate. It applied to their own situation as well. There was little he could do right now to change course, and she knew it. What Jamie wanted and his sense of honour about what he must do rarely came together in his life.

After his last visit, Tomas—with his usual lack of subtlety—had asked why she didn't press Jamie on the topic of their relationship.

"He loves you, girl, not that intruder he's got livin' in his house. You an' his son, an' these ones," he'd nodded at Conor, Isabelle and Kathleen, "are his family, an' he's yers. Press him on it."

She could, she knew, do just that—ask him, press him on it. Jamie had always given her the truth, when she wanted it. But for now, when she felt so fragile, and with Kathleen being so new, she just wanted peace and for Jamie to love this wee girl, without any fetters or demands on him beyond that. And she knew the truth—this man loved her, loved her children, and would do anything he could to keep them all safe and secure. If he did not speak, she thought she knew the reason for it, and knew the fault for that lay with her and not with Jamie.

For now what they had was enough; though she knew, that one day in the not too distant future, it wouldn't be—not for Jamie, and not for her.

Chapter Six

Travelling Man

KOLYA HAD SLEPT all the way home, and Jamie had merely carried him to bed, removed his shoes and coat and left the boy to his dreams. Around him the house was quiet, Maggie long gone to her rest and Violet in Paris for a few days. He was grateful for the quiet, for the space between leaving Pamela's house and returning to his own was never quite long enough to adequately make the transition from the man he was with her and the children, to the man he needed to be to deal with the situation within his own walls.

In the kitchen, he made himself a pot of tea and took it to the study, along with a cup and a bit of milk. It was late, but he wanted a moment to simply sit and let the traces of his time with Pamela and all the children linger a little upon him. It wasn't uncommon to feel this way—as though he'd left home rather than returned to it. Pamela and the children were family and had been for some time, but having Kathleen had served to forge those links into an even stronger bond. Had he a choice right now, he would have swept them all into his care and brought them to live here, in his house upon the hill.

Except, at times it felt to him that he was a stranger in his home now, despite knowing every inch of its structure, its particular nooks and crannies, the slope of the floors, the way the light looked against his bedroom wall first thing in the morning, and the sounds the house made late at night. His house had long been his refuge, but of late it felt more like an armed camp, where the enemy lived within the walls.

Despite all his years of spy work he wasn't suspicious by nature, and tended to trust with a certain amount of reserve until a person showed him why he shouldn't. Mind you, it wasn't that Violet hadn't done plenty to make him wary—wives who turned out to be KGB agents tended to sow a fair deal of distrust in their wake.

One thing had been abundantly clear; whatever love he had once had for her was gone. He had felt some guilt over it but not enough he thought, to take up a life with her.

Vanya had been blunt about it. "It's not any lack in you, Yasha, it's the simple phenomenon of camp love; you love who you can while you can. This is not so unusual. When you have choice though it's different—your heart goes where it will, and knows its home just as a bird knows to which bough it belongs. I believed you loved Violet as much as you could, but still it was camp love and she turned out to be a traitor. Once you were free to love, your heart returned to its place of home."

Vanya was right, his heart had returned to its place of belonging, and for three bittersweet days in Paris it had known what it was to love fully and without boundary. It was a privilege he'd known only briefly in his life—for a time with his first wife, Colleen, before the babies had begun to arrive and then to die, and with Pamela while they had occupied small islands of time and space over these last three years.

The sticking point, of course, was Kolya, who did not know his mother and had not warmed to her beyond the most basic interactions which he might have had with anyone. It was a source of both frustration and pain for Violet, and while Jamie sympathized with this he also felt it was his job to keep Kolya safe and comfortable. At four years of age, Kolya had the self-possession of a Cossack who has just ransacked a village—and so his lack of ease with Violet was both telling and a source of worry for Jamie, who had always trusted the instincts of small children and dogs.

It was in the midst of these ruminations that a loud knock sounded on the glass closest to where he sat, causing him to jump and slop a bit of hot tea on his pants before sending the cup tumbling to the floor. He cursed out loud, wishing he still had a pistol in a holster under his desk. However, Kolya tended to crawl under all the furniture and he'd felt it wisest to lock the gun away.

The face at the window was both grotesque and familiar—grotesque because its owner had pushed it up against the window and was grinning at him, with a smile that was more gum than tooth. Familiar because he had known this man for many years. Teddy—which likely meant trouble of some sort was about to show up on his doorstep, or at his study window, as it were.

"Jesus Christ almighty, man, were you trying to give me a heart attack?" Jamie said, opening the door into the little garden and stepping out, heart still hammering madly.

"For a spy, you're a wee bit jumpy, James."

"Spies are the most paranoid people on the planet, as you have cause to know," Jamie retorted, tone acerbic from the jolt his adrenaline had taken.

"Aye, that's true. I've got a fire goin' just down the hill. Come an' have a drink with me," he said, and then added in response to Jamie's look, "be civil, it costs ye nothin', an' I've a mind for somethin' hot to warm my bones."

"Fine," Jamie said, "just give me a minute." He went back inside to grab a sweater and shoes before returning to the garden, which was already glowing with the night's first bite of frost. He looked back through the study window with regret; the fire there was burning nicely and there was still tea steaming in the pot.

He followed Teddy down the hill into a hollow usually used by Yevgena as a place to park her wagon when she came to visit.

From the rear the man looked a proper shambles, with holes in his clothes, (which he always wore in several layers—canvas, denim, flannel, and wool) so that his attire resembled a patchwork quilt of various cloth and colour.

In the depths of the hollow the campfire glowed like an autumn chrysanthemum, darkness pooling around it in lapping waves. To the left was the piece of canvas the man used as shelter as well as the bits and bobs of the itinerant life: a small smoke blackened cauldron with a triangular handle affixed to it, in which was brewed everything from coffee to herbal remedies; a tin mug, a fork, spoon and knife slotted together, remnants of Teddy's former military life. A deerstalker hat—so old and disreputable that it looked like the molting skin of a raccoon hung over a bush—and a blanket roll tied with twine, which sat neatly inside the canvas shelter.

The cauldron with coffee in it was set upon the fire and there were potatoes smoking in the coals. Teddy sat down and took off his boots, emptying each one of a day's worth of tramping. Small bits of leaf and twig hopped into the fire and a cloud of dust arose when he beat each boot upon the ground before stretching his feet out—arrayed in three layers of woolen socks, red, blue and green and rife with holes—toward the flames. The unwrapping of his person began then—the removal of a layer or two, the shaking out and folding of each article, laid aside for the night or to be put back on if the air was particularly chilly.

Though he had known Teddy for many years now, he had never gleaned more than the basic details of his life. He didn't know where he was from, nor where he holed up when the winter descended. He didn't know if he'd ever had a profession, or whether he cared to have one. The one detail Teddy had let slip when he'd been deep in the drink one night, was that he'd once been a soldier. "I started walkin' after the war, an' then I just kept goin', haven't stopped since. I's a tramp, no more, no less."

Originally tramp had meant 'long and toilsome walk' which certainly applied to a man who had—as far as Jamie could ascertain—been walking for the last three decades of his life.

He'd come upon Teddy on his land one day, many years before, seated before a fire and making himself coffee in a soup tin with a welded-on handle. What had begun as a mild confrontation with a trespasser had culminated with Jamie having a cup of coffee with him, and then inviting him up to the house for a meal. During that first breaking of bread he'd learned that the man's name was Theodore, though he preferred Teddy, and that he'd walked all over Europe and the Americas, cadging a bit of work where he could and sleeping rough in all manner of places.

Jamie always offered him a bed and a meal, and while Teddy would take the meal with thanks he always refused the bed, instead holing up somewhere on the property with his roll of blankets and his bit of canvas for cover.

Many years ago now, Jamie had offered him a bit of work carrying messages—ones committed to memory, for Jamie never put anything on paper beyond stories and legal documents if he could help it. For the first six months of Teddy's employ he'd fed him false messages and laid deliberate traps so that he'd know if Teddy was indiscreet, or willing to sell his services to others for information he'd gained from Jamie. But he'd been utterly dependable and loyal for the entirety of that time and so Jamie had made it a long-term arrangement. It accomplished two things in his view—his messages arrived by a courier whom none would ever suspect and he knew the man had a small but steady income to keep him in boots and groceries.

Teddy could not be hurried, and so if he had information a man had to wait until the coffee was drunk and the potatoes eaten before said information would be passed along. Jamie drank the coffee with some trepidation, as he was never too certain what dark tincture might have been boiled in the pot before it returned to its main occupation of coffee kettle, and accepted a roasted potato, carefully peeling away the charred skin, and pulling apart the smoking meat of it. He wasn't hungry, as Pamela had just fed him, but he ate it for courtesy's sake. He'd learned the hard way that Teddy took offense if his drink and vittles were refused.

And so it was that Jamie, slightly overfull and with a thin twig stuck between two teeth—a remnant of the coffee, which had tasted distinctly gritty—waited patiently while Teddy rubbed off his utensils with the bottom of his shirt, changed his socks from day to his 'sleep woolens' and then, emitting a loud belch, stretched his feet out again so they almost touched the flames, and at last conveyed the words he'd brought with him over hill and dale, through sleet and snow.

"Mordecai wants to see ye. He's set a meeting for the usual place—wherever that might be—next month."

Jamie felt a jolt at that news. It had been a very long time since Mordecai had summoned him to a meeting. They'd agreed some time ago that it was best to keep their contact to a minimum unless it was an emergency. What contact they did have was achieved off the espionage grid, as Jamie was all too aware how closely they were both watched by the higher ups at MI6. Still, it had been years, and Mordecai's reemergence now likely wasn't a herald of good news.

"And that's all he said?" Jamie asked, though he knew that Mordecai, surly old bastard that he was, didn't waste words on anyone, not even his former pupil.

"Aye, that's all he said."

He would have to go, though he was loathe to leave Pamela and the children just now. He knew she wasn't coping anywhere near as well as she wanted him to believe.

"Maggie did say as you've a wee girl now, only newly born."

"I do," Jamie said.

"Is it Pamela that's the mother?" Teddy asked, displaying his rather fearsome ability to suss news in the manner of a dog seeking truffles. He only needed a thread of scent to sniff out what was going on.

"Yes, she is the mother."

"She's a true lady, an' those don't come along every day. She were right good to me when you were gone those years in Russia. Always made certain I'd warm clothes and a warm meal, an' a bit of silver in my palm on my way out the door. Will ye marry her then?" he asked, fixing Jamie with a look like that of an errant knight whose only code is chivalry to the fairer sex.

Jamie, wondering why he felt the need to explain, nevertheless did just that, keeping the details circumspect and knowing that nothing he said painted him in a heroic light.

Teddy wore a look of bemusement by the time he was done. "Hmm, so the gist of it is that ye live with the one ye married, but don't love, an' have a child with the one ye do love, but didn't marry."

"I suppose that is a fair summation," Jamie said drily.

"Well," Teddy said dubiously, scratching his belly through a circuitous hole in his layers, "I guess yer honour's intact, at least, though it's not a virtue known to keep a man warm at night."

Which was, Jamie thought, a rather succinct summation of his current situation.

After that, they spoke of general things—how the winter had been mild so far, which wool was best for keeping fungus away from a man's feet during the damp months—merino was their agreed choice—and whether or not vodka, applied internally through the ear canal was an effective cure for earache, a malady which Teddy often suffered from.

It was late when he bid Teddy goodbye and began the walk up the hill towards the house. The night was cold and the heat of the fire faded quickly from both clothes and skin. He was tired and longed for his bed, though the mere thought of it brought back Teddy's words about honour not keeping a man warm through the night. In his mind's eye Pamela's face rose as she told him to make a wish on that trembling bubble she'd held in her palm. He had told her the truth when he said he'd wished only to hold that moment, while on another level he'd thought that the bubble—transient and fragile—was a good metaphor for where they now stood; their relationship an amorphous sort of thing which they were both too afraid to define. Pamela for reasons very different than his own.

Honour, he reflected, might be a virtue, but it tasted like ashes in a man's mouth.

Chapter Seven

Awake and Dreaming

'I HEAR THE LARK *and the lark hears me,*' Pamela sang to herself, continuing on with the lullaby she had begun for Kathleen, as she made her way down the stairs into the warmth of the kitchen. *'Singing from the leaves of the old oak tree…'*

She paused to deposit a basket of laundry on the floor, hoping she would manage to get it washed, dried and put away before the indefatigable Pru returned from her days off. Kathleen was snugly asleep in her bassinette, and so she had a little time to attend to a few of the other demands of life.

'Oh let the lark that sings to me, sing to the one I love.'

It was a song she had sung to all her babies, even wee Deirdre, her first child with Casey. It still hurt to think of her at times, lying thousands of miles away across the sea, under the cold winter snows of Boston. She wondered if someone had sung it to her own self as a baby, maybe her father or one of the succession of nannies who'd helped to raise her.

'Over the mountains, over the sea, back where my heart is longing to be…'

She sniffed the air, reassuring herself that the scones she'd put in the oven before going upstairs hadn't yet begun to burn. Normally, she would put Kathleen in the cradle by the fire as she liked to keep her within sight. This afternoon, once her bookwork was done, she planned to have a quick whip-round with the Hoover though and didn't want it to wake the baby. She'd come so close to losing her to a madwoman, that she was still superstitious over the baby's safety, and knew it might be months before she could properly relax.

Kathleen, however, blissfully unaware of the events which had taken place during her last week in the womb, had settled in beautifully.

'Oh let the lark that sings to me, sing to the one I love…'

The words drifted away sounding slightly melancholy in tone. She looked out one of the kitchen windows at the sky. The day was a cold one and the odd snowflake drifted past the glass. Inside, it was warm and cozy with the fire lit and the Aga going full tilt, and yet she felt a sudden shiver run up her body. She had rarely been without company since she'd come home from the hospital, but today it was just her, Conor, and Kathleen. Isabelle was spending the day and night with Gert, and Pru had two days off and had gone into Belfast to visit with friends and would stay in the city for the nights. The girl, in pragmatic Maine fashion, had quickly found her footing in both city and countryside and already had a small group of friends with whom she spent her free days. While Pamela had longed for a bit of quiet, it suddenly felt too isolated here in the woods, though she had once loved this property for that very reason. It saddened her to know it wasn't likely she would ever recapture that sense of sanctuary she had once felt so strongly here. That was something she had been thinking about—whether to sell the property and move somewhere closer to a town or into the centre of one. And to consider that all this must be done on her own, and that she might well live alone for the rest of her life.

She breathed onto the window and drew three hearts there, putting her children's names inside. When the window frosted up, Conor and Isabelle would see them and be delighted. As the condensation melted away, a memory came, light-footed, to hover beside her. She'd been standing at this very window one night, ready for bed, but looking out at the night, where a quarter moon rode the sky, on a bed of drifting cloud. Her hands had rested on the mound of her belly, for she'd been six months along with Isabelle at the time. Casey had come up behind her and put his arms around her and then reached out a hand to the window. They'd had a sharp and unexpected late frost, and it had crept in under the window sills and put a light shimmer on the panes.

He drew their names together on the window, where the frost had settled fine as lace. He pressed his finger carefully, writing her name and then his. She pressed back against him, relishing the warmth of his body and turned her face up for a kiss. When she looked at the window again the frost had turned to water under the warmth of his touch.

"You've spelled my name wrong," she said, laughing.

"I haven't," he said, indignant, "it's only melted already."

He ran his hands over the round of her belly, and she felt the baby stir to his touch. She sighed and arched her spine, stretching her back and lifting her hands up to hold his.

"*What are ye thinkin' about?*" Casey asked, knowing the difference between her various quiet moods and when the quiet indicated that something was troubling her.

"*About the people who once lived here,*" she said, "*and all the things they experienced and the love they shared, gone now as though they never existed. Where does it go—all that love, all those moments?*"

Because he knew her better than any other, he answered the real question which she hadn't uttered out loud, but which he'd heard nevertheless.

"*It stays with us,*" Casey said softly, "*an' we hand it on to the next generation, just as the generation before did with us. I think it's always here, Jewel, an' it waits for the next person to take it, grasp it an' then one day release it. For now though, it's ours to hold for as long as we're able, an' then it will belong to Conor an' this one,*" he patted a small foot which kicked against his hand, "*an' through them it will go on.*"

She sighed. What he said made sense in the larger picture, but in the here and now she felt fragile, like a vase with a crack in it which was steadily widening over time, and so life and love felt fragile too.

"*It's never long enough, is it? No matter the time we get, and the love we have, it's never enough.*"

"*It makes me think of that quote from the Indian fellow—the one you told me last spring when we saw those blue butterflies all through the field we were walkin'.*"

'*The butterfly counts not months but moments and has time enough.*'

"*Aye, just so, darlin'. We're just blood an' love borne on butterfly wings. Nothin' endures but change.*"

"*Man's yesterday may be ne'er like his morrow; Nought may endure but Mutability,*" she said softly, for Shelley was always her touchstone in times when sorrow brushed her with its chill hand.

He kissed the top of her head, and then rested his cheek there, his stubble soft against her hair. "*That's true. He was a wise man, yer Shelley. For now though, my love, there is time enough.*"

They were silent then, standing in the night's embrace, the three of them connected by blood and love, and the fragile beat of a butterfly's wings.

She stepped back from the window, the memory had been so vivid that she half-expected Casey to be there behind her. Of course, he wasn't and never would be again. Their time had, indeed, not been long enough.

Sometimes she thought she ought to leave this house simply for that reason, so that she might cease dwelling in the land of memory. It wasn't healthy for her or the children.

"Pamela Riordan," she said sternly, "stop mooning about and get to work." The sound of her own voice snapped her out of her melancholy and she turned to face the pile of ledger books awaiting her on the table, neatly stacked and ready for the columns of numbers that needed to be entered and balanced. She would make a cup of tea and get down to work, while Kathleen slept. Conor was upstairs, happily occupied with his train set and would only come down when he got hungry.

While she waited for the kettle to boil, she drifted over to the shelf beside the stairs, pulled down her sketch-book, and leafed through it. She hadn't touched it in months, and she felt the pull of it suddenly, the want of a pencil in her hand and the flow of lines, both quick and slow, forming into something—a bee, a fairy, a piece of driftwood, Isabelle curled up asleep on the sofa with Rusty beside her. Her publisher had gently suggested that another volume of photos along with sketches as a follow-up to *Children of the Troubles* would be a good idea within the next six months, as the first one was selling surprisingly well.

Alas, she thought, turning her attention back to the stack of ledgers awaiting her attention, the construction business was not quite so straightforward. She had—painfully—acquired the knowledge of the business but she didn't have the passion for it that Casey had, that innate knowledge of wood and stone and earth that made for a truly great building, whether that building was the smallest of cottages or the grandest of public constructions hadn't mattered, he had made each of his projects a thing of beauty and sanctuary. When she had been engaged to Noah, she had given serious consideration to selling the business and she wondered now if she should just go ahead with that plan and devote herself fully to her photography and the books.

Ten minutes later she was well stuck into the ledgers, though half of her was listening for Kathleen's small cry, or for Conor to come rushing down the stairs looking for food. She glanced at the clock, five more minutes until the scones needed to come out of the oven. She realized then that Conor had come down to the landing on the staircase and was standing tip-toe on a three-legged stool looking through the octagonal window, which gave a view out over the yard.

"Be careful, I don't want you toppling off that thing," she said, knowing giving Conor a warning about potential bodily harm was about as useful as telling a bird not to fly.

"Mama, there's a man standing in the drive," Conor said, "he looks like he's lost."

"Hmm?" she was only half-listening, the numbers in the ledger book having snarled her thoughts into a mass of writhing snakes. She wanted to get the accounting done before Kathleen woke up and demanded her full attention.

"There's a man standing there, up where the tree fell down the day I was born," Conor said, his tone a touch impatient now. He always knew when she wasn't entirely focused on what he was saying. But now that the words reached

WHERE BUTTERFLIES DREAM • 61

her, she got up from the table, shoving the pencil with which she had been adding figures, behind her ear. It had better not be that bloody detective again.

She looked out the window up the long drive and saw the stump where the ash tree had, indeed, fallen the day Conor was born. There was, however, no man standing there now.

"I don't see anyone, sweetheart," she said, feeling a tad spooked. It was a thin day, the sort on which one might expect to see a ghost.

Conor heaved a sigh of impatience. "Mama, he's right there, he's walking down through the trees."

She looked again, along the line of Conor's slightly grubby hand and then froze in place. She couldn't breathe suddenly, and wondered if she was losing her mind.

"C-Conor, what does he look like to you?" she asked. Her son looked up at her, his eyes slightly grey just like his father's had been every time he was troubled.

"Mama?" he said, concern making his voice a wee bit higher.

"Conor, just tell me what he looks like to you," she repeated, aware that her own voice was scaling upward toward hysteria.

"He's big," he said, looking back at the tall figure who was now in the yard.

"Yes, he's big," she agreed faintly and went to the door, unable to feel her legs, breath stuck so hard in her chest that her lungs felt as though they were on fire. She lifted the latch and walked out through the door, certain there would be no one there, as there had been for so long now. She was afraid to look, afraid to open her eyes on an empty yard, or to find a man there who looked a good deal like another from a distance.

The yard was empty. She looked around wildly, trying to will the apparition back into being, for surely both she and Conor couldn't have hallucinated the figure coming down the drive, that tall man with the long strides and the dark hair. Her heart, beating wildly, plummeted in her chest. She was going mad; she was certain of it. And then she heard a soft sound, a man saying her name, as no man had said her name in three long years.

He was standing next to the byre, as if uncertain whether he should come any nearer. Standing there, tall, dark and with a presence like no other man in the world. She couldn't move, because she understood all too well how this played out—she would walk toward him and he would disappear, because she was certain now that she was dreaming, must be dreaming. And then he said her name again and shattered the still which surrounded them.

"Pamela?" His voice was hoarse, as though he hadn't spoken in a very long time.

She was moving, or at least she thought she was, for there was a strange aura around everything, as if her vision was drawing in. She could hear her son come out into the yard behind her, could hear him saying 'Mama' over and over in a panicked tone.

She kept walking and he was still there, still standing by the byre as if he was rooted to the earth.

"Am I awake?" Her voice was only a whisper, a thread so small that it was nearly inaudible.

"Aye, ye're awake, or we're dreamin' the same dream," he said, his own voice faint.

He stepped toward her, slowly, and she began to understand this was real, she *was* awake. Her son was standing behind her, her small boy who looked so very much like the man whose gaze was fixed upon him with such sadness and joy all mixed together.

"Conor?"

"Aye?" her son stepped up beside her, and took her hand, the mistrust in his voice evident. The man smiled, and tears came into his eyes.

"Ye'll have grown a great deal since I saw ye last."

"Ye know me?" Conor asked, and there was something way down in his voice, something frightened and angry at the same time, that told Pamela on some level, instinctual perhaps, he knew who this man was standing before him.

"Aye, I know ye, laddie. I was the first person to hold ye, even before yer mammy did."

Conor looked up at her, his eyes like smoke now, his hand clutching hers hard enough to bruise it. She was grateful for the pain though, as it was the only thing tethering her here, and making her believe this might all actually be real.

"Mama, who is he?"

She looked up at the man in question, her eyes dry and burning and saw the fear in his face struggling for primacy with a giddy joy, the mirror of which was roiling inside her own chest right now.

"He's your daddy," she said and then all the world went black.

She came around seconds later, vision slowly clearing to find two worried faces above her.

"Are ye all right, then?" Casey asked and she took a breath, spots still dancing at the edges of her vision. She sat up slowly, eyes glued to his face, still disbelieving this was real and that she wasn't having some particularly lucid daydream.

He reached out a hand but halted it inches from her, as though he was afraid to touch her. She was afraid too, but thought she might break down in front of him if she didn't touch him, didn't assure herself he was real, he was flesh. She put her hand out, palm up, and he reached back and took it in his.

Tears prickled at the top of her nose, just for the feel of that hand—big, strong and calloused—which had always been home to her.

"Will you come in the house with us?" she asked, not wanting to let go of his hand. Not wanting to take her eyes off him for even a second lest he dissipate, like the dream she still half-believed him to be, into the cold afternoon.

He nodded and she had the sense he wasn't quite capable of speech right now. He helped her to her feet and she looked at Conor, who stood with his eyes big as saucers, small fists clenched at his sides. She put her free hand out to him, but he shook his head, silent and clearly upset.

They walked in the house together, Conor going first and then turning in the doorway to give Casey a look which ought to have seared the ground beneath the man's feet.

Inside, the house was vaguely blurry and she wondered if it was shock, until she smelled the cause.

"Is there somethin' burnin?" Casey asked in a mild tone.

"Oh Lord, the scones," she said and ran to the oven. A great puff of smoke came rolling out as soon as she opened the door, the scones bearing a decided resemblance to charcoal. Conor, eyeing the big man in his kitchen warily, clambered up on the counter and opened the kitchen window.

"Smells like home," Casey said and smiled, and she smiled in return, sliding the scones into the garbage bin with one hand whilst waving smoke away with the other. A gust of cold air blew through the open window and alleviated the worst of the smoke.

There was a sudden ecstasy of grey wool in the kitchen as Finbar shot in from the outdoors through the door they'd forgotten to shut. He hit Casey like a rocket, causing him to stagger back while putting out a hand to fend the dog off. Finbar was one hundred and forty pounds of purebred Irish Wolfhound, and it was a little like trying to control a bucket filled with lit Roman candles.

Pamela laughed, tears clouding her vision. "He clearly remembers you."

"Down boy," Casey said, trying and failing to get a grip on the dog. Conor went over to the door, keeping a berth between him and his father and closed it, shutting out the cold afternoon. He returned to the kitchen to stand at her side, a look of ferocious suspicion on his face.

"Isabelle is with Gert and Owen," she said, feeling that she must say something, anything to make her feel that she was indeed awake and attached to the ground.

"Aye? I remember them a bit," he said. "I got yer letters, Conor." Casey stood by the hearth, Finbar still wiggling at his feet but settling now to a low-pitched whine of joy and the occasional shudder of canine rapture.

"Ye did?"

"Aye, I did, but only just a few weeks ago."

"I got the horse ye made me," Conor said, though his tone was slightly hostile.

"Did ye? I'm glad for that," Casey said gently.

"You *did* carve the horse?" Pamela said, "He found that months ago."

"Aye, I'll explain that if ye'll give me a chance," he said, slowly removing his coat as if she and Conor were skittish horses around which he was afraid to move too quickly. Skittish horse wasn't too far off the mark, mind you. Her entire body was tingling; it was, of course, shock and a terrible fear that this wasn't real.

"I think, if ye don't mind, I'm goin' to have to sit, my knees are just the wee bit wambly," Casey said, putting his coat down over the back of the sofa. She had forgotten how big he was and how immediate his presence felt to her. It was making her nervous, though whether with joy or trepidation she couldn't yet tell.

"Of course," she said, "go ahead and sit down, I'll make you some tea."

As Casey sat down at the table behind her, she braced her hands against the smooth wood of the counter and took a long and shaky breath, aware that he was watching her. She felt like she had toppled headfirst down the rabbit hole, only instead of strange creatures and bottles of magical liquid, there was a ghost in her kitchen who was entirely solid. She put the kettle on automatically, still feeling like she might faint again as she fumbled in the cupboard for the tea tin.

Despite the surreal feeling, she didn't think this could be a dream. Because in all those years of dreaming this exact scenario, the kitchen had never smelled of wet dog, and she had never slopped water all over herself, and Conor had not ever glared at his father with such suspicion that Casey probably felt the scorch of it across the room. Conor was moving with her, almost glued to her leg, and she was afraid she might trip over him. Casey was following the two of them with his eyes, and the look there both frightened her and made her weak in the knees.

"Where's he been then?" Conor said, sounding like a suspicious grown up. Casey politely pretended he'd not heard the question, as it was clear Conor wasn't looking to him for an answer.

"Sweetheart, I don't know yet, but he will tell us. Maybe for now you could go up the stairs and check on Kathleen."

Conor peered out around her hip, just in case Casey took a notion in his head to move or breathe too often. She swallowed a laugh, her wee son was a brave soul. She leaned over and kissed him and hugged him tightly to reassure him. "It's all right, Conor, he's not going to hurt us, just go on upstairs."

Conor shot a look at Casey that was akin to a cannon torpedoed across the deck of a ship, and then went up the stairs. She poured out the tea from the pot and placed the mug, warm-bellied, onto the table in front of Casey.

"Thank ye," he said quietly.

"You're welcome." She felt absurdly formal and as if she was in a play in which she did not know her lines.

"Ye've given me a cup of hot water," he said, looking into the mug.

"So I have. I-I forgot to put the tea in," she said and laughed, though it sounded more like hysteria than laughter.

"'Tis all right," he said gently, "perhaps ye could just sit with me for a minute while the wee man is upstairs. From the looks he was givin' me I don't imagine he'll stay up there long, he's protective of ye, aye?" There was a note of pride in his voice that Pamela did not miss.

"Yes, he is. He's small, but he's a Riordan through and through, thinks it's his job to look after me however he can."

"He's a good laddie," Casey said, and she felt the pain of the words even as he spoke them.

"He is," she agreed, hoping she wouldn't cry.

"I would tell ye why it is I've been away so long, an' I'd like to tell ye why I left in the first place, only I have no memory of it. For a long time, I had no memory even of you an' the babbies." He looked down at the mug, his hands braced around it as if it were the only thing keeping him steady. He looked up and took in the expression on her face. "Are ye all right?"

"I'm having trouble breathing," she said, still on the edge of the bubbling hysteria.

"I'm sorry," he said, "an' if that's not the most fockin' inadequate statement of my life, I don't know what is."

She laughed and he smiled and she felt the ice between them crack just the tiniest bit.

"I hardly know where to start," he said, twisting the mug round in his hands, "it's goin' to sound mad to ye."

"Just tell me," she said softly.

He told her then the story of his disappearance and time away and she simply listened and didn't interrupt. As he told it, she felt the pain of her last three years mirrored in his. At some point in the telling he showed her the dent in his skull, well hidden under his hair but easily felt by her fingers. Her hands tingled as she touched him, his hair still the same silky and springy mixture it had always been.

"Oh, Casey," she said, as she touched him, the words little more than a whisper but he nodded and reached up to take her hand, simply holding it in his. It felt like a lifetime lay between them in those three years. In some ways, she was all too aware, it was just that—a lifetime of change and other people and children who had grown and changed so that a man might hardly know them as his own.

"And so now, here I am," he said quietly, after he was done telling her of San Francisco, and a man named Eddy, a house with a tower and the dark and bloody world of bare knuckle fighting. She had the sense that this was only the bare bones of what he'd experienced but there was time to hear more of his life later.

"I have a million questions," she said, "but I can't think of where to begin."

"Just ask whatever comes up into yer mind, an' I'll try to answer it as best as I can."

She looked at him and felt a bubble of laughter coming up in her chest. It was partly shock but it was also real laughter. The kitchen around, familiar as the palms of her own hands had taken on the aspect of a Surrealist painting, as if up close the whole thing—hearth, Aga, mugs, table—had become mere blurred dots and the only real thing was this man looking back at her, the same dazed expression on his face that she was certain was on her own.

"Pamela, there's one other thing I would tell ye—" he began, only to be interrupted by Conor who had come back down the stairs.

"Kathleen is awake," Conor said, still wary of the big stranger seated in their kitchen.

"Kathleen?" Casey asked, an odd look in his face that told her he knew more than he had let on about just how much had changed since his disappearance.

"Yes, Kathleen. I have another child," she said.

"Jamie is her da," Conor said, no small emphasis on the name.

"Is he, indeed?" His tone was mild, but there was a tension under the words that made Pamela feel slightly sick.

"I need to go get her," she said.

"Aye, I'll wait." His gaze flicked back to Conor, who had taken up a stance near the stove, his arms crossed over his narrow chest, a dark scowl fixed to his face, his eyes the deep grey of true upset.

She went up the stairs, hoping that the situation in the kitchen wouldn't get too fraught in her absence. Poor Conor, there wasn't anything that could have prepared him for this. There wasn't anything that could have prepared her either, come to that. The shock of it prickled along every inch of her skin and she had to stop partway up just to catch her breath.

In the bedroom, Kathleen was working herself up into a fine temper, green eyes sparkling with tears, though a gummy smile split her tiny face when she saw her mother come into view. Pamela picked her up and held her to her shoulder, patting her back. Her snuffles started to subside and she nuzzled into Pamela's neck. The warmth and her smell—talcum, milk and lilacs—was reassuring. She could, standing here in the bedroom she had once shared with Casey, almost believe she had imagined that he had come home. That the last hour had been no more than a dream, something longed for but not real. She took a deep breath and put Kathleen down on the changing table. She got a fresh diaper from the stack and changed the baby out of her nap clothes into the clean diaper and a pale lavender outfit that Jamie had gotten for her.

Jamie. God, what would he make of all this? He had gone to London on business, but would return to Belfast tomorrow. He would be shocked, she should call and let him know, she needed to call Pat, too. She needed to get her nerves under control so that she didn't feel like she was about to fly in a hundred different directions all at once, from joy and fear and a lingering feeling that she was hallucinating. For a moment she sat, Kathleen in her arms, the warmth and tender flesh of the baby comforting her. She couldn't quite fathom that when she walked back down the stairs the man she had waited for an eternity would be sitting there, being glared at by his son, but there nevertheless.

Kathleen gave a small, impatient cry. She was hungry and needed to be fed. The idea of sitting in the kitchen feeding Jamie's daughter in front of Casey made her want to erupt in hysterical laughter or tears—she wasn't sure which emotion was uppermost at the moment.

"Come on, wee angel, there's someone downstairs for you to meet." She sighed and gathered up her courage along with her daughter, and went down the stairs, feeling a little like a Christian with a lion sitting in her kitchen.

Downstairs, father and son were still in a wary standoff of dark looks. Casey remained sitting and Conor had shifted position only as far as angling himself between Casey and the door, as though he had suspicions of an attempted bolt for the outside world.

Pamela sat in the far corner of the kitchen, by the fire, putting a blanket over her shoulder so that she could nurse Kathleen with some modicum of privacy.

"I'm goin' up to my room," Conor said, and turned on his heel and headed up the stairs, small feet making decided thumps on each riser.

She gave Casey an apologetic look, but he merely shrugged and said, "It's a shock to the wee man, I can't say I blame him."

"You said you got Conor's letters?" she asked, for that was where he'd left the thread of his story dangling. The fact that he'd known where they were for months now.

"Aye, I did. I came here last spring. I was walkin' the countryside, an' I came in over the wall because I heard an army vehicle comin' up the lane. Next thing I knew I was standin' next to a fairy house in the wood. I don't know what made me put my hand in the house, but I did an' then there was the wee cubbyhole an' the letters. I lost those," he said, and looked away from her for a moment, "an' then I came back later when I understood this had been my home, an' I checked again an' there was a letter. He told me I should come home. It was that night I found ye in the workhouse."

"That was you—the avenging angel was you?" she said, startled by the information and yet it all made sense now. Casey was the best shot she had ever known, and taking out the people in that horrible room had taken the skill of a sniper.

"Avengin' angel?"

"That's what Pat and I have been calling the shooter—well, you as it turns out. I'd be dead now, if you hadn't come along."

He smiled, though it was a strained expression. "Jamie would have saved ye."

"I don't think he could have against four men and a madwoman," she said. "We'd all be dead if you hadn't stumbled across us that night."

"For that alone, Pamela, I would be glad I've come back."

Kathleen had finished nursing and Pamela righted her clothes under the receiving blanket, feeling absurdly shy. The man had seen everything she owned—many times—but right now it seemed as if a stranger sat in her kitchen. She put the baby over her shoulder and patted her back until she let go of a soft belch.

"May I see her?" he asked, the strange look still upon his face, but something else there as well, a hint of longing for the children who had grown so much in his absence. Isabelle had not been much bigger than this when he'd disappeared. She stood and walked over to where he sat and placed the baby in his arms. Kathleen goggled up at him, green eyes wide. The sun had come out and the glow of it set her delicate web of curls on fire. Casey looked down at her, his face a study. She couldn't even imagine what he was thinking right now, but as her own mind was caroming around like a wobbly-kneed fawn on ice, she supposed he was in little better state.

"She's lovely, Pamela. She has the look of you about her. Her father as well." This last was said with a certain stiffness that didn't escape her notice. Kathleen did look a great deal like Jamie and just now that resemblance was exaggerated due to her nerves and Casey's careful observation of the baby's face. She took the baby back and held her snugly. She felt defensive, and ridiculously, she also felt guilty.

She put Kathleen in the cradle by the hearth and then set to making dinner. Regardless of a father come back from the putative grave, she knew Conor would be hungry. It gave her a feeling of having slightly solid ground beneath her feet to do something so homely as peel potatoes and carrots. Casey talked to her as she put a chicken in the oven and readied the vegetables. It felt as though she was trying to put a puzzle together as she listened to him, one that was missing many substantial pieces. Going from the little he'd told her, she realized the frustration that must have been his constant companion all this time, never knowing who he was, or where he belonged.

An hour later, as she put the food on the table, she could hear her own pulse pushing blood through her veins, her senses as alert as if a wolf was in her kitchen stalking her with the intent of having her for his meal. She called Conor to dinner and he came slowly down the stairs and walked to the table, only to pull his chair all the way around it, placing it pointedly beside her own. He got up on it, and kneeled rather than sitting, though she normally did not allow him to do that. It gave him a little extra height though and put him almost on level with Casey. Casey smiled at him, and got a scowl in return for his pains. Casey looked at her then and there was a suspicious twitch at the corner of his mouth.

Conor was the only one of them who did justice to his dinner. He was growing like a weed already and always hungry, and wasn't one to waste a meal simply because of an upstart father who returned from the dead at the inconvenient hour of his supper. Casey watched him as Conor removed his hostile gaze from him in order to tuck into his food. There was a look of pained longing on his face that made her heart hurt. She could only imagine what it was to see his son after so long, and for him to remember the toddler he had left behind and come home to find this young boy in his place.

She ate as well, but didn't really taste the food at all. She realized partway through the meal that she was staring at Casey, who had eaten half of his meal and then put it to the side. He gave her a crooked smile and she returned it with a hesitant one of her own.

"The supper is tasty," he said, "but I've no appetite. I just—I can't quite believe I'm sittin' here lookin' at ye across the table, as though I just went off to work this morning an' am returned home for the evenin.'"

"I know," she said softly. "I feel like I'm going to wake up from a strange dream any minute now, just as I did so many times when you were gone, only to find you *were* just a dream."

After supper she went about her evening routine. It seemed utterly ludicrous to do so, as if it was a normal night and yet, babies and children still needed all the things those routines were built around—feeding, changing, pyjamas and bed. Casey stayed downstairs while she put Kathleen to bed, who, thank heavens, went off to sleep easily. That was the beauty of a baby, as long as her tummy was full and her bottom dry, the dramatic events of the day couldn't cause a ripple in her life.

Conor was very quiet as he brushed his teeth, cleaned his face and put on his pyjamas. This wasn't unusual for him, but she knew her son well enough to know when he was upset. She got him tucked into bed, and then sat down beside him for a moment.

"Are you all right?" she asked.

He gazed up into her face, his dark eyes wide and suspiciously bright.

"I thought I would know him if he came home, Mama. But I don't."

"I know it's upsetting, Conor, but you will know him again and then it will be like he was never really gone."

He nodded but she could see that he was less than convinced. Poor wee man, she could hardly blame him, she knew she sounded less than certain herself, as much as she wanted to reassure him. She kissed him and smoothed the hair back from his face, stroking his head, just as she had done to soothe him as a baby. Normally he wouldn't have allowed it, but tonight he needed the comfort. Despite the day's excitement and upset he was asleep within minutes. She hoped what she had told Conor was true, both for him and Isabelle. For her and Casey, she knew, it was likely to be far more complicated.

Casey was standing by the fire when she came downstairs, his back to the room and his hands braced on the mantle. She caught a glimpse of his face in profile before he turned toward her and felt her heart sink. He was going to leave. It was there in the set of his face and the lines of his body. His tension was palpable even from several feet away.

"I can't stay here, Pamela. I'll come back tomorrow, if I may though. You an' I have things to discuss, no?"

"Yes, we do clearly, but I—I can make up Pru's room for you, she's away just now. I don't want you to go, I'm too afraid you will disappear again. Please, Casey," she crossed the floor and took his hand, tears blurring her vision, "please don't go away with things as they are right now."

"Oh, Pamela," he said, something broken in the two simple words and he moved toward her, hesitant and uncertain. She closed the remaining gap and suddenly she was in his arms and he was holding her tightly, that big body she remembered so well, there solid and warm, and she couldn't hold back the tears anymore. She cried all the tears that had been held back over this long, long time of thinking him dead, of longing for him, of looking forward to her own death, so that she might finally know where he had gone, what had happened to him, why he had not come back to her and their babies.

He carried her to the sofa and held her against his chest and it felt natural to put her arms around his neck. She held onto him tightly, her face in the curve of his neck, the force of her tears shaking her entire body. He rubbed her back, making soft soothing noises, until the trembling stopped and she lay against him, spent.

"Are ye all right?" he asked softly, the low hiss of the fire and the soft rumble of the Aga the only noises in the house other than her breath, soft and warm against his neck.

"I might be in a few more weeks," she said, the tears still there in her voice. "Are you uncomfortable? I can move if you need."

"No," he held her tighter, "I think I could sit this way with ye for the rest of time."

"We have time," she said, aware of the uncertainty in her tone. "We can talk about it tomorrow."

"Aye," he agreed, voice soft, "we can do that."

The thud of his heart echoed through her, warm and steady and real. Real. My God, he was real. There were so many questions in her mind, and no doubt in his too. Despite him holding her, and his body against hers feeling as natural as rain on her skin, she could also sense a fear in him and knew there was a large part of him held back. It was understandable; she felt shy and uncertain herself. And yet, oh and yet to be held by him again when she had given up hope of that ever happening again in her life, was a thing of wonder.

They sat so, silent, for some time until she heard the noise of small feet on the stairs and looked up. Conor stood at the bottom of the stairs, rubbing his eyes, and looking as angry as a crossed badger. He looked at Casey.

"Ye've made my mama cry," he said accusingly.

"Aye, I suppose I have, though I didn't mean to. 'Tis all right, laddie," Casey said, "yer mammy is just the wee bit sad right now, but she'll be fine come mornin'."

Pamela sat up, and beckoned to Conor. "Come here, sweetheart," she said, "I'm fine."

Conor scrambled up into her lap, putting his arms around her neck and hugging her tightly, and then Casey put his arms around both her and Conor, and held them until they fell asleep.

Chapter Eight

The Threads of Love

PAMELA WOKE ALONE, well covered with a blanket and warmed by the fire that blazed in the hearth. A thread of panic shot up from her stomach, spreading alarm through her blood. She sat up, the blanket spilling onto the floor. There was terror that she had dreamed Casey's coming home, that she was now going to wake up to the ordinary reality where he was forever gone.

He was by the fire, crouched down, poking up the blaze, the flames lending both light and shadow to his profile. She had forgotten how big he was, how large his presence was in any room he was in. He wore a grey sweater and worn jeans, his hair tied back with a leather thong. Living on a mountaintop he had said, left his grooming somewhat to be desired. He had beautiful hair though, and she had always loved it long, though he'd tended to keep it cropped short when they had been together. The contours of his face were changed somewhat from how she had held them in her memory, as though someone had taken a drawing and altered its lines subtly and while the drawing looked the same at first glance, the longer you looked the more apparent the changes became. There was another man in that face, a stranger of whom she was half-afraid.

His scent was on her, the scent that was so distinctly his and yet this too was changed. Just now though, watching him here in the house he had built for the two of them, she could pretend for a moment that he had never gone, and this was just another night for them, that there weren't the years in between and that they knew one another as well as they once had, and more because there had been the everyday between them.

He turned toward her and the spell was broken. When he looked at her she couldn't pretend there wasn't an abyss yawning between them, but she was still filled with a joy that felt like a delicate glass vessel in her hands. She wanted to clutch it tight but knew she could not for fear of being cut through by it.

"I took the laddie up to his bed a couple of hours ago," he said, watching her as she looked about for Conor.

"Did you sleep at all?" she asked, knowing too well the answer to that question. The house lay quiet around them, the fire hissing softly, the windows wreathed in delicate veins of frost.

"No," he said and stood, one hand bracing his right knee. "But that's no matter, I don't always sleep well these days."

She sat up and pushed her hair back from her face. "I could make you something to eat, are you hungry?"

He shook his head, and she felt her heart sink a little. He was going to leave, she could feel the need of it in his body clear across the room.

She excused herself and went to the bathroom, needing a moment to gather her wits. She brushed her teeth and splashed water over her face, and then gathered her hair up and tied it in a knot with an elastic band. Her face in the mirror was flushed and she looked like a woman who had been hit by a figurative truck. Her entire body still thrummed with Casey's touch. There was a dream-like aura to the previous day, and she felt a sudden shaft of fear that she would return to the kitchen to find him gone, and would once again face the bleak reality of life without him.

But he was there, solid and big, when she entered the kitchen, his face turning toward her and she felt her heart start to thump painfully just at the sight of him.

"Could you manage a cup of tea?" she asked, knowing she sounded desperate just to keep him here, beneath this roof under which they had once lived together, in love and passion and just the everyday things of life—meals and long talks and rocking babies and exchanging the gossip of each of their respective days. She was afraid—no, she was terrified—that if he left, he would not come back and she would have no way to find him.

"Pamela," he began and she could hear his need to leave simply in the utterance of her name, "I should go. I promise I'll come back, ye needn't fear that. I want to see Isabelle as soon as may be, after all."

"Only Isabelle?" she asked, knowing it was wrong to even say it, but feeling entirely heedless and, if she were honest, hurt.

"No, not only Isabelle," he said and came to where she stood, and touched the side of her face lightly. "Surely ye know better than that. Only it's hard, no?

To be here in the same room with one another, and have it be something other than what it was, than what we thought it might be. Or maybe it was only how I thought in my own head, imaginin' seein' ye again, touchin' ye."

"Have I disappointed you?" she asked, knowing it was a loaded question, but she knew she needed to give Casey the permission to be entirely honest with her, brutally so if it was what was needed.

He looked at her long, his expression unreadable, for the light was low, just the fire and the small light over the Aga that she had kept burning for him every night for three years. She had never, in all that time, imagined the two of them standing in the same room, and feeling as distant as if they were utter strangers to one another. Which, she realized, they were in no small degree.

"Oh, Pamela, I wish ye could know what I feel just to look at ye, after all this time."

"I do know, Casey, because I feel the same. As if no time has passed and yet it's like we're meeting one another for the first time."

"Pamela, I was a dead man for all intents and purposes. I'm broken in ways that I can't even begin to explain to ye. You will have changed a great deal as well. We are not the husband an' wife with the two wee ones that we were a few years ago."

"Then who are we? I have been lost from the day you disappeared, Casey, so if I'm not your wife, who am I?"

"You will always be my wife," he said softly, "only I don't know what that means anymore, do you?"

"I just want to kiss you," she said, "simply because I need to touch you, and because I have longed every day for three years to kiss you. Do you think you can allow me that? And then I will let you go."

He smiled, though it was not a smile filled with joy, but rather a wary uncertainty. Well he could damn well stand the kiss.

She moved toward him and took his hands, tears prickling at the back of her eyes just at the feel of them. She looked up to find his dark eyes looking down at her. Then she reached up and touched the side of his face, gently, and went up on tiptoe to put her mouth to his. He tasted warm and sweet and she leaned into him just wanting to breathe one breath with him, to clutch his scent to her so that she might smell his warmth on her after he left. He moved against her, his hands sliding from hers to cup her face. The kiss deepened and the fire of it moved like lightning straight down to her belly and parts lower. She felt Casey's breath catch and then he released her, stepping back from the kiss and detaching his hands from her.

He took a long breath and then smiled at her, sadly. "It seems some things have not changed, no?"

"No, clearly they haven't," she said, a flush rising hot through her face.

He swallowed and took another step away from her. "I'd best go, Pamela before we both do somethin' that we'll regret."

"I wouldn't regret it," she said softly.

He took another deep breath and put his hand to the back of the chair, retrieving his coat.

"I'll call ye later today, an' ye can let me know when it's a good time to come see Isabelle."

She nodded, afraid to speak, for fear she would yell at him if she let so much as one word slip past her lips.

After he left, she went upstairs to check on Kathleen. The baby was stirring a little; she would want feeding soon. Pamela changed out of the jeans and sweater she'd fallen asleep in, in Casey's arms, and into her nightgown. Then she sat down in the chair in the corner of the bedroom. Kathleen would need a few more minutes to properly wake and until then she could use those moments to catch her breath. Here in the dark of their bedroom, it was hard to believe he'd been in the house just a few moments ago. And yet she still felt his kiss on her lips, and smelled his scent on the sweater she now held to her face.

Kathleen began the small snuffle which was the precursor to her true cry of hunger. She would be awake enough to feed now. Pamela picked her up, relishing the baby's warmth and sweet smell. She quickly changed her diaper and then sat down with her in the rocking chair, baring one breast before Kathleen could work herself up to a full howl of outrage over her empty tummy. The sight of the tiny red head at her breast, soothed her. There was nothing more grounding than feeding a baby. She could feel her body slowly relax along with the insistent pull of Kathleen's mouth.

The calm was welcome, for her thoughts settled a little, along with her body. Logically, she knew that there was nothing she could do about the situation right now, or perhaps, ever. It had been clear to her that Casey felt like a stranger here in his own home. With the injuries he'd suffered and his three years of wandering in the wilderness of memory loss, he might never truly return home to them.

She switched Kathleen to the other breast, hoping she would finish before falling back to sleep. Otherwise, she would have to pump the breast as it was overly full. In her arms the baby was a small boneless weight with a heartbeat as light and rapid as that of a hummingbird. Pamela merely sat, feeding her child, and watched as the light slowly crept in from the edges of the room, slipping in over the windowsill and reaching out with slow winter fingers to touch the furniture and blankets. The bed sat in a softly gathering pool of the ashy light, the quilt glowing with cut blocks of amethyst and rose. She had only recently begun to sleep in the bed again. For a very long time after Casey had disappeared, she hadn't been able to bear being in it alone. During their marriage though, it had been a place of passion and joy. When all else had failed them in the troubled spots of their relationship, they had been able to put aside their differences and find peace with one another here in the dark of their marriage bed.

Jamie's grandmother, Finola, had once spoken to Casey of that very matter and her words now echoed in Pamela's head—words that had been a simple observation but had been entirely true as well.

Don't turn yer thoughts from it, it's why ye're here, man—the hold yer body has on hers. It's love but it's the physical aspect too. Ye're bound to her by a million threads, but this is one of the strongest. 'Tis at the centre of the web an' binds the two of ye fast when other things have failed. Ye know it well enough.

Yes, they'd had passion but they'd also had love, a love that had weathered so many storms and been more resilient as a result. She had wanted to simply blurt it out to him today, to tell him that she loved him still and have him say the same to her. But there had been a raw hesitancy in his face which had stopped her. For here she was with another man's child in her arms, a man whom she also loved and while that love was made of completely different threads, it was just as real and Casey knew that all too well.

The strands of love were a tangled and complex thing, and rarely did a whole cloth come of it. In her own case the cloth had been cut and torn more than once and whether it could be mended and made strong again, remained to be seen. She cut off the thought, it wouldn't serve her just now to go down that path. With a joy so freshly born and so terribly fragile, she would rather just let it be for a time. And so, she sat, with the warm pulse of Kathleen in her arms and allowed that fragile joy to sit in her heart like a warm fire.

When she made her way downstairs a short time later, the house was already stirring. Finbar was whining to get out and Conor was sitting at the kitchen table, small hands busy gluing leaves and acorns together. She made a mental note to wipe the table down later before the glue hardened into a permanent part of it.

Pamela went to Conor and put an arm around him, dropping a kiss on his frowsy head. "Are you hungry?" she asked, knowing the question was rhetorical, for Conor was always hungry. He was growing like a weed, and showed signs already of one day being the same size as his father.

"Yes," Conor said, and then looked up at her. "Is he gone?" he asked.

"Yes, he's gone for now. He'll be back later though," she said, uncertain if Conor needed reassurance or if he was simply feeling territorial about her and his sisters.

"He's really my daddy?" Conor queried, his small chin stuck out in a fashion that couldn't have said 'I'm a Riordan' more clearly had it been stamped on his forehead.

"Yes, sweetheart, he is really your daddy."

"Then why did he leave?"

"He hasn't lived with us for a long time, Conor. A lot of things have happened to him since he left, and so he feels strange with us just now." She felt sick even as she said it, because it was true, they had both been uncomfortable and uncertain. She felt like someone who had wandered out onto a great sheet of ice without realizing it, and now was having a terrible time keeping her footing. Casey had been right, in all the years of imaginings, this scenario wasn't one that had occurred to her. They were strangers to one another. And yet, last night in his arms she had felt like she was home for the first time in so very long.

She set about making Conor sausage and eggs for his breakfast, the homely task centering her in the here and now. Kathleen, with luck, would sleep for another hour or so, and the day would roll on as the days before it had. And yet, she knew, despite routine and babies and household duties, nothing would ever truly be the same again.

Chapter Nine

Without Prejudice

OUTSIDE, CASEY TOOK a deep breath of the cold morning air. He eyed the sky, noting the narrow band of silvery grey breaking over the hills. Dawn was on its way and he needed to be on the move. He walked into the pine copse, grateful for the dark shelter of it. He stopped a few minutes later and put his hands to a tree, feeling the rough bark and smelling the chill amber scent of winter pine.

He was completely overwhelmed in a way he hadn't been in a very long time. Just to be there in the house he'd built, with Conor and Pamela, had felt like a dream he'd wandered into without understanding quite what he was meant to do or say. Even so, when he'd held her in his arms he'd felt a sense of belonging such as he'd not felt since the day he'd disappeared from his old life.

The doctors had warned him about this long ago, that emotion would never be as easily contained for him again and that he would have to avoid things that overstimulated him if he was already in a heightened state. He doubted they could have foreseen an event such as the one he was experiencing right now.

He put his forehead to the trunk, feeling the silken tickle of tree beard. A thread of turf smoke wound past his nose, someone's morning fire had been lit. In the distance he could hear the stream which cut across the corner of their land, and the noise of tree limbs in the morning wind—a sound like loose bones rattling against each other. A few deep and measured breaths and he began to calm; he needed to move on, it would soon be full light and he couldn't risk running into someone on his way back to his truck.

The snap of a twig reached his ears just a fraction of a second too late. Had he not been distracted the men would never have gotten the drop on him. As it was, they had a hold on him before he could even understand what was happening.

Casey fought, trying to hit his way clear of the men and make a run for it. He landed a couple of good punches, but they had caught him unawares and before he knew it, he was down with his hands shackled behind his back, rope biting into his wrists. They tied his ankles then and threw him into the back of a vehicle—a van he thought—trussed up like a turkey on Christmas Day with a bag over his head, tied securely round his neck. There was no way to get the bloody thing off without risking choking himself and he'd be damned if he'd help them out that much. A moment later the van began to move. He could smell hay and horse manure on the floor beneath him. Pamela's scent was on his clothes as well—that soft green scent that was so unique to her. *Christ, Christ, Christ!* He should never have gone home. He knew better, but he'd given in to the temptation to see her and the children. And if he died for that bit of weakness? He banged his head against the van floor, cursing himself inwardly. He would die with her touch upon him and for that alone he would be glad he'd gone, but her suffering would only start again—fresh, new and as sharp as a knife still hot from the grinding stone. He had been selfish, and she and Conor would pay for it.

He drew in a breath, forcing himself to get his panic under control and take in his surroundings as best as he could—blind, bound and in a window-less van. He started to count as it was a good way to calm himself and also to get an idea of how much time was passing and how far they were travelling. They were going at a good clip, without much stopping and starting. A half hour later he was certain they were skirting the city for he couldn't hear the noise of people or busses nor the general buzzing bustle of a city. Even the cars they passed were few and far between, just a quiet thrum of noise there and then gone. He tested the ropes on his wrists to see if there was any give and any possibility he could somehow wriggle free of them. The bastards had done their work thoroughly though and the knots were such that the more he wriggled and twisted, the tighter they got.

Where the hell were they headed? The van had slowed and turned onto a road that was very narrow, for he could hear the sound of tree branches scraping along the sides. Clearly, they were in the woods, somewhere remote no doubt and where there would be no one to hear the sound of a gun.

The van stopped a few minutes later, coming to an abrupt halt and throwing Casey sideways into one of the wheel wells.

"Bastards!" he yelled, knowing they couldn't hear him but taking satisfaction in voicing his feelings anyway. A moment later the van doors opened and they pulled him out. Even through the hood the air was cold and raw. One of the men leaned down and untied the rope around his ankles. Then they grabbed him, one on either side and pulled him, stumbling, along with them. He might be able to make a break for it, if he could get the damn rope off his wrists and get the bag off his head. The crunch of snow overlay a thick layer of leaves. A forest then, composed mostly of hardwoods. The grade of the hill beneath his feet ran steeply down causing him to trip over unseen roots and rocks. His knee, never fond of abuse, was complaining loudly.

At the bottom of the grade, they stopped and Casey had the sense that they stood in a small valley—no doubt so heavily treed that his body would never be found. It was hard to believe that only a few hours ago, he'd been sitting warm and safe with his wife and child in his arms.

Once, long ago, when he'd thought he was about to die, he had felt that this was how he'd want it had he a choice about it—out in the open air with an Irish sky above his head and the scent of earth and wood in his nose.

I'm so sorry, Jewel and I'll never be able to tell you just how sorry I am. Nor how empty my life has been these last three years without you and the children. I'm sorry to you too, Patrick, so very sorry for letting you down once again. He could see Pamela's face in his mind, as she'd looked when he was leaving—like she couldn't quite believe he'd go and was angry with him, and filled with sorrow at the same time. She'd been right, he ought to have stayed or at least explained himself better than he had.

They pushed him to the ground, face-down, hands still secured behind his back, and kept him there with a well-placed gun barrel to his head. He'd survived bullets twice before, but he doubted the fates would be so kind as to save him a third time.

His senses were all on high alert, everything magnified by the adrenaline coursing thickly through his blood—the cold scent of earth and leaf mold in his nose and the poking of an unfortunately placed stick and the wet of snow melting against his legs. His heart thudded like that of a panicked rabbit in his ears. It would be an ignominious end and he was all too aware of the irony, for it was the exact ending all his loved ones had believed he'd suffered three years ago. There was no tragedy so farcical as an Irish one.

His skin began to prickle, as if small shocks were running along his arms and legs and he realized someone else had entered the valley. The boss of these two thugs presumably. He wondered if he was the one meant to kill him? If so, he wished he'd bloody get on with it, as all this waiting to be shot wasn't doing a great deal for his bowels.

"We found him walkin' on Mrs. Riordan's property," said the man holding the gun to his head, "an' when we asked him what he was about he refused to answer."

"Let him up," a voice said curtly, and he felt a shiver of premonition go through his bones. He knew that voice.

They pulled him to his feet with more force than was strictly necessary and then one of the men pulled the hood off him. Casey looked up, blinking at the onslaught of light, and thought that death—all things considered—might have been the easy way out.

"Jesus Christ," said Lord James Kirkpatrick.

"Aye," Casey said drily, "ye can say that again."

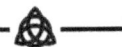

"Amnesia?" Jamie asked. An hour had passed, and in that time, they'd retreated to a small hut somewhere, he presumed, on Jamie's land. It was little more than a rough hunting cabin, and Casey wondered what its true purpose might be. Right now though, he was grateful for the shelter. He was even more grateful for the heat being thrown out by the potbelly stove in the corner and the flask of whiskey Jamie had stuck in his hand for fortification. The man sat across from him, clad in a dark blue sweater, jeans and a shearling coat. He'd removed his gloves after the hut had warmed, and his hands lay relaxed on his thighs. He appeared so cool and unruffled that Casey wondered if he'd imagined the look of shock in the man's face such a scant time ago.

"Do ye doubt me?" Casey asked, still feeling nettled, if not outright furious at his abduction.

"No, I know you well enough—or did—to know there's not much else on earth that would have kept you from Pamela and your children this long, apart from death. Does she know?"

"Aye, I just spent several hours with her."

"And then promptly left her." The statement was blunt, but no less true for that, Casey supposed. He remembered this about the bastard—he had never been one to mince words.

"Funny, I didn't see *you* there. Bein' that ye have a child with the woman an' all."

"You've been back for more than a year, and you're only now letting her know you're still alive?"

Thrust and parry, it was like playing chess where a wrong move could result in the loss of a limb, at least figuratively speaking. He was feeling bruised in spirit, and remembered this too was a feature of his encounters with this man.

"I didn't know who she was, I wasn't even certain I had children, nor where it was I'd lived. It was why I came here—to Ireland—to see if I could find who I'd once been."

"And so you did," Jamie said softly, though there was a steel-edge to the words that was as chilly as the frost melting away from the logs next to the fire.

"Aye, an' so I did," Casey replied, his words matching the tone of Jamie's. "An' arrived home to find that my wife has most assuredly moved on."

"Is this not," Jamie said, the same edge there in his voice, "what you wanted?"

"No of course not," Casey said indignantly, "that's a damned stupid question."

"Really—shall I give you a direct quote from your own hand?" Jamie asked, though Casey knew the question was meant rhetorically. "*Love my children well, you're the one man who has the heart for it—to accept another man's children without prejudice. If I cannot be there to raise them, I want it to be you. Give her time, and take what time you need yourself, it will not, in the run of things, be so very long.*"

"Aye, well, I likely thought I'd be dead by the time ye read it, an' followed through on it. Ye were maybe a little quicker off the mark than I thought ye might be."

"Three years is not so much time in the ordinary run of things, but for a heart that's grieving it's a lifetime. If she hadn't moved on when she did, she might well have died. She was making herself incredibly ill at that point."

Casey took a swig of the whiskey. In the last twenty-four hours he'd once again seen his wife and son, he'd held the child of the man across from him, he'd been assaulted and kidnapped and now was having a conversation that made his brain feel as if was being gleaned for chaff. Altogether, the drink was probably not wise. He took another swallow.

"I took her and the children away to Maine for the summer just over a year ago. Things changed for us there—she came up for air, both literally and figuratively."

"Is that where it began then?" Casey asked. "Or is that a naïve question? Because maybe it really began all those years ago when the two of yez first met."

Jamie eyed him rather coolly. The bastard always had this ability—to hide his emotions regardless of how disturbed he was. It was rare to know what the man was feeling and thinking unless he flat out told a person. It struck him that he remembered the tension between them, and all the attributes of the man which had always annoyed him. Quixotic as his memory might be, it seemed quite clear on how it felt about the chilly bastard in front of him.

"I would ask how it was between the two of yez, an' how it is now?"

"I think, perhaps, that's a question you'll have to ask Pamela, rather than me."

"Ye know I can't ask Pamela, because she is a woman, an' she won't understand. She'll think it's the wrong question. But ye're a man an' ye know it's the only question."

"Do you really want an answer, Casey? Because, were I in your shoes, I don't know that I would."

"Aye, I do. I need to start from a place of truth, if I'm to rebuild my life."

Jamie gave him a long and assessing look. The words, when they came, were spoken quietly, but what they lacked in volume was more than made up for by the force of their impact.

"I don't know what you remember of her, but when she loves, she can never give less than all of herself."

Casey nodded, trying to ignore the shaft of white-hot jealousy that bolted through him at the man's words. "I do recall that much," he said tersely.

"And yet, even then," Jamie said, "there was something of her held back, something that belongs only to you."

"And somethin' of her that has always belonged to you," Casey replied.

It was here that they reached an impasse. They both knew it for truth and it had long been the sticking point between them—that they loved the same woman and that she, despite making vows with one, had always loved them both. Casey could feel it creeping toward him, like a cloth wicking water through its weave—the complications of his old life. He knew in his life with her, he'd accepted Pamela's relationship with Jamie, though he'd always had issues with it. The man had long been her best friend, and now clearly he was much more. Before he had been things to her which Jamie was not—husband, lover and father of her children. Jamie was two of those things now as well. And he—well he was uncertain of everything just now, including the wisdom of venturing back into said old life.

"What will you do now?" Jamie asked.

"I don't know, if I'm bein' honest. I need to find out who tried to kill me three years ago. I don't want to put Pamela and the children in any sort of danger because of my presence. An' I don't expect to simply walk back in an' take up my life as if no time has passed."

"Did you not speak to her about it?" Jamie asked lightly.

"No. She's feelin' defensive an' she's in a wee bit of shock too. I can't blame her for any of that. She needs time. I don't want to make things worse for her. I saw her in that workhouse an' I have an idea of what that must have done to her."

"You have an idea but that's all. She's incredibly fragile right now, she won't admit it, but she is. She's been thoroughly traumatized. She spent a week thinking she was going to die and that the baby was going to be stolen."

"I'm not goin' to hurt her," Casey said.

"Aren't you? You've come back and let her see you, and yet you say you don't know what you plan to do. If you're not going to stay, if you're not here for her and the children, that is going to hurt her terribly. I'm not sure she could recover from it."

Casey could feel his anger rising. "An' what of yerself? Ye have a child with her, after all, an' yet Pat tells me ye're married."

"Things are complicated right now. But the thing that isn't complicated is that we have a daughter together; she and Pamela are my main priorities. The other conditions of my life are problematic, but they won't interfere with my care of them."

There was a challenge in there which Casey did not miss. There wasn't much he could say to it just at present, though. Father Jim had told him what he knew of Jamie's past and Casey knew what this child must mean to him, and of course, he had long known what Pamela meant to Jamie.

"You are still her husband, in the eyes of God and the law. What does that mean to you? Have you come back to be her husband again, or only to tell her you're still alive?" The question was asked mildly enough, but there was a flame burning deep in the green eyes that told another story entirely.

Casey had always appreciated this about the man—that he never cut him any slack. It was a sign of respect and one of the most goddamn maddening things about him at the same time. The lack of sympathy always made him feel like an equal in the man's presence. It might have been the one thing that made him answer with utter honesty.

"It means everything to me, an' yet I felt like a stranger in the house today. I owe her something, only I don't know what that is exactly. I am not who I was. Neither is she. I have little to offer her—some of my memories have come back an' some haven't, an' there's no way to know if it will ever all return."

The emotion was threatening to swamp him again. There were things he could not say, not even to Pamela. How holding Jamie's daughter had caused a hollow sensation beneath his ribs. How he felt such envy that Jamie had held Isabelle so, and watched her and Conor grow these last three years. The fear and distrust in Conor had been palpable, and while his logical side understood it, his less rational parts felt the sting of it like a lash across his soul. There were some things a man lost, that he could not regain, not even given time and hope.

The look on Pamela's face when he'd asked to see the baby had stung as well, but she needn't have worried, he had merely wanted to hold the wee one and have a proper look at her, for Pamela had held her with the baby's face away from him, defensive and no doubt afraid of his reaction. Well, he could hardly blame her for that, he supposed.

He had meant it when he said Kathleen was a beautiful baby. Delicate skin, fine as the petal of a newly opened rose, with the soft blue-green tinge beneath of vein and blood, and deeper the opal of bone, holding the promise of both mother and father in her face. But what had hurt most, like a knife without a hilt sunk deep in his belly, was how he had known—looking into that tiny face, haloed with the fiery shimmer of red hair ablaze in the setting sun—that he was looking into the face of a love made flesh.

He looked up to find Jamie watching him, the green eyes bright and unreadable.

"Do you have somewhere to stay?" Jamie asked, evenly.

"Why do ye ask?" Casey was made wary by the question; he wasn't ready for anyone to know where he was living. It was a caution well-exercised. Going to see Pamela and the children had been his first mistake in three years and it had already created a rather disastrous ripple effect.

"If you want to use this hut, you're welcome to it. None will bother you here. There's fuel for the fire and I can have food brought down to you."

Casey considered it for a moment. He understood Jamie well enough to know his word was good. If he said none would bother him here, none would. It was tempting, but he did not want to owe this man anything more than he already did; he needed things to be as clean and uncomplicated between them as possible.

"Thanks, but I've accommodation elsewhere." It was going to mean facing the long drive back to Wicklow tonight, and then the turnaround to-morrow if he meant to see his daughter. And he did mean to see her.

"I'll have one of the men drive you back," Jamie said. "I assume you have a vehicle somewhere?"

"I do," he said, shortly. He'd left the truck on an old abandoned farm track not far from the property. Crossing the border in a vehicle was always a risk but there were old roads which were blocked by little more than move-able barriers or spikes. He'd sussed a few out some time back. The border had always been more porous than the British had hoped, and if a man knew the countryside, there was always a place to cross unnoticed.

"Do you want the lift then?"

"Aye, that would be appreciated," he said. Part of him wanted to walk the distance, rather than accept a favour from this man, but it would take at least a few hours and his knee was paining him badly. He wouldn't make it all the way to his truck without assistance.

There was one last thing he needed to say. For despite the feelings he had toward this man, which were confused to say the least, there was one thing on which he felt very clear.

"Jamie."

Jamie stopped in the doorway, morning sun blazing upon his fair hair. He simply stood and waited for Casey to speak.

"Thank ye," he said, almost choking on the words but knowing he must say them, nevertheless.

"For what?" Jamie asked, a small crease in his forehead denoting his puzzlement.

"Everything," he said, and meant it.

Chapter Ten

Time Enough

"MEIN GOTT!" GERT SAID for what had to be the tenth time in as many minutes. She had come by to return Isabelle, and also to bring food, as she had done every day since Kathleen's birth. Worried about Pamela's lack of rosy cheeks and general robustness, Gert had cooked every nutritious dish she could think of, hoping to somehow endow Pamela with the health of a German valkyrie. Today's effort was *spaetzle,* along with a roasted chicken in its entirety. Both items were sitting upon the table, completely forgotten, as Gert stared at her in disbelief over the words Pamela had just spoken to her. She was fanning herself with a copy of *Hop on Pop*, which had been the only thing within reach when Pamela had imparted her shocking news. For the ten minutes since Pamela had told her about Casey's return, she had interspersed breathless gasps of 'Mein Gott,' with rigorous questioning.

Gert and her husband Owen, were the children's honourary grandparents and had loved Conor and Isabelle from the day they were born. They had included Kathleen in this love, making it clear she was every bit as much family to them, despite having a different father. They had loved Casey too, and so, knowing the children would let it slip and having conferred with Casey on the matter, she had told Gert the news of his return.

"Vere has he been? Vhat has he been doing, that he leaves you and his *kinder* alone for all this time? *Lieber Gott,* to think you almost married *that* man too! *Mein Gott* if Casey had come home to that! Can you imagine the scene?"

"Yes," Pamela said a little drily. "I *can* imagine it." A thrill of horror had shot through her when that very thought had crossed her mind. Imagination, regardless of how vivid or well-exercised, fell somewhat short when she tried to picture Casey arriving home not just to a new baby, fathered by Jamie, but to her residing in Noah's home as a newlywed, with Noah as her bridegroom.

"And vhat about this little one?" she'd asked, pointing at Kathleen, "Vhat is he thinking about her?" Gert's tone was defensive on behalf of Kathleen, as if she was ready to do battle with anyone who had so much as a conflicted feeling toward the baby.

"I don't really know. He held her and said she was beautiful, but beyond that we didn't talk about Kathleen."

"Vell, he vas always good vis the babies, no?" Gert said, softening immediately with the knowledge that Casey hadn't outright condemned Kathleen. "He is stubborn, but a man of good sense in the end. If he is still that man, he vill accept her."

If he is still that man. There, in that small phrase, lay the crux of the matter.

"I do not like you being here alone," Gert said, moving onto her next topic of worry. "Vy is Vanya not here, or that nanny of yours?"

"Vanya has been staying at the pub, pulling double shifts and I told Pru to stay in Belfast for a few more days. I felt Casey deserved to have his first meeting with his daughter privately." While the information about Vanya wasn't strictly true, she didn't think Gert needed the details of his whereabouts at present.

"*Ja,* that is good. Still, I do not like you being here alone at all. Not after these last months."

"Jamie has men watching the house," she said, thinking it was a miracle Casey had made it past them the day before.

"Vell, that is very vise of him, seeing as he is not," she sniffed, "here himself."

"He's here as often as he can be," Pamela said, giving Gert a warning glance to let her know she wouldn't tolerate any criticism of Jamie. Gert was fond of Jamie, but she was very protective of her and the children, and unhappy with him for having a wife turn up after three years of silence.

Just then, Owen came in with Conor and Isabelle, saving her from any further commentary on her rather complicated family life. Isabelle flew across the floor, pine needles caught in her curls and a smile on her face.

"Mama! Kaflee!" she said, and grabbed Pamela around the knees, hugging her lower legs energetically. She peered up over the edge of the rose-pink blanket her sister was wrapped in. "Kaflee 'wake?"

"No, she's sleeping, sweetheart, so we need to be quiet."

Isabelle rose up on her tiptoes so that she might see her sister's face and assure herself that Kathleen was indeed, asleep. She put one hand on Pamela's arm, and Pamela felt the distinctly sticky residue of pine pitch. Isabelle often collected tiny chunks of it, and tucked them in her pockets. This had led to more than one laundry day mishap.

"Kathleen will be awake soon," Pamela said. "You can help me change her when she wakes, if your hands and face are washed." Isabelle, like most three-year-olds was not terribly keen on washing, but in order to help with Kathleen, she would endure scrubbing of all sorts. She scampered off to the kitchen sink, where Pamela had a step for her, so that she could reach the big old stone sink. The area around it would be puddled enough to support a small family of ducks by the time she was done, but she would be relatively pitch and mud free.

Conor would usually come check on the baby too, right after he dumped whatever insect/vegetable matter/amphibian he'd found, in a spot where she usually discovered it after he went to bed. It wasn't unusual for her to make a trip outside in the dark, with either a frog or beetle in hand, to restore them, with apologies, to their natural habitat. Today though, Conor was unnaturally subdued, and went up the stairs without his usual tearing energy. He had been very quiet since Casey's visit and Pamela had taken advice Pat had given her long ago about dealing with male Riordans, leaving Conor to think things through on his own without troubling him further with questions a child his age couldn't possibly answer.

"The laddie was awful silent out there," Owen said. "Is there somethin' amiss with him? He's usually tellin' me the name of every plant an' bug we come across, but today he barely said three words."

Pamela and Gert exchanged a glance. Owen, wise to the silent conversations women often conducted while men were in the room asked, "What is it?" He looked from one woman to the other. Gert looked at Pamela, who nodded. She wasn't sure she could repeat the tale yet again, and Gert would be more than happy to share the news.

Gert filled him in, briefly, which was unlike her, and managed to only say *mein Gott* three times during the telling. Owen looked surprised but kept in his shock, unlike his wife. He sat for a moment, just looking at the two of them and then a smile rose in his face, transforming his gnomish features into something quite beautiful.

"Well then, isn't that a grand an' lovely thing?" he said.

"Yes, it is," Pamela said, smiling back at him.

Conor came downstairs then, with a knapsack packed and bulging. He went and stood beside Owen, and gave her a look which reminded her forcibly of his father. Looking at the knapsack, she knew there were likely a few tools in it, a chunk or two of wood, and probably some snails—hopefully in a jar, and hopefully with a lid on said jar. Clean underwear and a toothbrush were far less likely. With the wisdom of motherhood though, she always kept a change of fresh clothes and a spare toothbrush at Gert's house for each of her children.

"I'm goin' with Owen," Conor said stubbornly, as if challenging her to say no at her own peril. "He said I could."

Owen flashed her an apologetic glance. "Now, laddie, ye know I said ye could come only if yer mammy said 'twas all right with her."

"If it's all right with the both of you," she said.

"Aye, of course, the laddie is always welcome to stay with us. Ye know that, Pamela."

"You can go, Conor, but I want you home by the day after tomorrow," she said, knowing he was stubborn enough to stay with Gert and Owen until they made him go home.

She gave him a hug and a kiss, so that he would know she wasn't upset with him. Conor, never one to hold a grudge, hugged her back and gave her a slightly gritty smack on her lips. He leaned down and kissed Kathleen too, with the careful gravity he'd treated her with from the minute he'd first met his baby sister. It was hard not to gather him up, and tell him he had to stay home with her and his sisters. It would be neither fair nor right, though.

He went out the door then, small self held stiffly, and she knew he was fighting tears. It might be best if he did go and wasn't home when Casey came for his visit with Isabelle. He got in the car and shut the door, waiting for Owen and Gert with a look of resolution on his face.

"Poor little *Mausbär*," Gert said. Gert had called Conor 'Mousebear' from the time he was born. Isabelle was *Leibling*—darling, and Kathleen was *Mäuserl*—tiny mouse.

"He's upset about Casey," she said, keeping her voice low despite the fact Conor couldn't possibly hear her.

"Aye, well, I imagine that's to be expected," Owen said. "It's likely upset his apple cart pretty well. He had an image in his head, an' then the man comes back an' is real an' not some imagined hero. It's a lot to take in. He'll manage though, he's a steady little fellow."

"He is that," Pamela agreed. It was true, Conor was a little rock for the most part, and could navigate any upset with an aplomb and dignity that was near to unnatural in a child his age.

Gert bustled about putting the food in the refrigerator. It was a measure of her shock that she didn't bother to instruct Pamela on how to warm it properly, nor give her opinion on the dozen or so things she usually did before departing. She simply kissed Kathleen's face, and then looking down at Pamela with some sympathy, touched a hand to her head, as though in blessing, and then went out to the car where Conor waited.

Owen hung back for a moment, taking her hand in his and giving it a squeeze. He was normally not an outwardly emotional man, so it was a measure of how moved he was that he spoke as he did.

"I'm right chuffed that the boy is alive, an' has come home. Ye could knock me over with a feather, I'm that delighted." Moisture glinted in Owen's eyes, and she squeezed his hand back in a show of empathy. Owen was right, it was a lot to take in. Conor could hardly be blamed if he needed time to find his balance in this situation.

"Me too—both the happy bit and the feather knocking bit," she said, and laughed, thinking what an enormous understatement this was, and yet she still couldn't put the fact of his return far away enough from her to look at it properly. Her feelings had been a muddle of both joy and trepidation and she felt rather like a fever patient, cold one minute and boiling hot the next.

She watched as Owen drove away with Conor, feeling a pang in her heart for her son. Walking back into the kitchen, she looked around her trying to see the house through Casey's eyes, wondering if it appeared changed to him, or the same place he'd left that November afternoon three years ago. Or did he simply not remember, and all this—the house, the property, the things which were the routes and maps of her daily existence and the life she'd once shared with him—merely just a building and some land which belonged not to him, but to someone he barely knew—his former self? For what was a house without the memory of the love and laughter, the joys and sorrows which had been shared within its walls? It was merely a beautiful shell, a house with good bones and possibilities. And yet the echo of it must remain within him, for he'd managed to find it on his own, even without a conscious memory of it. What had been home must live somewhere within his cells.

Two hours later, she was changed into a pale pink sweater and a pair of old jeans, which despite being rather worn, were still flattering even to a body which wasn't quite one month post pregnancy. She'd managed to have a bath and wash her hair and even put a touch of mascara and lipstick on, as Isabelle had fallen asleep after her lunch and Kathleen was happy to lie in her bouncy chair beside the bath. Around her, the house glowed in the afternoon light, the winter sunshine wonderfully bright. A fire crackled in the hearth, the flames merrily leaping sprites, clothed in gold and violet. Kathleen had been put down for her afternoon nap a half hour before, and would likely sleep for another hour or two before needing to be nursed again. Any calm she'd managed to cultivate earlier in the day, had now fled and she felt both anxiety and anticipation running amok in her body.

Isabelle was playing happily with a box of Conor's outdoor treasures. Pamela sighed, knowing she ought to take it away from her, as Conor knew every item in the box and if anything went missing would protest over his sister being allowed to play with it. However, she didn't want Isabelle to fuss just now, as Casey was due to arrive and she wanted their daughter in a good temper when he first saw her.

Casey arrived a few minutes early, knocking on the door and causing her to jump a little. It felt odd, despite his absence, to have him knock on his own door, asking permission to enter rather than just coming in.

She opened the door, pulse racing as if she'd run up and down the stairs a dozen times, when all she'd done in reality was walk across the kitchen and lift her hand to the latch. He smiled at her, then stepped into the house, and with him came the scents of his walk—the wet green of the woods and the slightly smoky scent of winter earth. She fought the urge to step back—as well as the opposite—to simply throw her arms around him, and hold him until her heart stopped hammering at the mere sight of him. She settled for taking his coat, and placing it near the fire to warm it. It took a great deal of her self-control not to just crush the coat to her face and breathe in the scents of him. It was as though she could only take him in, in pieces—the smell of him, the touch of his hand, the sight of his smile and the warmth it flooded her body with. To try and take him in in his entirety was too much right now, and more than her battered senses could seem to manage.

When she turned back Casey was standing behind her, holding out a small pot of palest pink cyclamen, the delicate flowers looking like a drift of butterflies about to take wing.

"Oh, they're beautiful," she said, touched by the tiny bouquet. "You used to only give me flowers on anniversaries."

"Did I?" he asked, and she felt a pang for mentioning it. What it must be to him not to know the smallest details of his previous life, to be tripped up by small comments, which were ultimately meaningless, but would hold a wealth of hurt and confusion, simply for the not knowing about them.

"Yes, you did. You gave me other things which were just as wonderful all the time, though," she assured him.

"Did I then?" he said, and smiled. A small coil of pleasure unfolded in her stomach and she looked away, feeling overwhelmed.

He looked over to where Isabelle sat amongst a mass of crumbling leaves and took a deep breath, like a man facing an unpredictable firing squad.

"Isabelle, someone is here to visit you," she said, trying to keep the anxiety out of her voice. Isabelle got up and poked her head around a chair back and then, intrigued by the tall dark stranger, walked over to where Pamela stood. Isabelle was not one to hide behind a leg nor to play shy. She planted her small self in front of Casey, and looked up at him, a set to her face which was all too reminiscent of the man in front of her.

Casey looked at his small daughter, his own face a study. Isabelle had been not quite four months old when he'd disappeared and now, she was three and precocious and possessed of a bold nature, much like, Pamela thought, the man she was now eyeing with suspicious ferocity. Her hair was a tumble of black curls and her eyes the same brown as her father's—so dark as to be almost black—it was as though Casey was looking at a small female version of himself. In nature, Isabelle was even more her father's child than Conor was.

She put her hands on her hips, "Who be dis, Mama?"

Casey hunkered down, meeting his small daughter's fierce look with a gentle one of his own. He appeared caught somewhere between laughter and tears.

"I'm yer daddy, Bella," he said softly.

Isabelle shook her head and backed up a little. "No, my daddy is gone. I want Jamzie be my daddy."

Pamela winced inwardly, she knew it had to sting hearing such words from his daughter's lips. Casey, however, took it in his formidable stride.

"Aye, I know Jamie has been a good friend to you an' yer mammy, an' he's Kathleen's daddy too, so it makes sense that ye're very fond of him. But I should like to be yer friend too, Isabelle. Do ye think we might be friends? It'll be up to you, but I should like that very much."

She narrowed her eyes, as though assessing his offer. Isabelle was a tough customer, and Pamela held her breath, her heart aching for Casey and all that he had missed.

"Ye can come see my dolls," she said finally and put out her small hand to him. He took it and Pamela breathed out, a small flicker of hope in her heart that it was going to be okay.

Father and daughter came back down the stairs an hour later, during which time Pamela had done every random task she could think to do, as well as nursing Kathleen and changing her. She warmed up the *spaetzle* and chicken, hoping that Casey would stay to eat. Casey was carrying Isabelle, and her arms were around his neck. He raised an eyebrow at Pamela and smiled. It had been a good hour, clearly.

"You'll stay to dinner?" she asked. Isabelle clapped her hands together, "Stay, stay." Isabelle loved company and would insist that anyone who happened by stay for dinner, but Casey's face lit a little at his child's words.

"Aye, I'll stay," he said, and Isabelle gifted him with a smacking kiss to his cheek. He laughed and looked at Pamela, his eyes glowing with moisture. She felt a little in her own. Isabelle had been her daddy's girl from the first minute he'd held her and she hoped that there was some memory, deep inside their daughter, which would allow Isabelle to know that, even if she couldn't remember it consciously.

"Can I help ye with somethin'?" he asked.

"Sure. Would you make tea for the table?" The teapot and kettle were out, as was the tin of loose leaves. He wouldn't need to ask where anything was, and so she felt it was the best task to give him.

They sat to eat a few minutes later—Kathleen in her cradle and Isabelle sitting beside Casey and staring at him with great interest, rather than attending to her meal. Getting Isabelle to eat had long been a challenge and Pamela sighed, knowing she would need to isolate her so her attention span was greater than that of a bee in a field of wildflowers. Casey took in her look, and started to feed Isabelle off his own plate, rather than hers. Isabelle, always of the opinion that other people's things were more interesting and therefore more desirable, ate everything offered to her. Casey lost half his meal in this manner, but he seemed well pleased that Isabelle was happy to be fed by his hand.

Once she was done with eating, Isabelle got down from her chair and went to play with her brother's building blocks, something Conor allowed when he was home, but only with supervision. Pamela decided it wasn't worth the upset to stop her though, and mentally apologized to her son. She got up and refilled Casey's plate and put it back in front of him.

"Thank ye," he said, and then looked down at the plate as if he wasn't sure what to do with the contents.

"Is something wrong?" she asked.

"No, it's just I'm not used to someone lookin' after me, even in such a small way. It's nice."

"Oh," she said and flushed a little, pleased that something which was no more than habit to her—refilling people's empty plates—had such an effect on him.

He looked up, his eyes meeting hers and causing the heat in her cheeks to rise even higher. "Christ, ye're beautiful. I remembered that, but thought maybe my mind had exaggerated ye. Even my dreams never did ye justice, though."

"You dreamed about me?" she asked, just as Isabelle poked a tiny and indignant face over the end of the table.

"You did a swear," Isabelle said in her best censorious tone, glaring at Casey. "You hassa put money in de jar now."

"Ye're right, I did," Casey said, taking her comment with the seriousness a three-year-old expected to follow such a pronouncement. He stood and dug in his pocket. "Here, I've a pound note. Will ye help me put it in the jar?"

"Dat's too much, right, Mama?" If a stickler for the rules, Isabelle was also inherently fair.

"Yes, that's right, Isa-bit. We'll give daddy his change, though." Pamela held her breath a little to see if Isabelle would protest at having Casey called daddy, but Isabelle merely said, "A-wight," and let Casey pick her up so that she could tuck the pound note into the jar. She grabbed a small fistful of change from said jar and offered it to Casey.

"Mama say you haffa take da change," she said, in her best bossy tone.

"Well, I'll not know how much a swear costs, so I don't know how much change I'm meant to take."

"Mama says one pee for lil words, five pee for the badders an' ten pee for willy bads. Yous is a willy bad, cuz it Jesus's last name."

Pamela bit her lip to keep from laughing and noted that Casey was having trouble keeping his own face straight.

"Willy bad?" he asked.

"Really bad," Pamela translated for him.

"Ah, I see," he said, with a quiver in his voice that told her he was making a heroic effort not to laugh. He picked the coins out from Isabelle's hand, counting them out loud, so that she would know he was taking only what was owed and no more.

"You is a good boy," Isabelle said when he was done, and kissed his cheek when he'd taken the last coin.

"Well, thank ye for that," Casey said, raising a questioning eyebrow at Pamela. Isabelle, however, was more than happy to explain.

"Dat's what Mama says when I do sumfin' bad, an' she kisses me. Mama says dat you did a bad fing, Isa-bip, but you iz no a bad people."

"That's good to know," Casey said, and she thought the quiver in his voice this time wasn't from laughter.

"You play now?" Isabelle asked, briskly moving on to more important matters.

"Aye," Casey said, "what would ye like to do?"

"Play wif Conor's blocks. Conor likes billin' fings."

"I like buildin' things too," Casey said, clearly already becoming fluent in his daughter's language. "Do you?"

Isabelle shrugged. "Suntimes. I like playin' wif Conor's fings."

Pamela smiled wryly. "She's honest, at least."

He smiled in return. "I believe she takes after her mother there, no? I remember ye bein' rather straightforward about things."

"You were no slouch in that area either," she said.

"Blocks," Isabelle said, impatient with the conversation.

Pamela took the opportunity of Isabelle having her own company to bathe Kathleen. Normally Isabelle wanted to wash Kathleen and dress her, both things she was too small to do, though Pamela allowed her to do little things, so that she might feel the importance of being the big sister to Kathleen. Still, it was nice to just bathe the baby without having to clean up puddles of water and soap afterwards. It seemed a good indication to her that Isabelle was already clearly quite comfortable in her father's company. Conor was another matter entirely, but as Owen had pointed out his apple cart had indeed been upset and in a way Isabelle's hadn't and could not be. Small as he was, Conor had been a rock for her, as much as a child his age could be. He was wise beyond his years, and Owen was right, he had likely built his father into a mythical hero who could not be recognized when presented in the flesh.

Gathering Kathleen up in her arms, she went down the stairs, hearing Isabelle's chatter and Casey's briefer and gentle responses. At the bottom of the stairs, she halted and watched them for a moment. Casey was patiently building a rather impressive house from the Meccano set, while Isabelle sat in his lap, giving out orders like the tiny Hussar she was. Just watching the two of them made her throat ache like a sliver of glass was caught in it. The sliver of glass grew as Casey closed his eyes and bent his own head over that of his daughter, clearly overcome with emotion. Another night, long ago, swam up before her eyes, of Casey dancing in the low light of the old kitchen, Isabelle in his arms, warm and glowing like a tiny rosy pearl, and she felt it again—the cost of his time away from them.

She cleared her throat before stepping down from the last stair, giving him warning so that he could compose his face before looking toward her.

"Mama," Isabelle chirped, "come see a house we builded."

"It's beautiful, sweetheart," she said, walking over to stand beside them, and making all the appreciative noises a mother made when shown her offspring's creations.

It *was* beautiful—due to Casey's skill. Clearly, he had lost none of his aesthetic sense when it came to the art of building things. He had always had this ability, one he'd passed on to Conor, to take a few things—bits of wood, bark, moss, shells or even building blocks—and turn it to something magical, something into which he'd imbued a bit of his soul.

"It's bedtime, Isa-bit," Pamela said, patting Kathleen's back. The baby was wriggling, and would soon need to be nursed. "You need to get your pyjamas on and then bring your toothbrush to me, so we can brush your teeth."

Isabelle drew her small face into a frown. Never a fan of bed time, she was even less so when she had company. "I's not goin'. Is not p'lite to go bed wif a wizitor."

Casey bit his lip to stop himself from laughing, and Pamela sent him a stern glare, feeling the need to laugh bubbling up irresistibly in herself. Proximity to him was making her feel a little drunk, as if she'd imbibed far more than was wise.

"Daddy will come again to visit you, Isabelle. You are already way past your bed time."

"I can do those things with her, if she doesn't mind," Casey said.

Pamela looked at her small recalcitrant daughter. "Can Daddy help you with your pyjamas and teeth?"

"Yes, him can help me. Him has to read wif me too."

Pamela smiled. "Isabelle don't be bossy, you know you have to ask, not tell people what to do."

Isabelle tipped her wee face up toward Casey. "You read wif me?"

"Aye, I'll read to ye, if yer mammy doesn't mind givin' up the readin' for tonight."

"Go ahead," she said, feeling that she desperately needed a moment to pull herself together.

Isabelle gave her a kiss, tasting rather strongly of humbugs, clearly she had found the secret stash Pamela kept in the pantry, or Casey had some tucked in his pocket. Isabelle took Casey's hand then, and said, "You haffa read *Sleepy Sheeps* fee times," illustrating her point with three raised and rather grubby little fingers. Pamela felt a slight qualm, *Sleepy Sheeps* was a handbound book which Jamie had written for Isabelle, and Pamela had illustrated it with numerous sheep, some sleepy and eager to go to bed, some not so eager and needing a variety of rituals to finally get off to their slumber—one small black and curly-wooled sheep in particular. Jamie had filled the book with words designed to soothe and calm, and Isabelle sometimes didn't even make it through the first reading, much less two subsequent ones before succumbing to sleep.

Father and daughter set off up the stairs together, Isabelle still telling Casey what had to be done to execute her bedtime ritual in full, and Pamela heaved a sigh of relief, knowing she would have a good half hour to herself. She settled on the sofa to nurse Kathleen. Just looking at the tiny face at her breast, haloed in fiery wisps of hair, steadied her a little. Pamela breathed in all Kathleen's lovely and complex baby scent and felt something let go in her core a little. Tears began to slide down her face, and she simply let them fall. There was no one to see but Kathleen, and babies were beautifully nonjudgmental.

For the last three years, something inside of her had been frozen, still and waiting, like a pond in winter, and she had been terrified of it one day thawing and bringing her to a place where she fully accepted the loss of Casey. Now it was no longer still, it was in melt and shock, because the one thing she had been almost certain would never happen, had. He was here, he was whole, he was home, and yet she felt a huge amount of uncertainty and a bit of terror around all of it. What if it never felt like home to him again? What if they could not bridge the gap of those three years? What then? And what of Jamie? Her relationship with him was mending, and though she hadn't anticipated it moving forward in any appreciable way as long as he was married to Violet, still she knew his feelings and she knew her own. Right now, she didn't even know what Casey wanted, and thought it likely he didn't know either.

The sound of his step on the stairs jolted her out of her reverie. She wiped any trace of tears from her face and righted her clothing just as he came off the last stair.

"Wow," he said, sitting down one of the chairs by the table, and letting out his breath. "She's a force of nature, that one."

"She is, in both nature and action," Pamela said drily, "entirely your daughter."

He laughed. "I'm thinkin' that's not intended as a compliment. She looked at me when I finished readin' her book to her, an' said, 'I like you, youze can come back again.'"

"She doesn't hand that out lightly, so take it for the compliment it is," Pamela said.

"Oh, I do," he assured her.

They sat quietly for a few minutes after that, a strange awkwardness arising, until she became aware of his regard, his eyes resting on her with an unfathomable expression. Once she had known his various moods, and could guess what he was thinking merely by the look on his face. Now, she wasn't so certain, though he'd always had the ability to hide his emotions, when he so chose.

"What is it, Casey?"

"Nothin' much, I'm just thinkin' how lovely the two of ye look, sittin' here in the quiet. I remember ye sittin' just so with our two in the same way."

"You remember?"

"Well, it's more of an impression than an actual memory. Only seein' ye there with the baby in yer arms, I can feel that I've seen ye so before. Could ye maybe do with another cup of tea?"

"That would be grand," she said.

He banked the fire and made another pot of tea. To see him moving around the kitchen, stacking wood on the fire, checking the hasps on the windows as if it was second nature to him, was greatly comforting as well as an emotional grace note which threatened to make her cry again. It was also a chance to simply watch him, and take in the sight of him.

There were changes in him. And yet, he was still Casey, still the man who had always made her weak in the knees and had given her a family both in himself and the children they had created together. The man who had built the home in which she had found sanctuary, and then lost it when he disappeared.

"Will I put her in the cradle for ye?" he asked.

"Yes please," she said, and held Kathleen up so that Casey could scoop her into his arms. He did it as he always had, with great care, so as not to wake her. He'd the knack of it—handling babies—and she thought it was that he simply liked babies and so was relaxed with them, and sensing that, the babies felt secure in his arms and thus behaved well for him. Kathleen didn't so much as stir as he walked her across the floor, and placed her gently into her cradle.

She joined him at the table, the tea steaming between them. And then it was just the two of them, the house quiet around them, Finbar snoring lightly by the fire, and the children asleep. It recalled other evenings, when they had sat so, content to just be with one another.

"Can I ask where Conor is?"

"He's gone to Gert and Owen's for the night."

Casey nodded. "He's not comfortable with me, is he?"

"No, not yet. He's upset right now, but he missed you a great deal. He was old enough to remember you when you disappeared, but not old enough to merge that memory with the man who showed up in his house the other day. He's small, but he thinks of himself as the man of the house in some ways, as ridiculous as that might sound—and he's right. He will come around, he just needs time. He's like all you Riordans, stubborn as stone."

Casey smiled at her last statement, a quick flash of white in the dark of his stubble, the indent of his dimple sending a ripple of pleasure through her body, just for the sight of it.

"It's different to be in yer presence," he said quietly. "Mind, it's not like I had a clear picture of ye for a long time. Every now an' again, I'd dream about ye, though. The dreamin' was both a comfort an' a disturbance."

"You mentioned that before—that you'd dreamed about me," she said softly, feeling oddly shy.

"Aye, though ye were more a presence than someone I could see. When I dreamed of ye, it was like tryin' to clutch at mist—beautiful an' all filled with light, but in the end no matter how much ye grasp at it, ye're left with empty hands. I'd be unsettled for days after."

"I'm sorry," she said, feeling as guilty as if she'd stolen into his dreams purposefully in order to agitate the man.

"Ye're sorry? What on earth are ye sorry for?"

"Only that you were disturbed, but couldn't remember. It must have been very frustrating for you."

"Aye, it was, an' yet I wouldn't have traded those dreams for anythin'. They were the one thing reassurin' me that you were maybe out there some-where in the world. An' sometimes ye came to me when I felt especially low, an' that helped a great deal." Something of that time lingered in his eyes, and he seemed to know it, for he turned his face from her.

"Casey, you don't have to look away from me. You can tell me anything. I'm glad if the dreams helped, but God I do wish I'd been there for you, had been able to touch and hold you when you needed me."

"Of late I had remembered some things about our life together, but to actually be here an' see ye move about an' to watch ye with our children again, an' see how well ye've loved them an' the perfect trust they have in ye—well, it takes a man's breath away." He took a shaky breath as though to underscore his words. "I forgot," he said, his eyes deep with emotion, "how it was with us."

"I did too. I knew and yet to be in your presence and feel how it is again—it's a little overwhelming."

"Aye, it is," he said, giving her the tentative smile he'd been using since his return. "There's somethin' I should like to ask ye, if ye don't mind."

"You can ask me anything," Pamela said, thinking perhaps that wasn't the wisest statement on her part. Casey had never been a man to shy away from difficulty, and there were definitely some questions he might ask which could prove to be explosive, considering how tense things felt right now.

"In one of the letters that Conor left me, he mentioned that ye were no longer goin' to 'marry Noah.'"

A waterfall of ice-water ran through her intestines. She hadn't thought he knew this and while she realized he would have to be told at some point, she had hoped it wouldn't be this soon. She'd wanted firmer ground beneath their feet before the subject of Noah was broached. As if he'd read her thoughts, Casey said, "I think we have to have the truth between us—all of it, no matter how uncomfortable."

"I was engaged to Noah Murray. I don't know if you remember him or not," she said, keeping her voice even. Even in so plain a statement it gave her a sharp pang to say Noah's name, she had avoided speaking of him for so long.

"Noah *Murray*? Kate's brother? The Noah Murray that once threatened to kill ye? The biggest murderin' bastard in the Murder Triangle—that Noah Murray?"

She swallowed. "Yes, *that* Noah Murray. It was," she said aware how defensive her tone sounded, "an arrangement between us. I needed protection and he—" she stopped short, realizing Casey wasn't going to be best pleased by what her end of the deal had been with Noah. "How do you remember that—that he threatened to kill me once?"

Casey waved a hand in the air, as if dismissing this bit of memory. "I do remember some things, Pamela, bits an' pieces, this just happens to be one of them. I'm thinkin' it left an impression on me when the PIRA boss threatened to kill my wife. Anyway, please continue with what ye were sayin'. What was it Mr. Murray needed?"

"Companionship," she said stiffly. "He was a good friend to me, Casey. He kept us safe and that was what he offered to me and our children—safety and protection. It seemed a fair enough bargain."

"Companionship, is it?" he snorted. "Is that what he called it? He wanted ye in his bed, an' if he had to make a legal arrangement to get what he wanted, it probably seemed a small enough price to pay."

"You're making me sound like a paid whore," she said angrily.

"I'm not sayin' any such thing. Are *you* sayin' sex wasn't part of this arrangement?"

"No, it wasn't. He gave me the option of a platonic marriage."

"An' did ye take him up on that offer?"

"No, I didn't. I didn't think it would be fair. He had made it clear that he did desire me, but he wouldn't have married me just for that. It didn't matter in the end, because I broke off the engagement."

"Why?"

"Because I just couldn't go through with it. I couldn't marry anyone, Casey. I was still married to you, regardless of the fact I thought you were dead." She shook her head. "I just couldn't."

His hands lay loose on the table, though the strength in them was clear. Big hands, beautifully defined by bone and muscle and vein. Hands that could cradle and comfort, hands that could kill with one well placed blow. Hands that had touched her with tenderness and love, with passion and frustration and that could make her shiver with desire just looking at them.

"You still wear your wedding ring," she said, quietly, uncertain as to why she was bringing it up with him, as loaded as even the simplest statement seemed to be between them.

He shrugged. "I never took it off unless I was fightin'. It was one of the things I carried with me from my life before. Even when I didn't have a clue who I was, Pamela, I still felt married to you. I still *am* married to ye, come to that."

She swallowed, throat prickling with tears suddenly. "I only took mine off when I was engaged to Noah. It didn't feel right to wear your ring and his at the same time. When I broke off the engagement I went home and put your ring back on. I wasn't even sure it was the right thing to do, but my world felt more balanced with the bit of silver on my hand."

She put her hand over his, nervous to make even so small a gesture. Something that had once been as natural as breathing to her, now seemed to hold a terrible weight of meaning. He moved his hand so that his fingers wrapped around hers, holding them firmly. She dared to take a tiny breath at that point, relieved by this small sign of affection between them. He looked at her then, and she stiffened her spine a little, bracing for what he might be about to say.

"I want to say this one thing to you. It was you, Pamela, that kept me goin'. Just the idea that I might one day find ye, kept me alive at times."

"And now here you are," she said softly, feeling the joy of it even as she said the words.

"Aye, here I am, throwin' yer entire life into disarray." He smiled and yet she had the sense there was some truth to those words for him.

"If it is disarray, it's the most wonderful sort."

He put his free hand out, but then stopped as if he was suddenly uncertain he should touch her.

"What is it?" she asked.

"I think I'm scared to really touch ye. I'm afraid ye'll disappear like a soap bubble—there an' then gone."

"I won't," she said, and took the hand, pressing it to her lips. The familiarity of it—the calluses, the scent of earth and smoke and that darker note—brought tears to her eyes. She turned her head and laid her cheek against his palm, closing her eyes.

"I do understand that I have thrown things into an unholy mess, Pamela. I don't expect—"

Pamela looked up and touched her fingers to his mouth, halting his words.

"No, don't say it, Casey. For three years, I've prayed and dreamed about this—you sitting here, with a cup of tea in front of you, looking back at me. What do you think my life without you has been?"

He looked at her for several seconds, pain in the dark eyes. "Empty, if it was anything like mine."

"Empty, lonely, and terrifying. I couldn't sleep most nights wondering if you were out there, or if you'd been killed and if you'd needed me at the end, and I wasn't there for you. Horrible things," she choked a little on the words, "would play over and over in my head, and I'd wonder if those things had happened to you, if you'd been in pain, if you'd been afraid, if you'd—"

"Hush," Casey said and got out of the chair and came to kneel down at her feet. "It's all right, Pamela. We don't have to talk about it just now. I was wrong to even start this conversation with ye."

"No, you weren't. We will have to talk about things, and you're right, we need to have the truth between us."

"Aye," he put a hand up and cupped her chin, his eyes warm, though a lingering trace of sadness could still be seen in his expression. "We do, but there's time enough for truth, an' it's likely best we don't speak it all in one go."

"There *is* time enough, now, isn't there?" It was a risky question, but she could not seem to stop herself from asking it. Time enough for truth and revelation, time to come to know what those shadows in his eyes were made of, time for her to tell him all the truths of what had happened while he was gone. Time enough to see how strong their marriage was, despite the years apart and all that had taken place. Given enough time anything could be absorbed into the stream of a life, could be taken in and made part of the structure of love, making it stronger even as it changed the shape of it.

She leaned down and kissed him and then put her forehead to his, just to feel the warmth and life in him.

"Casey?" She said it softly, so that he might answer or not, as he chose.

"Aye, Jewel, there's time enough now."

Chapter Eleven

Order and Justice

THE ROYAL IRISH Constabulary had been the brainchild of British MP, Robert Peel, and the formation of it had been in response to a country which was, at the time, in a state of rampant lawlessness.

For the one hundred years previous to the establishment of a police force, the countryside of Ireland was held in the grip of bands of violent men. Their picturesque names—Ribbonmen, Thrashers, Peep o' Day boys, Whiteboys, Carders—belied the terror which rode the wind everywhere the men went. These gangs were a direct result of the agrarian grievances of the peasant class, who had seen their small tenant farms—which many families had lived upon for generations—torn out from under them by landlords who saw a chance to improve their own lot by turning the wee plots into pasture for cattle. Violence and retribution were their calling cards, and anyone who dared to whisper a word against them in witness to their deeds, suffered a terrible fate at their hands—beating, pitchforking, shooting, tarring and stoning—and so the people learned to look away and keep their tongues silent as the grave. This was a rule applicable to the North unto the present day.

The only law available at the time was that of the 'baronial constables' mostly a force of old men, who were there to enforce the landlord's wishes and rule. While these old 'barneys' as they were called could serve writs or officiate when court was in session, when it came to real trouble the military had to be called upon. However, when Robert Peel arrived in Ireland, most of the army was away fighting in the Napoleonic War and it was in this absence that he saw the opportunity to establish a national police force.

Peel's hope was to have salaried magistrates brought in with a force of trained constables under their command, to areas of the country which were identified as 'troubled'. Enacted into law, it worked well, with lawless counties finding a great decrease in unrest and disorder within the first several months. Still, despite Peel's efforts to circumvent patronage, the force was largely identified as the protectors of the landlords and gentry, and distrusted by the peasant class.

Signing up to be a constable in those days had been no small commitment, for the men had to live in barracks at night and couldn't even consider marrying for at least seven years, and even then, their wives had to be fully vetted and approved by the Royal Irish Constabulary. There was no official rota of duty, rest days or leave.

Eventually, it became clear the force needed a centralized command, and so Dublin Castle—the seat of British power in Ireland—would become that centre, issuing orders from a lofty perch to the countryside of a land they didn't understand, and never would.

After the partition of Ireland, the Royal Irish Constabulary would morph into the Royal Ulster Constabulary in the North and into the Garda Siochana in the Republic. The force in the North would remain largely Protestant, aligned with the Protestant community, right into the present time, with the odd Catholic accepted into the force as a token gesture against the charges of prejudice towards the Nationalist community, and favouritism toward the Loyalists.

One of those token heathen Catholics was Detective Will Holroyd, who was currently sitting on the ledge of a crumbling windowsill of a long-abandoned workhouse, eating a green apple and musing over his own role in the aforementioned force. Will sometimes thought the monk-like existence of that early force, without home or wife, quelling the savage countryside, would have been more in his line. He was a being of order and absolutes. This trait was one of the reasons he'd pursued a career with the police.

While Will no longer graced any church with his presence, he had been raised a Catholic, and that was all that mattered in this country. As far as his fellow officers were concerned, he might as well have hung a picture of the pope in his cubbyhole of an office, and wore a rosary around his neck. They also resented him for what they saw as an end run around regular duties to get where he was in the hierarchy of the force. He'd worked for the Met in London for ten years, before the transfer home. Before that he'd done his time in the streets of Belfast though, clad in bulletproof vest and carrying an automatic weapon, always certain he was about to be shot or blown to kingdom come. When he'd left Belfast, he hadn't looked back and had thought he'd never return for more than a brief visit. But when his mother got sick, he felt that as her only living child he was obliged to come home. He'd been transferred home at his current grade, and been slotted in above men twice his age, which went down about as well as a pickled pig's foot that had gone off.

The result of being Catholic on a mostly Prod force was that he was twice as determined to never show favouritism to his own, and to pursue the order and absolutism of justice, as much as possible in a country rife with injustice and chaos. Of course, as it turned out, his work had little to do with either order or absolutes of any sort. He found this greatly frustrating at times.

In truth, Will wasn't great at bowing down to authority, and preferred to do things at his own pace, and within his own understanding, which made him, he was aware, a great detective but a terrible policeman.

Today—his day off—he'd driven down here to South Armagh. The windowsill in which he currently sat, chewing his apple, was in the room of the workhouse where Noah Murray had died. If his superiors saw him now, it was likely he'd get an earwigging and possibly a boot in the behind, kicking him down the ranks back to a plod on the street. Which was something, Will thought, jumping down from the windowsill and throwing his apple core into the woods that clustered close around the rotting building, he couldn't countenance.

The room around him was cold, and it still smelled of blood. He thought maybe it always would. Long drifts of ivy hung through the holes in the roof, and the dark shadows of trees bent in the window, tracing their crooked boughs upon the floor.

When he'd first returned, one of the names he'd heard a lot, coupled with some truly colourful invectives, had been that of Noah Murray. Despite living well out of the territory of Belfast, the man had been considered enemy number one of both the police force and the British Army. It had been clear to Will that his colleagues were afraid of the man as well as determined to find a way to take him out permanently. The attrition rate for a policeman in South Armagh was extremely high, and that was in a country which was considered the most dangerous place in the world to be a police officer. Will had wanted to take the man down legally and bang him up for life, and so he'd drawn a bead on Noah Murray, even during the time when he, Will, was still going through a baptism of fire within the force, heathen Catholic that he was.

He'd watched and waited, but there had never been a chink through which he could find a weakness in Noah Murray's territory or person, and he'd begun to believe the myth which surrounded the man of someone who was both invincible and untouchable. Then one day a fellow officer had disappeared, and Will's senses had pricked like a hound with the scent of blood in its nose. Following the scent had been a challenge, but he had both the determination and the single-minded focus of the aforesaid hound. He'd just felt he was starting to get a little traction when word had come down from his superiors to quit poking his nose into this matter. Noah Murray was dead, and that was an end to the case his boss had said.

A month had passed since he'd first stood in this room. This cold room, stinking of blood, this room which would be imprinted in his mind's eye for the rest of his life. There had been blood everywhere that day, and bodies—five of them. There'd been a filthy, blood-soaked mattress, and a chain attached to the wall beside it. This was the mattress where Noah Murray had died, and this the chain which had bound Pamela Riordan to the mercy of a madwoman and her three henchmen.

Calling off the investigation meant one of two things—Noah Murray was still alive and in hiding, or Special Branch was demanding an end to the investigation. Already on thin ice with his commander, Will had stopped the investigation out in the open, where his superiors might realize he hadn't given up on the hunt. He'd been one of two detectives to follow up on the carnage they'd found in this workhouse, and so had heard Pamela Riordan's story firsthand. Judging by her clear and present trauma in the aftermath, he wasn't putting money on Noah Murray being present amongst the living. Which left Special Branch. Was Special Branch covering for the woman? And if so, why?

He walked over to the fireplace, his steps echoing in the cold afternoon. The ashes of the fire were still heaped high, but they too were cold. No mortal had disturbed this place since last he'd been here. Still, there was a presence. Will didn't believe in ghosts, which he supposed was rather un-Irish of him, but he'd never seen one and therefore didn't put much stock in them. Still, a place didn't need ghosts to be haunted, merely the energy of some great shocking event left hanging in the air, with neither time nor place for the energy to dissipate into, was more than enough to haunt a place.

Noah Murray's men had scattered to the four winds in the wake of their boss' death. Except for one, a man he'd managed to track down through a series of painstaking leads. It was this man who had told him that Pamela Riordan had, indeed, been at Noah Murray's farm the night Constable Blackwood seemingly disappeared into thin air. The interview was there in his mind, though he'd had the foresight to get it on tape as well.

"I let her in the gate, then I called up to the house on my radio to let him know to expect her. She had blood all over her coat, that much I saw when I spoke to her."

"Did she stay long?"

"She spent the night."

"Was she involved with him romantically?"

"Later she was. At that point, I don't know. It was what he wanted, though," the man had shrugged, "an' so if she wanted somethin' from him, maybe it was a trade of sorts that night."

"A trade?" He had, of course, understood what the man meant, but he wanted it clarified for the recording.

"She gets in his bed, gives him what he wants, an' he kills a man that she's findin' increasingly inconvenient."

"You have reason to believe that Mr. Murray had Constable Blackwood killed?"

The man shrugged. "No, ye're the one who suggested it, I'm just givin' a possible argument for that scenario. Whatever happened that night had the woman good and scared. I saw her face when she arrived, an' I know."

Will didn't doubt it. He had known Blackwood in passing, and had not liked the man a great deal, and knew it was certainly within the man's character to harass a woman to the point of terror. Possibly to even kill her. So if the woman had felt the threat to be that great—well, he could see why she'd go to Noah Murray for help.

"Beyond her arrival there that night was there anything in particular that made you think she might have asked him to kill the constable?"

Fear passed over the man's face, light as a ripple of air over water but Will caught it and knew this next bit of information would require a little prodding. Someone else had clearly been there that night, but who he wondered, would make this man fearful of speaking about the person?

Will's mother used to say 'prick a man's pride, and find his weakness.' He chose his next words carefully.

"I know Mr. Murray was famed for his ability to keep a lockdown on information; I heard he kept most of his men on a need-to-know basis, and only his inner circle knew what was going on from one minute to the next. If you weren't part of that inner circle, then clearly you wouldn't know what happened that night and no shame to you."

The struggle was brief, and Will knew he'd hedged his bets correctly by focusing on the man's vanity.

"There was a man did work for him sometimes. Usually Noah did his own work, mind, but now an' again, he'd farm it out, so to speak. I never did see the man up close, so what I say next is only an impression, an' not a description."

Will nodded, not wanting to interrupt the man now that he was started on the flow of information.

"Noah never let the rest of us meet him, I don't even know how the fella would enter onto Noah's land. I think usually they'd meet elsewhere, but that night he came when Noah called. I think he must have been nearby to arrive so swiftly."

"Nearby?" Will raised an eyebrow in question.

"Well, somewhere close enough that he arrived only a few hours after she showed up, lookin' like she'd butchered a hog. Anyway, I did manage to see him the once or twice, just a glimpse, but I'd the impression he'd maybe been a soldier, or maybe still was."

"What caused you to think so?" Will asked, feeling that curious prickle at the base of his skull that he sometimes got when a thing was true.

"Just the way he held himself, he seemed like a soldier to me. Also, in our business we're wary of soldiers, so I was surprised. Thought maybe that's why Noah kept him away from the rest of us."

A soldier who was a hired killer? Will knew it had happened, but it always felt like a bit of shock, though he knew one should never underestimate the variety of things humans would do for the sake of a coin or two in the hand. A soldier made this whole scenario more interesting and far more dangerous. He knew if he was to prove that Pamela Riordan had asked Noah to have Constable Blackwood killed, he'd have to find this soldier and crack him. It was fortunate that he enjoyed a challenge.

"What about James Kirkpatrick—did you ever see him at the farm? Or near Noah Murray at all?"

"I only saw the two of them in the same space the once, an' that was on the woman's property. I don't think they'd met before, but I'll tell ye this, Noah didn't like findin' the man there. It was early mornin' an' it was clear the man had spent the night. There was talk amongst the men, when he decided to marry her, bein' that she was carryin' Kirkpatrick's bastard."

It was one of those oddities Will had found with these hard men—this dour, almost priestly attitude toward sex and women. And yet, he had a sense that the man in front of him had found Pamela Riordan attractive, and resented her for it. Well, men did sometimes, didn't they? Resent a woman they wanted but knew they'd never have. Watching his boss with her could have spurred that resentment into something more. It was also possible that he could simply want to punish her for existing beyond his reach. Will had seen such things before, and knew not to underestimate the bitterness of a man who understood there would always be things he was not allowed in this world.

"You didn't like her?" Will asked.

"It wasn't that I didn't like her, didn't know her really. Noah kept her well away from the rest of us." The man couldn't help himself it seemed, for there was a slight sneer in his voice, and Will knew he'd pegged it right. This was a man filled with resentment, and therefore he was malleable to manipulation of the mildest sort. Knowing that he wanted to vent his spleen, Will merely fixed a polite interest upon his face, and maintained his silence. It only took a moment before the man swallowed the bait.

"A woman like that is going to cost ye, isn't she? Noah was a lot of things, but stupid wasn't one of them. He knew there'd be a price, an' it wouldn't have exactly curdled his wame to kill a man or two should she require it."

"You didn't like your boss?"

The man shrugged again, face impassive. "It doesn't much matter whether I liked him or not, he's dead."

Will sometimes found these men uncomfortable in their matter-of-fact attitude toward death, and yet he'd also found them capable of a great deal of sentimentality. It was an odd mix, he thought, and it always made him chary of the lot of them.

"Noah was hard, in the way ye need to be to get things done in this country. I never met a man who wasn't afraid of him, but that wee bit of a woman didn't fear him in the least. It was a great deal of what he liked about her, I think. But still, aye, I think she's capable of all sorts."

Will thought this was likely true, though he suspected her morality was far more intact than that of the man sitting in front of him. Still, this business of his required that he wade through the mud to get to the truth, for justice was often buried deep and one let the small fish go in favour of the hope of snaring the big one. Not that he thought the woman was a big fish, but she was certainly attached to a few. James Kirkpatrick not being the least of them.

After the interview, there were many questions to ponder and inconsistencies to brood over. That was why he'd come here to this workhouse today—to ponder and brood a bit. If indeed, Pamela Riordan had asked Noah to kill a policeman for her, it was his job to prove it and see it through to the court. What happened beyond that was not within his control.

Will had always loved puzzles from the time he was old enough to put them together; he still loved a good crossword and had the Sunday edition of the New York Times delivered to his local corner shop every week, so he could spend his evenings poring over it. When he was ten an uncle of his had given him a puzzle with three thousand pieces. The picture was of a beautiful Japanese girl in a pale blue kimono standing in front of a temple. He'd loved it, and even developed a bit of a crush on the unknown Japanese girl in the picture.

Then his little sister had taken a few pieces of the puzzle outside and lost them. The puzzle had been ruined for him after that, the Japanese girl no longer worthy of his love, and the picture incomplete and therefore a source of pain to him. His mother had even cut out bits of cardboard and coloured them into a good approximation of the missing pieces. But the puzzle was still no good in his eyes, because he needed the real pieces, otherwise the picture was just a fake. He felt the same about a mystery with missing pieces. This mystery had a few, and he needed them to complete the picture.

The missing pieces in this mystery were, by his reckoning, three in number: who was the shooter, where was Noah Murray's body and how was he going to find the soldier who was hiring out as a killer?

He believed the Riordan woman's story about what had happened here, despite the fact that there'd been no trace of Noah Murray's body. There had been a lot of blood, though, too much likely for a man to have survived the loss of it. Still, a lie by omission was still, in Will's books, a lie. And he was certain there were things Pamela Riordan was not telling him.

So to begin—who had shot the five people found dead in this room? Will had run the crime scene photos through his head ad nauseam, trying to get a fix on the trajectory of the bullets, and where a shooter would have to be placed in order to hit targets so cleanly and swiftly. He'd come to the same conclusion again and again—the bullets had come from outside and the trajectory told him that the gunman had been placed on a level with the window in order to shoot with such deadly accuracy. Heart shots for the four men, one to the head for the woman. So he'd been in a tree, which told Will the man had an uncanny amount of self-possession. Plus it had been dark and raining, not ideal conditions under which to kill moving targets. Someone with military training, or possibly a sniper for the IRA?

Will went down the stairs and out into the chill of the afternoon. The blue light of December had turned everything a cold pewter, and tendrils of fog moved amongst the wet black boughs of the trees. It was time to get out of here. Will wasn't superstitious, he'd seen far too many crime scenes for that, but something about this old workhouse put the hair up on the back of his neck. This place had seen too much death and despair right from its inception. Still, he stood for a time, at the base of an oak tree. He'd climbed it several times already, and had a good idea of exactly which crook the shooter had braced himself in, but he'd left behind him no trace, no clue. It bothered Will. He liked filling in puzzle pieces, supplying answers, understanding how everything fit, even if the official investigation was over.

His boss had told him to let it go. "Look, Noah Murray is gone, and the woman is no threat. You don't want to cross James Kirkpatrick either, he's got connections on levels you can't even dream about, boy."

"Why is it that *he* wouldn't want to see justice done here?"

His commander had sighed. "Jesus, Will, what is justice? You've got some tit-for-tat notion of it. You saw the state that woman was in, those bastards kidnapped her with every intention of killing her once her child was born. Someone made sure that never happened, and I can't say I blame them. What happened to the four in that room *is* justice, and the sooner you learn what that looks like in this country the better off you'll be."

He'd held his tongue, but the commander took in the stubborn set of his face and sighed. "Your problem is that you get obsessed, you never know when to let things go, never know when to close your eyes and stop up your ears. That's why the boys at the Met didn't shed any tears when you left. Obsession never leads anywhere good, Will. Mark my words, it's going to get you killed one fine day."

Thinking about the words now, he felt a sinking of his spirits. Maybe the commander was right, and the answer didn't mean more than the people involved. He kicked at the ground under his feet, feeling a flare of temper. But damnit, the answer did matter—the answer was what made this work he did worth it.

It was then that a small spark in the thick forest loam caught his eye. He must have dug something up with his kick. It looked like the glint of brass. He bent down and brushed wet leaves away. The glint became a gleam, and a smile spread across Will's face. He grabbed a stick and pried the gleam out of the cold earth. Then he fished a handkerchief from his pocket and spread it across the palm of his hand, dropping the gleam into its starchy white folds. A shell casing. He'd been right, the shooter had been up this tree, and he'd left a memento behind. He likely hadn't meant to, but it had been a dark and stormy night, as the line went, and odds were the man had been in a hurry to get clear of the area, and hadn't been able to find the casing. With luck, he'd left a fingerprint behind, a small map by which to trace him.

His commander's words echoed in Will's head as he tucked the shell casing into his pocket. *Mark my words, boy, it's going to get you killed one fine day.*

Maybe, maybe not, Will thought, but first he'd see that justice was done. There was a missing body and two killers who were roaming the wilds of South Armagh, and he didn't plan on dying until he'd found all of them.

Chapter Twelve

The Man He Used to Be

CASEY RIORDAN STOOD on the doorstep of his old home, filled with a strange hesitation. He had been here only two days before, but somehow this day—Christmas—felt as though it held an import the previous days had not. The people on the other side of this door were his family, and yet the ways and rhythms of their world were unfamiliar to him, and he felt a little like a man who has entered a dance where he doesn't know the steps.

"Courage, man," he muttered to himself, and knocked on the door.

The nanny, whom he'd met twice now, opened the door, wee Kathleen over her shoulder. She stood aside for him to step in, eyeing him with a certain amount of distrust. Certainly her name—Prudence—fit her character. He couldn't fault her loyalty to her mistress, nor to the children. For that alone he liked her.

As though summoned by his thought, Pamela stepped off the last of the stairs into the kitchen, fussing with her curls, which refused to succumb to the restraint of pins. She wore a lovely dress which somehow managed to convey the notion that she was clothed in heather-coloured smoke. She looked up at him and smiled, a soft flush lighting the pale skin. His body felt a thud of recognition, and the discomforting grab of possession. While he might have doubts about coming home to this woman, his body clearly did not.

"Can I take your coat?" she asked, and he realized he was staring, simply standing here on the woman's well-polished floor with snow melting from his boots, like some great oaf who was seeing a woman for the first time. Well, his feelings for Pamela had never been of the subtle sort, and clearly that had not changed.

He gave her his coat, and took off his boots, setting them to the side of the door, with the strange echo inside of him which told him he'd set them just so many a time before.

"I've a couple of things here, can I give them to ye before we go in?" He could hear the bustle in the kitchen and knew that Pat and Kate were in there, and Prudence had joined them with Kathleen. There was a boy in there too, tall with ears that stood out from his head, and a smile on his face that lit all the space around him.

Of course," she said, and he felt it again—how the very air vibrated between them, making him both nervous and painfully aware of her.

He handed her a box, which he'd tied with twine, not having made it to the shops in the last few days, and so having to rely on what was to hand for wrapping.

"Tis for wee Kathleen," he said and watched as she opened the box. Inside lay a mobile to hang over the baby's crib, of starfish and shells, each carved so that they were whisper-light and would dance on the finest of breezes.

"Oh Casey," she said and lifted the mobile out, the starfish and shells moving in a swirl of violet and celadon, azure and lemon, and a pink as soft as an apple blossom. "I can't believe you had the time to make this."

"Aye, well," he shrugged, making light of the work, "I don't sleep much these days, an' the nights are long. I thought with yerself an' Jamie for parents, this wee one would have sea water runnin' in her veins rather than blood, an' so the shells an' such seemed fittin.'"

He reached into the box he'd placed upon the floor and withdrew another parcel. "This one is for you."

She took the parcel from him, soft colour flooding her face, and opened it. Inside was a shawl, near to the colour of her dress but soft as swansdown and as ephemeral as smoke and mist. She wrapped it around her shoulders and looked up at him. "It's absolutely lovely, Casey. Thank you."

"'Tis nothin' grand, only I did remember this colour looks well on ye, an' that ye've always needed a wee bit of extra warmth in the winter."

"We can't all have our own internal furnace," she said, clearly touched by the gift. She leaned up and kissed his cheek, and a waft of her scent, soft and feminine, enveloped him. He put his hand to her back and gave her a light hug. The constraint between them, even in so light an exchange, was palpable. And yet, to touch her, to be able to do so even with restraint, felt like a miracle.

"I have something for you too," she said and went over to the cupboard by the fireplace and pulled out a package wrapped in brown paper on which someone—Conor he assumed—had drawn a copious amount of fir trees and elves, with the occasional and inexplicable chicken thrown in for good measure.

He looked at Pamela in surprise. "I wouldn't have thought ye'd time to worry about a present." He opened the gift carefully, untying the string, rolling it up and sticking it thriftily in his pocket. It would have been an indication of how bare bones life had been for him in the last few years, had he not always been so, keeping small bits and pieces and knowing he'd find a use for them at some point.

Inside the brown paper he found a sweater, a heavy garment which fell like silk from his fingers. It was a deep burgundy, and he thought it looked vaguely familiar.

He shook the sweater out and held it up against his chest. "Did ye knit this yerself?"

She shrugged. "I was making it for you when you disappeared. I finished it a while back. It was a sort of act of faith believing you'd come home to wear it one day."

"Ah," he said, and felt a prickling in his throat. "Well, thank ye, Pamela."

"You're welcome," she said and took off the shawl so she could go and attend to the dinner. Watching her remove it gave him a small pang. He had to admit to himself that seeing something he'd given her, on her, gave him satisfaction. He knew too well exactly what that emotion was about, and it had nothing of restraint to it.

"You look very handsome," she said, and he felt suddenly self-conscious. It had been some time since he'd worried about his attractiveness to a woman, but he found himself thinking about it now, particularly since he'd become reacquainted with just what James Kirkpatrick looked like. He'd taken care with his appearance today, and had bought a new set of clothes for the occasion—a red sweater and a nice pair of charcoal dress pants, and had shaved just before he'd left Finn's place early that morning, though he knew a hint of stubble was already shadowing his jawline.

"You look lovely, but I imagine ye know that," he said and smiled.

She returned the smile. "Thank you. It's always nice to hear it, especially from you. Come into the kitchen, your brother and Kate are already here."

The kitchen was a hive of activity, with pots covering the top of the Aga, and the windows fogged with all the steam from the cooking. Pat looked up from his position on the floor with the children, and smiled. A wave of gratitude for his brother passed through Casey—with Pat there was no strangeness, it was almost as if they'd simply picked up where they'd left off three years ago.

He walked over to where Conor and Isabelle were sitting with their uncle, a set of spiral drawing wheels scattered on the floor between them. He lowered himself to the floor, hoping his knee wouldn't give way. Conor eyed him warily, though his look wasn't one of outright hostility, and by this small token Casey felt slightly encouraged that his son might be coming around a little.

Isabelle had no such compunction, and got up and threw her arms around his neck, planting a rather sticky and peppermint-flavoured kiss on his lips. He hugged her to him, closing his eyes for a moment against the emotion that swept him each time he looked at his children.

Isabelle plunked herself down in his lap, and Pat's eyes met his over her curly head. He read there the joy his brother took in seeing how easily Isabelle had accepted her father back into her life.

For her he had carved a small troupe of fairies, in a variety of poses—one skipping merrily, one standing on its head with its eyes crossed and one giving a sly wink as it prepared to do a cartwheel. From her gasp of delight, he guessed that she was pleased, and felt that every moment of lost sleep these last two weeks had been worth it.

"Fank you, Daddy," she said, and tilted her wee face up for a kiss, which he happily gave her. She then stood and scampered off to show her mother her gift.

Last, he handed a box to Conor, the contents of which had cost him both sleep and several cuts, and no small amount of cursing. He'd finished it only this morning, and had hoped to heaven the paint would dry before he had to pack it up.

The boy opened the box warily, as though he half-suspected there might be a bomb hiding in the cardboard interior. He drew out the contents, and then looked at Casey, his dark eyes a puzzle. Casey couldn't tell if Conor was pleased, or otherwise. Which, he thought, certainly made him a Riordan through and through. In the boy's hands was a miniature carriage, drawn by black horses, gleaming with stain and a good coating of wax, which he'd rubbed in until his shoulders ached.

"It's the story ye told me," he said, though in truth it was more that Pamela had relayed the story, thinking perhaps Conor would jump in and finish the telling, thus effecting a bit of a thaw in the boy's feeling toward him. "The one with the Queen of the Fairies an' her six black horses, an' her wee carriage. I loved it, an' thought ye might like somethin' to remind ye of it."

"Thank ye," Conor said, turning the small carriage and horse over in his hands.

"Look inside," he said, and showed Conor where the door opened to reveal a miniature interior. "I'm carvin' ye wee footmen to go on the carriage too, only those aren't quite finished."

Conor nodded, and Casey noted the boy's expression. He was half-afraid, half-hopeful but for the first time since his return, Casey felt his son was a little bit open to forming at least a friendship with him. He would take that and be grateful for it.

Conor stood, and placed the carriage on the mantel, arranging the horses just so, and fussing with the leather reins Casey had fashioned for them. Casey took this gesture to mean the boy was pleased with the gift. It was progress, and he'd take it as the gift it was. He stood then, and followed his brother into the heart of the kitchen, where Pat was now helping Kate with something which steamed aromatically. Kate turned and beamed him a smile. He liked his new sister-in-law a great deal; she had acted toward him as though he'd only been gone a few days on a trip, and was now returned and, as a result, felt his presence only required a minimum of fuss.

There was a knock at the door just then, and Pamela turned from the stove, curls damp with steam and her face flushed with the warmth.

"Would you get that for me?" she asked, "It's just Tomas."

He went to the door and opened it, feeling some trepidation at finally encountering this man. Casey knew he meant a great deal to both Patrick and Pamela, and it was clear even in the few things they'd said about him, that he was protective of the two of them, but of Pamela in particular.

On the doorstep, stood a sharply dressed man, with piercing blue eyes and a shock of silver-white hair. He held a whiskey bottle in one hand and a bag in the other.

"Hello, come in. I'm Casey, I'll imagine ye've heard me mentioned," he said, feeling immediately on the defense merely from the assessing look the man was giving him, eyes sweeping him from head to toes and back again.

"Ah, the absentee husband," he said, blue eyes sharp with a challenge Casey knew it was best not to rise to.

"Aye, I suppose that is me," Casey said, feeling the invisible hackles that every man had, rising along his backbone.

The man was slightly portly, and had the flush of a heavy drinker to his skin but there was nothing about him that suggested he would be slow on the uptake, or lacking in acumen. Casey knew his reputation was that of a once brilliant barrister who'd wasted much of his talent and opportunity, due to a penchant for the bottle. Pat, however, respected and admired him, and that, in Casey's view earned him some benefit of the doubt. Pamela clearly loved him, and that too weighed heavily in his favour. Casey suspected favour and benefit of the doubt were two things *he* was not going to be getting from the man in front of him.

The man had taken his measure and, he was certain, found him sadly wanting. He didn't really blame him, most days he wasn't certain he trusted himself, never mind expecting a stranger to.

"Just so ye know, I'll be keepin' an eye on you. If ye so much as turn a hair on that girl's head, I'll make certain ye rue it, d'ye understand?"

"Finn will know me well enough to give ye a reference on my behalf," Casey said drily.

"My cousin is a good man, but maybe a wee bit naïve. Trust is a personal thing, an' as ye've given me no reason to trust yet, I'll take yer measure as I see fit. Ye're not my long-grieved husband, nor my brother."

"I've not given ye reason not to either, bein' that ye've been here about ten seconds altogether." Dark eyes met blue, and did not falter before the steely glare.

"I'm a barrister, I'm skeptical by design, ye'll have to prove that ye're worth trustin', not the other way round."

Tomas, having made his position clear, moved off into the kitchen, kissing the women on their flushed cheeks, giving Pat a hearty hug and then moving to the children, who were clearly both familiar and comfortable with him. There was laughter, and chatter, and the sound of it rose before Casey like a wall, one he knew he stood outside of. None of this held familiarity for him, he was a being apart from this group of people, for their lives had moved on and now included new people, new cares and worries, and new patterns of which he was not a part. As if she sensed his thoughts, Pamela looked up then, green eyes bright with concern.

"Can you uncork the wine for me?" she asked, and he knew that she'd sensed his dislocation, and was trying to pull him into the invisible space which existed in a grouping of people who knew each other well, and moved in their own distinct rhythms which could not be understood by outsiders.

He did as she asked though, coming to stand beside her, his very skin aware of her every movement, her scent filling his senses even over that of the food and drink. There was nervousness in them both today, and he wished they were alone, even for a few moments, so that he could touch her, and know again that sense of belonging he'd felt so strongly the first night in this house.

"Is there anythin' else I can do?" he asked, uncertain whether he was asking for a task, or if there was something he could do to mend what he sensed in her body. He could tell that she was hurt by his discomfiture, for the flush had deepened on her face, and her eyes were dark, something he thought he remembered happened when she was upset. His memory had such a fragmentary quality at times that he didn't know what was real, and what might be something his brain had manufactured in order to build a story from a single thread.

"No, I think everything is ready. I just want you to sit in your chair and enjoy the dinner," she said. She turned away from him swiftly, but not before he saw the glint of tears in her eyes. As much as he was overwhelmed, he thought perhaps, with all she'd been through, it was even more difficult for her.

"I can do that, only I don't know which chair I'm meant to sit in," he said. He felt slightly dizzy, which was how he often felt when something which ought to be familiar simply wasn't, and he had no clue as to the answer.

"Well, in *your* chair of course," she said, looking slightly surprised at his question, "at the head of the table."

"Ye're certain no one will mind?"

She looked down, busying herself with straightening the silverware, which had already been perfectly aligned. "It's your chair, no one has sat in it since you disappeared."

"No one has sat in it for three years?" he asked, voice quiet, as he didn't want the children to overhear. Absorbed as they were in their gifts though, they weren't paying attention to the adults, even if Conor did cast a wary glance in his direction every other minute or so.

"No, as I said, it's your chair. I couldn't bear to see anyone else in it."

"Oh," he said, nonplussed. She continued to fuss with the napkins and candles, refusing to meet his eyes. "Pamela, would ye look at me please? Please," he repeated.

She turned and looked at him, the green eyes glittering with tears, and he felt it suddenly, what these years must have been to her and how much the empty chair was symbolic of that pain and desolation.

"I'm sorry," he said, knowing the two words were horribly small in the face of what he'd just glimpsed in her eyes.

She shook her head, and turned from him again, and he saw that her shoulders shook a little. It frightened him, the thought that he might never be able to make up for what had been taken from her during his absence.

He sat in the chair, because that was what she wanted, but he had the odd sense of taking another man's place at the table, though he smiled and laughed and made talk and hoped that he fooled her at least a little. He feared he hadn't though, for he saw her looking at him with worry more than once. He felt half made of fear since his return—fear that he would never find his way back to who he'd been, fear that his family would no longer see him as necessary to them. His greatest fear though, was that the man Pamela needed was the stranger who'd sat in this chair—the man he'd once been, but no longer was.

The dinner was—mostly due to Kate's efforts—delicious. And yet Pamela found herself unable to eat more than a few spoonfuls. More than one worried look had been cast in her direction, and while she appreciated everyone's concern, she was beginning to find it irritating. Despite all that had happened, she thought she was functioning rather well, and wished people would stop fretting, or wanting her to talk about it. Because they clearly were waiting for her to say something about the workhouse and all that had happened there, yet she knew she couldn't and maybe never would be able to.

Still, the faces arrayed around her, were those she loved, and she was grateful for their presence. Pru had invited Ambrose, and she watched their two heads bent together—one rose-gilt and the other with a cowlick of tawny brown. She noted the flush on Pru's face, and the look in Ambrose's eyes, and realized with a dart of worry that the two of them were falling in love. It seemed ridiculous, they were only babies, after all. Mind you, she'd been only a few months older than Pru when she'd fallen in love with Casey. Ambrose was one of her subjects from her first book, and as such, she was very fond of the boy but also felt responsible for Pru and anything which concerned her.

Tomas was chatting with Pat, but she noted his shrewd gaze moving to Casey every few minutes. She thought Tomas had accepted her invite in part so that he could take Casey's measure. So far, it had to be said, he seemed less than impressed, and looking at Casey's face, she thought the feeling might be mutual. Casey was wary, and as such, not at his most charming, and Tomas was suspicious of Casey's story of his lost memory. If he knew Casey at all, he'd understand that he never would have left them, unless something as cat-astrophic as his loss of memory had happened, but he didn't know him, and was therefore more than a little dubious about the reasons for his absence these last three years.

Looking at Casey, she knew he felt he was a stranger in a strange land. His fears were hers, but she wasn't certain how to tell him that without scar-ing him off. He'd looked as wary as a cornered cat throughout the meal, and she'd sensed his discomfort when everyone was talking and laughing. Such things were, of course, communal, and without a memory, or with only bits and pieces of it to clutch at, none of it would mean anything to him.

She had been excited about this day, simply because Casey would be here with her and the children, and Pat and Kate too, along with Tomas. But now she felt overstimulated, and everything was overly bright and loud, with something strangely hollow underneath, and she had a sudden fear that none of this was real, and that it was all about to burst like a balloon and she would wake to find herself in the workhouse, her baby taken from her and Casey no more than a dream she'd had. She could feel the panic rising, the way it did, like she was in a swift rising sea, and would soon be under water and unable to breathe.

"You'll excuse me, I need to feed the animals," she said, hoping to get outside before anyone saw her face. She dressed hastily in her wellies and thick sweater, throwing a scarf around her neck and then stepped out into the night. She took a deep breath of the cold air, and looked up. The sky was frosted with a scrim of stars, as though they'd been tumbled there by Old Man Winter's hand, like dice scattering ice and fire in their wake. She walked briskly toward the byre, not wanting anyone to look outside and see her lollygagging. They were all worrying overmuch about her and she'd had enough.

The byre was warm and snug, though not so warm that she couldn't see the fog of the animals' breath on the air. Khamsin whickered joyously at her arrival. He knew her appearance at this time of day meant it was meal time. Paudeen even let out a small and happy bleat. She fed Paudeen first, as he was wont to *baa* the rafters down if Khamsin got fed before he did.

She set to mixing Khamsin's feed to the formula Jamie had taught her long ago. The warm scent of molasses and the slightly acrid scent of the beet mixture drifted up to her and she took a deep breath of it. Horse, sheep, feed and hay, it was a smell that always calmed her and made her feel a bit more centered in her world. She put Khamsin's feed in his trough and gave him a rub between the ears as he set to his meal.

The horse snorted slightly, though he didn't deign to lift his head, as cold air rushed into the byre. It was Casey, she knew before she even turned around. If he'd been gone thirty years instead of three, she still would have known him, the energy with which he entered any space would always be un- mistakable to her. Khamsin whickered softly and Casey walked over to stand beside her, an apple in his hand which he presented to the horse. Khamsin cast a suspicious look at him, and then took the apple gingerly as if he suspected Casey of trying to slip him some poison.

They stood there silent for a moment, listening to the soft sounds of the animals eating. Finally, Casey looked slant-wise down at her.

"I wanted to check on ye—ye seemed a wee bit overwhelmed in there."

"I'm just tired—the baby, and," she waved a hand, "everything, I sup- pose. I find I can only manage so much and then I need a minute alone."

"I can go," he said, and moved back toward the door.

"I don't mean you, Casey. Just come sit with me in the quiet for a minute, would you?"

"All right," he said, and pulled down two of the neatly stacked hay bales so that they might sit on them. "I brought ye some food. Ye scarce touched yer dinner in there. I can't imagine that's good for you or Kathleen."

"I am a bit hungry," she said, surprised to find it so. Casey unpacked the small bag he'd brought out with him. Bread, cheese, thinly-sliced ham, pickles and a couple bottles of stout. He took the lid off one of the bottles and handed it to her.

"I remember ye drinkin' stout when ye nursed our two," he said, matter- of-factly. She took a swallow of the drink, relishing the dark and grainy taste of it. Just being here alone with him, looking at him, gave her the sense of rid- ing a roller coaster she had no memory of getting on. And once the ride was underway, she'd discovered that the rails were rickety and she wasn't belted in firmly. And yet, oh and yet, there were moments of such intense joy, like this one right now, simply looking at this man sitting across from her and watching the movement of his body and hands as he put together a rough sandwich for her. He'd always functioned with an economy of movement, as if every action had a purpose which he'd already predetermined, and yet there was grace to that movement as well, an echo of the sheer raw strength held in check until he needed it. She wondered what it was like to face him in a fight—seeing all that power unleashed and bent on beating you, had to make his opponents more than a little frightened.

"Is somethin' the matter?" he asked, taking in her regard of him.

She shook her head. "No. I just like looking at you. I imagine it will take quite some time before I'm used to seeing you right here in front of me."

The few swallows of stout went straight to her head and a wave of exhaustion passed over her. She leaned back into the stall door with a sigh.

"Would ye like me to ask people to leave?" Casey asked, looking at her steadily. "I think they'll all understand if ye're not quite up for the day this year."

"I just want them to enjoy themselves. I'm fine. Did Pat send you out here?"

"No, I made the decision to come after ye. Pat's worried—mind, they're all worried about ye."

"I know, I just can't talk about things yet. I feel like if I do it will stain this time with Kathleen, and with you coming home. And I am so happy about that, Casey. To know you're alive, after such a long time of thinking you—" she choked on the word. "Well, I can't even explain what I feel every time I look at you."

"Aye, I feel the same. I worry that I'm starin' too much, an' that I'll make ye uncomfortable. I feel like I have to drink the sight of ye in, like I'm afraid I need to store the look of ye against another drought. Now, quit starin' an' eat yer bit of food, woman. I'm not lettin' you out of the byre until ye're done."

Her stomach welcomed the food as she realized just how hungry she was. She ate everything, shocked that she had such an appetite. It had come to her attention that everything had a sharper edge to it since Casey's return home—food and drink were fuller flavoured, everyday scents were sharper and warmer, and when he occasionally touched a bare bit of her skin, it felt like a warm fire had been set within her blood.

"What did you do these last Christmases?" she asked after swallowing her last bite of sandwich and finishing off the bottle of stout. She had the sense Casey would make good on his threat to keep her here until she'd eaten to his satisfaction.

"The first one I was in hospital, an' not awake. The second one I spent at a soup kitchen with my friend, Eddy. The third one I was up on the mountain in the wee hut."

"I hate to think of you alone like that."

He shrugged and looked away from her, as he did at times, to hide, she thought, just what those three years had been like for him. "I don't imagine yers were terribly merry either, Pamela."

"No, they weren't. I tried to keep them light for the children, but I barely remember the first two, they're a blur for me now. Last year, Jamie had every-one to his house and it was a good day, especially for the children. And then it wasn't," she said, remembering how the day had ended, and the man with whom she'd spent those last hours. She shrugged as Casey looked at her ques-tioningly. "It's a story for another day."

Fortunately, Casey had always been a man to know when to move on to another topic.

"What I said before, about bein' sorry for the pain I've caused ye—I meant it. I am sorry, Pamela."

"It wasn't your fault, Casey, you have nothing to be sorry for."

"It doesn't much matter whether it was my fault or not, it still hurt ye terribly. An' for all we know it *was* my fault. That's what I need to find out—if I did somethin' that led to my bein' near killed."

"How will you find out though, without putting yourself in terrible danger?"

"How will I get on with my life properly, Pamela, if I don't find out?"

"I don't know the answer to that, Casey, but I will not be able to bear it if anything happens to you again. Do you understand that? I won't be able to bear it."

"I know. I'll be careful, only I do need answers. Ye understand that surely?"

"I understand it, but don't expect me to like it."

He smiled. "I'm not that foolish, woman."

A brief silence fell between them then, but it wasn't uncomfortable. She looked up from packing away the stout bottles and dishes for the food, to find him watching her. It was one of those soft searching looks he'd been giving her since his return. There was no hiding from it and she wondered if he even knew what he was doing to her with that look.

"Thank you for coming today. I know you weren't entirely keen on the idea."

"To tell ye the truth, I wasn't goin' to, but that didn't seem right, so here I am."

"Well, I'm glad you did."

He nodded, but didn't say anything further and she felt it again, that yawning abyss into which their marriage would tumble if they couldn't bridge those three years.

He stood then, and she noted he put most of his weight onto his left leg to lever himself upright. It was clear his bad knee was giving him grief today.

"I have a salve for that." She nodded toward his knee which he was rubbing now. "I used to put it on you, before bed each night, you swore it worked a treat."

"Did I then?" He smiled, a flash of white and dimple amidst the darkness of his whiskers. The intimacy of those times rose up in front of her, and she ducked her head, feeling a flush light along her skin which she feared might be visible even in the low light of the byre. She stood, brushing the straw from her clothes, and checked Khamsin one more time, though the horse didn't need checking, and Casey likely knew it.

She cleared her throat, just to break the silence and stepped toward the door, only to find herself standing right in front of him, so close that she could feel the warmth he always emanated.

"Pamela?"

"Yes?"

He opened his mouth to speak and then hesitated. She was half-afraid of what he might say. "Can I hold ye, just for a minute while we're alone? Would that be all right?"

She nodded, feeling both relief and a slight onset of nerves. He took a breath and then drew her in gently, holding her as though she were a glass vessel he fully expected to shatter in his arms. She put her head to his chest, and closed her eyes. He was so warm, and she was pulled to his heat, feeling the comfort and familiarity of it. As they stood there breathing, his warmth becoming hers, she relaxed against him with a small sigh and felt a rush of overwhelming gratitude for the moment that held them right now.

"Casey?"

"Aye?" His voice was a warm rumble where her ear rested against his chest.

"Merry Christmas."

Chapter Thirteen

Infinite While It Lasts

THE CHAPEL STOOD apart in the cold winter afternoon, lit within by dozens of flickering candles. It was a familiar place, for Pamela had been here with Jamie some years ago, on a night when they'd witnessed a man die by a violent hanging and she had lost a baby after jumping from a burning byre. Little had changed, for it was a place where time held scant sway, and the years passed softly over it, only touching here and there in the smallest of ways. One of the noticeable ones was marked in the faces of the priest and two monks in attendance at the christening. Father Lawrence had more white salting his temples, while Brother Gilles was moving much more slowly than he had been the last time she'd seen him.

They were a small grouping, just Jamie and herself, Kathleen, Patrick and Kate, Gert and Owen, Tomas, Vanya and of course Conor, Isabelle and Kolya. They had asked Patrick and Kate to be godparents before Casey's return, but then had given them the choice of opting out after, being that the situation could prove quite awkward for Pat, and she knew he would not want to hurt his brother for the world.

When she'd approached him about it though, he'd merely given her what she thought of as a true Riordan look. "She's as much family to me, Pamela, as Conor and Isabelle are, an' that's all I'm goin' to say on the matter." And so here they stood, Pat handsome and stalwart in his dark suit, Kate resplendent in the full bloom of late pregnancy, Conor holding his uncle's hand, and Isabelle twitching like a fairy who'd had too much dandelion wine.

Casey was not in attendance, though she had made a point of inviting him, not wanting him to feel left out of a family event. He had thanked her but said no, that Kathleen ought to have a christening free of tension and the drama that his mere presence might occasion at this point. It was, she knew, much more than that.

She was dressed in a green wool suit, appropriate to the season and the solemn setting, but fashionable enough to feel festive. Jamie wore a beautifully cut suit in a deep grey, with a green tie to match her dress. Kathleen lay in his arms, resplendent as a tiny empress in the yards of pearl-grey satin and Brussels lace which made up the Kirkpatrick christening gown. Jamie had worn it and so had many generations of Kirkpatricks before him. It gave her a lovely feeling of continuity knowing that Kathleen had those ties going back so many years. She had sometimes envied Jamie his history, for her own had felt rather truncated once her father died.

Around them, the candle flames flickered softly, reflecting like small swarming fish in the depths of the font. There was a great hush and even Kathleen was silent, eyes huge and round in her face, as if she too felt the sanctity of where they stood. Father Lawrence held out his arms, and Jamie kissed Kathleen's forehead before passing her to the priest.

There was an ancient beauty to the ritual—the processional, the hymns and verses and the actual baptism itself, with Father Lawrence smiling down at wee Kathleen, as he poured the water on her and then anointed her with the chrism oil. After this, she was returned to her father's arms, where she lay looking up at him, green eyes wide with wonder.

Conor and Isabelle had both been baptized by Father Jim, and there had been this same sense of beauty and solemnity, only of course a different man had stood by her side, holding their child. She felt one of those small moments of dislocation that sometimes came over her, from the woman she had been a few short years ago, to the one who stood here now, beside Jamie, as mother to his child.

At the last, they lit their baptismal candles off the long-burning flame of the Paschal candle, and the scent of beeswax and incense rose all around them. Christ's eternal light brought into baptism so that the one baptized might be protected by that light. She looked at her daughter, so small and fragile, and prayed that evil would never touch her and that joy would follow her steps all her life, and the only sorrows be those that came to all women in order to temper the joy, and make of it an even sweeter thing. Conor lit his candle with such an air of gravity that she felt the clutch at her heart she so often did when it struck her how fast he was growing. Isabelle, on the other hand, danced up to the front and back, as though her feet were possessed by mischievous fairies. She then returned to Jamie's side, wrapped one arm around his leg, and leaned into him. Jamie put a hand to her head, and stroked her mad furze of curls. Isabelle adored Jamie, and Pamela suspected, always would, and was under the assumption that she now had two fathers, and was quite happy with that development.

'For by one Spirit are we all baptized into one body, whether we be Jews or Gentiles, whether we be bond or free; and have been all made to drink into one Spirit.'

Her eyes met Jamie's over the fiery head of their daughter, and she smiled through her tears. For a moment she saw the life they might have had together, that ephemeral castle in the air which had always, on some level of time and space, existed between them. And she knew he saw it too—both the transcendent beauty and the utter impossibility of it. It passed through and over both of them, like the shadow of some golden dream which had never quite made it into being.

There was one last prayer for the safety and blessing of all who gathered that they might protect and teach this tiny girl as she grew, and keep her safe from the dark of the world, by providing the light of the spirit.

And then it was over and Pat was shaking Jamie's hand, and Kate was hugging Pamela, the round of her belly hard, taut and wriggling with life. Isabelle was tugging on Pamela's dress, needing the facilities and Conor was asking if she had food in her purse.

Ten minutes later she had both children sorted, though it had been a struggle to convince Isabelle to keep her woolly tights on, which she insisted were 'suppocakin' her, and Conor had lamented that she'd only packed sandwiches and oranges for him and not thought to bring cookies. It had the effect of placing her solidly in the here and now, which was the wonderful tonic cure of children.

It was time then, to head to the dock for the return trip. Outside, the winter afternoon was fading quickly into night, all the dips and hollows of the land gauzed with blue shadow. The sky was clothed in silks of pearl-pink amid cottony grey overclothes, which was always snow's herald.

They had come in two boats, but when they got to the dock only one awaited them. It was the larger of the two crafts but didn't have the capacity for all of them.

"Engine died on the other boat," their erstwhile boatman said, "I can try to make a run back later, but it's startin' to snow, an' should it get any thicker—an' it will, for my elbow is painin' me mightily, an' it only does so when the weather is about to get a bit on the crazy side—I'll not be able to get back until tomorrow."

"Why don't you two stay the night along with the children?" Father Lawrence said, looking at Jamie and Pamela. "There's room, and then Joseph won't have to return until the weather has cleared off. Besides, James, if you can spare the time, I should like to speak to you about a few matters."

Jamie looked at her, a question in the green eyes. She knew the exact thoughts running through his head, for they were circling through hers as well. Father Lawrence added a final two cents.

"Forgive me for saying so, Pamela, but you look about ready to drop where you stand. I think a hot fire and something warm to eat might go a long way to restoring you, rather than a cold trip across the lake."

Pat stepped forward. "He's right, Pamela. Ye need some warmth an' sustenance. Owen will run over an' check on the animals."

"Mama," Conor said, "can I go back with Uncle Pat please? Tomorrow is Kieran's birthday party an' I can't miss it."

Pat spoke before she could say no. "It's fine by me, Pamela. 'Tisn't a problem to get him there an' back. The laddie shouldn't have to miss out on his fun because of a boat engine."

"Why don't ye let us take Isabelle too, an' ye can come get her when ye're back an' settled," Kate said, giving Pamela's hand a squeeze.

Isabelle clapped her wee hands together. "Go wif Aunnie Kate, Mama."

It was a measure of Isabelle's love for Kate that she was willing to forgo time with Jamie in order to be with her.

"Bring Koly too," Isabelle said, linking her arm through Kolya's and looking up at Jamie.

"I don't think—" Jamie began, but was interrupted by Kate.

"Jamie, it's fine, he'll be lovely company for her and make the whole night more fun for the lot of them."

"Please, Daddy," Kolya said, bright blue eyes appealing to his father.

"All right," Jamie acquiesced. "Be on your best behaviour, laddie, d'ye hear me?"

Kolya nodded and after giving Jamie a hug and a kiss went off with Isabelle to board the boat.

"Are you certain? Three children is a lot," she said to Pat. Pat clearly saw the other question which was likely printed on her ever-transparent face, though, and answered to that.

"Pamela don't look so, it's not a scandal to stay out here with Jamie an' yer wee girl. Might be that the two of ye could use a bit of time out of the world, alone with yer baby. Such a time might not come again, so take it while ye can."

"Oh, Pat," she said, overcome by his grace as she so often was.

"Here, give us a hug; I didn't mean to make ye cry."

Pat's hugs always shored up her spirit, though it didn't prevent a few tears from spilling down her face. They were right, much as she hated to admit it, she was exhausted and the emotion of the day, not to mention the last several weeks, had caught her up hard, and was threatening to lay her flat.

Pat drew back a moment later and looked down at her.

"Will it be all right if Conor and Isabelle spend a bit of time with Casey? Only he's meant to come up for a day or two, an' I know he'll want to see them."

"Of course it is," she said. "He doesn't need permission to be with his own children." She knew her voice was a little stiff, but she couldn't help but feel the sting of hurt that he'd not contacted her since Christmas night.

"He means to come see you as well, Pamela. I think he needs a bit of time to sort his feelins' out, an' get his bearings around this life of his. He's overwhelmed, an' I know you are too. But I think for him, he feels like a stranger in a strange land, like he's a wolf runnin' about the edges of a bunch of circled wagons, afraid he's about to be shot or reviled in some way."

It was true, she knew, his discomfort whenever he stayed more than a few hours, had shown her that clearly. She understood and yet it hurt deeply when once he had been the other half of her whole, and she had felt he was the person she knew best in the world, and knew that he'd felt the same.

"We've got to go now," Joseph said, rubbing fretfully at his elbow, and glaring at the air as though he could see the weather forming in front of him, and what he saw clearly didn't please him.

They stood long enough to wave them off, Jamie, Father Lawrence and herself, before turning to seek warmth and shelter. Joseph's elbow was apparently no mean prognosticator for the snow began to fall thick and steady before the boat was entirely out of sight.

"Let's get in out of the weather, and see about preparing rooms for you," Father Lawrence said briskly, rubbing his hands together. They followed him into the old living quarters of the monastery, Jamie holding Kathleen snugged tightly to his chest so that the cold could not touch her, Pamela following in his wake, feeling a strange sense of relief to have this small time out of the world with both him and Kathleen.

It was as Pat had said—this time might not ever come again, and she knew well enough to hold it while she could.

Brother Gilles showed her to a sitting room, where she could feed Kathleen by the comfort of a roaring fire. She sat in the chair next to the hearth with relief, taking off her shoes and wiggling her toes in the heat. The chapel had been chilly, and her feet felt like blocks of ice. Brother Gilles ducked out to give her privacy, but returned shortly thereafter, with a mug of warm broth for her.

"Tea is lovely, but broth heats the bones," he said, which seemed to Pamela a very French and very accurate sort of observation.

"It is so wonderful to see you with a healthy baby in your arms, and two other healthy children running about as well," Brother Gilles said, stretching his hands out to the fire, as he settled in across from her in an ancient leather armchair. Brother Gilles had attended to her, in the wake of her miscarriage, here at the monastery, all those years ago.

"Yes, God has been rather abundant with me since you saw me last." Pamela said. "Oh, good girl," she added as Kathleen let out a small belch. She tucked Kathleen into the corner of her arm and gazed down at the baby's face, feeling the melting love that one did with babies, as if their flesh was still one with your own. It was different for fathers, she supposed, for having never carried their child inside, they wouldn't feel that insistent aching tug which came once a child was outside your body, and yet still entirely dependent upon you for sustenance and life.

"That is wonderful, no? Children are God's greatest blessing in this life—I am glad to see he has been so generous with you."

"He has been indeed," she said, thinking Brother Gilles had no idea just how generous the universe had been of late with her blessings.

"The last time you were here, you were married, no? It was clear to me that you and Jamie had a great deal of love for one another, but that your heart belonged to a different man."

"Well, that's a rather long story," she said, "but the situation is much the same now."

Brother Gilles feathery eyebrows shot up. "I believe I have time for you to tell me, if you so wish."

So she told him, sketching it in briefly in some spots and filling things in more fully where she felt it was warranted—Casey's amnesia, Jamie's situation with Violet and why and how he'd married her. She touched carefully on her relationship with Jamie and just how far back it went. It fell short though, for there were never adequate words to explain how entwined this man was in her life, and how complicated it all seemed now that they had Kathleen. And then, the miracle of Casey's return, and how it felt like it should be simple, and yet it was anything but.

Brother Gilles was silent for a moment, once her story came to an end, his hands steepled in front of his face, hiding his expression so that she could not tell if he was shocked or dismayed by her recounting.

"Well, that is wonderful in many ways, and yet as you say, rather complicated. I see why you chose such a small and private christening."

"Yes, well we did give Casey the option of coming, but he, not surprisingly, declined."

"Then you have been as fair as you can be in this situation. May I ask where James is in all of this?"

She sighed. Explaining her and Jamie's situation was a bit like trying to give directions in an overgrown labyrinth. This man, however, had known Jamie since he was a child and loved him as well.

"You know what it means to him to have a child whom he can love without fear." Even Kolya, blessed with the rude good health of a Russian peasant, didn't come entirely without strings—as had been evidenced by Violet using him as a pawn to hold to her marriage with Jamie.

"I do," Brother Gilles agreed.

"For now, we're just happy being parents to this little girl," Pamela said, kissing the top of Kathleen's silky red head.

"And yet, I still see a great deal of love between the two of you."

She looked up from the baby, and knew that her face was transparent with a truth that was undeniable. "Of course you do, has anyone ever stopped loving Jamie once they've started?"

"No, I think not. But he loves you as well. I have not witnessed such emotion before in him, as I have today."

She looked away and swallowed. The day was threatening to overwhelm her, and her throat tightened with the tears which had hovered throughout the christening. Tears of both joy and sorrow.

"You can speak of it, if you wish. I have been told," he smiled, long nose twitching slightly, "that I am a good listener."

"I feel like no matter what I do, I hurt someone. It's like I can't put a foot right in this matter. I love them both, and the laws of man and church say that's wrong, and a sin."

"And what is it you are asking me?"

"How do I reconcile the laws of man with those of my heart?"

Brother Gilles leaned forward, placing his elbows on his knees, a contemplative look in his brown eyes.

"Perhaps if I were a different sort of priest, you might get a more traditional answer but as I am not, I will simply tell you what I think and not quote doctrine at you."

She nodded, shifting Kathleen so that the baby was over her shoulder.

"Love is what we all come to this life to experience. Love in all its many variations with its myriad faces and complexities. Love with all its beautiful complications. To love is not a sin, not if you do it with a full heart and good intent. The good Lord does not say, 'love this one, but not that one' does he? And so should we say thusly? It seems to me that the two men whom you love, have come to a certain peace with this situation—if your husband could live with the knowledge of it before, can he not reconcile himself to it now? I realize that circumstances are somewhat different than those which he left behind when he disappeared, and yet might he not come to view this *petit chou* as a further blessing, and a being who will only enrich his life that much more?"

"I do not think he sees it in quite such a..." she hesitated, searching for an appropriate term, "shall we say—divine light, as you do."

Brother Gilles laughed, and Kathleen burbled as if in agreement about the humour of her mother's comment.

"It could be that the Creator felt that after a lonely childhood, you deserved what love he could bring to you. Perhaps the love of both men was a pattern laid down in your being before you were even born. The Creator might occasionally make monsters, but he does not make mistakes."

"How did you know I had a lonely childhood?"

Brother Gilles looked across at her, his homely face lit by the fire so that he appeared almost angelic, and said, "There are those of us who are stamped with it, and we recognize another from our tribe. But now here you are, blessed with an abundance of love—I think perhaps the true sin here would be turning any of it away. The choice there is already made, you are bound by the bonds of marriage to your husband and so must only have the ties of the flesh with him from here on out—that is if he chooses to remain in the marriage."

"And therein lies the rub," Pamela said ruefully. "I don't think he knows what he wants and I can hardly blame him, can I? He comes home, not knowing entirely who he is, or where his place is, only to find the life he left behind is no longer recognizable."

"There is still love, and surely that *is* recognizable to him and to you. Or are you telling me his feelings are not as they once were?"

"No, I believe he still loves me. He's not said as much, admittedly, but I think maybe he's afraid to."

"And you love him, so I believe the path is clear. In the eyes of both the church and the law this man is still your husband, and I believe it is so in your heart as well."

"It is," she said softly, "and yet…"

"Oh yes," Brother Gilles agreed, "and yet. Jamie is not a fancy to be taken lightly, and I'm sure you above all others know and feel this."

"What I feel for him is, I believe, for life. It is my burden to bear, and I would do so happily if I did not feel that it also hurts others."

"Perhaps it need not be a burden, for love takes many shapes and forms and what you give Jamie is no less because it is not given within the bounds of marriage."

"I'm not sure he would agree with that."

"Perhaps not now, but his love for you is, I believe, something with a great capacity for understanding."

She nodded, for this was true but it didn't lessen the pain of hurting Jamie.

"There is a sadness in you, something beyond I think your current situation—if you will forgive the observation."

Pamela shifted a little in her chair, adjusting Kathleen's blanket around her face. The baby stirred, her mouth making a small moue of protest at this fidgeting on her mother's part.

She looked up at Brother Gilles, and saw an endless well of understanding in the warm brown eyes. A certain melancholy had lingered with her since the workhouse and Noah's death. It wasn't something she felt she could speak about freely with either Jamie or Casey.

"I often think," the monk said carefully, "that sitting beside a fire is a bit like being in a confessional. Something about the warmth and light, with the darkness all around, seems to make it easier to say the things of our hearts, both the good and the bad."

She laughed, though she heard the hollow note in it, and was certain Brother Gilles heard it too.

"I lost a friend a couple of months ago," she said, and thought how small and bald the sentence was in contrast to what she felt about the loss of Noah. Brother Gilles nodded, encouraging her to go on.

"His name was Noah," she began, and then she told the priest about the man who had been her friend, and then something more, and who had also been the anchor in her life in ways no one outside the two of them had been able to understand. She told him about Noah's death in the workhouse—the blood, the pain and the horror of it, and how she had helped him to slip the knot of life that night, so that he might have at least some choice in his death, small as that choice might have been. All during the telling, she could feel something cold rising through her core, like a needle made of ice, a truth which she could not quite grapple with just yet. And still she said it, for the monk was right—the fire inspired confession.

"I—it was my fault. I had a hand in his death because there was no way he wouldn't come to their summoning once he knew they had me."

There was a silence as she finished, broken only by the soft hiss of the fire and Kathleen's even, steady breath.

"First of all, I am sorry for the loss of your friend. If you will permit me to say, it sounds very much as though he felt his life for yours was a more than fair exchange. Love is like that, knowing neither boundary nor limit in what it will give or trade in order to save or redeem the loved one."

"He did feel that way, but that doesn't change my role in how things played out."

"No, perhaps not, but I think you need to allow his sacrifice to be what it was. If you feel regret and guilt around what happened, you diminish what he gave you—your life. Still his loss deserves your mourning. If he was a man you were willing to marry, your feelings for him must have run quite deep."

The words caused the tide of tears she'd been holding in all day to surge near to the surface again because they echoed too closely something Noah had said to her long ago in reference to Casey.

"*I didn't know yer man well, it seems to me, though, that he would not think it a waste of his life, did he die protecting those he loved.*"

"I know what you are saying is right. It's only…" she hesitated, unable to find the right words to describe how she felt inside, and the terrible sorrow which seized her at times. The good brother seemed to understand, though, for he filled the space with his own words, gently spoken.

"It is natural. I have found this time of year to be a liminal space—that place between what was and what comes next. There is a quiet in these days winding down from the solstice toward the new year. We celebrate but we also meditate on what has changed, what is lost and at times we wander the hinterland of all those other paths life might have taken us down."

"Memories do feel closer this time of year. I think of my lost babies, just as I know every parent who loses a child does. Somehow things are just a wee bit sharper this time of year. You, of course, understand this better than most."

Long ago, Brother Gilles had told her his story of loss, of the children and wife who had driven away one bright day, many years ago, never to return.

"Yes, I do. It was long ago, but I remember their faces as if they only just now, walked from this room. Such is a parent's love."

He was right. For she held within her own heart, the image of a tiny girl, with a face like a flower and bones like pearls, brought to being in a primordial sea. The second daughter that she'd lost, she had never seen and so there was a hole there, and a small face which was more spirit than substance.

"And now, if you will allow an old man a long-lost pleasure, I should like to hold your sleeping child for a little while."

"Of course," she said, and stood, transferring Kathleen carefully to Brother Gilles' upheld arms. "If you don't mind watching her for a bit, I'd like to step out for a breath of air."

"*Certainement,*" Brother Gilles said, "this little lady and I will be just fine together. Come fetch her when you are ready, but don't hurry. It's been far too long since I rocked a child by the fire."

She left the good brother and Kathleen alone, departing with the sound of Brother Gilles soft voice in her ears, singing a French lullaby.

L'était une petite poule grise
Qu'allait pondre dans l'église
Pondait un p'tit' coco
Que l'enfant mangeait tout chaud

L'était une p'tit' poul' noir
Qu'allait pondre dans l'armoire

There was a small grey hen
That would lay her eggs in the church
She laid a little egg (1)
That the child ate while yet hot

There was a little black hen
That would lay her eggs in the cabinet...

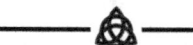

It was the trick of an artist's eye—to see something as it would look in a sketch before seeing it as it was. The monastery, caught suspended in the falling snow, presented as such, when she stepped out of the living quarters into the night. With only torches to send small beacons into the night, the entire set of buildings was cloaked in shadow and snow, the flare of each small fire an oasis of golden cheer. The stillness was such that it seemed as though time itself was caught fast, held unchanging in a glass globe where the ever-revolving world might look in, but not intrude.

The world was entirely transformed. When they'd entered the small stone building there had been a light skiff of snow upon the ground, now it was a few inches deep and falling so heavily that she couldn't see the lake despite it being no more than twenty yards away.

She had a good notion where Jamie would be, and so she walked down to the lake, picking her way through the snow, glad she was now wearing warm boots. He stood by the shore, his back to her, gazing at the edge of a thick wood.

"Jamie?" she said, not wanting to startle him.

"Come look," he said quietly, and put a hand back to guide her over the snow to his side.

The deer stood perfectly still, so that she might have mistaken it for a statue excepting that she had seen it before. A white deer, barely visible in the white landscape which surrounded her. She had seen her once before, on that night so long ago.

"I didn't know if she was still alive. The monks haven't seen her in some time, so I assumed she had died. She's nearly eighteen, that's a long life for a deer."

There was a flicker of movement, a ripple of shadowy brown pelt and then a stag stepped out from under the boughs of an oak and stood behind the doe, his antlers lightly frosted with snow. The two animals looked across the expanse of ground between them, and Pamela felt that strange, prickly feeling she sometimes had with wild animals, the feeling that they were communicating in a language as old as the world, a conduit through the ether, before time had been counted and measured.

"Mate or son, do you think?" she asked.

"I don't know. I would think she's past her fertile years though, so more likely a mate. I'm just happy that she isn't alone, that she has one of her own kind to keep her company. Mate or son, it doesn't matter, just another creature who is of her kind is enough."

She shook her head, attempting to turn away, but she ought to have known better, Jamie always saw and knew even when no one else did.

"Hey, come here, it's all right."

It was a comfort simply to be near him, to smell his scent and feel the familiarity that was Jamie. For the last three years, this man had been her safety in the world. He was, and always would be, her dearest friend.

"You don't have to worry about me. I'm tougher than you seem to believe."

"I know that, Jamie. But I also know the other side of you, the one you rarely let anyone see, and I…" she faltered for a moment, "I don't want you to be alone."

He smiled down at her, brushing her hair back from her face. "Have you been in my house lately, Pamela? I'm hardly alone."

"That's not what I mean."

"I know that, sweetheart. I am no more alone than you are just now, though. I don't want that for you, either."

She took a long, shaky breath, blinking away tears. Jamie smiled down at her, his hair wreathed in a diamond dusting of snow.

"Do you know what I was doing out here? I was praying in gratitude. I was thanking God for a beautiful healthy child and I was thanking him for her mother as well. I am not sad or sorry for any of it, though I could wish it wouldn't bring you grief with Casey."

"I am so glad you can feel the joy of her, Jamie. It's what I've always wanted for you."

"This is where I've always come to pray, or rail at God, depending on my mood," he said, and while the words were light and humorous in tone, Pamela understood the darkness which lay behind them. He'd told her once that Father Lawrence had brought him here, the first time he'd had a manic episode, and how angry and lost he'd felt at the time. "I've prayed here many times, both in sorrow and anger, but today is the first time I prayed with a heart filled with joy."

"Oh, Jamie, I'm so glad." She reached up and took his face between her two hands and kissed him softly.

"Pamela?" he said, clearly surprised by the kiss.

"We just had our daughter baptized, and regardless of what has happened since or what may come, Kathleen is a child who was made with great love. This might be the last time I can do that without feeling as though I've betrayed someone."

"You're right," he smiled, and reached out to move an errant curl away from her face. "She was made with great love."

"Remember that story I told you in Maine—the one about the time I jumped in the sea at night because I believed a full moon and sea water were all I needed to grow scales and become a mermaid?"

"Of course I remember," he said, and there was an echo there even now, of what that time in Maine had meant to him. That echo lived within her too and, she knew, always would. It only made the place they now dwelt, that much more painful.

"I've been like that mermaid for years now, Jamie, escaping to the sea every chance I got. You are my sea, and now I have to get out and live on the land again."

And then because she was overcome with emotion, and a deep dwelling sorrow for those ephemeral castles she'd glimpsed so briefly in the chapel, she simply put her forehead to his chest, snow-covered though he was, uncaring of the cold. He put his arms around her and held her tightly.

"Pamela, I am not a fool. The day I first saw him I knew what would happen. He was drawn back to a world he didn't even know because of his love for you. That kind of love changes the very atmosphere around it, and you love him no less."

"I don't know how to explain it adequately," she said, "he is my husband, but it's not just that I made vows to him, either. It's that when he's here, when I know he's alive..." she trailed off, shaking her head, causing a rain of fine crystals to shimmer around her.

"It's just that he is the love of your life," Jamie said, a hint of wryness in his tone.

"Yes," she said softly and looked up at him, "he is, but as I told you once, Jamie, you are my soul and that will never change for me."

He smiled. "I can never quite decide if your damnable honesty is what I love most or least about you."

"I don't know what will happen with him, only I have to give him the chance to rejoin us as a family. He's been through so much."

"Pamela, I would never expect you to turn him away. He is, indeed, your husband in all senses of that word, and at the very least," he added drily, "I don't think you'd be able to keep from his bed."

"And you accuse *me* of damnable honesty," she said.

"Is it not the truth? I've seen you with him, I understand the sort of fire that burns between the two of you."

"As it did between us; it was only a fire of a different nature," she said, speaking her own damnable truth.

"In its moment it was infinite," Jamie said, and she felt the knife cut of his words deep inside, because, of course, they were true. A fleeting few days in a house in Paris, a summer in Maine, a lifetime of feeling and wanting to clutch what had been, what would always be, as one clutched at smoke from a fire abruptly tamped. Even though one understood the burns which would come and last. It was too late to avoid pain, one understood that and accepted it as best one might.

She shivered involuntarily, and Jamie quickly took off his coat and wrapped it around her. It smelled of him, the scent of comfort—lime and sandalwood, and that indefinable note that was simply Jamie—a faintly smoky note, with hints of something crisp about it: a first fall of snow, a night by the sea, a madcap run through the winter streets of Paris.

"Let's get you inside," Jamie said. "You're shaking like a leaf in a storm. It's not good for you to get chilled like this. Then I'm going to get us something hot to drink."

Inside, she found Brother Gilles still rocking Kathleen by the fire, his eyelids drooping, whereas Kathleen's were wide open. The minute Pamela hove into view, the baby started to fuss. She would need feeding and to be changed before bed.

"I believe a room has been prepared for you and *la petit* here." Brother Gilles stood and handed Kathleen to her, and then led the way out of the sitting room and down the hall. The stone corridor was perishing, and she felt the cold drive up through her feet, despite the boots.

The room was one with which she was familiar, and she had a moment's pause as Brother Gilles stopped and opened a heavy wooden door. The last time she'd been in that room, she had lost a child—wee Grace, whose face she had never seen, lost while Casey was interned on a prison ship. She found the memory was still there, but much of the sharpness had gone out of it, and she looked down into Kathleen's face, and snugged her baby a little more closely.

The fire was built high and hot, and the light bloomed out golden as treacle over the room. The bed was heaped with a feather quilt, and four neatly-placed pillows. On the bed, laid out, was a nightgown and a sweater and a woolly pair of socks, along with sheepskin-lined moccasins. The good brothers were apparently well prepared for stranded wayfarers who needed overnight lodging.

Someone had made a nest for Kathleen in an old drawer, deftly lined with a cream-coloured sheepskin. Between that and the blankets she'd brought along with her, it would provide a cozy place for the baby to sleep.

She put Kathleen on the bed, and then swiftly changed into the warm nightgown and sweater which had been left out for her. The woolly socks completed her outfit and she sighed with bliss as her feet began to warm. The outfit, while not terribly flattering, was extremely practical and warm.

Kathleen, by this point, was making it clear she needed to be fed, or her mother would soon regret her tardiness. She quickly changed the baby, something she thought she could do one-handed and in the dark—were it necessary, at this point in motherhood.

By the time Jamie knocked on the door, Kathleen was fed and tucked into the fleece-lined drawer and Pamela was sitting on the bed, the feather quilt tucked in around her legs. Despite the fire and the warm clothing, she still felt chilled, though sometimes she thought it was an interior chill rather than an outside one, a residue of the cold she'd carried with her since the workhouse.

Jamie entered, putting a halt to her ruminations, a grey velvet bag in one hand and a tray with hot drinks balanced on the other. She got up and relieved him of the tray, placing it on the low table next to the fire. He wore a thick navy blue sweater over top his dress shirt in an effort to fend off the cold.

"You look tired," he said, "get back into bed and I'll pour you a cup. Brother Gilles made you a pot of restorative chocolate, and he sent along some food as well. I thought you might well be hungry."

Jamie poured them each a cup, and brought one to her, where she now sat on the bed, feeling suddenly very weary. The day had been a lovely one, but long, and the exhaustion had caught up with her. Kathleen was, after all, only six weeks old, and the doctors had warned Pamela she was likely to feel the effects of her abduction and the stress it had caused for some time to come. In moments like this one, she understood just how right they'd been.

Kathleen, no doubt sensing her father's presence, started to snuffle a little. Jamie scooped her up from the makeshift crib and put her to his shoulder, speaking lovely nonsense to her, as he always did, and the baby calmed immediately, small red head burrowed into the side of his neck.

Jamie eyed the spindly chair next to the fire rather dubiously. It looked like a medieval torture device, and Pamela had discovered after sitting on it, it felt like one too.

"Just come sit with me on the bed," she said, "it's by far the most comfortable spot."

"I'm sorry about the weather," Jamie said, settling in beside her, and handing her a roast beef sandwich. "I know you hadn't planned on having to stay the night here."

"No, I hadn't, but in truth, I'm glad," she replied, "it's nice to just have some time with you and Kathleen. When Casey was gone, it seemed often that time stretched itself out to unbearable lengths, and then it would rush past when I realized how much the children had grown and changed in his absence. Now that he's back, I feel like things are running pell-mell toward an unknown destination. If I could make time stop, here and now, just for a few days, I would."

Jamie nodded. "I wish we could do just that. What you said about time stretching out to unbearable lengths reminds me of a story my grandfather used to tell me on Christmas Eve, to help pass the time and, no doubt, keep me out of my parents' hair for a bit. When I was little, I used to get rather keyed up around Christmas time, as you might imagine," he said wryly.

"Yes, I think I can imagine," she said, having seen Jamie in his manic state a time or two. She had also seen him in the opposite state, when things were so dark, he could not see the light. "Will you tell it to us now?" she asked.

The night invited a story—the great hush of the monastery, the snow falling thick and silent outside the ancient stone walls, and the fire burning high and bright in the hearth. It warmed her to know Kathleen would have a lifetime of this man telling her stories, and it hurt her heart to know she herself would no longer be a part of that enchantment. Except tonight, when she might grant herself one heart's wish.

"Of course," he said, and settled back into the pillows, Kathleen now fast asleep on his chest. One hand cupped Kathleen's bottom and the other rubbed her back. Pamela, having already polished off her sandwich, leaned back too, clutching her mug fast between her hands, a fine thread of anticipation running through her as Jamie took a moment to begin. She loved to watch him in such times, as he gathered the gossamer threads of story from his memory, and gave thought as to where he would begin. He kissed Kathleen's shimmery red head, and then started, his voice low so he wouldn't disturb their sleeping child.

"One Winter Solstice when the world was still quite young, and Time not so old as he is now, there was a great storm such as had not been before, nor since, if truth be told. Snow covered the world from pole to pole, and the storm raged on for weeks, freezing cattle in the fields and birds in the air, so that they hung suspended in flight and their songs congealed right there in the ether, bright notes like shards of coloured glass, which could be seen but not heard. It was so cold that the world actually stopped turning and was stuck firm on its axis. Time knew if he didn't get out there and un-stick the world, he would be caught fast and not be able to move—neither forward nor back—ever again. And if Time couldn't move, nor could anything else.

"Now the axis of the world was at the crossroads between east and west, where the Zephyr wind met and mingled with the wind of Eurus. Time knew it was there he'd find the axis, and unstick the world so that it might once again turn and roll forward. He began his travels in the teeth of a terrible gale, which screamed like a thousand witches abroad on the night. He wore a coat of wolf hide, made from the long-toothed wolves which used to hunt the land both high and low, in the far country from which he'd come. Leagues passed under his feet, as he walked for days and nights all together, never stopping, though at times he slowed due to the cold and the dark.

"Many moons passed over his head, and many lands rose before his coming, and fell after his departure, as he journeyed toward the axis of the world. He saw both wonders and horrors along the way, and found his mind much occupied by both, so that often he had to stop, retrace his steps, and begin his journey anew. Sometimes he almost came to a complete halt, for he carried eons within him, the weight of hours, days and decades, as well as heartbreak and joy. Beginnings and endings were in him, like an unfurling spiral which had no limit to it, and his heart was pained with the heft of these things.

"Finally one morning, he saw a strange light upon the horizon, the colour of a rose flushing through the great lashings of snow. He knew he was getting close to the end of his journey. The axis of the world was the point from which the light rose each day and so he walked toward that rose-lit sliver of light, which became just a bit bigger with each league he walked.

"It was dusk by the time he came upon the inn. It loomed up out of the dark, a tall, crooked building that leaned whichever way the wind happened to blow. It was built of great creaking timbers culled from the first forest and had stood at the crossroads between East and West, from before even Time could remember. Therefore, he knew it was terribly, terribly old.

"He approached the building, mesmerized by the thought of warmth and food. The windows shone a pearly gold—small orbs of fire caught within each frost-thick pane. He cleared a small patch on one window, so that he might peer in at the firelight and determine if this was a right place to stop. Staring back at him was his reflection and he stumbled back in shock. He had travelled so far and so long, and yet had not felt his age, and so it was a great jolt to look in the glass and see himself an old man, with a great mossy beard, and hair that hung around his wrinkled face like great hanks of seaweed. He didn't want to enter the inn, fearing that others would shrink back from him in terror—an old man, covered in wolf skins, with a slightly crazed look about him from all the days and nights and years, which he had passed alone. But go in he must, for he was in need of sustenance, warmth and rest before he could finish his journey, and unstick the axis of the world.

"The inn was a snug one, with several travellers seated about the great fire, for many had been caught out by the storm, and had taken up residence here at the inn. Time's presence caused curious looks, but little more, for the visitors were a motley crew. Both men and women clustered around the huge, roaring fire—people of every race and colour, from the palest of frost-whites to an ebony so deep the skin held tints of blue. Rough-hewn tables were scattered about the room, and travellers of all descriptions sat at them, eating and drinking, and to judge from the noise, making merry despite the circumstances which had landed them here. Time was curious about all these folk, but first he must eat and melt a little of the ice from his bones, and see if he couldn't make himself just the tiniest bit presentable.

"There was a small table in one corner, empty, where he might sit alone and sort his thoughts before engaging with anyone. He was barely seated, when a serving maid brought him a tankard of spiced wine to warm his blood, and beef on the bone, as well as a wheel of cheese and a loaf of bread.

"After he had sated the worst of his hunger, he felt the prickle on his skin of someone's observation. He wiped his face with the rough cloth the serving maid had provided along with his meal, and attempted to tidy his hair, not wanting to appear a wild man complete. When he turned, he could not tell at once, just who was observing him. Was it the girl with the amber skin and the eyes as dark as sloes, whose net and trident made her occupation clear? Time knew of the famous pearl divers, those with the courage and stamina to dive deep, deep into the dark and bring back the tears of the angels. Whose breath, it was said, held until it turned to silver threads, which slowly wound out as the woman surfaced, an oyster in her mouth, with a pearl in its belly. Or was it the man who wore on his wrist a contraption which made a most annoying and steady noise, back and forth—*tick tock, tick tock.* Time had heard of such a creature, one who attempted to capture *his* essence—Time's essence—as if such a mad thing was possible. Why the creature might as well build a rope from sand and expect it to lead a mule. They called such fools 'horologists'—an ungainly name, he thought, but apt for such a ridiculous occupation. Perhaps the one watching him was the man who was moving shells about on a make-shift table, a hat tilted down over his left eye, with a grin built to distract all around him? Or the tall woman with the carriage of an empress and skin the colour of a raven's wing? No, none of them, and yet the gaze remained. Then he saw her, seated furthest from the fire, and partly hidden in the shadows. It was because he realized, she was constructed equally of both light and dark. He knew, without doubt, it was she who watched him, she who observed. And so he returned the scrutiny, cataloguing her appearance.

"There was about her, the clasp of the sea's chill embrace, her dress the scattered green of ocean brine. Within the dress she sat like a stone goddess, still and watchful. Around her neck were circlets of shells—pale lavender, watered green, blush pink. Her eyes were the colour of the first spring he'd ever known, back when even Time was so new the world barely moved. Furs wrapped her shoulders, the silver-white of them in contrast to the tumbling smoke of her hair—the coils of it as dark as the night held within the window glass.

"Despite her chill gaze, there was a great allure emanating from her, and he was up on his feet, moving toward her before he understood what he was doing. The woman was both old and young, barely more than a girl in one glance, and then a shift in the firelight and he could see there was an old crone hidden within the very bones of her. With one graceful wave of her hand, she indicated the space beside her, and that he should come and sit for a spell.

"He put out his hand as he neared her, and she received it in a grasp which was surprisingly strong. "I am Time," he said, keeping his voice low so that the horologist, ready with his glass funnels and cogged wheels, would not hear him, and attempt to capture that which could not be held.

"I know who you are," she said softly, and smiled.

"Do you?" he asked, feeling a sudden urge to laugh, not for what she had said but for the joyous upsurge in his blood at the sound of her voice.

"You are the lost beaches turned to stone so very long ago, the stars gone wayward on their courses, now hidden from view. You are the rock which rises and crumbles, the forests which grow and decay, the tides that change the very shape of the world."

"And you are the thread which binds it all together," he replied, recognizing her for just who and what she was.

"I am the thread," she acknowledged, with a graceful tilt of her head, "and I am also that which cuts the thread. My story is an old one, though perhaps, not so old as yours."

"Tell it to me," he said, "for there's fire and wine, and a very long night ahead."

"She nodded, and let slip the silver-white furs from her shoulders, her sea silks rustling around her, and the gold of the fire outlining her form with heat and light.

"I come," she began quietly, "from when all the world was water, and I lived amongst the mountains of the sea, fathoms deep, where the moon seemed little more than a small pearl, aloft in the dark of night. One day, though, I came upon a bit of land, and crawled onto it, not entirely understanding what it was. I knew I needed to get back in the water, but I was terribly tired and fell asleep. I think I must have slept for a very long time, for when I woke, I had legs and not a single scale left on my body. I could not swim and so I could not return to the water. The land seemed so small in comparison, and I felt parched and angry much of the time."

"Time had heard tales of such—creatures that were part fish, part woman and had been known to lure men into the great tides beyond the horizon, from whence no man had ever returned. He understood she was both this, and something far greater in and of herself, and of all the things beyond that boundary.

"Then one day," the woman continued, "many moons later, I felt a strange surging in my body, and then things began to grow around me and on me, roots and vines and flowers. Seeds fell from my hands, and were taken away by the wind, and sprang up in far lands. I still had my great need of water but I could live away from it, because it was within me and I realized I carried it everywhere I went."

"And it did, he saw, for a trace of salt glimmered both in her hair and in a thin veil over her skin, but he saw too the other part where small leaves grew within the weave of her gown, and vines coiled around her narrow wrists, and flowers bloomed, petal by petal, within the cool sheen of her skin.

"I had many, many children and of course, not all survived. I knew a mother's sorrow, and a mother's rage. I knew love and hope and despair and decay. I waxed old, and knew great pain in my bones and then I was new again, fresh as the dawn, and just as unknowing. The tides of my body were the tides of the great oceans, and I knew the pull of the moon and the fertility it brought to all things.

"I knew too all the dark places of the world, that territory out beyond the memory of man—the ice fields and forests, the land untouched by anything other than the wild, and the rules of tooth and claw. I tasted death more sharply than any other can, and knew the darkness of it upon my tongue, always. Blood was coin and dice to me, and the game was eternal—rife with winners and losers, and no way to tell who was which."

"Her story wound on, and it *was* an old one, one which every creature knew, and yet he was held rapt by it nevertheless. For it was both painful and yet exquisite in the telling.

"As Time had pointed out, it was a long night and the jug of wine never seemed to empty, and the fire burned high and hot. They spoke of many things that night—of the movement of the stars and planets and the great winding world, and the places of spice and sand, where snow had never fallen until the storm, and the herds of animals and their migrations, creating thunder with their hooves and wings and fins. They spoke of all the people who had come, built their fragile empires, and then disappeared with barely a trace left behind, their cathedrals and temples now dust or crumbling to ruin in a far jungle.

"Some time in the small hours, the pearl diver told her tale, and the trickster entertained them with sleight-of-hand and illusions built upon light and movement. And then, as the soft hours approached only Time and Life—for Time had understood who she was from the minute she began her story—were left awake. Outside, the wind still howled and the snow hissed against the frosted windowpanes.

"Between them flowed something more than just conversation, something ancient which had existed even before either of them had. As though they had been engaged in conversation of the silent sort long before this night. Time felt he had both lost and gained by the hours spent with her.

"Morning arrived, as it is wont to do, in a slow fan of light, pinking the horizon and sending a trembling wave of rose-gold through the inn. The storm had, at long last, ended.

"We have talked of all since the world began, and long past its ending," Life said, eyes now the colour of the sea on an autumn day, a green so fathomless, there was no proper description for it. "We have said all we must, and now will go our separate ways."

"I feel as though I lost something," Time said, "something I was before, now no longer is."

"The horologist stole bits of you during the night." she said, rather matter-of-factly, considering the news she was imparting.

"But I never felt it," he said, "the night went by so quickly, and there was so much to say that I never noticed a thing."

"No one ever does feel it."

"You might have stopped him," Time said, indignant.

"There was a great sorrow in her face as she replied. "The horologist steals Time, whether we will it or no. It is inevitable."

"They broke fast on simple things—bread, cheese and a dark ale which tasted of apricots and amber. Then together they moved out into the day, which was bright and fair, and into shoals of melting ice and snow, so that the rush and roar of moving water could be heard all across the land. Ahead the crossroads sat, small bunches of green pulsing through the snow, clustering at the base of the sign. One road was his, and the other was hers. She was right, the horologist had taken, as thieves always do, and the cost of that was their separation.

"Her eyes, as she looked at him, were all the contrary colours of the ocean, and held within them the tides of the universe, the lost souls of men without number, and his own soul now too, he knew, and did not mind it being so, as long as she was the keeper.

"The axis has shifted, you needn't search any longer," she said. "All that was required to make the world move again, was for the two of us to meet and touch in passing.

"She stood on tiptoe and kissed him, holding his face between her two hands, the scent of green growing things all around her. And for a moment, he felt his youth again, and the joy of simple existence.

"He took his leave of Life there at the crossroads, and watched with regret as she walked her own way, plants springing up in the footprints she left behind, and birds dropping their bright glass notes all around her as she moved.

"Something of Life had followed him, just as he thought a bit of his own self had gone with her. For as he walked, all around his feet were great melting puddles, in which small frogs swam and sang, and here and there bluebells shot up through the patches of snow, and the glass notes of bird song, drifted down through the air. The long season of loss, while it had been beautiful in parts, was over, and the land rejoiced. Time never did return to the crossroads, except once many, many moons later. By then the inn was gone, and the only trace remaining was the skeleton of its tall and crooked frame, with roses growing up and around the old timbers—roses, pale as the innards of a shell, glimmering with a skiff of salt, bending this way and that in the wind, with the perfume of Life drifting all around them."

There was a long silence as Jamie finished, the only sound in the room that of the fire and the soft breathing of their sleeping daughter.

"I think," she said softly, "that's not quite the tale your grandfather told you."

"No, but the story adjusts to the listener as it sees fit."

"Does it?" she asked, a pain in her throat as fine and piercing as a silver needle.

"The horologist steals whether we will it or not, Pamela. There is no earthly way, despite what we wish, to make time stop."

He was right, of course, but oh how she wished that in this one case, he wasn't.

"This is for you, I had it made while you were pregnant." He handed the grey velvet bag he'd brought in with him to her, as his eyes met hers. She set her mug to the side, and tugged open the drawstring. She reached into the bag and felt the cool weight of stones against her fingers. Once in the light, she saw just what it was—sea glass, formed and wrapped in a cord of freshwater pearls, and anchored by a beautiful moonstone, which glowed in the light of the fire with flushes of rose and silver.

"Oh, Jamie," she said, tears filling her eyes and rendering her blind for a moment.

"The sea glass is from our time in Maine. The moonstone is for Paris. One day you can give it to Kathleen. And you can tell her, if you so choose, what it represents."

She looked up at him, understanding the deeper meaning of his words, the necklace a-glow in her hands.

"What would you have me tell her?"

"Tell her that her mother and father loved each other very much and that one magical morning in a beautiful old house in Paris, they made her out of that love. Right now, though, we have to face our immutable truth—time moves on for all of us, Pamela, this you know, as do I."

"I do not want it to move on without you," she said, a tear spilling and slipping down her face. Jamie cupped her jaw in his hand, and turned her face toward him.

"It will though, sweetheart. It's simply how things are for us. But in other ways it won't. We have this beautiful child between us now, and she is our link to the infinite. Pamela, look at me—what else can you do? Turn him away? It would break you and you know it. You love him as much as you ever did, can you deny it?"

"No, nor would I want to deny it. But I love you also, and sometimes that feels as though it's tearing me to pieces. I didn't have expectations, Jamie, I know you're married, but I believed that one day…" she trailed off, hesitant to put her feelings into words, uncertain that it was even right to do so. And yet the night and Kathleen's christening had created a sacred space where she might, this one last time, speak truth to this man.

"One day we would pick up where we left off in Paris? I thought so too, Pamela. Since this little girl was born, things have felt easier between us. And the love never went away. It never will."

"That was not to be," she said, nearly choking on the words, *"though I wanted it so.* Oh Jamie, I am a ridiculous fool."

He took her hand in his and said, "If you are then I am as well." And then, because he was Jamie, he answered poetry with poetry and knew, without doubt, she would understand.

> *"Be not immortal, since it is flame*
> *But be infinite while it lasts."*

Voices rose from the distant chapel, a soft chant of faith, hope and love. Love which had endured for centuries, love for a man who was only present in the spirit of belief and grace. Yes, love could survive anything, could overcome obstacles and could even live without the physical presence of the loved one. If it must.

This moment here, holding his hand and listening to their daughter breathe, was not forever, but it was, indeed, infinite.

Part Two

A Bit of Ground to Stand Upon

Chapter Fourteen

A Wee Bit of Ground to Stand Upon
January 1979

ONE THING ABOUT having your husband return from his putative grave was that it rather put all the other aspects of your life into sharp perspective. Since Casey had walked out from the edge of the wood, Pamela hadn't given much thought to her status as a single mother—which, she supposed, she no longer was—her contractual obligations to her publisher, or the ledgers from the construction company. In fact, she hadn't been able to think with much coherence at all, as her thoughts were entirely scattered and reeling around like a drunk on a patch of ice.

The single thing she had managed to maintain focus on was the children and how Casey's return was affecting each of them. Conor in particular. Old enough to remember his father and also to remember how much he'd loved him, she had thought his acceptance of Casey might be an easy thing for the lad, but it was proving to be anything but. Her first instinct had been to give him some leeway and time in which to sort his feelings out, but as a sort of stubborn intransigence seemed to have seized the boy—which ironically reminded her in no small part of Casey—she thought it was time to confront the lion cub in his den.

Conor was an early riser and was usually up and about before Isabelle. So when she heard him stir, she went and sat on the end of his bed, wanting to talk to him before the day began. He sat up when he felt her presence, his dark curls sticking up at a variety of angles from his head, his eyes still only half-open and a wary look on his face. She could see that he knew what it was she wanted to talk about, and that he was already digging in his metaphorical heels.

"Daddy is coming to visit this afternoon, Conor, and I think it would be nice if you talked to him, maybe showed him your train—we could set it up downstairs if you'd like. I know he'd love to see it."

Conor merely said, "Mmphmm," in an echo of his father. She sighed inwardly, Conor was every bit as stubborn as Casey, and about as tractable as a mule when he took a notion in his head.

"You have to think about how hard this is for your daddy, Conor. As hard as it is for us to have him come home, and feel like we don't know him like we used to, think how it must feel to him to come home and find everything strange. Imagine," she continued, picking up the edge of his baby quilt, which sat folded at the bottom of his bed, "that one morning you woke up and nothing looked right to you—not your bed, or your room, not your sister or me, or even Finbar or Rusty. You didn't recognize anyone you loved, or anything that you see every day. And you couldn't remember the things you used to know how to do—like feed Khamsin, or where to catch the bus, or even the school you go to. Or what if you fell asleep at school, and when you woke up, you couldn't remember where home was. How might all that feel to you?"

"Scary, I guess," he said.

"It's a bit like he's lost, Conor. Remember that time you wandered off from me at the church picnic and then didn't know where you were, even though there were only a couple of trees in between us?"

He nodded, small face still set in a stubborn expression.

"Well, that's how it is for your daddy. He's home but there's still trees between him and us, and he can't quite see us the way he used to."

"What if he never does, Mama?"

This echoed her own fears—what if Casey never truly regained his memories? What if he never could remember how things had been, and what it meant to share the sort of home they once had? Conor did not need to be prey to her own fears, and so she answered with reassurance tempered with a bit of reality. Conor wasn't one to be easily bamboozled.

"I believe he will, and if there's some small chance he doesn't, we'll make a new life with him, built on the foundation of what we used to have."

"Ye mean he'd live with us?" Conor asked, a dubious note in his voice.

"Hopefully one day, yes, we'll all live as a family again. Would you like that?" she asked.

Conor's face was a study, and he took a moment before he answered, fine black brows drawn down in thought.

"I think maybe I would like it," he finally said, "but sometimes, Mama, I really miss Jamie comin' to visit, an' I think that when Daddy lives here, Jamie won't be able to visit anymore."

No one could ever accuse her son of not being astute about the goings-on around him.

"No, he won't in quite the same way but he'll still come to see Kathleen, and you know if you want to visit him, he said you can go to his house any time he's home."

"Will that make Daddy mad?" Conor asked.

"No, it won't, Conor. He understands that Jamie has been our very good friend and that he took good care of us when Daddy was gone."

Casey wouldn't be angry, but on the other hand she wasn't entirely certain how comfortable he would be with it.

"What if he decides not to live with us, Mama?"

She smiled, attempting to look reassuring, threads of anxiety winding through her veins at his comment.

"Then we'll manage, won't we? We did it for three years, Conor and we're still doing it now."

"But I don't want you to be sad anymore."

"I'm not sad, Conor. You don't have to worry about me, baby."

Conor merely gave her a look which said he didn't really believe her, and so she changed the topic to the one subject sure to distract him—food.

"Do you want sausage or bacon with your breakfast this morning?"

"Can I have both?" he asked hopefully. Normally he wouldn't ask because he knew he could have one or the other on weekends, but not both. But this morning she wanted to keep him as sweet as possible in the hope that he would be more relaxed when Casey came to visit.

"I'll let you have both today, but only as a treat."

The lure of bacon and sausage had Conor down the stairs and sitting at the table expectantly by the time Pamela dished the food onto his plate.

Pamela, used to having her meals interrupted, took bites of toast and bacon in between wiping down the counters, and filling the sink with soapy water so she could wash the dishes.

Conor ate steadily, but she noticed his dark eyes gazing at her often, as though he had a question he would like to ask, but wasn't sure he should.

"What is it, baby?" she asked. "You know you can ask me anything you want to."

Conor had clearly only needed that wee bit of encouragement, for he asked his question then without hesitation, though his wee face looked troubled as he spoke.

"Does he want to be married to ye still?" he asked, forking up more eggs even as he spoke, and eyeing her in that frank, open way which was a trait of all the Riordan men in her life—Conor, Casey, Patrick.

"I don't know, Conor. I don't think he knows right now. He needs time to readjust to his old life, and maybe time to remember some things, enough that he feels comfortable with us again."

"That's not how bein' married works," Conor said. "Sister Mary Frances says that once ye're married ye're married for always."

"Did she then?" Pamela asked, feeling less than charitable toward the nun, whom she normally liked. "Have you been talking to people about Daddy being back?"

"No, but Kieran knows an' he told people," Conor said, and Pamela mentally cursed Kieran, who at six, had the ability to gossip like a pensioner in a tea shop. "What if he doesn't like bein' married anymore?"

Pamela suspected this was yet another observation of Kieran's, who was also possessed of many opinions—or rather, she suspected, his mother was—which Conor tended to repeat at home.

"I don't think it's that he doesn't like it, it's only that it's strange to him. It's like what I said to you upstairs, he needs time to find his way with us."

Conor, never one for long conversations, hopped down from his chair. Having put paid to the bacon and sausages, as well as a good-sized serving of eggs and two slices of toast, he was ready to get dressed and head out-of-doors. He brought his plate over to her, and then gave her a quick hug before he was gone up the stairs with Finbar—like a woolly mammoth pulled along by the gravitational force of a small comet—in his wake. Despite his seeming acceptance of her answers, she knew he was bothered more than he could likely tell her by their whole situation. Conor had always liked things to be black and white, and slotted into their correct positions.

He was too young to have to worry about her situation with Casey and so she'd been careful about how much she said to him. Her son was nobody's fool, though, and she had caught him watching her worriedly several times when Casey was visiting. In truth, she was nowhere near as fine with things as she had tried to make Conor believe.

Every time she saw Casey she was torn between throwing her arms around him and just holding him as though she was trying to keep him in place, and a fraught reserve which she supposed was only natural considering how strange they were to each other now. And yet, when he touched her the reserve fled. She knew it was the same for him because she'd seen the surprise in his face when he'd held her that first night. His body remembered her, even if the man didn't entirely—that much was clear.

Conor's words came back to her now as she stood over the dishes, thinking she ought to have been in the bath a good twenty minutes ago, for Kathleen would be up looking for her first feed of the day any minute now.

"What if he doesn't want to live with us again?"

Just the thought made her feel slightly sick, and yet what she had told Conor was true—they would manage. Regardless of what did or did not happen between her and Casey, the children had their father back, which was no small thing.

Yet still…she sighed, pushing a stray curl back with one soapy finger, she had never thought to find herself at this sort of crossroads with Casey.

"What if he doesn't like bein' married anymore?"

What if, indeed.

If Conor's attitude toward his father had softened at all in light of their talk, it wasn't immediately in evidence when Casey arrived that afternoon, though he wasn't overtly hostile either, for which small grace she was thankful. Isabelle, who had already accepted her father back into her life, as though he'd merely been gone a few days, had blithely gone off with Gert for an afternoon of biscuit making.

Conor had bolted into the house when he saw Casey pulling down the drive.

"He's here," he said and then took up his stance beside her, his little body nearly thrumming with nerves. Conor was normally an unflappable child, able to deal with any situation that came his way. He'd had to deal with a lot, things he shouldn't have had to, in his father's absence. And now that the one thing he'd most devoutly wanted had happened, he couldn't seem to deal with it in any sort of reasoned fashion.

She had left the door open for Casey and told him to simply come in. She'd given him a key the last time he'd visited as well, because whether he felt it or not, this was his home and always would be.

He came in out of the bright day, a box of groceries in his arms, which he deposited on the table. Though she had told him it wasn't necessary, he brought something each time he came: food, fuel, boards to repair the roof on the shed, treats for the children, flowers for her. Despite the loveliness of it, of having him care for them in a variety of ways, she couldn't shake the feeling that he was trying to earn his spot amongst them, instead of realizing he'd always belonged, and always would.

"Hello," she said, slightly breathless, and wishing she'd brushed her hair one more time before his arrival. She still felt ridiculously twitterpated every time she saw him. Casey smiled and kissed her cheek, and she wished he would just hold her for a few moments and still her shaking. He'd always been able to do that—make her feel safe and provide the ground beneath her feet that she'd needed to feel stable. She took a deep breath in, filling her senses with the scent of him before she stepped back, not wanting to overwhelm him. It was almost as if they were afraid to touch each other too long, for fear that they might lose control. Well, she amended, *he* seemed worried about that, she felt it might be just what they both needed.

"Hello Conor," he said, in a mild tone. He had adopted a patient attitude with Conor, neither pushing their relationship, nor stepping away from the possibility of it.

"Hello," Conor said, his own tone slightly less stiff than what he'd been using with Casey since his return. Such small things made her hopeful for the future.

"I made you a plate for lunch, if you're hungry," she said to Casey. Conor had already made short work of his lunch, and was trying to slip out the door before doing his homework.

"That would be grand," he said.

"Sit down then and I'll get it for you."

She fetched the plate from the oven, and placed it along with a fresh pot of tea in front of him.

"It's only last night's leftovers," she said apologetically.

"It's hot an' fillin', an' that's more than I manage some days. Will ye sit with me while I eat?" he asked.

"Of course," she said and sat down, feeling the same odd combination of nerves and singing joy she'd felt since his return.

It gave her pleasure to look after him even in so small a way as this—feeding him with last night's ham and potatoes. These last three years he'd had no one to care for him, and she was determined to somehow make up for the lack of that, if he would allow her to.

"I might be around a bit more regular-like this next while," he said suddenly.

"Oh?"

"Aye, Tomas asked me to come an' have a look at his fireplace. Apparently, he's interested in havin' me do some restoration work on it."

Pamela's eyebrows shot up at this statement.

"Are you going to?"

Casey took a swallow of his tea before replying.

"Aye, I can use any work that comes my way, an' if the man can get past his dislike of me well enough to ask me to work on his house, I suppose I can do the same in order to put a few coins in my pocket."

"You can stay here if you'd like to," she said, her heart racing a little just suggesting it.

Casey didn't answer at once, but she could sense his hesitation at the mere suggestion, and tried to hide the hurt it caused her. She could understand why he might not be ready, but it stung all the same.

Conor had taken advantage of their distraction and was attempting to sidle out the door back to freedom, when she glimpsed him out of the corner of her eye.

"Get back here, young man, you promised me you'd get your history worksheet done before you went outside again."

"I'll do it after supper, Mama, I promise," he said, even though he'd promised the same thing the night before and had fallen asleep promptly after his dinner was consumed.

"Conor," she said in the tone she used to signal that he was launching himself onto thin ice, if he kept protesting.

Conor sighed. As far as he was concerned homework was something designed by the nuns to punish small boys who wanted to be outside every minute of their weekend.

"I could help ye with that, if ye'd like. I know a bit about history," Casey said, his voice neutral, as though it didn't matter one way or the other if Conor accepted his offer.

Conor gave him one of his assessing looks which was similar in content to looks she'd seen on Pat's face when he was deciding upon the criminality of a potential client.

"All right," he said finally, though the words were grudging in tone.

Casey looked at her over Conor's head and smiled, though he made sure Conor didn't witness it.

She went about her work, listening as Conor read the questions, slowly but surely to Casey, and heard Casey's quiet responses. Occasionally, she looked over at them, the two dark heads bent in absorption over the rather grubby homework sheet. The dirt was compliments of Finbar walking over the paper, as it had been flung on the floor by Conor when he unpacked his schoolbag the day before.

She left her two men to their own devices while she went upstairs where Kathleen was stirring from her nap, and would soon need changing and feeding.

It seemed peaceful enough downstairs while she picked up the few things scattered over Conor and Isabelle's floor, and then hearing Kathleen start to make the soft noises she did upon awakening, she went to her own room, entering just in time to hear a full-throated cry.

As soon as she put her face over the side of the crib, Kathleen gave her a gummy smile, green eyes sparkling with tears. She changed the baby and then sat to feed her, enjoying the few moments where she didn't need to worry about anything other than nursing her baby, and resting for a few moments.

Casey and Conor wouldn't come to blows in her absence—or at least Casey wouldn't.

Twenty minutes later, she put Kathleen to her shoulder and descended the stairs. Halfway down, she heard Conor's voice and sighed. Whatever conviviality he and Casey had managed a few short moments ago, it now seemed to be over. "How do ye remember *that* but you don't know where you lived?" Conor was asking.

Pamela came off the last stair, and felt a qualm deep inside when she saw the expression on her son's face, for it was the look of a boy who wanted answers and assurances that his father could not give him. His face was tilted up towards Casey's and his wee chin stuck out in an accusatory fashion. While mostly even-tempered, Conor at times, had been known to explode when he finally let his feelings out.

"Conor," Pamela began, thinking she should gently steer him off this track, but Casey turned to look at her, and shook his head.

"No, it's a fair question, Pamela, an' the lad has a right to ask it."

He turned back toward Conor, an echo there in his dark eyes of what the last three years had cost him—had cost all of them.

"I read a lot of books about Irish history, both when I was livin' in San Francisco and when I came back here. Ye see, all I really understood about myself was that I was Irish, an' so it seemed the sensible thing to read up on the country an' see if there was anythin' there which might give my mind a jolt. The doctors seemed to feel that my memory wasn't so much gone, as it was sleepin', an' that if I could find a way to wake it up, the memories might come back to me."

"Did it work?" Conor asked, suspicion still written clearly across his face.

"No, not as I would have liked it to, but it did give me a stronger sense of myself. It was as if I'd only had air under my feet for a long time, an' then suddenly I had a wee bit of ground I could stand upon, an' take a look about me. Then I came back here, an' it only made that sense stronger. The wee island I was standin' upon grew so that I could walk a ways on it, before feelin' lost."

"So what did wake up yer memories?" Conor asked, slightly less hostile in tone.

"Yer letters, an' seein' yer mammy's face." He glanced up at Pamela, and she saw there the utter desperation which had imprinted itself upon both of them that night, and yet that horrible time had recalled him to her, and so something wonderful had been borne of so much darkness. Conor had asked many questions about what had happened to her, but they'd kept the details sparse, and merely said someone had kidnapped her by accident. The truth was more than a small boy needed to know. The truth, she thought, was more than she could manage most days. It hadn't fooled Conor, for he'd merely given her a look of great dubiousness and left off with the questions.

"Where did ye see Mama?"

Casey looked at Pamela, a question in his face. They had both agreed to give Conor what truth they could, but letting him know his father had been there that night at the workhouse, and that the only reason she, Jamie or Kathleen was still alive and present was because of this man here would only lead to more questions. What Casey had to do to free them from the clutches of five mad people, was not something Conor could be told now, or perhaps ever. So they had agreed on a story that was simple and which they both could remember the details of.

"One day I happened upon the property. I didn't know then that it was my home as well. That was when I found yer letters in the wee hole in the tree." That far the story was true, what he said next was the white lie they'd decided upon together. "I came back later, an' saw yez outside with yer mammy. Just the sight of all of ye was enough to make me understand who ye were to me."

"Why didn't ye come see us then?"

"I was afraid," Casey said simply, and Pamela knew this part was the bald truth. "An' I wanted to give ye all a bit of time to adjust to Kathleen bein' here."

Casey looked over at her, and she felt it—all the things that couldn't be explained to Conor because they existed within the grey lexicon of adult doings. For him, it was simple, his father had returned and yet had not, and he wasn't happy about it.

"Ye don't want to live with us," Conor said, a note in his voice which alerted Pamela that the small thundercloud which had been hovering around Conor since Casey's return, might be about to burst. He'd clearly heard the offer she'd made Casey, and had noted his father's silence.

"No, that's not so, Conor. It's not so simple as that."

"Is it that ye don't want to be married to Mama anymore?"

"No, it's not that either, Conor," Casey said, gently. "It's not that at all." He flicked an apologetic look at Pamela, who thought that Conor had rather succinctly stated all her own concerns without so much as a fig for his father's comfort. While her heart hurt for her boy, she was also proud of him for being so courageous.

"I'm goin' outside," Conor said, and Pamela could tell that he was on the verge of tears, in part because he hadn't liked Casey's answers and in part because the emotions roiling around his father's reappearance in their lives had fully caught up with him.

"Would ye mind if I came out with ye?" Casey asked, his tone neutral.

"Suit yerself," Conor said and slammed out the door, after ramming his feet into his galoshes.

Casey looked up at her, and sighed. "Probably best if I give him a minute to cool off before followin'."

"I'm sorry," she said to Casey, "he's just been a little…" She put her hands palms up to indicate she couldn't quite find the right words to describe Conor's state of emotion.

"He's just been," Casey said wryly, "a little bit of a Riordan is what ye mean."

Pamela laughed. "Yes, I suppose that *is* what I mean."

"It's all right, I do remember that my daddy always said my own childhood stubbornness would return to haunt me one day, an' I suppose this is the day. If ye have no objection, Pamela, I think it's time Conor and I had a bit of straight talk between us. I'll go carefully with him, ye needn't worry that I won't. But I think it's best if it's just the two of us. I think maybe the fact he's willin' to be honest about how upset he is, means now is the time to talk with him."

She nodded, knowing he was right and also knowing that he and Conor were going to have to map the geography of their relationship between the two of them, and she would have to leave them to it. She trusted Casey to navigate that with his stubborn son.

"Well, here I go. Wish me luck," Casey said with the air of a man about to mount the gallows steps, and then stood and followed his son out the door.

Outside, the afternoon had grown chilly and shadows were beginning to drift in and settle around tree roots and the base of the stone wall which divided the property from the road above.

Casey didn't see Conor at first, but he could hear him. He followed the sound to the other side of the byre, where he found Conor hammering away at a chunk of wood, ostensibly driving nails into the fort he was building, but Casey had a feeling that the hammering was frustration, and the wood possibly symbolic for his own head.

As it was wont to do in such situations his father's voice sounded within him just then. Brian had warned him about moments like this, and had said that he hoped to witness him with a son as stubborn as himself one day. Well, here that day was, and while his father was not in attendance, Casey had a feeling he was somewhere having a good laugh. Why Brian's voice should be so clear in his memory when more recent voices and events weren't, was a mystery to him, but he was grateful for the paternal advice, nonetheless, as he had a strong feeling he was going to need all the help he could get in the coming years.

"Listen to me, son," he began, only to have Conor turn, small face red with anger, eyes a smoky grey which Casey had seen in the mirror more than once in his life.

"Don't call me son! I wish ye'd leave, I wish ye'd disappear again!"

Casey stepped back. The words stung far more than he could have imagined. He understood his child's anger though; he was going to have to take whatever it was Conor needed to dish out.

"I could see how ye might feel that way. I'm sorry I was gone so long, wee man. Ye know it wasn't of my own choosin', don't ye?"

"I heard Mama say you were gone longer than ye had to be. That ye were here for a long time before ye came home." Conor's wee fists were balled up and Casey felt grateful that the boy had let go of the hammer.

"Aye, she's right. I don't suppose ye were meant to hear her say it, though."

Conor glared at him, though he looked slightly shamefaced. "I wasn't supposed to be listenin', she thought I was asleep. She was talkin' to Uncle Pat. Uncle Pat was mad at ye too."

"Aye, I know that. Can't say I blame him either."

"Why did ye stay away longer?" Conor asked, looking like he might be on the verge of tears. Even so, he wouldn't cry. Casey knew Conor didn't trust him enough to cry in front of him yet. He wasn't one to cry much, anyway. The laddie was a tough one.

"Ye know how sometimes, ye're so sad that ye just can't be around other people? Because ye don't want to cry in front of them, or ye just need to be alone until ye feel a wee bit better?"

"Aye," Conor said warily.

"Well, I didn't remember you all for a bit there. Ye know when I showed ye the dent in my head—that's where my brain was hurt, an' for a long time I wasn't me, an' it took a very long time to come back and be myself properly. I didn't want to come to you an' yer sister an' mammy if I wasn't goin' to be right as a father an' a husband. Do ye understand what I'm sayin'?"

"I think so," Conor said, though his eyes were still that smoky-grey that said his anger hadn't dissipated in the least. Casey knew there was only one thing for it.

"It seems to me, boyo, that we have to do somethin' about our situation here."

"What do ye mean?"

"Well," Casey rubbed a hand over his stubbled chin, "ye could hit me, that might make ye a wee bit less angry."

Conor narrowed his eyes in suspicion. "Uncle Pat let me hit him once when ye were gone."

"Did he then?"

"Aye, he said sometimes women don't understand that men need to hit things, an' even sometimes people."

"Aye, our own daddy taught us that," Casey said, thinking Conor had probably simplified things down somewhat from the lesson his uncle had been trying to teach him.

"I—I don't think I want to hit ye," Conor said, his lip trembling a little. He was fighting to hold on to his composure. Casey was proud of him, but his heart ached for his son at the same time. Making up ground together was no easy task, he thought wryly, for either of them.

"Ye might not want to, but I think ye need to, boyo, so just go ahead and do it. Put yer anger into it."

Conor took his advice at face value, and walking over to him let fly a punch that winded Casey and caused him to stagger back a little, eyes watering. He felt a rush of pride as well; the laddie had one helluva punch on him. He caught his breath and then nodded at his son, so that he might know he was fine. He sat down on a stump that was used as a base for chopping wood; the boy really had winded him.

Conor's eyes were bright with unshed tears. "I don't want ye to leave. I'm sorry I said that."

"I know ye didn't mean it, laddie. But I wouldn't blame ye a bit if ye did. It's all right to be angry with me, Conor. I love ye no matter what, so ye can be as mad as ye need to be an' ye can say what ye feel, an' I'll not be angry with ye for it. Now d'ye think I might hug ye?"

Conor nodded, tears slipping down his cheeks and Casey drew him in gently. He wrapped his arms around his son and held him tightly, knowing Conor needed it and knowing he needed it too. They sat so for a long time, as the light changed slowly toward evening, and the sun turned the land around them gold and lavender.

"I thought I would know ye, but then I didn't. I told Mama, I thought she told you."

"Ah, no. Yer mammy will be careful about what she tells me, an' unless ye told her she could, she's not one to share confidences that way. She'll worry the wee bit too much about hurtin' my feelin's' too. Women are that way, no?"

"I don't want to hurt yer feelin's' either," Conor said, small brow furrowed in worry.

"All I want from ye, Conor, is that ye tell me the truth. Even if ye think it might make me sad. I'm a grown man, an' I'm yer father, so I just want ye to always tell me what ye're feelin', an' not what ye think I want to hear. D'ye understand what I'm sayin'?"

"Aye," Conor said, though he still looked a little doubtful about the notion of unbridled honesty. Considering some of the revelations this policy had brought about between Pamela and him, he tended to think the lad had a point. Still, he knew Conor needed the freedom to tell him what was in his heart, even if it was things that were bound to hurt. That could not be helped, but it might at least begin a process of healing for the boy, and for himself.

"I know ye're worried about yer mammy, but she an' myself have things to work out between the two of us, an' that will take a little time. Do ye understand that?"

Conor nodded.

"Here's the thing though, Conor, I *am* yer daddy, an' ye're goin' to have to come to terms with that, because I am not goin' anywhere. Okay?"

Conor nodded, and then slid down off Casey's knee, offering him a hand. "I'm hungry. D'ye want to come back in the house with me?"

Conor's hand was grubby and still damp with tears, but Casey took it gratefully, and then went back into the light and warmth of home, holding his son's hand.

Chapter Fifteen

Spy Game

THE PALLADIAN FAÇADE of White's Club in St. James rose above Richard's head, its dormered attic windows and famous bow window where Beau Brummell had once sat and allowed London to gaze upon his magnificence, giving it an air of far more raffish times. Originally a chocolate house and then an infamous gambling den, it had, over the years, morphed into one of the most exclusive gentleman's clubs in the world. It was also—and more pertinently to Richard's visit this afternoon—the unofficial meeting place for members of the British Intelligence community.

His observation of the building itself was strictly a matter of memory, for the entire building was shrouded in a thick February fog. As Dickens had once said—*Fog everywhere*—fog up the river and down, on the marshes and in the yards, fog wrapped in tendrils around the sails of ships, fog sheathing bridge and boat alike, fog hovering near firesides and settling in the lungs of pensioners. There was so much fog that Richard felt like he was wading through the streets in a clog of wet wool. He stepped in through the doors of White's, happy to be out of the fog and into the warmth and luxury of the club.

Richard had long been a member of White's, his entry into it having been guaranteed by his boss's endorsement. In theory, he rather objected to the snobbery of a private gentleman's club. In practice, it was a good place to conduct business.

The man he had come here to meet waited for him in the coffee room, where the fog, thick and creamy, curled and purred against the long rectangular windows and gave the room an aura of cozy secrecy. He sat in repose, though in truth Richard had never seen the man ruffled in the slightest degree. Beautifully-cut suit, neatly-cut iron-grey hair, body as lean and well-ordered as that of a whippet, and a look of studied bemusement on his ascetic face. Not many men put the fear of God in Richard these days, but this one still did. A holdover, he supposed, from his training days.

He wended his way through the plush chairs and small tables. One could almost hear the conversations which had been conducted here over the last few hundred years—conversations which had changed the balance of global power, had seen empires rise and fall and had, he thought, tugging at his tie a little, likely resulted in the deaths of more than a few people.

When he arrived at the table, the man indicated the chair opposite, and then proceeded directly to the point, as was his usual way of doing business.

"I want you to bring one of your agents in from the cold," he said.

"Which one?" Richard asked, undoing his suit jacket before sitting down across from the man he privately referred to as the Grey Man, for his ability to blend into his surroundings regardless of the environment. The man took a sip of his pink gin before replying.

"Our little Irish golden boy."

Richard felt a spark of panic. There was only one man to whom that description could apply, and he was only a slightly less difficult bastard than the man in front of him. James Kirkpatrick, who had been off their radar for three years, and Richard had hoped, off their books for good. He supposed he ought to have known better. James Kirkpatrick had been one of their best operatives. Charming, intelligent, ridiculously good looking, with connections to a variety of spies, crooks, thieves and shady operatives all over the continent, as well as overseas, he'd been an asset the service couldn't resist recruiting. They'd used a woman to draw him in, and the result had been rather mixed, to say the least. They had landed James Kirkpatrick, but they'd also had to cover up an affair with a Tory MP's wife, and a child who had learned only a few years ago—at the age of twenty—no less—that James Kirkpatrick was his father.

The second James Kirkpatrick—Jamie's grandfather—had worked for them also, during the war years, though Richard, despite spending near to a fortnight going through old files, had never found out exactly what it was the man had done for them. Which told him it had been highly classified, and likely highly dangerous. There had been a scandal surrounding him as well, for he'd left his wife and lived with a Gypsy woman until his death, but hadn't ever divorced the wife.

The man sitting across from him now knew all this firsthand, for he'd known the grandfather as well as the grandson, in fact he'd been Jamie's first handler. Something had gone awry in the relationship though, beyond the scandal, for he knew neither man felt warmly toward the other. Richard held the man's gaze—which was needling its way over his face now, assessing, he thought, how much Richard knew about Jamie's current circumstances.

The man's name was Felix Plum, and within the SIS, he was legendary. He was widely considered one of the greatest spies British Intelligence had ever put out in the field. He sat back now, pinstriped suit immaculate, red tie a rare blaze of colour for him. Richard considered that he must have received the tie as a Christmas gift, though trying to imagine this man with a home and a family, sitting down to a Christmas meal was frankly beyond him. He thought of him as always here, in this club, pink gin in hand, flawlessly-cut suit always the same, the man himself only animating when someone needed something, or when, God help them all, things went cock-eyed. The latter of which was, Richard feared, the reason for his summoning.

"He broke off all ties with us, he wants nothing to do with this business anymore," Richard said, taking a sip of the brandy which he'd ordered as soon as he'd arrived. He took a second to savour it, before continuing; it tasted like a golden apricot dropped from the tree at the perfect moment. "I think we owe it to him to leave him alone, after his time in the Soviet Union."

"Owe him for what? He got out of Russia alive, after all. He's had three years to lick his wounds, and from what I can tell he's not been idle during that time."

Richard merely lifted an eyebrow at this, though he knew exactly what it was Felix referred to. Jamie had spent two years in a Russian gulag, and come out with a son, leaving behind a wife who turned out to be a KGB agent. A KGB agent who had appeared again in his life, just when he was moving on with another woman—one with whom he'd had a daughter, now only two months old.

"He doesn't want this life anymore. I'm not certain he ever really did."

"It's James, he finds peace boring. I suspect he's good and bored by now, after his stint at playing house these last three years with that American girl."

Richard rather thought Jamie loved that American girl a great deal and hadn't been merely playing house with her. That they had a daughter together he knew, but beyond that he wasn't quite sure about the parameters of their relationship. What he did know was that Jamie had put in a great deal of effort to find the woman's husband when the man had disappeared some three years previous, even to the extent of tapping his old connections on the continent and in America.

"I'd think you'd have a better notion than me. You had the training of him, after all."

"No, I didn't. His first handler was Mordecai."

Richard's heart sank a little closer to his toes. He had a feeling he now understood just why this man wanted Jamie pulled back in from the cold.

"Mordecai?" he said, the dismay evident in his voice.

"Yes, Mordecai. He plucked Jamie out from under my tender ministrations right at the beginning, and took him under his crooked wing."

Mordecai was the stuff of agency legend, half-chimera, half-tall tale, and yet still *the* greatest spy the SIS had ever laid claim to. Mordecai—he'd only ever needed the one name. If you asked ten different people about him, you'd be the recipient of ten different stories: he was a Sephardic Jew who'd lost his entire family in the Holocaust, he was an Israeli assassin who'd been instrumental in the Six Day War, he was the Nazi hunter who'd hunted down escaped Nazis and killed them in the streets of Buenos Aires, or—and this one was Richard's favourite—he was a lost royal from the Romanov family and the only one to survive the execution of the family in that bloody basement. Richard had no doubt Mordecai had planted the seeds of all those stories because that was how Mordecai operated. He was like a ghost, more story than substance. Of late though, he'd heard rumours that Mordecai may have gone rogue. Gone over to the Soviets, hiring himself out to the highest bidder. Even that could be a story fabricated by Mordecai himself, and then diffused through his elaborate and very effective grapevine which ran through both Europe and Asia.

"I didn't know Mordecai ever ran agents," Richard said. Mordecai had operated by his own rules, and was always rumoured to be in some obscure corner of the globe, but he'd never heard of him handling any other agents.

"Officially, he didn't. But he knew Jamie's grandfather, and when he heard we were trying to recruit the grandson, he slipped in at the last minute with his usual sleight of hand and spirited the boy off."

Richard paused to take another drink, and to forestall any look of amusement that might cross his face, due to the very idea of something not going this man's way.

"Needless to say," Felix continued, crossing one leg over the other in his usual fastidious manner, "this has caused James to have some rather unique ways of going about the intelligence business. But of course you know that, having been his handler these last ten years."

"*I'm* not his handler any longer though," Richard said, putting a slight emphasis on the personal pronoun, so that Felix might understand that Richard knew he was being manipulated. "He was serious about being done with the service."

Felix smiled, and it was not a pleasant thing to witness.

"It's not a job one can quit, as you well know, Richard. Besides we still have uses for His Lordship."

"How do you propose to keep him chained to the business, when he wants out?"

"In the time-honoured fashion," Felix put his glass on the polished mahogany table. It glowed with the delicate rose flush of the gin. Richard had never seen the man finish a drink. "Blackmail."

Richard set his snifter down, not caring for the direction the conversation was taking.

"And with what exactly would we be blackmailing him?"

Felix bared his teeth once again, but Richard was certain this time it was not meant to be a smile.

"Our boy has an illustrious past and he has not always been circumspect in his amours."

Richard did not comment, there was no need, he knew Jamie's past as well as anyone did, or as well as anyone had been allowed to except perhaps his small circle of intimates with whom he lived.

"I don't think there is a woman at present."

"Oh? Richard, there is always a woman, or in our Irish boy's case, several. But for our purposes, we only need one. The Russian woman, who is, after all, still his wife."

"Why?"

"So I can expose him," Felix said. "He'll put his head up at some point, and then we'll be ready."

"Expose him?" Richard suddenly understood just what Felix was driving at. He shook his head. "No, not Jamie."

"Richard, the man spent two weeks in Lubyanka and came out alive. What exactly do you think that means?"

"You think James Kirkpatrick is a double agent for the Soviets? No, I wouldn't believe it for a moment."

"That's because you've never been in the basement of Lubyanka, with the reek of your own fear and pain, day after day, night after endless night. Not many men survive that, and if they do it's because they made a deal with the devil. If you believe otherwise, then you're overly attached to the man and perhaps not best suited to run him anymore."

Richard stiffened slightly, but didn't let it show in his face. "If you think anyone else can or will run that man, you're mistaken. He won't work for us again, I would bet my career on that."

"Would you indeed?" Felix smiled, but it was not a pleasant expression, but rather a baring of teeth to a potential foe.

"I would," Richard said, thinking he'd bet on James Kirkpatrick against pretty much anyone, even this man. "Do you have a man on him now?" Richard asked, fearing the answer a little.

"We did, but he lost him. He must have used a decoy, which means he knows he's being followed. He went to see the priest in Paris, went in the front door of Notre Dame and then disappeared somewhere within its bowels, because there were men on all the exits and no one saw him leave."

"I've never had anyone successfully follow him. He runs on Moscow rules when he needs to, keeps it simple, doubles back on himself, takes buses and trains, wearing one disguise and then another. I have never run another spy that had such unerring instincts about when he's being followed."

"What I want to know, Richard, is just who set up a meeting between him and Mordecai? Because someone must have. We've been watching Mordecai when he puts his head up above the parapet. It occurs to me now that he was likely making himself conspicuous of late, to lull that idiot I had following him, into a sense of complacency. We lost track of him somewhere between Moscow and North Africa. Jamie was meant to be in New York, but he's not. So what do you think two missing spies might be doing?"

"Meeting somewhere in between those two locations."

"Exactly. Now where, knowing James as you do, do you think that location might be?"

"It's Jamie," Richard said drily, "if there's one thing the bastard isn't, it's predictable."

"In some ways that's true, but the man does have a streak of sentimentality in him for his old haunts."

Then, suddenly, it clicked into place. "Marrakech," Richard said.

"Yes, indeed," Felix replied and saluted him with the glass of pink gin, "Marrakech."

Chapter Sixteen

Mordecai

THE KOUTOUBIA MOSQUE rose against the African dusk, a towering rosy pearl washed with bands of smoke lavender, dust gold, and the first faint shiver of night's indigo. The Mosque of the Booksellers, so called because the second iteration of the mosque—the first had been torn down due to not being strictly aligned with Mecca—had been host to a hundred booksellers, who hawked their wares near the entrance of the mosque and amongst the gardens which flourished there.

The call of the muezzin sounded then, echoing across the rooftops and rebounding off the stone walls. It was of such a piercing sweetness, this final call to prayer for the day, that Mordecai, tough-as-nails old Jew that he was, felt a blossoming pain in his chest. The sound was not unlike the Hebrew prayers of his youth—those prayers sung by the cantor, which even now he could hear in his heart, when he chose to listen. His youth had been spent in a tiny Polish village, near to the Russian border. But that had been before the Nazis, when the entire face of the universe had changed for Jews and their God. Once there had been a thriving community of Jews in Marrakech; his people had been here from the time of Carthaginian rule, but that community was now no more than a handful of aged men and women, whose children and grandchildren lived in far-flung lands—Israel, Canada, France, America.

In Marrakech, there was no fog. It was warm, and it was a Friday, which meant the souk was crowded. Mordecai, dressed as a Bedouin in dark robes and a headdress, moved through the crowds smoothly, though inside he seethed a little at how difficult Jamie had made it to find him. Well, he supposed he deserved it, he'd trained the lad to be a trickster, and now he was paying his dues on that.

He stopped on the edge of the Jemaa el-Fna—the vast central square of the city—to catch his breath. Twenty-five years of chain-smoking had taken a toll on his lungs.

Mordecai took a moment to light a cigarette and then dragged in a hit of nicotine, looking around him at the stew of life which existed in the square—the snake handlers, fortune-tellers, healers, witches, jugglers, and a blind storyteller with a small brass bowl for those who had gratitude for his tale. He drew in a little to hear the storyteller, for many were gathered around the tattered blanket the old man sat upon, faces bent down toward his voice. All his life Mordecai had been drawn like a moth to a flame to a good story. The man looked ancient, his face and hands grained with years of hard work and filth. Poor beggar likely lived on the streets. Storytellers didn't make a lot of money these days, and the few coins gleaming dully in the bowl at the man's side seemed to pay testament to that. It wasn't for lack of talent though, for the man had a voice like red honey—a brew that was both sweet and bitter, resulting from bees feeding on rhododendrons high in the mountains of Nepal, the ingestion of which had been known to result in fits of madness and a divine sort of intoxication.

"There once was a man named Kadour, who was a sweet seller who wasn't at all good at selling sweets. Each day he sold less and less, until he could no longer afford tea for his kettle, nor the honey to make sweets. Finally, the day came when he had no money for food or lodgings and he was cast out into the streets of Marrakech to sleep in the cold and beg for his living. But Kadour was too ashamed to take up begging and so he thought to himself that he might find his fortune in another place.

"Kadour packed up his belongings, which consisted of his old tea kettle, the moth-eaten *djellabah* on his back, a parrot that could only speak in rhyming couplets, and a tiny lantern made from tin and red glass.

"It was a cold morning when Kadour set out for the snowy reaches of the Atlas Mountains, with the parrot singing ancient Persian love songs in rhyming couplets on his shoulder."

The story was an old one, but the man told it well, in the sort of flowing Arabic which reminded Mordecai of a nomad he'd once known, a Kuchi man from Afghanistan, who'd done a little work for him now and again.

The words flowed on into his ears, as Mordecai scanned the crowd for the man he was here to see, as the storyteller described a land of magic carpets and delicate silver minarets blooming upon a midnight velvet sky, and of a sultan so wealthy that it would require two thousand camels to carry just his gold. The storyteller paused every now and again to hack and spit into an extremely grubby handkerchief which had clearly been used in this fashion many times without the courtesy of a washing.

He turned in a circle, running the possibilities through his mind. Sometimes he thought he'd trained the boy a little too well. The man in the straw hat with sunglasses? No, too short and too fat, there was only so much a man could do with prosthetics after all. The man hawking sugared almonds and prayer mats? No, a bit too tall and swarthy. He looked back at the storyteller, with his crooked frame and tuberculotic lungs. Too old and too crooked, not to mention the man had the humble aura of one long used to poverty.

Could Jamie be late? Not likely, Mordecai knew, the man tended to be punctual to a fault. Had something happened to him? Not likely either. Mordecai had rarely known such a slippery bastard when it came to evading tails. Also, he thought with a bit of pride, he had, after all, trained him, and Jamie could evade the wind when he so chose.

The storyteller wound up his tale, the words ribboning out into the space around him, sweet and lingering as roses on the tongue.

"You comb of a castrated cockerel, smoky-coloured, bent and crooked."

Mordecai's Irish was rusty, but he knew a good Gaelic insult when he heard one. He looked back at the storyteller, with his crooked frame and tuberculotic lungs, and saw a very white flash of teeth and the gleam of green eyes. Bastard, he'd always been good at camouflage, though it shouldn't have come so naturally to him, considering his looks. He'd never fooled Mordecai quite this well before, though. The storyteller stood, and tidied up his blanket, picking up the basket with the coins in it, and walked off into the teeming market. Mordecai waited a few beats and then followed him.

It wasn't simple keeping him in sight, for the boy had always liked to present him with a challenge. But he managed to keep close enough to catch a flash of the dirty green *djellabah* disappearing around a corner, or slipping across a street, caught in the light of the smoking braziers of the souk. Right and left and then two rights, and around him the scents and sounds of the market rose: smoke, dust, warm African spices in fragrant red and yellow mountains, frilly drifts of orange blossom in a tea seller's stall, and long dark pods of vanilla, wafting the alluring mists of a far continent. Donkeys brayed, their panniers jostling against the tide of humanity which infested the alleys of the souk. Small fires were lit in glass globes, and he saw all the faces one did in this flotsam and jetsam of the tribes of the world: the wandering flower children who had gotten lost along the way and never returned home, the nomads of every skin colour, who were simply moving through this crossroads of the earth, the drug addicts who had fallen down a rabbit hole long ago and never re-emerged. All the silken roads of the world met and mingled in Marrakech, and even a golden-haired man with singular talents might blend in and lose himself in such a swarm. But Mordecai managed to keep him in sight, though often it was no more than a flash of cloth, or the sense of the man having turned this way and not that.

He made one last turn down a narrow street lined with plain-faced buildings with only one or two windows facing into the street, and doors—painted with the colours of Marrakech—ultramarine, saffron orange, greens with the depth of the ocean—bright spots of colour in the stone walls. The street was empty, and he knew he would have to guess at the door. He walked slowly, gazing down at the ground, if there was a sign he would know when he saw it. The door at which he stopped was less than prepossessing, a narrow wooden one, painted a faded green, the walls around it roseate stone that was chipped and crumbling in spots, with a harp carved into the stone at some point long ago. Curb appeal was not something the people of Marrakech ascribed to. Home life was inward, and meant to be intensely private.

His knock was answered by an old man who did not speak to him, but merely nodded and bowed, flourishing one long, bony hand in the direction Mordecai was meant to take.

Like many homes in Marrakech this one was a traditional riad, built around a courtyard, with many rooms leading off into more private quarters. He stood now in the setwan—the small receiving room which held two couches, a beautiful cochineal dyed rug, and a few plants; a spot where an unexpected guest might wait while the master of the house was notified of his arrival. He was not, however, required to wait.

"You are to come through, sir," the man said and walked on silent leather soles ahead of him. Mordecai removed his shoes before following the servant down a long corridor which led into the centre of the house. There before him was a set of elaborately carved cedarwood doors, beyond which lay the courtyard. Mordecai stepped from the dim light into the open space, the sound of the fountain filling his ears like aqueous chimes. The courtyard was the centre of the house, and the fountain was the centre of the courtyard—for in a desert land, water was the epicentre of life, and thus the epicentre of the home.

What he saw before him was something straight out of *Alf Layla wa Layla—A Thousand and One Nights*. During his traverse from the square through the markets, the moon had risen and shimmered now over the courtyard like a scimitar made from rose quartz, glowing in the mirror of marble that was the fountain, and caressing the tall cypresses which grew down each side of the courtyard. Sprays of water caught the light from small jewelled lamps, hung low in the branches of lemon trees, where the fruit glowed like oblong suns. A breeze stirred the scents of honeysuckle and jasmine, and the soft white smell of gardenia.

At the far end there was a raised dais, scattered with rugs, pillows and a low table. On the table was a silver filigreed coffee pot, and thin cups from which to drink the coffee. Rising now from the cushions, no longer clad in the filthy *djellabah*, was Lord James Kirkpatrick, golden hair a bright cataract in the river of moonlight and trees.

Mordecai crossed the room, the mosaic tile chill beneath his feet. Jamie came down the stairs to greet him, the cool façade giving no indication that he'd been in the square only moments ago, spinning tales like a spider spins its web, to draw in the curious and unwary.

Mordecai threw back his hood, and gave the man in front of him a look which had reduced others to quivering masses of jelly, but which had little effect on Lord James Kirkpatrick.

"You might have given an old man a break, hustling around Marrakech like a donkey with a flea on its tail. I'm getting too old for this nonsense," Mordecai grumbled.

"Sit, you old curmudgeon and have some coffee. The food will be along shortly."

Mordecai lowered himself slowly onto a large velvet cushion. Arthritic knees made this a hard feat, but he eventually gained the cushion and found it surprisingly comfortable. He half-expected doe-eyed *houris* to slide in from the courtyard arches, and drape themselves over the cushions and divan. It certainly wasn't beyond the scope of what was possible with James Kirkpatrick.

"It has been a time, James," he said, taking a first appreciative sip of the coffee. It was made in the Arabic fashion, with saffron and cardamom to spice the strong brew.

"It has. When was the last time—'67 in Reykjavik?"

"No, '68 in Cairo—right after you moved that completely unsuitable American girl into your home."

"Ah yes, I remember now," Jamie replied, completely ignoring, Mordecai noted, the statement about the American girl.

"I have things about which we need to speak." Not one to waste words, Mordecai never took long in coming to the point of their meetings.

"I am here to listen, but I have to warn you, Mordecai, that I am done with the world of espionage. I came when you called because of friendship, and the loyalty I owe you."

"Done with the spy business—you? Oh, James," Mordecai gave a dry laugh. "You'll die of boredom within the year."

Jamie merely smiled and shook his head. "My concerns have become more local these last years. What concerns me is my own country, and her unending strife. I should like to be part of the solution there, to build something better for the generations who come after."

"Ah, and why is that, old friend?"

"I have a daughter," Jamie said softly, "perfect, healthy and whole, and only two months old. I should like to be around for the raising of her."

"May God guard her from evil, and grant her a long and fruitful life," Mordecai said solemnly. "I am happy for you, Jamie."

"Thank you."

"And her mother?"

"Her mother is that completely unsuitable American girl you mentioned earlier," Jamie said, laughter in his eyes.

"Well then, love at last, James?"

"Oh yes, love, but not without its complications," Jamie said, but didn't offer further information.

"Have you married her?" Mordecai asked, genuinely curious.

"Had I married her I would have made bigamists of us both."

"Ah, complications indeed," Mordecai said, "I thought perhaps you might have managed a divorce in the last few years."

"More coffee?" Jamie said, tone light, and Mordecai knew he wasn't going to answer any more questions about the woman. The food arrived then, brought by the man who had shown him in. There was a pot filled with tagine, a bowl of fragrantly spiced couscous, and a platter of vegetables, swimming in a clear broth. Mordecai's stomach growled loudly. He filled his plate, and took a few bites before addressing Jamie's last statement.

"So Ireland? Why the worry now? Like my people, yours have been at war for such a long time, I imagine you'd all feel naked without it."

"It's likely Thatcher will become the next prime minister of Britain, and that won't bode well for my wee country," Jamie said, forking up some of the succulent lamb.

"You are thinking that she'll have something to prove, and she'll go harder than a man might in order to prove it."

"Exactly," Jamie responded.

"So no more spy games for you?"

"Whatever I do these days is off book, so to speak," Jamie said. Mordecai knew this had been true for some time, but especially so since Russia.

"They don't like it when you colour outside the lines, James, you better than anyone know this. If they slap your hands, it could be permanent. I don't want to hear about you getting stabbed in the leg with an umbrella, and then having a mysterious death a few days later."

Jamie's expression sobered. "I was sorry to hear about Markov—you knew him, I believe."

"Yes, briefly. The service thought about recruiting him at one point, but he was considered too volatile in the end. Journalists make poor spies, they want to shout truth from the rooftops even when the price is life itself."

"Was it true about the umbrella?" Jamie asked.

"Yes, they did use an umbrella, though I think it was a distraction and they used some other means to get it into his leg—a pen maybe. Drop the umbrella though, get him to look at it and then step up and stab him in the leg. They did it on Zhivkov's birthday, not a coincidence I am thinking."

Geory Markov had been a Bulgarian dissident journalist who had been one of the loudest critics of both his own government and of the Soviet regime in general. It was rumoured that the Bulgarian and Soviet secret services had colluded in his death, which had been effected by the insertion of a ricin pellet into his leg via some sort of stabbing instrument, be it umbrella or pen was of no matter, dead was dead, and a much needed voice had been silenced.

"This is ridiculously delicious," Mordecai said, spooning more of the tagine and couscous into his bowl.

"It's the preserved lemon," Jamie replied, "I find it makes all the difference."

"You cooked this?"

"Yes, I occasionally cook. I find it relaxing between bouts of espionage."

Mordecai sat back, relaxed, his belly comfortably full and the wine giving him a nice buzz of well-being. He could almost forget why he was here. Almost.

He surveyed the man in front of him, thinking back to when they'd first met. Jamie had been a young boy at the time, on a trip through France with his grandfather. Mordecai remembered the senior James with great fondness. They'd had some escapades, and several close shaves during the war, but he'd never had a colleague he'd trusted more, with the exception of the man now sitting before him.

Jamie was no longer the young man Mordecai had once trained. There was a great deal of his grandfather in him, and it showed now as he aged. But this man was also something more, something fine and set apart. Jamie had always felt things too deeply, something Mordecai no longer had the capability for himself, and while he admired this in the man he also knew it to be his greatest weakness.

"Is Yevgena well?" he asked. He had great respect for the Roma woman who was also a Jew like himself, and who also, like him, had lost everything to the Holocaust. She had been the great love of Jamie's grandfather's life, and he hers. He thought it likely she'd been devastated by the man's loss.

Jamie nodded, and then as though he'd read Mordecai's thoughts, spoke to confirm them. "Yes, though she is not who she was before my grandfather died."

"I had heard that your Russian wife was returned to you," Mordecai said quietly, aware he was kicking a hornet's nest with the simple statement.

"Returned to me?" Jamie said. "That's a curious turn of phrase."

"Is it?"

Jamie contemplated him for a moment, and then sighed. "It would be easier if you just voiced your suspicions, Mordecai."

"She wouldn't be the first asset who was turned, and if she's been turned, there's a limited number of people she can possibly be working for. Particularly as they've planted her in your home. So I ask you, James, are you harboring a viper in your own nest?"

"Quite possibly. I was a fool with her once, I don't want to repeat that."

"So it's the age old conundrum, do you let her stay in order to keep your enemy closer?"

"I don't know. If her story is true, then what do I owe her?"

"Not your life, Jamie, not that space in the world which is closest to you."

"That space is filled," Jamie said, "for this lifetime and beyond, and for that I have no regret. Still, I married Violet and that is no small commitment. I need to know if she is, indeed, spying on me, before I decide how to proceed."

"You want that I should find out?" Mordecai asked.

Jamie contemplated him for a moment, the green eyes bright. "You have better connections in Russia these days than I do, Mordecai."

"It is not her Russian connections I'd be poking at, so it could cause you some trouble, but this you know."

"Yes, this I know."

Mordecai nodded, lit another cigarette and then got down to the reason for this meeting.

"Dmitri was recalled to Moscow."

"What do you mean *was* recalled?"

"He went. Two weeks ago now."

"Why in hell would he go? He should have contacted one of us."

"Yes, he should have but he didn't, which tells me they must have threatened those of his family who are there."

"Christ," Jamie said, letting out his breath on the one syllable.

Dmitri Malenkov was a highly placed diplomat whom Jamie had managed to recruit some years before. He was the Russian ambassador to Britain, and as such had been considered one of the greatest coups in espionage history. He had played the game with great skill, even though he was balanced on the razor edge of discovery at all times. Dmitri had another aspect to his life which had made him very attractive to British Intelligence—he was a KGB officer, who had been sent as ambassador to Britain, as a cover for his real job as a Russian spy.

Born into the KGB elite—both his parents had been spies—Dmitri had never really considered any life other than that of working for the Russian secret police. He was considered the single greatest source of information both by the British and by the Americans, who were fed what the British felt was necessary via the CIA. This had bothered the Americans, who'd insisted on knowing who the source was, and Mordecai had long suspected, were digging hard to figure out just where the source of the pipeline was.

They owed Dmitri, and Dmitri had known that only too well. Mordecai was right, his family must be under threat for Dmitri to answer that summons without a word to them. At this point, with two weeks having elapsed since he'd left, he would already be dead, if that was the intention in calling him home to Moscow. They would have taken him at the airport and driven him directly to Lubyanka. If they hadn't killed him, then the mystery still remained of why they'd pulled him back.

"You said there were two things. What is the other?" Jamie asked.

Mordecai had been blunt all his life with those he trusted, and so he went straight to the point. "I'm going to Moscow, and I may not make it back out. I have things I would give you for safekeeping should that eventuality come to pass."

"For Dmitri? Mordecai, if the security services get so much as a whiff that you're there, they'll kill you."

"I know that, but I am old, if I die it is not such a tragedy, even for me. If I can help Dmitri I will, but he is not why I am going."

"Then why now?"

"Because I have found Adsel."

Adsel. The two syllables held such a weight of meaning, of years of a life given over to the hope of vengeance. Only two people outside of Mordecai knew about Adsel, and that the hope of one day finding him and killing him, was the one thing that had kept Mordecai alive in those first years after the Holocaust. Mordecai had told him, one night when he'd had too much to drink, and he'd told Yevgena when he was stone cold sober. Because, of course, Yevgena's story was not so different from his in substance, it was only the details that differed.

Mordecai had grown and come to manhood in a little Polish town near to the border with the Soviet Union. He had been a labourer, building and repairing a variety of goods. His parents had seen to it that their sons were educated as well as could be managed in such a small village with limited means. He married the girl next door, with whom he'd been in love since childhood, and after two years of praying and hoping, their union was blessed with a son, a boy whom they'd named Dawid. They had believed themselves blessed, and Mordecai had been a contented man, even if he did worry more and more about the news coming out of Germany.

And then, the Germans had invaded Poland, and Mordecai had taken his small family and as many villagers as could be convinced of the urgency of their situation, and fled for the forests surrounding the village. Here they had organized and built shelters, foraged for food, and established a base where they could return after forays into villages, when they would hunt for food and supplies to keep their families fed.

He'd taken his entire family: mother, father, sisters, brother, wife and child. His mother and father were in their middle years, but the fear caused by the approach of the Nazis, coupled with the terrible stories coming out of eastern Poland and Germany, had taken their toll. His brother Ben was in his teens, his sister Adah, a late gift from God, was only four. The only person he felt worry about was his brother-in-law, Adsel. Adsel had once been a friend of sorts, but they had fallen out when Chana chose Mordecai for her husband, and not Adsel. Adsel had never truly forgiven Mordecai for that, though Chana did not care for Adsel and never had. Mordecai sometimes thought Adsel had married his sister to take revenge on him. Rebekah was a simple woman, and had always been a little slow. Adsel was a mean-souled man with a bad temper, and Mordecai was certain he took it out on Rebekah. Mordecai had never trusted him, and was reluctant to bring him along on their flight into the forest, but felt he had little choice.

Other villagers joined them, and so it was that a group of thirty-five souls fled their village and all they'd ever known, in the hope of staying alive. Mordecai quickly became their leader, and was the one who planned the food missions, organized the camp, gave jobs to people according to their strengths and hoped to God he could manage to keep them all alive through the hard winter which lay ahead.

Then one day, just as winter was beginning to make its presence felt, word had arrived that the Germans knew about their camp and were coming for them.

Mordecai moved his people deeper into the forest, even knowing that many of them could not possibly survive the trek. His own mother was one of the first casualties. Weak and sick, the lack of food and the chill nights sapped what little will she had left in her. She lay down to sleep one night, and did not wake the next morning. His father became an old man overnight, and the care of little Adah had fallen to him and Chana.

They paused for half a day to bury his mother in an anonymous forest grave and then continued on their journey. There was no time for mourning or its rituals.

He led his people to an island in the midst of a vast swamp, thinking that it would provide them with protection of a sort. It almost proved to be their undoing, however. The trek through the cold water had exhausted all of them, and Mordecai had to lead from the front and then harry from the back, much of the time carrying Dawid, and at times, Adah. By the time they found the island, everyone was completely silent, most collapsing shortly after their arrival, too tired to light a fire, or cook the little bit of food they had left.

For days they could hear the Germans tramping through the forest all around, the echoes of their voices and the shooting of their guns, moving around in such a way as to make them seem both at a distance and as close as the other side of the reeds behind which they crouched.

He was certain many times that hunger would kill them, or lead them into reckless behaviour which would surely draw the Germans to them like flies to a rotten carcass. He knew he would have to find food for them, even if the risk to his own life was great. They would all die soon anyway, if he didn't find them some sustenance.

He took two of the strongest young men with him, and left the others behind to keep the rest of the group safe. Knowing young men and their propensity for hotheadedness, he also left instructions with Chana and his father about where to lead the group, and where to wait for him, if they should need to move on in his absence.

The trip was not a successful one, unless one counted three scrawny chickens, a sack of half-rotted potatoes and a pie stolen from a windowsill as success. And then one of the men with him—a boy really—was shot by the German soldiers who were camped outside of the village they'd chosen to raid, after sneaking off in the middle of the night while Mordecai and the other man were asleep. They never knew just why he'd gone, only that he'd paid for his folly with his life.

Mordecai and the remaining man kept moving; cold, half-starved, and with their strength faltering with each step, it took two days more than Mordecai had planned. But when they arrived, with the meagre bit of food and supplies they'd managed to find, his family was gone: father, sisters, brother, baby Dawid and Chana, his beautiful Chana. All the other villagers were gone as well. There were clear signs of a struggle and drops of dried blood upon the ground. The other man had simply sat down, as though his bones had turned to water and stayed there. Mordecai had staggered around the forest all night, trying to find some trace of his family, but the drops of blood had petered out at the edge of the swamp and he couldn't find a corresponding trail on the other side. Near morning he too collapsed, and simply stayed there for two days, despite the cold and his own hunger. He never saw the other man who'd gone on the raid with him again, and never knew for certain what had been his fate.

Mordecai was found by a group of men who belonged to a Jewish resistance force and nursed back to health. After that he joined them in their efforts to save one Jew at a time from the black maw of Nazi Germany. It would be years before he finally traced the fate of his family—years of heartbreak and nightmares. The truth was as bad as anything he'd feared. They had all died in the Sobibor extermination camp, shortly after they had been taken by the Nazis who had come for them, two nights after Mordecai and the other men had left on their hunt for food.

For a long time, he had assumed that Adsel had been with his family when they'd been taken, and had gone to his fate in the gas chamber with the others. It was only during a chance meeting with an old neighbor in the streets of Tel Aviv many years later, that he would learn the truth. That Adsel had—during Mordecai's absence—gone into a village and told the German commander about the people hiding in the woods.

From that day to this, Mordecai's lodestar had been the promise to get vengeance on Adsel for his betrayal and for the murder of thirty-one people who'd once called themselves a village. Jamie's fear was that once that vengeance was quenched, there would no longer be a purpose to life for Mordecai, but only an empty hollow into which his family would never return. Justice, in such matters, often turned to ash in a man's hands. Jamie knew though, that Mordecai would not hear anything he might say on the matter, and in truth, he would do the same if he lost those he loved in such a way. And now, an old man, standing here under the dome of an African sky, reiterated the promise he'd made himself long ago.

"I will kill him. If I too die in the effort I should like someone to know where my bones finally fell. But you will leave my bones there, James, you will not seek to find that which is already lost. I only ask that you will say the Mourner's Kaddish for me, heathen Catholic though you are."

"I will," Jamie said, because of course he would. He knew he was the only person left in the world whom Mordecai trusted. Just before he left, the old man turned and touched his face. This bit of sentimentality worried him more than any of the words the man had spoken that night. Mordecai had been a tough handler, and he had never before shown Jamie this kind of tenderness.

"Perhaps," he said, "it is time to be happy, James. Only you know what ingredients are necessary for that. Give my blessings to your daughter."

And with that, Mordecai melted into the Moroccan night, no more than a slip of shadow and then nothing by which to tell he'd ever been there.

Jamie stayed for a time in the courtyard, taking a last swallow of wine and watching the stars flow overhead, like a great river of silver sand, their Arabic names drifting through him along with each glittering grain in the sky.

'We are stars wrapped in skin…'

The line of Rumi came naturally, as poetry always had, and he felt it as he sometimes did—that this was true, that he and those he loved were just stardust blown in from a far galaxy, wrapped in the joy and pain of human existence.

He turned his thoughts then to Dmitri, and the question which was uppermost in his mind. Why, if Mordecai wasn't going to rescue him, had he brought him up at all? Mordecai never wasted words, and so Jamie feared that he knew all too well what it was Mordecai intended him to take from what he'd said.

Dmitri was that rare creature, a spy who operated from a place of ideals and conviction. He didn't see himself as a traitor to Russia, but rather to the inhumane and corrupt system of the Soviets. If they'd lifted Dmitri and taken him to Lubyanka, he was either dead or wishing he was by now. Jamie shivered, despite the warmth of the night. The hungry ghosts of Lubyanka could be summoned by merely thinking the name once you'd been a prisoner there. He drew in a long breath and pushed the memories away.

This house had belonged to his grandfather, and had been left to him in his will. It was a place of memory for him, of exotic summer retreats, of adventure in a strange land, which had seemed the stuff of fairy tales to him, and he as a child, of the romantic frame of mind to embrace it as such. This house, like the one in Paris, was dear to him because of all the memories it held of times with his grandfather. In the pattern of his life, it was one of the threads that shone with the gold of happiness. He had thought that he would like to one day bring Pamela here and show her this piece of his history. That was not to be, however.

In an echo of what she had once said to him one fire-lit night in Paris, he wanted her happiness more than he wanted his own, and so he had been, in most ways, filled with joy that Casey had, by some miracle, been returned to her and that they had another chance to live their lives together. And the arrival of Kathleen had given him a joy he could still barely fathom. He had told Pamela the truth that night in the snow; he was filled with gratitude for the existence of their daughter.

For a time—in Maine, in Paris and after Kathleen's birth—there had been a sense of the world being held at arm's length, a finding, once again, of that which mattered, and a forgetting of those things which did not. But the world had returned, and he knew there were now meetings he must keep in both London and Paris. He was looking forward to neither.

He took a breath, turning his attention from the stars to the scene around him. The dishes had already been gathered, the table now unadorned, the wine drunk and the lamps burning low. It was time for bed; it had been a long few days and he was owed some sleep. He walked from the courtyard, the scent of lemons and thyme drifting about his senses. Before he went through the carved doors into the house, though, he paused, looking back to where the oil lanterns guttered fitfully like dying stars in the night, and the water sounded softly, as though chimes moved in the wind. Something fluttered near his face, drifting westward—silent, winged and belonging to the air. Memory stirred, and he found himself surrounded suddenly by the scent of tall firs, the air of the sea and the touch of a woman who had stood at his side. It had been one of those days so bright with clarity that it seemed a man might drink it, and keep it for the times less clear, less filled with light.

"Jamie," she had said, voice soft, "look there."

Before them—tumbling, drifting, fluttering—was a butterfly, bright as a bit of floating sunshine, caught in the vagaries of moving air. They didn't speak, but merely watched as that winged creature held aloft on the wind, flew bright as dawn, out over the sea. The moment held them, just the two of them, despite the children in the sand at their feet and the noise of the gulls and the lapping waves. And when the tiny winged light blinked out upon their horizon, she had said, so quietly that only he could hear, "It won't come this way again."

He had looked at her then, and noted that she had tears in her eyes, though he did not comment upon them. He understood, as she knew he would. Indeed, the butterfly, in its brief and beautiful struggle with life, would come no more this way. And so, remembering it now, he took the moment of beauty for what it was—ephemeral, wrought fine in the clear light, and piercing with the pain of that which passes too soon.

He understood their situation, he knew the love they shared was only changed and not truly diminished, and yet, oh and yet, how he missed all the things which they had so very nearly grasped, now gone beyond their reach.

Chapter Seventeen

Dearly Departed Friend

IT WAS LATE in February before Pamela was able to pay a visit she'd been putting off for some time. Conor was at school and Isabelle was spending the morning with Gert, with the understanding that Casey was coming by to take her for the afternoon. Kathleen was with Jamie for the morning and she was free for a few hours.

The previous day she had taken the children and gone up to Belfast to see Kate and Patrick, and to visit with their new baby. Lily had been born on Valentine's Day, seven pounds and eight ounces of baby perfection, with a mop of dark hair and eyes of a deep blue that Pamela thought might eventually turn to the striking gentian of Kate's eyes—the same shade Noah's had been. Pat was over the moon, utterly in love with his new daughter, and Pamela had been overjoyed to see such happiness in the man. Pat and Kate deserved every bit of joy that came their way. She wished that Noah had lived long enough to see his sister so settled and happy, that he'd been there to hold his niece and to look into her face and see the promise of a new generation.

She stopped the car at an old stile, nearly invisible under a covering of ivy and moss and walked the rest of the way into the property. In her hands she carried a delicate spray of blue freesia. Vanya was working at a greenhouse which grew flowers to supply florists and she'd managed to procure the delicate blooms through him.

There was a great hush over the land. The animals had been sold off in the weeks after Noah's death; Kate and Patrick had seen to that with the help of an auctioneer who knew which farmers might be interested in buying the various livestock. The house and byres had been cleaned out and locked. There wasn't so much as a footprint to mar the snow that had fallen the night before. The fields were dusted with snow as well; the tilled rows softly frosted on their peaks and set to sparkling diamonds in the morning sun.

She stopped when she neared the house, and leaned against the stone wall which girded the old kitchen garden. The last time she'd been here with Noah had been the morning she had told him she could not marry him. He'd accepted her words with the strange grace he had so often displayed toward her. It was another night which came to mind now though—a time when the engagement had been new and she had wanted to give him something to mark it.

It was late evening, not quite twilight, as she came around the corner of the drystone wall into Noah's yard. She stopped the car and rolled down the window, taking in a breath of the cool night air. The house sat quiet in the dim, a light glowing from the kitchen window. Noah would be back from the evening care of the animals—bringing the cows in from the pasture and penning the sheep. Soon all these things would be her routine as well. Soon the house, sitting there foursquare and trim, would be her own. She would cook meals in that kitchen, bathe her children in the spartan bath, put them to bed in the empty rooms upstairs and then she would go to Noah's bed, and give to him what a wife gave to a husband in the night while the world around them spun along, unconcerned with the dramas of man and woman. She thought about the small, simple homely things of daily life with another person—the morning chat over tea, the bustle of getting out the door, the arranging of all life's details and how easy and lovely all that had been with Casey. She wondered what it would be like with Noah—would there be the melding of each other's days, the small talk late at night, the understanding of the difficulties each faced in the world? Would she, eventually, find a sort of sanctuary in his arms that went deeper than mere protection? She sighed and pulled the car the rest of the way into the drive, parking it in front of the house. She could see Noah moving about in the kitchen.

On the seat beside her was a small cloth-wrapped parcel. Tonight, she had come alone, leaving Vanya in charge of Conor and Isabelle. All three had been happily playing with modeling clay when she left. She had decided that she needed something to mark the proposal and her acceptance of it, so that she might feel it less a business arrangement, and more than one thing in exchange for another. She wanted to observe a few formalities, so that Noah would understand this was not merely a barter for her.

She had put a lot of thought into what to give him and had settled on something that had meaning to her, but would also touch something in him. It was a small volume, blue bound, the pages old and somewhat worn, but it was well-loved and Kate said the poet had long been a favourite of Noah's.

She got out of the car, and nervously smoothed her skirt down. She had dressed for the occasion, in a silk blouse the colour of the interior of an oyster shell and a grey skirt that complemented it. Pearls were in her ears and at her throat. Noah's sapphire was on her finger. Her hair she had left loose, the curls grown out now so that they touched her shoulders. She took a deep breath, pulse racing, filling the air around her with the scent of her perfume.

She tapped at the kitchen door, suddenly nervous, and wanting nothing more than to return home and make clay elephants and hippopotamuses with the children and Vanya.

Noah answered the door, a towel hanging around his neck, bare-chested, hair wet and face still sheened with water droplets. He always had a wash as soon as he came in from his work, and had clearly been in the midst of this routine when she knocked.

"I'm sorry, I wasn't expectin' ye," he said, standing aside to let her in.

"I—I shouldn't have come unannounced," she said, feeling a blush light along her cheekbones. She had never seen him this way before. His body was finely cut, lean but well-muscled, his chest covered with dark hair that ran down, sparser over his belly, until... she dragged her eyes away, aware that he was watching her with no little intensity.

"Don't be foolish, ye needn't stand on ceremony any longer. This will be yer home soon enough, ye may as well start actin' like it now. I'll get ye a key. Excuse me a moment, an' I'll go put a shirt on."

She nodded, feeling as though her face was on fire. Clearly he realized that his bare chest had discomfited her. It was ridiculous to feel like some virgin school girl in this man's presence.

She stood by the kitchen window, looking out over the fields to the edge of the wood. She thought of the time she had run into David Kendall here, and crossed herself as she always did when she thought of the British agent who had been her friend. She tried not to think about what had happened to him, he had been a gentle and kind man in many ways and he had not deserved the death which had come to him.

Noah returned a few minutes later, clad in clean pants and a nicely pressed blue shirt. His hair was still damp, but neatly combed back from his face and he smelled of the same cologne he had worn the day he proposed to her.

"I apologize, will ye sit? I was just about to get my tea, are ye hungry?"

"No, I'm not. I ate before I came here. I just came by to bring you this." She held out the package, feeling slightly ludicrous.

He took it, looking at her questioningly before unwrapping it and turning to the spine to read the title. He was silent, merely looking at the book, not opening it, just holding it there in his hands as though he wasn't quite certain what to make of it.

"It's a sort of engagement gift. It's Auden. My father gave it to me when I was thirteen. It's a first edition." She felt suddenly awkward, and wondered if this had been the wrong thing to give him. "I just thought…Kate said…"

"Thank ye," he said forestalling her stumbling explanation. "It's lovely."

He set the book upon the table and she had the feeling that she had upset him in some way.

"Noah, was it the wrong thing to give you?"

He shook his head. "It's just that I've not let anyone know me in a very long time, Pamela. Somehow, without my intendin' it, ye do know me, though. Know the boy I once was, an' that maybe he's not entirely gone from the man. It makes me feel a bit odd to know that."

"Odd, or vulnerable?" she asked, putting a hand on his forearm where it rested against the worn wood of his kitchen table, his sapphire burning deep against the white of her fingers. He turned to look at her and there was something in the forthright gaze that scared her. It wanted something, that look, something that she was afraid to give.

"Are ye certain ye want an answer to that question?"

"Yes," she said, though she was anything but certain.

"That British medic, the one who was my friend, he told me something once an' it has stayed with me all these years. He said that life was a great deal like a battlefield. That ye had yer regular soldiers that did as they were told, who marched in straight lines right into the mouth of a cannon if told to do so, an' then ye had yer guerrilla warriors, who hid in the shadows an' came out to fight an' then withdrew until the next battle. An' last he said there were the people who got caught in no man's land, between the lines, an' that they lived there in the wastes because they had neither the courage nor the want to leave such a place. They lived half lives because they were afraid of anything more. He called it the land without breath, where a man was neither alive nor dead, but somethin' in between."

He took a breath, and put his hand over hers, the sapphire hard between their respective flesh. "An' that's where you an' I live, Pamela, in that land without breath. The difference is I think ye're content to stay there, an' I am not."

Noah had been right. She had been content to stay there in that land without breath. It had seemed the safest place to live at the time. Casey's return though had jarred her out of that territory. There were moments when she felt the pain of it again—feeling so alive that she was aware of every heart beat and every pulse of blood through her skin. It was, by turns, uncomfortable and exhilarating.

Standing here now, looking out over Noah's land, she realized he had been right about more than one thing that night. She *had* known the boy he once was just as he had known the girl she once was. They had recognized the lonely child which dwelt inside each of them.

"I miss you," she said quietly. It was the truth. She did miss Noah. Some part of her always would. He had been a very good friend to her and then he had been more. What they'd had between them had been, in some ways, terribly intimate. In part, she knew, it had been because their relationship had been solely theirs, and hadn't really involved anyone else until they'd gotten engaged.

Thoughts of their last few days together rose up, dark and bloody, and she pushed them away forcibly. She would not allow those thoughts today, not here on his farm.

Suddenly movement caught her eye near the byre closest to the house. A man walked out—tall, and with a bearing that gave him away as someone with a military background. She stiffened, startled but knowing she had to stand her ground, as there was nowhere to run. He walked across the yard and then halted about ten feet away from her, clearly sensing her apprehension.

"What are you doing here?" he asked, suspicion writ large over his features. Up close she could see he was older, perhaps in his late fifties with the close-cut hair which confirmed her original thought that he was military.

"I just came to talk to Noah," she said. This statement caused the man to raise his eyebrows a bit. "I know he's dead," she continued, "I was engaged to him for a little while. He was very dear to me."

"Ah, you must be Pamela," the man said his expression changing from suspicious hostility to a welcoming smile. "He spoke of you often."

"He did?" she asked, shocked. Noah hadn't been one to confide in others and she had thought, other than Kate, it wasn't likely anyone in his life had known about the two of them.

He walked forward and offered her his hand. "My name is George Mitchell. I knew Noah when he was a boy, and we still kept in touch from time to time, particularly over these last few years."

"You're the British medic he spoke of," she said, twigging suddenly to just who the man must be. She took his outstretched hand and shook it.

"That would be me," he agreed. "And if you're Pamela, you not only know he's dead, you were actually with him when he died."

She nodded, words failing her for a moment. The tight feeling returned to her throat and she had to fight for a breath before she could answer. "Yes, I was."

"I'm very sorry for that. It must have been truly terrible."

"It was," she said, voice barely above a whisper. "And yet, I was glad he wasn't alone, which is ridiculous because it was my fault, at least in part, that he was there. They used me as bait to lure him."

"Someone would have gotten to him eventually. You must know that. People had been hunting him for years. It was a miracle he lived as long as he did. It was only because he kept to his policy of being more ruthless than any of his enemies that he made it so far as he did."

"That's just it, though, having me in his life made him more vulnerable."

He looked down at her and shook his head. "Because of you, he had a wonderful last few years to his life, consider that before you beat yourself up. He wouldn't want it, and you know it."

She nodded, understanding the truth of what he said, but unable to truly let go just yet. Perhaps it was as Brother Gilles had said, and she must let her grief over Noah run its course.

"What are you doing here?" she asked, curious, for she'd never seen the man while Noah had been alive, though she was aware of just how compartmentalized Noah's life had been.

"I'm here to see to the selling of the farm. Kate asked me if I'd handle it, and I said I would."

"Oh," she said, feeling a sudden sadness that didn't really make sense, and yet was there, nevertheless. There was a time she had thought this farm would be her home. Or at least she had thought she would live here, because home was Casey. But Noah had loved the farm, and so for the loss of it, she grieved. It was strange how quickly all the traces of a person's existence could disappear, as though they'd moved as lightly as a bubble on the wind, and then one day were simply taken away by that wind, which scoured all traces in its wake.

"Was he afraid at the end?" he asked, and she saw that it was a thought which haunted him. That the boy he'd loved might have felt fear near the end, might have suffered enough pain to lose his rationality.

"No—at least not for himself. He wasn't afraid of anything, I don't think. I suppose that's why he dared to have a British soldier as his trusted advisor."

"And the wife of an apostate IRA man as his fiancée."

She laughed. "Point taken. No, fear wasn't one of his downfalls."

"Did he tell you how we met?"

She nodded. Noah had told her a soldier had come across him and his father one day, while his father was beating him out in the field. The soldier had stopped the beating and he and Noah had become friends after that. She hadn't realized the friendship had continued to the end of Noah's life though. This was the man who'd taught Noah his medical skills so that he'd been able to deal with simple wounds on his own, and others that weren't so simple, she thought, remembering the night he'd stitched up a bullet graze in her side.

"Kate told me a bit, because I asked how he'd died. She said none of them really knew what had taken place in that workhouse because you hadn't spoken of it much. Both she and her husband seemed to think that given time, maybe eventually you would tell them the whole story."

"I don't know if I will," she said quietly, "I haven't found the words for it yet. I don't want to talk about it, or relive the details. It was awful, so awful that maybe there *aren't* words for it, maybe there are some things that happen in this world that simply defy being quantified in language. And there are things," she added, "that I don't think Kate should know."

"She's imagining them anyway."

"I know, but it's possible that it's actually worse than what she's imagined. I did have to tell her what happened, but I didn't tell her everything. I know the images that play through my own head at night, I don't wish that on anyone else."

"It might help you though to share it with someone. There was a man who rescued you and took you out of that place, wasn't there?"

"Yes, and he knows most of it. I can talk to him, if I need to." She could talk to Casey too, the man had made that clear, but she thought talking to him about those days with Noah was bound to be a bit of a minefield.

"Did you love him?" the man asked. The bluntness reminded her of Noah.

"I did, just not in the way he wanted me to."

"I think maybe that doesn't matter so much, only the fact that you did care for him. That was rare in his life, as you likely know."

"I do know. He had my friendship though, and he knew that."

"Outside of Kate, I think you and I might be the only people he ever trusted in his lifetime."

Pamela didn't say anything, for the man's words weren't a question, but simply a statement of fact. Noah's life had not been easy, and to be numbered amongst those he trusted was a mark of how deep the man's feeling had run both for her and the soldier standing beside her.

"I'll be around for a few more days. I just want to make sure all the details are sorted so the sale can go through smoothly. It seems a shame to have the farm go. Noah worked so hard to keep it and it was something he truly loved. But Kate doesn't want it, and I can't say I blame her. I don't think this was a happy place when their parents were alive."

"No, it wasn't. I think Noah tried to change that for her, and for himself. But there's only so much a sixteen-year-old boy can do."

"Sometimes I think," he said, "that there's only so much darkness a human being can see and experience before it destroys something essential in them. It's a bit like having a limb amputated, only in the sense of spirit or soul. It can't be regrown once it's gone and a man can never be whole without it."

"He still had poetry in him, and he still counted the stars," she said, causing the man to look at her. He didn't ask for an explanation though, and seemed to understand well enough what she meant.

"Perhaps love had changed him," he said.

"Perhaps it had," she agreed, feeling the terrible hollow behind her ribs that always opened up when someone spoke of Noah to her. Love hadn't been enough to save him and sometimes she thought that was the only thing that mattered.

The man turned toward her. "I'm glad we met, even if only for a few moments," he said. "I admit I was curious to see what sort of woman it was who'd made Noah want to marry."

"I'm glad we met too. I'm happy to know he had your friendship all that time." She put her hand out and he took it between both of his.

"My granny had a saying—pain shared is pain divided. You might want to consider that."

She nodded and then stood watching as the man walked off toward one of the smaller byres—the one Khamsin had lived in when he was a colt.

Long ago Noah had brought an old man needing a night of refuge by the fire to her home. And that man had said something to her which she now remembered.

"Noah's like that, he'll take a piece of yer soul, an' not return it to you. Only it will be because of his own hunger, not because he's enchanted it away from ye, girl."

The words echoed in her head. The old man had been right in a way. Though perhaps anyone you cared for in your life took a piece of your soul and kept it with them always. If that was so, then she did not mind if Noah had taken a piece of hers away with him, when he died there beside her in that old dark building. Casey too had taken parts of her away with him when he'd disappeared, and now that he'd returned she wasn't entirely sure how to restore what had been lost or how to patch up the holes from the pain and longing of those years.

It was time to go. Noah was no longer here and there was little comfort to be found in the empty house and buildings and the silent fields which had once buzzed with activity. But then suddenly she realized there was something she needed to say. She turned, and behind her the old farmhouse glowed in the light of late morning.

"Thank you for being my friend, Noah."

A few freesia petals had drifted down into the cold embrace of the snow and earth, and lay there softly luminous with blue light. Stooping down she laid the rest of the flowers there along with the fallen petals, and then she walked on, leaving the flowers behind in the snow.

Chapter Eighteen

A Philosophy of Building

CASEY EYED THE structure in front of him with a certain amount of trepidation. He let out a long low whistle as his eye travelled over it. He'd been wary when Tomas first called and asked him to come and have a look, as he'd a fireplace which needed extensive repairs. He could still feel the sting of their Christmas encounter and wasn't inclined to trust the man. Pat had assured him, however, that Tomas truly did need someone to repair the fireplace in his library before the place burned down around his ears.

He took the house in, his mind automatically cataloguing certain things: 16th century, solid oak beams, an addition or two from other time periods, though none which jarred with the overall personality of the house. Structurally, it appeared mostly sound, though the roof needed replacing, and clearly there were issues with an oak tree growing through said roof on one corner. It was how he thought, he realized, with a builder's mind—always seeing the design and flow, and how it might be improved, what needed fixing, the details which required care.

The door opened as he approached, and Tomas stood in the entry, blue eyes veined with red, with the look of a man who doesn't have a clear recall of the evening before. He held a cup of tea in one hand, still steaming from the pot. Casey smiled and tried to keep his immediate reaction to the man in check, which was that of a riled porcupine with all its quills up. Tomas merely gave him a rise of one grizzled eyebrow and motioned that he should come in.

Casey stepped in and bent to remove his shoes.

"Ach, don't bother with that, man. The floor's not been swept since last Pamela was here, that old harridan I get in to clean spends more time tipplin' than she does sweepin' or washin'. Come on, the fireplace is in the study."

The study had been updated at some point, Casey thought, taking in the big windows which framed a view out to a small wilderness of ferns and briar roses. The floor to ceiling shelving was part of the update, and was chock-a-block with legal tomes and dusty piles of paper. If the man wanted him to do this job, he would have to sheet the whole room and tape it down. It would still be a mess though, mortar dust was absolutely insidious in its ability to get into and under everything. He walked over to the task in question, and took stock of it. It was big enough for a man to lie down in, and Pat had told him Tomas had indeed slept in it, or passed out in it—as it were—more than once. He hunkered down and ran his hand over the floor. Then he peered up the chimney and poked at the masonry a little.

"I can repair it but ye might be better off tearin' it out an' rebuildin' it from scratch. Most of the brick has crumbled, an' isn't safe. If it is crumbling all through, ye could end up with one helluva chimney fire. It's possible that the floor joists are saggin' a wee bit too. D'ye know if they've ever been replaced since the house was built?"

"Not in here, no. Tell me, can ye do that—rebuild the fireplace from scratch?"

Casey rubbed the tip of his nose thoughtfully. "I don't know to be honest. I think I can, but I can't be certain until I start workin' on it. Ye may want someone more qualified than myself to take on such a big project."

"No, ye'll do," Tomas said shortly. "Yer brother says ye can fix anythin' an' Pamela agrees with him, so I trust they're tellin' me the truth."

Casey wisely kept his tongue, while hoping the man didn't intend to be around supervising the work once it commenced, because he might be tempted to bury him under some brick work if he did. He wanted the work, a house like this was a dream. One that was a huge challenge but a dream nevertheless. He had all sorts of ideas already about how things could be done and what could be fixed with new materials while still maintaining the integrity of the house's history. It would be a challenge to just keep to the fireplace and not start drawing up plans for the rest of the house.

He'd be doing this job alone. Pamela had managed to keep his wee company intact while he'd been gone, but only just. It had been down to a skeleton crew of two men by the time of his return. They'd had two projects on the books, one of which had finished within his first month home and the other which he'd sold off to one of the remaining men. The second man had moved on to another project with another company. Casey wanted to start fresh, just himself and his two hands and whatever work he could find. Just now, he didn't want other men depending on him for wages and work. Maybe one day

in the future he would want to rebuild the company and take on other workers, but for now he preferred the simplicity of being on his own.

"Well, what do ye think? Is there work enough for ye to take it on as a
project? I'd not like to waste yer time," Tomas said, voice prickly as a goose-
berry bush.

"Work enough? I thought ye were only lookin' to have the fireplace
rebuilt."

"Aye, I want that done, but I'd like the rest of the house seen to as well. If
ye can draw up some plans, an' give me an estimate on costs, then I should like
to hire you to do the whole house."

Casey didn't bother to hide his surprise. "It's a big project, are ye certain
ye want me here for that long? You an' I haven't gotten off to the best start after
all."

"No, but maybe we need to fix that for Pamela's sake."

"Well, I'll not argue with ye over that," Casey said, "though I was under
the distinct impression ye thought me next door to a killer of baby animals. So
ye'll forgive my surprise at ye wantin' me meddlin' about yer house every day
for months. An' make no mistake, this *will* take months for me to complete."

"Aye, I'll admit, I've reservations about ye. Yer brother has a soft side to
him, fortunately he is able to hide it in court for the most part, though occasionally I'll grant it works in his favour. You, on the other hand, I'm not so
sure about. Pamela loves ye though, so I'm willin' to give ye the benefit of the
doubt. My question is—are ye the same man that disappeared out of her life
three years ago? Or have ye changed too much to give her the kind of love she
deserves?"

"Ye're every bit as nosey as my brother says ye are," Casey said.

"Aye, I am. I never had children of my own, my wife an' I couldn't. Pamela
and the children have graciously allowed me to claim them as the daughter
an' grandchildren I never had. I love them every bit as much as if they were,
indeed, my own."

"Aye, well they *are* my own," Casey said, nettling at the man's tone.

"The children are, certainly," Tomas said, blue eyes like ice. "Pamela is a
free agent though, would you not agree?"

"She's my wife, but aye beyond that she is a human bein' with her own
will an' way about her."

"Ye've not treated her as a wife since ye've been home, so perhaps ye
shouldn't be too surprised if she chooses not to be one of these fine days."

"It's between Pamela an' myself, an' if she decides not to be with me,
that's somethin' I will have to learn to live with."

"Can ye live with it?"

"Do ye ever stop bein' a lawyer?" Casey asked, thoroughly vexed by the man and his probing questions. His main talent seemed to be finding a man's sore spot and then poking at it until it bled. To his surprise Tomas laughed.

"No, man, I don't suppose I do—ever stop bein' a lawyer that is."

"We'll get back to the fireplace then," Casey said, putting just enough force in his tone to let the man know he was done talking about his wife for the time being.

"I can take a hint."

"Can ye?"

Tomas laughed. "Oh aye, when it's delivered forcefully enough. Ye would have made a good lawyer, ye could have intimidated judges an' juries into doin' what ye want."

"I'll leave the legal manoeuverin' up to yerself an' Patrick. I know how to build things, an' that's about it."

"Well, lend me yer expertise then. Is the fireplace worth savin', or does it need to be rebuilt from the ground up."

"I'd keep the original facin'; ye'd be hard put to find anythin' like the carvin' on this nowadays. I can take it apart an' sand the scratches out of it though, if ye'd like, an' then stain it to somethin' fittin' to the period."

Tomas nodded. "Go on, man."

"Well, I'd take the main structure down, keep the bricks but rebuild it with new mortar. I'd take up the floor too, an' replace the joists. I'm feelin' a little sag as I walk on it."

It always came to him this way, what might be improved, made stronger and more beautiful, while still retaining the core integrity of the structure. "It's possible I could set up a ventin' system so that it pulls the cold air from the room, an' pumps it back out warm. Most chimneys lose a lot of the warm air to the outdoors. I did it in my own house an' it's never cold, no matter how damp the winters get."

"Do ye have a philosophy of buildin'?" Tomas asked, surveying him with an expression of curiosity.

Casey shrugged. "It's nothin' so grand that ye could call it a philosophy, but I've a few things I try to abide by on any project I take on. With a house like yers—one with a history to it—ye always want to leave somethin' as it is, whether it's the stairs worn from the years of people climbin' them, or an old door, or a banister with scratches on it. It represents the love the house has known as well as its history. Mind, if ye don't want that, it's yer house an' I'll fix things as ye like."

Tomas looked at him over the top of his cup, the steam wafting up around his red eyes, giving him a bit of a Mephistopheles-gone-to-seed air. "No, ye do as ye see fit, man. I'll check in from time to time, but I'll not sit on yer shoulder twitterin' at ye either. I'd not take yer advice on application of the law, so I'll warrant ye don't need mine on restorin' a house. Come on, I'll show ye the rest of the place, an' ye can tell me what ye'd do with it, if neither time nor money was an object."

Tomas walked him through the entirety of the house, and Casey could feel the itch in his palms as they progressed room by room: kitchen, formal parlour, a forlorn room, with only a threadbare sofa gracing it and the buttery, a room filled with boxes and a cracked window which had let the damp in. Then came the long gallery, which ran above the stairs, and the bedrooms, most of them smelling of dust and disuse, but with an inherent beauty of line and form, like an old woman who had once been a great beauty, and still carried the memory of it in her bones and carriage.

The room with the tree was large with a loft to the ceiling which was unusual in a house this old. There was damp around the tree, but he was surprised to find the damage wasn't much worse.

"I have the roof repaired every couple of years," Tomas said, watching him as he pushed on the floor here and there, trying to gauge just how much water it had taken in.

"I've an idea which may save ye havin' to do that, but I'll need to sit with it for a bit before I try to draw it an' show it to ye. There's a bit of a gap sometimes between thought an' execution for me."

"D'ye remember at all what happened to ye?" Tomas asked.

Casey shook his head, and eased his way up to his feet. "No, sometimes I get snatches here an' there—a fist hittin' me, a gun to my head, but not anythin' more than that. I never see faces either, so I've no idea who might have done this to me."

"D'ye fear it happenin' again, if the same men should get wind of ye bein' home?"

"Aye, I do, but I can't let that keep me from life entirely. It might be that I'll never remember."

"I know a psychiatrist who does regression therapy. Have ye ever thought of tryin' something of that sort?"

"Aye, I tried it when I was in San Francisco a few times, an' all it did was give me a fierce headache."

"Might be now that yer memory's been loosened up a bit—ye remembered yer family after all, an' where ye lived—yer mind would be more amenable at this point."

"Could be," Casey shrugged. "I'm scared to upset the balance in my head, truth be told. Just remembering Pamela, the children an' Patrick was a huge blessing for me. An' yet, I feel like if I could find out who it was wanted me dead, the knowledge of it would set me free."

"Well, if ye think ye might want to try it, I can call her—the psychiatrist that is."

"Thank ye, I think not just yet, though."

Downstairs, Tomas offered him a drink in the drafty old kitchen.

"No thank ye, I avoid alcohol for the most part, it doesn't do my addled brain any favours. I am goin' to just board up the window in the buttery for the present, so that damp stops comin' in. I've got the materials in my truck, so I'll just nip out an' get them."

Outside, the rain was pelting down at a furious rate, soaking him to the skin in the few minutes it took to grab what he needed and make the dash back to the house.

Tomas handed him a towel, a soft blue article which looked familiar to Casey.

"Pamela gave them to me after she checked the state of my linen closets and told me the towels were 'more hole than substance.'"

Casey dabbed his face with it, and finding it clean proceeded to give his hair a good rubdown. He took the wood, a hammer and a handful of nails into the buttery, where he set to boarding up the window.

"Ye know, yer philosophy of buildin' would make a good philosophy for life too." Tomas hovered in the doorway, watching him work.

"Aye," Casey said, voice muffled by the four nails he held in his teeth, "how's that?"

"The idea of makin' somethin' new upon the bones of what was, an' yet leavin' somethin' there to remind ye of the past, an' its value. Ye might apply it to yer marriage."

Casey merely gave the man a look, and then returned to boarding the window shut. Tomas gave a small snort and turned back to the kitchen, leaving Casey in peace for a few minutes.

The man was right, and that was what rankled more than anything else. He did need to apply the same philosophy to his marriage. Build upon what was good between the two of them, understand that any relationship of length had scars on its underbelly, not always seen by those outside, but known to those inside. Mind you, his and Pamela's particular battle scars were fairly apparent to anyone who might care to look. Clearly, they were all too apparent to Tomas.

When he repaired houses he always looked at the foundation first, assessed the bones of the property and made his plans and adjustments from there. What he'd had with Pamela had been rare and quite wonderful, despite their particular house taking more than a few hits of damage. If he was going to extend the metaphor, he thought, perhaps, the time had come to dig deep and find his bedrock so that he might know, once again, how to build something both strong and beautiful upon it.

Chapter Nineteen

Mountain Ghost

MARCH THAT YEAR came in like a lion, with a storm of epic proportions, which felled more than a few trees throughout the countryside. By the middle of the month, however, March decided to settle into a lamb-like docility, with unseasonably warm days and placid weather, which made everyone feel just the slightest bit edgy, certain as they were that fickle maiden that she was, March was likely to drop an icy boot on all their heads before she was done with them.

However, the warm weather continued on long enough that Casey asked Pamela if he might take Conor to stay for a few days in the mountains, where he'd lived upon his return to Ireland. Pamela had said yes, knowing as he did, that while Conor and he had advanced in their relationship, there was still a bit of thawing to do. Casey felt this might be best accomplished by a few days away from the rest of the world, where they could do as they liked and not worry about bathing, eating vegetables, wearing clean clothes, or any of the other necessary rituals of civilization.

Casey had driven as far as there was passable road, and then parked the truck in a spot he'd used when he had lived on the mountaintop. From there, they loaded their bags on their backs, and proceeded on foot.

Two hours into their walk they came across a field dappled with mushrooms. Brian had taught his sons how to tell the mushrooms that were edible from those that were poison from the time they were wee lads. He'd said it had been imperative to make certain they knew the difference as Casey was wont to eat anything that came within his line of sight for a few years. This time of year though, was early even for the morels which were the only mushrooms which grew in the spring. Casey thought with the unseasonable weather, though, a few might have sprung up early. There were, however both true morels and false ones. Though the false ones weren't deadly to eat, they'd give a man a fierce bellyache. Even the real article needed to be cooked, or they'd cause stomach cramps.

They found a patch of shade provided by a stand of oak. Casey took off his sweater, and used it as a net for the mushrooms. He showed Conor how to tell a true morel, and then they simply ambled around the edge of the wood picking to their heart's content. Conor stayed close to him, though he stopped every few feet to pocket yet another treasure. Casey had been a magpie himself when he was small, and had a day to wander in the forest.

They chatted a little, though Conor wasn't a great talker, and preferred to show things, rather than tell them. When he did speak, it was because he had something to say. This was evidenced by the question the boy asked the minute they paused to take a drink of water.

"How'd ye know to come here, to come home, I mean?" Conor asked. Since the day Conor had hit him, Casey had been subjected to a barrage of questions. However, his son was talking to him, so he wasn't inclined to object to the interrogatory fusillade.

"I don't know entirely, but I have an idea about it."

"What idea?" Conor asked, and stopped to look up at him.

"I'll tell ye, but can we sit a minute, an' maybe eat our lunch?" Casey asked. His knee was twinging, but he also wanted to sit down and look in his son's face when he answered him. "Here let's sit on this tree," he said and pointed to an ancient beech which had fallen down some time ago, judging by the delicate green blanket of wood sorrel that covered much of it. He chose a clear spot, and sat down, easing his leg out in front of him.

Conor sat beside him, and Casey parceled out the lunch. Ham and cheese with a bit of mustard on thick slices of brown bread, apple cake that released a whiff of cinnamon when unwrapped, two oranges and a thermos of hot tea.

Conor set to eating with a hearty appetite from the morning's walk, intent on his food as only a hungry young boy could be. Casey's stomach was rumbling rather loudly, and he bit into the sandwich relishing the bite of the mustard against the smoky taste of the ham. He looked about as he ate, taking in their surroundings.

They were in a small valley, formed by a long-ago glacier scraping away a chunk of the mountain and leaving a depression behind. It was just past noon and the small valley swam in light, golden motes of dust creating a haze amongst all the tender bright green of spring. The sun was still directly overhead, and the warmth of it penetrated right down to his marrow. There was a pungent whiff of wood garlic somewhere nearby and he could see the delicate petals of a patch of wood anemone peeking out from under the log.

He looked over at his son, who was watching a wood beetle industriously burrow its way under a bit of lichen, while eating his sandwich. The light brought out the blue tints in his hair. Like Pamela, Conor's hair was so dark it held iridescent bits of green and blue, like a crow's wing seen in the sun. Conor had grown a fair bit in the few short months since Casey's return, his body just a wee bit leaner and his face a touch thinner too. He was going to be a big lad, much as Casey had been as a child.

After finishing off his sandwich, Conor fixed his father with an expression with which Casey was becoming all too familiar.

"Ye said ye'd tell me how ye found yer way back here."

"Aye, I did. Well, I had a friend who told me that his people believed we were all made of the earth an' so no matter how far ye drifted in this world, yer homeland would always call ye back, an' wait for yer return. I think maybe this land called me back because the very soil of it is in my bones. An' then I believe that you an' yer sister an' mammy had a great deal to do with it as well."

"Kathleen is my sister just as much as Bella is," Conor said, and Casey could feel the boy's tension telegraph across the narrow space between them. He understood what the simple statement meant. It was defensive but also a challenge.

"Aye, she is that. Ye're a good brother, lookin' out for her as ye do. I am right fond of the wee girl myself, just so ye know."

"Even though Jamie is her da?" Conor said. Casey sighed, this child was not backwards about being forwards, that was for certain.

"Aye, she's not to blame for who her daddy is, an' as fathers go, Jamie is a good one, is he not?"

"He's my friend too," Conor said, though his voice had gotten rather quiet.

"I know he is. Conor, I know ye may not understand this, but believe me when I tell ye that I like Jamie too. A great deal actually. I'm grateful to the man because he looked after yez in a lot of ways when I was gone. I'm grateful to him because he loved all of ye too. An' yes," Casey added seeing the next question queuing up on Conor's lips, "I'm even grateful that he loves yer mama."

He realized as he said the words that he meant it—he *was* grateful to the man. Grateful for so many things—nursing Pamela through an illness that might have otherwise killed her and giving Conor a firm foundation through both his presence and his stories, so that his son had not only survived his absence but grown during it too. Grateful that Isabelle had been secure enough in the man's love that she felt she had two fathers now. Grateful for wee Kathleen, with whom Jamie trusted him without reservation—that alone was an enormous gift. He was even—though granted this set of emotions was far more mixed—thankful that the man had given Pamela such security and comfort; it was the other things he'd given the woman that he was not quite so grateful for. He snorted a little and cut the thoughts off, as he'd been cutting them off for weeks now.

It seemed that Conor divined his thoughts for he spoke then of his mother. "She was sad a lot," Conor said, looking up at him. "When ye were gone."

"Aye, I imagine she was," Casey said gently.

"She hardly ever cried though," Conor added, "'cept when Phouka died, she cried then."

"I think she was afraid to cry," he said, reaching down to remove a beech leaf from his son's hair.

"She was. I heard her tell Uncle Pat that she thought if she started she might never stop. She said she couldn't do that to us—me an' Isabelle. But she could have cried, I would have looked after her."

Casey took a breath and looked his son in the eye. He put a hand on Conor's shoulder, though whether to steady himself or reassure Conor he couldn't have said.

"I know ye could have, but ye don't need to worry about that any more, son. I am here, an' it's my job to look after all of yez, includin' yer mammy."

Conor nodded, and then gave him one of those dubious looks that reminded Casey forcibly of his father, Brian.

"Do ye think she'll let ye look after her?"

Casey laughed; this son of his was wise far beyond his years. "Well that's the million-dollar question, isn't it, boyo? But maybe we won't give her too much of a choice in the matter. Only we'll be quiet about it, aye?"

Conor smiled up at him, leaf shadows flickering across his wee face. "Aye, it will be our secret."

They arrived at the hut in the late afternoon, and set to work to ready things without delay. There were the usual jobs to contend with when a place had been left empty for any length of time; a bird nest abandoned from the previous summer blocking the chimney, a coating of dust over everything he'd left behind, including his wee bits of furniture and tinned goods, and the few dishes he'd had.

The laddie was handy, and able to help him with every task, or do the less dangerous ones on his own with minimal supervision. He kept an eye on him at all times though, for a mountain wasn't a place a man could relax his vigilance.

By the time they sat down by the fire that evening for their meal, they were both exhausted. Casey had wisely packed tins of soup, cheese and bread, so that they might have something which would fill their bellies but not require much in the way of cooking for this first night.

"Ye're mighty good with the tracking," Casey said, "did someone teach ye?" Conor had shown him the track of a deer, which had been hidden in long grass, but Conor had easily followed it by other signs—broken twigs, missing bark, bent blades of grass.

Conor looked up at him, small face slightly troubled, giving Casey the answer before Conor voiced it. "Jamie did," he said.

"It's all right, Conor, ye needn't fear talkin' to me about Jamie. I know he's very dear to you, an' that's a good thing."

Conor gave him one of those slightly dubious looks. It was identical in expression to the ones Pat used to give him when they were small and Casey had a mad idea for their next adventure.

"It won't hurt yer feelins," Conor said, "or make ye mad?"

"No, an' even if it did, that would be fine, no? I'm a grown man, an' I'll feel things that aren't always reasonable, but I'll do my best not to make anyone else suffer for that."

"Even mama?" Conor asked. Casey sighed, the child was too quick by half.

"Aye, especially yer mam," he replied, knowing he'd not done well by that standard so far.

Conor was quiet then, as though he needed a bit of time to digest what his father had said. Casey let him be, knowing the boy would come to an acceptance in time, or he would not, which was of course the price of a three-year absence. There was neither fault nor reckoning to be cast nor understood, it was simply the cost of it.

It began to rain after their dinner, and so they took shelter in the hut, and played a round of Monopoly during which Conor exhibited the traits of a robber baron and stripped Casey of his meagre holdings more than once. Knowing how hungry the lad always was, Casey made him a snack before bed, and then settled in to read with him. It was cozy, with the fire and the smell of the soup he'd made them for dinner still lingering in the air, and the rustle of Conor's book as he turned the pages. He felt the peace of it right to the marrow of his bones, and turned his head slightly to watch his boy as he read. It had felt a little surreal at first, having the child he'd been unable to remember when he'd lived in this hut just two short years before, here with him.

It pierced him to the quick at times—the loss of three years of watching Conor grow, of answering his questions, of simply being there to read to him at night, and listen to his troubles. But there was a new comfort between them, and while their mutual bridge might be shaky, Casey thought it was likely strong enough now to bear the weight of their relationship. He tried not to dwell on the lost time, because he knew bitterness lay down that particular path, and he didn't want to waste the future with regrets.

The one thing that hadn't been lost to him though, was love for his family. Love for this wee man and his tiny fiery-tempered sister, and love for their mother. Love too for Kathleen, who was a part of each one of them and as a result, part of the warp and weft of him as well.

Once Conor was asleep, Casey went outside for a bit of air. The rain had stopped and the sky had cleared. Here on the mountain, it felt like the stars were right above his head, trembling in their splendor.

His eyes swept the tree line, though in the dark the woods were impenetrable to his vision. One night when he'd lived here, he'd seen a man standing at the edge of the wood, watching him, and there had been a sense there, even though Casey had been frightened, that the man had come to see him, to tell him something. When he'd gone down to confront the man though, he was gone, leaving no trace behind in the fresh fallen snow. At times he wondered if he'd hallucinated the specter, conjuring up company for himself because he'd lived in such isolation.

Something a doctor in San Francisco had said to him during a session came back to him now. He'd been telling her about the sense he sometimes had, of being outside himself, or at times being in the presence of something formless, which had neither name nor home, but was still undeniably there. He shivered a little now with the meaning her reply took on here, with that dark wood so close.

"It's something I've found in some of my patients who've experienced great trauma to the brain. They feel ghosts, even see them at times."

"Ye believe in ghosts—you, a woman of science?"

Her face looked vaguely troubled at the question.

"It doesn't matter what I believe, only what the patient knows. Have you seen a ghost?"

A strange sense had come over him then, that the doctor knew he had, and was merely asking for formality's sake.

"We all have a sense of the boundaries of self. We know where our body begins and ends, we have that knowledge of self as we move through the world. Only young children, and sometimes those with troubles of the mind, experience that feeling of a lack of boundary. Well, one might argue that drug users experience this as well, but it's not as pure an experience. So, what I'm saying is you perceive yourself as an entity with a physical boundary, consisting of your flesh and bone. But in patients with trauma to their brains, it's possible I think, that there's a gap, just a small one between that sense of self and sense of the other, so in that small bit of time, one senses something else, another presence. It could be the mind is doubling the spirit in a way, and that for those few seconds the *person stands outside their own being, and feels that. Or it could be that people with brain injury are able to feel and see things others are not."*

He thought now of Brian, and brought up one of those mercurial bits of memory which inhabited his brain. His father had oftentimes had trouble sleeping, and it wasn't unusual to find him up doing chores or reading in the middle of the night. This bit of quicksilver was a memory of a night when Casey had come down the stairs of their two-up, two-down looking for something to eat, and found his father sitting at the table, carving into wood the bones of a heron. They'd found a skeleton on their summer retreat to Donegal, and Pat had begged to bring it back though Brian usually preferred to leave nature to take care of her own. Brian had, through the whole of that summer, slowly carved it out in wood, recreating the skeleton in miniature as a gift for Pat.

Even for his restless father, the hour was late, and he'd asked him what he was doing, up so deep into the night, or early as it was, for there were pale streaks on the horizon outside their kitchen window. His father had looked up, his face almost dream-like in its exhaustion, and when he spoke his words were that of a poet.

"I'm holding the bones of the night together, to keep safe your dreams and those of your brother."

At the time, he'd thought it just another of his father's flights of fancy, but now he understood it was much more. And so he thought again of the doctor's words, about the brain doubling one's spirit, and making it seem a ghost stood right beside a man. Yet, he had the sense that it wasn't him he'd seen that night, at the edge of the wood, but rather something other—a man who held the bones of the night together in his hands, keeping his son safe.

That was his job now, passed down a generation, to keep the shadows at bay from the small boy who slept so soundly within those fragile walls, to guard his dreams, to follow the track of the moon across the night sky and be there waiting when his son woke to the dawn. To hold the bones of the night, so to keep safe his child.

Chapter Twenty

The Last Wolf in Ireland

THE CAVE ENTRANCE was narrow and hidden behind a screen of scrubby rowan. The ground tilted down sharply right inside the entrance, and Casey took Conor's hand in his to guide the lad down, playing the torch along the narrow path. It was a distance of about seventy steps on a steep descent and then the cave floor leveled out.

It was the third day of their time together on the mountain, and thus far the days had passed easily as they fished and hiked through the forest and meadows and lay under the stars at night with Casey pointing out constellations to his son. The weather was fine and while Conor had his quiet spells, he was in an amiable enough frame of mind and was clearly enjoying their time here together.

Casey had brought Conor here to a cave he'd discovered his first spring on the mountainside to show him something he thought the lad might like. It was the sort of thing he would have found magical at Conor's age, and still did come to that.

What he wanted to show him was at the back of the cave, tucked in an indent in the rock, where it wouldn't become prey to any scavenger that happened through. He shone the light of the torch on the walls, and saw the answering glint of a gleaming tooth.

"Right here." He gave the torch to Conor, and then knelt down in the sand which covered the cave floor, and removed the object from its hiding spot. "I was diggin' a bit, lookin' at rocks an' such, when I came across it."

The skull was old and huge, and belonged to a time far distant from this one. The bone had turned a soft grey-green, and had buff spots from the touch of time's long hand. A sharp tooth had remained fixed in the jaw, and Conor ran a small finger over it with great caution.

"What is it?"

"A wolf," Casey said, "a mighty big one, judgin' by the size of that skull."

"There aren't any wolves in Ireland," Conor said.

"Not now, no," Casey replied, feeling a shaft of sadness for all the lost beasts of the world, "but long ago, Ireland was called Wolf Land, for there were plenty of them here, roamin' the forests an' bogs. There's many a time they're mentioned in the old tales, an' lots of places are named for them too. Ye know the ring forts, like the one up on the Inishowen Peninsula, where ye told me Uncle Pat took ye last year?"

Conor nodded, small face serious in the oval of light thrown from the torch.

"Well, they were built in part as protection against roamin' bands of wolves." He thought too of the other stories, the ones of battlefields littered with hundreds of dead men, and great flocks of crows—*like a black and smothering tide,* as one book had put it—and packs of wolves, *a smoke of hunger and destruction,* swarming the bodies, eating their fill of carrion.

A breeze came through suddenly, one of those odd rushes of air one got in a cave at times. It ruffled Conor's hair, and made him turn toward the back of the cave.

"Where's the air comin' from?"

"There's a chimney through to the surface down one of the corridors; when the wind blows just right ye get a gust along there that billows out into the larger part of the cave. Ye never want to get stuck in a cave that doesn't have a source of air beyond that of the entrance, because if that one openin' gets blocked ye'll suffocate to death. An' that would be a long an' lingerin' way to go. Ye know the big cave we passed on the way here, the one near Kilkenny– Dunmore? Well, long time ago a bunch of men found a lot of skeletons in there, mostly women an' children. 'Twas thought they'd fled there for shelter durin' a raid by Vikings. The Vikings didn't want to follow them into the cave, so they set fires at the entrance, an' those fires burned so high an' so hot that they stole all the oxygen from the cave, an' all those people suffocated to death. So if ye go in a cave, ye must always check to make certain there's air comin' from at least two places."

"Did you ever stay here?" Conor asked.

"Oh, aye, a time or two, when I was out huntin' an' it was gettin' dark an' the hut was too far away."

What he didn't add was that he'd surveyed the place well in case he needed it as a hiding spot, lest someone came hunting him. He'd stored a few dried goods, some candles, a blanket roll, and a knife here. But Conor didn't need to know that.

"Why d'ye think he was away from the pack?" Conor touched the skull again, hand running over the crest, his face awed as though he could see the wild animal clothed once again in fur and flesh, in tooth and claw.

"Maybe he was old, an' the winter was particularly cruel that year. He'd have used this place for shelter. Maybe one night he simply fell to sleep, an' didn't wake in the mornin'."

Conor nodded, but he turned his face so that light no longer touched it.

"What is it, boyo?"

Conor shrugged a little. "Just that he might have been the last one, an' all alone when he died." He touched his chest as he said it, and Casey understood what that gesture meant.

"Aye, but maybe he didn't mind so much. Could be it was peaceful, an' just like fallin' into sleep at night. Maybe it was snowin' outside, an' there was the great hush that comes with it, an' it was almost like fallin' away into an old song he'd known from birth."

The nights he'd slept here, the skull looking down upon him from those ancient and hollow eye sockets, he'd thought about it, about simply falling to sleep and not waking to yet another day in a world that, at times, felt unfathomable in its intricacies. About what it might be to just go into those trackless wastes, soft-footed and solitary, wind ruffling his fur, his eye on the far horizon beyond this world.

"Did you feel like that sometimes?"

"Like what?" Casey asked, startled from his ruminations.

"Like the wolf, that maybe you'd just go to sleep an' not wake up, here in this cave?"

"Ah, no," Casey said quickly, discomfited by the lad's reading of his thoughts. "What makes ye ask that, son?"

Conor shook his head. "Ye just had a funny look on yer face, like ye remembered feelin' that way. Y-ye must have been lonely sometimes."

It wasn't really a question, but Casey knew his son needed an answer, nevertheless.

"Aye, I was, lonely for you an' yer sister, lonely for yer mother, an' Uncle Pat, an' for my old self as well, I suppose."

Casey stood then, thinking it best to change the direction of the conversation. "Come, let's go have a drink from the spring."

He led the way to the back of the cave, where it branched into two long corridors, one too tight for him to crawl into and one that he could walk in if he hunched over. The spring burbled out at the junction, just a small upwelling of water, which smelled of the depths of its origin deep within the rock.

He cupped his hands and drank, and Conor did the same, the water silver-bright on tongue and throat. It tasted of the deep things of the earth, dirt and rock and a cold as sharp as the edge of a freshly-honed blade.

"We'd best head back above ground, boyo, before the light fails us or we'll be sleepin' with the wolf tonight."

Conor took his hand, without being nudged to do so, and Casey smiled to himself in the dark, over the feel of that small hand, still cold and wet from the spring, but clasped within his as naturally as day folding into night.

Conor hesitated though, before they began the climb up to the world once again.

"What is it, lad?"

The light from the torch cast a dim glow over Conor's face, something like water, still and yet otherworldly. It was enough to see the expression on the boy's face, his brow drawn down a little, and his eyes troubled.

"Are ye still lonely?"

He put his hand down, and touched the small, worried face in reassurance.

"No, Conor, I'm not."

They arrived back to the hut late, and after a quick meal of stew and bread, decided to go fishing and see if they could catch a trout or two for their breakfast.

Conor was enamored of the tackle box, with all its bright feathers, floats and lures. He was leaning over it now, like a connoisseur trying to choose the right wine for the moment. He settled at last on a red and black one, and Casey hunkered down beside him, and helped him tie the lure to the line.

When they settled in beside the pond, the sun had begun its slow descent into the west, lending a fine line of gold to the rim of the mountain. They were quiet, merely enjoying the evening and the companionship of one another. It would be time to go in soon, for once the sun went down, the air turned distinctly chilly.

"Daddy, Daddy—look!" Casey turned swiftly, worried the lad was in trouble, but he was simply excited because he had a fish on the line. The line was spooling out at a terrific rate and Casey ran over to help him secure it, before the fish ran away with it.

He put his arms around the boy, fastening Conor's hand to the reel and feeling the jolt in both their bodies as the fish's run was abruptly halted. Conor was thrumming with excitement and Casey remembered that feeling, the thrill so big that it was almost frightening in its intensity. The pull was immense, and Casey wondered just what sort of monster his son had caught. His mind went back to a time on a lake with his brother, when Pat had almost drowned and he'd witnessed a being which he could not explain to himself, and had never spoken of to any other soul.

Casey tightened his grip over Conor's hand and gave the line one last jerk, hoping it didn't snap, and the fish broke the surface of the water—all gleaming and iridescent scale, and the smooth muscle of one which dwelt in water, water spraying as it rose, catching the fading light like drops of cascading bronze. He pulled Conor back, his hands still over his, trying to take some of the give out of the line, so that the reel would work once again.

"Now—reel it in, laddie!"

The fish, falling back into the pond, set off in a last blazing race for its life, streaking back out into the centre of the water, pulling the line. The rod was an arc of strain, and had it not been Conor's fish, Casey thought he might have foregone breakfast and let the beast go in sheer respect for its fight.

Conor lurched forward and slid, feet first into the pond, with his father right behind him. Through some dexterous handling on Casey's part they managed to keep hold of the pole. Conor's hand was still clutching the reel and once he got past the shock of the water, he began to spool it back as fast as his small hands could manage.

And then it was there, flipping and thrashing, swinging dangerously close to Conor's head. But Conor swung the line, and the fish landed on the shore with a thump. Casey bodily lifted his son out of the water and set him on the bank. He followed, streaming water and pond weed, and then stood beside Conor, who was looking down at the fish, which was gasping and struggling, sensing his watery home was within reach, if only he could get to it.

"Ye have to give him a knock on the head, boyo, an' finish it. Ye don't ever want a creature to suffer longer than is necessary. Here's a rock, just give him a quick knock, an' it'll be done."

Conor swallowed and then holding the rock tightly, hit the fish on the head. It lay still then and Casey gave it a good perusal to be certain it was completely dead, and not just stunned. He then turned to Conor, and grinned and Conor, wet, winded and thrilled with his catch, grinned back.

"Now we can have fish for breakfast, Daddy," Conor said, with a note of pride in his voice—that of the hunter who is providing food for others.

He knew Conor had called him daddy in the rush of pure excitement, but he was incredibly touched nevertheless. Just hearing him say the word put a lump in Casey's throat.

"Aye, we can. We'll fry it up with some potatoes an' it'll be a grand meal all together. First though we have to clean it."

"Can I do that?" Conor asked.

"I suppose ye can, though ye'll need to go slow an' canny about it, an' maybe don't tell yer mammy I let ye use a knife."

He made certain Conor had a proper grip on the knife and that the fish was secured with his other hand. Casey guided his hand with the initial cut but let the boy finish it, slowly and carefully with a sawing motion that meant the innards wouldn't come away clean, but he didn't mind a little extra work if it meant Conor understood he trusted him with this task. He looked at his son and felt a rush of tenderness. Conor's tongue was stuck out slightly in concentration, something he did himself and that his father before him had done. Genetics was a funny thing, and mysterious as well. There were things that skipped generations—a way of moving or thinking, eyes that were a particular shade of blue or green, the line of a jaw, laughter, or even something as random as the sound of a cough, and then showed itself strongly in a child four generations later.

"Uncle Pat said ye used to fish here with yer daddy."

"Aye, we did."

"When's the last time ye went fishin'?" Conor asked.

"With my daddy, or just the last time?" Casey asked, pulling the innards of the fish out and tossing them into the water. Such was life, that death provided sustenance, the dead swallowed—both literally and figuratively—in the ravenous churn of the living.

"Both," Conor said.

"I was fifteen last time my father brought yer Uncle Pat an' me up here for a fishin' trip. He was only alive a few summers beyond that. We had a fine time, it was the first time he'd been able to come with us in a few years. It felt like old times we'd had on the mountain with him, when we were still small like you."

"How old was Uncle Pat?"

"He's four years younger than me, just like yer mama. So how old would that make him?"

Conor thought for a moment, looking down at his hand and clearly squelching the impulse to use his fingers as an aid. He took a breath, his inky black brows drawn down in concentration.

"Eleven," he said triumphantly.

"Aye, that's exactly right."

"What about the last time ye fished here, not with yer da?"

"I was alone, just me. I was livin' here. I often fished for my supper."

"Do ye miss him?" Conor asked.

"My father?" Casey asked and Conor nodded, the narrow nape of his neck smudged with dirt, and drops of water glimmering in the soft curls of his hair.

"Aye, every day of my life," Casey said honestly.

The sun was below the mountain's horizon now, and dusk had begun its slow encroach. There was a raw edge to the air, the drowning light of the mountain rimmed in blue. Casey looked over at Conor. A last stray gleam of light gilded his jawline, which already held a certain strength to it, foreshadowing the man he would one day be. Conor turned his head, and looked up into his father's eyes and Casey felt the utterly helpless love of a parent wash through him.

"Daddy?" Conor said the word with a sort of reluctant delight, as if he was testing out the feel of it on his tongue.

"Aye, son?"

"I missed ye too. Every day ye were gone."

Chapter Twenty-one

Holding the Night

IT WAS THEIR last evening on the mountain. They'd had fried trout and pota-toes for dinner and were now outside, where Casey had put down a sheet of canvas to block the damp, with an old quilt over top to lie upon. It was just a time to be quiet or to chat as it pleased the lad. He felt regret at the thought of packing up and going back down the mountainside tomorrow.

It was a beautiful night with the moon just a sliver off the full, so that the night was etched around them, as though someone had taken a pen with both silver and indigo ink, and drawn a faint line around everything—trees, the hut, the rocks and his wee boy who stood on tiptoe in front of him, his arms outstretched toward the sky.

"What are ye doin', Conor?"

"I'm holding the night. Mama told me that sometimes the night is very lonely, and it needs to know it's needed an' loved."

There was a stitch in his heart, when he thought what Pamela might have meant by that simple statement, and yet she had turned it into something beautiful for their son. He thought about another boy then, from another time who had also loved the night sky.

"Mama said you used to pull the moon down for me," Conor said sud-denly, as though the dark and the silence had brought the memory up from his core, from a time when story held the place of remembrance.

"Aye, it was somethin' my own daddy used to do for me. He taught me all about it, an' how long ago, people would never say the name directly—ye

WHERE BUTTERFLIES DREAM · 211

know like I taught ye with the auld ones. So people would refer to it as a brightness, or as the Queen of the Night, for the moon is a womanly sort of bein' an' the Celts revered the female as much as the male. They knew one without the other was without balance."

He was learning Conor's expressions, and when the boy wanted to ask a question he wasn't certain he should. Conor's wee face held just such a look now.

"I can see ye've a question, so just ask it," Casey said drily.

"Well, ye're a boy, so don't ye need mama for balance?" Conor asked.

He'd been right, it was one of *those* sorts of questions, the kind of which Conor seemed to have an endless supply. He thought perhaps a little distraction was currently in order.

"A good friend of mine told me a story about the moon, would ye like to hear it?"

Conor gave him a look which told Casey this subject was not closed, but that Conor was graciously willing to move on from it for now. He came and sat down on the blanket.

"Aye, I'd like to hear the story," he said and moved a little closer to Casey, so that his warmth combined with his father's to create a cocoon against the chill of the evening, a metaphysical hut within which a story could be told.

"There are certain stories that are so special they must only be told in the dark," Casey began. "This is one of those stories."

He paused then, because a storyteller always did, paused for a few beats to let a little anticipation build. There was something more though, that happened in those beats of silence, where a bit of the other person entered you, and something of you entered them, and it was all as it should be. Casey could feel that shift begin, as the boundaries between him and his son dissolved, and the spiral between teller and listener, became a circle which enclosed the space, and made it other for the duration of the telling.

"Long ago, in this very lake, there lived a creature that was neither human nor animal, neither fish nor fowl. He was a great dragon-y sort of beast, but unlike a dragon he lived in water, an' while he was a great swimmer he couldn't fly at all. He was terrible fierce and could snort great clouds of hot water from his nose, an' the earth—when he chanced to walk upon it—shook beneath his feet. His mother had died long before she was able to teach him his manners, an' so he was a bit in the way of bein' a great wild thing. An' while it was grand to be such a creature, an' to be master of everythin' around, it was also a mighty lonely thing to be. He had no friends, an' no kin for him to hunt with, nor eat with at his hearth at the bottom of the lake. There was no one to tell his tales to when the day was done, no one to pat his scales, nor hold his great paw when times were hard. Why even the wee purple urchins in his lake had pearly oysters for their friends. The waves had the shore, the otters had the reeds, the stars had the grains of sand, an' the trees had the wind. But for the creature there was no one. There was truly none as alone as him.

"It was a night near to winter when he first saw the moon. Well to be fair, he'd seen it before, but he'd not really paid attention properly. On this night the moon was full, its belly round as a scryin' ball with starlight and honey, an' the sight of it stopped the creature in his tracks, an' he stood there upon the shore of his very deep lake an' gazed in wonderment at this great orb above. He lifted his head an' roared, for such measures had always worked for him before in attractin' attention to his wants an' needs. But this had no effect on the moon, an' in fact by the next night the creature noticed she'd turned her shoulder against him a little, an' despite all his roarin' each an' every night when he saw her appear in the sky, she kept turnin' that shoulder until her back was fully to him, an' she disappeared from the sky altogether.

"'Twas then he realized he needed to do somethin' spectacular in order to draw the moon's attention. Over the years, he'd collected many things—shiny things which had drawn him, for he was one of nature's natural magpies despite bein' a mythical an' monster-y sort of creature. An' so he gathered all his bits an' bobbles—shells an' gems, an' rings he'd found lost in the bottom of the lake, an' mermaid scales he'd collected every time he'd found them, lyin' abandoned where the mermaid had shed them.

"He waited, night after night, as the moon at first peeked out around the clouds, and then as she waxed into the shape of a bowl, tilted upon its side, and he bided his time, watching her as she grew and changed, until the night she rose like a great silver ship upon the tide of night. An' when he saw her set sail over the hills an' valleys, layin' out a shimmerin' path upon the sea, he rose out of that dark lake, gleamin' in scale an' claw with every precious thing, both silver an' gold, hangin' off him. He'd put it all upon him, decked himself out in gorgeous array, so to speak, so that the moon might notice him, an' be awed by his riches.

"That night the moon was very full, though, an' her radiance lit all the land around so that he saw every wee hill, every fold in the valley an' every berry upon the trees, an' felt a great sorrow that he would never be able to make the moon see him. An' because he was so lonely, an' had such great hopes that the moon would see him, an' love him in return, he cried then, great silver an' frost tears that began to freeze the water all around him. He didn't notice, for his sorrow was so great that it drowned out every danger. The next thing he knew he was caught fast in a great sheet of ice, an' could move neither forward nor back, neither up nor down. He had gills an' scales an' so not bein' able to swim meant certain death for him. 'Twas then he howled, cryin' to the very heavens, an' shakin' the wee urchins so that their pearly caps fell off, an' the trees round about in the hills shed half their leaves in fear. An' so it was that the moon, who was just gettin' ready to take her leisure amongst the hills, heard the sound and caught a little gleam of something from the corner of her eye. The moon did love shiny things, bein' one herself, an' was intrigued by the thought of somethin' bright enough to catch her attention when her belly was so full an' round. She tilted herself forward, so that she might see better, an' in response the sea rose, feelin' the moon's touch, an' sent a great wave toward the shore. It washed into the lough, nearly drownin' the creature, an' yet doin' little to free him from his predicament.

"The moon felt terrible about the creature's sorrow an' that it was stuck so fast that it was sure to die before mornin' came. The followin' night she'd been plannin' to shed a bit of herself as she did each month, until she disappeared from the sky altogether for several nights at a time. An' so she simply shed it then an' there, and dropped it light as a feather shawl from her shoulders. That light drifted down, down, down, until it touched the lake where the creature was slowly fallin' down death's door stairs. The creature's head was about to sink below the water, an' with his legs stuck fast, he was goin' to drown. But then somethin' warm touched him, so warm that he took all the strength left to him, an' raised his head an' saw that light dazzled all around him, glitterin' along great brown trunks of kelp an' spillin' diamonds all across the water. He opened his mouth, awestruck by the sight, an' in doin' so, he took in a great gulp of water, an' swallowed that bit of the moon.

"The warmth of the moon's light melted away the creature's frozen tears and set him free, an' the water all around him glowed like a silver pearl. The light inside him filled up his loneliness an' tempered his anger, so that he learned to make friends with the urchins an' the otters, with the kelpies an' the rocks, an' with the very stars an' the grains of sand upon the shore of his lake. An' he became known as a very kind creature, one which still carried pearls an' gems an' gold scalloped shells upon him, risin' an' sheddin' his treasure only once every seven years.

"But the years passed an' the creature grew old, as creatures always do, and eventually he retreated to his cave far below the deepest parts of the lake, an' his song was heard no more, an' he was sorely missed by the urchins an' the otters, the stars an' the sand, the kelpies an' the rocks, an' the shore of his lake."

"That's it?" Conor said, tone slightly indignant.

Casey looked over at the face of his son, and laughed. "Aye, laddie, sometimes that's how stories end, with a bit of sadness. Still an' all, though," he added hastily, seeing the look in Conor's eyes, "'tis said that on nights when the moon is full an' the creature feels the light of it all the way in his deep, kelp-y lair, he rises to the surface an' sings to the moon of his love, an' she spills a little of her light to fill all the cracks in his soul."

They were quiet after that for a stretch, each lost in their own thoughts and yet the silence was companionable, Casey thought, and he realized he was getting used to his son once again, and to the role—daunting as it was at times—of father to him.

During the telling of the story, they'd stretched out on their backs, and Conor's head was pillowed on Casey's shoulder, providing a feeling of warmth and security to them both.

"Sometimes, when ye were gone," Conor said, small voice so quiet that it seemed merely part of the night around them, "I would hear ye singin' to me."

"Did ye, then?" Casey asked, his voice calm for he did not want to startle the boy. His heart however had begun to thump rather painfully, for he'd dreamed such things—singing to wee children, whose faces he could not see.

"Aye," Conor said matter-of-factly as though it was nothing worth noting when your father sang to you across the divide of time and space. Well, Pamela was his mother, so the lad likely did take such things in his stride. She had always seemed to have a foot in each world, both the corporeal one and the one of spirit.

"Who taught you about the stars?" Conor asked.

"My daddy, who was, of course, yer grandda," Casey said, feeling a sliver of grief in his throat for his father. "Ye would have liked him a lot, I believe. He was a great deal like yer Uncle Pat."

"I love Uncle Pat," Conor said, with the sort of emphasis an adult might have placed on it, so that there could be no doubt.

"Aye, me too, laddie. We're both lucky to have him in our lives."

Conor yawned widely.

"Are ye tired? Ye can go to sleep, I can carry ye back to the hut later."

He could feel Conor's head getting heavier on his arm, the child's breath slowing to the beat of the mountain and the stars overhead. There was a small, glowing stillness in his heart just now, a warmth so sweet and peaceful that he wanted to grasp the moment and keep it so forever—a small snapshot distilled inside the crystal of emotion.

"Daddy?"

"Aye?" Casey said, brought up out of his thoughts by Conor's voice. He'd thought the laddie was asleep.

"I love you," his son said. The small glowing stillness burst into a bright and painful joy in Casey's chest. He snugged Conor a little tighter to him, relishing the warm and healthy feel of his child. He smelled of water, fried fish, potatoes and freshly-cut wood and Casey simply breathed him in, feeling a gratitude that went all the way to his core.

"I love you too, Conor-lad."

"Don't ye need mama for balance?" The question echoed in Casey's head and though he had not answered it for Conor, it was a question now insisting that he answer it for himself.

What he felt for Pamela, separate and beyond the children and the tie that came with them, was something which both grounded him and terrified him at the same time. He suspected that the terror had always been there to a certain degree. The grounding, he knew, had been something they had built together and given to one another in the creation of a home which had neither walls nor roof, but had still been their greatest shelter.

He had been as lost as a man could be without falling completely off the face of the earth, and yet he had remembered her, not her name, not even for a very long time, her face, but she had always been there inside him, and he realized that what he felt was an immensity of gratitude.

And what was the other side of gratitude's coin? Casey rolled over onto his back careful not to disturb Conor. What, indeed? He drew in a long breath, gazing up at the stars overhead.

Want, desire, lust—all true and all too simplistic to describe what he felt with Pamela.

He'd dropped by the other day to visit with the children, only to find they were out on a jaunt with Gert and Owen, and that Pamela was there alone. She'd come to let him in, clearly having gotten out of the bath to do so. She was wrapped in a robe and perfectly decent and yet…and yet, he'd been entirely aware that under the robe she was bare as an egg.

After, he couldn't remember much of what he'd said, or what she'd said come to that. It was possible he'd gone on about the agricultural practices of the 17th century for a good ten minutes for all he could recollect now. And she had known, because a swift soft blush had raced up through her skin to stain her face the colour of a hothouse camellia. That blush which had caused a riptide of lust in him as he remembered that her skin flushed that way all over when he made love to her. At that point, he'd felt a hasty retreat was his only option before he did something from which neither of them *could* retreat. And yet, he hadn't retreated, he'd simply stepped forward and kissed her as he used to do every time he parted from her, even just to go outside. She had been warm under his hands and his body had responded accordingly to the one woman it wanted and did not seem to understand it could not, at present, have. And she'd made a noise then, just a soft sound of surrender deep in her throat that sent a surge of lust through his body so strong that he wanted to take her then and there on the floor, and reservations be damned.

He'd stepped back, feeling dazed and hot.

"I-I'm sorry, I wasn't thinking."

"Perhaps you ought to try not thinking more often," she said tartly. The colour was still high in her face, and he could see she was torn between amusement and annoyance. He suspected this was not unusual for the two of them, though.

What he felt for her was more than desire though, as incredibly potent as that particular emotion was; it was that somewhere deep inside he knew she was his place in the world where he went when he was happy or sad, weary or excited. She was simply his home. It was fear that he might no longer be all those things for her, which had kept him this long from her bed. That and the sense that there were matters he must settle within himself before a full return to her and their marriage.

He sighed, Conor's question still hanging there in front of him, bright as if it were printed in bold across the sky. Aye, he needed her for balance. He needed her as the place where his heart lived and breathed.

Chapter Twenty-two

Children of the Troubles

MISS MARGARET LIVED in one of the many postwar council houses that lined the streets of Ballymurphy. Such housing was often dully uniform to the eye, and yet still people managed to make the homes their own in a variety of ways. Miss Margaret's way was clearly that of flowers. The postage stamp-sized front garden was already, even in these early spring days, a riot of green stalks and leaves and early-bloomers: pale lavender dogtooth violets, headily fragrant bunches of grape hyacinth and cheery-faced clusters of lemon-yellow primroses. A rose clambered up the bricks, newly minted with delicate green leaves.

The door was white and freshly painted, with a cast iron knocker on it. Miss Margaret was clearly house-proud and rightly so. Pamela stood with her sketch pad under one arm, her camera bag over the other, and watched as Finian clacked the knocker three times. It was Finian who had arranged this meeting when she'd mentioned she was starting work on the next volume in her *Children of the Troubles* series. Though series seemed a grand word for something with one published volume and a bunch of doodled ideas on sheets of paper, which was what volume two currently consisted of. Finian had been one of her very first subjects, and had featured heavily in the first volume.

Miss Margaret opened the door a few seconds later. She was a tiny woman, and every detail of her was neat and dainty, from her daisy-print dress to her crisply-starched apron to her immaculate lavender-rinsed hair. She looked like a fairy tale illustrator's vision of a kindly grandmother. Which she might well be, but Pamela had lived long enough in and around Belfast to know better. Any woman of a certain age in this city, who'd raised children in these streets, was tougher than old boot leather, dainty appearances notwithstanding.

"Miss Margaret," said Finian, "this is the lady I told ye about. Pamela, this is Miss Margaret."

"Come in, come in, or the necks will be cranin' out the curtains all up an' down the row. Come in, come in."

She hustled them through the narrow hall, and off into the kitchen, which lay to the right. Every kitchen in the entire street would be in the same spot, as every house had the identical layout. The kitchen was small and clean, and painted with bright blues and yellows, which glowed in the mellow sunlight of the spring afternoon. The delightful smell of ginger, butter and sugar hung in the air and Pamela's stomach rumbled a little in response.

"Please sit down," Miss Margaret said, untying the apron she wore and placing it neatly over the towel rack which hung by the sink. "There's tea almost ready, an' ginger biscuits an' a lovely Victoria sponge to go along with it."

"Thank you," Pamela said. She put her camera bag down and knelt to take the camera out. It was all ready with the lens she best liked for close-to work like this, where the subject was in a mix of artificial and natural light. Some of these houses tended to be dark as well, and it often depended on the time of day, and if it was overcast or raining. She ran a hand over the camera. It was her pride and joy—a Leica that Casey had found in a pawn shop in Boston some years ago.

"Ye'll be gentle with the lass, aye?"

Pamela looked up to find Miss Margaret with more than a trace of apprehension on her face.

"You don't need to worry," she said, quietly. "I won't push her on anything, and I won't put anything in the book—pictures or stories—that she's not happy with."

"She's a bit of a history, an' it's not been an easy road for her. She's a sensitive girl."

Pamela nodded. "She can take the lead, and I'll only talk to her about things she's comfortable with."

Miss Margaret nodded, and then called up the stairs. "Ciara love, come down, Finian an' the lady photographer are here."

There was the sound of feet padding down the stairs and then a girl came into the kitchen. She was small like her grandmother, narrow and slender and light on her feet. She wore a pale blue jumper and a pair of dungarees and she immediately reminded Pamela—rather painfully—of Sylvie, Patrick's first wife. She had large and very dark brown eyes, rimmed with thick treacle-gold lashes. Her hair was a pale blonde, as soft and ephemeral looking as dandelion fluff, and she had a delicate winsomeness to her, which would translate beautifully to paper. She was also clearly nervous. This, Pamela was used to, most people were shy when interviewed, as though they feared they might be asked to plumb the depths of their soul and offer it up for public consumption. Usually a little reassurance went a long way.

They gathered at the table together, and Miss Margaret put down a plate of the aforementioned ginger biscuits and a Victoria sponge which gleamed with a ruby filling of strawberry jam. Last came a large brown betty with a thickly-knit cozy wrapped around it.

Tea was poured all around in delicate cups, and Pamela realized the good china had been brought out for their visit. She took a few swallows and had a piece of the Victoria sponge and chatted with Ciara and her grandmother to give everyone time to relax. Finian, she noted, was unusually quiet. Usually the boy could talk the ear off a person's head with little trouble to himself. They spent a good thirty minutes in this fashion before Pamela put down her teacup and smiled at Ciara.

"I'll just ask you a few questions," she said, "and you answer me either as briefly or with as much length as you like. It's your story and I want you to tell it. I'll be just making a few sketches as we chat—are you comfortable with that?"

"Aye," the girl nodded, the delicate stalk of her neck little more substantial than the stem of the aforementioned dandelion. She smiled at Pamela, just quick, but a lovely flood of colour suffused her face, as though the wee dandelion had turned into a newly opening rose for a minute. She was a beautiful girl, and Pamela began to see why Finian—who was casting glances at her every few seconds—had been so insistent that Pamela interview and draw her.

She set out her tools—her pencils and sketch pad, the charcoal she used for shading and to rough in the outlines of bones and flesh. The more detailed sketches she would do at home, when she'd had time to muse over what would best represent the child she was drawing.

"Now then," Miss Margaret said, donning a scarf and raincoat with brisk efficiency, "I'm away to the shops for a bit. Ye'll be in good hands with Ciara, though. Ciara love, keep an eye out for Mrs. Porter, it's her meal day." She patted her hair one last time, and then was out the door, net bag tucked tidily over one arm, and formidable handbag swinging jauntily off the other.

"Ready?" Pamela asked, smiling at Ciara in reassurance.

The girl nodded, though she was still visibly nervous. Pamela had a few questions she used with most of the children she interviewed, just casual questions designed to get them to open up a little. People, even young ones, liked to tell their stories, they just needed encouragement to find the words to begin.

Thus far she had found the girls tended to be more forthcoming about their lives—they would express their hopes and dreams freely. They seemed to have the ability to see a way forward even when the boys did not, even if that way forward was a somewhat misty ribbon of road into the unknown.

The boys were far more reticent though, with the exception of Finian that is, she thought, looking fondly at the curly head which was bent over her sketchpad. Finian did not have any reservations about sticking his shapely nose into people's things and business. The lad had a roguish charm about him though that made people forgive him most of his sins. Still, she worried about him because she knew he was more susceptible than some to the siren call of rebellion.

Often for boys of his age the IRA was thoroughly romanticized, and if they had a family history within the republican world, then it could seem inevitable to them, it gave purpose to their lives, and allowed them a way to give voice and action to the pain of always being aware you were a second-class citizen in your own country. Most families would have chilling stories about the violence done to parents and grandparents by the other side. For them the IRA was an organic part of their world, it was made up of their friends, their neighbors and often their family. That had been the case for Patrick and Casey, and for Casey at least, the road to him had seemed both obvious and fated. His father, Brian, had not seen it in the same light, and she knew Casey's original forays into the world of republican rebellion had caused no small trouble at home for him. Finian ran with a rough crew, and he had an uncle in the IRA, so the door, as it had been for Casey and Pat, was just that little bit more open. She had become very fond of the children she interviewed for her books, but her original three—Finian, Ambrose and Bernie—would always hold a special place in her heart.

She picked up her sketchpad and looked at her subject, who gave her a half-hearted smile.

"What were you doing before Finian and I arrived?" Pamela asked.

"I was winding wool for my nan," she said, looking down at a basket of skeins on the floor at her feet.

"Then just keep doing that," Pamela said, taking the lens cap off the Leica. Ciara chose a skein of vivid red, the wool thick and soft-looking, and set to winding it around a small chunk of cardboard.

"I'm going to just take a few snaps, so I've got a record to refer back to and also hopefully get one or two for the book as well."

Ciara nodded, her fine skin flushed from the kitchen warmth. Pamela moved around as unobtrusively as she could, taking pictures from a few different angles. Over the years she had learned the art of disappearing behind the camera so that the subject wasn't aware of her as a photographer, but rather as just someone they could chat with, so that when she did have to issue orders about turning their head, or smiling, or not smiling they would do it without thought, and therefore the expression and pose would be as natural as was possible.

The scene hung in the haze of the mild afternoon sun, gilding Finian's hair, glowing softly in the teacups and pot, and making the wool in Ciara's delicate hands seem little more substantial than a puff of scarlet smoke.

Movement outside caught Ciara's attention and she stood to look out the kitchen window, pausing in her wool-winding. "Oh, it's Mrs. Porter," she exclaimed. "Finian, there's the basket on the cooker, Nan left it for her. Will ye run it out to her?"

Finian nodded, pleased Pamela suspected, to do anything the girl might ask of him.

Ciara lingered by the window for a moment watching Finian take the basket down the walkway. "My nan makes her a meal or two every week. She comes by to get it, but she never comes in and she never speaks."

"Do you know why?" Pamela asked quietly, getting up to catch the light as it lent a fine green-gold shimmer to Ciara's face.

"Her little boy disappeared from a bus stop just down the way about five years ago. She's not been right since. No one ever knew what happened to him. Well, him an' his friend actually, there were the two of them. They were there one minute an' simply gone the next. To this very day, no one knows what happened to them. At first, the police insisted they'd simply run off somewhere an' would eventually turn up, because they'd done it before, gone to the seashore for the day instead of goin' to school. It was thought someone ought to have seen somethin' as they'd disappeared off such a busy road but people don't talk to the police around here. Mind, the local 'Ra said as people should talk to the police if they had any information, but still no one came forward. It was like they vanished right into thin air that day." A small shudder shook the girl's slender frame and she returned to the table to sit, and took up her teacup, clutching it between her hands for warmth.

"His mam looked for months and months, an' the searchin' an' not findin' made her crazy, my nan said. I believe that don't you? That if you look an' look for someone ye love, an' don't find them, ye could go mad after a time."

"Yes," Pamela said, "I do believe that." She didn't just believe it, she knew it right down to the very marrow of her bones. There had been times when she thought she would actually go mad and never be fit for life again when Casey was gone.

Ciara looked over at her. "Finian told me about yer husband returnin' home after bein' away for so long."

Away. The term was one she'd used herself, for comfort's sake, as though Casey had only been away with the fairies, and would return to find years had gone by, while for him only a few hours had passed. In an odd way, it had been true. So much had happened in his absence and she thought he often felt the confusion and discombobulation of someone who truly had been taken away by the fairies and returned to a world he no longer recognized.

"Yes, he did," she said, still surprised by the reality of it. She had prayed endlessly for him to return to her and he had.

"That's a miracle," Ciara said without any hint of cynicism or wonder, but rather a plain statement of fact.

"It is," Pamela said, stopping herself from adding the fact that miracles were not entirely uncomplicated things. Still, every time the realization hit her afresh—that he had returned, that he had come home, that he was alive and relatively whole, she felt a sort of joy that was so sharp it felt like it cut something in her soul.

Ciara looked like she was on the verge of saying something in response but Finian returned just then, and she simply gave him a quick smile and said, "Thank ye."

Pamela began to rough in the parameters of the first sketch, placing a dot in the centre of the page, and then another below for where she would place the tip of Ciara's dainty nose.

The bones were always first, for to capture the bones—literally the skull beneath the skin—was always for her the foundation to a good likeness. The bones were the scaffolding, the flesh the plaster and paint. Ciara's bones were delicate, airy in design, and she immediately pictured the girl as a sprite rising up from a field of wildflowers, caught on a draught of spring air. The light was perfect, casting her in sun and shadow, highlighting the delicacy of her profile.

"I'm not sure where to begin," Ciara said, hesitantly, "only that I've lived here in Belfast all my life. I've not been anywhere, not beyond goin' up to Derry for a few days. You—you will have lived other places, an' travelled a lot?"

Pamela realized that the girl viewed her as exotic, having been to ports of far call, and having lived in a place as storied as America sometimes was portrayed here. "Yes, I was born in New York and grew up there. I lived in Boston too for a while. Belfast is home now, though."

"I should like that one day, to travel, to see things I've only read about or seen in picture books." There was a wistful look to Ciara's face, as though such things held a dream-like quality for her, and that she couldn't be quite sure it would happen.

"You will," Pamela assured her, hoping that her words proved true for the girl. It was too easy to get caught in the grind of life, to suddenly have mouths to feed, and an unemployed mate in a society where it was harder for a Catholic male to get and keep a job than it was for a Protestant.

"For everyone there is a place where your story truly begins. It's there in your mind, it's the one thread sticking out of the tapestry, and it's maybe a different colour than the others. Just close your eyes and you'll see it."

Ciara obediently closed her eyes. The girl's skin was so fine that the light seemed to shine right through it in places, and there was the purity of the novitiate about her. Her ears were softly pink, and two soft streaks of colour showed in her pale cheeks. Pamela thought this was more due to the girl realizing that Finian couldn't take his eyes off her than anything else. A moment later, eyes still closed, Ciara began to speak, slowly at first but picking up speed as she went.

"When I was five we inherited a house on Percy Street. The street was mixed at the time—both Prods an' Catholics. I was only wee, but before that we'd had a cramped flat in Sevastopol Street, an' so this house seemed a mansion. I had my own room, an' so did my brother. There was a big kitchen that got a lot of sunlight, when the sun did shine, that is. We had neighbours that were Prods, I played with Protestant children, an' didn't know any different. Maybe six months after we moved in there though, I got cornered by a group of girls—big girls, or big to me at least because they were nine an' ten. Ye know what a difference a few inches an' months makes at that age. They slapped me around a bit, an' scared the bejaysus out of me, as ye might imagine. Kept callin' me a wee Fenian whore. It was the first time I'd encountered raw hate like that, an' I didn't understand it. Well," Ciara opened her eyes, "there is no understandin' hate like that, really."

"No, there isn't," Pamela said, having been the recipient more than once of just that sort of hatred.

"We continued to live there, an' I simply avoided those girls. I had wee friends who were Prods, an' I think for most of us, we were too small to know we were meant to hate one another. It was nice for a time."

For a time. There was a wealth of meaning in those words, which she understood only too well. Time was always short in one way or another in this country.

"There were riots—well, ye were here in '69 Finian says, so ye remember how it was."

"I do," she said. It had felt like the world had gone entirely mad, shooting in the streets, fires everywhere. Her own home burning down and her locked inside it with a man who had once raped her and had clearly intended to do it again that night, until she had been rescued by a most unlikely saviour. Casey had believed her dead for a short time during that horrible twenty-four hours.

"My da knew it was likely to get bad, though there wasn't a great deal of warnin'. When he saw the Protestant businesses shutterin' their windows though he thought there was something bad in the air. So he made our house as secure as he could. We sat on the stairs, me an' him, mammy an' wee

Michael. We were holdin' pokers an' hammers, an' my daddy had a shotgun. Even at that we knew they'd overwhelm us quick enough should they get in. We could hear them poundin' at the door and windows, howlin' as if they were animals smellin' blood. My parents were tryin' to be brave, but even us wee ones could tell they were afraid, an' that terrified me more than anythin'.

"They couldn't get in, an' so they went after a house a few down. Ye could see the shadows of the flames leapin' on the upstairs walls. It was the first time I knew that somethin' so pretty could also be incredibly destructive. We survived the night, an' in the mornin' when we managed to venture out beyond our door it was like steppin' into the aftermath of a great battle. Some of the houses toward the bottom of the street were smokin' ruins, just shells of what had been homes the night before. There was glass an' bottles smashed all over the street. We could hear guns bein' fired just a block or two away. So we're standin' there in this hellish landscape, despairin', wonderin' if all of our neighbours survived the night when this woman came up to my mam an' said, 'Youse best be out today, because ye're getting burned out tonight.'

"We had to leave with just the clothes on our backs, an' what we could shove into a suitcase because there wasn't time for anything else. We holed up with my nan. My mam went back the next day, an' they hadn't burned the house out but took it over instead. People were in there takin' our belongins'—furniture an' such, everything my parents had worked so hard for durin' the years they'd been married. My mam yelled at them to leave her things alone, an' they just ignored her, kept haulin' furniture an' dishes out of the house. Finally, she just left. We had to start over, an' my da was never really the same. But I think he might have recovered eventually, if it hadn't been for my uncle getting killed."

And here, thought Pamela, they had come to the core of the tale. It was, in its roots, an old story. Old at least from the view of republicans in Belfast. Everyone had someone who'd died as a result of the conflict, in one way or another, that was what it always came down to. A small, dirty war provided a cover for all kinds of sins. If she'd been murdered by Constable Blackwood that terrible night two years ago, her death would have been chalked up to a Catholic woman caught out walking the streets of a neighbourhood she should have known better than to be in. In fact, her life had only been spared because she'd struck pre-emptively, going to Noah to rid herself of the threat of the constable. Yet another sin covered over by the unending fighting and blood that, at times, seemed soaked into the very ground they all walked upon. Except, she thought, recalling the interview with Detective Holroyd, not as well covered over as she'd hoped.

"My Uncle Jim was the quiet one in the family, an' da said he was a little slow. Not so much so as ye'd notice but it took him longer to take in directions or instructions and he often had to mull on an idea or suggestion for a few hours before he understood what it was about. He was harmless, an' he was always lovely with me an' my brother Michael. He'd take us out on Saturday afternoons, up the coast an' away from the city, an' he'd always buy us an ice cream. We'd go to the seashore, an' play for hours. I still remember lookin' way up the glens an' askin' my uncle 'What's that, does it have a name', an' him sayin' 'that's the wild deep blue yonder, Ceecee.' It was the Atlantic; ye know the blue changes that far north, an' ye sense ye're lookin' at somethin' separate an' altogether more frightenin' and fascinatin' than the water runnin' about yer toes.

"Uncle Jim always took the time to teach us the names of things, plants an' animals an' all the wee swimmin' creatures of the sea. They'd lost their parents—my da an' him—when they were young, an' it had just been the two of them for a long time. My da always looked after my Uncle Jim, an' made certain he got to work, an' had a bit of a social life as well."

Ciara looked down at the wool in her hands, but Pamela knew she was seeing something else entirely. A young man, someone well-loved, the way you loved a man who showed you the world as a child. Who showed you early and often, how gentle and kind a good man could be.

Ciara took a breath, the delicate line of her throat trembling as she resumed her story. "He got caught up on the edge of a riot. He'd only gone out to see if he could find his mates, an' have a bit of craic for the evenin'. People who were there said it was mad, lads throwin' bricks an' bottles, an' a few Molotov cocktails so that there was fire an' smoke everywhere. No one could see, an' there was confusion all over the streets, an' then the soldiers went after some of the boys. My uncle started to run, he would panic in situations like that an' just go, not even knowin' which direction he was headed.

"There were witnesses there who said they saw three soldiers run after him, an' one of them yelled *shoot him, shoot him!* And then one did, shot him right in the back, he just fell there, dead. Nineteen years old an' dead. An' for what?" Ciara asked, though Pamela knew she wasn't looking for an answer because there wasn't one, at least not a good one. The only answers were ones that could not satisfy, and never brought justice. Frightened soldiers caught up in the adrenaline of terror, too young and too inexperienced for the land which was considered the most dangerous place for a British soldier to serve in the world. Slippery trigger fingers without a moment's pause for regret, for thought of the life at the other end of your bullet. Warfare in Belfast didn't abide by the rules of regular combat. It couldn't when you were fighting in the streets with civilians on every side of you.

"I was too small to understand what had happened, and how a lack of justice can hurt the people left behind so badly. My nan said it corroded my da's soul, an' she was right. He was never the same. He was sad, he was angry an' there was never goin' to be justice through the courts. The peelers laughed in his face, an' said his brother had deserved to die. When ye're that angry, an' there's nowhere to turn, well, as my nan says, the anger will out somewhere."

"What happened then?" Pamela asked, though she knew, God help her, she knew.

"He killed a man, it's that simple really."

Pamela was careful not to show any surprise, and discovered she didn't really feel any. There was sometimes an inevitability about death here that made the means of it not terribly shocking.

"It was a long time before that happened, but he started into the drink shortly after my uncle's murder. My parents' marriage was never the same, an' often my da felt like a stranger to me. I remember before though, when he was still fun an' kind an' filled my world."

"I had a father like that too," Pamela said, feeling the pang in her heart that always came when she realized how long it had been since her father had died. "And where is he now?" she asked, softly, though she knew there were only two options.

"He's in the Kesh. He's been there for five years. My mam died of the cancer two years after he went in, so then I came to live with my nan. I see him on visitin' days, but he's not keen on me comin' too often."

Casey had felt the same way when he'd been interned on a British prison ship—he hadn't liked her seeing him there, caged, and unable to protect or help her with all that she faced outside. She understood it, just as she understood how Ciara's father might feel about his young daughter coming to see him in prison. Still, a woman needed to see her men—father, husband, brother, son—just to reassure herself that he still existed, that he hadn't become a ghost in a story she told herself for comfort when another night had arrived without his return home. Without that reassurance it was too easy to succumb to a certain hopelessness.

"Living here—has it changed you?" Ciara asked. Pamela looked up from her sketchpad, a little surprised by the question. It was hard to know where to begin to answer—yes, it had changed her, in ways both good and bad. She was not the somewhat naïve girl who'd landed on these shores nearly twelve years earlier, but she had gained much as well. Her children, Casey, Jamie, Patrick. All of them were her family. A non-traditional one to be sure, but she wouldn't trade them for anything simpler.

She opened her mouth to answer, but was stopped by the kitchen door suddenly swinging wide. A head poked in, swiftly followed by a body, and then two more bodies right behind. Three men, all in balaclavas, and all with rifles in hand.

Finian, Ciara and herself all froze in place, a tableau vivant arranged just so—Finian reaching for another biscuit, Ciara with the ball of wool mid-ravel, and her with a wee knife halfway through the charcoal, a curl of wood poised to drop. *Belfast, Art, Domesticity and Ginger Biscuits*—it might have been called. Or simply *Heart in Throat*, which certainly would have been, Pamela thought, her own heart pounding like a mad rabbit, the more accurate title.

"Is Miss Margaret home?" the first man asked sharply. Finian shook his head, apparently rendered mute by the mens' sudden appearance. The men, with barely a glance at the three of them, moved through and headed up the stairs. Over the clatter of their boots Pamela could hear the unmistakable rumble of army vehicles moving into the narrow lanes of Ballymurphy.

Ciara got up from her chair slowly, flapping her hands a little in distress. "Oh dear, I wish my nan was here."

Finian was looking more than a little peaky, and Pamela turned a glare on him. "*Finian?*"

He swallowed and gave her a weak smile. "This is a safe house for the 'Ra."

"*What?*" She hissed, trying to keep her voice down and not yell at the towheaded child in front of her.

"Miss Margaret keeps her doors open to any of the lads as need it."

Ciara nodded rather frantically, still flapping her hands like a distraught chicken. "She does."

"Finian, you might have warned me."

"Aye," he winced a little at the look on her face, "I'm right sorry about that. It's been quiet of late, didn't think this was goin' to happen."

The trucks had stopped outside, the rumble of the engines causing the house to vibrate and setting the teacups to rattling in their saucers.

Pamela reviewed their situation with what objectivity could be managed—the facts numbered only two, so the review was brief—they were stuck in a house with three armed-to-the-teeth gunmen just up the narrow stairs, and said house was surrounded by British soldiers, who were also, one had to assume, armed to the teeth. It turned out the objective viewpoint was much the same as the subjective one. As Casey might have put it in his succinctly poetic way, they were '*focked ten ways from Sunday*'. She felt a hysterical urge to laugh, though there was, admittedly, little humour in the situation.

"I think we'd best get down on the floor, in case there's shooting," she said, realizing she needed to protect the teens as best she might under the circumstances. The three of them hunkered down in the corner where the cabinets met, huddling together as if somehow being close to one another could provide a bulwark against the violence they knew was coming.

The door flew open again and then everything went a hollow white, as though the little house had been suddenly thrust into the core of a burning star and there was neither sound nor air. Then there was a great *whoosh* of wind and a noise like the end of the universe had arrived with an enormous thump, in the midst of Ballymurphy. There was a tremendously sharp pain in the side of her head and she found herself afraid to even reach up to touch it; the explosion had knocked her down onto her face on the floor and she could feel the crunch of broken glass beneath her. She didn't move though, because the soldiers were inside the house now. Sound became impression at such times, mixed up with all the other emotions and senses and there wasn't time in the scramble to sort one feeling from the next—shock, terror, fury, the booming and cracking as if the world had split like an overcooked egg, and the feel of wet pain on her head. And then the cold and unmistakable nudge of a gun to the back of her neck. She lay as flat as she could, knowing the slightest false move could result in a bullet right through her brain.

It felt as though an eternity passed as she lay there on the floor, soldiers shouting, though it seemed as though their voices were muffled and she feared something was terribly wrong with both her ear and the side of her head. A hand grabbed her roughly by the upper arm, and pulled her to her feet. A stream of something wet and warm ran down the side of her face—blood, she thought and wondered dazedly, if there was actually a hole in the side of her head. She wanted to look round and make certain Finian knew to keep quiet and that Ciara was in one piece but the soldier was shoving her ahead of him, and it took everything she had not to stumble over the bits of broken chairs and crockery.

All she saw was what was in front of her—dust everywhere, hanging in thick clouds in the air, the cooker a mess of wires and broken porcelain and one teacup with its contents still gently steaming, sitting untouched on the table. He pushed her outside ahead of him, where orders were being shouted and there was general chaos. Three army vehicles were parked willy-nilly, soldiers kneeling all around them, rifles cocked and aimed at the upstairs windows of Miss Margaret's home. Pamela was acutely aware of being caught between two sets of trigger-happy men.

Her heart was pounding in her chest, blood swooshing erratically in her veins, and there was a thumping panic in every cell which made her certain she was about to die. The whine of bullets split the air around her, the sound like that of a large and angry bee, and a soldier shoved her to the ground and yelled, 'Stay there!' A bullet hit the ground near her head, with the distinctive thunk of something moving at high velocity hitting an immovable surface. And then suddenly it was profoundly quiet, and she knew there were dead men in Miss Margaret's pristine home. It was a Belfast quiet—the sort that descended after violence tore apart the workaday noise of children and cars, and mothers chatting as they wheeled buggies. Everyone would be in their houses, curtains drawn, doors locked, hoping not to draw the eye of the god of war. She chanced looking sideways to check on the children. Like her, they were both facedown, but with, as far as she could tell, all their bits and pieces still in order. Finian even managed an abbreviated nod to reassure her that he was all right. She noted that he was holding Ciara's hand; ever the chancer, he'd seized his moment when it presented itself.

The ground beneath her forehead was wet and churned up from the soldier's boots, but it felt wonderfully cool and solid. The jolt of worry over how bad her injury might be shot through her again, leaving her queasy. She didn't dare move right now though, for fear a nervous soldier might shoot her.

"You can get up," one of the soldiers said, "but do it slowly with your hands up above your head."

Pamela wanted to ask how she was meant to get up off the ground without the assistance of her hands, but felt the point might be lost on the young man in front of her. She managed in the end and wished she had the courage to touch the side of her head, but she didn't dare bring her hands down. The soldier backed her toward the wall of the house opposite from Miss Margaret's. Both Finian and Ciara were lined up too, hands up, faces thankfully free of blood.

"Are ye all right, Pamela?" Finian asked, his face smeared with dirt and half of one of his eyebrows singed off.

"I think so," she said, blinking in an effort to clear her head. "Is—is the side of my head...can you look?" She couldn't put into words the thoughts she was having. Could she be lucid with a chunk of her skull missing?

Finian nodded. "Turn it toward me."

She shut her eyes, not wanting to see his expression.

"Ye're fine, it's not but a mess of stirabout."

"Stirabout?"

"Aye, oats, porridge—it must have been blown clear off the cooker. 'Tis fortunate the pot didn't hit ye—or did it?"

"Yes it did but it doesn't hurt terribly," she said, feeling much improved, porridge being so wonderfully benign in comparison to what she thought was dripping down the side of her head. "Are you and Ciara all right?"

"Aye, I think so."

Ciara didn't speak, but she nodded, her eyes trained on the soldiers.

Two ambulances arrived then, along with three police cars, all trundling down the narrow lane. Pamela felt her body freeze up a little. There were police in the RUC who did not wish her well, and one had threatened to kill her some time back. While that particular threat had been removed, she was all too aware he'd had friends on the force, and she wasn't entirely certain which ones had known about his enmity with her.

Thus it was to her great relief, to see a familiar and friendly face emerge from one of the police cars. Constable Fred, looking like everyone's favourite grandfather, rosy cheeks and laughing blue eyes at odds with the serious expression he wore just now.

A small, cold hand slipped into hers just then and she realized Ciara was frightened. The girl was shaking, but her lips were tightly pressed together as if she would not give them so much as a word.

"It will be okay," Pamela said, "just tell them the truth, but don't give them anything they don't ask for. Keep it to the bare minimum. If a yes or no answer will do, then that's all you say."

Ciara nodded, swallowing convulsively, her hand clutching Pamela's so tightly that she thought she could feel the bruises forming in her bones.

"Will I see you again?"

She nodded. "Of course you will. We'll talk later, I'll have you out to my house—you and Finian, it will be a bit quieter at least."

"Okay," Ciara said and giving Pamela one last frightened look, went off with a policeman to be questioned. Or at least that was Pamela's hope.

Constable Fred came to her. "Well lass, I'd as soon not be seein' yerself here today."

"All things considered, I'd rather not be here myself," she said.

"Are ye all right? Ye've a mess on the side of yer head there." He peered at the matted hair, which still held drippings of oatmeal despite her efforts to get rid of the worst of it.

"Yes, I think so, I'm shaky and I can't hear out of this ear, so you'll have to talk to the left one."

"We're meant to question ye, so try to look appropriately terrified by me, would ye?" he said, looking entirely stern, lest anyone was watching them. "Just give me the outlines of what ye were doin' there, because granted it doesn't look good bein' caught in a house with three IRA gunmen. So just tell me the why an' the how."

So she told him, why she was there, why the two children were there and how the gunmen had simply come in without a word of by-your-leave. Because it was the truth, and because he knew her, Constable Fred believed her. When she had finished, he nodded and said, "Now if ye promise me that I'll not see ye again any time soon, I'll let ye go. Dependin' on how things go here, ye may be called back in for questions, but I'll try to save ye that if I can. Before ye go entirely though, I want ye looked over by the attendants, ye've a nasty bruise on the one side of yer face an' ye'll need him to check yer ear for damage. Is that a deal?"

"Yes," she said, utterly grateful that Constable Fred had been on this particular call.

Constable Fred nodded and then handed her on to the medic. The ambulance attendant had the brisk efficiency about him which she had found in so many of the men and women who worked in the various emergency services.

"Vision blurred?"

"No."

"Ears ringing?"

"A little, I can't hear out of this one." She pointed to her right ear, aware the porridge was solidifying into a sort of glue in her hair.

"I'm goin' to put my finger up, an' I want you to touch the tip of it with yer own an' then touch the tip of yer nose as quickly as ye can."

Pamela did so, relieved to find the test simple to execute.

"All right then, I'm goin' to just check yer head over."

She nodded her permission and he checked her over with a swift economy which was reassuring. Working in Belfast, one of the worst places in the world for emergency trauma—the Royal Victoria was renowned for its trauma unit—she knew he had seen much worse than a bruised and banged up woman who couldn't hear out of one ear. He flicked a light in her eyes, peering into each one.

"That's good, yer pupils are both reactin' normally an' yer skull is intact. Ye don't seem to have any points where it's painin' ye in particular. Ye're goin' to have a goose egg on the side where ye got hit, though, an' it's possible ye're mildly concussed. Yer hearin' should restore itself in the next couple of days, but if it's not improvin' noticeably by tomorrow mornin' ye need to get in to see a doctor."

"I will," she said. The man gave her a stern look.

"See that ye do, a concussion grenade is naught to mess about with. Ye're lucky it wasn't worse. Have ye someone at home who can keep an eye on ye the next day or two?"

"Yes," she said, not wanting to go into her rather complicated living arrangements, nor the players who came and went on the stage of her home. She knew if she called him, Vanya would come stay with her for a night or two. Pru was at Jamie's looking after Kolya for the week.

"All right then, here's some paracetamol, ye're goin' to have a grand headache for a few days, but ye can't have anything stronger than that. An' absolutely no alcohol either. If ye feel faint, or the headache gets really bad, ye need to get into the hospital right away."

Constable Fred was waiting for her when the medic finished with her. From somewhere he'd managed to get her a cup of tea. She took it gratefully, realizing she hadn't eaten anything other than a slice of toast and a bit of Victoria sponge today. "The young ones are fine," he said, "the other paramedic checked them over, an' they've been sent down the road to the lass's aunt. The wee girl was shaken up, but the boy was just angry."

"Can you blame him? We were sitting there chatting and having tea when the men came in." She flicked a glance up toward the shattered window of the room where the men had holed up.

"Two dead, an' one taken into custody," Constable Fred said shortly. She understood his tone, it was no picnic being an RUC officer. Every single policeman had to check the undercarriage of their car each morning before setting off for work, lest a bomb had been attached to it overnight. Pat had to do the same, but not because of the IRA.

"They threw a concussion grenade into the kitchen. They might have hurt all of us much worse than they did, that might be why the boy is angry," Pamela said, not wanting to use Finian's name for some reason. It made little sense, as the police would have ascertained his identity right away, and yet in this world you kept what you could private, held tight against the various indignities that could be visited on a person.

"Oh, I know lass. I just hate to see it happen to another generation, this hate, this pain. You an' I both know where this ends up, an' that's with that young man in prison or in a body bag long before his time."

"Yes, I do know," she said, the situation was far more complicated and yet it was just this simple too—an angry young man, a police force with a few corrupt members, a trigger-happy bunch of scared soldiers and an organization that appealed greatly to an angry young man with no way to vent his frustrations other than through the perpetuation of violence and imprisonment.

"I've contacted yer brother-in-law to come pick ye up. Yer wee car's windows were shot out, an' I think it's best that ye don't drive until ye're feelin' better. He said he'll come get ye as quick as he can."

"Thank you," she said, wanting nothing more than to go home and have a bath. Kathleen would need feeding soon, as it was likely she'd gone through the bottles Pamela had left behind with Gert.

"Can ye hear yet?" he asked, pointing to her bad ear.

She shook her head, an action which made her dizzy once again.

"What did the paramedic have to say?"

"He had a look and thinks it's temporary. If I don't start getting my hearing back within the next couple of days though, I'm to go see a doctor. I—my camera is still in there, I don't suppose I could go get it?"

"No, I don't suppose ye can," Constable Fred replied. "But I'll see if I can't find yer camera an' things for ye later, if they'll let me in."

"Thank you, I appreciate it," she said, fearing that the camera might well have been broken in the explosion. She'd placed it on the table, when she'd picked up her sketchpad.

"Is that yer man there?" he asked, looking down the street to where a truck she recognized all too well had pulled up and parked. Sitting in the driver's seat, and looking like it would be no stretch for steam to start emitting in streams from his ears, was Casey. She swallowed down the bolt of fear that went through her, wondering where Patrick was.

"Yes," she said with the resignation of a prisoner about to climb into the dock, "that's my man." She wished suddenly that the police had chosen to arrest her. It might have been a great deal less fearsome than facing Casey, and in jail there might have been the hope of tea and a bun.

Constable Fred walked her down to where the barricade stood, and where Casey now waited, arms folded across his chest, for her.

"Thank ye for lookin' after her," he said to the constable, "I'll take over from here."

He took her arm, and steered her toward his truck, walking so swiftly she had to half-run to keep up. When they reached the battered truck, he opened the door for her and made certain she was seated before shutting the door and walking around to his own side. He got in, turned the ignition over and began to drive, all without speaking a single word to her.

"I-I thought he'd called Patrick. I'm sorry," she said, chancing a look at him as he drove through the traffic. He nodded curtly, and shifted lanes on his way out of the city.

"He did call Patrick, only I happened to be there droppin' off the toaster that I'd fixed for him, when the call came through. When Pat told me what had happened, I said I'd come fetch ye."

"Well, thank you," she said, resisting the urge to fall weeping into his arms. It was a move that would have been impeded by both the gear shift and the man's driving, but it was the look on his face more than anything that made her keep stiffly to her own side of the vehicle.

He remained silent and white-lipped until they were well into the countryside. When he broke his silence, he wasn't speaking directly to her and being that her right ear was the one facing him, she only caught occasional snatches of words, but it was enough to make her grateful for her lack of hearing.

"…most aggravating woman ever born…if ye live through yer next escapade, then let me tell ye… on the blessed green earth ye were thinkin', ye're a mother after all…an' if ye think…"

After much more in this vein, during which time she looked out the window at the fields and stone walls rolling past, he spoke loudly enough so that she could hear every word.

"Pamela, have ye listened to anything I've said?"

"I can't hear you on that side."

"What the hell do ye mean ye can't hear me?"

"It's only temporary, just the blast from the grenade rendered me deaf in my right ear. The medic assures me there's no permanent damage," she added quickly, seeing the storm clouds gathering with force in Casey's face. This, of course, was a bit of a lie, but it was a lie of self-preservation just at present.

"Rendered ye deaf? Jaysus Christ almighty, woman, *rendered ye deaf!* Do ye hear yerself? No, of course ye don't. Is it too much to hope it also knocked some sense into ye? Aye," he muttered, answering his own question, "I suppose it is too much to hope." He added something in Irish then which she was quite glad she couldn't understand.

A few moments later, Casey pulled the truck over in a narrow lane that petered out into a farmer's field. He turned to her and she knew she hadn't mistaken his mood. He was absolutely furious. He merely looked at her, the dark eyes as grey as smoke. She swallowed, feeling a choke of fear. She might not know him as she once had, but she was not unfamiliar with the expression he wore.

"Are you mad?" she asked, feeling it was better to get this over with.

He laughed. It wasn't a laugh filled with joy or humour though. "Am I *mad*? Jaysus Murphy, woman. I just found ye in a house surrounded by the bomb squad an' men wieldin' automatic rifles. Can ye possibly—maybe ye know just for the novelty of it—take a day off from gettin' yerself in life-threatenin' trouble?"

"I didn't…" she began hotly, and then stopped at his raised eyebrow.

"I know ye didn't get yerself in there deliberately, but I have never known another person with such a talent for findin' trouble."

"Except for you," she retorted. He opened his mouth to say something and then shut it.

"Ha," she said, "you've no comeback for that, do you?"

He shook his head. "I'm startin' to remember why I smoked," he said, still glowering. "Did I drink as well?"

"Rarely," she said tartly.

"Bit of a miracle, that," he grumbled and then turned and unexpectedly took her hand in his. "Ye scared me, an' I'm in a temper about it, but I'll get over it, as I have many times before."

"I'm sorry, but it's not like you haven't caused me a great deal of worry in your own time."

He nodded. "More than worry, Pamela, heartbreak an' fear, an' I'm sorry for it too."

"I know you are," she said, feeling the prickle of tears in her eyes.

She looked out over the field beyond and took a deep breath, trying to regain some composure. It was an edge place, this time, that carefully balanced set of moments between afternoon and evening, before the dark gathered up her skirts and walked softly over the horizon. There was a daffodil sunset, pale yellow and luminous, while far off to the east a silver sheen glimmered on the hilltops, heralding the rising moon. It was beautifully serene, and she felt some of the tension go out of her. She looked at the man beside her and realized he was, as of yet, untouched by the bucolic serenity which surrounded them.

"If you've something else to say, you might as well spare your spleen and get it out now," she said, resigned to a verbal pasting.

He sighed, and she stiffened her spine a little, bracing herself for the words she knew were coming. Therefore, she was very surprised by what he did say.

"Would ye mind if I kissed ye?" he asked, his words somewhat terse.

"Of course you can kiss me. I'm rather surprised that you want to though."

"I always want to, even when I'm mad," he said, in a rather aggrieved tone of voice. "Though, admittedly, biting seems a bit more attractive in moments like this or just turnin' ye over my knee."

She laughed. "Casey, both of those actions would lead to things far worse than kissing."

"Far worse or far better," he said, and gave her one of his old grins, a flash of white and dimple in the midst of his heavy afternoon stubble. He leaned toward her and touched his mouth to hers. The kiss, unlike his words, was soft and searching and made her ache inside for both the want of him, and the need to soothe his demons. She could give him that with her body, she knew, if he would just allow it. It would fix more than one issue between them, if he would just quit being so damn stubborn.

She put her hand to the back of his head, curling her fingers into the silk of his hair and pulling him deeper into the kiss with her. He drew in a sharp breath and then put his hands on her back to bring her body closer to his. It was an ignition of the chemistry which had always lain between the two of them, the recollection of a language their bodies had practiced with great fluency. Before either could comprehend what was happening, his hands were under her shirt and her head was reeling. He tasted warm and sweet and familiar, oh-so achingly familiar. His hands were creating a line of pulsating warmth along her skin and she wanted nothing more than to have a bed at her disposal and then he could reassure her all he liked.

He pulled away from her suddenly, with a sound that fell somewhere between a strangled goose and a thoroughly frustrated man. "Christ," he said and put his head to the steering wheel. "I could use one of those cigarettes about now."

"So could I and I've never smoked. We could—"

"No, Jewel. When an' if we do it'll not be in a car where I can't even move about properly. An' it's certainly not goin' to be with you concussed an' half deaf."

"Which is it, man? If, or when?"

"I think, Pamela, it's when an' well ye know it."

She was tempted to inquire further into just how far into the future *when* might be, but decided that restraint might be called for in this instance.

He took her face gently between his hands and looked her over, clucking a little over the bruising on her temple. "Jaysus Murphy, woman." He kissed her softly, once on her forehead and then on each side of her face, his hands cupping her jaw as though it was made of the most delicate glass imaginable. Which wasn't far off the mark, she thought, considering how sore it was. His hands slid into her hair and he kissed her mouth again, still careful with her, and she wondered if he knew, instinctively, that she needed this—the gentle touch from his hands and body to counteract the violence of the last few hours. He had known so much violence in his own life, far more than she had, and much of it had been inflicted on him with the intent to hurt or even kill him. How often had he needed her touch in the last three years? And had gone without touch or love of any sort?

"Pamela, what the hell is in yer hair?" he asked, withdrawing his hand from said hair with some difficulty.

"Porridge," she said.

"Of course it is. Stupid of me to ask really," he said and then began to laugh. He laughed until finally, gasping, he put his forehead to the steering wheel once more, now and again snorting or erupting in a bit of mirth.

"I'm glad you're amused," she said, tartly. "Though I'm failing to grasp just what is so humorous about this situation."

"It's us. I remember this, Pamela. The mad scrapes ye always get yerself in an' how angry it's always made me. I don't know, feelin' this way is like rememberin' a very large section of our relationship."

"*This* is what you remember?" she asked, feeling rather indignant.

"Well, it's not like I get to choose what comes back an' what doesn't, woman."

She sighed. "Well, it might be nice if you recalled our wedding day, or the day Conor was born, or how much we loved each other, rather than my mad scrapes as you call them."

"Aye, well I can see your point there," he said. "What else is upsettin' ye? Because I can see somethin' is."

"My camera had to be left behind," she said, trying to swallow back the tears that rose just at the mention of it. "They wouldn't let me back in the house to retrieve my things."

"It's a camera, it can be replaced."

"N-no, it can't…I just…it's irreplaceable because you gave it to me our first Christmas in Boston." She could feel the tears welling up, and knew she was powerless to stop them. "When you were gone, I was terrified I'd lose something you'd given me or made for me. The car stopped working at one point, and it felt like a link with you was dissolving. And I knew—" she choked a little on the words, "that one day all the links would be dissolved other than the children."

"To be honest, I'm surprised that damn car hasn't dissolved, it's a miracle it's still runnin."

WHERE BUTTERFLIES DREAM · 237

"It's not funny," she said, crying harder.

"Come here, woman. Ye're right, it's not funny." He pulled her back to him, cupping her head with one hand, while rubbing her back with the other. "If the camera is broken, we'll see if we can get it repaired, if not we'll find ye a new one, even if I have to travel to Boston to track another down."

"It's—it's not about the damn camera," she said, sniffing.

"Aye, darlin', I know, but we'll fix it all the same."

Two hours later she was bathed, dressed in a fresh set of pyjamas and tucked up on the couch, with Kathleen stretched out asleep beside her. Casey had picked up the children from Gert and Owen's and brought them home. He had then supervised her bath, stating that a woman with a 'dunt in her skull' couldn't be left alone in that much water. She'd left the door cracked open, re-sponding to his light chatter the entire time she was in the tub, realizing it was just his way of making certain she hadn't fainted, without impinging on her modesty. She sighed. She wished he *would* impinge on her modesty, it might speed things up a little.

Casey was making dinner now, with help from Conor and Isabelle. Al-ways self-sufficient, Conor, standing on a stool, was peeling potatoes. Granted there was a fair bit of peel left on the ones he was placing in the pot. Isabelle's version of 'hep' consisted mostly of asking Casey endless questions and hang-ing off his leg, begging to be picked up. Isabelle adored her father unreservedly, and Pamela was glad that at least one relationship had been simple for Casey.

Kathleen stretched, her hands splaying up suddenly like tiny pink star-fish. She sighed softly, clicking her tongue, and then subsided back into her slumber. The soft light from the nearby lamp was caught fine as gossamer in her curls, glimmering in strands of copper and cinnamon and gold. There were moments when she saw Jamie so clearly in Kathleen's wee face that it was like a small knife in her heart.

"Daddy, are ye goin' to stay here tonight?" Conor asked, and there was a note of hopefulness in his voice that caused her to hold her breath. In turn it also warmed her heart to hear Conor calling Casey, 'Daddy' with such natural ease. Their time on the mountain had healed things between them, and she was utterly grateful for both their sakes.

"Aye, Conor, I'm stayin'," he said. He flashed her a look and the next bit of what he said was directed at her. "I'm not the sort of man to leave a concussed an' deaf woman alone with three wee children."

It was clear that the only relationship which still needed a good degree of mending was the one he had with her. She was hopeful though, because despite his anger in the truck, things had felt open between them—it had felt wonderfully normal. When he'd kissed her he hadn't held back either, there had been both passion and tenderness in his touch.

She watched him now, moving about the kitchen, mussing Conor's hair, carrying Isabelle on one arm while he put dinner on with the other. From the minute she'd met him all those years ago, she had been sexually attracted to him to the point of not being able to think clearly in his vicinity. This was still patently true. She wanted him so badly it was like he was water and she'd been traveling in the desert without for weeks. The man, however, was acting like the most reluctant virgin in the world. It was a role to which he was eminently unsuited.

It brought back Finola's words to her on this very subject. *"Men always know when another man is in their bed, even if it's only the thought of him. There's not room for more than two, as ye well know, dear girl."*

There was a hard truth to it, and she knew it was, in some part, what held Casey back from returning to her bed. She could not blame him, and yet she wished Jamie's grandmother might have told her how you banished a man from your heart and mind, when you still loved him. How did you separate him out of the most intimate moments of your life, when he was part of your very bone marrow, when every day his child looked at you with her father's eyes? When he was the echo of your own soul? Jamie's words from their night at the monastery, said just before they'd both fallen to sleep, repeated over in her head.

"He is your husband, this I understand. It does not mean we don't love one another, and for me, that will never change. It is the one truth of my life that I know with certainty, my love for you and my children."

And then he had added a fragment—just two lines—from their poem, the one that recalled those days and nights in Paris. But these lines were not those which Jamie had spoken to her in that firelit bed. These were words of a different shade, which held in them something of ending.

> *True love in this differs from gold and clay,*
> *That to divide is not to take away.*

It was not Shelley, but a different poet, however, who echoed again within her own thoughts.

> *That was not to be though I wanted it so*
> *The world knows sorrows beyond those of love.*

And so it was, and yet it did not make the sorrows of love any easier to bear. Nor, she thought, looking at the man in front of her, the joys. Every emotion for her of late, was mixed, both with shadow and sun, with joy and pain. It was both sweet and sharp, because with gain had also come loss—a loss which had strange borders to it, and an unknown wood, in which the ghost of love so nearly grasped, so dearly bought, lamented what it could not understand—that that which had barely begun must now end.

Kathleen was crying. Pamela started up in bed, confused by the sound. She was used to it coming from the crib which stood at the foot of the bed. Some nights she was out of bed and reaching into the crib for the baby before she even fully woke. The sound was distant though, and already fading from a cry to the occasional snuffle. Casey must have taken Kathleen downstairs. Grabbing a sweater to throw on over her pyjamas, she went down the stairs, pausing partway as she heard Casey talking to the baby.

"Nasty things, teeth, but useful when all's said an' done. Now, don't tell yer mammy but I'm thinkin' a wee bit of whiskey might not come amiss for ye just now. Here's the bottle—we'll just get the cap off—yer daddy makes this stuff, did ye know that? He's damn good at it too. We'll just put a drop or two on yer gums, ah there, ye've a good bite on ye, don't ye? Now isn't that better, wee one?"

Kathleen gurgled in what sounded like relieved agreement, and Pamela continued down the stairs, to find Kathleen with her head on Casey's shoulder. He had one hand on the baby's bottom and the other was patting her back and he smiled at her over the red head and tear-streaked face of her baby.

"I'm sorry, I didn't hear her crying until just now," she said, sitting down on the sofa and putting out her arms for Kathleen.

"She's all right now, aren't ye, darlin'?" Casey asked Kathleen, who grinned at him around her drool-festooned hand. "Wantin' the company of yer mammy now, are ye? Wee turncoat, an' after I fed ye whiskey too," he said, kissing Kathleen's head before handing her into Pamela's arms. She settled Kathleen against her chest, smiling down at her as the baby started to fuss again.

"It's all right, sweetheart, just give mama a second here." She swiftly undid a few buttons on her pyjamas, baring one breast and getting Kathleen situated to feed. The little body relaxed almost at once, and Pamela sat back into the sofa, sighing with the comfort of feeding her child.

When she looked up it was to realize that Casey was staring at her with a flush to his face that was visible even in the low light.

"I'm sorry," she said, "I wasn't thinking."

He shook his head. "No, it's me should apologize, I shouldn't be gawkin' at ye like some gormless schoolboy."

"It's not like you haven't seen them before, so I guess it just seemed natural. I'm used to being here alone of late; I don't think much of baring myself when the baby needs feeding."

"Aye, it's just been a time since I've seen ye naked, even a glimpse at this point is somethin' to be grateful for." He smiled, and the tension eased a little.

Pamela noticed that her book on the Troubles was open on the sofa, turned to the middle. She recognized the page, and knew why he'd halted on that particular one. It had been the centerpiece of the book for her, and something which had given it a meaning it wouldn't have otherwise had. The sketches had been done both from memory and old photos she'd had of him as a child, and then as a stripling teen and as a young man, newly married. The small boy she'd drawn with flames for feet and with a cloud of dust and chaos in his wake, for Casey had been a being of movement from the day he was born. The teen sketch had been from a picture where he was leaning up against a wall, grinning at whomever had taken the photo, his dimple in evidence as well as the mischievous sparkle in his eyes, which no amount of trouble-making had ever quenched. The last one was of him holding Conor, when he was only days old. She'd snapped the picture before Casey had been aware she was there, watching him, and it had been a tender moment captured in the channel which existed between photographer and subject.

"There are more," she said quietly, "sketches that is. I became a little obsessed for a time. I think I was desperate to try and capture you, before you began to fade from my memory. They're on the top shelf by the hearth."

Casey gave her an odd look and then walked over to the cupboard and opened it. The sketches were in a worn green folder. He drew it out and opened it. He was quiet for several long minutes while he looked at the drawings, and then laid each in turn on the chair which sat by the fire. She knew what he was seeing, for each one was imprinted upon her heart. What she had felt while drawing them, was still hard to think about because there had been a desperation to those sketches, and a sense of profound loss as she'd finished each one.

Kathleen was asleep, the fiery head fallen back in utter exhaustion, her mouth open to reveal the pearly gleam of a newly sprung tooth. Pamela did her buttons back up one-handed as Casey continued to leaf through the sketches.

"This one," Casey said suddenly, "with the trees, ye put a wolf in it. Why?" His words were terse, and she felt a prickling on the back of her neck, as though a strange entity had moved into the cozy kitchen scene with them.

The picture he referred to was the last one she'd done; it was him standing on the edge of a forest, but part of the trees as well, with a wolf peering out from the long grass at his feet. The figure of the man was electric with movement, despite the static medium, and she'd drawn him with white spaces, irregular pieces missing, drifting off into the wind as sand or seed.

"It's because you've always had that wild side to your nature, something a little uncivilized, something raw. It's as if you belong to the land around you, are part of it, and that you're essential to it as well." She shrugged, feeling foolish, for Casey was looking at her now like she'd lost a few of her senses. "It's one of the first things that attracted me to you, that sense of wildness."

"And the missing pieces?"

"Because day by day I was losing a little more of you, like my memory was subject to every breeze that passed, and it would carry off something more of you—a gesture, something you'd said, how you looked at me, the exact sound of your laugh—all those things were getting harder to recall. The picture was how I felt."

He came to her and hunkered down at her feet, taking her free hand in his. "I want ye to know I'm proud of ye. How ye picked yerself up an' kept goin' with life. Ye've clearly been a terrific mammy for our two, an'," he waved a hand over the book, "ye're an' amazin' artist. I always knew ye were gifted with the picture-takin' but I'd no notion ye could do this. I swear some of those drawins' could come to life an' dance about the room. Ye've done a wonderful thing here, Pamela, allowin' these children to tell their story to the world."

"Thank you," she said softly, afraid that if she said anything more she would start to cry again.

"Now, about this sketch," he said, and held up the last one in the pile, a smile on his face.

"That one is from a picture you allowed me to take," she said, flushing from her neckline to the roots of her hair.

The photo had been simple enough. They'd been in the bed together when she'd taken it, and he'd been lying down, laughing at something she'd said, but there had been a look of such raw desire in his eyes which the camera had caught, that it had taken her breath away when she'd developed the photo. He was also quite naked in the picture. He'd protested at first, but had eventually given in with good-natured grace to what he referred to as her 'boudoir sessions'. Because she developed all her own photos, he'd occasionally allowed her to catch him in such vulnerable and as he put it, 'seriously compromisin' moments.

"Aye, I guessed that much. I suspect ye had me at a bit of a disadvantage at that particular moment though."

"Well, you may not remember this but we had a very happy marital bed," she said, aware that she sounded somewhat prim.

"Aye, even if I didn't remember it consciously, I'd know it now. I do feel what's between us, Pamela. I think that has not changed, no?"

"No, it hasn't."

The dark eyes were soft as he looked at her and she had that sensation of falling, almost like flying, that she'd always had when he looked at her so. It was an awareness of him, of his body which bordered on a kind of exquisite pain, it was so intense. She could feel the breath of him, as though it was her own, the heat and the desire which stretched between them like a cord, binding them to one another through time, distance and loss. He opened his mouth to speak, "Pamela, I—"

Just then, Kathleen stirred and Casey swallowed and looked away. It felt like a physical blow, and yet she understood just why he'd turned from her.

He stood, face now composed. "Ye should go back to bed, woman. I'll bring Kathleen up for ye."

It was on the tip of her tongue to tell him she could take Kathleen up herself, but as she stood with the baby in her arms, a wave of dizziness swept over her, causing Casey to snatch Kathleen up so she wouldn't drop her.

"Go on up, I'll follow ye," he said, patting Kathleen's back and making shushing noises though Kathleen had barely stirred, despite the rather rough transfer from one set of arms to the other.

She ascended the stairs, silent. There was a worry sitting within her, like a small caustic flame, that they would never bridge this final gap, the one where he could trust her with his entire self and his vulnerability once again.

In the bedroom, he placed Kathleen carefully in her crib, waiting for a moment to make certain she would settle, before he came and sat down on the side of the bed. "Do ye think ye can sleep a bit more?"

"Yes, I'm exhausted, and I always sleep better when you're in the house." And then, on impulse, she blurted out, "Will you lie down with me? Sleep here beside me. Would that be okay?"

To her surprise he nodded. "Aye, I can do that. I'll hear Miss Kathleen right away if she wakes again, this way."

He stood and pulled off his shirt and bent down to take off his socks. He took off his pants then, and slid between the sheets. She could feel his warmth and was immediately pulled toward him.

"I used to dream this, you know. I'd feel you get into the bed, and then you'd take my hand and simply hold it while I slept. Sometimes, I'm afraid I'm still dreaming."

"Aye," he said softly, "I feel the same at times. I think I'll wake up an' find myself back in San Francisco, or maybe in the hut on top of the mountain, an' it will just be me. An' I wonder what will I do if that's true, if I'm simply dreamin' this, an' ye're not real. Mind," he added in a different tone, "days like today make me pretty certain it's real."

'All that we see or seem, is but a dream within a dream,' she quoted to him. "I wonder that sometimes, if our lives aren't just a dream within a larger dream?"

"An' just who is dreamin' this dream?"

"I don't know—God maybe, or a whale deep in the sea."

"A whale? I'm thinkin' that's maybe the porridge pot to the head talkin'. "

She ignored this statement and took his hand, reassured by the gentle squeeze he gave hers. The darkness enfolded them softly, and just the proximity of his body, his warmth, made a profound gratitude roll through her, so that she felt tears forming once again. The day was catching up to her and her breath hitched, as the tears rolled down her face.

"Are ye all right, darlin'?" Casey asked, and then a white blot moved through the air toward her.

"It's ridiculous," she took the proffered hanky and wiped at her face, "when you were gone, I couldn't cry, now that you're back I can't seem to stop."

He simply gathered her in close to his body, knowing instinctively it seemed, what would give her comfort. He shimmered with heat, and she curled up into his warmth gratefully.

On the one year anniversary of his disappearance she had gone to a shrine belonging to St. Bridget. She'd prayed for a lessening of pain, but she had, at the last minute, asked for a miracle. And, against all odds, it had been given to her. Ciara had been right, this right here, this man lying beside her, holding her hand, was a miracle, pure and simple.

"Pamela?" His voice was soft, barely audible in the hush that surrounded them.

"Mmhmm?"

"There's something I would have ye know."

"Yes?" She felt a small tremor of fear. Sometimes she thought there was a great deal about his three years away that he hadn't told her and she worried there would be a revelation one day she wasn't quite prepared to handle.

"What ye said earlier about wishin' I'd remember Conor's birth or our weddin' day, or how much we loved each other? Just for the record, woman, I do remember that—how we loved one another, it's why I'm here. It's what brought me home."

In reply she reached over and kissed the side of his face, feeling the warmth of his skin and velvet plushness of his whiskers. They lay silent for a time then, the island of the bed a place of truce that allowed for a cessation of fear and worry and hesitancy. Long after she thought he'd fallen to sleep, Casey spoke.

"What if we are dreamin'?" he asked, voice no more substantial than a moth's wing brushing past in the dark. In it she heard the pain and fear of the man who had been lost and wandering in a wilderness for three years, a man who had barely dared to hope he would ever know home again. She put her hand to his chest, feeling the pulse of his heart echo through her and the response of her own blood to the call and rhythm of his.

"Then I never want to wake up."

Chapter Twenty-three

Irrational Emotion

THE WORK ON Tomas' house had brought back echoes to Casey of his time in California, and the house he'd both restored and lived in there, along with the woman who'd inherited it. He didn't reflect all that often on his time there, as it hadn't been the happiest period of his life. Most often, he'd found, he'd felt like a ghost—a spirit without a name or identity or roots to keep him in place. The house there, a big old Queen Anne in Marin County, had been the closest he'd come to having a home. It was certainly the place he'd most often laid his head down at night. He didn't think often of the woman he'd lived with there either, though he'd been fond of her in a way. Sometimes he wasn't entirely certain what it was he'd felt for Bridget—sorrow, pity, attraction, and a certain half-resentful kinship—because he'd known they were, in some respects, two peas in an undesirable pod. They'd both been lost, Bridget because of a history she would never discuss, and him because he hadn't a clue where he belonged.

Restoring her house, though, had also restored part of him, had given him a feeling of solidity, of actually existing, rather than just drifting. Now and again he'd dream about it still, and wake thinking he was in the tower room where he'd slept at night. Where Bridget too had slept. It had been an odd intimacy, to sleep beside a woman each night and yet never have sex with her. It had been an odd existence altogether—the fighting, living with a woman he didn't love but still cared for, wandering amongst the homeless and feeling more kinship with them than he did with anyone else other than Eddy. Mind you, Eddy had been rootless as well, as adrift as the population of the streets where they had distributed food, clothing and what little care the denizens of San Francisco's lost corridors would allow.

He'd wondered at times during those three years if he'd lost the ability to feel things properly, and then he'd found Conor's letters, seen his wife in that horror house, and come back and known from the moment he touched her that he had, most assuredly not lost the ability to feel. Oh yes, he thought, giving the nail he'd just fixed into the wainscoting a good smack, the woman certainly made him feel all sorts of things.

The last time he'd seen Pat, the man had asked him what exactly it was he was waiting on to go home, and stay there.

"I want to be certain the woman knows what she wants," he'd said.

"Well, why don't ye bloody ask her then?" Pat said, looking at him like he had a few bolts loose in his brain.

"Because she may be tempted to tell me what I want to hear."

Pat merely rolled his eyes, and snorted. "Ye're bein' a great eejit, man. If ye'd the sense God gave a goose, Casey, ye'd have taken the woman to bed about a week after ye got home. Now ye've turned it into somethin' it need never have been, an' caused a deal of tension to boot."

Sometimes Casey found his brother's calm pragmatism more than a little annoying. In the main this was because the wee bastard was, more often than not, right in his summations. In truth, though, he had felt it best to wait, just perhaps not quite *this* long. He hadn't wanted Pamela to make decisions out of a knee-jerk emotional reaction, and find herself saddled with a man who only remembered about a third of his life. She'd also been fragile, both physically and emotionally, and everything between them felt so tenuous and delicate that he knew to add the stress of lovemaking after a three-year dry spell, seemed like the act of a fool. A dry spell, admittedly, of his own making. For Bridget had taken every opportunity to offer him the solace and comfort of her body, and he had turned her down, rather reluctantly at times, but still he'd managed, despite the fact that—as Pamela herself had pointed out more than once—he was not one of the world's natural celibates. For three years, he'd managed. He snorted, and drove the hammer down a little harder. Oh yes, he'd managed all right, even with a beautiful woman tucked in the same bed as him more often than not and him thinking he might go mad if he didn't simply have sex with her.

He'd been like a monk, one who prayed constantly for a woman he wasn't even certain was real.

Bang! Bang!

Words Tomas had spoken to him the evening before resounded in his head. '*If Jamie Kirkpatrick was my competition, I don't think I'd be takin' my time about stakin' my claim to my own wife.*'

Bang! Bang! Bang!

The man had a point, and it was one Casey couldn't quite answer to. Yes, he'd waited all that time for her, hell he'd waited three damn years, worried that his feckless brain had made her up in order to give him a story with which to comfort himself. Frankly at this point three minutes felt too long to wait, and yet here he was—he hit the nail hard enough that the hammer slid from it and rebounded off the board, nearly hitting him in the face. He took a breath before resuming his previous train of thought, taking more care with the hammer. Yet, here he was with a woman he desired to the point of madness, a woman who'd made it clear he was more than welcome to her bed and her person, and he was half-living with a curmudgeonly old bachelor who he wasn't even certain he liked, and who he was damn sure, didn't like him. He was a bloody fool, and none knew it better than himself.

Bang!

It was past time, he knew, to be honest with himself about just what it was that was holding him back from the woman's bed, and that was the fear that what she'd found so briefly with Jamie might eclipse whatever fragile thing they had begun to build together. Pat's words sounded in his head again, and he snorted. Aye, he was an eejit in any number of ways and this wasn't the least of them, still there it was, jealousy—hard as an apple lodged in his windpipe.

No, he'd never been certain what he'd felt for Bridget, but one thing he'd always been clear on was that he didn't love her. And that was the crux of it, he knew. He hadn't loved Bridget but Pamela did love Jamie. Bastard.

Bang, bang, bang!

He looked down at the section of wainscoting with some chagrin; he'd given it a bit more of a beating than he'd meant to. He'd have to replace it, but the sacrifice was worth it as it had gone some way toward relieving his frustration.

Tomas might be a bit of a bastard, but he knew how to get his point across. It was time for Casey to get the hell off the fence and move forward. That was, he knew, going to mean letting Tomas set him up with the psychiatrist. Admittedly, the thought frightened him a little—having a doctor pick over the bruised and battered contents of his brain. It was necessary though. He needed to return as much of himself as he could to his family, and just at present this seemed the most viable way to do just that.

So lost in these thoughts was he that when the bell rang, he hit his thumb with the hammer, and in reflex kicked out, knocking over a can of paint.

"Jaysus Murphy!" He was going to have a time of it cleaning this up now, and he could feel blood dripping to the floor from his thumb. He'd have to answer the door, being that he was waiting on a delivery of brass hinges to arrive, and the man had promised to drive them over to him, as soon as they arrived in his store. He opened the door, mind still back in the room where paint was coagulating on the floor. Expecting the man from the hardware store, he was startled to find a woman there, slender, upright, with hair as dark as his own, and something about her face which reminded him forcibly of Isabelle. He was, he knew, looking at his mother.

She stood, holding her purse in front of her like a shield, and eyed him up and down. He felt just the wee bit like a bug under a microscope, pinned down by those dark eyes, and he was uncomfortably aware that his emotional age had been suddenly reduced to roughly six years. He knew he ought to say something, but found himself completely tongue-tied. And then the woman did something which took him by surprise. She dropped her purse and flung her arms about his neck, and started to cry. While he didn't remember everything about his mother, he knew this was entirely out of character for the woman.

He patted her back awkwardly, uncertain what else to do. Finally, she let him go and backed away to look up into his face. She touched his cheek, her hand cool and soft. "Ye look well, Casey."

"Thank ye," he said, feeling about as awkward as it was possible for a man to feel.

"Ye're bleedin', come on, let's get ye into the kitchen an' wash that off."

The next thing he knew he was seated at the table, and the woman was washing down his mashed thumb with a very good make of whiskey. He wasn't even quite sure how it had happened, but she appeared to be good with bossing a man about with a minimal amount of words.

"Will there be a wee kit about with bandages an' such? Ye'll need a bit of wrappin' for this thumb."

"Aye, I have one in my bag over there," he nodded toward the canvas bag he carried everywhere with him.

He watched her as she moved across the room, and rummaged in the bag until she came out with the little tin box which held the medical supplies he carried with him, for just such moments as now. It held bandages, a tube of arnica cream, a small bottle of ethyl alcohol and a few of his pain pills. She was slender and fine-boned, her hair still dark with only the odd thread of silver glinting in it. There was a bit of iron in her though, he could see that clearly. He wondered if it had always been there, and why she'd needed it. He felt the core of it in himself. Her movements, quick and light, felt strangely familiar to him, as though somewhere deep inside, in his cells, he did remember this woman, and knew her instinctively as kin. Such moments still knocked him out of place a bit, as though he'd passed out and woken part way through a play with no notion of the storyline.

"I can manage on my own, I'm used to dealin' with injury," he said, aware even as he said it that he was being ungracious.

"Aye, I'd heard ye'd taken up brawlin' as a way to make a livin'," she replied, clearly less than impressed by his pugilistic skills. Pamela seemed of a like opinion, and had asked at one point if he had been determined to knock what was left of his brain out his ears. Deirdre fixed him with a dark gaze, her expression one of a woman who feels tried by the obstinacy of the male half of the species. "How about ye let me be yer mother for a minute or two?" she said.

"Ye haven't been my mother since I was six years old, if I recall correctly," he said, feeling annoyed with her. The woman did have a point, though, he supposed. She was, after all, his mother in biology if nothing else.

"Ye're my son, from the day you were born until the day I die, that's one of the solid facts of my life."

"Aye," he said, "there's no denyin' that as a fact. Whether it's a fact either of us is fond of is another issue entirely."

"That may be true for you," she said, looking him in the eyes, "but it isn't for me. Ye're my son, an' I love you, that's not changed from the time I knew I carried ye until this day. I've not been a good mother, an' I'll not need tellin' it, for that's fact too. But I will tell you this, Casey, when I thought ye were dead, ye can't even imagine what that meant to me, knowin' we'd never found any sort of reconciliation, an' then there was no hope of it."

"Ye feel there's a hope of it now?" Casey asked, both curious and half-resentful that the woman assumed they could have a relationship.

"It's up to you now, isn't it? I should like it, but if ye decide against it, I'll respect that," she said, and patted his now bandaged hand. "That'll do for now. Make sure you check it every day though, in case infection sets in. Now, could you do with a bite maybe? It's near to tea time, an' I've a lovely batch of scones with me. I've just come from the shops, so I've tea as well. Will ye break bread with me?"

"Aye," Casey said, managing to keep his tone amiable enough, though the woman gave him a look over her shoulder that told him she wasn't fooled in the least.

While she made the tea, he escaped to the study and managed to scrape up the worst of the paint. Having had a few moments to congeal, it was simply a matter of folding up the plastic sheeting around the paint. Nothing appeared to have leaked through to the floor itself, though he'd have to check when the light was better in order to be entirely certain.

Deirdre called his name then, and he went to the kitchen with the odd sense of being a small boy called indoors from his play.

The tea was set out on the table, which had been covered with a well-starched and ironed table cloth, and the kitchen looked a bit brighter, as though she'd given it a quick clean and polish in the few minutes he'd been gone. On the table was the tea pot, cups and a plate with scones, butter and jam. Where she'd procured the clean dishes he wasn't sure, but he didn't think it was from Tomas' dusty cupboards. He cast a glance at the purse she'd brought in and wondered if it was a little like Mary Poppins' carpet bag, a down-at-the-heels receptacle capable of producing wonders.

They spoke of the children while they ate the scones and drank their tea, this subject feeling like the least fraught of all possibilities. It became clear to Casey, as he listened, that his mother knew his children well. Pat had mentioned that Deirdre had spent time with Pamela and the children, while Casey had been gone, in order to help in whatever way she could.

"She's a good grandmother to them," Pat had said, "an' I think maybe that ought to weigh a little in her favour."

He supposed it ought to, and in truth, his own history with her had left behind little more than a residue of resentment and the long scar of abandonment.

She put down her cup, and eyed him in a manner which put him on his guard a little. He'd the sense he was about to get some unwelcome advice. His fears were confirmed the moment she began to speak.

"I'm aware I've no right to hand out judgement or advice to ye, but ye didn't just get that stubbornness of yers from yer daddy, so I'm goin' to say something I feel needs sayin'."

"Aye?"

"Ye need to forgive Pamela. To my way of thinkin' she's not done ye wrong, at least not with intent of any sort. She grieved ye somethin' terrible, Casey, an' if ye love her still, ye need to get past what's changed while ye were gone."

"If she's done nothin' wrong, then what is it I'm to forgive?" Casey asked, feeling uncomfortable as this conversation mirrored too closely the thoughts he'd had while banging the hell out of the wainscoting.

"Even if she hasn't done wrong, jealousy is not so simple an emotion as that, an' none can blame ye if ye feel it. But still an' all, it's an irrational emotion, isn't it?"

Irrational emotion, thought Casey, was about all he'd felt since he'd returned home.

Tomas came in just then, saving Casey from reply. He was surprised the man was home so early, he rarely returned to the house before late evening, and sometimes slept in his office overnight. Pat said they had a cot for those nights, and Casey had concluded that the cot was for the times when Tomas had imbibed a wee bit too much and wasn't fit to drive himself home.

"Lovely to see you, Deirdre," Tomas said, and Casey had to stifle a laugh. The old reprobate was actually blushing.

"Yourself as well, Tomas," his mother replied, and then turned back to him.

"I'd like to come by and see you now an' again, if ye'll allow it."

Tomas looked rather pleased at this notion, and Casey was tempted to say no just for that reason alone. Unfortunately, he couldn't think of a good reason to deny her. When a man couldn't remember anything other than being angry, it was time to admit that was no longer a good enough reason. If he was sincere about making his way home, it would have to include the parts of his past with which he wasn't comfortable.

"Aye, I'll allow it," he said, aware that his tone wasn't entirely convivial, but it didn't seem to ruffle the woman's feelings in the least.

She leaned down and kissed his cheek, and then was gone in a rustle of poplin coat and umbrella, carpet bag tucked neatly under one arm.

Tomas still stood in the kitchen, looking at the door through which Deirdre had just exited.

"So ye know my mother then?" Casey asked, leaning back and folding his arms, and feeling a small bit of enjoyment in the man's discomfort.

"Oh aye. I've met her a time or two when she's come by the office to see yer brother."

"She sees Pat regularly?"

"No, I'd not say it's been all that often, but I know she visits Kate now an' again, an' of course Pamela and the wee ones."

"Aye, Pamela's said."

"I believe yer mother was a good bit of help to her at times while you were gone."

"I'm sure she was," Casey said, but in a manner that would make it clear that while he'd agreed to see the woman now and again, he wasn't willing to talk about his relationship—or lack thereof—with her.

Tomas cleared his throat. "There's somethin' I have it in mind to speak to ye about."

"Oh," Casey said, a little worried by the man's tone.

"I was thinkin'," Tomas began slowly, "that it would make more sense if ye lived here while doin' the work. Ye're without a home until ye settle yer business properly with Pamela, an' I thought here would be as good a place as any. Ye could have one of the rooms upstairs, there's a few to choose from, an' ye can take yer pick. Ye know that I work long hours, an' so ye'd mostly have the run of the place an' ye wouldn't have to make that drive down to Wicklow so often."

Casey was so surprised that he didn't say anything at first, merely looked at the man and tried to keep his mouth from dropping open.

"Well, what do ye think?"

Casey opened his mouth to say 'thanks, but no thanks', but found himself, much to his surprise, saying, "I think it's a good idea, an' I thank ye for the offer."

"Good," Tomas said, "it'll be easier to see yer brother this way, an' yer mother too. An' ye'll be a whole lot closer to Pamela an' yer wee ones. That's settled then. Ye'll stay to supper—it's late an' ye might as well eat."

"I'll stay," Casey said, surprised to find that he rather liked the idea of staying here, and having a few roots, however transitory, for a space of time. "There's somethin' I would like to ask ye to do on my behalf."

Tomas, already looking through the rather bare cupboards, turned. "What's that?"

"Yer friend—the psychiatrist?"

"Aye?"

"If ye'd contact her, I'd appreciate it."

Chapter Twenty-four

Where Hope and Memory Meet

TRUE TO HIS WORD, Tomas had an appointment with the psychiatrist set up for him within the week, and Casey, now sitting outside the woman's office, had a case of nerves akin to a virgin contemplating a shipful of lusty pirates.

He was just debating the wisdom of getting up and fleeing the office when a quiet voice told him to come in. He'd been expecting a grim atmosphere, maybe a dirty rug with a worn couch and a poe-faced woman with black-framed glasses who would peer at him like a bug under a microscope, and likely, he thought, assess him as a hopeless case. What he found instead was a grandmotherly looking woman, with apple cheeks and snapping blue eyes, whose office was a cozy sitting room, complete with peat fire hissing in the hearth and a well-worn couple of armchairs beside it.

"Please sit, make yourself comfortable."

Casey sat, thinking that comfortable wasn't on his list of possibilities when he was about to have his brain picked apart.

She threw a chunk of turf on the fire, poked it with the fire rod and then sat across from him, hands on the arms of her chair. It was as if, he thought, he'd sat down with someone's beloved nan for a chat.

"My name is Alice, if ye're comfortable with calling me that, then it's what I prefer. If not, Doctor Nolan will do fine."

"All right, Alice it is." He cleared his throat nervously, and thought he'd made a mistake in coming here. When a man couldn't remember much of anything, what was there to talk about?

"So, perhaps we can start with you telling me what it is that's brought you here today."

"Will Tomas have given ye the outlines?" he asked.

"Just that you had severe memory loss, and that you'd recently regained some of your memories, but not all."

"Aye, that's the sum of it," he said. "I suppose what I'm here lookin' for is help in findin' out what happened to me to cause the memory loss in the first place."

She nodded, the blue eyes thoughtful. "Have you given much thought as to why some memories have returned, while others have not?"

He nodded. "I have. I think I remembered what I needed to in order to return to my family, and it could be my brain feels the rest isn't entirely necessary."

"Is it possible you are afraid to know what happened?"

"Aye," he said, still wanting to bolt for the door. "It's possible I am." In fact it was probable, but he didn't add this.

"Do you have any notion about why you might be frightened to know the truth?"

"Aye," he said.

"Would you be willing to tell me what that fear is around?" she asked, her voice warm and casual.

"I'm afraid to find out I'm somehow complicit in what happened to me. That I brought it upon myself, an' that it's my fault my wife an' children were so long without me."

"I imagine," she said, "things will have changed for them in three years. Are the children very young?"

"Aye, they are. Our boy is six an' our wee girl will be four come summer. There's another child too."

"Not yours, I take it?"

"No, not mine," he said. "My wife had a child with another man—a man she has loved most of her life—while I was gone."

"Do you blame yourself for that as well?"

Casey took in the question, and gave it a little thought, and was surprised that the answer came to him so quickly. "I suppose I do."

"Do you find yourself resenting the child?"

"No," he said. This didn't need thought, for he truly didn't. "She's innocent in all this, come to that so are her mother an' father."

"I find it interesting that you don't mention yourself in that list," the woman said. "If you absolve them of responsibility because they thought you dead, then do you not have to extend yourself the same courtesy?"

"No," he said abruptly.

"That was a quick reply," she said, mildly. "Did you know that already?"

"No, I didn't," he replied, shocked at this admission, one he hadn't even made to himself before.

"You didn't know who you were, does that not absolve you of at least some of the responsibility?"

He shrugged, uncomfortable. "Does it? If I took actions which led to someone tryin' to kill me, then am I not guilty for what that caused?"

The woman gave him a long look, and he tried not to squirm like a guilty school boy.

"I suppose that will be for you to decide. Tomas will have explained what my specialty is?"

"Aye, he told me ye do regression therapy."

"Do you know anything about regression therapy?"

"Aye, I do, it was suggested to me by my doctors in San Francisco, but it didn't work for me. I," he hesitated, uncertain he should tell the woman this next bit but, thinking it might be important, forged ahead, "I also had a couple of sessions with drinkin' ayahuasca, which provided regression of a sort." He shuddered, remembering his final session with the old man, who he'd been sure was a witch doctor.

"I've read about it, but you're the first person I've met who has actually gone through the ceremony. Did it help you?"

"It gave me back my name," he said.

"Well, then it was clearly worth it."

"Aye, it was," Casey said, even though he'd been horribly sick at the time. Still, it had provided him with the first step back to the life which had been his. Mind, he was in no great hurry to repeat that experience.

"You'll know then that the theory is that those memories are simply buried so deeply inside your mind that your conscious mind doesn't have access to them. That's my job, to find a way to help you access them. Think of it like a jewel at the heart of a mountain of earth. We merely need to dig away at the earth until the jewel surfaces. Our minds are built to shield us, and to look out for us after trauma. The way the mind most often does this task is to simply take that event and drop it in a very deep pond, so that we needn't look at it, nor have to relive it. My job is to aid you in making the dive to retrieve that memory. Mostly I work with trauma survivors, but emotional trauma, more so than physical trauma. Clearly, you've experienced both, so we'll have to proceed slowly and with a great deal of care. To that end I have a colleague—a neurologist—whom I'd like to consult with along the way. I'd like for him to have a look at you as well, so he can help me decide what the wisest course is for you."

Casey nodded, images of electrodes attached to his head, dancing in front of him.

"It will be slow, and it may be in the end we won't find those lost memories, as there may be a reason your mind is so intent on keeping it hidden. Memory can be a very strange thing. There was an American neuropsychologist who did some studies with rats some time back. He trained them to perform a variety of tasks, things like running a maze. He removed various portions of their brains—areas we associate with holding memories—and retested them. They still knew exactly what to do. Eventually he found out that no matter which portion of their brains he removed, he could not eradicate their memories. Even when massive portions of their brains were removed, their memories remained stubbornly intact. So the conclusion was that memory must be spread throughout our entire brain, and not just stored in one little section. Either that, or memories were somehow externalized."

"Externalized?" Casey asked, intrigued but not really understanding what it was the woman was leading up to.

"Well, I'm not sure even now that I understand what he was saying, but I think it helps if you're familiar with the idea of holograms."

"Holograms?" Now he felt more confused, what sort of doctor had Tomas sent him to here?

"Here, let's make it visual, I think I'll find it easier to explain with a few props."

She went to the desk behind her, and grabbed paper, a pen and a couple of pebbles from a dish on her desk, leading him to wonder if this was a demonstration she gave often.

She pulled the small table by the hearth over a little, so that it sat directly between the two of them. A sheet of paper was placed neatly on the wooden surface, and then she drew a squiggly circle in the centre of it.

"If I drop one pebble into the pond I get a ring of concentric circles traveling out into the edges of the pond. But if I drop two simultaneously, what happens?"

"Two sets of concentric circles, makin' that same trip, but also crossin' the path of the other. I do understand the notion of interference, if that's where ye're leadin' me here," he said. "I imagine the waves in this pond are meant to be light."

She smiled at him. "Well, I'll cut to the chase then. Ye'll understand how laser light can show us a three-dimensional figure, by the light bein' split so that one half interrupts the other?"

Casey nodded.

"Good, well did you know if I were to take a picture of an apple with holographic film and then cut it in half, an' then illuminate it with a laser, each half would still show a full apple?"

Casey rubbed at the back of his neck, the bees in his head emitting a low-level buzz. It usually meant that one of his headaches was in his near future, or that his mind was resisting any interference with its current mode of operation.

"Even if I cut that picture up into several small strips, the laser would still project a whole apple just from a single narrow strip."

"I follow so far," Casey said uneasily, wondering if his brain was the apple or the strip in this story.

"What I'm saying is this, it's like your brain is that set of strips, and there's a whole apple in there, so to speak, we just need the right illumination, and the right strip to focus it on to give you back your three-dimensional picture."

"Even if some strips are missin'?" he asked.

"Even if three or four are missing," she said.

"So then it's just a matter of findin' the correct illumination?" He felt a tinge of hope work its way into him, like the first small green shoot of spring, which shows up despite the snow and howling winds.

"Well that, hopefully, is what the regression therapy will be. If we can show you the whole picture, then maybe your brain can find a way to remember. What is it that you are hoping treatment can give you?"

He considered for a moment, and then simply answered, because for him, the answer was right there and didn't require any pondering on his part.

"I want to be a whole man for my family. I want to know if the threat that existed then, is still alive now. I can't spend my life lookin' back over my shoulder, an' until I know exactly what happened to me, I feel I can't fully return to them."

"What brought back the memories you do have? Can you trace it to a particular moment? What was happening at the time?"

He froze for a minute, wondering how to tell her about finding Pamela in the workhouse and then proceeding to kill everyone in it, other than his pregnant wife and her lover/father of her impending child. It wasn't a straightforward sort of tale, particularly in the matter of implicating oneself in a quintuple murder.

He took a deep breath and then simply plunged into the telling. He spoke of finding himself on his own land and not knowing it, and then he told her of the night he'd stumbled across Pamela in the workhouse and the realization he was looking at his wife.

"I mean clearly I remembered somethin' or I wouldn't have kept goin' back to the property, but seein' her in such a state of distress seemed to dislodge what memory I needed to deal with the situation."

Doctor Alice didn't inquire as to exactly what he meant by 'deal with the situation', for which Casey was intensely grateful.

"It would seem your brain responds to emotional shock. It almost seems as if it's sleeping and the shock wakes up that particular area of memory. Obviously, we still need to take into consideration—very serious consideration—that your brain is injured physically as well. Therefore, I don't want to move too quickly with your treatment. This is good news, it means the memories are still there, they're merely dormant at present. I feel we can, with some work, get back at least parts of your former life. I can't make promises, but I do think your case isn't hopeless in any way."

Casey felt tears of gratitude forming and took a breath, hoping to forestall them. He didn't want to cry in front of the woman. His emotions tended to extremes, and he found he had to exert a great deal of control in order to keep them at bay at times.

He put his head down, pinching the top of his nose and taking a deep breath.

"All emotion is welcome here," Doctor Alice said, "this is going to be a rough road to travel, Casey, and a lot of it uncomfortable. Are you prepared for that?"

"Aye, I'm ready as I can be. As to rough roads," he looked up at her and smiled, "I don't know any other sort."

He was dreaming in red. Red at its most primal hue—blood. The movement of his body was that of dreams, slow and thick-moving, as if gravity bore down on him much harder than it did in the waking world. There were trees around him, and the very air seemed dark, red, and sinister with portents. Someone was following him, watching him—he could feel the prickle of eyes all along his skin. He began to walk faster, though he was headed away from the house, and there was no shelter anywhere near to him. He wasn't armed either, so he had nothing but his hands should he need to fight. Stopping, he turned around, looking into the trees. There was nothing to see but darkness though, and he shook himself a little, and continued walking. Still, the feeling remained, a sharp spot on his spine, where the nerves prickled with barbed ice. And then he heard them, and knew that death was coming, swiftly, and with little warning. Someone hit him then, hard and just before the world expired from his view, he thought of his wife and his children and felt a pain which dwarfed that of his physical body.

Casey sat up in the bed, heart pounding madly and his head on fire with pain. He thought he might be sick, and threw his legs over the side of the bed, only to be overcome with dizziness. His hands flew to his head, as though he could hold it together, and quell the sensation that it was about to crack open, spilling out its secrets, so that they would be lost to him forever. His lungs were burning and he realized suddenly that he hadn't drawn a breath since waking. He needed to get outside where the air was cold and would shock his body back into full wakefulness.

It was a clear night when he stepped out into Tomas' yard, his entire body still trembling. The moon was old, melted into a weary silver puddle just above the horizon. Goosebumps stippled his skin immediately, for his body was still damp with sweat. He looked around, half expecting dark figures to step out of the night, as though he were back there in that time, rather than in the here and now. There was a fear in him that if he stepped into the wrong spot, he *would* find himself back there and realize he had never left. Before he'd come home, he sometimes thought he had died, and gone to purgatory for his sins, but just didn't know it. Tonight that feeling overwhelmed him again. Perhaps this *was* purgatory—to not know, to never be sure what was real and what was not.

"Stop it, ye great eejit," he said out loud, just to steady himself a little. Instead it had the effect of spooking him, and a fine cold needling started along his spine. Around him the trees loomed close, the fountain silent, but water dripping one drop at a time somewhere in the yard. He should have stayed in the house, gotten himself a drink of water and tried to go back to sleep. Coming outside had set off all his internal alarms.

Could it be that the session with the grandmotherly woman had actually shaken something loose in his head? Was the dream what had happened to him? Did it help at all when he couldn't see any faces or identify any voices?

A memory rose in his mind, of a walk he'd been on when he'd lived high in the Wicklow Mountains. It had been coming on autumn with the season's flood of colour and mad rush toward decay. There was a spider with a large web in the hollow of a rotting log, and he'd often stopped on his rambles to check in on her, as she was the biggest orb weaver he'd ever seen. The last time he'd looked in she was carefully guarding a sackful of babies and he wanted to see if they'd gone. The image of small spiders borne aloft on what basically amounted to a parachute, made him smile. It was small connections to his landscape and to his day, such as this one he'd had all summer with the spider, that grounded him and made him feel that he was building some sort of a life for himself, one that would eventually include humans as well as arachnids and raggedy-arse cats.

But when he arrived at the hollowed-out tree, it was to find the web torn, the spider gone, either eaten by a predator or having taken her leave to wherever it was spiders journeyed come autumn's bite. The babies he hoped had found their ephemeral air balloons and gone to...well, wherever it was baby spiders wintered over until spring.

He had stood there feeling strangely bereft, as if one of those small connections had been torn loose and left him less moored in the world. Standing here now, in Tomas' garden, he felt instead the containment of it—this world of his. And he knew he was still caught in a web, one which he could not see beyond the boundaries of. He was no different than the spider, for like her he could feel the tugs of the outside world, the raindrops and winds, and the brush of a fluttering moth wing, but as soon as he tried to look at things straight on, they disappeared.

It was his biggest fear, that if he disturbed this web he currently sat within, he would expose his mind to the winds of chance, and maybe, like the spider, lose the small hoard of past events—of memory—that he guarded for the treasure it was.

He would have to take the chance, though, because as he'd said to the good doctor, he needed to be a whole man for his family. He needed to be the man his wife had once fallen in love with. For he knew eventually the day would come when they would both regret it if they settled for anything less.

The good doctor had pointed something out to him which ought to have been obvious from the start—his memory responded to emotional shock. With his finding of Pamela that night in the workhouse, things had come back, small glimmering bits of memory that he had grabbed out of the air and clutched to himself the way a starving child might hoard food.

So if a shock to his mind was needed, he had a good idea where he just might be able to find one.

Chapter Twenty-five

Poetry and the Price of Honesty

WHEN MAY ARRIVED, it was clearly in a mood. Wet and chilly, with low grey skies and a permanent raw feeling in the air so that they were burning fires well into the day. Pamela's counters were filled with seedlings which had grown lanky, as they waited impatiently to be set out in the ground. Despite the weather, despite the low and glowering sky—and the cold which had her still bundled up in sweaters and scarves when outside—the world felt verdantly alive and glowing about its edges with a faint tinge of green. It was, she knew, Casey being present, filling the house and her blood with a rushing sort of vitality and excitement. This feeling effervesced its way into the most mundane tasks of her day. Even something, she thought scratching the tip of her nose with a floury finger, as mundane as making bread—the task in which she was currently engaged—as she listened to the noise and chatter of the young people filling her house this raw, grey afternoon.

Finian, Ciara, and Ambrose had all come to visit Pru for the day and like all mothers of small ones, Pamela took full advantage of the time when her children were occupied by other people.

"Is Casey comin' by this afternoon?" Finian asked.

She spooned up a little butter from the blue crock in which it was kept, and spread it thinly over the round of dough. She then covered the dough with a damp tea towel, before turning to answer Finian's question. Finian and Ambrose were sprawled out on the kitchen sofa, Ambrose with a stack of poetry books to his left and Rusty curled up beside him. Finian, always restless, was tapping his heels on the floor and playing cat's cradle with Isabelle. Pru and Ciara were on the big rug by the hearth, fussing over Kathleen who was happily gurgling, taking in their attention with the air of a tiny empress.

"Yes, I believe he'll come once his work day is done," she said.

"Is he livin' here now?"

"No, he's not living here as such," she said, wishing Finian would cease and desist. "He's working on renovating Tomas' house, and staying there while he does the work." That ought to be enough, she hoped, to discourage him from further questions.

"Her man used to be the head of the Provies," Finian said to Ambrose, who flicked a glance up at Pamela and then over at the children. Right on cue, Isabelle asked, "Wass pobies, Mama?"

Ciara shot a glare at him over Isabelle's frowzled curls, and Pamela smiled to herself. Since Finian had taken up with Ciara she didn't need to curb his worst tendencies anymore, as the girl had them all well in hand.

"Oops, sorry about that," Finian said, though he didn't look in the least bit repentant. He'd met Casey for all of two hours when he'd dropped by for dinner one night and Casey had been in residence for the evening. Much to Casey's annoyance, Finian had seen him as a very glamorous figure—gone for three years, now returned from exile, former IRA member from a legendary republican family, with a stature and mien designed for command. Finian, born with a rebel's nature, was stymied as to why a man would leave the 'Ra behind to take up a domestic existence. He'd been after Pamela ever since as to when she expected Casey's return.

The girls had Kathleen well in hand, and Isabelle and Conor were now absorbed in a game of snakes and ladders with the two girls, and the bread would need a couple of hours of rising time before going in the oven. It was a good time to get dinner prepared, Pamela thought, pausing to survey the contents of her cupboards.

Behind her, Finian was tapping his heels harder, always an indication that he was getting restless.

"Will ye ever get yer face out of that book, an' join the conversation?" he said with some frustration, glaring at Ambrose.

Ambrose gave him a look which might have withered a more sensitive boy, but which did nothing to Finian. "Ye don't seem to require my help, ye've sucked up all the air in the room as it is."

"Well, tell us what ye're readin' at least," Finian said, undeterred by his friend's sarcasm.

"It's poetry, an' I know how ye feel about poetry," Ambrose replied, before putting his face back in the book. "I've read ye some an' ye always turn yer nose up at it."

"Well, how do ye know if it's a good poem?" Finian asked.

"Ye just know," Ambrose said impatiently, looking at Finian over the top of his wire-rimmed glasses. "It makes ye feel something—whether that's joy or pain, sorrow or disgust, it will make you feel it on a level you didn't know before. Poetry is the distillation of emotion, taking the best words to express that one feeling, whatever it might be. Here, listen to this one, it ought to be straightforward enough for ye."

Finian rolled his eyes, but he sat back to listen, nevertheless.

'His gaze those bars keep passing is so misted…'

The boy had a good reading voice, Pamela thought, listening as she put a salmon in the oven to bake. Ambrose knew Finian well, and he had chosen rightly with the Rilke poem. A panther caged, weary of its imprisonment, pacing in ever-tightening circles. Yes, Finian would relate, it was an apt metaphor for the anger and frustration of being a young Catholic male in this country.

Finian was sitting up, as though the words had been a string by which Ambrose had pulled him in.

"Now, there's somethin' more like it," he said, "I can understand that."

"Did ye read that book I gave ye?" Ambrose asked, causing Finian to roll his eyes again.

"Ye know I don't like history books, all that dry goin' on about people who've been dead for hundreds of years. How's it relevant to me an' my situation in the world?"

"Ye ought to educate yerself," Ambrose said. "Read the writins' of those men ye say ye revere. They weren't just names, ye know, they had lives an' ideas that still apply today."

Finian tilted his head to one side, as though giving due consideration to Ambrose's suggestion. Then he grinned, and jumped up off the sofa, nervous energy sparking off him.

"Ach, I'm goin' outside. C'mon, Conor, let's go look for frogs."

Conor never needed to be asked twice to go out-of-doors, and was up and out the door, with no more than his wellies on his feet, before Pamela could stop him.

"Don't bring any back with you," Pamela called out, knowing it was futile, but optimistically hoping for one amphibian free day in her home.

The girls followed Finian outside, taking Isabelle along with them. Kathleen was in her bouncy chair, happily gnawing on a set of large, colourful rubber keys. Ambrose lingered behind, up off the sofa now and scanning the book shelf next to the hearth.

"D'ye have a favourite poet?" he asked. "Only ye've so many books of poetry here, I wondered was one special to ye?"

"Shelley," she said, without hesitation. "I love so many different poems and poets, but he is my white night poet. His words are my comfort at three o'clock in the morning when I can't sleep and the world seems a very dark place. Here," she wiped her hands on a tea towel and then walked over to the books, reaching down a volume she kept on the top shelf, well away from sticky hands. She handed the slim, leather-bound volume to Ambrose.

"Th—this is a first edition," Ambrose said in a voice of awe.

"Yes, it is. I know how careful you are with books though, so I don't mind you looking at it."

"Was it a gift?"

"Yes, Jamie gave it to me for Christmas one year."

"Ye miss him?" Ambrose said, turning the pages of the book as though it were a sacred relic and he a worshipper at the altar.

"I still see him," she said.

"That's not what I asked," Ambrose replied, his voice quiet.

"I know it's not, but it's hard to tell the truth about this at times. The answer is yes, I miss him. I always will. It's a constant in my life."

"Finian was sayin' he felt for yer husband, because of the situation he's stumbled home to. I told him life isn't so clear cut, an' that none could blame ye for placin' yer love elsewhere when ye thought him dead. I think maybe it's you that has the hardest bit, havin' to choose between the two halves of yerself."

She looked up at the tall, gangly boy and was touched by the understanding in the brown eyes. He was a lad with a great deal of empathy and the ability which gave him that quality, which was to stand in another's shoes for a moment and understand how their reality might be. He gave her one of his quick and lovely smiles, and then returned his face to its habitual position—bent over a book.

Jamie had been by the night before, and they'd sat and had a cup of tea together after Kathleen had gone to sleep. It had been a time since they'd sat so together, and she was grateful to simply be near him and talk as they used to. And she had felt it, in the odd green-tinged twilight which had sifted in through the windows, the strange and inexplicable understanding which had long existed between them, and always would, regardless of time, place and proximity. It was a gift, and one she thought both blessing and curse. Because what she had said to Ambrose was true, she did miss Jamie, missed him in a way which went bone-deep and would, she thought, be with her for the duration of her life.

She ducked into the cold room to grab some potatoes for supper. As she came out, she looked over at Ambrose and saw that his lips were moving, just as her own did when she wanted to commit a line or two to memory; somehow the movement of the tongue and lips stored the words in her mind in a way merely reading them did not.

"What's caught your fancy?" she asked, transferring the potatoes from her apron to the sink and wondering if there would be enough to feed all these young people as well as Casey, should he show up in time for dinner.

"It's this bit—

'And many an antenatal tomb,
Where butterflies dream of the life to come.'

"That's dead gorgeous, that is. It's wee bits like those two lines that make me despair of ever writin' anythin' worthwhile myself."

"You will, you have already, Ambrose. You have a voice, and you have a country which needs that voice."

"That's what I want—to be able to make people see my words—like here, ye can feel the butterflies' longin' for that life they don't yet have, but they know it's there, they feel all the beautiful possibility of it. It's how I feel about Ireland, the one we dream about an' the beautiful possibility of it."

There was a bright spark in his eyes that chilled Pamela to the core. She knew that light, and she understood the pathway it often illuminated for young men and the sacrificial wheel it bound them to. She did not want to see this beautiful, dreamy soul enter that dark realm.

There was a brief knock at the door just then and Casey entered, a bag of groceries under one arm. He came into the kitchen, rain lightly beading his coat and hair. He bent down and kissed her and then put the groceries on the countertop before taking his coat off. She felt that frisson of excitement she still got every time he walked into a room, the disbelief that he was once again here. It felt like having small electrodes attached to her skin, that jumpy, near painful sensation that told her all she needed to know about her body's opinions on the man who stood in front of her.

He washed his hands, and then set to helping her with the dinner. In moments like this one, watching him peel the potatoes and set them on the stove, before he moved to setting the table, while she transferred the salmon to a plate and mixed butter and dill in with the carrots, things felt wonderfully ordinary, as though he had found his way once again into the stream of family life, and was slowly finding his footing amongst them.

The salmon did stretch to everyone though there was not so much as a bite left on the platter once dinner was done. There was a lot of laughter around the table, and the chatter got increasingly animated as dinner progressed, the topics ranging from car engines to a dress Pru was making for herself, to the best places to camp on the west coast. Pamela had a small pang, knowing it wasn't her place to deny Pru permission to go anywhere, but was worried all the same by the looks she saw passing between the girl and Ambrose. They were both so terribly young, and yet, she had been no older when she'd met Casey, and understood only too well the intensity that came with first love. She glanced over at Casey now, watching him as he ate, listening to the answers he gave when either Finian or Ambrose asked him a question.

There was a lovely ease between them at times, which had sprung up since that night when he'd slept in the bed with her. He'd stayed a time or two since, but not in the bed. He slept on the sofa and was always up and about before she rose in the morning. It was, to say the least, a bit of a frustrating situation—to have him so near, to know what it was they'd once had between them in the bed, and not be able to actually induce the man into said bed. It was enough to make a woman think she might go a wee bit mad. It was more than sex, though. It was also just the touch of him, to lie beside him in the night, and hear him breathing as he slept. To put her hands on him, and know the security of his body next to hers. To feel his naked body against hers, hard and needing. She shook her head a little, of late her thoughts always circled back to sex, and the lack of it between the two of them. She realized suddenly that Casey was looking at her, and she flushed, wondering if he'd read her thoughts. He raised an eyebrow at the blush, and smiled at her in a way that told her that he did, indeed, know exactly the track upon which her thoughts had been running.

She came back to the conversation, Finian's words catching her ear.

"It's only that the last time we took a bus, the army stopped it outside the city, an' we all had to get out an' kneel on the roadside while the Brits held their guns to our heads. It would have been fine—I mean it's happened before plenty of times—only Ambrose's sister, Gracie, was there with us that day, an' she told his mammy about it. An' now we have to go away for the summer."

"It's not such a bad thing," Casey said. "My daddy used to do the same with Pat an' me—send us away to the country for the summer months. It never did us any harm, an' we learned a great deal."

"Is that how ye ended up in the 'Ra?" Finian asked.

Casey gave him a long and considering look, before replying. When he did speak, his voice was low but carried with such authority that it stilled all the chatter at the table.

"Not in front of my children, boyo."

Said children had, thankfully, already left the table and were mostly oblivious, though Conor, sensing a shift in the mood had turned and was looking at his father, face slightly anxious. Pamela held her breath, while giving her son a reassuring smile. If Finian pushed it any further, which he was entirely capable of doing, she didn't know how Casey might react.

"I'm sorry," Finian said, red to the roots of his golden curls. Pamela let go of her breath, relieved that the boy had, for once, taken the safer path.

They worried her, these two boys. Finian had a quick temper, and was like a pinwheel rocket, his anger was a flash and bang sort of affair, loud and prone to do local damage, but ultimately it fizzled out rather quickly. Ambrose, on the other hand, was a slow burn and she feared if the day came when his fuse ran out, the explosion would be of the sort no one would be able to forget.

"Where are you meant to go?" Pamela asked, thinking Casey was right and that a summer away would do these two no harm. On the other hand it meant the boys would have a great deal of freedom, and the girls would also naturally gravitate toward that. She wasn't entirely sure where her authority lay with a nineteen-year-old nanny.

"I've an uncle up in Donegal, an' my mam has already called him to see if we can stay there. She thinks we get into more trouble in the summer, but I don't see what difference it makes when the Brits are pricks year-round."

Pamela opened her mouth to admonish Finian for his language, but Ciara beat her to it.

"I swear Finian Gold, ye need to keep a bar of soap in yer pocket to wash that dirty mouth of yers. Ye'll need," she smiled prettily, "to put money in the swear jar."

"Oh aye, I know. But still the British *are* just what I called them."

Casey rolled his eyes at her when Finian wasn't looking and she had to bite the inside of her cheek to keep from laughing out loud. These small moments were becoming more common between the two of them. Just little bits of shared humour and understanding, and she thought even if Casey didn't remember everything, on some level the memories of their life before were there, stored in his cells.

Once dinner was done, the girls left the table to go play with the children, Casey set to washing the dishes, and the boys hung about, drying the dishes and stacking them up in random spots around the kitchen. Pamela retreated to her rocking chair near the fire, to feed Kathleen. She could hear both the girls, and their lovely chatter with the children, and the boys as they engaged in political talk with Casey.

Tonight it appeared the topic on the table was the history of hunger striking in Ireland. Mostly it was Ambrose trying to explain it to Finian, whose mind kept wandering due to him gazing over at Ciara every other minute. Ambrose, realizing that his audience was short on attention, snorted in disgust and turned his remarks toward Casey.

"Ye'll know," Ambrose said.

"I'll know what exactly?" Casey handed Ambrose a rinsed pot and the boy held it dripping over her clean floor, clearly far more intent on what he had to say than the task at hand.

"The roots of hunger strikin' in Ireland."

"An' why is it ye're presumin' I have such knowledge?" Casey asked, clearly amused by the boy's passion.

Ambrose raised a skeptical eyebrow. "Because I know ye do. Now, will ye explain it to this thick-headed clot?"

"Well, he'd be better off gettin' a rundown of this from Patrick, but I can give ye the bare bones of it. Ye'll be familiar with the Brehon Laws, no?"

"Aye, *I* am," Ambrose said, with no small emphasis on the personal pronoun.

"Well, then ye'll know the roots of hunger strikin' go back to those laws. An individual havin' a just claim against another, particularly someone of higher rank, was obliged, as a condition precedent to assertin' that claim, to undertake a fast at the door of the debtor. After a reasonable period of time, if the claim was not satisfied, the fastin' claimant would be entitled to seize the property of the debtor in an amount equal to twice the value of the original claim."

"I knew ye knew," Ambrose said with satisfaction, and beamed a smug look at Finian.

"Now," Casey continued, gesturing with a glass he'd just washed, as he warmed to his subject, "as to how it applies in our own times, it's the same for the most part. Only it's about principle an' how that can be the basis of a claim. So should the claimant be injured or die in the course of the fast, the debtor—in this case the British government—would be held liable for such injury or death. In fact, if the fastin' claimant died as a consequence of the fast, the debtor fasted upon is considered guilty of murder. Provin' it in court might be tricky though. Particularly as we're subject to British law here."

"But under Irish law an' precedent, it *is* murder," Ambrose said, his voice distant and a look in the soft brown eyes which sent a chill through Pamela. Behind her the girls had become very quiet. She looked over at Pru, and saw the echo of her fear in the girl's face, a direct confirmation of her worries about Pru and Ambrose. "It elevates the struggle, an act of sacrifice like that."

"Aye, there's a power in such things. It becomes livin' myth, an' a martyred hero will always stir somethin' deep within the Celtic consciousness. But in the end, lad, that martyr is dead, he never lives to see the fruit of his own performance. An' that is an enormous price to pay in order to make a point. A point which will be lost on the debtor entirely."

"Ye must have run the risk of losin' life with the uh—organization ye belonged to," Ambrose said, voice steady, though there was a slight flush in the pale cheeks.

"Oh, I did. I was young an' foolish once too. There are other things in my life now which matter more, though," Casey said and cast a quick smile over his shoulder in Pamela's direction. "There are other ways to protest an' fight back, that don't require ye to sacrifice yerself on the blood altar of republicanism."

"I think ye can hardly claim to have done that yerself," Ambrose said in a matter-of-fact way.

"Ach, no," Casey said, "I was more the fightin' sort, not passive resistance, if ye can call somethin' that ends in yer own death passive. Patrick an' Pamela on the other hand, were always out marchin' an' carryin' the protest signs. Pat wasn't given to the violence, an' so he took his frustration an' channelled it into somethin' positive to help others. Becomin' a lawyer is just a further extension of that. Ye might take a cue from him, lad. Pamela tells me ye're smart as a whip."

"D'ye not think, though, if it rouses the country then it is worth the life of a few men—the way Yeats said it, *'The common people, for all time to come, will raise a heavy cry against the threshold, Even if it be the King's.'*"

"Poets are rarely the ones dyin' on the front line of this particular fight. Ye might want to give that some thought."

"Aye, I'll give it some thought. There's not really the money for school, mind. But I'll think on it."

Without warning, a sudden wave of dizziness swept over Pamela, as if her head had gone under water on a dark night. She couldn't smell the scents of the house anymore, but rather something cold, the sort of cold that emanates from dead leaves and frost, from the absence of warmth and light. The cold took root in her stomach and began to cast out tendrils, growing inside her like a sapling sheathed in frost. It was as if an entity had come into the room, something invisible, yet no less real for that. The chill of it emanated out through the cozy kitchen, reaching out with those tendrils to touch Ciara's delicate neck, Pru's capable hands, casting a shadow across Finian's gold curls and resting like a mantle, dark and cold, around Ambrose's shoulders. She blinked, thinking something was wrong with her eyes, but the darkness remained. She didn't dare to look at Casey, she didn't want to know if the touch of it was upon him. Her eyes swept down toward her children, and she saw they sat in pools of light, the strange dark not touching them.

She stood, patting Kathleen's back and fighting off the dizziness which continued to roll over her with the force of a returning tide. She took a step forward and felt the floor shift under her, and she stumbled sideways, clutching Kathleen's head to her shoulder. Casey crossed the room in three quick strides, and took Kathleen from her, then reached out a hand to steady her once he had the baby safe against his chest.

"Are ye all right?" he asked, and she looked up to find his face drawn in an expression of concern.

"I-I just need some air," she said. This was true enough. She needed to breathe fresh, cold air and have a bit of silence in which to gather her wits.

"Are ye certain ye're steady enough to be wanderin' outside on yer own?"

She nodded. "I am, I was just a little dizzy."

Casey gave her a dubious look as if he didn't quite believe her. "Aye, so ye say, but I'll keep the wee one with me, if ye don't mind."

Outside, it was raining, the drops driving down hard and cold, needling at her scalp and shoulders, drenching her in the matter of seconds it took to cross the yard to the byre. She leaned her head against the wall of the byre, and felt the rain as it ran in rivulets through her hair, and down her neck, until it gathered and became a small stream in the groove of her backbone.

The air was cold and raw, and a few deep breaths of it quelled the queasiness she'd felt inside the house, and slowly banished the dark feeling which had grown over her skin, and altered her sight. She knew it was real though, and wished she could talk herself out of the strange knowledge which had come to her in that moment. Knowledge of something coming for all those young and beautiful souls in there. There was no way to know what, nor any way to warn them, because it would do no good. Both Finian and Ambrose burned with a very particular fire, and she could not stop either of them from drawing near the blazing heat of it, regardless of the fact it might well immolate them. She was experienced in how difficult it was to turn a man away from a thing he believed in right down to the core of his soul. Casey had taught her that, but he had finally, as he'd said, found something more important. Still, her greatest fear was something more happening to him, some dark hand reaching in from the maelstrom that was life in this country and yanking him—once again—out of the weave of their world.

Courage was opening your eyes when you were afraid, when you didn't want to see what was directly in front of you. And so, just before she had stumbled, she had taken hold of her courage and looked at Casey, and saw no shadow upon him, but only the same clear light which gathered around her children.

"Is there anythin' that needs fixin' or mendin'?" Casey asked, eyeing up a small crack in the plaster over the kitchen sink. It was his way of looking after them right now, she knew, fixing anything he could find which had the smallest need of it. He had always done this, though, kept things shipshape and running smoothly.

"Nothing urgent," she said, thinking about the door of their bedroom and how sticky it had become in the last couple of days. Despite Casey's best efforts the upstairs floor had never been quite level, and the door had needed a little planed off the bottom each spring.

"What is it? I can see there's somethin' ye're thinkin' about."

"The bedroom door is sticking a bit, but it's not something I'm worried over, it can wait."

"I'll have a look," he said and was up the stairs before she could stop him. She could hear a few muffled thumps, and the sound of a hammer tapping out hinges, and then he came down the stairs carrying the door.

His toolbox was sitting in the small porch off the side door, and he fetched his plane, before spreading a canvas cloth on the floor to catch shavings. He sat, wedging the bottom end of the door between his knees, just high enough so that the plane wouldn't catch at his pants but low enough that he could put adequate pressure on it.

It was peaceful in the kitchen. The young folk had all left for the pub, shortly after she had come back inside, soaked to the skin and shivering, but relieved to find that the strange mantle which had clung around the four of them, was gone. Thinking about it now, in the warmth of the kitchen, with the scent of freshly-planed wood lending a note of comfort, it seemed as though she might well have imagined it. Some strange trick of light, making her see that which wasn't there.

She sat now, thinking of the dozen or so things she ought to do before bed, and yet feeling too relaxed and sleepy to get up and deal with them. She'd had a hot bath at Casey's insistence, while he put the children to bed. Even Kathleen was fast asleep in her crib upstairs. She was in her pyjamas herself, and ready for bed.

"Pamela, why do ye have rebar drilled right into the door frame of the bedroom?" Casey asked, startling her a little with the abruptness of his words.

"That was something I had done when all the threatening letters were coming in. It's the same in the children's bedroom. I thought it would buy us a few extra minutes if someone broke into the house during the night."

"Oh," he said, clearly a little taken aback at her answer. "Did ye hire someone to come in? There's real craftsmanship in the work."

"No, Noah did it for me."

"Oh, I see," he said, and while his tone was calm enough, she caught sight of his expression before he turned his head back to planing the door. The look there spoke volumes. "Was he upstairs much then?"

Her heart started to beat a little harder. She had known this moment must come, but like all completely unpleasant tasks, she had hoped to stave it off as long as possible.

"Is that the question you want to ask? Or are you asking if he was in our bedroom much?"

He took a long curl of wood off the bottom of the door, his aim and stroke meticulous even though she could see the tension in the set of his shoulders.

"An' what if that is what I'm askin'?"

"Then the answer is he was up there exactly once—and that was the day he put the rebar in."

"Were ye ever in his bedroom?" he asked, his hands still on the plane but his eyes meeting hers as he posed his question.

She swallowed, a cold thrill of anxiety rippling over her body. A lie might be the kinder course right now, but they'd made a vow of honesty to one another and in the end she knew it was the right course, even if it cost them dearly.

"Yes, I was. The first time was when I was shot and went to him for help. I was in no shape to go home that night, so I slept in his bed. Where he slept that night, I don't know." It had been that same night that she asked Noah to kill a man for her, but she thought just now wasn't the time to relay that information. Casey could only be expected to take in so much at once. The story of the shooting and having to hide in the pipe with a rat she had told him, the details of the rest of the night she had omitted.

"And the other times?" he asked, so still that he seemed engraved against the background of kitchen and hearth—a study in ink which held in it both tension and fear.

"There was only one other time," she said quietly.

"Aye?" he said. There was a certain regret in his eyes already, just for asking.

"Are you sure you want to know this, Casey?"

"It's all right. I already knew."

"Oh, I see," she said, voice so small that she wasn't certain he even heard her. "How long have you known?"

"Since the time we talked about ye bein' engaged to him, an' I asked ye what he was to ye. I could tell there was somethin' ye weren't sayin' at the time. I didn't want to know it, I think, an' so I told myself it was somethin' else. I believed ye when ye said ye cared for him but didn't love him, so I knew it must be that ye'd been intimate with the man an' wanted to spare me the knowledge of that."

"It was one time, Casey. I know that probably doesn't mitigate how you feel about it, but it was once. He came to me because he'd just seen a child killed right in front of him. He needed me, and I thought I was going to marry him. It was the next morning," she looked away from him, unable to bear the scrutiny of those dark eyes any longer, "that I broke off the engagement."

"He must have found that a little confusin'," Casey said mildly enough, but she caught the look in his eyes and knew he wasn't feeling mild about this at all.

She shook her head. There was no way to make him understand the strange, sad desperation of that night and how it had felt like the warmth and oblivion of her body was something she could give Noah, when she could not give him the one thing he truly desired—her love.

"Did ye love him?" he asked, and though his voice was quiet, it was neither soft nor gentle.

"No, not in the way you mean, not as I loved you, as I will always love you. But as a friend, as someone who understood me—in that way, yes, I loved him."

"So why did ye break off the engagement?" he asked.

"Because I just couldn't go through with it. I couldn't marry anyone, Casey. I was still married to you, despite the fact I thought you were dead." She shook her head. "I just couldn't."

She went to him and knelt at his feet, and took his hands. "I'm sorry, only then it didn't seem as if it would matter to anyone."

He looked down at her, the dark eyes soft with sorrow. "Did it not matter to you?"

"At the time, no, I can't say that it did."

"And now?" he asked, and she noticed that a small muscle jumped in his throat.

"Yes, it matters if it hurts you. If I'd had even an inkling that you were still alive, Casey, you have to know I would never have been with another man."

He shook his head. "It's only that sometimes I look at yer face, Pamela and I get an' idea of how much these last three years have cost ye. I fear I will never be able to repair the damage from that."

"It's not your job to do that," she said.

He put his hand to her face, thumb softly bracing her chin, forcing her to look up at him. "If it's not mine, then I should like to know whose it is."

"Mine, I suppose."

"Aye, yours but mine as well. I don't know that I can ever make up for the lost time Pamela, an' all that happened to ye in those years, but I should like to try."

"Are you upset? About Noah?" she asked, looking directly at him, knowing that bravery was necessary between them in this moment.

"Would ye believe me if I said I wasn't?" he asked, and while the tone was light, the look in his eyes was anything but.

"No, I wouldn't," she said.

"I'm sad, but I can understand it, an' I'm sorry too, that ye felt that way bein' with a man. I'm also jealous as hell."

What she had told him was true, she regretted it for the pain it was causing him, but for the act itself she did not harbor regret. Noah had, as she'd said, needed her and it was the one form of love she could grant him. Her body had merely been the vessel that night to give to him what he needed. It wasn't like making love with Casey, nor Jamie come to that, but it had been an exchange between the two of them which had been both intimate and reflective of the affection they'd long held for one another. There had been times when she'd felt shame around sex, but that night with Noah was not one of them.

The act had been one which was simply another step in a complicated and strange relationship, which had also been one of her greatest anchors over the three years Casey had been gone. There was no way to make Casey understand that, nor should he have to. Noah had mattered to her—he'd mattered a great deal. How to tell a man that and have him understand it didn't touch what you felt for him? There were things which Casey did not need to know, and how she'd felt about sex with Noah was one of them. He knew about the act, he didn't need to know about the emotion behind it.

"Will you stay tonight?" she asked.

He looked at her for several seconds, the dark eyes unfathomable and she wondered what exactly was going through his head.

"Aye, I'll stay if ye like. I can sleep on the couch, it's comfortable enough."

She drew back a little. While she understood that he might not want to make love when the thought of another man being with his wife hung so vividly before him—still, the rejection stung.

"You don't have to stay, Casey. I'm sorry, I shouldn't make you feel beholden." She meant the words, but she was aware that her tone was stiff.

"Pamela, I just don't think it's a good idea tonight. I'll stay, but I can't come upstairs."

She nodded, and stood, determined not to cry in front of him.

"I'll say goodnight then," she said, and turned toward the stairs. He stood though, and took her by the shoulders, turning her toward him and drawing her into his arms.

"Don't go upstairs angry with me," he said softly.

She shook her head, and then leaned her forehead against his chest. "I'm not mad at you. I'm afraid."

"Afraid of what, Jewel?"

"Afraid you don't want me anymore. That everything that has happened since you disappeared has destroyed what we had. I'm afraid that you don't trust me enough to give me your vulnerability."

"Oh God, woman. Do ye not know I ache to the marrow of my bones for you?"

She put her hands against his chest, unable to speak. His heart thudded under her cheek, and his hands were still and warm on her back.

"Pamela, will ye look at me?" His voice was a little hoarse. "Please," he added, when she didn't move.

She took a long breath and then looked up, frightened by what she might find in his eyes. But all she saw there was love, and a sorrow that went to the core of him.

"I want ye, woman. I need the love of yer body as I need water an' air, but I think tonight, with the thought of Noah bein' there between us, it's not a good idea."

He kissed her then, carefully, clearly feeling the very fragile balance which existed between the two of them, and she could not help but respond, starved as she felt for the touch of him, the need of him. He broke the kiss first, making a small sound of frustration and, she thought, pain.

"Pamela, I—"

"No," she said, cutting him off, thinking she couldn't bear it if he said anything more. "You're right, it's best that we don't tonight. I understand, Casey, I really do." She stepped back from him, and smiled, though she knew it wasn't a convincing expression. "I think I'll go up now."

"Aye, sleep well, Jewel."

She turned back on the landing, and faced him. He still stood where she'd left him, in the middle of the kitchen, wood shavings puddled around his feet and a look of bemusement on his face.

"Casey."

"Aye?" he looked up, half startled, as though he'd been lost in thoughts far from the place where he stood.

"I ached for you too," she said softly, "every moment you were gone."

Part Three

A Thousand Tiny Cracks

Chapter Twenty-six

Blood and Apples

"ARE WE LOST?"

Ambrose looked at the passenger seat of his car, where his best friend and major pain in the arse sat, a young gentleman also known as Finian Gold.

Ambrose, being male, subscribed to the point of view that one was never truly lost until one fell off the edge of the world, and so said, "No, I'll just need a minute to get my bearins' an' then we'll be fine."

The two boys were currently driving slowly along a very narrow lane in County Armagh. Ambrose's grandfather was away on a long-anticipated trip to visit his brother in Boston, and Ambrose and Finian were looking after his farm. They'd been away this evening to a dance, and it had meant a round trip of a few hours, between picking up the girls in Belfast, driving to Bangor for the dance, driving the girls back to Belfast, and then returning here, so he could be up to tend to the cows come morning, Ambrose felt it had been well worth it, just to spend those few hours with Pru.

Ambrose slowed the car even further, thinking it would have been wise to stick to a main road. Ahead of them, the track wound on up a hill. It consisted of a series of potholes nearly large enough for them to disappear into. The bits of macadam that were still intact were rife with tufts of grass and dandelions, which looked like floating globes in the moonlight. He supposed, though, if a man had to be lost, this was a fine place to do it.

They were in the midst of an old apple orchard, and the moon hung three-quarters full and was tinged pink—strawberry moon, he thought it was called—shedding enough light to bathe the countryside in a silver haze. The light fell through the apple blossoms, rendering the delicate blooms a translucent white, and making the trees appear like ghostly brides awaiting their bridegrooms.

Coming through the orchards of Armagh always put him in mind of the legendary Gaelic lovers Baile and Aillin. Heir to the throne of Ulster, Baile fell in love with Aillin, who just happened to be the daughter of the King of Leinster. The Druids, well knowing the match would start a war, ruled that the lovers would not be together in this world. Unwilling to live a life apart, Baile and Aillin arranged to meet and marry in secret.

Baile set forth from Emain Macha—which was the ancient name for Armagh—but was told on the way of the death of his beloved. At the very same time, the identical story was told to Aillin of her lover, Baile. Both were so overcome with grief that they died as soon as the last words fell from the deceptive messengers' tongues. The two were buried side by side, allowed to be together in death, if not in life. It was said that an apple tree was planted on each grave, and that the two trees had but one shadow, so entwined were their limbs. It was a tale as old as time, but it was no less romantic for all the retellings.

He wanted to bring Pru here—well, if he figured out where *here* was—while the blossoms were at the peak of their gauzy beauty, and tell her the old tale. He'd thought of apple trees the first time he'd kissed her, for her lips had tasted of cider.

"Are ye wool gatherin' again?"

Finian's voice had the effect of pulling him into the here and now again, with the realization that they had indeed gone astray and were now turned around on a bit of country road on the wrong side of midnight, in an area he feared might be predominantly Protestant.

He stopped the car and put on the brake, giving himself a minute to think, hopeful that if he paused for a bit he'd be able to pull up the mental map he kept in his head. Such a map was a matter of instinct, and instinct he'd found required silence and focus.

Beside him, Finian sighed, for he knew what Ambrose was doing, and that it could take several moments for him to access his 'mad mental map', as Finian liked to call it. It was a technique his grandfather had taught him when he was very young, and he always saw it in his imaginings as an old brass telescope of the sort they once carried on ships. He would put his mind's eye to the scope, and then he could either pull the focus in or dial it out, bringing up the landscape one piece at a time, or viewing the whole of it. His granddad always said landscape was personal; it was made up of the things you'd experienced in it, and so would appear different to your vision than it would to the next man's, because he would see his own experience imprinted upon it.

"Ambrose, not now, we can figure our way back to the farm, if ye'll just keep drivin'. I don't like stoppin' on these godforsaken roads in the middle of the night."

Later, he would wonder if Finian was a wee bit in the way of a seer, but just then he ignored him, and closed his ears to his friend's protests. He put his eye to that imaginary telescope, and waited for the map to show itself. It took a few minutes, during which he could feel every twitch of Finian's impatience, and every sound of the countryside at night: a small creature rustling in the hedge next to the car, a bird startled into squawking before settling back down, and the noise of the night itself, that pure velvet hum that was pricked with starlight, and like no other sound on earth. It was out of this hum that it came—the landscape he carried inside him—floating up from the dark water of the unconscious. It was like the old continent at first, just a mass of land, dripping with moss and agleam with its water birthing. He quickly brought his focus down so that it was a pinpoint in the midst of country, county, townland.

There was his grandda's farm with its stone walls and rippling fields, and there was the old beech, which stood at the head of the lane to the farm, one that his great-great-grandfather had planted, and which he'd spent many a boyhood day in, apples in one hand, a book in the other. He widened the map a little, and saw the narrow meandering roads, the route of which only made sense if you realized the roads here belonged more to cows and sheep than humans. Out again, and he saw old Widow Butterdean's neatly kept farm where he'd helped his grandfather bring in the hay one summer, and how he'd found a rare orchid fossilized in the midst of a tightly packed haycock. He had it still—the orchid—held between the pages of the first volume of *A Social History of Ancient Ireland*.

Beyond the widow's fields, was the silver pond where one day he'd found a woman floating face down—he'd thought at first she was a drowned swan—and had not understood when his grandfather told him that white, white thing with the streaming hair was dead and was a woman who had lived alone in a vine-covered cottage, and was known to harbour a great sadness that had something to do with a young man who'd never returned from a faraway war. His grandfather had said she'd chosen to sleep that way, with the green water pulled over her like a blanket, and lilies to cushion her head. He'd never forgotten the image, and while he'd felt sorry for the woman, for even then he'd understood it was no good thing to have a terrible sadness, he'd thought such a place might be peaceful as a final resting spot.

He widened the telescope a little more and saw the vine-covered cottage, which he'd believed haunted when he was small, tucked away in its wood, dreaming its old longing dreams of love, and of a soldier who, in another reality, did come home after a faraway war.

Then came the village, quiet and yet roiling with all the drama any human stage inevitably commanded. The wee shops—the butcher, the baker, the candlestick maker—all facing the tiny square which sat at a crossroads. It was from this crossroads that two roads wandered off from the village, and he was certain it was a tributary of one of these which they were currently on.

Both roads were lined with hedges, neatly trimmed to within an inch of their lives on the Protestant road, and gone adrift with the wildness of holly and ash, blackberry bramble and pools of white foxgloves, on the Catholic side. This last item was said to cure a man when worn as an amulet, should he step upon fairy grass and be cursed with itchy feet that caused him to travel without rest for the span of his life. And then suddenly he knew where they were, the location slowly opening to him, as though it had been hidden away and shy of being seen—the old Flynn orchard, abandoned long ago due to some family tragedy that he couldn't quite recall, but the family had never sold the land, and the apples had long gone wild, and while they were rumored to yield a cider which tasted like the first apple upon a man's tongue, no one ever picked them. His granddad had said it was because the orchard was haunted and no one willing to risk encountering the ghosts who lingered there.

This review of his map told him one thing—they were, indeed, turned around, but it was only a matter of taking the next three lefts they came upon to right themselves on their course.

"…and of course, I'm mad about her."

Ambrose realized suddenly that Finian was talking, though still looking around him as though he expected an Iron Age wolf to come bounding out of the trees, and drag him back to its dark cave. Finian was a city boy to the core, and nighttime in the countryside was, for him, beset with boojums of a wide and wild variety. In his usual form, he reverted to chatter in order to calm himself. He was, of course, speaking of Ciara, for whom he'd fallen like a weight of sand dropped from the top of a building.

"Aye, anyone with eyes can see that," Ambrose replied easily, not wanting to agitate Finian. "She's got ye wrapped 'round her wee finger."

"I'm happy to be there. What about you an' Miss Prudence? Are ye in with a chance there, or no?"

"Don't talk about her like that," Ambrose said sharply.

"It's serious, then?" Finian asked, as if surprised by this news.

In truth, Ambrose had been a little shocked himself by Pru's feelings for him, and his for her. After all, he wasn't handsome like Finian, and he'd never known how to spin shit into silver the way Finian could either, when it came to talking up the girls. But he'd liked Pru immediately. She was straightforward, honest and smart, and she had the prettiest hair—the colour of a wheat field with the sun setting over it. He could talk to her about anything—books, family, ambition, hopes, dreams and even just the most trivial bits of his day, and in turn she shared all those things with him.

"Hell's bells, man, I didn't know it was like *that*." Finian let out a long, low whistle. "*Goin' to the chapel, an' we're gonna get married…*"

"Shut yer gob, ye eejit."

"Come on, give over, are ye dead set on her, then?"

"Pru knows what I feel, an' that's enough for me," Ambrose said, hoping his tone sounded sufficiently prohibitive to put a halt to the conversation. He'd never been one to talk over his feelings a great deal, and he wasn't about to start with Finian, who was a terrible gossip at times, and entirely indiscreet. He wasn't certain he *could* put it into words because what he felt for her was completely out of his range of experience, and frankly, his understanding at times. He knew Finian thought she was a little plain, and that she had a bit of an edge on her, though compared to most of the women in Finian's life—his ma in particular—Pru was a positive marshmallow. Finian didn't know that Ambrose thought Pru was the most beautiful girl in the world and that she was, for him, the personification of poetry. All those beautiful strings of words that he so loved paled in comparison to how she made him feel. He understood it was more than an infatuation, and so he had taken his time and been careful with her. His mam had always said he was a canny lad, wont to think his way through things before committing to any sort of action.

He released the brake and put his foot down on the gas pedal. The hill ahead was steep and the car would need a bit of gumption to climb it.

He'd met Pru through his friendship with Pamela Riordan, and it seemed a bit of a miracle to him that in allowing a woman to take his picture one day, his life had been transformed. A friendship had grown with Pamela, around a shared passion for poetry, and he'd found a kindred spirit in her, and much to his surprise, also one in James Kirkpatrick, who he'd gotten to know a bit after the man grilled him in his study one memorable evening before he had taken Prudence out for the first time.

"Ambrose, look. There's a roadblock up ahead, an' it don't look like a regular one," Finian said, leaning forward, his hand clutching the dash.

Ambrose's heart skipped a beat, and panic swept through his body, turning his bowels to ice. Finian was right, for as they'd crowned the hill and turned a corner, vehicle lights bloomed into view and showed them a barrier across the road. Finian was right about it not being a regular roadblock either, for those weren't British soldiers up ahead, who, while annoying, weren't necessarily violent at all times. If this was a UDR patrol—and he thought, judging by the uniforms that it was—then it was a totally different story, as they were violent more often than not. Ambrose tried to think, and found his mind was racing around with about as much traction as a greased pig on ice. The lane was narrow, with ditches on either side. He could back up, but they'd chase them down, and odds were if they ran things would go much worse than if they tried to just calmly pass the barricade. As if sensing his thoughts, Finian said, "Don't back up, the fuckers are behind us too."

Ambrose glanced quickly up at the rearview mirror, to find that there were three men, all with rifles held at waist height, standing about ten yards distance behind the car.

"Shit," Finian said, which rather summed up the whole situation quite neatly.

The Ulster Defence Regiment was, in theory at least, part of the greater British Army. The idea had been to recruit locals, many of them ex-soldiers themselves, to 'defend the life or property in Northern Ireland, against armed attack or sabotage.' To say that the regiment took their remit rather broadly, was to severely underplay how corrupt and often violent they were. They didn't require anyone sabotaging or staging an armed attack either, in order to wreak their particular brand of havoc. Originally there had been a small Catholic contingent in the regiment, but the highest numbers still only totalled eighteen percent of the force. After internment it had dropped down to three percent. Catholics had long been aware that neither the Army nor any of its local regiments were their friends.

Ambrose slowed the car to a near crawl, he didn't want to startle the bastards in any way, shape or form. It was too easy for them to claim he'd done something threatening, and then simply open up on the two of them with their rifles.

"Fuck, fuck, fuck," Finian said. This bit of eloquence told Ambrose that Finian too understood who these men were.

One man broke from the cluster by the barrier, walked up to the driver's side window and rapped sharply on it. Having little choice, Ambrose rolled the window down.

"Step out of the car," the man said. He looked like a bulldog, short, compact and terrifyingly strong.

Ambrose hesitated. Were it daylight at a busy crossing this wouldn't cause him a great deal of worry, but on an abandoned road in the wee hours with no one around to hear them scream, it was another matter altogether. He thought rather wildly about just running the barrier, but knew they'd both be dead before they got near it, the car filled with bullet holes as well as their corpses.

"I said get out of the fucking car, ye fucking Fenian bastard."

By those words both boys understood just how dire their situation was about to become. Ambrose gave Finian a lightning quick glance, and saw his friend in the brilliant glare of the headlights from the military vehicles. He looked terrified.

"Are ye deaf or just stupid? I told ye to get out!"

The soldier wrenched open the door, seized Ambrose by his collar and yanked him out of the car. Ambrose fought to get his hands up, to pull at the shirt where it was choking him, to find his feet so that he could stand rather than being pulled hard and fast over the ditch, through a gap in the hedge and into the field beyond. Bramble caught at his clothes, and rocks cut his skin.

He heard a short, sharp scream and felt a flash of rage—what the hell were they doing to Finian?

Twenty yards into the field, the man threw him to the ground and then the beating that he'd known was coming began. The world was reduced and distilled down to blood, pain and the dread of the next kick, the next blow. It was the taste of grass, dirt and blood in his mouth. It was the knowledge that this was how he died—anonymous, for he was just a fucking Fenian, a fucking Taig boy to these men. He felt like glass, his flesh a completely inadequate shield between bones and boots.

He tried to retreat inside, as if there was an altar somewhere deep within his cells, where he might stop for sanctuary, and not be aware of what was happening to his body, but he was too terrified, and the occasional scream from Finian kept that sanctuary far from his reach. These men were going to kill both of them, it was only a matter of how long it was going to take, and how hard the dying was going to be.

Voices blurred together, so that he only heard snatches. "Feel that, ye fockin' Taig bastard, we'll set fire to ye, the way yer bastard friends did to Gus. Hey, get the petrol, Jack, bring it here. I'm goin' to burn this fockin' Taig until even his mammy won't recognize the ashes."

He thought he might be sick, the thought of burning terrified him. The dying *was* going to be hard.

Fleeting pictures touched him and fled: the old blue bunny he'd had as a baby; the feel of his grandfather's hand, calloused and hard and smelling of tobacco; Agnes, the sister nearest him in age, and only eleven months his elder, though they looked enough alike that they might well have been twins. And then Pru, as she'd looked only hours before, flushed and beautiful in his arms, her blue eyes speaking worlds to him with only a look. He'd not told her he loved her yet, but he hoped she understood it all the same.

He was still a virgin for Christ's sake—it seemed inordinately unfair to die before he'd ever known what it was to bed a woman. Particularly when Pru had offered only the week before, and he'd turned her down in a fit of what now felt like regrettable decency.

Jamie had loaned him a book of ancient Irish bardic tales, which he suspected might be worth a lot of money—he hoped to God someone would return it to the man when they went through his few belongings. It felt idiotic to be worrying about such things just now, and yet his mind was whirling all sorts of trivialities around and around.

The petrol was cold when they poured it on him, and he flinched, trying to pull himself into the ground, wishing with his whole being that he could burrow in like an animal, and disappear into the earth. Everything slowed down, so that the smallest sound was like a crash of cymbals in his ears: his own breath like a freight train, and yet a fragile thing which was about to be taken from him; the men laughing; the sound of bone cracking; Finian letting out a terrible howl; a match striking against stone, and then the smell of sulphur and death.

Please God, help. The words were on a loop in his head; they were the most efficient prayer he could manage as the petrol began to burn his skin. He hoped the pain would cause him to pass out, and he wouldn't feel the fire as it ate him to ashes.

A rifle shot sounded. Had they killed Finian? He wished his own end could be so swift. But then a voice, rough and carrying, cut through the night, like a call of redemption sounding from a hill.

"What the hell is goin' on over there?"

"Mind yer business, an' be on yer way!" The soldier spoke sharply but Ambrose heard reprieve in his tone, for he was unnerved by the intruder coming along to interrupt their fun.

Lights then and a vehicle bouncing across the field, headlights pinning the soldiers in their crime, like hunted hares.

"Finian!" He yelled it out and got another kick for his pains.

"Here," came the short reply.

"Ye're on my property. I'm armed an' so are my friends who are with me, an' don't think we'll hesitate to shoot yez. Now, leave those two lads alone, an' get back in yer jeeps an' get the hell out of here. Ye've ten seconds before we open fire on yez."

Ambrose felt a wave of hope, despite the petrol fumes choking him, and the certainty that his life was still hanging by a very thin thread. He waited, not even daring to lift his head, as time stretched out like hot taffy, so that it seemed to sag in the middle, and he thought he might be permanently suspended here, waiting for that match to fall and set the world on fire.

"Do yer masters know ye've chewed through yer rope an' gone off leash?" the man asked, voice genial enough but with an edge to it. The inference was clear. If their higher ups found out about this makeshift roadblock it could be that a fairly severe punishment would be in order. The UDR struggled to be seen seriously by the British Army, but it was no secret they weren't considered much more than a raggle-taggle group of rank amateurs.

The man above him let out a sharp burst of air. No doubt he was frustrated at being deprived of the fun of burning a Catholic boy alive. There was a hesitation—one that seemed to stretch into eternity—but then the soldier finally walked away.

Time began to move again, though he waited until he heard the vehicles start and drive away into the night, before he dared to take so much as a decent breath.

Ambrose pushed himself up off the ground cautiously, lest his bones had indeed turned to glass. A few ribs were likely cracked, for his breath caught upon the pain as he used the field wall as leverage to pull himself up. His legs were shaking as he stood, and felt about as likely to hold him up as poorly set cream, but he managed to keep to his feet, and face the man now approaching him. He was just in time to see several dark figures on the edge of the field fade silently into the woods from where they'd clearly been hiding. The man hadn't lied; he had not come here alone.

"Are ye all right, boy?"

"I'll do," Ambrose said warily, hoping they hadn't tumbled from the frying pan to the fire.

The farmer came within a few feet of him. He was an older man, slight, with a shock of grey hair that stood out all around his head. There was also an aura of no-nonsense all around him, and Ambrose thought it likely the man would have, indeed, shot the soldiers.

"Ye'll not mind me sayin' this I hope, but ye don't look as though ye'll do. The roadways are a bit wild back here, was there a reason ye were prowlin' about so late?"

Ambrose nodded. "We were just headin' home—we'd been to a dance out Bangor way, an' had taken our girls home, an' were returnin' for the night to my granddad's farm. I'm lookin' after his place while he's away, an' I thought I remembered a shortcut back. Turned out to be a mistake."

The farmer gave him a sharp once-over.

"Ye'd be Ambrose Turner's grandson, then?"

"Aye, that's me."

"An' how'd ye run into yon bunch?" The farmer nodded toward the road.

"They had a roadblock set up, looked like UDR to me."

"Oh, aye, likely was. Bloody bastards—it's a fine day when a couple of young lads can't go to a dance an' get themselves home without bein' half murdered. Come on, boys, the house is just up this way. I can have my son take my truck back, but I'll take the two of youse in yer car, neither of ye looks fit for the drivin'. Keys?"

"Left in the car—at least I hope so," Ambrose said. Pain was starting to throb in his various bits and pieces and he wanted to check his teeth, but was scared to as well. At least two were loose, he knew that much without touching them. He could still taste blood in his mouth, along with the thick, dark taste of the petrol.

The keys were—thankfully—still in the car, and they were soon in it, driving up the rather rough road to the farmer's house. It occurred to

Ambrose—belatedly—that this was perhaps not terribly wise. Mind you, if the man wanted them dead, he could have just given the UDR boys another five or so minutes more, and both he and Finian would have been finished.

There was a wife inside the farm house, and the kitchen was a warm and inviting place, and didn't look like the lair of a mad killer. Not that he knew what the lair of a mad killer might look like, but he thought it would be a bit spookier than a wife in an apron, the smell of bread in the air, and a nicely built fire in the hearth.

The farmer gave him a clean shirt and pants. "The trousers will not be long enough for ye, lad, but they'll be better than what ye're wearin'. Go have a wash an' change yerself."

He stripped out of his clothes, shivering in the cold tile of the bath and then gave himself a quick wash with warm water, the reek of petrol taking up the whole space of the small bathroom. The pants were too short, and they hung about his hips, but they were dry and warm and not likely to catch fire if he walked too near flame. There was a small mirror over the sink, tinged green with age, and he gave himself a quick glance, half afraid to look. It wasn't as bad as he'd feared, as the beating had mainly been contained to his body, though they'd managed a few blows to his head as well. His glasses would need mending again, but the damage to his actual face looked as though it would heal in a few weeks. The damage to his spirit, he knew, was going to be another matter altogether.

The wife looked after their injuries with minimal talk, just took care of them in a kind, if slightly brusque, fashion. The farmer helped her, though it was clear that if the family had a medical officer, it wasn't him. Finian, as it turned out, had a broken wrist, which the woman neatly bound while Finian bit down on a belt, and then told him he'd have to see a bone doctor as soon as he might.

Ambrose took stock of his friend, now that there was a moment to do so. Finian was pale and subdued, traces of blood still visible in his hair—crimson on gold. His face was bruised, and it looked like his nose might have been broken. Likely it would only add to his charm, for such was Finian's luck. They'd been friends since primary school, and as much as Finian made him crazy at times, still he loved his friend, and would have been utterly devastated had he been badly damaged, or worse yet, killed outright.

The wife made them tea and a plate of sandwiches, and to Ambrose's surprise he was able to eat, though he chewed exclusively on the right side of his mouth, as the molars on the left were most assuredly loose.

It was during his second sandwich that he became aware of an underlying tension in the room. He looked over at Finian, but he seemed unaware, his face white with pain as he sipped one-handed at a cup of tea. Ambrose felt it though, and thought he might have a notion of just what it was about.

"D'ye want us to call the police?" The farmer was looking at his face carefully as he asked the question, and Ambrose had the sense that it was a test of sorts.

"No," he said quietly, "that'll do no good, will it?"

"Maybe not, but still an' all if ye'd like me to call them, I'll do so for ye."

"No," Finian said, "Ambrose is right, it won't help. The police aren't the quarter to look to for help."

Ambrose flicked a look at his friend, realizing Finian had picked up on the tension, after all.

"All right then, lads, I'll not call the police. Is there anyone else ye'd like me to call?"

The question hung in the air. There were any number of people, and yet, Ambrose felt, it wasn't necessary to involve anyone else. He had the sense the farmer would prefer it that way. He'd be fine to drive home now, he thought, feeling fortified by the food and tea.

The farmer turned then to Finian, and asked a deceptively simple question, which was of course, anything but.

"How are ye feelin', lad?"

"Like shit," Finian said, "but I'll manage."

The farmer nodded, and then fixed his gaze on Ambrose, the blue eyes calculating and yet not unfriendly.

"And what about you, boy, what is it you feel?"

Ambrose considered it for a moment, as he felt his way over his internal landscape, looking for that steep-sided valley wherein he kept his emotions. A messy sort of map at best, but definitely readable. He'd always been one to sort through his emotional terrain before pronouncing a verdict on what he found there. The terror had faded a bit already, the shock was going to take a little longer, but there was one emotion that burned like a low flame, steady and ready to burn higher and hotter as it found fuel.

"Rage," he said.

It was an incremental rage, one born from long years of living as a Catholic in a city and a country where that was too often a very dangerous thing to be. It was born of all the streets he could not walk for fear of being killed, its root was in all the times he and Finian had to outrun a gang of boys simply because they'd strayed too close to an invisible tribal boundary. It came from the fact that he knew that regardless of how smart or capable he was, he was likely looking at a manhood pocked with unemployment. It lay in the knowledge that too many of his friends had died already, one shot in the street as he ran, a shy boy who had been all of twelve years old at the time. It was there, slowly building, each time he'd been stopped at a checkpoint, and had feared he would die, and it was there every time he'd been forced to his knees and had a gun held to his head. Tonight had merely brought the simmer of it to a full boil.

The farmer nodded, as though his answer had pleased him. "Good, ye should feel angry. Now," he continued, leveling a look at Ambrose which spoke clearly, "would ye like to do somethin' about that?"

Chapter Twenty-seven

The Scent of a Long-Ago Love

ONE SILVER NIGHT, when the moon was beginning to turn her shoulder to the world, Ambrose took Pru to the vine-covered cottage where long ago a swan had drowned. And there he told her about the old beech tree and the days he'd spent reading in it, about the swan who was a woman, one who had slipped into the pond one fateful night, and drawn it over herself like a blanket. Then they'd sat by the side of that very same pond, moon-frosted on this night, and he'd told her of the soldiers' attack in all its horror, and about how he'd felt afterward.

"Why didn't you tell me sooner?" she asked, voice soft.

"I didn't want to tell ye when I was so angry. I didn't want ye to see fear in my face either."

"You know you can share all that with me, we promised each other, remember? To speak it all, no matter if it made the other person uncomfortable or sad."

"Aye, I know," he said, looking down at the pebbles he held in his hand, as though he wished he could gather words with the same ease. "See, the thing is I want to be ten feet tall in yer eyes, Pru. I want ye to know I can be strong for ye." He plucked one of the stones from his palm and flung it out over the pond, and she could feel the frustration that burned in every cell of him. "Bein' beat like that, an' nearly burned alive, made me feel weak an' afraid."

"There was nothing you could have done, neither you nor Finian. They wanted to kill you, so there was no way to stop them. Just for the record," she said, "you are ten feet tall in my eyes, and you are strong for me. But I want you to know, if you need to be weak with me, it wouldn't change what I think of you at all. There's nothing that could ever do that."

He nodded then, his thin sensitive face in profile to her, and she wondered if he doubted her. Inside, she felt the horror of what had happened to him, and a fury so big she was shocked that she could contain such a thing within her skin, without bursting into flame. It wouldn't help Ambrose to feel any better if she showed him that fury though. Her anger she could deal with on her own, it was his that worried her. Though her residence in Northern Ireland was of short duration, still she understood how very contrary the rules could be here, and how life was a commodity in a political game where the rules changed daily, and even the participants didn't quite know where they were on the board. There was little she could say to change how he felt, there was nothing she could do to change the danger he faced every day in his own city simply because he was born on a particular street, in a world where something so small marked a man for life.

Descended from a long line of tough Maine fishermen, Prudence was a practical girl in many respects. Observation of Casey and Pamela these last several months, had taught her that there were ways far more effective than words to help heal a man. And so she put a hand to Ambrose's face and turned him toward her, leaning in to kiss him. It began softly, but as was their wont of late, the alchemical shift occurred that turned a simple kiss into something far more. Quicker and quicker it seemed, they reached that place now where a kiss became raw need, as though if one could kiss the other hard enough and long enough one might drown and submerge, and find that longed for shadow where two became one. It was getting increasingly desperate each time they were together, and she felt, with her usual New England practicality, that if something was an inevitability—and she knew this was—one might as well commence with it. And so she gently disengaged from Ambrose and stood, holding out her hand.

"Come to the cottage with me," she said.

He looked up at her, a question in his eyes.

"Ambrose, it's what I want."

He nodded, and stood, taking her hand in his, and walking with her to the cottage. It was only later that she would recall that there seemed to be an ineffable sadness there, moving like a breeze over his face—there and then gone, so that she thought she might well have imagined it.

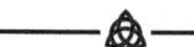

Since that night, the cottage had become their secret place. Somewhere they could hide from the world and its judgements, somewhere they could have a bit of life and love away from the troubles of the city. They returned whenever they could get away. At times, one would wait and the other might not arrive for some time, and sometimes, like today, they had hours where they need only belong to each other.

Various bits and bobs had migrated here with them—candles propped up in the neck of an old cracked vase, and a squat one stowed in an ancient blue mason jar, as well as two plates and two mugs which Pru had bought in a consignment shop. A few books—old, beloved, dog-eared—and a frayed map of the stars, which Ambrose had been given when he was six. They'd tacked up a set of old postcards they'd found in a shop of secondhand tat, along with the plates and mugs. Pru had bought an old perfume water tin, replete with images of dancing elephants and a mysterious woman peering through a curtain of jungle vine. The perfume water had been called *Rose of India*, and now held their tea, as well as any spare bits of food they wanted to shut away. While the tin had been treasure enough, inside Pru had found the clutch of old postcards and letters—now pinned to the wall—which dated back to the First World War.

The cards and letters told a story between two people named Edward and Maeve. And it was a story which had held Pru and Ambrose in thrall from the very first card—a picture of a soldier seated beside a campfire, gazing into the distance, with the figure of a woman hovering in the smoke from said fire. It was, of course the words on the back of the card—faded and nearly illegible, written in violet ink, with the scent of a long-ago love permeating each line—which made the cards such a find.

The cards and letters had been idyllic at first: the couple's first meeting when they attended the wedding of a mutual friend, Edward an aspiring architect from London, who worked in Belfast, Maeve a milliner's apprentice in Dublin. The story had wound through train rides and meetings, picnics in the countryside, ambles on beaches, and longing stirred by the briefest of partings. And then the letters had taken on a slightly frenetic air, for the dark clouds of the Great War were scudding over the world and overshadowing even the brightest of days. They would, Pru thought, have felt it coming, and would have known their time might well be cut brutally short, and so had needed to love as quickly and fiercely as they might. Edward had signed up right away, and Maeve, judging by the smeared ink on her response to this news, hadn't taken it with equanimity at first.

Pru and Ambrose had spent an afternoon, wrapped in blankets (yet another smuggled item, this time from Maggie's discard linens pile) putting the cards and letters into order, from the beginning of the love affair to where the writings stopped. They'd speculated on this and whether it meant the affair had ended, or that Edward had finally come home from the war, or that they were simply missing some of the correspondence. Since then they'd taken turns reading them out loud, imagining all the bits which weren't written down but existed between the lines. They argued amiably over whether Maeve had dark hair or light, whether Edward was tall or short, and whether either of them wore glasses. Ambrose thought Maeve was blonde, Edward was short and that neither wore glasses. Prudence was certain Maeve was dark-haired, Edward was tall, and that he wore glasses when doing paperwork.

"The sexual pull of glasses is highly underrated," she said, looking pointedly at Ambrose's own glasses, which admittedly, having been mended recently with electrical tape, were somewhat lacking in erotic allure.

Pru loved the correspondence. It provided a portal into a different time, and gave her small glimpses of another life, the details of which she enjoyed mulling over later, during Kathleen's nap times, or while supervising Kolya out-of-doors. Little pieces of that world—the lavender kid gloves which Edward had bought from Clerys for Maeve their first Christmas, the bottle of absinthe they'd gotten terribly drunk on one night, the straw hat trimmed with daisies which had fallen off Maeve's head when Edward had kissed her; the gate they leaned over to admire a field bright-sparked with cowslip; a quick, rough drawing of a house set down near a wood, which Edward said he'd build for Maeve one day—all these things would hover in her mind's eye for days. And, of course, all the words of love, ribbons and streams of them, from the light and playful to those of desire and pained yearning, mirrored what she felt for Ambrose and he for her.

Her own favourite was a card with a picture of a woman looking out to sea. The back was filled with the words, *My soul misses yours,* over and over, until the card was a tide of violet-inked longing. Then there was the one she was currently reading out loud to Ambrose, which made it very clear at which point Maeve and Edward's love had changed from that of the spirit to that of the flesh.

"*Oh my darling, I will carry last night with me through all the dark days to come. I will lie in my bed at night, aching with your absence. Come home to me. Come home now. I am no more than pure need, I am only the absence of you. Come home and fill me,*" Pru read, and then added, "Rather bold, just putting it on a postcard like that. They must have made the postman blush."

"Aye, well," Ambrose said, "readin' other peoples' love letters, I propose that he got what he deserved."

"Speaking of reading other peoples' love letters, isn't that exactly what we're doing right now?"

"Aye, but these two are likely long dead, an' I'm not havin' to look the woman in the face after readin' what she'd been up to with her lover."

"Does it show in *my* face? Do you recommend I stop talking to people until at least three days after?" Pru asked, laughing.

Ambrose looked up at her, the brown eyes soft. "Aye, I think it does, but then I know, don't I?"

"You do at that. Are you telling yourself, Ambrose, that you're looking at a satisfied woman?"

"I suppose only ye'll know that for certain, but aye, I'd like to feel ye were left happy." Even in the dim light that the candles provided, she saw the tips of his ears turn pink.

Pru laughed. "You couldn't tell?"

"It did seem ye were enjoyin' it as much as I was, but my oldest sister did say that women will pretend at times just for the sake of gettin' it over an' done with."

"Ambrose Turner, do I strike you as the sort of girl who would fake anything at all?"

"Ah, no," he said, "I don't suppose ye do. So ye really did like it?" The tips of his ears were still the colour of a peony but he was smiling now, brown eyes a-glow with reflected candlelight.

"Yes, I really did," she said, feeling a flush rise up in her face to match that of his ears.

"I'm glad of that. I'm still a bit gobsmacked about all this—you an' me. I'm a bit of a poor an' weedy specimen according to my sisters."

"You know how I feel, don't you?" she asked, worried that he didn't really know just what this was for her.

"Aye, when I'm with ye I can feel it floatin' in the air between us, but when I'm gone from ye I sometimes start to doubt things, ye know?"

"Yes, I do know. Your sisters—formidable as they are—aren't a reliable source for taking stock of yourself. You know in their eyes you're still about three and incapable of getting your shoes on the right feet. While to me, you're smart, funny and kind, and you're really rather wonderful at this," she gestured around them at the mess of blankets, and their own general dishevelment.

"I'll notice ye didn't put handsome on that list," Ambrose said, smiling. He had the sort of smile that transfigured his face into something which lit all the space around him.

"Handsome? That's a word for matinee idols—you know the square-jawed sort with lacquered hair, from back in the forties and fifties." She looked at him consideringly. "No, you're not handsome, but you're beautiful. Just the sight of you makes me tremble inside."

He snorted. "Beautiful? My ears stick out like an elephant's, my nose is canted a wee bit to the right, an' me mam has always said I'm about as brawny as a rake turned sideways."

"Your ears *do not* stick out like an elephant's, your nose has a charming dent and as to your body," she sighed and placed one hand on his chest, "it looks pretty perfect to me. Besides none of those people are seeing you naked. Just because they did when you were knee high to a grasshopper, doesn't mean their opinion carries weight anymore. You're mine," she continued, "and I wouldn't change a thing about you."

If there had been a way to simply have him feel what she did, so that he would know just how deep her feelings for him went, she would have done it because words always fell short, though she supposed words did when you loved someone with your entire being.

Ambrose smiled, stroking one hand down the shining length of her hair. "It's as though nothin' matters, but this, how this feels. Is it madness do ye think? Will we grow out of it an' become sensible at some point?"

"No," she replied, echoing all young lovers down the ages. "Do you think about this a lot when we're not together?" she asked, half-teasing, but also wondering. It felt to her at times, that since the first time they'd made love, she hadn't thought of much else. She lived and breathed for this stolen time with him.

He laughed, the sound warm and falling all around them through the green-gold scatter of afternoon light. "The only time I'm not thinkin' about doin' this with you, is when I *am* doin' it with you, an' that's only because I'm utterly incapable of thought at that point." He yawned expansively. "What time is it? Do I have time to sleep for a bit before I need to take ye home?"

"You do," she said, wishing they could stay through the night. Wishing that, like the Beach Boys song, they could just say good night and stay together.

Pru watched the late afternoon light as it washed over the room. Ivy blocked out much of the sunshine, but what did get through flickered like a living thing over the stone walls, giving her the sense they were in some underwater cavern, hidden so well that they might never be found. The cottage was so deep in the woods, that they might, in truth, never be found. It was what had made it attractive to them both—to have a sanctuary where no eyes could fall upon them. She wasn't a superstitious creature, so the fact that a drowned woman had been the last to live here bothered her not a whit.

Earlier, she had told the truth when she said Ambrose made her feel safe and secure. It lay in the strength of what he made her feel more than in any physical sense. She had always been a girl of firm convictions, but had grown up in what felt like a narrow sphere. Her parents had been loving but very strict; her mother was a devout Anabaptist, and had a very tight moral code. As much as she loved her mother, she had jumped at the chance to come live in Belfast and help out Jamie and Pamela with their various children. She felt like she could breathe here, despite the ceaseless conflict. If her mother could see her now, she'd probably think her a harlot. Pru smiled to herself, thinking she didn't mind the term so much; the benefits that came with it, she'd found, rather took the sting from the word.

Edward and Maeve had loved with this bright and wondrous intensity too. What had been their fate? Had they ever built their little house near the wood, or been able to say goodnight under the same roof? Were they somewhere now with a lifetime of love and shared moments between them?

"Do you suppose he came home?"

"Hmm?" Ambrose inquired sleepily.

"Edward from the postcards—do you suppose when the war was all over he came home to her?"

"If he lived, he must have. I can't see these two livin' a life without one another otherwise, can you?"

"No," she said, knowing at the same time that there was little surety in the world, even for lovers who felt invincible in the force of their feeling.

Ambrose fell to sleep after that. Today was a rare day off for him. He delivered milk in the mornings, and had to be up at the break of day. After that he worked at a petrol station until early afternoon, and then sometimes ran errands for Patrick and Tomas, work which he found fascinating and that was leading him to think about furthering his education in the direction of the law. Tomas had made it clear to him that if he was interested, the fees for school could be arranged.

She wasn't tired, and so simply lay content in the curve of Ambrose's arm, watching the flame dance in the blue glass jar, like the aqueous fire of a mermaid's hearth. The two long-ago lovers still occupied her mind, hanging vivid in the air before her, as though their time was suspended in a transparent golden ball, where they still lived on in some sort of alternate plane—eternally young, scented with Indian rosewater and adorned with lavender kid gloves and jaunty straw hats, while waiting with breathless anticipation as a train rolled into a station.

There was still one postcard left in the perfume tin, one she hadn't tacked up with the others. It had a stamp but there was no postmark, and there was a newness to it that seemed to say it had never been mailed, and that no hands other than Maeve's had ever touched it. The picture on the front was of a wood, with great old trees tangling their roots together, their branches intertwined over a weathered gate. Strangely, considering it was a postcard, there was no location printed on it, though Pru thought it might be the wood beside which Edward had promised to build Maeve a house.

On the back, the postcard held only one line.

'In dreams you are still with me.'

Chapter Twenty-eight

Truth Between Brothers

LISTENING TO HIS brother curse a blue streak, and rain down imprecations on the heads of blissfully unaware suppliers, Pat Riordan experienced a strong feeling of déjà vu. He'd known such times before with Casey, where the man was utterly frustrated by contractors and suppliers who functioned even a hair short of perfection. He listened to the next stream of invective and then voiced his doubt as to the likelihood of St. Colman actually putting boils on the arse of the man who'd been unfortunate enough to deliver warped beams to Casey Riordan, being that the saint in question was responsible for hanged men, horned cattle and horses. For this comment he received a very black look, as Casey's head popped through the hole in the ceiling, his face glowing blue from the tarp he'd erected over said hole.

"Fetch me the damn level would ye, man. 'Tis the one with the red ribbon tied to it."

There was a marked sarcasm in his brother's voice, which Pat chose to ignore. The man had bloody asked for his help, and he was going to get it, despite Pat feeling that he was functioning on the spark between his last two functioning brain cells. In terms of strict accuracy, though, it was Pamela who had asked for his help on Casey's behalf. Kate, accompanied by Deirdre, was in London for two days, having left him amply provided with food for both him and the baby, while she tidied up the last of Noah's business affairs. She had originally planned to take Lily with her, but Pat had thought that what was likely to be a bit of an emotional voyage for Kate, wouldn't be enhanced by the company of a teething, and therefore very fractious, little miss. Kate had given him what he felt was a somewhat undeserved look of great dubiousness at his suggestion. Still, she'd agreed to the plan in the end. Now, he felt that her dubiousness was well deserved.

Pat had, in the course of his life, dealt with thieves, terrorists, murderers, and he thought—listening to the cursing still coming from the roof—his brother. Yet, he was certain they'd all bow before the tiny reign of terror that was his daughter while she was cutting a tooth. Kate must have sensed his frustration last time they'd spoken on the phone, for Pamela had called him the previous evening and asked if he'd help Casey out at Tomas' house, while she watched Lily for the day.

The tiny turncoat, after staying up most of the night, had fallen to sleep on Pamela's shoulder, her entire being suffused with a beatific contentment within moments of arriving at the house. He'd left feeling an utter failure as a parent, but also, it must be said, feeling an overwhelming sense of relief that Lily was someone else's problem for a few hours.

He wondered if today would be a good day to broach the topic with Casey of the bequest Noah had left to Pamela. More cursing issued forth from the roof and he decided it was a subject best left to another day. Pamela he'd talked to already, and she'd merely nodded, the faraway look in her eyes which she always got when someone spoke of Noah. She had, however, requested that he fill his brother in on the details.

"Can ye fix it?" Pat asked, as Casey descended the ladder, still muttering in frustration. A spot of rot had made itself apparent in one of the weight bearing beams, and Casey had removed all the ceiling around it, in anticipation of replacing it quickly.

"Oh, aye, it's just the damn boards they've sent me are warped, an' that's goin' to put me behind. Bein' that the whole house is off true, I can't afford any compromisin' with the materials."

Pat wisely refrained from speaking aloud the thought that Casey never compromised on materials even when the house was straight as a die.

His brother eyed the ceiling above with an owlish glare, and then sighed. "Let's sit an' have a bit of lunch, it will give me a chance to get my thoughts sorted on which project to tackle until I can get decent lumber to work with."

Lunch was bread and cheese with a side of pickle relish, a thermos of tea and a salad filled with greens that were both bitter and sharp.

"Pamela insists on gettin' a peck of weeds into me every other day. I swear the woman is pickin' stuff straight from the hedgerows, I expect to turn into a hedgehog any day now."

"She likes to look after ye, an' that's not a bad thing."

Casey looked up from his forkful of salad, and gave Pat a narrow glance.

"I feel like that statement isn't meant to be as simple as it sounds on the face of it."

"Maybe that's because it's not," Pat said.

Casey put down his food. "If ye have somethin' to say, Patrick, go ahead an' say it."

"I do. Ye're halfway livin' with the woman anyway, why the hell don't ye go home?"

"I don't know," Casey said, sounding almost as annoyed as he had a few minutes previous on the roof. "I just feel it's not the right time. There are moments I think maybe it would have been best if I'd never come back. Maybe Pamela an' the children would be better off without me."

Whether it was from lack of sleep or utter frustration with his pigheaded twit of a brother, Pat felt a wave of incandescent fury sweep through him. He threw his sandwich down, and reached across and took Casey by the front of his shirt. "Don't you fockin' dare, you bastard! Ye don't get to waste yer life on bitterness an' what ifs, do ye understand? Ye don't get to."

"I wasn't plannin' on it," Casey said, clearly taken aback at Pat's reaction, "but why is it I'm not allowed?"

"Because our father sacrificed his life so that you wouldn't end up in an early grave!" Pat regretted the words the moment they rushed from his tongue, and felt himself go cold all over as he realized what he'd said.

Casey's face had gone blank, and Pat took his hand away from the man's shirt, feeling sick, his blood thumping hard in his face.

"What do ye mean by that, Patrick?" Each word came with slow deliberation, and Pat wondered if on some level, way deep in his subconscious, this was knowledge Casey had long had.

All the blood in his body seemed to have pooled in his toes. He shook his head. "I shouldn't have said that, it was only a moment of temper."

Casey merely looked at him, one of those looks which reminded him how well his brother had always known him. Casey was rarely fooled by a lie, and truth be told, Patrick knew himself to be a miserable liar.

"No, it wasn't. Don't do that, Pat. Just tell me the truth."

Pat sighed. This was not a truth he wanted to tell, nor did he think it would serve anything to give this knowledge to Casey.

"I really shouldn't have said it, it's only somethin' I know because I overheard a conversation I wasn't meant to."

"What conversation?" Casey asked. There was that curious stillness to him just now, a trait he'd inherited from their grandfather their da had always said. A stillness like that before a terrible storm, something that held a warning in it.

"I heard Daddy talkin' to Uncle Des one night. 'Twas that last summer we stayed with them. I was comin' down the stairs in the middle of the night, lookin' for food as usual," he smiled, "an' about halfway down I caught a bit of their conversation, an' realized it was somethin' serious, an' not likely somethin' they'd take kindly to me hearin'."

"I don't imagine that stopped ye from eavesdroppin', though," Casey said drily. Pat couldn't dispute this, for curiosity had often led him into trouble when other concerns did not.

"No, it didn't," Pat said. "What I learned that night was somethin' that made my blood run a wee bit cold. Daddy went back to the 'Ra, so that they would take down Denys Moran, for then the man could not own ye anymore." Pat had told Casey this bit of his history some time back, a history which had put him on the bad side of some very dangerous men.

"Oh," Casey said, looking like a man who'd just been heart shot. He shook his head. "All these years, an' ye never told me, Patrick. Why? When ye saw that road I was goin' down an' all the mistakes I was makin', an' yet ye never breathed a word."

"Once Daddy was dead, would such knowledge have made a difference to ye? Ye were mighty angry for a long time after he died, Casey. There were times I was grateful ye'd only ended up in prison, an' not dead in a grave beside our da."

"Have ye been angry at me all this time?" Casey asked, and though there was little emotion in his tone, Pat saw the look in his eyes, and knew it had taken no little bravery to ask the question. Unfortunately, he knew he was going to have to tell his brother the truth, a lie would not serve just now.

"Aye, I suppose I have been. I don't dwell there, but aye, I've been angry at times. When ye went to prison, after the sacrifice our father made, I hated ye a little, even while I went on lovin' ye."

"I took our father from ye, just when ye most needed him."

"Ye took him from yerself as well, man. Maybe ye don't remember him as well as ye once would have, but when he made that choice, he made it knowing what could happen. He would have thought the sacrifice worth it. He loved us more than he loved himself, an' now, havin' yer own children, ye know what that's like. Should Conor need ye to make such a deal to give him a chance at a happy life, would ye hesitate?"

"No, I wouldn't, but I trust Conor will grow to be a far more sensible boy than I was."

Pat gave him a sideways glance which spoke volumes. "Aye, the odds do seem in favour of that."

"I owe ye an apology, because he wasn't just my daddy, he was yers as well."

"I don't need an apology, just go an' live yer life the way he hoped ye one day would if he secured it for ye. Love yer wife an' yer children an' make a good life for the lot of yez. That's what he'd want for ye, an' ye know it. He wanted it enough to trade his own life should it be necessary. If ye feel ye need to talk to the man, go out to his grave. Take some whiskey with ye; it's somethin' ye did now an' again before."

"I did?"

"Aye, ye did. I did too. I still do, come to that. Sometimes a man just needs to talk to his father, no?"

"Aye," Casey agreed, his face still blank with shock, "sometimes a man does."

Chapter Twenty-nine

Breaking Bread with a Ghost

HIS MEMORY WAS like a drowned mosaic, one of those sometimes found in Britain, sunk into an underground stream, the beautiful tiled floors with leopards and roses which the Romans had put in their bathhouses. The places where the tile had risen to the surface, and where the water was clearest were those moments—edged in crimson, leaved in gold—which were his life with Pamela and the children. The darker bits where the water was murky, were other things, things that were crucial to him.

He hadn't gone into the city during daylight hours, only a few times at night or near to it, the dusk hiding his face, his turned up collar, whiskers and low-brimmed cap, keeping his face hidden from those he passed. His size was a problem, not many men were as tall or broad of shoulder as he was. Still, he'd managed to pass unnoticed, if one didn't count those that crossed the street to avoid him. With the collar, the cap, and the general nature of his presence (Eddy had once called him a forbidding fucking bastard) people did tend to avoid him.

So, what did a man do then, if he felt he needed that sharp shock in order to see the other pieces of the mosaic—the dark parts, which would give him the full truth? The only answer which had come to him was to re-visit those murky pieces of his past.

He eyed the door in front of him. Battered with Belfast's history, it was a door he'd gone through a few times before—the Four Leaf Clover Club, a notorious republican haunt, a place which had seen murder, bombing, beatings and stabbings. It wasn't family friendly, and he'd never truly cared for the establishment, but he felt that if one wanted darkness, one had to walk into the heart of the maelstrom that was republican Belfast. This club, with its bloody history, was that heart.

He pushed open the door, hoping that the simple act wouldn't get him killed. Inside, the club was slightly dark, and he took a minute to blink and adjust his vision. As far as aesthetics went, it wasn't a place to please a man. At some point, someone had the notion that a hideous green indoor/outdoor carpet was a good idea in a place where people drank, smoked and occasionally spit tobacco when the proprietor's back was turned. As a result, the carpet under his feet felt distinctly sticky as he crossed the room to the bar. The publican was a stocky, bullet-headed man who looked like he regularly ate nails for breakfast, and he merely stared at Casey and then grunted to indicate he should order or leave.

Casey ordered a pint, and got it in a rather dirty glass, which he took with a smile and a curt nod of thanks. He then took a seat at a table in the corner, the chair wobbling slightly as he slid onto it. The pub was murky, but he sat where the light would hit him well enough that others could see him; it was, after all, why he was here—to be seen, and possibly draw a reaction.

Men were turned in their seats, eyeing him, a certain hostility in every gaze. That, he'd expected, as this wasn't the sort of pub a man idly wandered into for a drink and a chat. In fact, unless one was well known in the republican community and had family ties to the IRA, it was highly inadvisable. He understood the risk he was taking but felt if it provided an answer, it would be worth it. Well, unless he got killed for it. Granted this whole idea was a calculated risk or, he thought, just entirely mad. He suspected that Pamela would feel that the latter summation was the correct one. It was fortunate that the woman didn't know he was here.

He took a sip of his drink, enjoying the dark taste of it, aware as well that one man had stood and was crossing the sticky carpet. He swallowed and then looked up, keeping his expression neutral. The man before him was short and wiry, and reminded Casey of a banty rooster—small and confrontational with a confidence way beyond his pay grade. Behind him stood a tall man with straw-coloured hair.

"There's a deal of clubs in Belfast, d'ye mind if I ask why ye've chosen this one?"

Casey heard the man's question, while understanding that it was not so much a question as a threat. His attention however was riveted to the man with the straw-coloured hair, whose height was near to his own. He was staring at Casey without blinking, and was white to the gills. As though, Casey thought, he was looking at a ghost made flesh. That he'd once known the man he could feel, for the bees were buzzing lightly at the base of his skull.

"Have I made a mistake, then? I only wanted to wet my throat."

"Aye, I do believe ye have. Finish yer pint, an' don't take too much time about it."

Casey nodded, holding the man's gaze in a pleasant fashion. He knew better than to challenge him. He assumed he was unknown to most these men, and he was vastly outnumbered. Men had died for just so little in this city.

The music began when he was about halfway down his pint. It was a quartet—two fiddles, a squeezebox and a bodhran. He kept the music out at the edge of his hearing, carefully scanning the club to see if anyone else had recognized him.

A few of the men still watched him carefully, but none with the shocked aspect of the man with the straw-coloured hair. So it appeared that one man in here knew him.

He drank the rest of his pint slowly, knowing it was deliberately antagonistic to such as the banty rooster man, but needing a bit of time to be sure his appearance had the necessary impact. He watched and he waited, and his patience paid out, for he saw the man with the straw-coloured hair rise and walk over to the musicians, a tensile quality to him that said this was no simple request. He bent down over the shoulder of the fiddle player, said something, and received a nod in return. He then stood, looked directly at Casey and then walked back to his table. Casey was certain the look held a significance which was, admittedly, somewhat lost on him.

One of the fiddlers stood and began to sing. The melody tickled at his memory, but he couldn't quite place it.

'Her head was bare and her grey hair over her eyes hung down
Her neck and waist, her hands and feet with iron chains were bound...'

Two more verses into the song, and it came through his brain like a flood—a minor flood, but a flood, nevertheless. Music was sometimes this way for him, he only needed a phrase, a chorus, a set of notes to set off a cascade in his head. This one he knew.

'From that day down with chains I'm bound, no wonder I look pale
The blood they've drained from every vein of poor old Granuaile.'

The song seemed an odd choice for a republican bar but, then again, a woman pirate was most certainly a rebel, so maybe it was apropos. Then his brain made the leap—pirates were smugglers and in the Mournes there was an old smuggling route. The man was most certainly conveying a message, but Casey knew he was missing the fine details because the Mournes encompassed a very large area, and the tracks ran for long distances through them. He hoped there was a way to get the remaining information out of Patrick, without tipping the man off to what he was doing.

At song's end the straw-haired man rose, and made his way over to him. "Ye're done with yer drink, I'd advise ye to go now." He paused, and then spoke in a lower tone. "Three days, mid-mornin', ye'll know where."

Casey reached up and scratched his ear without thinking, and saw an answering spark in the man's face. His ear wasn't itchy and he had simply done it without thinking. Judging from the man's look, it was the right answer to what he'd said—how he knew this he wasn't certain, only that his doctors had said much of a person's knowledge was instinct and that some memories would resurface if he simply got out of the way and let them. Of course, there was the small detail that, contrary to what the man believed, he did not know *where* at all, but there was little he could do about that here and now. He hoped he might be able to wrangle the information out of Pat without raising the man's suspicions.

He took his time about donning his jacket and swallowing down the last of his drink. As he crossed the space between his table and the door, he felt the eyes of all the men upon him. He simply kept moving and did not look back.

Outside, the night was cool, and there was a fine mist of rain coming down, but he felt warm and slightly elated. For despite the chilly reception he'd just received, he felt suddenly that he was hanging onto a thread, something which—if he could maintain his grasp on it—would lead him back into his past, and let him know why someone had so clearly wanted him dead.

'They don't sow potatoes nor barley nor wheat
But there's gangs of them diggin' for gold in the street…'

Casey whistled his way through an old tune about the mountains in which he currently climbed. The words rolled through him as he went, the land opening up around him as he came over the crest of a ridge.

'…I might as well be, where the Mountains of Mourne sweep down to the sea.'

The final notes died away upon the air as he stopped to take his bearings. Below him stretched a vista of myth and legend, and being Ireland—song. The Mourne Mountains had once caused the Belfast-born writer C.S. Lewis to proclaim that in certain lights, it was the one landscape where he expected a giant to pop its head over a ridge at any given moment. It was certainly of a scope where a giant might feel comfortable.

It was three days since Casey's night in the club, and he only hoped that he'd understood the man's meaning as to location. The man wasn't to know his memory only existed in patches. He'd had to question Pat as to places it might be. He'd referenced the song, hoping to have the area narrowed down to something smaller than an entire range of mountains.

"It's a song about the pirate queen, Granuaile," Pat said, fortunately distracted by Lily spitting up down his shirt at that moment.

"Is there a place in the Mourne Mountains that was particular to her?" Casey asked, earning himself a suspicious look from his brother, who was still engaged in mopping the front of his shirt. Casey had lifted the fractious Lily from her father's arms, soothing her quickly with a few words in Irish.

Pat had sighed. "I swear that child settles for anyone but me."

"'Tis only because she feels yer anxiousness, if ye calm down so will she," Casey said. "So, the Mourne Mountains, an' Gráinne O'Malley?"

"Well, the Brandy Pad, I suppose," Pat said, and Casey repressed a sigh of his own.

"Was there a place we went up there?" Casey asked, trying for a casual tone, certain he had failed miserably. Pat, changing his shirt, answered in a muffled tone.

"Aye, there was a cave up there, where ye took me once when we were in our teens. Right off the Brandy Pad it was."

The Brandy Pad was an old smuggling route, which ran up through the Mournes. During the 18th century the area around Newcastle was a favourite spot for landing contraband—brandy, tea, coffee, tobacco, soap and wine were just a few of the things which would be landed on shore, loaded onto pack ponies and then trekked from the Bloody Bridge through the mountains and then down to their destination in Hilltown.

"I was mad at ye later because ye used it for assignations when ye were in the 'Ra. I felt like ye'd betrayed me."

With a little more prodding, under the guise of re-living boyhood memories with his brother, Casey had been able to get the location of the cave, and he realized it was a place he'd visited during his first year back in Ireland. As if his cells knew the places of his life, even if his mind no longer did. Then he'd told Pat that he'd run into a tall man with straw-coloured hair who clearly had known him well.

"If he was nearly of a height with you, it can only be Dacy."

"Did I know him well?" Casey asked, feeling the terrible void which still, at times, yawned right next to his feet.

Pat nodded. "Aye, outside of Robin, he was probably your dearest friend."

"I'd say you were my dearest friend, then an' now," Casey said, handing Lily, now blissfully asleep, back to her father.

"Aye, an' you mine, even if ye are a pigheaded fool at times," Pat said, smiling.

"Did I trust him?"

"Aye, ye did."

"An' did you?"

Pat shrugged his shoulders. "I don't know, I don't suppose I gave it much thought. I did go to him after ye disappeared, an' asked if he knew anythin'. He had no answers for me then. He did go visit Pamela at some point, but she didn't seem terrible keen on his company, though she never said why."

He hated lying to Pat in any degree, and he meant what he'd said, his brother was his dearest friend and he was grateful that their relationship was so easy. He would do what he could to prevent anything damaging that.

He stood now, catching his breath and surveying the land around him. The day was typically Irish, mist drizzling clouds to one side of him, cloaking the mountains in a thick fog, and a cerulean sky on the other side—a broad sweep of watercolours against a background of granite and sere mountain-top. Running up the mountain, like an exposed spine, was a low stone wall which had been built a long time ago. It served the same purpose it always had though, keeping livestock away from the reservoir it enclosed. He followed it up, and then climbed over a stile, and let himself down on the other side. He crossed the ground, taking care not to trip on the rock-strewn surface now that he was off the main track.

A narrow path led up from the base of the rock face, and from there it was only a matter of about a hundred steps. The opening to the cave was narrow, but afforded a panoramic view over the pass. It was why the location had been chosen in the first place, he suspected—no one could sneak up on a man here. He could literally see for a mile in every direction.

Land carried story—deep in his cells he knew these boulders, that dark cave opening, the line of light which rimmed the mountains, and the sound of the wind here, singing its way through granite. If a man listened deeply enough, he could hear the words of that old song, and know his connection to the world of stone and ice, of fire and water. This land was his story, and he remembered well enough to know some chapters had been dark, and were not ones he cared to re-read. But if he wanted to be whole, he would have to know all of it, even the pieces which pained him.

Before he went into the cave, he uttered a short prayer that he wasn't about to enter a trap and get himself killed for his foolishness.

The man was already there, sitting back in the thick shadow, on what looked like an upturned keg. He was alone. He stood and walked forward and then engulfed Casey in a hug.

"Christ man—*Christ*—ye could have knocked me down with a feather; I thought a ghost had risen an' walked into the club."

Casey merely nodded, and stepped back. He wasn't comfortable with the familiarity the man displayed, and didn't know if that was a result of having little memory of the man or an instinct which told him to be wary.

Dacy pulled a bottle of whiskey out from under his coat. "Will ye have a drink with me, man? I did think if I ever drank with ye again, it'd be at yer wake, but this is a far better occasion."

"Never drink with a man ye aren't certain ye can trust," said a voice in his head. If Pamela didn't care for the man, then he wasn't going to discount the woman's instincts.

"Thanks, but no. I don't drink the hard stuff these days, have enough trouble with my thinkin' as it is, I don't need to addle it further."

"Time was ye'd not turn down a drink with a friend," Dacy said, and something rippled over his face, a dark thread in the light tone. Casey wasn't sure if he'd imagined it or if the shadows in the cave were playing tricks on his eyes. "We did think ye dead, man, an' though ye may not remember, we were good friends once."

"For all intents an' purposes I was dead," Casey said, not wanting to take a trip into the twilight of nostalgia with this man, mostly because he didn't remember him beyond those broken tiles which had surfaced for him in the club.

"Are ye sayin' ye lost yer memory?" Dacy asked, picking up a tin mug and putting a little whiskey in it. The raw amber scent of it made Casey feel slightly sick.

"Aye, I did."

"All of it, or only parts?" he asked.

"All of it," he said shortly. "I was beaten and left for dead. Someone saw fit to put me on a boat bound for New York though, an' that's where I woke some six weeks later. Bits an' pieces have come back to me, enough to return me to my family. Things further back too, wee bits of my history with the Provos an' such. But of the time around the beatin', I've no memory at all."

Dacy's eyes were wide with surprise, and Casey wondered if his shock was genuine or something put on as easily as a mask. It had been so long since he'd trusted his own judgements about anything, that he wasn't willing to make a decision one way or the other.

"I suppose ye'll want to know if I've any information on who tried to kill ye?"

Casey felt a lurch of hope. "Aye, that's what I want to know. Only I thought perhaps it was somethin' I'd done, crossed someone in the 'Ra without realizin' it."

Dacy nodded. "Ye mean maybe, when ye were passin' along names off the targeted kill list? Do ye remember that?"

Casey nodded. His deal with David was something Jamie had filled him in on, as well as any other information he'd felt Casey needed to know before he ventured back into his old world. David had been a British spy, and part of the 14th Intelligence Company. He'd passed names along to Casey which were on the kill lists of both Loyalist paramilitaries and various other organizations which were under the umbrella of British Intelligence. Casey, in turn, had passed the names along to his old contacts within the republican world. Between Jamie, Pamela and Patrick, he had a bit of a patchwork quilt of knowledge around these matters. But it had become clear to him, as they attempted to help him rebuild his backstory, that he'd kept plenty of things secret in his old life.

"No one was angry at ye for that. Ye saved several lives. I did wonder if that was what got ye killed—when I thought ye dead, that is—is passin' those names along to the boys. I figured someone high up on the other side, might want ye gone for that. Maybe someone in Special Branch, or in one of the intelligence units."

"I just thought it possible that there was someone in the organization who maybe was workin' for the other side, an informant say, an' they ratted me out."

"Had someone known it would have come out, man. When Noah Murray wanted information, men gave it to him. So if there had been anything to tell, someone would have told it to him. He pushed hard on the Belfast cells, an' while some of the lads are foolhardy, I don't think any were mad enough to lie to Noah Murray. He made it clear he wanted information if there was any to be had."

"Aye, Pat has said," Casey replied shortly. The other words his brother had spoken still lingered with him too, like a stain he wanted to rub away. *'He'd have done anything she asked, Casey. And this was what she asked, that someone help her find out what had happened to you.'* Ah, but what price had she paid for that request? He knew, and knew the weight of it belonged directly on him.

Dacy was giving him an odd look, and Casey had a good notion of just what it was the man was thinking.

"I know she was in a relationship with Noah Murray," he said, forestalling any new information the man might want to give him on his least favourite subject. He knew too bloody much as it was.

Dacy nodded, and he could tell the man wanted to say something about it but understood by the look on Casey's face that it was a topic best left alone.

"I asked around as much as seemed wise, after Patrick had come to me seekin' answers, an' this much I do know—someone was paid to do it. Who hired them an' why I never was able to find out, just that a fair bit of money was offered through some back channels. But someone wanted ye killed, or at least disposed of. How ye ended up on that ship instead of dead is as much a mystery as who hired those men to kill ye."

Casey felt the rising tide of frustration which was so often his companion. Always these half-hints, tiny glimpses of something larger but never enough to call it a clue, or something that might actually one day lead to an answer.

Dacy opened his mouth to speak, and then closed it as if he'd thought better of whatever it was he'd been about to say.

"What is it?"

Dacy shrugged. "Well, I don't know but it did occur to me that maybe ye're lookin' at this all wrong. Everyone has assumed from the outset that this was somethin' political, somethin' to do with the Brits or the IRA, but what if it was personal? That would mean everyone was lookin' in the wrong direction this whole time."

"Aye, I did consider that, but I can't recall havin' any enemies, not to the degree that they'd want me dead."

"People get upset over some funny things; I knew a man who killed his neighbour simply because he'd chopped down a tree on the shared property line. Ye'd not think that would be reason enough, but if someone is off their nut, a little thing is sometimes a big enough spark. Besides, it's Belfast, bein' in the wrong street is reason enough. Could be someone was jealous of yer life, an' ye'd not even a notion of it. Maybe someone ye trusted quite well. Yer wife has always had a close relationship with Mr. Kirkpatrick, no?"

Casey shook his head. "She has, but it's not Jamie, an' I'll thank ye to never suggest such a thing again."

"So ye don't remember anything about the day it happened?" Dacy asked. Casey felt a cold ripple along his backbone at the words. He'd already answered this question, and knew he was being tested to see if he'd slip up and maybe reveal more. What if the man wanted to know because he needed to ascertain if Casey held the slightest thread which could unravel the tangled ball of the events of that day. There was a time he'd trusted this man, but now he did not know if he'd been a fool then or was one now.

"No, not a thing," Casey said, assuming a bland expression. It was the truth, and it was the thing least likely to bring him trouble. If they believed him to be a man without memory or knowledge, he was no threat.

"Well, maybe given time it will come back to ye."

Casey simply nodded, not wanting to give voice to any hopes he had around regaining his memories.

Dacy left then, after hugging him again. Casey waited while the man walked down the path from the mountain; he'd go down the track in the opposite direction but he wanted the man well away before he did so. Did he trust him? He didn't know, and that frustrated him. Much of his life these last few years had been ruled by instinct, but instinct didn't serve when you needed information that was specific.

The cave yawned behind him, chill and dark, and he stepped forward a little, feeling as though someone stood at his back, ready to put a cold and heavy hand upon his shoulder. He knew what it was—the recollection of a dream he'd had one night when he'd slept in the wolf cave.

Cave dreaming was something altogether different, it was underworld dreaming, dreaming without time—thick dreaming which laid a mantle of stone upon you, so that it lingered for days. The dream had felt real, more real than his daylight life often did.

He'd been out hunting, and had been caught away from the hut when dark fell. The cave had been less than a mile's tramp, and so he'd gone there seeking warmth and shelter for the night. He'd lit a fire, but it had still been cold, and he always dreamed strange dreams when he was cold. Still, the dream had been so lucid that he felt the cold didn't quite explain it entirely.

In the dream, a man had come from the back of the cave, simply emerged from the stone, and then sat down beside the fire Casey had lit. The fire had been hours old, burned down to glowing coals and there was bread on it, toasting, and the scent of peat and butter. He had reached down to grab the toast, and break it in half so that he might share it with the silent man, but when he'd looked up again, the stone man was him. His reflection was right there in front of him, like that in a pool of water, inexact, with something of that other world laid over it—a very long passage of time, a man who could walk through cave walls because he was made of stone, a silence that could drown the world.

Nevertheless, he'd handed him the bread, his movements slow as though they were both under that pool of water. He'd watched as the man had eaten it, one bit at a time, and found he'd eaten his share as well, though he didn't recall chewing, and the taste of the bread wasn't in his mouth. And then, suddenly, in the way of dreams, the man was simply gone and the glowing coals of the fire were quenched.

He'd awakened slowly, coming up from the dream like he'd journeyed through miles of cave passage to emerge. He was cold too, straight through to his marrow. The cold feeling had stayed with him all that night and through the next day, for he'd the sense that he'd broken bread with a ghost—his own ghost—and that he no longer walked in the world of men. Living so far from other human beings, it wasn't always easy to keep the boundaries of time and self.

Two days later, he'd headed down out of the mountains, knowing he needed the company of tribe and hearth. It had been the right thing to do, but he'd still had the feeling from time to time that he was a ghost, moving through other people's lives, but never really attaching to them or their worlds.

And now here he stood, on another mountain, with everything changed. He once again had tribe and hearth. He had more than that, he had family and love. There was much to lose now, and he felt the fear of that, what it was when your heart moved outside of you in the forms of wife and children.

He took a deep breath, for he knew well enough to let the mountain work its magic on his fears. There was an old Irish word—*aisling*—which roughly translated meant dream vision. It was the ancient concept of forty nights on the mountain top, of sinking deep into place and the wild and waiting for the spirit of the land to arrive. Usually the spirit manifested as a young woman, for when men told tales their own dreams interwove with those of the land.

Ireland had long ago been divided into five parts—Leinster, Munster, Ulster, Connacht and Mide. Over time Mide was absorbed into the other provinces so that now, only four remained. But Mide was also an idea, a place which was neither physical nor bound by time, another dimension that existed outside of these things. It was this he felt in the mountains, for it might have been today or a thousand years ago, the rocks paid no mind to the passing of such small movements on the scale.

He was a man though, and time mattered, for there was no going back and changing events or unspinning that which had been spun in his absence. For a long time, he'd been like that stone ghost, walking through eons, dreaming of old things he could not quite grasp. He'd been stone, blood, dark, granite cracked with cold. But now he'd emerged from that cave, found fire, warmth, sustenance and a love that made him feel as though there was no stone left, only a melting core and a need that went to his centre, to never lose that love again.

He turned from the cave mouth, and headed down the old track. He was done breaking bread with ghosts.

Chapter Thirty

A Thousand Tiny Cracks

THE GARDEN HAD long been a place of peace and calm for Pamela, and so it was where she retreated when she felt troubled or upset in any way. It was a beautiful day and normally the sunshine and the rhythmic and satisfying work of turning soil, transplanting and pruning the winterkill off her various herbs would have soothed any ills she might have. However, it did not seem to be working its usual magic today.

Tomas had been by to visit two evenings before, and had mentioned in casual conversation that Casey had gone seeking after his past the week before, in a location that wasn't exactly known for its savoury crowd. She'd grilled him after that, and he'd finally told her what he knew. Since that visit, her emotions had been ruffled in the extreme. Casey had been busy at Tomas' house the last few days, and thus she hadn't seen him since learning of his asinine trip to the Four Leaf Clover Club. All things considered, she felt this was probably quite fortunate for him and his well-being.

She rubbed her hands through the lavender, though it was not giving off a great deal of scent just yet. Holding her palms to her face, she breathed in the smell, which was there but mostly in its green, spring notes and not the heady floral days of high summer. It was not imparting any calm to her either, though it was likely she could *eat* the plant and not feel any of its soothing qualities, as mad as she was at the man.

What the hell had he been thinking? He might have been killed then and there. It still wasn't outside the realm of possibility that he had a price on his head. She knew much of his willingness to risk his neck was a result of his utter frustration with not knowing what had happened to him that morning when he'd disappeared, and that he felt he couldn't fully rejoin his old life with her and the children, without knowing what dangers lurked in the shadows of his memory.

"Reckless bastard," she said through gritted teeth, and picked up a rock from the soil, flinging it with all the frustration she felt. She picked up another and threw it. "Pigheaded fool!" she yelled, and scored a hit to the side of the shed, startling Paudeen out of his afternoon slumber. He gave her a dirty look—as dirty as a sheep was capable of giving—and let out a very peeved sounding *baaa*. The next rock was the size of a small potato and had a very satisfying heft in her palm. She threw it toward the trees this time, not wanting to upset Paudeen any further. "Buck eejit!" she yelled, starting to feel some small lessening of her anger in the verbal abuse of her absent husband. The rock, sailing in a glorious parabola toward the trees, just missed hitting said absent husband—now suddenly present—in the head, as he emerged from the edge of the wood.

"Jaysus Christ!" He dodged to one side as the rock sped past him, landing hard against a branch and ricocheting back toward him, causing him to duck and put his hands up over his head.

"Is it safe now," he called out a minute later, "or are ye plannin' to launch more missiles at me first?"

"Yes, it's safe. That wasn't meant for you," she said, though that wasn't strictly true. He crossed the yard toward her, and she admired his stride even as his physical presence revived the anger she'd just been relieving. "What are you doing lurking in the woods anyway? Where's your truck?"

"I came through the trees because I wanted to check on the stream where it got dammed up last month. I parked down the lane a ways, an' then walked in through the wood."

"Hmmphmm," she said by way of response, and then bent her head back to her work of clipping the lavender plants, studiously ignoring him as he entered the garden.

"Where are the wee ones?" he asked, his tone neutral, no doubt in response to her pointed silence.

"Conor's at school, Isabelle went shopping with Gert in the village and Kathleen is with Jamie today."

He picked up the spade from where she'd left it, propped against the garden fence, and began to turn the soil where she'd stopped off to tend to her wee herb garden. He attempted some light chatter with her, but when she made no reply beyond the occasional 'hmmpmm', he continued his work in silence. She finished the lavender and had moved on to the bed of rosemary and Casey had done two-thirds of the garden, when he finally spoke again.

"What's stickin' in yer craw, woman? Because it's clear somethin' is."

She sat back on her ankles and looked up at him. "I know what you did," she said tightly, the cauldron of fear and worry bubbling to the surface in a brew of anger, "or rather where you went."

"Where I went?" he asked, tone light. There was a wary look in his eyes, as though he knew exactly what she meant.

"Your visit to the Four Leaf Clover Club."

He went very still. "Aye, an' how is it ye know that?"

"I was told about it," she said.

"By my damn interferin' brother, no doubt."

"No, not by Patrick."

"Oh, was it Jamie then?" he asked, and she could see he was immediately upset at the thought.

"No, apparently both Patrick and Jamie saw fit to keep it to themselves. If you must know, it was Tomas who told me."

"Oh well, him," Casey snorted, "he'd be happy to see ye wind up with Jamie when all's said an' done, so I'm not surprised at his interferin'."

"It has nothing to do with Jamie, you fool. It's about you walking into one of the most notorious republican clubs in Belfast without so much as a word of warning to the rest of us. You might have been killed."

"Aye, admittedly, it was a calculated risk."

"Do you have anything to show for that risk, other than some of the most dangerous men in the city now being aware that you're alive, and once again available for the killing?" she asked hotly.

"Well, I'm still alive, so I suppose that's somethin'," he said and smiled, clearly trying to make light of the situation. The man could forget about relying on his charm today, however. She viciously snipped at the rosemary, stems flying everywhere, the blades of the pruning shears a blur of destruction.

"Ye might want to stop before ye take the entire plant out," Casey observed mildly, only to receive a withering glance in return. He held up his hands in truce and returned to digging up the soil.

"It's true what I said before about Tomas, ye know," he began, as though he were casually picking up the thread of a previous conversation, though she was not fooled by the tone at all. "He does favour Jamie for ye."

"No, he doesn't. Tomas is just protective of the children and me, that's all. He raked Jamie over the coals more than once when he thought—" she stopped abruptly, realizing the reason he'd raked Jamie over the coals wasn't going to help this conversation take a more genial turn.

"When he thought what? That ye were goin' to marry Noah Murray?" Casey stopped digging and turned to face her. One hand was draped casually over the top of the spade handle, but she wasn't fooled by his stance. There was a charged electricity coming off him that told her he'd been wanting this conversation for a while.

"Yes," she said.

"Because he thinks Jamie's better for ye, an' maybe he's right there."

"What the hell is that supposed to mean?" Her heart started to thump rather painfully. It wasn't the first time he'd said something which made her think he was leaning toward leaving the marriage.

"Do ye deny that ye have feelins' for the man?"

"Do I have feelings for him? Yes, I do. But it's you I'm married to."

"Oh well, that can be fixed quickly enough. I'll not have ye with me because ye pity me, woman."

"*Pity you*? I can't talk to you when you're like this," she said, standing and brushing the dirt from her knees to give herself a few seconds without looking at him. "You're irrational."

"Irrational? *I'm* irrational?"

"Yes, you are." She folded her arms across her chest, so that she wouldn't give in to her urge to fly across the garden and smack some sense into the man. "You know what I feel for you, Casey and pity isn't any part of it."

"Aye, so ye say, but there were certainly plenty of men—young an' old—mindin' the shop while I was gone."

"Minding the shop?" she said, her voice icily calm. "What exactly is that supposed to mean?"

"Ye know what I mean," he said, shoving the spade into the earth with such force that the handle snapped in two.

"Now look what you've done," she said, feeling a huge frustration which had little to do with the spade. "That will have to be replaced."

"I'll replace it, don't worry yerself about it," he said shortly and threw the handle to the ground.

"You needn't bother, I can look after it myself," she said, the frost still thick in her tone.

"Aye, well if ye can't, no doubt some hapless man will come along an' fix it for ye."

"You bastard," Pamela said, "why don't you just cut to the chase here and say what you really want to."

Casey took a long breath in through his nose, his eyes the colour of heavy smoke. "No, I think it's best if I don't."

"Oh no, please go ahead, I'd hate for you to stifle any of your thoughts," she said in a calm tone, which belied the fury that lit her very nerve-endings. "Meanwhile, I'm going in because I have a meal to make for your children."

To her surprise Casey followed her into the house. When she gave him a look on the doorstep, which he interpreted correctly, he merely said, "I promised Conor I'd mend his wee radio for him. I need to fetch it an' then I'll get out of yer way."

"Fine," she said shortly, walking into the house.

Casey went upstairs to retrieve Conor's radio and when he came back down she was peeling turnips with more vigor than skill. She had half a mind to simply keep her back turned and let him go without any further words between them. Since his return though, she had promised herself that she would never allow him to walk out the door with harsh words hanging between them.

She turned to find him standing by the table, turning Conor's radio over in his hands with a pensive air, as though he too had words he would say.

"Look, I realize how it must seem to you not having been here, but I was lonely, Casey, and scared almost all the time." She tried for a conciliatory tone, hoping to defuse the situation between them a little.

Casey's response, however, made it clear he was not in a conciliating sort of mood. "Aye, an' Jamie was here waitin' to pick up the pieces, just as he's always been."

"Would you have preferred it if I'd had no friends and no support?"

"No, obviously not—must ye be so contrary with me, woman?"

"I'm not trying to be contrary, but Jamie was my friend even before you disappeared. He stepped into the breach and looked after us in whatever ways he could."

"I understand that, but it was clearly a whole lot more than friendship," he said, the fire rising in his eyes once again.

"Yes, I loved him. That's a fact, and I can't change it."

He snorted and set Conor's radio down on the table with a decided thump. "Loved? Bullshit, ye still love him an' ye always will. An' it's maybe not just Jamie I'm talkin' about here."

"Oh, isn't it? Is it Noah Murray you want to discuss then?" Her hands were fisted by her sides, and anger caused her to speak recklessly. "You want to know what I did with him, how it was, is that it? You want to know what it was like to shag the biggest criminal in the county?"

"Pamela Madeline Riordan," he said with no small fury, "if ye don't quit talkin' like that, I am goin' to be forced to walk away from ye."

"Yes, damn you, Pamela *Riordan*, your wife! If you want a divorce, if that's what you're saying with all this ridiculousness, then you're going to have to file for it yourself, because I'm not going to."

"Did I say I wanted a fockin' divorce? Is that what *you* want, is that what ye're sayin'?"

"I asked first," she said defiantly, realizing she sounded ridiculous but with the anger pulsing through her hot and crimson, and she didn't give a damn how idiotic she sounded.

Casey paused for a second, as if checking in with his better nature, and then he clearly decided to abandon that notion and let fly. "I'm here an' I'm single. I am not the one who was engaged to fockin' Noah Murray, nor fockin' Noah Murray, as it happens."

"You bastard!"

"Better a bastard than a—" he clamped his lips shut over the next words he had been about to utter.

"Than a what—a whore?" she asked coolly.

"No, I'd not call ye that."

"Really, well what would you call me then? Maybe hussy, trollop, strumpet—do those sit easier on your tongue?"

"Pamela, stop it, those aren't words I'd ever use for you."

She seized then on what she thought was the salient point.

"So you're single, are you? How nice for you."

"That is not what I meant, an' ye know it."

"Do I? I have no idea what you've been up to this entire time."

"I'd prefer that myself," he said with no small heat, "for it's bloody clear what you've been up to, havin' a baby with one man an' plannin' a weddin' with another."

"One baby," she said tightly, "and one engagement, which I broke off."

He shook his head and walked toward the door. "I'm goin' before I say or do somethin' I'll regret."

"Do you have any feelings left for me?" she asked, regretting the words even as they left her tongue. It was a loaded question at best and it had been unwise to ask it right now.

He turned to look at her, disbelief written clear over his features. "What? How can ye even ask that?"

"Because I need to know—are you here only for the children, or are you here for me as well?"

Casey drew in a long breath and she quailed a little as he walked back across the kitchen toward her.

"All that time I was gone, wanderin' in the wilderness of my own head—alone and so fockin' lonely that I could hardly stand it at times—all that time an' I was faithful to you. To a woman I didn't even know, a woman I wasn't sure existed an' yet I couldn't bring myself to touch another, despite aching for the feel of a woman's touch. I crossed the ocean hopin' to God I'd find you, Pamela. Hopin' there was still a place for me in yer life. In the children's lives. An' now ye have the nerve to stand there an' ask do I *feel anything* for ye? For fock's sake, woman, I can't believe ye have the nerve to call me irrational when ye're the walkin' definition of it today."

"Do you think it's been a fucking picnic for me? I hung onto hope for so long I thought it might kill me. It became a millstone around my neck, hoping day after day that I'd find out anything, even the littlest hint about what had happened to you. Even if that hint pointed toward you being dead. I was alone with a baby and a toddler when you disappeared, in case that fact has slipped your mind."

"No, I'm well aware just how *busy* ye've been in my absence," he said, and there was no mistaking his meaning.

She gasped. "You have the nerve to even say that? You disappeared, walked off into the morning one day and never returned. What the hell was I supposed to do—stay celibate for the rest of my life?"

"Ye're blaming me for this?" He drove a hand through his hair.

"Jaysus God, ye're the most unreasonable woman alive. I was beaten nearly to death, shot an' thrown on a ship an' didn't know who the fock *I* was, never mind *you*—for three fockin' years—but aye, I see yer point, that's *my* fault."

"Is it mine, then? You told Jamie to look after me, to love your children and that's what he did."

"Oh, aye, I suppose that bit *is* my fault but I imagine when I wrote those words I knew how easily it would all take place," he said calmly, but the expression in his eyes told her he'd entered what she privately referred to as his 'slightly homicidal' phase.

"You—you," she sputtered, "are the most infuriating man!"

"Well, woman, ye don't do a whole lot for my own temper either," he retorted. He drew in a long, shaky breath. "Look, this isn't gettin' us anywhere. It's probably best if I go."

"You're not going anywhere. We're going to have this out," she said, trembling with fury. "You've been wanting to say something since you got back. So say it."

He looked at her and she saw something deep in those dark eyes, which made her doubt the wisdom of asking him to be totally honest with her. The next words out of his mouth, only confirmed her foolhardiness.

"Ye want to know? All right, here 'tis—I feel like ye cheated on me."

"Oh, I see," she said. "I thought it might be something like that."

"Ye see, do ye? No, I really don't think ye do, Pamela."

"Then please," she said through gritted teeth, "feel free to enlighten me."

He rubbed his hands over his face in frustration and then took a deep breath. She could see he was making an effort to calm himself before he said anything further.

"Were you completely faithful to me, Casey? Weren't there women you wanted, desired? You slept beside that woman you lived with in California every night for months. Are you telling me she never touched you? Are you saying your body didn't ache to have sex with her?"

"Aye, I did want her, an' aye she did touch me, but I never made love to the woman. So unless ye're goin' to quote Proverbs as law, an' say to even think of an act is to commit it, I don't see yer point here."

"Well then, I guess you're just a better person than I am. I had the gall to seek comfort with another man, so I suppose that gives you the moral high ground."

"Comfort?" he said, eyes narrowing to a hard glare. "Is that what we're callin' it now—*comfort*—Jaysus Christ, woman, ye do have a way of prettyin' things up."

"What would you like me to call it, Casey?" she asked coldly. "Would adultery suit you better?"

He shook his head, like a horse trying to shake off dozens of annoying flies. "Logically I know that's not the case, but emotionally yes, it feels like cheatin'. I've got all sorts of feelins' roilin' around in me over this, woman, but I've spared ye most of them."

"All sorts of feelings? Frankly, you don't appear to be anything but angry right now," she said squiffily, wishing that the man didn't arouse her own ire quite so easily.

"Yes, I'm fockin' angry, I'm furious as hell an' aye—ye needn't look at me that way—I'm well aware how unreasonable it is, but I'm still angry."

"Why?" she asked, so agitated she couldn't think clearly as to what the man might be trying to say.

"Because…because…" he spluttered, so upset that he couldn't put words to his feelings.

"Because what?" she said, gripping the edge of the table in an effort not to hit him.

He brought down his fist and hit the table so hard that all the cutlery bounced and the tea from her lunch spilled over, flooding off the edge onto the floor.

"Because ye're *my* wife, goddamnit!" he roared.

"Nice of you to finally notice," she said and turned away toward the sink to retrieve a towel for the mess. He grabbed her by the arm, whirling her back toward him, his eyes burning black.

"Do I feel anything for ye?" He snorted. "Jaysus Murphy that ye can even ask that, woman. Yes, goddamn it, I do!" He pushed her against the cupboard and then he kissed her, his mouth hard and demanding. She bit his lip, causing him to curse and draw a sharp breath before he put his mouth back on hers, flooding her tongue with the copper salt of blood. She put her arms around his neck, pushing against him with her body, uncertain if she was trying to push him away or pull him closer. She was furious with his words, furious with him. She had forgotten how strong the man was though, had forgotten that if he chose to exert that strength she was utterly helpless against him. He was exerting it now, holding her to him, so that there was no mistaking that he was both angry and aroused. She was in much the same state, every inch of her skin aware of the man next to it, touching it.

Her hands were under his shirt and she could hear buttons popping off. The feel of his skin, the hair on his chest, the contours of his muscles were like a map she'd followed a thousand times, always leading to the same destination. Someone's shirt ripped, she wasn't sure if it was hers or his and didn't give a damn. They lurched sideways, and she felt something fall with a loud splash and remembered the pot of turnips she'd left on the edge of the counter when he'd come down the stairs.

Her knee clipped a chair as they went down to the floor, his body on hers, both of them immediately soaked in the spreading puddle of water.

She tore his shirt off, wanting nothing more than his skin against her own, the feel of him inside her, even as she fought the urge to slap him. His hands were fumbling with the clasp on her bra now, fingers made clumsy by anger. He managed in the end though and then his hands were on her breasts, hot and hard, causing her to cry out at the sensation.

The entire world had become this—the hot fury of desire, the chill of the water, the heat of Casey's hands and mouth, the fiery intoxication of his body pressed hard against her own, the spinning want of it that made her both dizzy and as clearheaded as she'd felt in months. She reached down, fumbling at his zipper, just wanting him inside her, wanting him as she always had from the day they'd met. She tore her finger on his zipper but didn't feel the pain, her body coursing with the adrenaline of lust. He gasped as she touched him, and then said, "*Christ!*" on a rush of breath.

His name was in her head, repeating over and over, and it took a moment to realize she was saying it out loud, a litany of raw desire combined with the longing of the last three years. And then, suddenly, Casey stopped. He put his hands to the floor and pushed away from her.

"Not… not like this," he said.

He stood up slowly, his shirt in the pool of spreading water, pants unzipped and she simply lay there dazed, shirt rucked up, bra undone, and face stinging from the rasp of his whiskers. She sat up finally, adjusting her clothes, soaked to her skin with the starchy water. The kitchen looked like it had been ransacked by Vikings or pirates, or maybe just a Viking pirate she thought looking up at Casey—dark, dripping wet, partly naked and chest heaving with the exertion of the last several minutes. She took stock of her own emotional state, only to find she was completely discombobulated and not a little frustrated. Her finger was bleeding where she'd torn it on his zipper and she had cold turnip water dripping from her hair down her back.

Casey picked up his shirt and wrung it out over the sink, before putting it on and doing up the few buttons that were left. He did all this slowly and deliberately, like a man caught in a strange dream.

He looked at her and shook his head. "Go on up an' change, I'll clean up this mess," he said, his voice sounding as dazed as she felt.

She went up the stairs slowly, dripping all the way, and changed into a fresh pair of jeans and a sweater which would have made her old grammar school nuns proud.

True to his word Casey had the kitchen cleaned up when she returned to the bottom floor. He also had his coat and shoes on, and was clearly bent on leaving.

"You're going?" she asked, though the answer to that question was clear, being that his hand was on the door knob.

"Aye, I think that's best, don't you? I'm not thinkin' clear right now, an' neither are you. I don't want to say anythin' more that I'll regret once my temper has cooled."

"Is it because you can't forgive me," the words were little more than a whisper, "for sleeping with another man?"

"No, Pamela, it's not that, it's that I maybe can't forgive ye lovin' another man. That's my weakness, mind ye, an' not any fault of yers."

"Maybe so, but we both have to live with it."

"Aye, we do," he said softly, his voice drained of its former fury.

"I can't change the past, Casey. There's nothing I can do to make it better for you, it's up to you at this point."

"An' if I can't get past it?" he asked, sounding unutterably weary.

"If you can't, then there is nothing more for us here."

He nodded, and she fought the desire to go to him and take him in her arms, to take back her words and tell him a comforting lie. She knew to do that right now would be to compromise what they might have going forward—or not have, which was of course, the risk of it.

"I'll be away for a bit," he said, looking down at the floor, so that she could not catch his eyes. She didn't reply because she was, at this point, without words. He looked up for a moment and what she saw in his eyes broke her heart so that she felt it like a thousand tiny cracks shivering through glass.

And then with a soft click of the door, he was gone.

Chapter Thirty-one

Brotherly Advice

"CHRIST ON A CRACKER, this damn car is goin' to blow up on ye one of these days," Pat said, his words slightly muffled, coming as they did from deep under the hood of said car. Pamela winced a little, hoping this wasn't the death knell of her battered, bruised but much loved Citroën. Casey had bought the car at an auction years ago, where it had landed after its elderly owner had died. It had never been the world's greatest or most reliable car, but it had been through a great deal with her—including babies, getting shot, transporting a British spy and on one rather memorable occasion, going through a roadblock with an IRA member in the boot. For the last three years, Noah had kept it in working order, though he'd suggested mildly a few times that it might be time to find a more reliable vehicle. He'd even mentioned getting her a new one after they were married. More recently, of course, she'd had to have the windows replaced after the shootout at Miss Margaret's home.

All of that was now moot, though clearly Casey felt the car needed replacing as well. She couldn't quite explain what it was about the car that made it so hard to let it go to its rest in a junkyard somewhere, but it felt like a very old and dear friend, and so she kept having it repaired, though the cursing Pat had done since putting his head under the bonnet didn't bode well for its future longevity.

"Can you fix it, do you think?" she asked.

"Maybe, but it'll be a temporary patch at best." He poked his head out to look at her. "I know the car is symbolic of a lot more than just a bit of machinery that gets ye around, Pamela but I don't think it's safe anymore. An' maybe now that Casey's home, it might not be so hard to let it go."

She shrugged. Pat took in the look on her face, and sighed. "Hand me a socket wrench, would ye?"

She poked through the jumble of tools, and presented him with what she hoped was the correct wrench.

"Why didn't ye ask Casey to look at it? He's better with mechanics than I am. Our father taught us both, but Casey had the natural talent for it."

This was, she knew, Pat's way of opening up the subject of his brother, lest she wanted to talk about him.

"I don't think Casey is in the mood to do me favours right now," she said.

"Grab me the set of pliers with the red handles, please."

Digging in amongst the scrabble of tools, she extracted the red-handled pliers and passed them over to Pat.

"What's goin' on with the two of yez?"

"I don't know to tell you the truth. We had a fight the other day and he left, said he was going to be away for a bit."

"He's down in Wicklow, but I imagine ye sussed that for yerself."

"Yes, I figured he'd either gone to ground at Finn's or up in the mountains."

"He's coverin' in the pub for Finn for a few days. Finn is havin' some minor surgery, an' asked Casey if he'd mind takin' over for him while he mends."

"I'm not sure what to do regarding him; I don't suppose you'd care to offer any advice on dealing with a Riordan?" She asked the question in a joking tone, but she truly did want Patrick's take on her situation.

Pat looked up at her, a smear of oil on his nose. "Do ye want my honest opinion?"

"Yes, I wouldn't have asked otherwise," she said.

"Well," he said, in the practical tone he sometimes used, which told her she was about to get some very succinct advice, "as I see it, there's one simple solution to this. Take the man to bed. Talk to him afterwards."

"What?"

Pat gave her a pointed look. "I've seen the two of ye together of late. Ye're like a couple of caged cats circlin' one another. Take him to bed, an' talk after, otherwise ye'll just keep fightin' with one another."

Pamela smiled. "You have a point. I'm not sure the man will allow me into his bed just now, though."

Pat raised an eyebrow and Pamela laughed. "All right, were I to catch him in a weak moment, I admit he might be persuaded."

"Then persuade him, because neither of yez will see nor talk any sense until ye have."

"Do you know when he's coming back? Or if," she choked a little, recalling the look on Casey's face as he'd left the house that day, "he's coming back?"

"No, I don't know but I don't see why ye need to wait for him to return. Go down to Wicklow an' confront him. He's got a wee place to himself, ye'll have the privacy ye need."

Pamela briefly considered the impropriety of discussing all this with her brother-in-law, and then realized Pat knew all her dirty laundry, such as it was, from the last few years, and had never judged her nor made her feel the slightest bit uncomfortable about it.

"Ye know," Pat turned toward her, dark eyes soft, "I don't know him entirely, not in the way I knew him when we were boys, an' maybe I never will again, but I can say one thing with certainty—he loves you an' the children, Pamela. He needs to stop bein' stubborn an' let that be his guide. But," Pat sighed, "as he's the most obstinate bein' I've ever had the misfortune to meet, I think he could use a little persuadin'. He's raw an' he's hurtin' an' every time he looks at wee Kathleen, he sees proof of what you an' Jamie had when he was gone. So I think it's up to you to shake some sense into him. That is if ye're certain he's who ye want. I do know what ye had with Jamie, an' it's clear the two of ye will always have feelins' for one another."

She nodded. "We will. Jamie is part of my soul and to erase that or deny it would destroy some piece of me. And now with Kathleen, he will always be in my life, no matter what. But your brother is my husband, and when I say that I mean he is really and truly my husband in every sense of the word. I won't marry again if he leaves me."

"Tell him that, Pamela. He needs to hear it an' know that ye mean it."

Pat wiped his hands and looked back down at the engine somewhat dubiously. "Well, it ought to run for another week or two, I'm not layin' favourable odds beyond that, though."

"Thank you, Pat. I really appreciate it."

He gave her a hug. "It will be all right, Pamela. The two of yez are like magnets, ye can't be in a near space an' not be drawn together. He'll settle himself if he knows he's the man in yer life."

"I hope you're right, Pat. I'm not just so certain of that myself."

"That's only because ye have as much to lose here as he does."

Conor came out from the side of the house then, with Isabelle in his wake, both of them thoroughly grubby and no doubt looking for food. She looked down at her watch. It was mid-afternoon, and they'd need a snack of some sort.

Knowing they were in good hands with their uncle she went inside to make them sandwiches, cut up a few apples and got them each a glass of milk. Isabelle, who had the appetite of a fairy, would likely eat a slice or two of apple and then go back to her play, but Conor always needed something more substantial or he'd be looking for his supper within the hour.

Pat's words echoed in her head, as she made the children's snack, and then tidied away the cutting board and crumbs. There were still plenty of apples left, and they needed using before they turned brown. She'd make an apple crumble for dessert, as it was Conor's favourite, Casey's too come to that. She sighed; Casey would not be here to eat it.

Pat's advice had been practical and to the point, and she thought it was likely the best thing to do. It was just a matter of convincing Casey it was the wisest and most inevitable course. She took the food outside, along with a cup of tea for Pat, and then sat on the steps and watched her children as they hovered around their uncle, asking him endless questions, and peering with fascination into his toolbox. Pat was so like his brother, and yet he'd always been more measured and apt to err on the side of good judgement. If she was being entirely honest though, neither she nor Casey was great at being measured, nor had they always erred on the side of good judgement. In fact, she thought ruefully, they had rarely done so.

After Pat left, she sat for a long time on the step, watching the children play. Conor was constructing a small fairy house out of moss, twigs and rocks for Isabelle, who was running around finding more material for her 'hwouse', though there were more twigs in her hair—and Pamela thought despairingly, a good chunk of pine sap as well—than there were in her hands.

She would take Pat's advice and go see Casey, but before she could do that, there was one bit of business she had to deal with. Just the thought of it made those fine, shivering cracks in her heart spread outward like delicate shards of ice forming upon a pond.

Chapter Thirty-two

Come Home to Me

PAMELA TURNED IN the mirror, checking out her side and back view. She'd decided a new outfit was in order for her plans, and had bought an outrageously expensive and beautiful red silk dress. It was like a lick of flame in the cool afternoon light of the bedroom. The sleeves were long and sheer, rendering the skin beneath a glowing ivory. The neck was cut just low enough and the waist was nipped in tightly. The skirt fell two inches beyond her knees, flaring out in a soft waterfall of silk, which blazed from scarlet to crimson and back as the light flickered amongst its folds. Her shoes were a matching red silk, with a narrow strap that crossed her instep. Her hair was loose, the curls clustering around her shoulders and as usual, not really behaving. She dabbed a little perfume on her pulse points—throat, wrists and just a touch behind each ear. Coco Chanel had once said that a woman should wear perfume wherever she wanted to be kissed. Pamela added a drop to her décolletage.

It was ridiculous to be as nervous as if she was about to go on a first date with Casey. After all she was married to the man, and they had two children and had, for years, shared all the events of daily life together—meals, talks, arguments, sex, chores, jobs, and all the other tiny details that had made up the warp and weft of their world. They'd had their rough patches, certainly, rough enough that she had believed their marriage over at one point but they'd always managed to find each other again. And yet, she was as nervous as though she'd never slept with a man in her life.

Downstairs, Pat was sitting at the table waiting on Conor and Isabelle to finish packing up their few things to take with them for an overnight visit with their aunt and uncle. This visit had long been planned, for Isabelle wanted a sleepover with her new cousin, and Pamela after some nudging from Kate, had finally agreed to allow it. Kathleen was with Jamie for the next two days, and so it seemed to her that if she was going to broach the lion in his den, it was now or never.

"Wow," Pat said, taking in her attire, "goin' somewhere special tonight, are ye?"

"I've decided to take your advice," she said, sounding resolute. "I'm going down to Wicklow to seduce your pigheaded mule of a brother."

Pat laughed. "Despite yer mixin' of metaphors that's a very apt description of my brother. May I just say, it's about damn time."

Conor and Isabelle came clattering down the stairs then, Conor's bag thumping on each riser. They both came to a dead stop, eyeing their mother up and down. As used as they were to seeing her in jeans and sweaters and work clothes, they stared at her as if she had suddenly transformed from a pumpkin into a princess.

"You iz goin' to see daddy?" Isabelle asked accusingly, narrowing her dark eyes at the red dress.

"Yes," she said, "I am going to see daddy, but you can't come this time, sweetheart."

"I wants to see daddy too," Isabelle said, lower lip trembling alarmingly. Pamela suddenly saw all her plans going up in smoke.

Pat stood and swung Isabelle up into his arms. "Yer mammy an' daddy have a date, an' that's the sort of visit which is only for the two of them. Besides, Lily is expectin' ye an' she'll be awfully sad if ye don't come home with me, and," he added, "Auntie Kate has made ye those chocolate biscuits ye're so fond of."

Lured by the notion of disappointed babies and chocolate biscuits, Isabelle promptly forgot about her father and clambered down from Pat's arms, headed for the door. She ran back and gave her mother a quick hug, and then looked with impatience at her uncle.

"Gots to go, Unka Pat."

Pat laughed. "All right, darlin', let's be off then. Conor give me yer bag, so ye're not draggin' it all over yer mother's floor."

"It's heavy, Uncle Pat," Conor said, and then dropped the handle of his bag and flitted out the door after his sister.

"Jaysus Murphy has the boy packed stones in this thing? It weighs as much as a good-sized pig," Pat said, hefting Conor's small bag onto his shoulder with a grunt.

"Yes," Pamela said, "he likely has. I know there is a chunk of wood in there at the very least, and possibly a hammer. He likes to be prepared to build things given any opportunity."

"I just hope the wee beggar knows I've not his father's skill with the wood an' tools."

Pat leaned over then, and kissed her cheek, taking one of her cold hands into his own and giving it a squeeze.

"Wish me luck," she said nervously, returning his squeeze.

He smiled. "Ye'll be fine. He'll come round, ye'll see. It seems to me that dress isn't likely to fail ye." He was off out the door after his niece and nephew then, who were already waiting beside the car, Isabelle clutching her tiny pink suitcase, and Conor looking back at the house to be certain his uncle had his bag.

She locked the door behind her. Finbar was stowed with Gert and Owen for the night, and Khamsin had been turned out in the field. Owen had promised to check in on Paudeen at least once, and Rusty, being a cat, would be fine left to his own devices for a night.

She kissed Conor and Isabelle, waved Pat off, and then stood in the drive watching them go. It was a warm afternoon, and Pat's car windows were rolled down, and she could hear Conor say, "Uncle Pat what does 'seduce' mean?" She laughed, glad not to be in the position of explaining that particular word. Then she took a deep breath, put her bag in the Citroën and got behind the driver's wheel. It was time to face her future.

The long drive down to Wicklow gave her time to find her resolve sinking a little under a strong case of nerves. Even at that she found herself arriving in the village which had been home to Casey for a short spell, in what felt like minutes.

The village sat right at the base of the Wicklow mountains, and was of a size that a person might miss it entirely if they blinked on the way through. That would be a shame, though, Pamela thought, slowing the Citroën to a crawl, for it was set in absolutely gorgeous countryside. Patchwork fields of vivid green fell away toward the horizon, while on the other side of the road, thick woods of pine rolled up the mountainside. She could see why this particular corner of Ireland had caused Casey to halt in his wanderings and settle for a short while.

Egan's Pub was at the far end of the village, and she had to cross a small and precarious bridge first in order to reach it. The pub was neat and tidy, with window boxes filled with jewel-bright geraniums blooming cheerily out front, and a petrol pump gleaming with a recent polish, at the side. Ivy clambered around the windows, and up over the thatch of the roof. She parked the car, in need of both directions and a little fortification. She smoothed down her dress and took a deep breath. Casey might be behind the bar, and she needed to get her nerves under control before seeing him.

It gave her an odd feeling, not knowing just where in this village her husband lived. She walked into the pub, which was just as Casey had described it, clean and homey feeling, with a fire crackling in the hearth and neat snugs lining the outer walls, a few of which were filled. It was mid-evening, and only a few farmers were here having a pint before their nightly chores. They eyed her curiously, over the tops of their glasses and then returned to their drink and their chatter. Of her husband, there was no sign.

She hopped up on one of the stools at the bar, which was a long length of well-polished mahogany. No one appeared to be around so she leaned across the bar trying to peer into the back, just as a round and mostly bald head popped up in front of her.

"Can I help ye, miss?"

She clutched at her heart, startled by the man's sudden appearance and then she broke into a smile. "Finn," she said, as the man smiled in return, bright blue eyes disappearing into the folds of his cheeks.

"Well hello, Miss Pamela," he said. "What brings ye into my pub on this fine evening?"

"I'm looking for Casey," she said. "But first I need a drink. Something strong, Finn."

Finn nodded, "I've just the thing for ye, dear girl."

She took a deep breath and waited for Finn to get her drink. Now that she was here, she didn't feel quite so confident about her approach to this particular situation. Her pulse was thumping quick and hard, and a cloud of Diorissimo rose around her.

"I thought maybe he'd be here tonight. Pat said you'd had surgery recently and Casey was looking after things until you were healed up."

"Oh, aye, but the lad looked after the place all day, an' all the last week too, he needed an evenin' to himself. He's just over across the way. I can show ye, when ye've had yer drink."

Finn placed a glass on the bar in front of her and filled it from a small bottle. The smell was delicious though she feared if she sniffed it too deeply she'd be knocked unconscious.

He set the bottle beside her glass and nodded. "Courage in a bottle that is, but careful how much ye drink. I make the smaller bottles for the ladies, but it still packs a bit of a wallop, so go easy. Ye want to be able to stand when ye're done."

"Thank you," she said and took a swallow, gulping in her nervousness. "This stuff is delicious," she said, picking up the bottle and tipping a little more of the dark liquid into her glass.

"An' why is it, may I ask, that ye're needin' the courage?" Finn asked.

"I've come to lay down an ultimatum with Casey, so to speak," she said, thinking it was one thing to tell Pat she was bent on seducing his brother, but quite another to confide this to a near stranger.

He eyed her dress, and crooked an eyebrow at her. "Have ye then?"

"Well," she said nervously, "what do you think?"

Finn cocked his head to one side as though giving the question serious contemplation. "Well, it's my opinion the poor man doesn't stand a chance."

"He's a tougher nut to crack than you might think, Finn," she said, feeling a sudden depression of spirits.

Finn finished polishing the glass he was holding before responding to her statement. "Well, all I can tell ye is this. When he lived here there were more than a few who would have been happy to be the woman in his life. He weren't interested though, an' when I inquired about it, Nosy Parker that I am, he said it was because he was a one woman man, an' that woman was an' is you. I think ye need not have any fears about the man's feelins'. He loves ye, that's clear."

"Is that enough, though?" she asked, voicing her greatest fear.

"It's all there is, dear girl. Sure an' yer situation is a wee bit more complicated than most but he's a choice—he can live with it or he can live alone. Ye thought he was dead, an' so he can hardly blame ye for the fact ye moved along with yer life. An' he does understand that more, perhaps, than what ye're givin' him credit for."

"Does he? He's making it rather hard to tell these days."

"I don't suppose I need to tell you how stubborn the man is, Pamela. The truth though—if he could bring himself to admit it to ye—is that he'll be broken if ye let him go."

She took a deep breath. "I think it's time to beard the lion in his den," she said, hoping the drink would give her the last bit of bravado she needed.

"I'll walk ye over, 'tis only across the lane but it's gettin' on toward the dim, an' I think ye've maybe," he looked at the bottle, "had a wee bit more than was advisable of the drink."

The walk was just across the lane, but Finn took her right to the door of a wee cottage, where the light of a fire glowed in the windows.

"Wish me luck," she said, feeling that any luck she might have accrued by asking Pat for it, had likely dissipated by now.

"Ah, darlin' girl, I don't think ye need luck. Just go easy on the man, eh?" And with that he smiled and was gone into the night.

The knock on the door startled Casey, for he had been reading and the night was so quiet around him that he'd nodded off over his book.

He opened the door a crack, his foot braced on the bottom of it, so that if someone was about to force their way in, he would have a prayer of stopping them. When he saw who stood outside, he stepped back and opened the door wide.

"Pamela?" he said, more than a little surprised at her appearance after their last meeting.

"Are you going to invite me in? It's cold out here."

"Of course," he said and stepped back. She walked in past him, wobbling ever so slightly. He thought he caught a whiff of whiskey. He raised an eyebrow. "Are ye drunk?" he asked, nonplussed. The woman was normally a teetotaler, rarely having more than one drink, as it usually went straight to her head. And, he remembered, watching her drop her coat on the floor, parts lower.

"No, I am not. Or rather, yes I am, but not so much that I don't know what I'm doing, Casey Riordan."

He rubbed a hand over his face, wondering if perhaps he was still dreaming. "Did I accuse ye of not knowin' what ye're doin'?"

"No," she said drawing the one syllable out with the careful gravity of the inebriated, "but you will in a minute."

"Aye," he smiled, "why is that?"

Why became clear as she fumbled with the tie on her dress and then dropped it to the floor and stood in front of him in only a lacy bra and panties, stockings and high heels.

He looked about for something to cover the woman with, but short of throwing a blanket over her, there was nothing to hand. Besides, despite the fact that she was clearly three sheets to the wind, he was enjoying the view immensely.

"I am here to take you to bed," she said, sounding rather brisk and business-like despite the wobble to her walk.

"Are ye, then? Forgive me, Jewel, but ye don't look as though ye can stand, much less take a man to bed."

"Well, I don't need to stand for that, do I?" she said and so saying sat down on his bed and proceeded to kick off her shoes, one of which landed near to the fire, and then went on to roll down her stockings. Casey swallowed, torn between the desire to laugh, and just say to hell with it and do as the woman told him to. The desire was like a punch in the gut it was so strong.

"Are you coming or not?" she said, squinting up at him through a tangle of curls.

"Well call me old-fashioned, darlin' but I don't think I should take advantage of a woman who is clearly worse for the drink."

"Just because I've had a tiddly bit to drink, doesn't mean I don't know what I want. Now come to bed, would you?" One bra strap had fallen down, and the curve of both breasts was on full display. Her skin glowed like pearls seen through water, and her panties were sheer enough that he could see the shape of her. No, decency was not what he was feeling just now, not even a little bit. The smell of her—heat and desire and that perfume that was only her—was making him dizzy.

"At least kiss me," she said, clearly irritated with him, but still he could see, very determined. He knew exactly what she was up to, but it was pure bad manners not to kiss a woman when she asked you to. Especially when she was pretty much naked in your bed, and your wife.

Casey sat down beside her and took her face in his hands and kissed her softly, but at length. She was all velvet fire beneath his hands and when he felt her lean into him, he thought his morals could go to hell in a handbasket. He broke the kiss a moment later, his senses reeling, and drew back a little to catch his breath.

"Do you not want me?" she asked, and the hurt in her voice cut him to the quick. Christ, he was almost blind with restrained lust.

"Not want you, Pamela? Jaysus woman, I can hardly breathe an' I sure as hell am not thinkin' clear right now."

"Then why won't you just make love to me?" she asked.

"Because it's not right when ye're still tryin' to make up yer mind about what ye want."

She took a deep breath and closed one eye so that she could bring him into better focus. He wondered if Finn's brew had ever given anyone alcohol poisoning.

"There's something I need to say to you," she said slowly and carefully, articulating each word. "So, I'd appreciate it if you would just listen to me for a minute." The solemnity of her statement was somewhat ruined by a small hiccough.

"All right," he said, feeling vaguely uneasy.

"Here's the thing—you're my man. Come what may, hell or high water, as long as you're here on earth, you are my husband and my mate. Even if you decide you'd rather divorce and live apart from me, I still won't re-marry. As long as you're alive, I will always be married. To be with another man would simply be a lie. But if you can't be happy with me anymore, if you can't accept Kathleen as part of our family then I will let you go and I won't make it difficult for you."

"Ye won't make it difficult for me? I find that hard to believe, woman."

"No, I won't, not if you really want to go. I'll give you your freedom."

"Pamela, I will never be free of ye, even if I were to go live on the far side of the moon."

"If that was meant to sound romantic, I have to tell you," she hiccoughed daintily, "that it most certainly did not."

He laughed. "Well no, it wasn't meant to sound romantic, just honest."

For this statement he was treated to an owlish glare. "I know you'd like me to leave but I can't go home as I'm too drunk to drive. The room is tilting too," she finished in a rather accusatory fashion, as though he were moving the cottage about on its foundations. "There's nowhere to sleep but in this bed, so will you let me have half for the night?"

"Aye, ye can have the bed. I can kip on the floor," he said, fully aware that if he got in the bed with her all bets were off. He grabbed one of his clean shirts and tossed it to her. "Ye can sleep in this."

He turned his back to give her privacy, and to give himself the fortitude to stick with his morals, shaky as that particular handhold was.

He made himself a bed on the floor with two blankets and a pillow. It was the nocturnal equivalent of a hair shirt, and about as comfortable as said article.

"Mmmmm," Pamela sighed above him, "this shirt smells like you."

"*You* smell like eighty proof blackberry jam," he said. "Have ye been in Finn's whiskey?"

"Yes, I have," she said and hiccoughed. "I had a bottle of it."

"Ye drank a bottle of that stuff? Jaysus woman I'm amazed ye can move at all. A glass of it almost paralyzes me."

"He makes smaller bottles for the 'leddies,'" she said and giggled. Small bottle or not, a man needed little more than a thimbleful of the stuff to knock him on his arse. A woman—well, he was duly impressed with her capacity just now.

"Casey?"

He looked up to find a pair of big green eyes looking down at him.

"I'm cold, man."

"Well," he said, trying to sound censorious and not laugh, "ye ought to have thought about that before ye arrived half-naked on my doorstep."

"I wasn't half-naked," she said indignantly. "I am now though, and it's perishingly cold in here."

"No, it isn't, the fire's high as a kite an' it's warm as toast, woman. Ye never could stay warm when ye were in the drink."

"I didn't have to warm myself when I was in the drink, you always did it for me. You weren't," she hiccoughed, "so mean then."

"Mean, is it?"

"Yes, mean. You rejected my advances, I wouldn't call that gentlemanly conduct, would you?"

"No, I suppose it's somewhat ill-mannered on my part, but maybe not so ill-mannered as takin' advantage of yer legless state."

"Casey?"

"Aye?"

"Could you please come lie with me? I promise not to sully your honour. I'm just cold and it's lonely up here."

He sighed, appealing to the ceiling beams in the hope that they might give him some sort of divine restraint. They simply sat there being beams though, phlegmatic and silent.

He got in the bed, and she scooted over, making room for him. He noted that she hadn't had much success with buttoning up the shirt. The bed wasn't big and he wasn't small, the result being that he found himself within a couple of inches of the woman.

His body, as it turned out, didn't give a damn for his principles. It simply knew the woman it had longed for all these years was within touching distance. He put an arm around her, painfully aware that she was going to know him for a liar in about two seconds flat.

"Oh God, you're gorgeously warm," she sighed and snuggled along his length.

He put his face to her hair and inhaled her scent. She did smell like blackberry jam, enough that he had a strong desire to lick her just to see if she tasted of it too.

Suddenly she was still, and he had a good notion of just why.

"You do want me," she said quietly.

"Of course I do, ye wee eejit. Did ye imagine that I'd gone off ye?"

"You could; I don't take anything for granted between us, Casey. Not anymore."

He smoothed one hand down the side of her face, and along her shoulder.

"Pamela, turn over, I need ye to look at me."

She turned in his arms, and looked up into his face, and he was shocked to find her eyes filled with tears.

"Oh Lord, woman. Do ye not know what ye are to me?"

"I'm not certain of anything just now."

He kissed her forehead and then brushed his thumb gently under her lashes to take away her tears.

"Ye can be certain of this, Pamela Riordan—I have wanted ye from the day I met ye, an' I expect to feel the same on my death bed. An' I have loved ye almost as long as that. That is not goin' to change for me, not ever. I know that much, even if I know little else."

"You left though, after that afternoon in the kitchen. I thought maybe that was your way of saying you couldn't do this, you couldn't be with me anymore."

He stroked back her hair with one hand. "No, darlin', I just needed a few days to clear my head. Finn needed the help too, an' I thought maybe ye could use the time an' space yerself. Ye didn't ask for this after all, me droppin' back into yer life like an ill-timed bomb. I want ye to have a clear head an' the time ye need to make a decision."

"Do you think I would be here if I hadn't made a decision? For heaven's sake, man, my decision was made the day you walked into the yard," she said.

"Ye had to get drunk to come here, though, doesn't that tell ye somethin'?"

"That's because I needed Dutch courage. You're my husband, but you're not quite the same man I lost three years ago. I find this new version of you a little intimidating at times."

"Oh, Pamela. Surely ye know ye need not ever be afraid of me."

"I'm not scared of you, so much as I'm afraid we won't find our way back to one another."

"We seem to have a harder time stayin' away from one another, so I think ye needn't worry on that account," he said, a hint of wryness in his tone.

She kissed him then, softly, a kiss that held a question in its hesitancy. He kissed her back, wanting to still her uncertainty, wanting her to know what it was he felt.

She sat up and undid the two buttons that were all she had managed to do up, and let the shirt slide off her shoulders.

"God, you're beautiful," he said, feeling as though there was no air left in the room. The firelight gilded her, lending a beautiful gold to her skin, her hair furled over one shoulder, shining softly where it touched her breast. He reached out a hand, trembling, and she took it guiding it the rest of the way so that his fingers touched the top of her breast. He slid the hand around, cupping the weight of it, feeling how she trembled now, her body already arching toward him, her eyes sparkling with tears. He took her hand then, and pulled her down so that she lay along his length. The minute he'd gotten into the bed with her he knew he had gone past the point of no return.

She leaned down and kissed him, her mouth warm and sweet and tasting of tears. He ran his hands from her thighs up her back and then tangled his fingers in her hair. He groaned low in his throat, just to touch her so was almost more than he could bear.

Memory spoke softly at first, the arch of her spine under his hand, the taste of her mouth against his own, the spill of her hair through his fingers, like night-black silk. And then it spoke with force as she said his name, soft as a whisper and yet filled with demand. She put her hands against his chest, breathing in and out against his neck, trembling along her entire length. God, the desire was beyond his expectations, he felt as primal as a caveman, wanting to put his imprint on her; his scent, his want, his need, wanting to plant his seed in her belly as he had done before, so that all might know this was *his* woman. He stroked her back and she arched toward him, breasts pressed to his chest.

"I feel drunk just with the look of ye."

"I could look at you all night," she said, "just to get my fill of you."

"I'd as soon we didn't take up the whole night that way," he said, slightly breathless as she touched him softly, so that his cock sprang eager to her hand, wanting the fit of her, warm and needing. He rolled her under him, feeling the arch of her toward him, feeling the completion of the two of them, within his reach. Here it was—love and need and want, and an understanding that this was why he had never been able to settle somewhere else, that he had always, even without a memory, been fated to find his way back to this woman and this love. Still he stopped for a moment and looked down at her beneath him, brushing her face with one hand. "Are ye certain? Once we do this, there's no goin' back. This is us, Jewel, for good an' all."

She looked up into his eyes, her own glittering with unshed tears. She reached up and kissed him, took his mouth with tenderness and felt his response and pulled him down to her so that he was in her arms, their hearts thrumming against each other. He knew she sensed the sliver of hesitation he still felt, even as his need pounded hard against her, her own body arching in response.

"Just come home to me, man."

And then he was inside her, as her body opened up to him, bringing him home in the one way which had never failed them.

It was both tender and rough, for they were too hungry for one another to have finesse, though their flesh understood their urgency and carried them where they needed to be. Until at last they lay quiet, blood still coursing hard so that he could feel every beat of her heart against his chest. He lowered his head to her own, and kissed her forehead softly, his lips lingering there, so that he felt her breath slow. They simply stayed there for a long time, grateful for the feel of one another.

Finally Casey rolled to the side, and then pulled her tight to his body so that his warmth enveloped her. His entire body was in a state of stupefied happiness. He brushed the hair away from her neck and then ran his tongue from the hollow of her shoulder to the lobe of her ear.

"*Aagghh*, what was that for?" she asked, shivering.

"I wanted to see did ye taste like eighty proof blackberry jam, as much as ye smell like it. An' ye do, the stuff has come out through yer pores. I think I'm just the wee bit drunk off ye."

"Well, *I* am definitely drunk," she said.

She turned in his arms so that she was facing him, her head tucked in the curve of his shoulder.

There was a murmur of voices going past on the narrow lane outside his cottage door. Some of the regulars from Finn's heading home. Beyond that the night was silent, with only the soft hiss of the fire to disturb it. A warm peace had stolen over him and he felt like he could just lie here forever.

He wasn't naïve, he knew there were still difficulties to overcome. Between his own history in the IRA, the holes he still had in his memory, and his admitted jealousy in regards to Jamie there would be times, he knew, which would try them sorely. But right now, none of that mattered, because just the warm smell of her, the heat of her skin, the scent upon the nape of her neck… she was his home in this world and he understood it with a profound clarity that was like a bell resounding through his marrow, and just as surely he knew, he was hers. The rest did not matter and would fade with time.

He thought she'd fallen asleep, so even and slow was her breathing and so when she spoke he was surprised.

"Casey?"

"Aye?"

"I love you, man."

He bent his face into the curve of her neck, and breathed in her scent, feeling gratitude in his every cell.

"I love you too, woman."

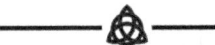

Pamela woke in the wee hours, when the dark still held sway but was of a quality that spoke of it giving way to dawn's light. Casey wasn't in the bed, and she felt a small beat of panic, before realizing he was poking up the fire and adding a few bricks of peat to it.

Watching him now, as he finished building up the fire, she realized she hadn't exaggerated before—she *could* just look at him all night. There was a terrible longing for him within her, which she thought might take a very long time to sate, or perhaps it would never be sated. From the day she had met him, there had been this—this invisible thing which existed between them, which insisted upon his touch, his body, which insisted upon *him* as what she needed to heal and become whole.

This man had been entirely unexpected in her life. When she'd met him it had been like being hit by a wave when you were simply out for a nice walk on the shore. From the first time he had touched her, she had never truly belonged to herself again. It hadn't mattered though, because he'd felt the same way. Still, regardless of their time together, and even the years apart, she had never been able to put into words just how intrinsic this man was to the well-being of her body, her heart and her very life.

Casey's eyes met hers, and he smiled, and she felt herself flush under his gaze, feeling suddenly shy. He seemed to sense this for he got back in the bed, and drew her to him, using one hand to smooth back the hair from her face. He kissed her forehead, and she felt her body relax at the touch of his hands. This was their most reliable language, and she was relieved to find they still spoke it with great fluency.

She ran her hand down his back, feeling the scars, each one imprinted on her memory.

"I longed for this every night," she said, "just to be able to touch you again."

"And I you," he said, running one hand down her side, his palm coming to rest on her hip. "It's good to have yer hands on me again, Jewel."

"Do you remember the first time we made love? We were out in the countryside, near a slab of rock where your family has always gone to carve their names. I'm sorry," she said, suddenly realizing how such a question might strike him, as patchy as some pieces of the past were for him. "I shouldn't ask you that."

He smiled, the dark eyes soft in the firelight. "There are other kinds of memory, an' this—us, my body remembers quite well. An' yet, what it is to touch you—I had forgotten the power of it, an' I do not have words adequate for how it feels. I remember that first time in my cells, though, even if I don't recall the details."

"I went there once," she said softly, "when you were gone. Long ago, you told me that if you died before me, you'd wait for me there. So I went." Her voice caught a little and Casey stroked her back, soothing her so that she might continue.

"Oh, Pamela," he said softly.

"I left the children with Gert and Owen for the day, and drove out there. It was overcast and the place seemed a lot more foreboding than when I was there with you. I walked down to where your family's names are and sat there, waiting. I thought if you were dead, maybe you'd give me a sign, something, just anything so that I could maybe start breathing again, and move on with my life. I spent a few hours there, watching the light move across the land, and waiting. And then I said an old prayer, meant to summon a ghost."

"An' did a ghost arrive?" he asked.

"I think so, though it was not quite what I expected," she said, earning a raised eyebrow from Casey. She shivered a little now, remembering that day.

It was a mistake, coming here, knowing what her memories of this particular place were. Sometimes she thought she was going a little mad, and that days like this just served to prove it. Still she found herself making her way down the embankment to the valley where a chunk of slate stood, with the names of too many Riordan men carved upon it. Casey had made her a promise long ago, and though she knew it was more than a bit crazy to expect a dead man to keep promises made while living, she had to see for herself.

She sat down on the length of dark rock, and put her hand to the carved letters. It was then she noticed that Brian's name had been added, and felt a shock go through her body at the sight of it. Casey had brought her here long ago, and that night had been the first time they'd made love. Here on this rock.

There were times she wondered if they'd cursed themselves, consummating their relationship in this location.

When, she wondered, had Casey done this carving—for it was his hand which had cut his father's name into the stone—of that she was certain. The only other person who might have done it was Pat, and his hand for carving was nowhere near as skilled as Casey's had been. She traced a finger over the letters, as if by touching something his hand had made, she could conjure him up, feel his touch as though it resided here in this rock.

"Hello, my love." Her throat caught on the words and she bit down on the tears she could feel aching at the back of her eyes. She took a deep breath, knowing she had to get the words out before she dissolved, before the pain took her in the wave that had been out there threatening to roll over her from the day she had come home to find him gone. Missing him was like a raw wound that never seemed to heal over, nor did it seem to ever get less painful.

"I-I don't know what to do with the plans we made, man. Not even the little ones like the addition we talked about building, or the big ones like how many more children we wanted. We said two more, remember? I thought they might both be girls and you and Conor would be besieged with women in your lives. But I also thought there wasn't a man more capable of dealing with that and finding joy in it."

"I'm so mad, I'm eaten with it sometimes that we will never get to live out those plans. That I will never know the touch of your hands on me again, never hear your laughter or have you tell me a story, that you won't be here to guide Conor and Isabelle, to simply watch them grow and to love them…" she trailed off feeling the great silence which held to the land here, and how small and futile her words felt within it. Her pain, after all, was not unique, it was simply what life served up on a regular basis to anyone who lived long enough.

"You promised me, man, that if you died before me, you'd wait for me here. I just want a sign, anything, that you can hear me, can feel me across the divide."

He had made the promise and then named this place so she'd know where to find him. Her words hung on the air, the sound taking a moment before it died away.

Casey had always teased that she was at least half witch, and would have been burned at the stake in earlier times for her beliefs, and the premonitions she occasionally had about things to come. To her, much of it was common sense—working with nature and inside of its cycles, rather than against it, fighting a battle one could never hope to win, and listening when your instincts gave you warning of danger drawing near to you. There were other things too, about which she was less certain, and yet knew there was a power to old ways and old words—words spoken in a certain order for a certain purpose. This didn't fall under the heading of common sense, and as such, felt a bit more dark and uncertain to her. But it was worth a try, she thought, even if one had one's doubts about dabbling in what amounted to dark magic. One never knew what one might summon across the divide between life and death. Still…she took a deep breath and closed her eyes. There was an old prayer, a simple call from one soul to another, across the boundary which separated her from Casey. Yes, it was worth a try, the desperation in her heart would allow no less.

She said the prayer out loud, shaking a little with fear, as the valley held a very odd feeling today.

"You who lived yesterday, I call you from my mind to yours,

Come back from the shadows into the light and show yourself here."

It was a cold day, and the afternoon was waning even as she said the words. She had come here for a purpose though, and as ludicrous as it seemed she must see it through. Her body was trembling and not just with cold, but with the fear of disappointment.

She opened her eyes, though she felt almost sick with fear. There was nothing, and no one. Around her the winds of longing still blew, and the landscape was just as empty as when she'd arrived. She was a fool—a ridiculous fool. What had she expected—a ghost to materialize out of the rock? Or had she come here only to touch the memory this place held, this bit of rock and carved letters, this place where she'd first understood that she loved the man she'd since lost? Still, she stood for a long time, watching the light fade, and feeling the wind grow colder, until she knew it was time to go home.

"But, of course, I never came to you," he said, and there was regret enough for a lifetime in his voice.

She stroked the side of his face. "You couldn't, I know that now. I never stopped hoping that you would, though. I would have this dream sometimes, and I'd see you walking on a road, away from me. You would always stop at a bend, and look back at me. I thought, at times, you were asking me to let you go, to promise you we'd go on with our lives. That we'd honour the love you'd given us by doing so. But I couldn't seem to do it. I even thought it wasn't fair to you, to hold onto you that way. I'd worry I was holding you in purgatory by my need for you. There was a prayer beating inside me all the time, asking you to come home to me. It was like a brand in my heart—*Come home to me.*"

"I heard ye once," he said, looking vaguely troubled.

"What do you mean?" A prickle went down her spine, and she shivered a little, causing him to pull the blanket over her.

"It was one night in a church. It was just after Christmas the second year, an' I was there lightin' candles. I lit seven, though I didn't know why, just that the number felt right. I would suppose the candles were for yerself and our children, Patrick an' Kate, an' my parents. Then though, I didn't know. I was just standin' there puzzlin' at all that light when I heard a shout. A woman's voice that said '*wait for me.*' I knew the voice was yers, somehow. I promised ye then that I would—that I'd wait for ye."

"When I was sick, Jamie told me I kept saying that—*wait for me*. He said I thought I was seeing you. My fever was so high that I was hallucinating." She shivered again, clutching his hand, as though that winter's night when she had almost died, still hovered near.

"It breaks my heart to know ye were so ill, an' I wasn't there to look after ye. It also makes me the wee bit jealous to know it was Jamie who was carin' for ye. Yet I'm also grateful because if I couldn't be there, there's no one better to look after ye."

"I'm sorry," she said softly.

"Aye, so am I, darlin'." He kissed her hand, closing his eyes for a moment. "Now finish yer tale, woman. Did ye get yer sign or not that day?"

"I did. As I stood to go a bird landed in a holly bush," she said.

"A bird?" he echoed, clearly puzzled.

"When we first lived together, you carved a song thrush for me because I told you how much I loved their call. It was the first gift you ever gave me, and it's something I treasure. You put a holly berry in its mouth, one you'd carved obviously, because of course, holly is the guard between this world and that. You always said I had a foot in both worlds, and so that's why you put a berry in its mouth."

"Aye well, considerin' the conversation we've just had, I'm thinkin' my opinion on that bears out. Ye ought not to be dabblin' with dark things, woman—one of these times ye're goin' to get more than ye bargained for."

"It's lovely to have you scold me again," she said.

He laughed. "Well, it's lovely to be scoldin' ye again, though a man might wish ye'd simply learn to behave yerself. Now finish tellin' me about yer wee bird."

"So there was that bird, sitting in that scrubby little bush, its roots hanging onto the rocks, with a few of the last season's berries still clinging to it. The thrush sat there for a bit, and then it took a berry in its mouth and looked at me for what seemed a long time, then flew off. It was the sign I was looking for, and I had thought," she said quietly, "it would be a comfort, but it wasn't. I thought it was you, saying goodbye."

He drew her closer to him, and kissed her gently on the forehead. "Oh darlin', even if I had died, I don't think I could ever say goodbye to you. There were times I thought I *was* dead durin' those three years, like I'd slipped from life to purgatory an' just didn't know it. All that time I was gone from ye, I was no more than a ghost. I didn't come back to life properly until I saw ye that day in the yard. I am not sure I'm whole even now, but all the pieces of me that still exist, Pamela, are yers," he said, voice slightly hoarse.

Tears were rising to the surface, and she swallowed hard, keeping them at bay for the moment. She took his hand and put it to her chest, so that he might feel the beat of her heart, and then did the same with her hand, his pulse warm and slow against the skin of her palm.

"I will take you in all your pieces, man, as you take me in mine. Together we are whole."

This time it was slow and measured, each touch a grace note, each spoken word a healing. The fire between them, never tamped even through three years of separation, built quickly, taking them within its shelter and heat, and then guided them whole into the redemptive flames of love.

Chapter Thirty-three

The Fixed Point of the World

CASEY SLIPPED BACK into the stream of domestic life without a ripple. The children were well used to seeing him on a daily basis, having him eat meals with them, read them bedtime stories, and help them with their various woes, so that now having him stay the night was just another step along the way.

For Pamela, it was a slightly different experience. It was a bit like being on a honeymoon with three children in tow, which was, ultimately, a rather frustrating experience. And yet, just to have him there each morning when she woke, to reach across the bed in the middle of the night and find him there, warm and solid, put her in a state of giddy joy.

Isabelle, who was not used to seeing a man in a state of undress, had presented Casey with a t-shirt the first morning he'd come down the stairs bare-chested.

"Not be naked in da house, Daddy," she'd said in stern admonition.

Casey had merely laughed and shrugged the t-shirt on over his head before getting Isabelle the milk she'd demanded.

This morning marked two weeks since he'd returned home, and settled back in with them, so that there were moments she felt like she'd simply dreamed him being gone. Though, she supposed, watching him put Kathleen in her highchair, and setting her bowl of oats and applesauce in front of her, that might make her wee redheaded girl a bit hard to explain.

It was a beautiful morning, and the kitchen basked in a general feeling of drowsiness and goodwill. Even Isabelle was eating her breakfast, rather than running amok about the house as she normally did in the mornings. The scent of sausages and eggs, and oatmeal and honey permeated the air, and Pamela could taste the tart sweetness of rosehip syrup on her tongue. Isabelle had somehow managed to open a jar of it on her own, and spill half of it on the floor before Casey could catch her. Now they were all partaking of the bounty that was left.

After making certain everyone had their breakfast, she sat down and tucked into her own food, finding she had a good appetite.

"Ye look tired this mornin', Jewel. Up late were ye?" Casey gave her one of those quick, beautiful grins which drove his dimple deep into his whiskers. He returned to spooning food into Kathleen's mouth, but his foot nudged hers under the table.

She flushed, knowing full well what the grin was about. The night before, he'd woken her in the wee hours, and taken her by the hand, leading her down the stairs. The room had been lit silver with moonlight, and Casey had opened a window to let the scent of the night flood in. Then, still wordless, he'd taken her down on the hearth rug, and they'd made love without ever exchanging a word. The strange light had given her a sense of weightlessness, and yet the whole experience had been so intensely physical that she was aware of every inch of her body, as well as every inch of Casey's. After, he'd taken her hand again, and they'd walked back up the stairs and fallen into bed, where she'd slept, deep and dreamless, for the rest of the night.

She got up and re-filled his plate, and then returned to the table to put it in front of him. She kissed the top of his head, lingering for a moment to breathe him in. He put up one hand and took the one she rested on his shoulder, turning her palm to his face and kissing it.

There were times she wondered, especially in simple moments like this one, how it all felt to him. The house, the children, the animals, the routine of it all. Were there moments he felt strange and out of step, as if he'd awakened in a dream, and wasn't sure what it was about?

"It's lovely," he said, looking up at her. She startled a little, realizing he'd read her thoughts as clearly as if she'd spoken them out loud.

"How did you know what I was thinking?" she asked, intrigued that a man with holes in his memory could be so attuned in other ways.

"I don't know really, only my body seems to remember the various moods of yers, an' knows when ye're worryin' on somethin.'"

Tears stung at the top of her nose, and she buried her face for a moment in his shoulder, overcome with gratitude for what they had regained, or perhaps never truly lost. Casey gave the hand he still held a squeeze of reassurance.

She stood upright a moment later, and Casey handed her a handkerchief with which she mopped her face, before the children noticed her upset. Conor had finished his breakfast, and was on the floor, carefully gluing together a mass of sticks, which meant that she was going to be peeling dried glue off her floor for the next few days. Isabelle was sporting shiny, sticky lips, proof of her enjoyment of the syrup, and was now hopping about the table singing, *'Frosty Weather, snowy weather, when the wind blows, we all go together.'* Finbar was industriously cleaning the floor beneath the chair Isabelle had just hopped down from, and Kathleen's beautiful red hair was glazed with oatmeal. Rusty was peering through the kitchen window, and she realized to her dismay that he had a good-sized mouse in his mouth. She sighed, he offered her such gifts on a regular basis, and had almost imperiled her life by dropping one on her toes the other morning, right after she got out of the bath. It was, she thought, smiling through her tears, just an average morning in the Riordan household.

"I imagine it might be overwhelming at first." She gestured around the kitchen at the children, the dog, the mouse killer peering in the window, and the porridge which Kathleen had just upended onto the floor.

"Not overwhelmin', no but there are moments when I think it can't be real, and then others when I feel like I never really left."

He took the hand he held and pressed it to his face, so that she felt the soft springiness of his morning whiskers, like plush velvet against her hand.

"All that time without ye, Jewel, I was adrift. I had no anchor, no fixed point in the world to call my own."

"And now?" she asked softly.

He looked up at her, the dark eyes peaceful. "And now," he said, "I'm home."

Part Four

Children of the Troubles

Chapter Thirty-four

Field of Fire

AMBROSE HAD BEGUN working with Casey on Tomas' house a few weeks previous, and it had come—other than his hours with Pru—to be his favourite time of each day he was lucky enough to spend here. Originally both he and Finian had been hired to help out during their free hours, but Finian had a tendency toward the slapdash and be done with it school of carpentry, and after a few dressing downs from Casey, he'd abandoned the idea of working for him. Casey, Ambrose had observed, was visibly relieved by Finian's absence.

He'd been a bit relieved himself, for he and Casey had established their own rhythm of work, and he truly appreciated what he was learning by the various jobs Casey set out for him. Watching the house come back to life through each painstaking recovery of the various woods, ceramics, tiles, copper fittings, glass and lead latticing, made him understand the man was an artist and that working with him was like being granted an apprenticeship of sorts. Casey always managed to find a way to replace the materials that needed replacing with something which fit the house, and was as close to the original as possible, but also provided the house with a soundness it had been lacking for some time. Ambrose thought the house felt the care, and appreciated it, for it seemed to almost glow when he came down the drive, when once it had appeared on the verge of ruin. Pamela had said it was a disappointed house, but that it now seemed to hold out hope for a revival of its former glory.

"Pamela mentioned that you an' Miss Prudence might be considerin' a move across the sea?" The words were spoken casually, but Ambrose knew if

Casey was bringing it up, it was because Pru had been talking to Pamela about it in a serious fashion.

"She's mentioned it a time or two, an' the idea has its appeals," he said, for that was merely the truth, it did have great appeal. He and Pru had been reading Henry Beston's *Northern Farm,* during their stolen afternoons in the swan woman's cottage, and they'd talked about maybe doing just that, finding a small farm in Maine, not too close to her parents, but somewhere away from the world, where they might have a bit of livestock, a small house, and where the blue-white fire of the winter skies would burn all around them, and summers would come creeping gold and green, with the sound of peepers and owls echoing up from the pond. For there was always a pond on this mythical farm, no matter how much the other details morphed and changed as their fancy spun the brightly coloured yarn of what might be.

"Then I'd ask what's holdin' ye back?" Casey asked, while scooping out a glob of beeswax from the tin at his side. They were waxing the overmantel of the big library hearth and were just now focused on the fan-shaped crescents which decorated the width of it. It was painstaking work, and Casey required a level of perfectionism which Ambrose found he rather enjoyed. It was easy to get lost in such work, in the fine detail of it, and the result, he'd found, was always very satisfying. Casey trusted him enough now not to triple check every task he set him to, and so they'd settled to a comfortable mode of working together, where they might talk, or they might not, depending on whether the task allowed it.

"I don't know," he said slowly, "only I feel like it's a matter of absence rather than presence, of bein' away, when my life has always been here in this place. I'd be foreign in America, an' I'd always feel some part of me was still here—always a migrant, livin' between two places."

Casey paused, giving him a considering look. "I understand what ye're sayin', I've been there myself. Pamela an' I lived in Boston for a time, an' I felt a bit like a square peg tryin' to ram into a round hole much of the time. But what ye need to know, lad, is that if ye go, ye'll always carry Ireland with ye, the good bits of her, while ye leave the bad behind."

Ambrose finished up the fan he was working on and moved on to a rosette, one with a poppy carved into it. There were, in fact, dozens of poppies scattered about the house, sometimes in the most unexpected spots: under the worm-eaten cushion of an ancient chair, on the inside of a cupboard listing from its hooks, and etched into the deep framing of the upstairs windows. He'd asked Casey if that was often a feature of Elizabethan homes, and if the poppy in particular had some significance to it.

Casey shrugged. "It's hard to know for sure but the poppy has long been a symbol of peace, death, an' sleep. Times were hard then, an' often children didn't live long, so maybe it was merely a reminder that those ye'd lost would have peace, wherever it was they might be. Then again, maybe the man who built the house was an opium addict."

"Was opium in use durin' that time? I've always associated it with the Romantics."

"Oh aye, it was part of the medical literature of the time. The pills they made from it were black an' called Stones of Immortality; 'twas made of the particularly strong bits of the opium, an' they added a bit of lime juice an' gold just for good measure. Though, other than the lime juice, I can't see it havin' much in the way of restorative powers."

"Ye know the oddest bits of information," Ambrose said, for Casey had a treasure trove of strange factoids, particularly when it came to buildings, land and plants.

"Ye spend enough time with my wife or Jamie, an' ye'll know all sorts of odd bits an' pieces too."

Seeing poppies all over the house, had brought to his memory another thing, something so powerful that it had, long ago, become metaphor in his life. When he was a boy, his grandfather had taken him to Donegal for a holiday by the sea. There had been a field there, long abandoned, with the traces of human habitation gone to decay in the form of bits of wall and old foundation stones thickly overgrown with grass and ivy. But what had drawn them to the field in the first place had been the colour of it. From a distance, he'd thought it was on fire, but it had been the flame of poppies, thousands of them, growing thick as sheaves of wheat, so that the field shimmered in the late afternoon sun. His grandfather had told him that once there'd been a village near to this very field, where more than a hundred souls had lived.

"It was a lively place, with families who'd lived here generation upon generation, and knew the land down to its every dip an' hollow, an' all the stories that went with them." His grandfather shrugged. "But then came the Famine, an' after there were none left to tell the stories, an' so they were lost to the wind, as surely as the people who once lived here."

In his mind, that field had become a symbol for the country and for the diaspora of the Irish, as though all of Ireland was that field, and the flowers, her people. Then a great blight had come over them and turned those burning petals to seed pods rattling in the wind, until the storm of time and tide blew those seeds across the world, landing them here and there, some perishing during the crossing, some taking root in the new land, some never quite finding that spot to make roots, grow leaves and shoots and spread out ever further. Even when they did flourish and grow, and become once again those bright, burning flowers, they fell in foreign lands, and never again knew that old field by the sea.

The vision of the fiery field was there in his mind, and he wondered if he could be one of those seeds flung far to another field, there to root and live, never to return? What if he couldn't flourish? What if he was only truly himself here in this land? But if he didn't leave—if *they* didn't leave—what would a future here look like? The Troubles weren't simply going to dissipate, nor were his current connections going to let him go in peace to play happy families with his American girlfriend.

He was jolted back to the present with the realization that he'd dripped a glob of wax onto the stone flagging, earning him a censorious look from Casey. The man was carefully wiping it up so that it wouldn't discolour the stone, while still speaking to him. He'd travelled further along the natural route of their conversation, as though he sensed exactly what was going on in Ambrose's mind.

"D'ye think Miss Prudence is goin' to stick around while ye spend years in prison, or mourn ye after ye died because a bomb went off prematurely, or ye got shot in the streets?"

Ambrose considered it, and had to reply in all honesty.

"Aye, I think she might, but I'd not do that to her."

"But if ye join the 'Ra I guarantee ye will do one of those things to her. Pru is no one's fool either, so if ye think ye're foolin' her, think again. Women are uncanny when they love ye, they seem to suss a man's thoughts before he's even had time to think them."

Ambrose thought the man had a point there. He'd watched Pamela and Casey together and thought he'd love to one day have what the two of them had clearly built together. There was a lovely flow and movement to their relationship which was apparent to all around them.

"My advice—move, an' ye can keep yer jaundiced look to yerself, I'm well aware of my own hypocrisy. Go to America with her, an' get a law degree. Fight for justice in the courts. Have some babies, have a good life. Not every man is lucky enough to have a woman love him the way that girl loves you, so I suggest ye don't look a gift horse too deeply in the mouth."

"Ye're that lucky," Ambrose said.

"Aye, I am, an' do ye see me joinin' back up to the 'Ra? No, ye do not." Casey paused in his waxing, putting the cloth to one side and fixing Ambrose with his dark gaze. "Ambrose, I mean it, this road has one fork in it, one path leads to prison, the other to an early grave. I'd like to see ye avoid both." Casey smiled, as though to take the sting from his words. "Now get back to yer work, before I'm forced to fire ye."

Standing here now, on a chilly mountainside, while bullets whizzed around his head, Ambrose recalled the conversation, and thought Casey had a very good point.

Despite the date on the calendar—that of mid-June—it was a raw and cold day, and all around him men stopped in their activity to blow on their hands and loosen up their trigger fingers. To each side of him stretched a line, shooting at targets set at some distance across a field. Around them rose the mountains of Wicklow, cutting them off from the rest of the world. The mountains were sufficiently remote to hide both the traffic in and out of the men and the noise of high velocity gunfire.

Behind the line walked a man in dark pants and sweater, light brown hair ruffled in the wind. His eyes were a dark brown, and he was a deceptively amiable looking sort. Someone Ambrose thought—aiming once again at his target—a man might not look at twice should he pass him in the street. That would be a mistake though. The man paused behind him, and Ambrose felt the prickle of his observation all along his skin.

"Ye're a fine shot, boy, who taught ye?"

"My grandfather," Ambrose said, sticking to his own rule of giving out as little information as possible. He wanted to keep what space he could around the mental fortress he felt was necessary to him during these meetings. He understood just whom he was speaking to though. His name was Cormac Dennehy and he was known throughout the entirety of the republican world. What Ambrose knew didn't necessarily make him comfortable with the man's command.

Less feared than Noah Murray had been, but just as widely respected within the more militant echelons of the PIRA, Cormac Dennehy had a family history within the republican movement which was both legendary and tragic. The Dennehy family roots in the IRA went back to Cormac's maternal grandfather who had fought with the Tyrone IRA in 1920. The family had retained its membership in the various incarnations of the IRA ever since. One of seven brothers, Cormac had joined the IRA in his teens and had been incarcerated twice, had lost two brothers to the cause—one because of a bomb which went off prematurely and the other when he was shot by the UVF in the family's green grocer shop. An uncle had been killed that day as well. All of this had merely hardened Cormac's will and convinced him that militant force was the only language the British understood.

The death of Noah Murray had left a power vacuum in the PIRA, particularly in South Armagh, and any man brave enough to try and fill that vacuum was going to be painting a target on his back, drawing both the enmity of the Army, the police, and the warring factions within the IRA itself. From all accounts, this was the man who intended to fill that vacuum. It had been whispered amongst the men gathered on this mountain today, that something big was in the offing. That made sense to Ambrose, as he thought it was likely the man wanted to do something so big that it could not be ignored, defining himself as the hardest of the hard men and thus as heir apparent to Noah Murray. Ambrose had never met Noah Murray, but he knew that Pamela had been friends with the man, and had even been engaged to him for a short time. Which to Ambrose meant that Noah had been a man of some substance far beyond his actions on behalf of the PIRA. The man currently standing at his shoulder, causing his bowels to turn to ice water, might not have the same substance, but he certainly had force of personality.

The man stayed, watching, and Ambrose squeezed off a few more rounds, hitting near to dead centre each time. He was a good shot, mostly accurate and not afraid of guns. He didn't particularly care for the feel of one in his hands, but he did understand how to use it. Finian on the other hand, loved guns, but in keeping with his personality tended to shoot wide of the mark more often than not. It had been noticed, Ambrose knew. Finian didn't realize it, but Ambrose understood what it might mean for him in an organization as tightly run as this one.

A halt was called to the target practice a few minutes later, and Cormac nodded to two men who retrieved several thermoses of tea from where they'd been stowed behind a large rock. The tea was passed around and the men huddled together, near any of the boulders in the field which might provide a bit of shelter from the stinging wind.

Once the men were settled, tea cupped between freezing hands, Cormac stood in front of them, fair hair still flying in the breeze, his stance military in its bearing. A hush settled over them all, expectation rising as the man began to speak.

"The force of England is entrenched and fortified. You must draw it out of position; break up its mass, break its trained line of march and manoeuvre, its equal step and serried array…nullify its tactic and strategy, as well as its discipline; decompose the science and system of war, and resolve them into their first elements." He paused for a moment, making certain he had their attention. The quote was an old one and most of the men here would know it, being that it was in the Volunteers Handbook, but it served the purpose it would have when it was written more than one hundred years ago, and that was to remind them that they had never and could not fight by normal rules.

"Those words are not mine," Cormac continued, "but those of the great patriot James Fintan Lalor. They are as true now as they were when they were written, however. We are David and the British Army is Goliath. Therefore we need to make certain every stone we throw is thrown with deadly aim, because there are no second chances in this war."

Every eye was trained on the man, and Ambrose felt his nerves rise a little. He had a feeling he knew what was coming, and it wasn't designed to calm a man.

"It's our aim to establish Green Zones," the man continued, "within the occupied territory of the six counties. Zones where the British are completely banished, which means their counterparts need to go as well. If we can create those pockets, then we can slowly enlarge them, until they occupy entire counties, and eventually the country. The way to begin this is to take out the hard infrastructure: police stations, army barracks, equipment stores, tanks, and occasionally the people who shore up that infrastructure."

By counterparts, Ambrose knew that the man meant the RUC, and all the various Loyalist permutations on 'security' forces: UDA, UDR, UVF, and the B Specials. It seemed an utter impossibility to Ambrose, but he thought perhaps that was only because he'd never really known a world without a foreign army patrolling the streets and fields of his country. The Protestant side of the divide necessarily saw the British Army as their allies, while the British used those forces within the Protestant community as they saw fit, and then discarded them when it was convenient for them to do so.

This was not the Belfast wing of the Provos. This side of the PIRA was less about politicizing and more about waging the war as a military campaign. As such it was possible they were a very great threat to the Belfast command, who saw them as a danger and as traitors for not supporting their undercover machinations with the British. It occurred to him that neither he nor Finian had really understood just what they were entering into that night in the farmer's house. These were the hard force men, whose politics were simple, straightforward and utterly ruthless.

"To that end, we're goin' to bomb the peeler station at Loughall. It's goin' to be a good-sized bomb, so we'll need a digger to carry it. We'll use the digger to smash through the security gates, an' then leave it there with the bomb. That particular station is only open durin' the mornin' an' afternoons, it's not likely anyone will be there at night, but we will need to do a bit of surveillance to that end. It's a small start, but if we take out their infrastructure one piece at a time, eventually the whole will crumble."

Ambrose wondered if the man was mad, and yet he could see the plan's merits. The station was in a rural area and so to have someone trundling past in a tractor wouldn't arouse any undue suspicion. The huge bomb in the bucket would be the bit that someone might notice, mind you.

After that, the men were divided up with either Cormac or his right-hand man Tommy briefing them as to their role in the upcoming event. Cormac clearly ran on a bit of a cell model—each man knowing what his unit was doing, but not what the role of the others was. It was a smart way to lead, and had served other legendary commanders, such as Michael Collins, well. Small armies had to run on different rules. This man clearly understood that.

When it was Ambrose's turn, Cormac beckoned him forward with a quick movement of his hand. Finian stepped forward with him, but Cormac held up his hand. "No, just Ambrose for now."

He felt Finian's eyes on his back as he walked toward the man, and knew a tiny seed of distrust had been sowed between them there in that simple moment. He suspected it had been done with purpose.

Cormac was sitting on a boulder, a lit cigarette in his left hand. Even in such a casual pose, Ambrose felt the threat of him. The man, clearly not one to waste either time or words, got directly to the point.

"It's been said to me that ye spend a deal of time in the Riordan household." The words were spoken casually, but the brown eyes were as hard as the rock on which the man sat.

"Aye," Ambrose said, keeping his voice steady, "their nanny is my girlfriend."

"They have a nanny? That's a bit upmarket for their bit of the world, no?"

Ambrose, fully aware that this man would know all there was to know about Pru, no doubt down to her preference for lemon in her tea and her dislike of tomatoes, merely nodded. This wasn't about her anyway.

"Casey Riordan made a vow an' then walked away from it. He's been gone to God knows where for three years, an' then he returns from the dead. Who knows what he was doin' for all that time? To say tongues are waggin' doesn't quite do it justice. So I'd say choose yer friends wisely, an' keep yer mouth closed around the man. That's just a friendly word of warnin'."

Ambrose nodded, sticking with his policy of saying as little as possible. He was relieved that the man hadn't suggested that he stop seeing Pru, because that was something he could not and would not do. Cormac's words had told him something though, and that was that Casey Riordan, despite keeping his distance from the Provos, was still considered a threat.

"Ye're a man of few words, Ambrose Turner, that's a good thing in our world. Ye might want to mention it to yer friend. Now to business."

The man paused to stub his cigarette out on the rock next to him. The tiny stream of smoke curled up into the chilly air and then dissipated, leaving only the ghostly scent of snuffed fire behind.

"Ye'll be watchin' the station for the next few weeks. Ye'll note down the times particular peelers leave, an' when the station has its turnovers. We'll want to know when the station is unmanned. We'll want a chart of their movements. Ye'll get pictures with names so ye know who it is ye're lookin' at. Memorize it before ye start yer watchin'. Ye'll take yer friend with ye, an' Paddy there," he nodded toward an older man who bore a marked resemblance to a cadaver, "will be with yez as well. He'll be takin' the lay of the land, an' figurin' out the weak spots in the perimeter."

Ambrose went hot and then cold. He'd thought, being so new, they'd be given a smaller role, not something that carried such weight, and people's lives in the balance. Something of his thoughts must have shown in his face for the man then said, "Freedom carries a price tag. Ye'll know the quote by Padraig Pearse about such things, no?"

He knew it, he'd seen it on the way here, engraved on a board beneath a 'Sniper at Work' sign. The words were long familiar, but they didn't seem quite so romantic to him as they once had. He nodded, but the man spoke them anyway, his eyes taking on a bit of a fanatic gleam with the utterance.

"Life springs from death and from the graves of patriot men and women spring living nations."

"Blood is the only thing these people understand, boy."

Ambrose thought while it might be true of the other side, it was perhaps even more true of their own. Casey had been right, this path he was on only had two destinations. He would have to find a way to forge a new path. The thought brought to mind words about St. Columba—*He turned away from Ireland, he entered a pact. He crossed in ships the sanctuary of whales.*

He loved this land, it was his, but he was afraid now that it might well take his life, or force him to take that of another. Leaving—crossing that sanctuary of whales—might be the only road left to him.

Chapter Thirty-five

Blood Echoes

IT SEEMED TO CASEY that therapy was the sort of thing designed to make a man mad, rather than cure him of said madness.

"You need to exercise patience with yourself, and also come to an understanding that the memories of the man you were might never return—at least not in their full form." These words came from Doctor Alice, who sat across from him, imperturbable in her cheery yellow sweater, with her glasses tip-tilt on the end of her nose. Casey liked her a great deal, but just now he found her calm and capable manner somewhat annoying.

"I just feel like all my memories are dammed up behind a sluice gate that's stuck fast. If I could unstick the damn thing, it seems it would all flood out. I swear, I can feel them strainin' against that gate at times."

"Is it the end all, be all? You have your family back, your wife loves who you are as much, it seems, as she loved who you were. Is that not enough, should some pieces of who you were remain in the darkness?"

Casey gave the suggestion a little thought. "I know it ought to be enough, but I feel that I'll not be solid in myself until I know the truth of who I was, an' until I feel like that man and *this* one," he pointed to his chest, "have merged into one person again."

Doctor Alice gave him one of her shrewdly assessing looks which made him feel a bit like a rotten apple and her a crow with an especially sharp beak.

"Well, shall we begin then and see where the staircase leads you today?"

"Aye," Casey said, feeling weary at the very thought, but knowing it was the only road open to him which might offer some answers during the walking of it. He lay down on the lounge she had just for the purpose of this particular kind of therapy, and took several slow, deep breaths.

And so they began, the pattern familiar to him now—eyes closed, breathing deep and slow, body relaxed until he felt he was drifting out of it, and then the long imaginary staircase which he still had some trepidation about descending. Down he went though, feet more certain on the stairs with each trip, and into the long hallway of doors. This was always the worst bit for him, choosing a door, which one to look behind this time, never knowing whether he'd find darkness or light, love or hate, joy or a depth of loneliness that felt like a desert wasteland. Never knowing if there would be peace or violence. It was like reading a book for the first time, one you were tempted to shut and put down, so that you didn't risk so much as another page of it.

The hall was dark this time, and he had the sense he was stepping off into a void, and that he might fall down a great hole, and never be able to climb back up into the light. He walked slowly, peering through the gloom, only to see that this time there was only one door in the hallway and that was at the very end. Well, it would save him the choosing at least, he thought and moved forward, legs eating up the space between him and the portal to that misted land of memory.

The door was old, its paint long faded, though he could see that it had been red, for a few flaking chips remained. He put his hand to the latch, which was cold with frost, and pushed. Inside was utter darkness, and he halted, worried lest the room be filled with traps. The rooms of the mind forced a man to be wary, and to attempt to determine just where those traps lay, and how deep their teeth might bite into his psyche.

*He stood still for a moment, getting his bearings and slowing his breath, so that the panic would not rise and muddy the waters of his subconscious. The dark dispersed slowly, until he could see that there was another door across the room, this one swaying a bit in the wind, creaking with a long low **screak** which raised the hair on the back of his neck. He knew he had to go through that door, and yet he felt something truly terrible might lie on the other side, something he wasn't ready to see. It was why he was here, though, to go beyond the door and see what he might find of his other self.*

Beyond the door, it was night. A breeze stirred through the opening and he smelled the cold in it. Winter? He put his hand in front of his face and saw the glint of silver on his ring finger. He was already married then, and just the knowledge of that small fact was enough to firm his will and push him out over the doorstep.

The dark had a quality to it that told him it was just past twilight. An early evening in winter then. The damp, clear smell of countryside filled his senses, and he took a deep breath of it. It was like a long draught of cold water from a stream, the sort that came down from a mountain peak and was strained through peat and tasted strongly of cold and earth.

He did as Doctor Alice had taught him and looked down to see his clothing. Boots of the sort he might wear on a construction site, but far more worn than the ones he currently possessed, denim pants with a hole in one knee, and a sweater with the cuffs unravelling. Not the clothes he'd worn to the session, and so this was definitely another time.

He walked out into the land and felt, beneath his feet, the give of the earth, and somewhere in the distance the scent of animals and feed. There was a sense of purpose in him, though, and he understood there was a reason he'd found himself here.

It was countryside of the sort he was used to—narrow winding lanes, high thick hedgerows, and soft hills in the distance. But it was different too, in a way with which he was also familiar, for it was blood land. The trees were dark, their boughs twisted and rough, and their leaves long fallen. It was winter and yet everything was tinged red, as though a fine spray of blood had settled over the land, and would not soak into its soil.

He was following someone—the sense of it was there in the prickling of his skin, and the way he felt himself looking up the road and yet trying to remain hidden at the same time. Understanding came suddenly—as it sometimes did in these sessions—and he knew just where he was and why. The man ahead was prey, and Casey was hunting him. The man ahead, along with three of his friends, had raped Pamela. Oh yes, he understood now just what he was doing on this remote country lane—he wanted to get the man alone, a good ways from any who would help him, to a place where none would hear him scream.

Four men had raped his wife and nearly killed his brother. Two were already dead. One neither he nor Jamie could find. The two who were dead had simply disappeared, and he was certain their fate had rested, in the end, in Jamie's hands. He didn't envy either of them.

Three had lived within the city boundaries in estates which were Protestant strongholds—Sandy Row, Newtownards and Tiger's Bay. But this one lived on a miserable little farm outside of Lurgan in Armagh. The only other occupant of the farm was the man's mother, and she rarely ventured outside the farmhouse door. She wouldn't be a worry.

He'd brought a knife with him, and he could feel the cool sharpness of the blade against his ankle. There were easier ways to kill a man, but a knife was a personal weapon, and this matter was very personal, indeed.

The man turned off the lane ahead of him and started down the narrow, muddy drive to the farmhouse. Casey kept on walking along the lane, for he'd already taken the lay of the land here, and knew the man's routine and when the best time was to take him unawares. The best time and the best place. Hiding in the byre was a risk, but it would put him where the man was most *vulnerable—within the confines of a big old stone building where the sound wouldn't carry. He waited in a small cluster of trees, just past the drive, until he was certain the man was in and settled down to his tea, before scaling the stone wall where the fields met a copse of beech, and made his way from there to the byre.*

Being that it was winter, the cows were in for the night. The animals rustled about in their stalls as they heard him enter, but they didn't make any fuss further than that about the intruder in their midst.

He hid at the far end of the byre, slipping in behind a stack of cream cans and coiled rope. The knife was in his hand now, slick and warm; his palms were sweating, and yet inside he was strangely calm. He carried within him the look on Pamela's face when she'd finally admitted to the rape. He could barely touch the surface of his thoughts there, for they were akin to a mad roil of snakes in a boiling cauldron. What had been done to her was something which stirred up a black and terrible rage in him, and at the same time broke his heart in two for what she'd endured at the hands of those four animals.

The man came into the byre after he'd had his supper, just in time for the evening milking. Casey crouched, keeping as still as his trembling legs would allow. He waited for the man to be done with the milking, not wanting bellowing cows to alert the woman in the house any earlier than was necessary. He was clearly ready to go out for the evening, for Casey could smell his aftershave even over the ordure of the byre and hear his anticipation in the jaunty tune he whistled. After the milking was finished the man lingered a bit, just inside the door of the byre, taking in the evening about him, and Casey had one small qualm about what he was here to do. The man looked so normal, milking his cows, thinking about the night ahead, relishing the thought of that first pint of ale, or imagining the girl whose eye he might catch across the room. This last thought sobered Casey and firmed his resolve, for surely a monster such as this one would have no compunction about raping the next vulnerable woman to cross his path.

Just then, the man turned back, his eyes small points of light, and Casey worried that he'd sensed him there hidden amongst the cream cans. So he stepped out, because there was no more need for subterfuge. The man saw him at once, and fear flared hot and wide in his eyes as he scrabbled back across the floor, his boots sliding in the muck. Casey's senses were so heightened that he could smell the blood pulsing hot and bright near the surface of the man's skin. His rage had been replaced by a cold fury at the very thought of this man touching Pamela, violating her and beating the hell out of his brother so that Pat had been near to dead.

He grabbed him before the man had the chance to yell, though it wouldn't matter if he did, for there was none to hear him. His hand was on the man's throat, and his face so close that he could smell the chill scent of peppermint on his breath. The man fought back, trying to claw at his face, to pummel his arms, desperate to get free of his grip. It was what Casey wanted, and he felt a visceral surge of satisfaction, an emotion so deep that it filled him to the brim. He wanted the hand-to- hand grapple because he was very good at inflicting damage in that manner. And because he wanted it to be personal for this man, for him to understand what a loss of power over what was done to your own body did to a person.

The punches were meant to hurt the man, but not kill him. Casey could deliver a punch that might well be fatal—he wouldn't, though. He wanted something quicker and more lethal than that.

But first he wanted the blows—both the ones he gave and the ones he received. He felt he deserved them for not being there to protect her that day. Physical pain was a small thing, but it was a tithe he could pay on what he owed her. The grief over what had happened to her was so powerful that killing this man seemed the only way to assuage it in some small part. It could not give her back what had been lost, but the blood debt would be paid.

Black blossoms of rage opened inside of him, growing so rapidly that he could only see through a narrow aperture, his focus down to the one thing that mattered in the few moments before him. Later, he would never know how long he'd hit the man, only that when the black blooms slowed a little, his hands were slick with blood and his body was roaring with an adrenaline so potent that it had cut off his hearing and feeling, leaving only his sight, which allowed him now to see the man on his knees in front of him. There was blood running from the man's mouth, like a slick of oil glistening in the night; one of his eyes was swollen shut and he was clutching his chest like his ribs were broken.

"Why—why are ye doin' this?"

Casey took in a long rasping breath. He didn't owe the man an explanation, but he would give him one, nevertheless. It was important that he know which sin he was about to die for.

"Ye raped my wife. You an' yer fockin' friends raped my wife on a train, an' then ye beat my brother nearly to death. Now get up an' fight me."

Casey reached down and hauled the man to his feet. The man clawed out at him, trying to get to his face, hoping, Casey thought, to buy himself a little time before the inevitable happened. Casey shoved him away, and then the man rushed at him, and really began to fight. It was then that Casey feared that he might lose control of the battle, for men are strong when they know they are about to die. But a man filled with a fury that sat like black tar in his veins, had a strength too, one that ignored kicks and punches, and a body writhing like it was on fire.

*The black bloomed again in a great billowing cloud, and though he heard the man begging for his life, it seemed to come from a great distance, as though all he heard was an echo from a far land. It seemed simple after that, even though it was anything but. Men did not die easy, no matter how quick the killing. And it **was** quick, a flash of blade, a rush of hot blood, slippery as jelly pouring over his hand, and a bubbling hiss of air and then, **sin sin**, the man was dead.*

After, he stood for a moment, rasping air into his lungs and trying to still the spots which danced in his vision. There was a moment where he could catch his breath, and then he needed to go, move the body further away and hide it.

There were men who would have done this job for him, and gladly so, knowing it was a Loyalist bastard they were taking out, but this murder had nothing to do with politics—this was profoundly personal.

Quite suddenly a wave of nausea overtook him, and he managed to stumble away from the body before he was sick. But then he was very sick, indeed. On his knees in the wood, the damp spreading through his pants, and yet he could not find the will to stand just yet, even though he needed to get clear of the place soon.

*He had expected to feel regret, or something far stronger but for which there was no real name. There **was** regret for the necessity of the act, but for the act itself—no, he did not feel regret. His uppermost emotion right now was a fear around the satisfaction he'd taken when he'd felt the life go from the man—the deep visceral sense of justice served which had come over him. It was that satisfaction which had driven him here onto his knees and made him so furiously sick.*

Brian's voice sounded suddenly in his head, and he tried to push it away not wanting his father's words of wisdom just now. But the voice persisted, insisting it be heard.

"It's only that I see my father in ye at times, Casey. Ye have many of his ways about ye, ancestry bein' the strange river that it is. A lot of what I see in ye were the things I admired about the man—his strength, his sense of justice an' his immense capacity for love. But there are times I see the darker side of him in ye as well. An' he was a man of violence. He didn't like it, an' he strove to keep it tamped, but he also knew it was deep in him in some way he could never root out. I loved my daddy, an' he was one of the finest men I ever knew, an' I see the same in you, laddie. But I'd add this one thing—you can't bring about justice by creating fear an' pain in others. Violence won't bring back whatever it is ye feel ye've lost."

He stood up and drew in a long, shaky breath, the scent of blood heavy in his nose and on his hands. He understood now, exactly what it was his father had feared in him. But then his father had not known what it was to have the woman you loved brutalized and know there was neither justice nor comfort that you could give her. All you could do was try to keep her safe, even if it was far too late for such measures.

He came back to himself in pieces, feeling utterly ragged and as though he'd been through the actual struggle he'd seen in his head. He looked down at his hands, certain they were covered in blood and that Doctor Alice was going to be horrified.

"Are you all right?" The doctor's voice was gentle, as though she knew he needed a soft touch just now.

"I'll do," he said, though he knew his abrupt tone belied the words.

"Was it the day you disappeared?"

"Ah, no," Casey said, "it was somethin' from another time."

"Something disturbing, clearly," Doctor Alice said, eyeing him with no small worry in the bright blue eyes.

"Aye, ye could say that." He put his hands to his face and rubbed it, hoping the friction would go some way toward banishing the visions in his head. His hands were shaking, and he could still see the blood—Christ, he could still *feel* it, hot and slick upon his hands, and that terrible rage which had been in every part of him, every cell and beat of his heart. There had been a dark and fierce joy in the killing, which had left behind a hollow feeling in his body.

"Do ye want to talk about it?"

No, he did not want to talk about it. He did not want to remember it. It was everything he'd feared—that he was not only a man of blood and violence, but that it had also been natural to him, as natural as the breath he drew into his body.

"What is it, Casey?"

He looked up, feeling as though he'd aged a good deal since his entry into this room today.

"I'm beginning to remember the sort of man I was, an' I'm very much afraid I wasn't a good one."

By the time Casey reached home, he had one of his headaches. It was just the nibbling edge of one, but this was always how they started, slowly building until he lost a bit of his vision, and ended up prostrate and nauseous in a dark room.

He sat in the car for a moment or two, taking a few breaths and letting some of the fear slide away. The nibbling in his head was becoming more of a gnawing.

Inside the house, he stopped in the entry for a moment, taking in the scene before him. Conor was on the floor with Isabelle, patiently showing her how to string a cat's cradle, and Pamela was in the kitchen, Kathleen on her hip, humming happily as she attempted to start dinner one-handed. For a moment the strange sense came over him that he sometimes had, of being a man standing on a deserted shore, watching something wondrous retreat from his vision, and make its way out to sea. As though his family were merely a mirage, and if he were to reach for them, the vision would go up in smoke and vanish on the breeze.

Isabelle saw him then and shot up and across the floor.

"*Daddy, Daddy*," she screeched, and jumped so Casey could catch her and swing her up into his arms. She planted one of her rather wet and exuberant kisses onto his lips. "Daddy, what's you get when you crosses a cat wif a ghost?"

"I don't know, wee darlin'—an elephant with twelve toes? A bat with three ears? No? What then?"

"A scaredy-cat," she said, laughing her growly little belly laugh so hard that she almost tipped out of his arms. Casey laughed with her, for her joy in the joke was infectious. She gave him a hug and then wiggled to be let down, so she could return to her play.

"Daddy, come look at what I did with the house today," Conor said, and he went to see his son's handiwork—a small scale model of their own house which they'd been working on together in the evenings—and felt himself swept into the tide of home, no longer standing afraid on the shore.

Pamela came over then to where he sat with the children, Kathleen still on her hip, and a flush lighting along her cheeks, which told him she'd had a long day of it. Kathleen was teething, and wasn't terribly thrilled with the process. The baby automatically reached out her arms for him, a gesture which never failed to melt his bones within him. Her affection for him hadn't seemed to replace her affinity for her own father, for which fact he was grateful. He loved Kathleen as though she were his, but he'd no wish to replace Jamie in the constellation of her affections.

He took Kathleen from Pamela, the warmth and scent of the baby filling his senses and banishing, in part, the darkness he'd carried home. She smelled warmly of talc and blackberries, the latter of which stained her small mouth, giving her the look of a fairy who'd strayed into the human realm for a day.

Pamela gave him a worried look, and then leaned down to kiss him, putting a hand on his arm as she did so. Just the touch of her gave his body and mind a bit of peace, and he smiled up at her as she drew back from him.

"Head aching?" she asked, and he laughed. It still disconcerted him a little, that she was so attuned to his bodily ills.

"A bit," he replied, "but it'll go on its own; I'll not need the pills. D'ye need help with the dinner?"

"Just keep an eye on Kathleen, that will be more than help enough."

He sat down at the table with a sigh of relief, Kathleen on his lap, and proceeded to speak soft nonsense with her. She rewarded him with one of her big smiles, featuring two bottom teeth, four top teeth, and plenty of drool. It struck him to the core—how swiftly babies grew and changed, how life itself rushed past like a river in full spate. He knew this too well, for he'd missed so much in three years with Conor and Isabelle, and even with Pamela, for she'd grown and changed too, only the transformation was less visible. It was what made love so hard, all the change coming at a person so rapidly and without respite. Love like this was frightening, love like this could crack a man in half and leave him little more than ash on the floor. He knew, because that's how he'd felt for three years, a man whose substance could be scattered to the four winds by the slightest breeze.

By the time dinner was on the table, Kathleen had fallen asleep on his shoulder, the breath of her soft against his neck. How any baby managed to slumber so blissfully through the racket Conor and Isabelle made he'd no notion, but he was grateful the wee lass was able. Pamela came and lifted Kathleen from his arms, and put her on the couch, braced with pillows and easily seen from the table. His lap wasn't empty for long though, for Isabelle hopped up and proceeded to eat much of his meal. Pamela normally admonished her for doing this, but he never minded. He'd missed so much time with his children that the knowledge they were already so comfortable with him, still felt like a gift.

There was a flash in his head suddenly, of the blood he'd seen on his hands during his session with Doctor Alice, and suddenly the feel of it was there too—slippery, hot and viscid on his skin. He wanted to put Isabelle from his lap, so that she wouldn't be tainted by his touch. It seemed like it would divide his mind at times, this knowledge—that he was a man of violence and blood, and yet also a father to these tiny people who depended upon him to be a good person.

Under the table, Pamela's foot pressed softly against his. He looked up, brought back from his musing to the present, where Isabelle was now attempting to feed him, but was succeeding only in dropping a good amount of mashed potatoes into his lap.

"Are you certain you're all right?" Pamela asked, the green eyes looking him over as though she was checking for wounds. Which she might well be, as the woman seemed to be able to see into his very psyche and understand things about him before he did.

"I'll do, Jewel," he said, and reached across to take her hand.

"Daddy," Isabelle prompted in her imperious little voice, which had, when it was warranted, led to him calling her Bella Napoleon.

"Aye, Miss Bella, what is it?" he looked down at the tiny face, and smiled. Big dark eyes looked back at him with great seriousness. This gave him a momentary qualm, for the last time she'd looked this serious she'd been about to tell him that there was a newt in the bathtub that she'd forgotten to return to its rightful domain.

"I love you," she said, and he felt it again—that terrible vulnerability which love gave a man.

"I love you too, wee darlin'," he said and leaned down to kiss the top of her head. He took a breath, closing his eyes for a minute. Isabelle's hair was like silk against his lips—dirty silk, he amended, feeling the grit of sand against his mouth. The prickle of tears threatened, just for the feel of his little girl. The therapy session had cracked something open in him, and he felt raw tonight—exposed to every emotional draft that moved through him.

Pamela squeezed the hand she still held and he looked up to find her eyes filled with sympathy. "You'll get used to it again," she said softly, "and you won't as well, that's how it is. Now eat what's left of your dinner before it gets cold, man."

After the dishes had been done and the children all safely stowed in their beds for the night, he sat down at the table once again, the onyx length of it glowing beneath his hands. The touch of the wood was reassuring, as if that ghostly presence could be banished by the solidity of something he'd fashioned with his own hands.

Pamela came and stood behind him, laying her hands lightly upon his shoulders. A shudder went through him, as though her touch were the key which would cause the Pandora's box of emotion and confusion inside him to fly open, spilling everywhere and showing her the tangle of snakes which his thoughts and feelings were at present. There was a fear in him that if she saw the darkness inside him she would leave him, and be right to do so. She moved her hands from his shoulders to his scalp, gently rubbing, the soft green scent of her soothing his raw nerves.

"Do you want to talk about it?" she asked, and he breathed deeply, letting her touch do its work. He let his head fall back, resting it against the warmth and softness of her breasts.

"I do, an' I don't, Jewel. I want to just forget it all, an' then I know that's what I've spent the last three years fighting against, so I can't."

"You can't help that, it's not as if you can remember what happened."

"Well, there's the thing," he said. "I do have an idea, as it turns out."

"You've had a memory about it?"

"No—or yes. I see things but only in flashes, an' not always in context. The doctor thinks I might never recall exactly what happened, despite regainin' a lot of my memories from before. She says that might be for the best, an' I tend to agree with her. But there was a night on the boat, on my way home that I do recall."

"Would you tell me about it?" she asked, and he heard the hesitancy in her voice, as though she were afraid to push him lest his fragile memory lose its recall.

"Aye, it's not a terribly excitin' tale, but it might take a bit of time in the tellin', so let's go sit by the fire."

Casey added a few bricks of peat to the fire, warming his hands and taking a breath, as the evening settled around them. He sat on the couch, near to the fire, and stretched his legs out, relishing the heat of the flames.

Pamela came to join him then, tendrils of steam curling out of the mugs she held in each hand.

"What's this?" he asked, sniffing the mug she handed him.

"It's for your head, just drink it."

He took a tentative sip. Last week she'd given him a concoction that he thought might well remove the hair from his chest, it had tasted so vile. This one tasted mildly pleasant though, and he took another, less cautious, sip.

"It's not poison," she said, smiling at the look he'd given the mug, "it will help relax you a bit. Now, take down your pants."

Casey raised an eyebrow. "I was goin' to tell ye my story, but if ye'd rather ravage me on the sofa, I've no objections to the change in plans."

She laughed. "I'm going to rub oil into your knee, but if you behave yourself, I'll take the rest under consideration."

He sighed and stood, stepping out of his pants and laying them to the side. He sat again, eyeing her as she knelt down in front of him, and opened a bottle which glowed a deep thick amber in the firelight.

"I've had weeds in my dinner, tinctures in my soup, bits floatin' in my tea, an' ye grease me up like ye're readyin' a pig for the chute every night."

"Yes," she said serenely, "and how are you feeling?"

"Green as a pond frog," he said.

"And other than that?" She poured a thin stream of gold into her hand and then set to work on his knee.

He gave it a moment's thought and realized that other than his headache, he felt good, in fact he had a sense of well-being that he'd not had in a very long time. The woman had worked her usual witchcraft, even if he did have the diet of a rabbit some days. Thinking on it now, he couldn't remember the last day his knee had given him the sort of grief it used to give him every blessed hour.

"I feel good," he said. "Though I tend to think it's yer touch on my body that's done the healin'." She kissed his knee, and then wiped her hands on the rag she kept handy for just that purpose. He put his pants back on, lest any of the children took it in mind to come down the stairs.

She sat down at the far end of the sofa from him, and gestured that he should take his ease in her lap.

"Lie down," she said, "sometimes I think it's easier to tell a tale when you're not looking your audience directly in the eye."

He did as bid, settling his head on the cushion she'd placed in her lap. She put one hand to his head, pulling gently at his hair, knowing that it relieved the tension in his scalp.

"It's not the sort of tale that will make it hard to look ye in the eye, darlin', though I take yer point. Still, it's always about findin' those first words, isn't it?"

"Just speak it," she said softly, "and I'll listen." She laid her free hand on his chest, and he felt the last bit of tightness go from his core. And so then the words came with ease, as they so often did with her.

"I smelled the land before I saw it," he began, "and I think I knew even then that I was home."

He smelled the land before he saw it. They were still a day out from Cobh when he felt the change in the wind—a change of scents, something less salt, something softer and sweeter, the smell of refuge and sanctuary. There was a soft thrum of excitement in his blood merely from that whiff of land, and a hope, caught in his chest like a needle, that this land would give him back his memory, or even just the end of a thread which he might follow through the labyrinth of finding out who he'd once been.

The fog had gathered in, thick as a wet wool blanket, just after noon. Sea smoke it was called by some, making it sound far more romantic than the reality. Casey had been twitchy ever since the smell of the land had invaded him, his blood pulsing in quick, bright sparks and making this last day at sea near to unbearable. The restlessness had driven him out onto the deck, to peer through the thick draperies of fog, straining for a glimpse of shoreline.

Suddenly he felt movement in the water below. It was instinctual, he supposed, that prickling uneasiness which came over a man as he sensed a great body sliding through the waves. He could see it in his mind's eye—a phantasmagorical creature rising from the depths of the abyssal plains, to emerge in this world of smoke and illusion. He felt that way himself—as though he was just now emerging from the bottom of the sea—not, he thought peering down toward the water, that that was a particularly attractive metaphor for his life, but it was, he supposed, as apt as any. A long time of submersion, and living in a place where no light could reach, and sight more a thing of instinct rather than knowledge. And then to emerge in a world filled with light, and yet find it foreign and strange, as though he was a wild creature who had to relearn the ways of man.

The sound of the whale surfacing came a moment later, that great watery exhale which carried the scents of the sea within it—fish and plant, salt and dark, and echoes of a mystery as old as the planet itself. The scent niggled at him, like an itch beneath his skin that he could never relieve—that this too, this breath from the deeps, was memory, and spoke in some way of that other life, and the man he'd once been.

The whale lingered upon the surface of the sea, and then slid back into the depths from which it had come, silent as dark stealing over the land. The breath lingered upon Casey's skin and in his nose, condensed into fine droplets of mist.

'*…and I shall broadcast, saying nothing*
The starry echoes of the waves…'

The scrap of poetry floated through his mind, and yet he did not know the poet, nor the voice which spoke the words in his mind. The voice still there, just a faint echo lingering. A woman who had loved poetry? Echoes. That was all he had, bloody echoes of a life that might have been real, or merely something he'd conjured up like a Potemkin village in his head. A beautiful façade but when you peeked behind it, there was only a yawning space.

He stood there for some time, staring into the fog and sea, until the soft disturbance of a gull passing through the mist, moved against his skin. He hoped the poor thing wasn't lost, flying blind wasn't advisable even for a seabird.

"'Tis said," a voice emerged near his elbow, startling him from the reverie of fog and leviathans, "that seagulls are the souls of Irish migrants who died overseas, an' return home as birds or the mist off the waves."

"Is that so?" Casey asked, the hair prickling along his arms and chest, and rising stiff on the back of his neck. He'd not heard the man come up beside him, and his defenses were now on full alert.

"Aye, that's so. We're romantic fools, we Irish, no? When ye're dead, ye're dead, an' there's no comin' back as a gull or a bit of fog. Ye're merely rottin' in the ground, providin' a bit of food for the worms. Still, sometimes it's wise to pay heed to the old superstitions. My nan used to tell the tale of a young girl who died of fever while away from home, an' her father thought it best to bury her there, an' not risk carryin' the fever back to their own place. An' so she was buried in the nearest churchyard, an' the father then made his way home. A few nights later he heard a scratchin' at the window, an' then a mournful cry of 'I am alone, I am all alone in my cold grave.' An' he knew what it meant an' that he must bring his daughter home, or she'd never rest easy. So off he went an' had the coffin of his dear daughter dug up, an' then put in a cart. An' he took her home then, all the way from Wicklow to Kerry, an' buried her again, there amongst her own, for the dead can only rest peacefully when laid down with their forefathers, for 'tis ill to perish amongst strangers."

A chill chased down Casey's spine, spreading out like a fan of ice to his very extremities. There were times he had felt this, that he was a dead man making the journey home, where he might find rest amongst his own.

There was the sulfuric hiss of a match catching fire, and then the tiny glow of it, like a coal hovering in mid-air. The scent of smoke tickled his nose, and he suppressed the desire to sneeze. He had the oddest sense that he musn't move, as if he was a rabbit and this man a venomous snake, waiting for his slightest twitch.

"Been on the sea a long time," the voice continued, "seen some funny things—things I couldn't explain, most not terribly interestin' other than in a metaphysical sort of way."

"Aye," Casey said, wondering what exactly the man was leading up to.

"There's a story I have that I feel might be of interest to you. Do ye have any objections to me tellin' it?"

"No," Casey replied, the feeling of dread in his stomach growing with every word the man spoke.

"Would ye care for a cigarette while I tell ye my tale?" The man asked, blowing out a long stream of smoke which dissipated into the fog immediately.

"No thanks," Casey said shortly, wishing the man would find his point, if indeed he had one.

"Suit yerself." There was a pause while the man took a long drag on his cigarette, the coal casting a reddish light onto his face. Casey recognized him, though he'd only seen him once before in the mess. It wasn't a huge ship, and odds being what they were in a contained world, he ought to have seen him more often than that. Which meant the man hadn't wanted to be seen, and that put Casey's hackles up, rigid and invisible, all along the length of his spine.

"So one of these strange things that wasn't in the realm of metaphysics, was on a voyage two years ago, near to this time of year. There was a man brought aboard at the last minute. I wasn't meant to see it, but I did. He was unconscious, they brought him on in a sheet, wrapped up so as none could see his face. At first I was wondering what sort of shenanigans were takin' place—thought it was a dead body. But then I saw somethin' more, money changin' hands, an' a bargain bein' struck. Didn't see the face of the man settin' the terms of the bargain, but I did see the one takin' the bag of cash off his hands. 'Twas the ship's surgeon, an' that money was meant to motivate the man to keep what was in that body bag alive."

Ice water was beginning to circulate through Casey's veins, and his heart was pounding so hard he could feel it in his ears.

"So I thought it was interestin', no? Some man beaten nearly to death—an' clearly left for dead an' yet not dead, an' someone willin' to pass over a great deal of money to make certain he survives. But a man that badly beaten, a man who's had that sort of harm done to him, well, he'd not escape unscathed, now would he?"

Casey was quite certain the question was rhetorical and so didn't bother to answer. The small bit of solidity he'd felt moments before was gone now, and he felt as porous as a figure made of sand and subjected now to the sea which whispered just there, mere feet away, waiting to drown him.

"It's not so uncommon to want a man dead—there's reasons aplenty in the world for that—debt, jealousy, hatred, a woman. But why would someone so badly want a man to live, an' yet not take him to a hospital but rather bundle him on to a ship, where he might die far more easily."

Condensation was purling on the back of Casey's neck and rolling cold down his back. He didn't move, though, merely watched the man through the fog which wrapped around them.

"I'm a curious man, an' I wondered who this person was that the surgeon was protectin'. So I wait until one night when the good doctor has been drinkin'. I know he sleeps sound as a bear in a winter's cave when he's had too much of the rum. An' I find my way to this mystery patient, an' it appears to me that whoever 'twas that wanted him dead, came very near to gettin' their wish because he looks the next thing to it. Both feet in the grave, an' the rest of him near to slidin' in. Skin the colour of ashes, where it's not bruised. But a big man, an' I'm thinkin' to myself that to take a man like that down, there had to be more than one person who came at him."

Casey kept his face carefully blank, though he trembled all along his body, wishing he could recall what the man was describing and more importantly wishing he understood just why the man was telling him, for the story did not seem to be a friendly one.

"Maybe a few more particulars would help ye. He had a tattoo on his left bicep, like a band 'round about his arm—said Erin Go Bragh in fancy Celtic script. Just thought such a man might seem familiar to ye."

"And if he does?" Casey asked, his voice no more than a slipstream of syllables in the fog.

"I'd say ye might want to warn him. Because, it seemed to me that someone very badly wanted him dead, an' that someone might still be lookin' for him, should he step upon the land."

"Well, if I knew who that someone was, it might help me avoid him in the future," Casey said, the cold breath of the whale still clammy against his skin.

"Who knows?"

Casey felt rather than saw the man shrug, for the fog was so thick now that the man only emerged here and there, like a puzzle with pieces missing.

"Ye'll mind what I said though, about folk returning home for burial amongst their own." And with that the man left, the pieces of him floating off into the fog, silent as though he'd simply been a ghost.

There was a long silence after Casey finished telling his tale, broken only by the soft hiss of embers falling apart in the hearth.

"Was it a warning?" Pamela asked, and Casey came back to the present to find his wife looking down at him with some consternation.

"Aye, I think it likely, Jewel. I'll not know whether it was meant in a friendly manner or not, though. The man did put the chill in my marrow, that much I can tell ye. I didn't sleep that night at all, but sat up keepin' watch. We docked at Cobh the next day, an' I didn't linger about once my feet hit the land."

He shivered a little, but it was visible even in the low light of the fire and he felt Pamela shudder in response.

"Did you ever see him again?"

"No, not that I was aware of, an' I was on edge for some time, so I think I would have noticed had someone been around me."

"I don't know who your guardian angel was—the one who took you to the ship, but I'm grateful to him."

Casey looked up at her. "Oh aye, but I would have been more grateful if he'd left me in Ireland alive. Still, I hope that one day I know who he is an' just why it mattered to him to keep me breathin.'"

"Sometimes I think maybe it's best if we're left in ignorance," she said, "what if finding the answers to what happened puts you back in their sights, and they decide to finish what they started?"

"What if they do anyway, Jewel? An' then I will have brought that home to you an' our children."

She took his face in her hands, the scent of green herbs warm on her skin. "Don't say that. I can't bear the thought of you being alone still, I can't bear the thought that you might be here in this country, and yet not with us—with me."

"I can't bear the idea of it either, but it was maybe selfish of me to come to yez when I still don't know what happened to me."

"I just think of you here, sometimes only feet away from us, and yet completely alone, and it hurts me," she said softly, her eyes unreadable in the dim ember light.

He shrugged, feeling slightly uncomfortable with the topic. "I think I needed it—the time of walkin' the countryside, an' the time in the mountains too. I needed a space in between to clear my head, or at least get it on a little straighter." He smiled ruefully. "Besides, the walkin' about led me to you. I was goin' to the workhouse to sleep the night I found ye."

A shadow passed over her face, the way it often did when there was mention of that night. She didn't speak of it, and he wondered again just how deeply the darkness had touched her during his absence.

"It makes sense that you'd find your memories here. That you knew enough to return to Ireland."

"Aye, I suppose so."

"The land would always call you back; it's your place in the world, after all."

He sat up and looked at her, putting his hand to her face and gently turning it so that she had to meet his gaze.

"Is that what ye think? No, darlin', it was you who called me back, no bit of earth could have brought me back to life the way you an' the children have. For a long time, I was a man without a soul, an' that soul didn't return to me until I found you again. I meant what I said before, Jewel. Yer touch heals me, in all the ways—physical, emotional an' mental. *You* are my place in this world."

"Damn it, man," she said, turning her head so that he couldn't see her face. She took a deep breath and then returned her gaze to him, smiling, though her eyes glittered with tears.

"'Tis only the truth, darlin'."

"How's your headache now?" she asked, sniffling a little.

"It's near to gone."

She gave him a slightly doubtful look; the woman knew just how bad the pain was at times. He'd meant it though, just a light touch from her was enough to bleed some of the tension from his body.

"I've not had so many headaches since ye returned to my bed either. I just thought," he grinned, "it was worth the mentionin'."

She stood and turned to face him, pulling at the drawstring of her nightgown. It was pale lavender, dusted with a print of forget-me-nots.

"Is that so?" she asked, a light in her eyes which never failed to rouse him. She let the loose neck of the nightgown slip off one shoulder, and arched an eyebrow at him.

"Aye, that's so," he said, and rose, pulled like a magnet to his own true north.

She shrugged the other shoulder and the nightgown fell to the floor. Her eyes still shone with tears, and the last light of the fire touched her skin with a patina of rose-gold. "Then you'd best come and get healed, man."

Chapter Thirty-six

Liminal Space

THE HOUSE GLOWED with firelight, and the scents of an August night came in through the open windows. Seated near to the fire, in chairs and sprawled on the floor were Pru, Ambrose, Finian, Ciara, and Father Jim. With Pru helping them out still from time to time with the children, the group of teens had become a regular fixture in their home, and often stayed to help with meals and then to eat them, and to make conversation afterwards, which ranged from heated political arguments between Finian and Ambrose, and wide-roaming rambles through history, myth, legend and poetry between the entire company. Father Jim came for dinner once a month, and his company was always welcome, for he added a note of gravity and a more objective view on politics and history.

Tonight the conversation had veered toward how the Irish mentality was different than that of other races—who might be presumed to be close kin—and yet in so many ways, simply were not.

"I think ye'll find," Casey said, patting Kathleen's back as she settled against him in what had become their nightly routine of Casey rocking her to sleep, "that it's to do with havin' a Celtic sort of mind, rather than a traditional Western viewpoint. There's always room for the liminal in the Irish mind."

"Aye, agreed, but wouldn't ye say that space can be a dark one too?" It was Ambrose who asked the question, and who had, indeed, begun the conversation.

"Absolutely," Casey said, shifting Kathleen from one shoulder to the other, her hair a spark of copper fire in the dimly lit room.

Pamela loved the light of fire, both in the hearth and in the few candles dispersed about the room. It gave a softness to things, a full-bellied roundness to the sharp angles visible in daylight. The shadows about the room were thick, but gave a sense of the night wrapping around the house in protection. People were both less seen and more seen in firelight. As a photographer it fascinated her, even though it was a light by which one could, of course, only take limited pictures.

She looked around the room taking in the details: the red glow on the dark jug which sat on the sideboard, the dance of light on the cauldron that was kept on the fire, the flickering glow like leaves dancing across the polished pine floor, the lick of flame on the rim of Ambrose's glasses; the copper-penny gleam as it caught the fall of Pru's hair, and Father Jim's dog collar a white streak amidst all the moving shadows.

"Shall I pull a story from the twilight?" The voice was like a distant bell, but it gave her a pang, for it was her father's voice. It had been he who'd given her the original love of story, and also the love of looking deeply at the world around her. Those words were how her father used to ask her if she wanted a story along with her bedtime. The answer had, of course, always been yes. Back then, she had truly believed stories dwelt in the twilight, in the shadows, there at the edges of her childhood bedroom—small smoky wraiths that would emerge at the sound of her father's voice and begin to breathe and live and caper across the stage of the teller's tongue.

"Stories cluster in the shadows," she said softly, touching her father in memory and feeling the echo of a long-ago loss, before returning to the conversation at hand.

"Now, Pamela's an American like myself," Father Jim said, "but you can't deny that she's rather familiar with that liminal space."

Casey snorted. "She has as much Irish blood as anyone in this room, which makes her a poor example. That one," he winked at her, "has always been an edge-dweller, she puts my wee bundle of superstitions to shame."

She watched him then, as he continued to listen and speak in turn, the air around the entire company warm with laughter and ideas, facts and fancies. Kathleen's head was tucked so deep into the curve of his neck that she could hardly see the silken fire of her daughter's hair, or the tiny ivory fingers pale against the green of his shirt. Casey was mostly in shadow, the fire touching blue to his dark stubble, and the strong bones of his face softened by the dim.

A warm blush travelled over her just for the sight of him, and he glanced toward her, a smile on his face, as if he had seen her thoughts on a screen in front of him. Even here in the midst of company, there was a space which belonged only to them. It was a gift, she knew, to have such a thing between them again after so much had contrived to make them strangers to one another. And yet, he might have been gone a hundred years and then come back to her and she would still know him for her man. How she felt about him, and how he, in return, felt about her, seemed as inevitable as the waxing and waning of the moon, or the returning of the sea to the shore, and like those two things, it was still a thing of wonder.

"What I mean," Ambrose was saying in that slow way he had which indicated he was thinking his way through what he wanted to relay, even as he said it, "is to be so far gone into that liminal space, that it's a world unto itself, an' ye could easily wander it for years, like Rip Van Winkle did, but it's so vivid that ye can't tell where the divide between worlds is. Have ye had that experience yerself?"

"Aye, I have," Casey said. These few words were an understatement, Pamela knew, for he'd experienced more than one strange supernatural sort of event. That it should be so was an irony, for he was a strongly pragmatic man. And yet, there was that in him which spoke of those long-ago Celtic ancestors, a sort of primitive connectedness to the world around, and an understanding of the circles of existence, rather than the linear rule of the purely rational Western mind. "What happened is somethin' I've never quite understood, but it certainly will speak to yer talk of liminal space," he continued, though she noted his face looked slightly troubled, as though he wasn't entirely comfortable with the memory. "An' I agree with ye, that we do exist in those liminal spaces more often than other races, but the thing that I question is just what are those edge places, which are neither here nor there? Are they contained within our minds only, or is there—as ye said—a real physical space one crosses over in order to have the experience?"

"Will ye tell us about it—the experience?" Ambrose asked.

"Aye, I'll tell it," Casey said, easily enough, yet Pamela could see that the skin of his forearms was lightly stippled with goosebumps. Holding Kathleen firm with one arm, he leaned forward and threw another two bricks of peat on the fire, causing the flames to flare bright and hot. Then he did the thing she had seen both he and Jamie do countless times—pull inward to find the story, while also casting out a gossamer net to capture their audience. She never quite understood how it was done, and yet both men had the gift of it. Story itself was liminal space, and with Casey's first words they stepped over into that place between worlds with him.

"The first winter I was back here in Ireland, I had occasion to be drivin' through the Glenshane Pass on a winter's afternoon. The light was startin' to fade by the time I neared the summit, but the air was calm an' clear an' there was a beautiful sunset bannerin' the western sky. Then without warnin', I drove into a snow storm. It was as if one minute it was clear for miles, an' the next I was drivin' blind an' cursin' up a storm. To be sure, storms can come up sudden in mountain passes, but this one seemed to drop down out of no-where. The road disappeared from in front of me, an' the wipers on my wee truck couldn't keep up with the snow comin' down. I knew I couldn't go much further, an' that there was no way on God's green earth I could go back the way I'd come.

"There was the worry too, that if I went off the road, I might well sink through into the bog—the blanket bog stretches for miles in that area—an' simply vanish from the face of the earth. I was in a bit of a quandary though, for I couldn't stay in the car all night either, as I'd be certain to freeze to death. 'Twas then I remembered there was a wood a small ways back, an' I thought if I could get inside of it, it might provide enough shelter to get me through 'til mornin'. I had a sleeping bag, an' the means to make a fire. I figured my odds weren't greatly improved by leavin' the truck, but at least it might be fifty-fifty, rather than a certain death in a cold vehicle.

"I got out of the truck, an' realized my mistake about two minutes into my slog through the snow. It was up to my knees, an' blowin' so hard in my eyes that I wasn't certain of the direction I was headed. It would be easy enough to stray off the road, an' end up on the bog—an' that would be a sure death on such a night. Night was fallin' an' the snow so thick I couldn't even see my own tracks to retrace my steps. I floundered about for a few minutes after that, an' I could feel panic start to race through my blood like a hare an' a fox were facin' off—an' suffice it to say, I wasn't the fox. There's no direction in snow like that, an' to be honest, I wasn't just that sure how to regain my bearins'. 'Twas then a hand touched my shoulder, sendin' a terrible jolt through my body. When I looked behind me though, there was no one to be seen. It wasn't a light touch either, for I could feel that it was turnin' me in a different direction, an' every finger on my shoulder felt like it was outlined in fire. I thought for certain my shoulder would be burned from the touch, but when I checked later, there was no mark on my skin. I'd no choice about changin' direction, an' so I did, an' that was when I saw the light through the snow. It puzzled me, because I'd come up that stretch before the snow began to fall an' I was certain there'd been no buildins' to be seen. But I wasn't about to ignore what seemed a great turn of fortune, an' so I made for it at speed, or as fast as I could through drifts of snow.

"The buildin' was low to the ground, and the roof was thick with snow already. I could see a bit of light shinin' through the windows, though they were thick with frost. The light I'd seen was a lantern hangin' outside the front door—just a little lantern with a strugglin' flame inside—in fact I'd no no-tion how it had stayed lit with such a moil of snow an' wind beatin' on it. But I wasn't of a mind to stay out in the weather ponderin' on it, so I pushed the door open and walked in, an' immediately felt that everythin' was wrong about the scene before my eyes. Had the weather been fine, I think I would have turned back, gotten in the car an' driven down the mountainside even in the pitch of night. I'd no choice though, so I simply shook off the snow, an' walked into the place. It was a pub, the sort that's ten a penny, just small with a worn old slab of oak for the publican to stand behind, and rickety wooden stools to sit upon. An' the same weathered faces ye might see in any country drinkin' establishment.

"At first I couldn't put my finger on what it was that seemed so out of place. The clothes were old-fashioned to be sure, but they were a rough lot of farmers, and ye know how country folk are—waste not, want not, so if they'd tweeds handed down from their granddads who was I to judge them? The pub too was old-fashioned, an' bare bones—like a step or two up from a shebeen, but there's plenty of country pubs that are like that. They didn't seem all that perturbed by my presence, nor my clothes which were wildly different than their own. It was just a strange sense I had, like I shouldn't be there, or that I was seein' them all through a skim of water, as though every one of them, an' the pub itself were slightly displaced, an inch over to the left of where they ought to be.

"I went up to the bar an' asked for a shot of whiskey an' a pot of tea, for I sorely needed the warmth of both, but the publican, despite bein' only a foot or so away from me, didn't seem to hear my request. I thought perhaps he was hard of hearin' but then an old man who was standin' watchin' me, leaned over an' tapped the publican an' gave him my order. The publican got the whiskey an' the tea, an' then set it before the old man, who pushed it down the length of oak toward me. I thanked him, thinkin' the publican clearly didn't care for my presence in his pub, but not havin' much choice about holin' up there out of the weather, I took my drinks an' went an' sat down on a rickety wee stool. I was wonderin' if I was havin' a strange fit of hallucinatin', an' was maybe still wanderin' about out in the snow, in danger of imminent death. I even pinched myself a time or two, tryin' to prove that I was, indeed, awake an' seein' the scene before me. I took things in slowly, tryin' to commit each detail to memory, but there was little to tell me if I'd just done a hop out of time or not. There's a timelessness to the countryside which ye'll not get in the city, an' so it was harder to suss such a thing. I thought perhaps the whiskey would help, an' so I swallowed it down, an' topped it with the hot tea to see if it would steady my mind a wee bit. It took the edge off things, an' I relaxed a little.

"It was then the old man approached me—the one who'd been observin' me an' who'd ordered the tea an' whiskey for me. He'd clearly seen a deal of hard road in his life. He'd the sort of face so seamed by the years, that 'tis like a mask of oak bark, so that ye can't tell their thoughts nor their years entirely. He asked if he might sit with me, an' I nodded. So he settled himself across from me, before sayin', 'Ye're a stranger to these parts, young man, no?'

"I nodded. 'Aye, I just got caught out in the snow, an' saw the light by the door here.'

"'Twill be a desperate night to be out an' about, 'tis sheer Providence that ye saw the light, an' brought yerself in out of the cold. The weather has changed a bit these last years, 'tis warmer than it used to be, though ye'd be hard put to know it tonight.'

"'It's changed, has it then?' I asked, genuinely interested. I knew these old country men understood the weather and watched its patterns in ways that were as old as time. Their lives depended upon it after all. An' to speak of somethin' so normal an' everyday as weather gave me a sense of groundin' myself a wee bit.

"'Oh aye, winters were perishin' cold when I was a lad. Things started to warm shortly before the potatoes failed. Sure an' the country has never been right since. I were only a young lad at the time, but I remember it well.'

"Well, as ye might imagine that kerflummoxed me, because there was no way someone alive durin' the Famine was still breathin' an' in workin' order. Normally I might have questioned the man's sanity outright, but the atmosphere of the place made me afraid to inquire as to the date. He looked like he was maybe near on seventy, which meant it might be some time in the early part of the century. Still, I doubted my own understandin' of things—their clothing was out of date to be sure, an' the buildin' itself straight out of the last century, but as I said before, those things are not so rare in the countryside.

"'It's right pretty country here,' I said, though it seemed a ridiculous thing to say given that the scenery was at present completely covered in snow. Yet, I knew the land, or I had at one time and the sense of it was there within me.

"'The land don't look as it used to,' the man said, "twas entirely different before the Hunger. It were smaller somehow, an' less lonely, maybe a little softer too. The Famine changed that ye know, the softness of the land, an' of the people for a long time after as well," he added, eyes clouded with memory. 'All the cottars were gone, all the wee farms, bits of land that had supported generations of a family, now grazin' land for sheep, an' the family lost to America or the grave. In truth, all things were lost to America or the grave—our language, our stories, our politics an' the very foundation of the country—its people.'

"He shook his head, and looked at me, but I knew he wasn't seeing me but rather something which lay far beyond me.

"'I didn't come from hereabouts, though,' he said, 'I were born down Munster way, an' the hunger did hit hardest there.'

"He took a sip of his drink then, an' I blinked a few times, wonderin' when it had appeared on the table. I'd offered to buy him a drink when he'd ordered mine, but he'd said no thanks. I could have sworn he'd not had a drink with him, when he'd come to sit at the table. He'd not left the table, and none had approached us either.

"He asked me then, if I'd ever smelt a quickset hedge in bloom?

"'Aye, a time or two,' I said, for there was a bittersweet scent in my nose of a sudden, and I was flooded with melancholy. I'd no notion if the scent was that of a quickset hedge, but it seemed I knew it *was* all the same.

"'Before the hunger came,' the old man said, 'I loved that smell. To me it was spring an' new beginnins', but after it was the scent of death to anyone who survived, for branches of it were set over the doors in the homes where people had died. I will take that scent to my grave.

"'We lived high on a mountainside above the sea, my mother an' father, my wee sister an' a set of twin brothers, scratchin' a livin' from the bit of soil there, addin' manure an' seaweed to it several times a season, the hillsides quilted with the lines of lazy beds. Terrible name for them, for they're bloody hard work in the buildin'. It were the method what worked best for that sort of soil—the thin' an' weak sort.

"'It weren't a bad time before, none of us were rich to be sure, an' most of us were poised on the edge of a knife that we had no understanding of, but still it were a sort of golden age, as much as peasants ever manage leastwise, before the blight came. There was enough to eat, a pig to fatten, babies to be had an' a community which was woven tight as a bit of tweed. That a funny mist floatin' in over the land one mornin' would rip that to shreds wasn't somethin' anyone could have fathomed.

"'Granted there were a number of things that came into play—the rundale system of parcellin' out the land into smaller an' smaller bits, the dependency on one crop to feed millions of mouths. An' the fact that all our cereal crops, an' our butter, cheese an' milk—what they did call 'white meat'—went on ships to England. The British saw the Famine as an opportunity, an' so did the owners of the larger farms—it must have seemed entirely providential to them, havin' the blight clear their land of the pauper tenantry.

"'Ye'll know yer history, boy?' he asked then, an' I nodded for there seemed little point in tellin' him that I'd not much in the way of memory, an' that what I did know came from books.

"'Well, then ye'll know that the blight came again an' again, until people were certain it was a curse from God for some sin we weren't aware of committin'. I was the oldest of four children, an' I was the lone survivor by the summer of '47. The little ones had gone first, an' then my father an' mother, last was my sister who was next to me in age. An' then there I was, fourteen years old, an' entirely alone in the world. I couldn't even shed a tear over it either, for by then I'd not the strength left in me for cryin'.

"'After, the hardest bit was the quiet. It was so horribly silent, no children laughin' nor cryin', no families talkin' next to the fire at night. Not even a songbird in the branches of the trees. It was as if even the air itself was dead. I envied the departed, for the horrible struggle was over for them, that fierce an' terrible battle to stay alive each day. I buried my family in the fields above the sea, for there was, by then, none to stop me from doin' so. An' then, because a man cannot live backward, I took to the road, for to move forward was my only hope of survival.

"'The first few days were both terrifyin' an' exhilaratin' or as close to exhilaration as a starvin' child could come. There were berries here an' there, though most bushes an' brambles were well picked over already, for as ye might imagine, much of the countryside was scoured clean. But for a small lad, willin' to crawl into holes an' under fallen trees there were wee bits of food to be found. Mind there were a few things I ate which made my stomach burn with cramp, for my guts felt like a twisted rag at that point. At night, I slept curled up in the hedges, diggin' a bit of a hole in the leaves an' dirt, an' coverin' myself up with a threadbare bit of blanket I had. Such disguise kept me well hidden, so that only the foxes an' rabbits could find me in the night.

"'I managed those first weeks on my own, always hungry, but findin' enough to keep me on my feet an' movin'. There were times I was certain that if I lay down other than at night, I'd not ever get up again. To lie down in the light would be a sign of defeat, an' the Grim Reaper would be sure to sniff my weakness on the wind.

"'One night, when the moon was high an' near to full, I spotted a hare in a bowl of land in the midst of a grove of ash trees. I'd been sittin' upon the edge of this bowl, waitin' to see if any rabbits might come out, an' watchin the moon rise until it lit the whole of that landscape to pure silver. I'd not eaten more than a handful of berries an' some old hazelnuts I'd found in an abandoned squirrel nest, for the past three days, an' I knew I had to find somethin' before I'd no strength left to hunt. But I was terrible tired an' weak that night. An' so the thought of just lyin' down in the grass an' lettin' slip my hold on life was mighty appealin'. For I had the sense then, watchin' that hare, of how little my life mattered, an' that I was merely a single tear in an ocean of them. The land seemed to speak to me, an' tell me that what had been would come again—lost kingdoms, lost lives, all just part of the wheel which kept on grindin' regardless of heartbreak an' joy, hate an' love an' all the wee dramas of our lives. To the land though, we were no more than the wave that sometimes passes over her, or the call of a flock of geese, returnin' in the autumn. An' so what matter to her, if I simply lay there an' became part of her soil, my bones her bones, an' my blood hers to take.

"'Then the hare moved, an' I took after him, for I knew despite the futility of it, I wanted to live. The want of it blotted out all else—if I wasn't to die, I needed food in my belly. An' there it was, part of the round—from philosophy to brute survival, in a matter of moments.

"'I ran, as I'd never run before, through that silver field an' into the edge of the dark wood. An' then I stopped so quickly that I nearly toppled into the dirt. For there stood a boy, tall an' ragged, an' my hare was danglin' from his hand, kickin' its legs, terrified, knowin' its fate in the way only prey can. The knife moved so fast, I didn't even see it, only one second the hare was still strugglin' an' the next there was a wash of black runnin' from its neck through the white fur. My eyes followed the blade then, for the tall boy was liftin' it to his lips. He made certain I was watchin' and then he licked the blood from the shiverin' length of it.

"'I can still see him as if he stood before me only yesterday—barefoot, threadbare, with blood stainin' his lips black, an' I knew I was lookin' at a creature who were no different than a fox facin' a mouse. He showed me clear in the months that followed that some men lose their soul long before they lose their life.

"'There were two smaller boys flankin' him, one to a side, an' it was one of these piped up an' said, 'Will we kill him then, boss?'

"'I don't know,' the tall one said. His eyes were dark as ripe sloe berries, but there weren't nothin' shiny nor pretty about them. He looked at me for a long time, as though he were gleanin' the chaff from the very corners of my soul, an' there was a warnin' there in his eyes, somethin' cold an' hard. It were no idle sort of look. He'd kill me an' feel no remorse over it. My life was no more than a rattle of the bone dice to him. But he seemed to decide that day was not the one, for he said, 'No, he's not worth the killin', he's just a bit of rag an' bone. What do ye say, rag an' bone boy, will ye join us for dinner?'

"'It were food, an' I still felt the hare had been mine, despite him bein' the one to slit its throat. An' so I went with them, an' got my share which was as much as the smaller boys, but not near what Fergal ate. For that was the tall one's name.

"'I took to the road with them, after that, an' while I were afraid of Fergal, still it was good not to be alone all day an' night. We were protection of a sort for each other, even if I saw them as a pack of rabid dogs. I was only fourteen an' had lost everyone I'd loved, so I threw in my lot with those hard boys, because 'twas either that or die. We walked the country that winter, the four of us. We were little more than staggerin' skeletons, feet wrapped in rags, an' without a coat to even share amongst us. We knew that to survive we would need to keep movin'—town to town, hedgerow to hedgerow. We ate what came to hand—rose hips, nettles, wild garlic, seaweed, mussels an' what few rabbits we came across. We stole a rifle from a cabin one night, where only one old man lay dead. It made it easier to find food, we even got a deer one night, while trespassin' on a lord's estate, but even deer were terrible scarce in those years.

"'It were a night in the spring when we come across a clachan where there wasn't even one soul left alive. There was no more than a few scattered cottages, on what had clearly been a very small farm, broken up into numerous smaller fields, for many tenants subdivided their land into bits an' pieces, until a man might be lucky to have a quarter of an acre to feed his family. It was terrible still that night, an' I think we all held our breath walkin' into that wee village. We could smell death as we walked over the fields. There was a narrow moon on the rise, one as sharp-edged as a dagger. The place felt haunted, as if the dead were very recently departed, an' still there hoverin about their wee cottages an' blighted fields. Still, we'd go through the cottages, for the dead have no use of corn meal or weapons, an' we'd need of both.

"'The atmosphere of the place got to Fergal even, for he ordered us to check a buildin' apiece, so that we might be done an' quickly take our leave.

"'The first cottage I checked was empty, the roof fallin' in, an' nothin' to say who the occupants had been. Had they died, or emigrated, or were they part of the walking dead who stalked the roads, fields an' shores of the land? In the second cottage, there was a family—all dead. Two small children, a mother an' a father. I looked them over, barely takin' in their faces. There was a coat lyin' over the two children—a coat which made me wonder if it had been stolen from someone else, maybe someone who'd died an' had no need for warmth. It was a fine thing, an' somethin' I knew they'd have sold long ago for food, if they'd been able to. Such a thing—a coat with a seal skin collar—was a bit of an anomaly there in a wee village out on the edge of the world.

"'An' so I took the coat. The children had been dead some time, so the smell on the fabric was bearable, though only just. I picked it up an' swirled it, watchin' the moonlight shine on that collar, before I wrapped it around myself, my skin ripplin' with the pleasure of such luxury.

"''Twas then I saw the girl. The one who weren't dead. I thought her a child at first, for she weren't much bigger than one of ten or so, though I'd come to find out she was fifteen. She'd not grown as she should have the last years, simply from lack of food. I stood starin' at her, as if she was a wild thing an' I'd no notion of how to approach or speak to such a creature.

"'Come on out where I can see ye," I finally said, low as I could manage, for I knew I wanted a moment to think before the others became aware of her existence.

"'There was a slice of moonlight layin' upon the floor of the cottage, an' it was into this she stepped. She was terrible thin, with eyes huge in her face, an' hair the colour of a newly-born fawn. I could see that she would be delicate lookin' in bone and movement though, even if she weren't half-starved. Her dress was little more than a rag, an' one shoulder stuck out with a collar bone ye could cut yer hand upon, so thin was she.

"'Ye should go,' I said to her, low an' quick, so she might have the sense that it was urgent. She shook her head, an' I wondered if she was mute maybe, people had been known to lose their voices from the shock of so much death around them.

"'Go,' I said again, feelin' that I needed to get her away before the other boys saw her. There was somethin' fine about her, even as she stood there in her rags with her dead lyin' round about her. Too fine for a pack of rabid dogs, too fine by far.

"'Go where?' asked a voice, an' I knew it was too late, for Fergal was standin' behind me, an' he wasn't goin' to let a bit of a girl go on her way, an' it wasn't because he was worried about her safety.

"'She merely stood there, shakin' a little, as his eyes roved over her. He were bold about it, an' though she was small, still there was a swell of bosom to her dress and a curve to her body, that Fergal was clearly seein'. He smiled then, an' ran his tongue over his lips, an' I think I realized in that moment that one day I'd have to kill him, before he killed me.

"'Things changed after she came with us, as things always do change when you put a sparrow amidst a flock of vultures, an' that's what a girl is in the midst of a few feral boys. It were subtle at first—one of us givin' her a share of our food, or a small clutch of berries we'd happened across. But we were competin' an' we all knew it. It was there in the hostile glances we'd catch from each other, an' the way we'd silently arrange ourselves at night, hopin' we'd be the lad she'd choose to lie nearest. It was natural enough to be sure, but I didn't like the way Fergal looked at her. 'Twas like that fox lookin' at an injured hare, knowin' the kill will be an easy one.

"'We were a month on the road with her, when it happened. We'd all bedded down for the night near to the edge of a wood. She'd taken to settin' her coat—for I'd given the coat to her, feelin' it was her right—down near to me. I think she knew she could trust me more than the others. I was so exhausted that night—it had been two days since we'd had any sort of food with substance—that I fell to sleep the moment my head hit the ground. I woke some time later to the sounds of muffled cryin'. I looked to my side, but she was gone, her father's coat a crumpled smudge in the dark. I got up, heart poundin' like a mad thing in my chest, an' listened again so that I might know which direction he'd taken her. The other two were awake, alert like dogs who didn't do the killin' but want their share of the spoils all the same. I knew what would happen if I didn't put a stop to all of it now.

"'I ran into the woods blind, bangin' my feet on tree roots, an' stumblin' over every stick an' stone, but I was focused entirely on those small sounds of distress.

"'They were no more than a shape upon the ground, him on top of her, her strugglin' underneath, thin white legs pushin' against the ground in an effort to heave him off of her. He was bigger an' far stronger than me, so I cast about in the dark for a weapon, knowin' I couldn't tackle him hand to hand. I found a rock, an' picked it up and then I brought it down over his head, over an' over, not even aware that she was screamin' at me to stop. The other boys had scarpered for the trees. When I came back to myself, I saw what I'd done an' was sick. Yet there was little regret in me, for if I hadn't he would have hurt her in a manner that would have lasted her a lifetime.

"'We buried him in the wood, an' covered him over with moss an' leaves, but no stones, for we didn't want to mark it as a grave.

"'After, we simply walked off into the woods. We washed at the first stream we happened across. We never spoke of what had happened that night. An' then it was just the two of us wanderin' overgrown laneways, where small huts were collapsin' back into the earth from which they'd come, an' the abandoned fields so quiet a man could hear his own breath even at mid-day. All around us the country was no more than a skeleton of its former self, the heather an' bracken re-takin' the hillsides, and unmarked graves pockin' every inch of countryside. We travelled Famine roads that had no destination, an' saw the ghosts peerin' out the windows of the workhouses.'

"'How long ago was it?' I asked him. 'I took a hit to the head some time back, an' dates don't stick in my head so well anymore.' I figured this was a good way to find out the date, an' what I'd said was true enough as things went.

"'Be fifty-five years come this September since the blight floated in over the sea,' he said, as I started rapid math calculations in my head. 'Imagine that—that something invisible could float all the way across the sea from America, an' lay waste to a nation.'

"That made it roughly 1900, give or take a year or so. Maybe the man was mad, an' caught in some strange time warp in his mind. Or maybe I was, for as holey as my mind was, it was a bit hard to know at times, just who was the mad one. Still he'd caught me with his story, an' I wanted to know what had happened to the girl, for I sensed he'd not had a great deal of time with her. So I asked him.

"He looked up from his drink, an' I thought I could see somethin' there of the boy he'd once been, and the girl he'd clearly loved.

"'It were the typhus. We'd come across a village one day, an' gone in to see if there was any food to be scrounged. She found a wee sickly child in the ruins of one of the cottages, still clingin' to the dead body of its mother, but clearly not long for the earth itself. I begged her to leave it be, the wee thing was goin' to die whether she was there or not but she said she'd not leave a child to die alone, an' sat there rockin' it until it took one last terrible breath, an' then lay there in her arms with that awful blank look what comes with death. It took me some time to pry her away, an' then I made her wash in a stream, though we'd no soap. Still, I thought maybe she'd be able to wash off the taint of that place, wash away the death. It wasn't to be though, for she fell ill about a week later with a fever, an' spots on her chest. Mayhap if she'd been stronger she'd have survived. We were in a forest when the fever come on, an' so we stopped because she could not go on, an' it was likely we'd be driven from any village or town we might come across. I built us a snug shelter out of branches an' moss, an' found a spring where I might fetch fresh water, for she was terrible plagued with thirst. I knew the sickness might pass to me, but I didn't care, for death would be a welcome visitor as far as I was concerned. I managed to forage for food, though she'd no appetite by then. It's a terrible disease is typhus, for she swelled near the end, an' her skin turned dark, an' the pain when she swam up out of her delirium was fierce. I was terrified, an' would have happily switched places with her if only to bear her pain.

"'It were the longest ten days of my life, an' yet the swiftest as well. I knew well enough that she would die, an' I thought it likely I'd sicken an' go shortly after. Road fever was that way, spreadin' fast an' scythin' folk down without any sort of final mercy. She got terrible warm near the end, ravin' about her petticoats havin' caught fire, an' how she must run into the water to put the fire out. Well, we'd neither a fire nor petticoats at that point, but I brought water from the stream, an' wiped her down with it, hopin' to bring her even the smallest bit of relief. Death came on the evenin' of the tenth day. She'd been quiet all that afternoon, an' I'd checked her more than once to see if she was still breathin'. Then near the time when dusk would begin to gather she said I must take her outside, I must let her die with the sky overhead, an' the leaves of the trees wavin' at her. I carried her, though I knew it caused her terrible pain. I put her down on a flat bit of ground, an' then I lay beside her, my hand touchin' her own, so that she might know she was not alone here at the last. She died before the hour was out. An' then all that was left to me was to wait for the fever to begin. I was afraid, but strangely peaceful too. Death had felt inevitable for a very long time, an' I thought maybe he'd come as a friend of sorts, bein' that I was very familiar with him by then. An' come he did, but not for many years, for many more miles of road were meant to pass beneath the soles of my feet. Why that should be, I still don't know but I took the years as they came, for so many had lost all theirs.'

"His tale ended there, an' there were so many words I wished to say, questions I wanted to ask, but it was as if all words an' thoughts were caught fast in cold honey, an' could not be dredged out from their amber comb.

"Then suddenly, I felt his hand on my own, an' the strange sight came over me once more, as if everythin' was a little askew from where it ought to be.

"'If ye remember nothin' else of what I've said—remember this one thing—we mattered, we weren't just a bunch of filthy peasants who died because our food rotted in the fields, or because we caught diseases we didn't understand. We mattered, we loved music an' our children, we fell in love an' out, we had feuds an' hatreds, disappointments an' moments of glory. We loved the land, for it was our very breath an' blood, an' we knew every hollow an' fold of it. It shouldn't be only our deaths that matter, because we lived, lad, we lived.'

"I nodded, lookin' into his eyes, which were a rare sort of blue, both ice an' fire at the same time. It seemed I could see all the things of which he'd spoken—the roads travelled, the small cottages razed to the ground, the dead an' the dyin' huddled tight for a last bit of warmth, the fields quilted with lazy beds, the fever sheds with their cargo of the damned, an' the girl who died under a leafy sky. An' as I looked into his eyes, it came upon me slowly that none of the other men seemed aware of us, as though we were invisible to them. The publican hadn't responded to me either, but I'd chalked that up to him maybe bein' hard of hearin'. I was certain I hadn't voiced this thought out loud, but the old man answered as if I had.

"'No, lad, they don't know ye're here, only I saw ye when ye came in.'

"This made no sort of sense to me, but if he was a dream there was little point in questionin' him about it, an' if he wasn't, well I'd the sense it was best if the other men didn't notice me.

"A quiet fell over the man then, an' he seemed almost as though he was fadin' out of my vision, his edges just the wee bit fuzzy.

"'Ye'll remember what I've told ye, ye'll remember that we lived?'

"'Aye', I said, for I was hardly likely to forget it. Then he reached across the table, touched my face an' said, 'Ye need to wake up, lad.'

"And then suddenly I woke to find myself sittin' in the truck and the petrol had nearly run out. Had I slept much longer I would have died."

The end of the story coming so abruptly had the effect of shocking Pamela into the here and now. The feeling was echoed in the expressions around her, as though he'd thrown a bit of cold water in their faces, and left them without a proper ending.

"So what do ye believe then?" Ambrose asked. "Did ye dream it, or did ye wander into a liminal space?"

Casey looked long at the boy before answering, and Pamela had the sense there was another conversation—albeit a silent one—going on between the two of them.

"In truth, I can't say. I've heard that people freezin' to death will often have extremely lucid dreams. Could be the mind's way of tryin' to make death come soft an' easy, I don't know. It did feel as if I was *meascán mearai*—it means bamboozlin' but it also means goin' astray in another dimension. An' I suppose that's what those edge places allow a body to do—cross the border between this an' that, between here an' there. Who is to say what a dream is? Perhaps it is only that—the space we tread between here an' death."

Ambrose nodded, but Pamela had the sense the boy was disappointed in some way by Casey's answer.

The little party broke up after that, with Pru and Ambrose heading back to Belfast, where Pamela had a sneaking suspicion they would find somewhere to spend the night together.

Casey came up behind her and put his arms around her. Clearly her worry had communicated itself to him, for he spoke then to her fears for the young couple who'd just departed.

"Darlin' if there's one thing you an' I know all too well, it's how short an' fragile life can be. Let them love while they can."

"So *was* it just a dream?" Pamela asked, leaning back into the pillows at the top of the bed, and taking in the view before her with great appreciation. Casey was stripped down to his briefs and was washing in the basin she kept on the bureau.

He finished washing his face before he turned to her, wearing a thoughtful look.

"I don't know, Jewel. It didn't have the feel of a dream, for I couldn't shake it off when I came back to myself. An' that's the thing, I had the sense of journeyin' back to the present place an' time, not merely wakin' from a dream-addled sleep."

He skimmed off his briefs, and slid into the bed beside her, still damp from his ablutions, but pulsating heat like a well-stoked furnace just as he always did. He drew her in immediately, and she snuggled into his side with a sigh of relief. It was one of the best times of the day this, just relaxing for a few moments alone with him, before they drifted off to sleep. Tonight though, she still felt the chill of the story he'd told by the fire, and could not rid herself of the image of him sitting in that truck, nearly freezing to death.

"What is it?"

"What?" she said, slightly startled by the man's percipience.

"D'ye think I don't know when ye're stewin' over somethin'? My memory is full of holes, but I'm not blind to ye, woman."

"It's only I might have lost you that night, and I would never have known. Just the thought of that unsettles me."

"It was a strange feelin', Jewel. The notion that if I did disappear into that bog, there was none to know I was gone. For all intents an' purposes, I'd disappeared long before. It was the first time I truly understood just how alone I was in the world."

His words were little more than a bit of ether scattered upon the air, but they struck her to the heart, nevertheless.

"I told ye before that there were times I wondered if maybe I wasn't in purgatory, an' so it seemed to me that time an' place might be a bit slippery in such a realm."

She leaned up on one elbow to look him in the face. "I hate that you ever felt that way. I want to take it all away from you somehow, but I know I can't."

He reached up a hand, cupping her face, running his thumb along the line of her jaw. "Oh but ye do, darlin'. Ye've always given me that edge place in which to seek shelter."

"I'm glad for that," she said softly, "though after the story you told downstairs just the idea of an edge place is giving me chills."

"Liminal doesn't necessarily need to be spooky, it could apply to us right here, right now."

"How do you mean?" she asked, sliding her hand along his arm to link her fingers with his, two ghostly silhouettes in the dim light.

"When I'm with ye in the quiet, I have that sense of steppin' out beyond the ordinary of my day, to a place that only exists when the two of us are together. It can be as simple as ye lookin' at me across the breakfast table, or when it's just the two of us in the bed at night, an' suddenly everythin' around fades away, an' I'm in that country only you an' I inhabit."

"Come with me, and I will go with you," she said softly, echoing words he'd said to her once, long ago. He moved over her, the firelight playing across his body and his shadow leaping high on the wall. She drew him down to her, for here all around them was life, and together they crossed the border into a land known only to the two of them.

Chapter Thirty-seven

That I Should Rise and You Should Not

THE GRAVE WAS near the north end of the cemetery, with a simple stone to mark where his father lay.

He recalled his father in feeling more than specific memories—though he had a small handful of those too—the sense that he'd always felt safe when his father was near, that the man had filled up the space around him with his presence. And that he'd always felt loved when Brian was in the world.

He knew his brother was right, and had felt it too—that until he was right with his father, he wouldn't be right with himself, and wouldn't be the man he wanted to be for his family. And so here he was, about to make amends with a spirit, clutching flowers in one hand and whiskey in the other. The flowers were a spray of anemones, for his father had loved the delicate blooms and he'd wanted to leave some with him. The whiskey was Connemara Mist, which he now took from the bag he'd brought it in, along with two small glasses. The tumblers were Waterford, for his father had always said good whiskey tasted better in a fine glass. It was a frustration to him at times, that he remembered small details like this—his da's love of anemones, and telling him about drinking from crystal but not the larger events of their relationship.

He poured the whiskey, the burnt sugar and oak scent of it tickling his nose and then set one glass upon the stone.

"Hello, Da," he said simply, feeling a bit of a fool for speaking out loud to a bit of stone and grass, but also feeling that this had once been as natural as breathing to him, this speaking to a spirit and a memory.

He swallowed hard, emotion rising in him as it always did when thinking of his father. If recollection served, his daddy hadn't been one for small talk, therefore he wouldn't bother the man with it now. So he simply dove in. "I'm so sorry, Da. I'm sorry for bein' reckless an' stupid, because as it turns out it wasn't just my life I was bein' careless with, it was yers too. What's worse is I think I knew down deep that ye'd done somethin' ye shouldn't have for me. That ye'd had to because I'd been a pigheaded fool."

He put his head in his hands, overcome by grief for a man he'd lost twice now, once to death and once to memory.

"Oh, Christ, Daddy, I hate that I did this to ye. An' I was too ignorant to know or understand the sacrifice ye made."

Something stirred down deep in his mind, like a fish had moved in a winter pond—a flash of silver scale in dark water, there and then gone, so that a man would question whether he'd ever seen it at all. But the echo of that silver flash still reverberated, and he managed to hold it for a few precious seconds, so that he heard his father's voice in his head.

"Ye are a blessin' to me, boyo, don't ye ever forget it. Go out into the world an' be as happy as ye can, as often as ye can, an' don't hurt others if it can be helped. That's all I ask of ye."

He knew it was possible that he'd conjured the words from a pool of false memory, simply because he so desperately needed them just now, but somehow he thought it was not so, and that these words were ones spoken to him by a father who'd loved him enough to sacrifice his life for him.

"I'm goin' to spend the rest of my life makin' up for this. I'm goin' to try to be as good a father as you were, an' a good husband too. The way ye would have been to Aibhlinn had ye been given the chance."

Aibhlinn had been his father's girlfriend for a time, and he wondered now what had happened to her—was she still alive, still out there somewhere with memories of her own, which might help fill in the cracks of his?

He sat quietly then for a time, with his father, that sense of security and warmth rising in him which Brian had always given him and which he now—God willing—would give to his own children.

He poured the whiskey from his father's glass into the grass beside the grave, and a few lines from an old Irish song floated through his head.

> *…But since it falls unto my lot*
> *That I should rise and you should not…*

He wished at times that crystal balls truly worked, and that he could find one to give him back pictures of his past. What he had now was incomplete, bits filled in here and there, but never the complete picture. There was one thing, however, that he didn't need a scrying glass to remember.

"Ye were the best father a boy could ever have wished for. I miss ye always."

He stood, the taste of whiskey still strong in his throat. His father had been a man of great character, and one who would forgive easily that which others could never move past. So the question for him now, wasn't if Brian would have forgiven him, but rather whether he could ever forgive himself.

Chapter Thirty-Eight

The Cost of Violence
October 1979

IT WAS NEAR DARK. The sunset came early this time of year, and was even now hovering like a great bruised pumpkin on the rim of the horizon. Casey had hoped to get home for supper, but that wasn't going to happen. Around them the countryside glowered in the thick brown-orange light. Darkness gathered at the edges—over turnstile and gate, between the blades of grass, coiling around the roots of trees, waiting impatiently to flood the land all around. There was a shiver at the base of his spine, a feeling he sometimes got when something was about to happen.

Casey and Conor had been down near Tandragee in Country Armagh for the day, and were only now making their way home. Casey had needed to deliver blueprints for a minor renovation job, and Conor had asked to come along for the ride. It had been a long day for a wee lad, but a pleasant one as well. The weather had been fine, so they'd stopped for an impromptu picnic in a field, where Conor had shown him a curlew's empty nest, and he'd had to explain the stallion that was 'hugging' a mare in a field.

"Daddy," Conor said, after a long spell of quiet, shortly after they'd passed into County Down, "my tummy is feelin' wambly."

"Is it then?" Casey asked, wondering if Conor was actually sick, or if this was simply his way of asking for a packet of crisps. Pamela swore by the curative qualities of crisps for nausea, and he'd found, to his own surprise, that it worked rather well. "All right, we'll stop up the way an' get ye some crisps."

There was a wee pub just ahead, and it only required a short reroute of their journey. The village was so small that the pub was its lone gathering place outside of the steepled churches which stood opposite one another over the lane which bisected the town. As a result the pub was the least sectarian drinking establishment within a hundred miles. Forced to choose between their political ideals and having a drink of an evening, the population of the town chose to leave their beliefs and political aspirations at the door. It was a small space but the publican was a friend of Finn's who Casey had met more than once, and when he needed a stop on his way through, he usually stopped here. He knew the man wouldn't mind him bringing Conor into the pub.

They pulled up to the building ten minutes later. There were a few cars out front, and the noise reached them even inside the truck. Clearly it was the place to be this evening. It was then he remembered that tonight was the All Ireland final.

He turned around just before they went in, looking back up the lane they'd driven down, that low hum still in his spine. It was likely just the time of year. Pamela always said she could feel eyes watching from the 'other side' this time of year because the barrier between worlds was as thin as a whisper.

The pub was no more than a tiny front room, which felt crowded when there were half a dozen people in it, never mind the fifteen that clustered in it tonight. Conor went off to the washroom, and Casey watched his small form go down the hall. He was no more than twenty feet away, and yet Casey felt a small tug of worry. Fatherhood was not for the weak, that was for certain.

He bought two bags of crisps and a Fanta for Conor, drinking down a glass of water while he stood at the bar. Overhead on a small screen the game was well into the first half. It was Kerry versus Dublin and it looked to be a good game. Kerry was a tough team, and if Casey had to put money on it, he'd put it on the lads in green and gold, but Dublin looked to be giving them a good run for their money.

Conor came back then, and stood by his leg, looking up at the screen. Beside them sat an old man, whom Casey had met a time or two before. He turned and smiled down at Conor, his face wrinkling into a fine network of lines, like an apple which had long ago fallen from the tree.

"Here, lad, look to me," the old man said, and then flourished his hand in front of Conor's face, before fishing a coin out from behind the boy's ear. "Now, hold yer hand out," he said and dropped the coin into Conor's palm when he obligingly held out his hand.

"Thank ye," Conor said, and then leaned into Casey's leg. Casey reached down a hand and touched the boy's forehead. He was running a bit of a fever. The laddie was definitely coming down with something, and he'd best get him home. Conor's next words confirmed the wisdom of this decision.

"Daddy, my tummy still hurts."

"I got yer crisps, maybe eat a few an' see if it helps."

Conor turned a shade of pale green at the thought of crisps, and shook his head. "I need to go outside."

"All right, let's go," Casey said, feeling that he'd be a vastly unpopular customer if his son threw up on the floor, no matter how dirty it was. He cast one last glance back at the television screen and then followed his son out the door.

A car was coming down the narrow road to the pub with its lights off. The hair on the back of his neck prickled, and he narrowed his eyes to catch a better glimpse of it, but then Conor moved off ahead of him and he ran to catch up, his attention diverted.

"Let's go round back, lad. There's trees out there, an' ye'll have a bit of privacy." He led Conor across the back lane to a small wood where he could empty his stomach if he needed to.

Conor darted into a patch of shrubs, and leaned over, retching. The prawn sandwich he'd had for his picnic lunch, had clearly been a mistake.

"Are ye all right, lad?" he asked. Conor's answer was muffled by the sudden crack of gunshot and Casey dove into the wood, pulling his son down hard and fast, and lying over top of him. The sound went on, splitting the air with the sharp *pock, pock, pock* of bullets leaving the chamber.

Conor must have heard the shots too, for he didn't protest and merely lay still under his father. Casey could feel his small heart beating steady as a drum, if a little fast.

He lay there for a moment, a stick poking into his side, twigs raining down on him and Conor, and felt both terror and relief. The gunfire had stopped, but that didn't mean the shooters—for he'd heard at least two guns, possibly three—didn't know they were about. If they did, they would come looking for the two of them. If they moved off deeper into the wood, they risked the inevitable noise attracting the shooters' attention. A moment later, he heard a car engine revving and the sound of a vehicle driving away in great haste.

"Daddy, ye're squishin' me," Conor whispered, wiggling a little.

"Aye, I know," Casey said, and moved off Conor, his own heart still pounding with the knowledge of how close they'd both come to being killed. He stood and brushed the twigs and leaves off his clothes and then checked Conor over from head to toe, to make certain the lad wasn't injured.

"Conor, listen to me. I need ye to stay here hidden, an' low to the ground. Don't ye come out for anythin' or anyone except for me. D'ye understand? It matters that ye do as I say."

Conor nodded, small face white and set, his dark eyes huge in the dim light cast from a lone bulb, just to the right of the pub's back door.

Feeling rather sick at leaving his son behind, Casey walked to the edge of the tree line. The light was almost gone, the world turned from brown-gold to a dusky liquid blue. The silence was thick and unsettling. The pub windows glowed, and yet the quiet had the quality of a great darkness. Despite having heard the car drive off, he stood and scanned the landscape before moving into the open. There was always a chance someone was lingering, waiting to pick off a straggler.

The back of the pub seemed best for entry, and so he crossed over the yard, his spine tingling with the thought of a rifle sighting in on it. The back door stood ajar, a hand propping it open. A hand which was red with blood, and terribly still. He took a breath and opened the door. A young man lay on the other side, dark patches on his back, some fresh and bright, telling Casey he was likely still alive. Bending down, he put two fingers to the man's wrist. At first he felt nothing, and then the tiniest thump against his fingertips, so light that he thought he might be imagining it.

"Just hang on, man," he said, "I'm goin' to get help for ye." He patted the man's hand, and then walked on down the narrow hall, and into the pub proper.

His eyes noticed innocuous things—a tiny split of champagne, a pack of cigarettes with one cigarette pulled halfway out, a snifter of brandy, trembling gold. And then there was the blood and the bodies. First though, he needed to call for an ambulance, and then check for signs of life.

He made the call, and then braced himself to check the bodies. The first man was the elderly gentleman who'd pulled a coin from Conor's ear. He'd been closest to the door, and had probably been hit first. The bullet had gone into his back; it was likely he hadn't even had time to turn round and see the killers.

Then there was a young one, lad looked like he was barely fifteen, though it was likely he was older—nineteen maybe, but with a face smooth as butter-cream. The bullet had taken him in the side. He'd probably been turning at the sound of the men entering. Boy was likely a farmer, he'd the look of it already, strong and capable and a bit lonely-like, the way farmers sometimes were. Casey passed a hand over the boy's eyes, closing them, for he already had the strange far-seeing gaze of one who has passed through to a far place, and no longer sees anything in this realm.

Others he knew—one had sold him hay, one he'd helped with a build-ing question, another he'd changed a tire for and yet another had simply been a man he'd enjoyed a chat with now and again when he'd stopped here for a drink or a bite. Each wrist and neck yielded up no pulse, not even one which was erratic and faint, like the bar keep at the back door. Within minutes he understood that young man was the sole survivor of this massacre, and the odds of his survival were likely slim at best.

"Daddy?"

Casey swung round, startled, slipping in a pool of blood, his bad knee giving way. He caught at the edge of a bench on his way down, but it only halted the fall for a second before he fell full length into a puddle of blood. He got to his feet carefully, a feeling of horror rippling through him as he felt the blood run down his chest, and soak into the waist band of his pants.

"Conor, I told ye to stay in the wood," he said, voice harsher than he'd intended.

Conor swallowed. "I—I'm sorry. I was scared somethin' happened to you. Is—is everyone dead?"

"Aye, all but one. Don't be sorry, laddie. Come on," he walked over to his son, sidestepping blood as much as was possible. He wiped a hand quickly down his trousers to get rid of the blood on his fingers, and then took Conor's hand and led him out of the carnage. There wasn't anything further he could do for those in the pub and he didn't want his son looking at dead bodies any longer than he already had.

Outside, it was full dark, and in the distance Casey could see lights approaching. Please God, let it be the police. He knelt down and put his arms around Conor, who was shivering uncontrollably. Conor stood, staring at the open doorway of the pub, as if expecting someone to burst forth from it, guns blazing, or a reanimated corpse to shamble out, still bleeding.

Three police cars pulled up then, with ambulances right behind. People from the village were beginning to gather too, milling around anxiously, some with frantic looks on their faces. The village would be devastated, a loss such as this would leave no life untouched in a place so small.

"There's one alive, round the back door," Casey said, as the medics hopped out of the ambulance. The police went inside as the medics went around the back and Casey prayed rather fervently that the young man was still alive, giving this village an island of hope in a sea of hatred and blood.

One policeman had cut away just short of the door, and came back to where he and Conor stood.

"Are ye the one who called this in?"

"Aye, I am," Casey said, trying not to give in to his instinctual distrust of the police.

"What happened here?"

"The pub was packed for the game. A car drove up. My son an' myself were out back of the buildin', an' heard gunfire." He knew his voice was curt, but he wanted to keep his information to a minimum.

"Why were ye out back?"

"My son was sick, he needed fresh air."

The policeman gave a curt nod. "Don't go anywhere just yet. We'll need to talk with ye."

The policeman stepped away and then turned back, eyes narrowed and a speculative look hovering about his face, as if he was trying to place him. Casey felt a cold wind cross his soul, and he worried that the man knew him from before. How, of course, was the question? These moments always left him feeling like a man at sea in a boat without oars.

Another policeman approached them then, and began asking questions. Casey gave what information he could, explaining that Conor had not seen anything. He provided what description he could of the car—four doors, lighter in colour—possibly white. The number of guns he believed he'd heard—two, possibly three. Why he'd been here in the first place, at which point Conor piped up.

"It was me, I had to stop for the washroom," he said, and Casey could feel the boy brace himself, as if he was worried the police might suspect his father of nefarious doings, if he'd been the one who needed to stop.

The policeman looked up at Casey, a question in his face.

"We were outside, because he was going to be sick. He thought fresh air would help."

"An' did it help?" the policeman asked Conor.

"No, I threw up in the woods over there," Conor said and pointed to the trees. The policeman nodded.

"Can ye show me where ye got sick?"

Conor looked up at Casey, and Casey nodded. It would corroborate their story, and let the police know they were being honest. The policeman walked them back to the woods, and then shone a flashlight into the spot where Conor said he'd been sick.

"All right, lad. So ye were sick, an' then what happened?"

"My daddy was right behind me, an' suddenly he jumped on me an' I could hear the sound of guns. When the guns stopped my daddy told me to stay where I was, an' not come near the pub. But I did, an' that was when I saw." Conor looked down at his small shoes. They were canvas, and Casey could see they were stained with blood.

"An' what did ye see when ye went in the pub?"

"Everyone was dead, even the nice man who gave me the coin."

"How did ye know that—that they were all dead?"

"My daddy said so," Conor replied.

"An' how did yer daddy know that they were all dead?" the policeman asked, voice deceptively gentle.

"Because he checked to see if he could help any of them."

The policeman nodded, and then looked back up at Casey. "I'd say ye're lucky that yer wee lad was sick," he said. He hunkered down then so he was on eye level with Conor. "Are ye all right then, lad?"

Conor nodded, his hand clutched fast in Casey's, holding onto his fingers so tightly that Casey winced a little. The policeman stood and nodded. "I'll take yer information down, as we'll likely have more questions for ye, but after that, I think ye'd best get yer boy home."

Casey wasted no time getting Conor settled into the truck once he'd provided the policeman with his name and phone number. He then went to the box in the back of his truck, where he had an old sweater. He took his shirt off, and mopped his chest with a dry corner, trying to get rid of the dark smudges. The chilly night air stippled his body with goosebumps. The sweater stunk of oil and wasn't entirely clean, but it was preferable to the scent of cold blood. A cry suddenly pierced the night, a long terrible note of utter grief, and the jolt of it shot through his spine. The living had begun to learn of their dead.

"Are ye warm enough?" he asked Conor, before putting the truck in gear.

"Aye, I'm okay," Conor said. Then he turned to Casey, a look of worry on his face. "Daddy, is this a secret from Mama?" he asked.

Casey shook his head. "No, Conor, this isn't the sort of thing we can keep from yer mammy. She has to know. Besides, with me soaked in blood, I think she's goin' to see that somethin' bad has happened."

Conor nodded, and then laid his head back against the seat. They drove in silence for a time after that, the countryside around them shrouded in darkness, despite a narrow moon drenched in mist, rising just over the hills in front of them. Casey was aware of the tension in his boy though, it emanated off the child as though a storm cloud, filled with electricity, surrounded him.

"Is there anythin' ye want to talk about, Conor?" he asked, gently, not wanting to push the boy if he didn't want to talk, but needing to be certain Conor knew he *could* talk if he wanted to.

"Can...can I ask ye a question?"

"Ye know ye can, laddie. Ye can ask me anythin'."

Conor took a breath and then asked the question.

"Have...have you killed people?"

"Why would ye ask that?" Casey said, thoroughly startled, and not a little dismayed by the question.

"Kieran's da said ye used to belong to...to the 'rah', an' that made ye a murderer," Conor said, voice shaking a little.

"Ah well, Kieran's da doesn't know me from a hole in the ground, lad, so ye'd be advised not to listen to him. No, I've not murdered anyone, Conor."

Conor nodded, and visibly relaxed, and Casey realized this was a question that had been in his son's mind for some time.

They continued the drive home, Conor mostly silent, small face still a stark white. Casey felt somewhat sick, though whether that was a result of what they'd just witnessed or the fact that he'd lied to his son, he wasn't entirely certain. He hated to lie to the lad, however he felt the truth in this instance was a bit much for a boy of his age to deal with. How to explain to him that you'd killed five people to save his mother and sister as well as the man he adored who'd looked after him while Casey was gone? Or that you'd killed in vengeance, and sometimes dreamed your hands were bright with blood? How to explain that you weren't a murderer, when actually you were? Was there ever such a thing as a righteous killing? And what would righteous mean to a wee boy, who'd just seen a sea of blood and dead bodies?

It was with great relief that he turned into the drive of their house. He parked the truck, and then sat quiet for a moment to take a couple of breaths. The house sat warm in the hollow, windows spilling a welcoming light.

"Daddy?" Conor asked, his hand on the door, his face in shadow.

"'Tis all right, laddie, I just need a minute to catch my breath, before facin' yer mama."

Conor nodded, and then followed Casey as he exited the truck.

They stepped into the kitchen, where warmth and light immediately surrounded them. Casey found the light harsh, after the dark safety of the truck. He hadn't been able to see then, see the blood on his clothes and still on his hands, had not been able to see the smudged fingerprint of blood on the back of his son's neck—that small stalk of a neck, barely bigger than when he was a baby. It was from where he'd touched him, trying to shield him from the terrible scene in the pub. It chilled something in him to know that even a touch given in comfort and love, could stain another with blood. Heat spread through his body, and a fury that those bastards might have killed his child, as they'd killed the other innocents there in the pub—slaughtered them and for what?

Pamela turned, a smile of greeting on her face, which swiftly vanished as she took in the sight of them. Conor, who'd held himself together so well the entire journey, ran to his mother and, wrapping his arms around her waist, started to cry. Casey understood exactly how the boy felt.

He gave Pamela a look, one of those swift and silent telegraphs which sometimes passed between married couples. It communicated what was necessary for the moment—that her son was fine, that he was uninjured, that immediate physical concerns were not a worry.

"What on earth happened?" she asked, sitting down and pulling Conor into her lap and cradling him to her chest.

"Where's Bella?" he asked, realizing suddenly that he shouldn't have come inside like this. Kathleen was with Jamie, thankfully, though she was too small to know what these red stains on him were.

"She's asleep, it's late," she said. "I was getting worried about you two, and clearly for good reason." Her eyes swept over him, and he knew she was trying to ascertain if any of the blood was his.

"We're not hurt, either of us," he said. "I need to get out of these clothes though, an' Conor could use a bath—he's runnin' a bit of a fever. I think it's best if I tell ye the details later."

She nodded, rubbing Conor's back with one hand, her cheek laid to the boy's head. Conor had stopped crying and only emitted the occasional snuffle, made secure and calm now by his mother's reassuring embrace.

Casey ran the tub for Conor, putting in a little of the wash Pamela made for the children, thinking a dose of lavender wouldn't go amiss for the boy. When he turned off the taps, it was to find Conor behind him, unbuttoning his shirt, small feet bare.

"D'ye want me to stay?" he asked.

"No, Daddy, but could you leave the door open so I can hear you an' Mama?"

"Of course, laddie. Ye just give a shout if ye need anythin', even if that's just me sittin' by the tub while ye have a wash."

Conor nodded, and Casey left the room so the lad could have his privacy. It seemed so little time had passed since he used to take him into the tub with him as a newly-born baby. Now here he was nearly seven years old, and already showing signs of a self-possession which Casey found remarkable in a child so young.

He returned to the kitchen where Pamela was doing the last of the evening tidying. Like his son had done a few minutes before, Casey wanted to wrap his arms around her and crumble into pieces.

"Are you sure you're okay?" she asked, turning toward him and putting out a hand.

"Don't touch me, darlin'. I don't want this on you."

She nodded. "Do you want your dinner? It's still in the Aga's warmer."

"I'm not hungry right now, but leave it, I may eat later on."

"If you get out of those clothes, I'll wash them," she said. She'd brought a bag for him to put the clothes in, and put it on the floor at his feet.

"No, Jewel. I'll get rid of them. I think if I were to wear them again, I'd just see the blood on them."

She nodded, and left the bag on the floor, to use for the clothes and then went to check on Conor.

Sitting down at the table, he attempted to collect his wits. He could feel one of his headaches nibbling at the edges of his vision, and thought he'd best take a couple of his pills before it got any worse. He rubbed his hands over his face, wishing he could erase the visions on a loop in his head. He was so weary. Violence held a terrible cost, and he felt, at times, that he owed more now than he could ever possibly hope to pay. There was a terrible coldness in the very marrow of his bones, and he worried that it might become a permanent feeling. The lie he had told Conor was part of it, and he wondered—had he done it to save the lad knowledge he was too young to bear, or to allow himself to remain a good man in the eyes of his son? Both, most likely, and so that latter bit made him something of a coward.

For so long, he'd been alone, and not known vulnerability like this. Days like today terrified him, because there was so much to lose now and with it came a stark awareness of how fragile life was, and just how swiftly it could be taken. He could not banish the knowledge that if Conor had been even a minute later in wanting to go outside, they would both be dead now.

"Casey?" He startled and lifted his head, to find his wife looking down at him, a line of worry puckering her brow. In her hand she held two of his pills, and in the other, a glass of water.

"I could see you had a headache coming on," she said in answer to the look he gave her. He took the pills, washing them down with the water. Then, setting the glass aside, he simply leaned his head into the warmth and comfort of her.

"I'm all right, Jewel, just a bit done in."

"Are you going to tell me what happened?" she asked.

"Aye," he said, and then proceeded to tell her, leaving out the worst bits, but realizing the horror of it was only too clear in what he did say.

"Oh, dear God," she said at the end of his recitation of the ugly facts of what he'd seen and just how much their son had witnessed. She didn't say more than that, but simply cradled his head to her breasts. He put his arms around her waist, and breathed in her scent. It was the smell of home, and he drew it deep into his lungs, hoping to banish the copper stink of blood which clung to him.

"I'm sorry," he said softly.

"What on earth are you sorry for?" she asked, though he thought she knew.

"That he saw what he did. I hate that he was there, that he witnessed all that. He's too young for such a thing. I worry that he's going to carry the memory of it with him for the rest of his life."

"He might, Casey, but he's still awfully young. He's also a very resilient child, so it's not likely to affect him as much as it will you. It was pure happenstance that you were there in that exact moment. That's no one's fault but the killers."

"On the way home, he asked me," Casey said quietly, "if I was a killer, if I'd murdered people."

She went still, her eyes dark and troubled. "And what did you tell him?"

"What I thought was advisable for someone so small," he replied, keeping his ears trained for any noise from the bath. "But ye know I lied to him, an' that's somethin' I don't feel good about."

She nodded. "Casey, you know full well, there are things he's not old enough to know. There are things parents keep from their children their entire life, and for good reason."

"Aye, all the grey parts of life—which seem to make up about ninety-nine percent of it."

She looked down at him, smoothing his hair back. "Go and have your bath, man. I'll look after our son."

When he was done with his bath, he went to check on the children. Isabelle, blissfully unaware, was fast asleep, curls in a mad halo around her tiny face. Casey bent down and kissed her forehead, smiling at the flushed cheeks and round open mouth. She was the picture of innocence, which wasn't something she could be accused of when awake. Just looking at her soothed his jagged spirits a little.

"Did ye manage to eat somethin', laddie?" he asked Conor, who lay wide-eyed in his bed, quilts drawn up to his chin.

Conor nodded. "Mama gave me some broth."

"D'ye want me to read with ye for a bit?"

"No, mama read with me already. I'm okay, Daddy."

"It's fine if ye're not okay, son. What ye saw today is hard for an adult to comprehend, never mind someone as young as ye are."

Conor simply hugged him then, his arms tight around Casey's neck and Casey held him for a time, so that the boy might feel his strength and know he was safe.

"I love you, wee man," he said, and tucked the blankets loosely around the boy, knowing Conor couldn't bear too much constriction at night. He rose then, and with one last touch of reassurance, as much for himself as for his son, he left the boy to his dreams, and hoped to God they wouldn't be ones of blood and gunfire.

On the threshold of his own room, he paused for a second, taking a breath, steadying himself before facing his wife. It was late, and she was waiting in the bed for him, her face pale and drawn as she watched him cross the room. He got in, smelling the lavender water she'd ironed the sheets with, overlaid with the scent of burning peat.

"Come here, man," she said and he moved across the bed to her, still feeling that terrible cold right down to his marrow. She put her arms around him, and held him tightly, as though she would take his body into her own, to both shelter and heal. It was something she could and did do for him, though tonight he felt both the refuge of her as well as the fear which went bone-deep for what might have been lost today. The softness and warmth of her body, and the sanctuary those things offered called to him the way water called to a man with a great thirst. He wanted to push up her nightgown, root himself between her thighs, and just succumb to blind need in order to erase the images in his head for a few moments. He knew the instinct, the way a man lost in the dark, would try to drown his pain in a well of light. She understood, for he could feel the shift in her body, the small movements which told him in the language of dark and skin, that she would give him whatever he needed for oblivion's sake.

He heard a noise then, a small step on the threshold and he took his hands reluctantly off Pamela. Conor stood just inside the door, clutching his blanket and a stuffed lamb which had been his constant sleep companion up until six months ago, when he'd decided he was too old for such things. Clearly, tonight he needed the comfort of the beloved familiar.

"Can I sleep with you?" he asked.

"Of course ye can, lad. Come on," Casey said, moving over and patting the bed next to him.

Conor, who, through habit and a trust which had been forged on the day he was born and never broken, usually turned to Pamela for comfort. Tonight though, he clambered up into the bed, curled into Casey's side and, worn out by the day's events, fell promptly to sleep in the manner that only a young boy possibly could. Casey was glad his son was able to sleep, for he knew slumber would be elusive for himself tonight.

Pamela rolled onto her side to look at him. "Are you all right?" she asked softly.

"Aye, about as all right as a person can be after such a thing."

"Do you want to talk about it?"

"No, I don't know what I'd say. Ye've been there yerself, Jewel, some things beggar a person for words."

"Yes, I know, but if you find there are things you need to say, you know I will listen."

"I know, darlin'. I feel like ye often know what I want to say though, even when I can't speak the words."

She reached over Conor and touched Casey's face, and he turned his head so that he could look at her. The only light was that of the fire, so that she was cast in both cinnabar and shadow. There was worry in her eyes, and he wished there was a way to stop the violence of this land from ever touching her again. Her hand traced the lines of his face—cheekbone, orbital arch, forehead, lips and jaw. He felt the tension begin to leave his bones and as the knots in his shoulders eased, he drew in a long breath, realizing it was the first full one he'd taken since he'd heard the shots ring out.

Silence held between them, and yet there was another form of communication taking place which spoke of many things—of how during every hard time, there was this—the two of them, and the invisible thing which existed both between and around them, and sustained them when the world encroached with all its strife and pain. He felt the tension in his core begin to melt a little, for her touch had woven a fabric around them, so that the very air seemed to distill, holding the firelight like embers in honey.

"I love you," she said so softly that it was no more than a slight ripple in that distillation of air and fire.

"I love ye too, Jewel," he said, feeling the sweep of gratitude which often came to him in these moments. He took her hand and put it to his lips, kissing her palm and then holding it to his face, feeling as though he could dissolve into her touch.

A few minutes later, he turned onto his back, careful not to disturb Conor, though once the boy was asleep little could wake him. Casey looked up at the ceiling, where the fire was reflected in a dappled rose glow. Exhaustion pulled heavily at him, but every time he closed his eyes, he saw the interior of the pub, and the lake of blood which had covered the floor, along with the bodies. Little details seemed to be tattooed on the back of his eyelids: the old man's watch chain with a line of blood running down it, crimson drops like rubies strung upon a silver string; the ghostly blue tip of a man's thumb where cue chalk lingered; the amber drip of a shattered bottle of whiskey and the gold-flecked hazel of another man's eyes, before he had brushed a hand over them to close his blank gaze upon the world. Around all this was the echo of his daddy's voice in his head, telling him long ago what the price of such things was.

'Violence is like a chained beast, boyo, an' if ye feed it too much it will just want more. An' then one day when it gets strong enough on all ye've fed it, it will break that chain an' there will be no controllin' it after that.'

He understood the warning his father had been giving him. His daddy had always seen him clearly, and the dangers which his nature posed. And now, he was a father and understood more deeply the fears his own father had held for him. To witness violence cost something, to trade in it with your own body and soul, cost something more, as he knew all too well. He did not want his son and daughters to one day have to pay such a price with their own bodies and souls.

"Pamela," he said, and though his voice was quiet, he knew the tone in the few syllables had disturbed the fabric which her touch had wrought. He still held her hand, and he felt the sudden tension in it.

"Yes?"

"We need to leave this country."

The silence from the other side of the bed was long, but he didn't regret saying the words, they were merely the deepest truth of his heart in this moment. They could not raise their children in this land. When she finally spoke, her voice was both sad and tired.

"I know," she said.

Part Five

The Book of Heartbreak

Chapter Thirty-nine

With Apologies to Mr. Keats

THE NIGHT WAS COLD, and the walk down to Finola's cottage had left her thoroughly chilled. She waited outside, nevertheless, too anxious to go in just yet. Above, the moon was just three days off the full, trembling like the paper cutout of a silver galleon, adrift on a sea of black velvet. There was a strange lack of depth to the scene, as though she was looking at a child's picture book in two dimensions: silver galleon moon; hedges of construction paper with ragged tops where the scissors had slipped; a small fox with thumb-tacked limbs moving through the landscape; vines made of coiling wire and decorated with bits of jewel for leaves, and a woman, with hair made of winding ribbons, gazing at the page in front of her. It would make a good scene for a child's book. The sort of book she might have proposed to Jamie, something which they could collaborate upon—her drawings, his words.

Casey's words from that night three weeks previous, echoed in her head. *We need to leave this country.* They hadn't spoken of it much since, but still she knew that Casey had meant it, it wasn't something he'd said only in the heat of the moment. It was understood between them now. She was going to have to speak with Jamie about taking Kathleen to live elsewhere. It wasn't something she looked forward to, for any number of reasons, not the least of which was Jamie being parted from daily contact with his daughter. Tonight, however was not the night for that particular talk, and she was coward enough to be grateful for the small reprieve.

Casey emerged from the edge of the wood then, wrapped in a red muffler and his navy pea coat. "Christ, it's pure desperate out here tonight. Jamie here yet?"

"I am now," said a dry voice from behind Casey. "You're right, it is desperate out here, shall we go inside?"

"Yes," Pamela agreed, following Jamie in, Casey right behind her.

Jamie had summoned them to this meeting a few days before. He'd left a rather cryptic message with her, via Vanya, and she'd understood she wasn't to call or discuss it with anyone outside of Casey. The result of which was that she stood now in Finola's cottage, feeling rather mystified.

The three of them took off their coats, gloves, mufflers and boots and then settled in by the fire where four chairs sat waiting for them.

"Finola will be joining us in a moment," Jamie said, noting her glance toward the extra chair. "Meanwhile, let's get something warm in us."

That Jamie should choose this cottage for a secret meeting didn't surprise her. His grandmother's cottage had been a place of refuge for him when he was a child, escaping a home which hadn't been entirely happy. It was a homely place, with herbs hung from the rafters, and well-worn chairs placed near to the fire and open shelves filled with mismatched china. If one came here with a worry or an ailment, Finola always had the remedy on hand for it, and Pamela knew that when he was young and still willing to show his vulnerability, this was where Jamie had sought those balms for both body and soul.

The door opened just as Jamie poured out tea for each of them. Pamela took hers with gratitude, wrapping her hands around the pot-bellied mug and savouring its heat. Finola came in on a gust of cold, damp air, nose and ears tipped in red, green eyes bright with vigor.

Jamie poured another mug for his grandmother, who took it after hanging up her coat and gloves. She settled in beside Pamela, smelling strongly of herbs as she always did. Pamela sniffed the air delicately, detecting the slightly dusty fragrance of chamomile, the sharp clean of lavender and the warmth of lemon balm. Finola must have been grinding herbs to make a tincture for nerves. She looked again at Jamie, noting that he did seem a little tense, but nothing beyond what might have been expected when he'd called a secret meeting. His grandmother flashed him a look, and Jamie nodded in return.

Jamie then put his cup down and leaned forward taking in both her and Casey with a rather serious gaze.

"I have a rather large favour to ask of the two of you."

"Aye?" Casey said, the same wondering in his voice which she was currently feeling.

Jamie took a breath. "I should like the two of you to look after Kolya, if something should happen to me."

"Is something going to happen to you?" she asked, tone sharp.

His gaze was level, the green eyes dark. "No, I just want this settled. I am going to be leaving on business, and I may not be back for a while; should something happen during my absence, I'd like to know Kolya has the security of a good home. All three of us know too well how chancy life is. Take your time and give it some thought. I just want to know he has the best parents I can provide him with, and I can't think of anyone I should prefer over the two of you."

She looked toward Casey to find him looking back at her. He shook his head, returning his gaze to Jamie. "We don't need to think on it, we'll do it, won't we, Jewel?"

"Of course we will," she said, looking Jamie in the eyes so that he would know his children, regardless of mother, would always be hers as well. "Where are you going?"

"I owe a favour to an old friend, and it may take some time to complete said favour."

"Which tells us exactly nothing," she said.

"It's all that I can tell you at present."

"Why don't you want Violet looking after Kolya?"

"Because, quite simply, I don't trust her not to use him as a weapon."

"I rather thought she was already doing that," Pamela said.

A fine tension strung itself between them, as invisible as a cobweb in the dark, and yet felt all the same. The two men glanced at each other, and then their gazes held for a beat or two, during which Pamela held her breath. It felt as though a deeper communication was taking place between the two of them, where something was asked and answered. She knew she was right, when Casey gave the barest of nods, and Jamie visibly relaxed in response.

Finola sat back observing the two men, a curious look in her eyes. A shrewd observer of human nature, she no doubt found these particular two men fascinating to watch. Pamela would have given a bit to know what track her thoughts were currently running upon, given that one of the men was her beloved grandson and the other she'd seen in the altogether during a ritual which Casey had, at the time, sworn was some sort of black magic.

As for herself, to be in the same room with both men didn't feel as fraught as it once had. She had made her choice, and looking over at Casey now, she felt a peace in her core around it. What she had said to him that night in the cottage was the truth—once she'd seen him that day last winter, the choice had been made.

"To that end," Jamie went on, "I've had Tomas draw up papers to grant you legal custody should Kolya need care. I'd like you both to sign them to-night, so that the legal knots are properly tied."

She couldn't rid herself of the sense that Jamie was tidying up loose ends in this moment because he was laying odds on his business needing to be in order before he left. But she could not do other than what he asked of her, and so she sat, reading through the lines of legalese, the words so terribly dry compared to the human transaction of emotion and promise that they represented.

There was a strange solemnity to the sound of the pen against paper, as she signed her name to the documents and then Casey followed, his bold letters a dark scrawl across the bottom of the page. After he was done, he stood, nodded at Jamie and then touched her gently on the arm.

"I'll wait outside for ye, Jewel," he said.

She nodded, and then had a quick word with Finola while Jamie sorted the papers into their various piles. Everything was in triplicate, and there was a separate envelope with both her and Casey's names affixed. She didn't like the feel of any of it, despite understanding the necessity.

Jamie handed the envelope to her, then another to Finola, who then, never one to make a fuss over anything, took it and slipped up the stairs without so much as a word.

She donned her coat and muffler, boots and gloves, tucking the papers into the inside pocket of her coat. There was a small safe in her dark room at home, where she kept important papers, and this would join the others there as soon as they arrived home. She turned then, to find Jamie standing by the door, as though he would reach for the handle and escape into the night as well, before she could ask any questions. She knew full well that Casey had gone outside ahead of her in order that she could have a moment with Jamie.

"Jamie, is this favour you need to do in Russia?"

"Why would you think that?" he said, his eyes still dark.

"So it is Russia," she said, angrily. "Are you completely mad?"

He smiled, but it was a brittle thing. "My doctors certainly seem to think so."

"It's not funny, Jamie, we have a daughter to raise."

"I know that, Pamela. I have no reason to believe this thing I need to do will be particularly dangerous. I just want to be certain that Kolya has a place to go should I be indefinitely delayed."

"Violet won't like it one bit. He is her son, after all."

"I'm fine with her looking after him in my absence. I have her watched to make certain she doesn't try to leave the country with him, and she knows that. But if something should happen to her, I don't want Kolya to become a ward of the state."

"Jamie, you're scaring me. Why might something happen to her?"

He sighed. "It likely won't, but she is ex-KGB, and that's a tenuous role to play. I think it's best for me to have things settled for Kolya."

"Please, Jamie, be careful. You're needed and loved here by too many people. We can't do without you. I don't want you to be a story I have to tell Kathleen. I want her to have her father."

"Pamela, I will come back, I promise."

She shook her head, tears prickling behind her eyes. "We both know it's not always possible to keep those kinds of promises, Jamie. So be careful, please."

"I will," he said, and she nodded, and then put her arms around him, giving him a quick hug before heading out into the night, where her husband waited for her.

Jamie stood for a moment after the door closed behind Pamela, feeling slightly lost. He had been aware of her careful observation of his face, and knew that she suspected he was poised on the razor's edge right now—a razor dipped in honey, but still capable of shredding a man to bloody bits. She was right to be worried, for he had long been familiar with the signs when his psyche was getting ready for one of its mad flights far too close to the sun. He needed to hang on for a few more days, he needed his blood to continue to stream with fire, and his mind to make those leaps it did in this state. Just a few more days, that was all he needed and then he would hole up somewhere and ride out the dark part of this particular storm.

"There is a hollow in the universe where she has stood for the last three years," his grandmother said, jarring him from his musings. He had not heard her come back down the stairs. "It's neither more nor less simple than that. She left something behind for ye." Finola nodded toward the table. "She brought it by some months back, but she said she'd tell me when to pass it on to ye. To-night she told me it was time. I'm goin' back upstairs, an' to bed. Don't forget to lock the door behind ye when ye leave."

He nodded, summoning up a smile from his reserves, knowing it did not fool Finola in the least. She was going upstairs so that he might have a moment alone with the package sitting on the table. She squeezed his hand, and looked into his face. "She loves ye, an' so do I, so heed her words, would ye?" She went up the stairs then, and he noted how slowly she was moving this evening. Usually she was spry as a pisky, but she was getting older, and this cottage was isolated, and damp in the winter. It was one of the things he needed to deal with when he got home, talking to her about possibly moving up to the big house, where she'd be warm and properly fed, and he could take care of her better than the present circumstances allowed.

He sat down at the table, and then rose again. He was both exhausted and agitated at the same time. What he needed he could not have, but this was nothing new. Still, there were times during which this sort of abstention was much harder to bear.

The letter was in a white envelope, with just his name across the front. Jamie—in the way she wrote it, with the up-tilted round at the top, and a falling slash at the bottom. It was tempting to leave it, simply not open it and therefore remain ignorant of the words she'd written. Even as he thought it, though, he was pulling the paper from the envelope and unfolding it. The paper held her scent—that combination of green things and a deeper note like clear amber, which was all her own and defied description. The letter was dated during the time she had been pregnant with Kathleen, just when she would have been preparing to marry Noah. He wondered why she had thought to give it to him now.

Dear Jamie,

I am writing because I am a coward just now, and feel I cannot say the things I must to your face. With apologies to Mr. Keats, I had thought to send you a note, something brief along the lines of 'I love you too much to venture to Hampstead...' knowing of course that you would understand that there is a terrible truth in those lines. I know what Keats meant when he wrote those words so long ago. Seeing a face you love can burn like fire. To borrow once again from Keats, to see you at present would be 'not merely paying a visit, but venturing into a fire.' And so I will not.

Even as I put pen to paper, I am not sure it is wise to tell you these things, but still I feel I need to.

I find it hard to believe at times, that there will be no more evenings in your study where our talk would rove from snails to stars and everything in between. A part of me has always believed that eventually we'd be a family, and the long conversation we began when I was a lonely girl of thirteen and you a heartbroken father of twenty-five, would simply continue on until one of us departed from this world. It's an old dream, and as such, it is dying a slow death, the remnants of it hovering still, like smoke from a long quenched fire.

And so I will say what I must. I am who I am because I've loved you so long, Jamie. That love lives in my core, to try to kill it would kill me. I need you to know that—time and distance will not alter that for me. It is simply woven too deeply into the threads of who I am.

Always,
Pamela

There was a postscript, clearly written much more recently.

PS- The book I made for you when I was pregnant with Kathleen. Both letter and book belong to you, and so despite all that has changed since I first put these words to paper, I would, nevertheless, see both lodged with their owner.

The book was large, with bits of ribbon and cloth bulging out of it. He walked over to the table and looked down. The cover was made from a fine leather, embossed with golden leaves. The title was there in pale green letters, embossed as well. It was a piece of art made, he knew, by her hands, for he recognized her style of sketching even there on the cover. The title caught at his breath—*The Book of Heartbreak*. He understood then, without even turning to the first page, just what she'd made—it was their story, and it was her own version of a love letter, the sort that tells the recipient goodbye.

He opened the book, hands trembling slightly, as they did sometimes with her. The narrative was clear—markers in the book of their relationship, those places where the story paused for a moment, the paragraphs and sentences, where they'd taken time to stop for breath, and for love.

The first page was a blaze of colour. It held a tiny woman constructed of felt, clad in strips of cloth, feathers in her hair, dancing beside a red silk fire; it was the memory of a night which felt like it had taken place a thousand years ago. She had attempted to seduce him that night, and there was a part of him, he thought, which would likely always regret that he hadn't accepted her offer. He turned the page.

On this page there was a white deer, glimpsed beneath the bough of an oak, with a lake shimmering beyond, and two small figures in a shelter, with the words inscribed upon the scene—*When the dark night seems endless, Remember me.*

He kept turning pages, and saw the last ten years of their time together unfold. Here was their summer in Maine—scattered sparkles of sand and a house made from bits of grey wood, stretching its wings out toward the sea. Across this page was a small drift of sketches, miniature illustrations of their time there, as well as bits and pieces of the stories he had told all that summer through. And a sail boat with a mermaid beside it, head above water. Jamie remembered only too well what that particular scene represented. It was too painful to linger here, and so he turned the page.

The next one made him pause for remembered joy. It was a simple background of lavender cloth and upon it lay a sheaf of delicate white silk, torn and shaped into a nosegay of narcissi, small diamond drops of glass gleaming upon the silk, like the snow which had kissed the petals of the real flowers. He closed his eyes for a moment, seeing so clearly that morning in Paris when he'd given her the flowers, and her eyes had filled with tears, those of a happiness newly born and barely touched. He took a breath, and opened his eyes, turning the page and laughing out loud at the scene which greeted him. It was a miniature of Montmartre rendered in plaster; bits of stone and glass, forming buildings; wire twisted and woven into wrought iron balconies; brilliant washes of paint, and a set of stairs with tiny tumbling felt *boules* cascading down them, caught frozen in the act of memory; an umbrella with a wickedly sharp silver tip made from a thick needle—here he rubbed the spot on his head where the old woman had whacked him, as they ran through her *appartmente*. She'd had good aim, for he had a scar where she'd repeatedly hit him with a much larger umbrella than the one rendered here, as they scrambled to get out of her abode. And last, tucked into the corner of the page, a tiny pair of red boots, made from bits of suede. The real pair he remembered fondly. He'd paid an exorbitant amount to a prostitute for them, so that Pamela would have something to wear in the Paris snow.

The next page was, of course, the fruit which Paris had yielded—a sea of blue feathers, waves cusped with pearl beads, and a tiny mermaid with a shock of red hair, deposited on a shore of translucent shells. Kathleen—their love made tangible and infinite. He smiled, running his fingertips over the waves, for though there was, indeed, heartbreak, they'd also had joy and laughter and family.

And then the last page—a tower set amidst pines—a small conical structure of bark and clay needle, and a stream—peat brown silk with waves of velvet water-weed beneath, and two horses grazing in long grass beyond. An owl, made of grey felt with gold bits for eyes, gazed from the tower window and a small bat flitted across the background of a starry night. And there were words woven faint as the traces of starlight round about the tower window, and into the boughs of the trees beyond—

...and the owls flit round the evening tower, and the young stars glance
Between the quick bats in their evening dance...

Shelley, Shelley, Shelley—their first poet, and their last.

And finally, placed just so, against that starlit sky, was a moth, wings translucent grey and dusted with a fine shimmer of powdered silver light. The moth desiring the star, and finding itself immolated once it grasped that which it had sought. She had been wrong about one thing that day, for it wasn't her who was the moth, it was him and she, of course, the star.

It was, he knew, no mistake that she had placed this scene last—*Step then to this world, which might be a beginning, or more likely an ending, which in it contains a beginning, and so on, world without end.* A damn fool had said—or rather written—it first, but it was, he thought, no less true for all that. He would remember it always—that day—a field filled with flowers and a young woman offering him all she had within her grasp to give, and though he'd refused her, he understood now that she had never truly taken back anything which had been given that day.

He traced a fingertip over the words, the small trembling rise of each a note of both passion and pain. Shelley had been the poet of both these things for the two of them. And so, of course, she would close with him—a two line coda to all they had been to one another.

True love in this differs from gold and clay,
That to divide is not to take away.

Chapter Forty

Open Your Eyes and Let Go

PAMELA STEPPED THROUGH the door of Egan and Riordan, Partners at Law, wondering if a woman's blood could actually boil in her veins. If so, steam ought to be emitting from her own ears just now with the regularity of a whistling tea kettle.

Earlier that afternoon she'd answered the telephone at home, an act simple enough in itself, but the conversation which had ensued was what had brought her here, with an urgent need to see her brother-in-law.

Miss Dervla Mundy looked up from her desk, which was a position akin to that of a sentry in a tower, in that one risked being shot if one didn't state one's business to her immediate satisfaction.

Her expression softened a bit at the sight of Pamela. "Hello, Mrs. Riordan, are ye here to see Patrick or Tomas?"

"Patrick," she said firmly.

"Will it be urgent, then? Only he's on a phone call at present."

"It will be, because if I don't speak with him soon, I may run off and kill his brother."

Miss Mundy stood, straightening her relentlessly starched blouse and nodded, as if to say none understood the ability of men to madden a woman as well as she did. Working as she did for Tomas, Pamela thought there was likely some justification in the woman's expression.

"Right then, I'll just go let him know ye're here."

A minute later, Miss Mundy beckoned her down the hall. "Go on in, he's waitin' for ye."

Pat was just placing the receiver back in the cradle when she entered his office. He looked up at her with a question in his eyes, though she suspected he already knew what she was going to say. So she simply launched in, not bothering with any preamble.

"Someone called me this afternoon to tell me, and I quote 'I'll be late for the fight, but tell Casey I'll see him after, bein' that I've a great deal of money ridin' on him.' You wouldn't know just what the man who called me might be referring to, would you, Pat?"

"Um, well—" he began, but she cut him off by raising a hand.

"Do you know where the location of the fight might be?" she asked. Pat, as she had half suspected was the case, did not look anywhere near as shocked as he might have been by this news.

"Erm," Pat tugged at his collar as though he was in need of air. From long experience she knew this as a Riordan tell. Casey and Conor both did it, and so did Pat any time they, and he, were forced into an uncomfortable corner.

"Patrick?" she raised an eyebrow at him.

"Well, he thought it best if someone knew where he was goin' just in case he needed help, or didn't turn back up when he's meant to. Kate did say as I ought to tell ye, but he was determined to take the fight, an' I thought it was only likely to cause discord for the two of yez."

"Oh, so Kate knows."

"Aye, she knows but only because the woman winkled it out of me, she has some sort of sixth sense when it comes to anythin' troublin' me."

"And does Kate know the location of the fight?"

Pat stood up from behind his desk with an air of resignation. "Aye, she knows. An' yes if ye call her she'll tell ye."

"You appear to have a choice then, either come with me, Patrick, or I'll call Kate and then I'll go on my own. Now, which is it going to be?"

Pat sighed. He wore the look of a man who was well used to stubborn women, and occasionally found them trying. "Come on, we'll take my car, we're not goin' in that damn rattle-trap of yers. I should like to make it there alive. Ye know," he turned and smiled at her, "just in case ye need a witness to the murder of my brother."

During the drive, neither she nor Pat spoke much. What was there to say, after all, when your husband or brother, as the case may be, was a buck eejit of monumental proportions?

"If it helps at all," Pat ventured cautiously, a good twenty minutes into the ride, "he's very, very good at the fightin', Pamela. He's so good that, years ago, his trainer wanted him to work towards becomin' a professional."

"It does *not*," she said, putting a point on every word, "help at all. And frankly it only points to him being more of a fool than I thought."

Pat coughed slightly. "Ah, how's that?"

"Because he might have done it professionally but chooses to go the illegal route and get his brains bashed out by another amateur."

"Ah, I see," Pat said, and then ceased to speak, which seemed wise on his part, Pamela thought, all things considered.

As they drove, the dark began to flood the land, a chill silver twilight turning to full night as they navigated narrow country back lanes, well beyond the reach of city lights. She would have never, despite her threats to Pat, been able to find this place on her own. She glanced over at him, grateful that he'd agreed to bring her, despite knowing his brother wasn't likely to be best pleased about it.

They were out beyond Ballygally, when Pat stopped the car on a narrow track, and then backed it into a leafy recess in a clutch of young aspen. Pat appeared to know exactly where they were, whereas to her they appeared to have arrived in the literal middle of nowhere.

"We'd best walk in from here," he said, sounding a trifle grim. "Ye don't want to come upon a group of drunk an' fightin' men too quickly. Stick close, an' let me do the talkin'."

"All right," she said, feeling suddenly nervous about just what she had dragged her brother-in-law into. Still, she was immensely grateful for his presence. Pat always had the effect of calming any situation into which he entered. She followed him up the road, which was as hard as concrete beneath their feet, for there had been several hard frosts in the last week.

Ahead of them, there was a man standing beside a gate, a jaunty hat on his head, but positioned so that he was blocking the path beyond. The man stepped forward, and there was clear menace in the way he moved. He eyed Pat up and down, and then said something sharply in a language she didn't understand.

Pat put a hand back and pulled her close to him, before replying at some length in the same language. The man looked him over once again, and her as well this time, before nodding and standing aside to let them pass.

"What was that?" she asked, certain that it wasn't Gaelic.

"'Tis the Cant," Pat replied, "or ye might know it as Shelta. 'Tis what the Travellers speak. I doubt he would have let us through if I couldn't speak it."

"You know Shelta?"

"Aye, I speak it a little; it comes in handy with some of my clients. Casey's more fluent than I am, though."

"What?" she said, truly surprised. She'd had no notion that Casey spoke anything other than English and Irish.

"Aye, some, like I said, more than me. He needed it in the past, but I'll let him tell ye about that."

"Yes," she said grimly, "we will be having a talk about it—all of it."

Pat took her arm, halting her. They had come out on a plateau of sorts, and she gasped at the scene laid out in front of her. There was a great fire and a lot of men, voices like something from another age—a pagan chant over a blood sacrifice upon the altar of nature and her whims. The fire backlit the night, and the people around the two combatants were outlined in the flames, their skin and hair glowing red, as if they stood at the portal to hell.

The cold had settled upon the land, and where the fire touched rock, and grass, it was silver-shot and glittering. Beyond, she could hear the sea, and smell the sharp, cold salt of it.

In the centre of all this, were the combatants. One her husband, at whom she was afraid to look, and the other a man of a size that caused her to gasp in horror. He was, quite simply, a giant, a being beyond the bounds of normal human breadth and length. He looked like something out of one of the ancient Irish legends—a man who might walk across the sea between here and Scotland in a few steps, leaving earthquakes and tidal waves in his wake. A man who could kill another with one well-placed blow. She thought she might be sick.

She turned then, and looked at Casey. He was in a fighting stance but emanated a strange calm, as though he stood in the eye of a hurricane, in that strange still place where nothing could touch him. Even with his hair plastered to his head, and with blood streaking his body and face, he somehow stood apart. His very being emanated the dark joy of the fight—the brutality and its partner—the risk of death, of standing near its threshold and laughing. Both men were clearly catching their breath, before one or the other of them rushed in and continued the violence.

Casey wiped a trickle of blood from his mouth and laughed, giving the other man a flicker of his hands, as if to say, 'Come on you son-of-a-bitch, come and try me.' Reflexively she crossed herself, throat dry with fear as the other man closed in on Casey, surprisingly swift for a being so large.

Pat grabbed her by the arm and pulled her behind him, as they drew closer to the crowd. "I don't think he should see ye, Pamela, or he'll get distracted, an' that can be dangerous in a fight like this."

"I'll hide behind you, but I'll be damned if I'm going to go sit in the car like some obedient mouse, Patrick Riordan."

Pat turned and gave her a wry look. "I'll not ask the impossible of ye, Pamela, just keep yerself out of his line of sight."

While she suspected Pat was trying to spare her the worst of the carnage, she knew he was also right, Casey could not afford even a millisecond of distraction. They drew as close to the fire and the two men fighting as Pat seemed to think was wise, and then stopped just beyond the edge of the crowd. Even from this vantage point, she could still see more than she wanted to.

Her breath was stopped in her throat, her chest tight with fear as she watched the man respond to Casey's invite, rushing at him like a bull or a boulder going full tilt downhill. Casey was waiting for him though, and caught him with an uppercut, but not before the man hit him with a bone-crunching cross that took him hard in the right eye. It pulled the power from Casey's blow, and he went down to his knees. Pamela let out a small cry, turning her face into Pat's chest, so she wouldn't have to see anymore. Pat put his arms around her, and patted her back.

"He'll be fine, Pamela."

Pat smelled comfortingly of ginger biscuits and *eau de baby*—talcum, pureed apple and nappy rash ointment. She inhaled a whiff of it, and tried not to count how many heartbeats it had been since Casey had gone down.

"He's up," Pat said, a few seconds later, rising a little on his toes, an electric vibration coming off him. Men and fighting, Pamela thought, resolutely keeping her eyes shut. Even a peace-loving soul like Patrick was susceptible to the lure of it. Then again, Tomas had said Pat was quietly ferocious in court. Perhaps it was in their genetics—to fight in whichever arena presented itself as most suitable.

Fighting the urge to stop up her ears with her fingers, she chanced a peek at the fight and saw the two men were now clasped in a bloody embrace, pushing at each other, exhaustion clearly encroaching on them both. Then Casey reared back with an effort of will that was visible in every line of his body. She hid her face in Pat's coat sleeve again. After that it was just sound—the brutal wet smack of flesh on flesh, fists hitting resistant force, and the occasional grunt of either pain or effort.

A narrow eternity passed over her then, time both compressed to this bloody bit of ground, and expanded so that it seemed it might never end, and she would be here hoping Casey survived, so that she might have the pleasure of killing him herself.

"It's over," Pat said, unable to quell a certain jubilation in his voice. "Damn, that was a fight!"

"Is he okay?" she asked, not daring to look up yet.

"Aye, he won, he's fine. He's knocked the other fella down, an' the man's not gettin' up."

She looked then, and saw Casey standing, blood and sweat liberally coating him, but standing, nevertheless.

"Oh, thank God," she said, rather fervently. Black spots danced in front of her eyes and she bent over to catch her breath and alleviate the dizziness.

"Uh-oh," Pat said, putting a hand to her shoulder. "He's seen me."

She stood up, edging back in behind Pat and peeking out around him. Casey was walking toward them, a questioning look on his face. When she moved out of Pat's shadow, shock transformed his features and he started to walk faster, long legs eating up the ground between them.

She suddenly wished she had taken Pat's advice and stayed in the car.

"Patrick, what the hell were ye thinkin' bringin' her out here?"

"Have ye met yer wife, man? I either came with her or she was comin' here alone. Which would ye have preferred?"

"All right, point taken." Casey turned to her at this juncture, a hint of worry playing about his eyes. "Are ye all right?" he asked.

"Yes, I'm fine," she said, tightly.

"Are ye, then?" he asked, and his tone was not quite as gentle as it had been a moment before. "The both of yez, come with me, if ye don't mind."

Pamela's eyes met Pat's and he shrugged and smiled. It was reminiscent of the times when they'd first met and found themselves in hot water with both Casey and Jamie for one of their escapades.

He led them away from the fire and the crowd of men, to the side of an old Bedford truck which had been converted into a caravan of sorts. A sign hung over the door of the box, bearing the name *The Flying Tortoise*.

"I really wish ye hadn't come here," Casey said, looking over his shoulder at the crowd of increasingly rowdy men, some of whom were clearly already deep in their cups and spoiling for violence of their own. He shot a look at Pat, who merely looked back at him, though Pamela sensed there was a silent communication taking place, a method of one understanding the other which had been established when they were young boys. Casey's spoken comment, however, had been directed at her. And it was to this she responded.

"And I really wish I hadn't found you here."

Casey shook his head, the distant fire touching his face with its light, a battered warrior freshly emerged from battle. "I'm well used to these sorts of crowds, an' know what to expect from them. But it's not a right place for a woman, particularly not you, Jewel."

"But it's a right place for you?" she asked, a fine, needling anger pushing up and out through her fear.

"Aye, in the moment it is. But we'll talk about this later, if ye don't mind."

"Later?"

"Aye, later. I've a bit of business to attend to, an' I'd like ye to wait, if ye don't mind."

She crossed her arms over her chest and took a long breath in through her nose. "What is it I'm waiting for?" she asked.

He leaned toward her then and the smell of blood and fire and a body put to its physical limits hit her in the face. It was an utterly primitive and male scent, and her skin rippled in response to it.

"Me," he said, "will that do?" The dark eyes locked with hers, another question in them which had more to do with the night, and what he could all too clearly feel from her body.

"Yes," she said, backing up from him a little, "that will do."

"Good, I'll only be a few minutes. Use this key, an' let yerself into the trailer. An' try to behave yerself while I'm gone." Casey cupped her face in his hands, gave her a lingering kiss and then was gone back into the crowd of blood-thirsty men.

"Are ye certain ye're all right?" Pat asked, looking after his brother, who was now making his way through the crowd, hands slapping his back, others trying to hand him drinks. "I think I might head back, it's clear the two of ye need some time alone. Do ye need me to pick up the children?"

"No, Pru is with them, so they'll be fine. If you could maybe call her, in case I don't make it back home until late, that would be much appreciated."

"I'll do that," he said. "Are ye certain ye're all right, then?"

"Yes, I'm fine. I wouldn't put odds on your brother's health by night's end, though," she said grimly.

"I hate to leave ye here, if ye're upset," Pat said, taking one last stab at keeping the peace.

"Lord knows, I'm used to it. Then again, so is he," she said, in an attempt at charity, thinking Pat was more likely to leave her if he thought she was of a mind to forgive his brother.

"Well, if ye say so," Pat said, a note of wry amusement in his voice. "I'll just have a word with Casey, an' then I'll be off."

She hugged him, grateful as always for her steady-as-a-rock brother-in-law who was also her dear friend. Without Pat, the last few years of her life would have been far more difficult.

Pat went then, into the night beyond the fire and the scents of blood and smoke. She found herself oddly nervous once he left, and so used the key Casey had given her to let herself into the caravan.

Once inside, she sat down in the hope of stilling her jumpy nerves. When that didn't work, she rose and peered out the window over a wee sink, bracing her hands on the smooth wooden counter. There was little to see, however, just the fire and the odd man who walked through its light, there for a few seconds, and then swallowed by the night. The sound of motors starting up and then growling their way off into the night began. People were leaving. She supposed that was the way of it with fights—always the worry that police might arrive to break it up, for she knew a lot of money exchanged hands at these events, if something so brutal could be called such, and she had no doubt this was Casey's reason for risking his neck by participating.

She looked about and found matches in one of the drawers, then lit a small kerosene lantern which hung on a hook near to the bed. It was laid out in a similar fashion to other caravans she'd been in, with the bed built into the overhang, which sat on the roof of the Bedford's cab.

Once the lantern flared into life, she took a good look around. Creamy yellow curtains, flocked with tiny red poppies hung over the windows, and a deep red quilt, embroidered all over with tiny bees, covered the bed. The inside of the box had been lined with pine, stained a warm and mellow amber. Everything in the trailer fit just so: the perfectly proportioned cupboards, the narrow windows which flanked the door on either side, reflecting the small flame of the kerosene lantern which was now well caught and dancing merrily. In one corner was a blue enamel heater, something from the Victorian age, set up on a riser, with a surround of blue delft tile, to protect the rest of the trailer from the heat. It was a very cozy space, and she wondered to whom it belonged. Perhaps the man Casey had gone off to see, no doubt to collect on his winnings, she thought.

Casey came into the caravan then. The look on his face was one of wariness, the brutal man out by the fire, seemingly gone. He was wet, and had a shirt on now, crumpled and damp but covering up some of the blood and bruising. His hair gleamed blue-black in the light of the caravan, droplets of water still caught here and there in his curls. He'd clearly had a wash during his absence.

"I'm sorry," he said, standing back by the door, "that ye had to witness that."

"Really?" she said, her tone as tart as a green apple. "You didn't look the least bit sorry out there. You looked like you were having a helluva good time."

Casey smiled at her, splitting his lip and causing a rivulet of blood to flow down his chin. He wiped it away, reminding her of the gesture out by the fire.

"Aye, I enjoy it, but I don't like you seein' me like that."

"I guess that's why you didn't bother to tell me about it," she said, trying not to give in to her temper.

"Aye, that's exactly why I didn't tell ye. I didn't want ye here."

"Oh, I see. Well, I'll go then."

"Will ye? How are ye plannin' to get home? I believe Pat took the car ye came in. Besides, now that ye're here I'd just as soon keep ye."

"Would you?" she asked, partly in challenge, as her fear had now turned to a full-blown anger with him for the stupidity of fighting. He couldn't afford those blows to the head, and he knew it.

"Aye," he said, and stepped forward, "I would. D'ye mind that?"

There was little point in lying to the man, for he had long known the effect he had on her.

"No, I don't mind that," she said, voice still somewhat testy.

"D'ye think ye'd feel friendlier if ye had a drink?" Casey asked, his own voice slightly acerbic.

"No," she said shortly. "Now, sit down because your wounds need tending. Is it too much to hope that there's alcohol and a few bandages around here?"

"There's a medical kit in the drawer beside the wee sink," he said, as he sat on the bench near the table, "but I'm fine, I don't need bandages. The whiskey is in the cupboard above me—a shot or two of that wouldn't go amiss right now," he finished, putting a hand to his eye and prodding it experimentally. No doubt, she thought, to see if the bloody thing was still attached to his head.

"I'll decide that," she said briskly, opening the drawer he'd motioned to and pulling out a small canvas bag. Inside was tape, a bottle of witch hazel, a few rolls of bandages, a small pair of scissors and a bottle with what appeared to be painkillers. She poured some water—the sink as it turned out was attached to a full tank—into a basin which she'd found under the aforementioned sink and wet the corner of a towel, in it. "Now, take your shirt off—and you needn't grin like that, you're not going to enjoy this next bit."

"Oh, I know, Jewel, but a man lives in hope."

"Jesus Christ, Casey Riordan," she said as she looked over the variety of injuries he'd incurred in the fight.

"Is it really so bad that ye have to blaspheme?" he asked, only half in jest.

"You have to ask? Or is it a case of no sense, no feeling?"

"I didn't mean to scare ye, an' don't bother denyin' it either. Ye only get this mean when ye're good an' frightened."

There was a light rap at the door just then, and Casey called out, "Come in."

A head poked in and a smile lit up a face that was rather battered looking, but nonetheless charming. Three gold teeth winked at her in the lantern light and the owner of said teeth nodded his head to her in greeting, though he looked rather startled to find that Casey wasn't alone.

"Ah, I see ye're well looked after," he said, clearly drawing inferences as to her presence here with a half-naked Casey.

"Come on in, Llew," Casey said, peering around the cloth Pamela was dabbing his eye with. "She'll not bite ye, though I'll not give odds on whether ye'll get hit."

The man stepped up into the narrow confines of the trailer, and tossed something into Casey's lap. "There's the purse, man. Thank ye kindly because I made a small fortune off ye tonight."

Pamela felt Casey stiffen as the words came out of the man's mouth. She took a long breath in through her nose, and poured some witch hazel onto the towel. Casey exclaimed as she applied it to the bruise over his ribs.

"Jaysus woman, I think the bastard out there was gentler with me than ye're bein'."

"Sorry," she muttered, and didn't miss the raised eyebrow Casey directed at her.

"Pamela, this is Llewellyn Ward, also known as Gypsy Boy. Llewellyn, this is my wife, Pamela."

"Yer wife?" Llewellyn's eyebrows shot up in surprise. "Well, I'm right pleased to meet ye, Mrs. Riordan." He took her hand and bowed over it, kissing it and then standing up with a graceful flourish. He grinned then, flashing the gold teeth at her. A charming rogue—it was little wonder, she thought with a bit of cynicism, that he and Casey got on so well.

"Llew saved my life one night in San Francisco. I'd not be here now, if it wasn't for him."

"Well, yer man here gave me the fight of my life," Llew said, "I figured I owed it to him to save his life, an' keep his skin for another scrap like that one. Didn't care for the man tryin' to kill him either, so it was really no kind of decision at all."

"And why was someone trying to kill you?" Pamela asked, seeing this as the salient point.

"Ah, well, that's a story for some other time," Casey said, realizing belatedly, it seemed, that he had taken the lid off the worm can, and that several worms had wriggled out, leaving them on view and open for discussion.

"Well, then, I think I'll leave yez to it," Llew said, with an air of a man relieved to be exiting the scene, "Casey, if ye want any more fights ye know where to contact me."

Casey looked up at Pamela, giving her a look of not terribly convincing contrition. "Aye, I know, but I'm thinkin' this will be my last fight, Llew. Best of luck on yer travels, man."

Llew smiled at Pamela. "Oh, I think ye're the one needin' the luck just now, man. Good night to you, Mrs. Riordan, sure an' it was a pleasure to meet ye."

"You as well," she said with what grace she could summon up, though in truth she could tell he was someone she would quite like given more than a glancing acquaintance.

"If ye have somethin' to say, darlin' it's probably best ye go on ahead an' say it. I'm beaten to a pulp here, ye might as well get yer licks in too."

Pamela's only reply to this was a rather haughty, *"Hmmphmm."*

Casey sighed, sounding a bit like a man thoroughly taxed. "Go ahead an' say it. Ye'll damage yer spleen otherwise."

"Say what?" she asked, though she knew full well what he meant. She was just unable, as of yet, to find the exact words she needed to fully express the mixture of emotions she'd felt out there watching him take punches that might have killed another man.

"I'm thinkin' the gist of it would be that ye consider me a buck eejit an' a few other choice adjectives as well. I've no doubt the list of names ye have for me is a long one." He braced himself as she moved toward him with a pad for his eye.

"You can put ridiculous on that list," Pamela said, applying the pad which she'd soaked in witch hazel with more zest than was strictly necessary, causing Casey to draw in a long hissing breath. "And while you're at it—idiotic, bull-headed, masochistic lump-headed fool."

"I believe," Casey said mildly, "ye'll find most of those words mean the same thing—stubborn an' stupid."

"If the shoe fits," she retorted and poured more witch hazel onto the cloth. She cleaned the two abrasions he had on his left shoulder—one looked like the other man had gouged him with his nails, and Casey drew in a long hissing breath as she cleaned it out. Then she carefully rubbed a bit of arnica cream into the spots where she could see bruises rising, red and black. He held himself stiffly, but remained silent through the rest of her ministrations.

Once she was done, she came around the front of him, and eyed him up, assessing if there was anything she'd missed which needed immediate attention.

Casey looked up at her and spoke. "Will ye touch me, Pamela? Without the witch hazel or the towel—just touch me." There was a look of such intense vulnerability in his face that she bit back any sharp retort which might have sprung to mind.

"Of course," she said, softly, and put her hands on his shoulders before bending over and kissing his face on each bruised and bloody bit.

"Come here," he said, and pulled her into his lap. "This moment right here is what I used to want after fights."

"This?"

"Aye, you sittin' near me, touchin' me. I always longed for ye, Jewel," he said softly, "but sometimes after a fight the feelin' was particularly sharp, just wantin' to be touched with tenderness an' love. Wantin' a woman's touch—well, *my* woman's touch to be exact."

"I'm sure there were women who would have been happy to provide that touch," she said, and her tone, like the witch hazel, was more than slightly astringent.

"Well," he gave her a dark look, "that was my point. There were but it didn't matter because it was you I was needin' not them."

"Oh, there were other women, were there?"

"Aye, but it doesn't signify."

"It might signify to me," she said, wriggling a little in his grasp.

"No, it doesn't," he said and took her mouth with his, giving her a practical demonstration of his words about just how little she need worry about other women.

She leaned her forehead against his, breathless, her entire body tingling. The swift pulse of his blood echoed in her veins; to touch him was to know her own truth.

"Only you, for all my life," he said softly. "It's that simple for me, Pamela."

"I meant what I said to you that night in Wicklow," she replied, "you're my man, no one else, just you."

He kissed her again, and she tasted blood on her tongue. The fear fluttered inside her, the way it used to all the time when he was gone—like a black-winged bird, trapped within her chest.

"Did you do it for the money?" she asked, worried that he felt he couldn't look after them until he had enough put by to cover all the bills, and finish paying out the house.

"Aye, it's partly the money—there's somethin' in particular that I need it for, an' I'd like to talk to ye about that some time soon. The other part of the answer is that I like it, I like the way it feels in the moment. It's a rush, I don't even feel the pain until afterwards."

"Casey, you know I am making money now, enough for us to cover all our bills and maybe with the next book, we'll even be able to pay out our house and property."

"I know ye do, but that's not quite the point, Pamela."

"Then what is the point?"

He shrugged, and then winced as the movement caught his ribs. "It's just that I'd like to look after ye, if ye'll let me."

She looked at him, surprised at his words. "You have been looking after us," she said, though she hesitated under his gaze.

"Aye, the children but not you, Jewel. Ye haven't quite let me all the way back into yer life, an' ye know it."

She opened her mouth to protest, and then considered their vow of honesty.

"No, I haven't," she agreed.

"Will ye look at me, darlin'? I mean really look at me, an' let me say what I need to say to ye."

She met his eyes, feeling oddly nervous.

"I want ye to trust me as ye once did, Pamela. I want ye to see me as yer husband, an' the place in the world that is yer sanctuary an' home. We had that once between us, an' I don't think either of us can accept less."

"I'm afraid," she said, tears rising and spilling down her face.

"I know ye are. I am too. I had no memory, no place in the world, an' not even a name to call my own, an' yet I never felt as vulnerable then as I do when ye look at me as ye are right now."

"It's not like either of us are butterflies that have been cocooned for the last three years, Casey. We've both changed and in my case, it's likely not all for the better. I felt like something hardened in me when you were gone," she said, looking down and away from him. "I'm afraid that if that core melts and you don't stay, I won't survive it this time. I have three children to raise and I can't afford to break."

"Oh, Pamela," he said and sighed. "*We* have three children to raise—and in the interest of full accuracy, when I say *we* I mean you, me an' Jamie."

"You're truly fine with that?" she asked, uncertain it was wise to ask, but needing the truth from him, nevertheless.

"I'll not say I don't have my moments, but he is Kathleen's father, an' I would not take that away from any man—I know too well the pain of it."

"You were always their father, even when you were gone, Casey."

"But I can't grab back those years, I wasn't there for the changes and troubles those three years brought to you an' them. That is lost an' always will be."

She took his face in her hands, and looked into his eyes. "We'll find it again, it's not lost, it was only misplaced for a bit."

"This is it, Pamela, us stripped down. You an' me. This isn't about the children, or Jamie or anything else. It's just us an' I need ye to trust me with yer whole self. Even the terrified bits of ye."

"I do, Casey. I always have. I need to learn to trust myself again, though, and that may take a little longer."

"Aye, I understand that, only ye can allow me to be strong for ye now an' again, no?"

"I think it's going to be the reverse," she said, dabbing at his lip, where a bright drop of blood was forming. "Just now, you're the one who needs looking after."

"Ye've a point there, but by tomorrow I ought to be able to at least drive ye home."

"Tomorrow?" she said. "I need to get back tonight. Besides, where would we stay?"

"Right where ye're sittin' woman. There's a bed an' food, an' a fire—not much more we could need. I spoke with Pat before he left, he'll let Pru know we'll be home tomorrow."

"Don't they," she nodded toward the few people still left outside, "need to take this truck with them?"

"Ah no," Casey said, "it's part of my winnins'. This is ours, Jewel."

"It's ours?"

"Aye, I thought it might be wise to have a movable home for the present time, an' I thought the children might find it excitin' to travel in it. As it turns out, it comes in rather handy tonight, because there's no bloody way I can drive this beast all the way back home on dark country roads. I need to have a quick chat with Llew—an' no, it's not to arrange any more fightin'. After that, I am goin' to need to eat. Would ye care to join me for a late supper?"

She realized, now that her initial worry had died down, she was starving. "Yes, I would," she said.

"All right, wait here for me. The kettle's there if ye want tea an' ye'll find all ye need in the cupboards, it's well kitted out. An' ye know where the whiskey is if ye think that might take the edge off yer nerves."

He gave her a quick kiss, and then was out the door.

What Casey had said struck her as deeply as a knife without a hilt—that while the children trusted him and had accepted him back fully, she had not. What she had said about not trusting herself was the truth; she was so afraid to simply let herself be within their relationship. Fear always wanted a corner, a bit of her held in reserve, as if somehow that would save her were something to happen to him again. It wouldn't—she knew that well enough. How he felt was also, she thought, in part a reaction to what he'd seen pass between her and Jamie in Finola's cottage. His history from the last three years wasn't on display for her constantly, hers was, and she understood how difficult that must be for him some days.

Casey was back within twenty minutes with an air of tension around him, which set her worry to spinning once again.

"We need to move down the road a ways. I know a wee bit of forest we can tuck up in for the night. It's only about five miles away, but that's likely far enough. I've got food too, but we'll eat when we arrive." He set an aromatic box upon the table, and her stomach growled in response. "Llew's mother made it."

"Far enough?" she echoed, worried now that they were courting danger merely by their presence.

"Aye, everyone else is movin' out, an' I don't want to be here alone, an' have the losin' man's family return an' find us on our own. I don't think they'll come back, but it's best to be safe rather than sorry."

Normally she thought, the drive might have taken fifteen minutes but in the Bedford it took double that. She was driving as Casey had hurt one of his wrists badly enough, during the fight, that he didn't trust it for driving any distance.

The truck lumbered down the narrow roads like a hippopotamus taking its sweet time walking a river bottom. Pressing her foot onto the gas pedal did little more than make the truck grumble and snort at her, before it settled back to its preferred speed. Casey, thank heavens, knew exactly where they were headed, and managed to guide her there with simple directions.

"Right here," he said, pointing to what appeared to her a solid wall of dark and murky forest. "I can manage from here, Jewel. Just switch seats with me, an' I'll drive it in."

He slid toward her, clearly intending that she should just climb over top of him, rather than get out of the truck. She merely arched an eyebrow at him, and got out of the truck, staying well within the arc of the lights so that the Bedford wouldn't accidentally wallow over her.

It was an oak forest with a smooth understory, and he pulled the truck in under a set of boughs that gave good shelter and camouflaged the vehicle from the road, lest anyone should happen past. That Casey had known this place, and seen it as a good hiding spot gave her a frisson of unease. She had noted this more than once since his return—this understanding he had of the landscape in terms of boltholes. Hiding out tonight seemed a wise idea, she had to admit, particularly considering the purse of money Llew had paid out to him, and she was glad to be away from the field where the smell of blood and fire had lingered in the air.

There were times she thought that another land, another home was, indeed, what they needed, a fresh start in a place where Casey could relax his vigilance. Yet, the very notion of leaving their wee house in the hollow—the first real home Casey had known since he'd lost his father and gone to prison all those years ago—made her heart ache. It wasn't just Casey, of course, about whom she had concerns.

Casey jumped down out of the truck, wincing a little as his feet hit the forest floor. He went around to the sides of the box, and closed the shutters, fastening them against any telltale gleam of light. Then he opened the door to the box, and gestured to her to precede him in. She got in with relief, grateful to be away from the field where the fight had taken place, and to have shelter from the night. Casey re-lit the lamp and then set to making a fire in the blue enamel heater.

Now that they were alone and safe, it had a bit of a fairy tale feel to it—the caravan interior with the shutters closed and the lantern lit, the stove humming away, taking the chill from the interior. Their dinner had chilled on the drive, but it was the work of a few moments to warm the food—colcannon and sausages, brown bread with butter and a bottle of ale for each of them. She found tea in the cupboard above the sink, and made it while Casey parceled out the food onto two plates. Then they sat across from one another tucking in with good appetites.

She watched him as he ate, assessing his bruises now that he was relaxed and her anger had cleared off. She felt vaguely troubled still, as it struck her that he had always been this man—a man for whom fighting was innate, a man for whom blood and pain were mere matters of course. This just happened to be one of the few times it had been right there in front of her where she could not avoid the understanding of either act or consequence. It disturbed her and yet she had always known it, lived with it, and accepted that the man he was out in the world, was only a small part of the man who came home to her at the end of the day.

He looked up suddenly, expression apologetic. "I'm sorry, I'm bein' a wee bit singleminded about my food here. I never eat before a fight, my stomach is too wambly. After though, I'm starvin'. What is it, Jewel?"

"What do you mean?" she asked, startled out of her thoughts.

"Well, I might not know ye as well as I once did, but I think I remember that particular look on yer face, an' it's not the expression of a woman thinkin' pleasant things."

"There are just times when I feel the gap of our time apart. All the things you were going through, all the experiences that I wasn't there for," she shrugged, "and it hurts because I can't change it, I can't turn back the clock and mend what's already gone."

He reached across the table and took her hand. "I know, it's a bit disconcertin' at times, isn't it? I feel the same. All the worry an' fear an' pain ye've struggled through these last few years—an' all of it because of me. I wasn't here to help ye or hold ye, an' there's times it gives me a hollow feelin' in my stomach just thinkin' about it."

"Me too," she said and didn't need to explain further what she meant.

The air around them shifted suddenly and she felt an overwhelming desire to just take him to bed, and heal him in that way if she couldn't in any other.

"Casey..." she began and then halted not knowing quite how to put into words what she was feeling.

He took the hand he still held and brought it to his mouth, kissing it, dark eyes locked with hers. It was the first time since the cottage in Wicklow that they'd been alone, and she saw the awareness of it in his eyes, just as she felt it throughout her body.

"I...shall we..." she began, feeling ridiculously self-conscious.

"Aye, let's," Casey said and rose, pulling her up with him.

The space was small, and so there was little room in which to maneuver. Casey made to take his shirt off, wincing as he raised his hands to his buttons.

"Let me," she said softly. She undid his buttons and then slid the shirt off his shoulders, running her hands along his arms. He smelled warmly of the soap he'd used to wash, though there was a faint tang of the fight on him still—fire, sweat and blood. His scent had always been a primal call which caused a fierce response in her body.

She turned then, giving herself a bit of elbow room in which to remove her clothes. She shimmied out of her pants, and then raised her arms to take off her sweater.

"Allow me," Casey said gallantly, and slid the sweater off over her head.

"Do you need help?" she asked, looking over her shoulder, as he attempted to unclasp the tiny hooks holding her bra together.

Casey gave a slight snort. "My wrist is injured, not broken, woman. I can manage." He did manage and in short order too. He leaned over then and kissed her shoulder, hands resting gently on her waist.

She shivered, feeling the heat of him all along her body.

"Are ye cold, darlin'?" he asked.

"No, not cold," she said.

"Well, ye've come out in goosebumps, so I think we should get ye into the bed."

She got in under the blankets, feeling strangely nervous, as though this man getting into the bed beside her was a bit of a stranger. It was, she thought, seeing him fight, and the raw brutality of that, and the clear hot joy he got from it, which had made her feel this way. And yet, as always, despite the nervousness, she was pulled to him, and lifted her face to his as he stretched out beside her.

He cupped her jaw with his good hand, running his thumb along the crest of her cheek and then pulled her toward him and kissed her softly. She could taste the blood on his lip, warm and salt, her tongue touching his lips gently. He drew in a sharp breath and she pulled back a little. "If you're tired—or just hurting," she said, "we don't have to do this." She was aware her words were less than convincing as her body arched toward his touch.

"Don't blaspheme, woman. Lord only knows the next time we'll be alone with the freedom to do as we like for a few hours."

They did, indeed, have the luxury of time, and yet there was still a fierce urgency in her just to join with him, and surrender to the furious blood-rushing tide of it. It reminded her of their first months together, and how she had been both frightened and giddy with the intensity of what they had found together in bed. She had asked him then if it was normal—what they had—and remembered now his answer.

"Will it always be this way, do you think?" she asked quietly. "I mean I don't know, I haven't ever been with anyone before, but this—us, how things are in bed, can it possibly stay this way?"

He regarded her in the dim. "I love that ye can look me straight in the eye an' ask such a question, an' yet ye blush over the simplest things. An' the answer is—I don't know, but I'll be honest, usually it settles a bit an' the fire dies back enough so that ye feel like ye won't get burned whole in it. But I don't think that will happen with us. I know ye don't have anything to compare this to, but it's somethin' else altogether, I've never known it to be this way. I feel like I could make love to ye thousands of times, an' still want ye like a man on fire wants water."

"I used to dream about this—havin' ye touch me after a fight." Casey said, pulling her back to the here and now as he settled into the pillows and drew her over on top of him. "D'ye mind? I don't think my wrist will bear up with me bein' on top."

"No, I don't mind," she said. "You did—dream about this?"

"Aye, I'd lie in bed at night an' try to will ye back to my memory, an' recall what yer touch felt like on my body. Though it's clear to me now that whatever memory I had, is a pale thing in comparison to the reality."

"Well, you don't have to remember now," she said, lowering herself onto him with a sigh made of equal parts desire and longing—longing to go back in time and take his pain between her two hands and so banish it from him forever.

"Remember?" he said, putting his hands to her hips and looking up at her with his good eye. "Darlin', I can't even think right now, much less remember."

"I should have put the light out," she said, then took in a sharp breath as he moved under her. She reached out for the lantern, but Casey took her hand, halting her.

"No, don't, Jewel. I want to see ye. I went such a long time without ye, let me look my fill now."

She touched his chest, careful to avoid his ribs. It was still a wonder to have him once again, and she felt a profound gratitude for it as she ran her free hand from chest to stomach. A wonder to touch his flesh and feel the muscle and bone beneath it that worked with such grace-filled symmetry. The brute display of which, tonight, had been shocking, and yet at the base of her shock had been this—desire, pure and unfettered—desire for this strength moving inside her, causing her head to fall back on her neck and her body to become pure sensation. Casey's hand still held hers, and the other was on her hip, guiding her with sure possession.

"Pamela, I need ye to look me in the eyes." His voice was soft and yet the demand there was clear.

She looked and immediately regretted it. Looking in his eyes was like gazing into a mirror which went down forever—a mirror of the last three years, and it was all there for her to see so clearly—the pain it had caused him and the pain she had felt during his entire absence. The sensation took her breath, piercing her to the heart. She closed her eyes again, wanting to simply be lost in their physical joining. But Casey was not one to be denied what he wanted.

"Let go," he said softly, so softly she thought she'd misheard him but then he said it again, moving against her with force. "Let go. Ye need not be afraid, for I'll catch you when ye fall."

A small jolt of anger shot through her—he *would* push her beyond the boundaries of self, he had always known how to do this with her. But she understood how to do the same with him. It was part of what made this so difficult.

"Jewel," he said, even more insistently this time, "look me in the eyes and let go."

It was clear to her what he was asking with those simple words. He wanted her trust again, absolute and complete. He wanted *her* completely and it was his right. He had never lost her trust but he was reaping the harvest of her grief and the two things likely felt much the same to him. And so she looked down.

His eyes shimmered in the low light of the caravan, and she couldn't tell if it was her tears or his that she saw. Those dark eyes had always seen too much and now they held her fast, pinned like a butterfly to this page of their life together. He would have her back whole, or he would not have her at all.

"I'm afraid," she said, holding his arms, the pulse of his blood swift and warm against her palms.

"Aye, love, I know. I am too, but there's no other way forward for the two of us. Ye know that just as I do."

She nodded, wanting nothing more than to turn her gaze away from his, but knowing she was powerless to do so. Despite her worry she wanted what he did. To let go of the fear and fall into this and find herself whole in his arms once again.

Even as his eyes kept faith with hers, he kept moving, touching, driving her before him on a peak of desire so sharp it bordered the line between pleasure and pain.

"Oh God, Casey," she whispered, and felt the old fear blossom red and full inside of her—fear that she would lose him again, and this time would die from the pain of it. "Promise you'll catch me."

"I promise," he said, and then she let go, the fear swept away in the deluge of both love and desire, and knew herself stripped before him, in both soul and body, as he was to her. And then the current took them both away, so that they might find the shore together.

Chapter Forty-one

Impenetrable Night

THE HOUSE UPON THE HILL was dark, and Pamela felt a shiver of worry pass over her merely at the look of the place. Mind you, the house always seemed a bit cold and lifeless when Jamie wasn't in residence. Maggie tended to keep to her section of the house during the evenings. She had a set of rooms off the kitchen—a bedroom with a sitting room and bathroom, kitted out for her convenience and comfort. She couldn't hear the doorbell though, so Pamela thought it best to go round the back of the house. If Violet was at home, she would rather not run into her. In fact, just at present she wanted to get back in the car and drive home, but she knew Kathleen would be inconsolable without her blanket and giraffe, and so needs must and all that, when the tiny red-headed teething devil was in the driver's seat.

However, when she knocked on the back door there was no answer and the kitchen was dark, as well as the windows in Maggie's rooms.

She trekked back around the house to the front, girding up her courage lest Violet answer her summons. Jamie had long ago given her keys to the house, but she didn't feel it was right to use them when another woman lived here.

Much to her consternation however, a key was not necessary, for the front door was ajar; the hall beyond it as dark as fifty black cats in a bag. The shiver of worry was now a full shudder and it pushed her into the house.

She called out as she entered, peering into rooms as she passed. A terrible hush held the house, and she thought perhaps no one was here. Which made the open door that much more troubling.

There was a faint light coming from the far end of the house, where Jamie's study sat. She breathed a sigh of relief, and made her way along the hall, the stones freezing beneath her feet.

The study door was half-open, the glow of light a tiny oasis in the dark house. She stepped through the door, spotting Kathleen's blanket and giraffe immediately. Both items were on the chair which Jamie and Kathleen sat in to read at night. She crossed the room to grab the blanket, stuffed the giraffe into her coat pocket and made for the door, worry at being caught here flaring her nerve endings like matchsticks against flint. But something halted her before she could step back out into the hall. This had long been her favourite room in the house and where she had felt safe and secure, though that was down to Jamie's presence more than anything constructed of stone and glass. It had been both a space of refuge and sanctuary to her, but tonight it felt off, wrong somehow, as if a dark being, something squat and glistening, sat upon the shelves, hidden in amongst the books.

The small lamp Jamie kept on his desk was burning, the light pooling across a ruffle of disordered papers. This in itself was odd, as no one used the room in his absence. Generally he kept it locked when he was away, and she had often teased him about it being his own version of Bluebeard's chamber.

She walked over to the desk, the papers striking a note of familiarity—Jamie's writing, that elegant scrawl something she'd seen almost every day for years now.

Something Jamie had once said to her long ago, came back to her now, about how the poet's job was to write sanctuary for the suffering of others, to give them a map out of that blue chamber of mind, and ease their pain. He'd laughed at the end of the conversation and said, "The problem is I forgot to make a map for myself. I don't know the way back anymore."

The scattered pages held random lines of poetry, small boldly-lined sketches of a boat, an owl, a bog pimpernel. Diagrams of things—a plane engine, a cutaway of an *amanita muscaria*, a plan for a treehouse. Lines of story—bits of silver and gold, amber and sapphire, flung upon the page; a rain of stars and coal fallen at the same time, making for something both brilliant and dark; strings of equations, in long, arcing lines. Jamie found math comforting, though personally she had never understood the allure. There was correspondence begun and not finished. And it struck her then, none of it was finished—not the equations, not the poetry, not the drawings. Most of it was haphazard—jewel-bright with brilliance, but unfinished—unfinished and disordered. She thought back to the night he'd had her and Casey sign the papers, and sat down in his chair with a thump. He'd been right on the cusp of hypomania and she'd merely thought he was tense. Because, of course, that's what he'd wanted her to think.

Now, he was God only knew where, ready to take a tumble head first into the darkness of the abyss.

"Oh, Jamie," she said softly, and the mere sound of her own voice spooked her. The house was far too still. A shadow flickered across the opposite wall, as though someone had moved behind her, swift and light on their feet. She stood, whirling around, but there was only the study windows, the outside filled with impenetrable night, with a tiny flicker of gold in the centre of each pane, reflecting the lamp light on the desk. Still, she was certain someone was out there, someone who could see her standing now in the pool of light, outlined against the dim of the study. It felt as though the air turned gelid around her, and she wanted to turn away, to run as fast as she could for that open door out into the night. A ripple ran from the crown of her head to the soles of her feet, along with the sensation that she was looking into a pair of eyes she could not see.

And then the feeling was gone, as if whoever stood out there had moved on into the dark. Her eye fell upon the telephone which sat on Jamie's desk, an article which was more ornamental than strictly useful, being that trying to hear someone on the other end, often felt akin to using string and two tin cans to communicate across the Atlantic. Still, she picked it up and was greeted with dead silence. Her sense of dread grew and she put the telephone down, rising with a wrench that was more mental than physical. She moved out from the study and down the dark hall. Nothing stirred, not so much as a mouse, and the cold clung to her skin, settling in wintry feathers at the base of her spine.

"Maggie?" she called out. "Violet?"

The kitchen was cold and dark, two things she'd never before known it to be. The cold feathers in her spine had turned to frost, sheathing her nerves and climbing in cold lattices up her back.

Maggie wasn't in her comfortable rooms off the kitchen. Her bed was neatly made, her ancient sweater hung on its hook behind the door, and everything else was in its usual order, but the rooms spoke, in both temperature and energy, of its occupant having been gone for a few days at least. That explained the chill in the kitchen and the sparkling clean counters and sink. Still, Violet and Kolya ought to be using the kitchen, though perhaps, they too, were not in residence.

If it wasn't for the front door being ajar, she might have left then, just minded her own business, taken Kathleen's blanket and giraffe and gone home to security, warmth and light. Instead, she found herself mounting the stairs, the chill of the house grasping with cold fingers, deep into her stomach.

The upstairs was dark too, and just as cold as the lower floor. A bit of light spilled through the doorway of Jamie's bedroom. His room looked out over the yard, and so caught a little of the paddock lights. She moved toward that bit of light, clutching Kathleen's blanket to her chest.

That was where she found her—Jamie's wife. Violet. The light from the window touched her hair, a deep ruby in the dim. She lay at the foot of the bed, skin white as marble. When she drew close, Pamela saw that her hair was deep ruby because it was soaked with blood. It pooled out around her, wicking into the weave of the cerulean blue rug. Pamela leaned down, numb with shock, and touched her fingers to the woman's neck. It was futile though, for the neck had been cut, nearly to the backbone. Here in the strange twilight created by the distant lights of the paddock, the bone glowed like pearl in the midst of such savagery. The flesh was cold and flaccid. Through her work photographing corpses, she'd long been familiar with the things death wrought upon the body. First cold and the pooling of blood, and then rigor mortis, and finally this, the chill and inert flesh that came when the soul flew free of its earthly confines. Violet was gone. Jamie's wife was dead.

Pamela felt a surge of sickness, and stepped back from the body.

Kolya. She had to go find the boy. Please God, let him be asleep and blissfully unaware of what had taken place under this roof. She half ran, half stumbled down the hall, the distance to Kolya's room seeming ridiculously far. Her hand was trembling when she touched the door knob, but she turned it and went in, knowing this was no time for hesitation.

He was in his bed; she could see the glimmer of his hair in the aurora of the nightlight. He lay perfectly still, his mouth a round 'o' of deep sleep. Please God, let it be the stillness of sleep. Kolya, she knew from long experience, tended to toss himself all over the bed at night, ending up at the foot with his legs hanging off. Just now, he was tucked perfectly under his royal blue quilt, without so much as a tiny pink foot sticking out. She swallowed, and reached down to touch the perfect little face, her heart hammering so loudly that it felt like it was outside of her, a great echoing drum. He didn't stir to her touch, but he was warm, and she felt breath upon her hand. She pulled back the covers, her eyes scanning him for any sort of injury. The child appeared whole, perfect, and unharmed.

"Kolya, sweetheart, wake up. It's Pamela, you need to come with me. I'm going to take you for a sleepover with Isabelle, all right?" She spoke carefully, not wanting to betray so much as a note of panic in her voice.

Kolya's eyes fluttered open, and he smiled at her, clearly still lost in dreams. Perhaps that was best. She wrapped him in Kathleen's blanket and then lifted him up. He put his arms around her neck, and tucked his sleep-heavy head into her shoulder. Kolya was a solid child and she hoped she could get him down the stairs and out of the house without needing him to walk.

They passed Jamie's bedroom on the way to the stairs, and she forced herself past the open doorway without so much as a glance. She didn't need to look, after all, the sight of Violet's open throat and eyes were burned into the synapses of her brain.

Down the stairs she went, one arm firmly around Kolya's bottom, and the other cradling his head. The door was still ajar, cold air streaming through it, and the land outside as silent as the house.

She made it to the car in record time, puffing a little as Kolya was about as easily carried as a sack of cement. Thankfully, the back doors of the Citroën no longer locked, so she didn't have to fumble with keys to get Kolya into the car. He slept through it all—laying him down, pulling the blanket up around his ears, and then her futile attempts to start the car. For the car, having seen her through bullets, bombs and narrow escapes, had now decided to pack it in.

"You bloody bitch, not now!" She pounded the steering wheel in utter frustration. She was alone on this mountaintop with a small child, and a dead woman. The police needed to be called, but she remembered the dead silence of the telephone in Jamie's study. The line had been deliberately cut, of this she was certain, so going back to the house—something she would rather cut off her right hand than do—wasn't even an option. She turned the key four more times, and each time the car gave the same abbreviated cough before choking.

The drive down the hill normally took a good fifteen minutes, the walk carrying a child, would take the better part of the night. There was no choice about it, though, she needed to get herself and Kolya off this mountaintop.

She took the sleeping child out of the car, hefting him over her shoulder and starting down the drive, trying hard not to look behind her where the house loomed, and shadows flitted outside the windows.

It was cold, and snow started to fall before she was even fifty yards down the drive. Her breath showed in small, huffing clouds as she hurried along as best as she could, Kolya feeling as though he weighed as much as a good-sized log now, rather than a small bag of cement.

It would be best, she thought, to get off the drive, and out of plain sight from both the house and any traffic which might come up the road. The woods to either side of the drive were thick, but this near the road they were at least passable, though it was going to make the going that much slower. She couldn't risk the drive though, lest the person who'd killed Violet was still lurking on the property.

The little ditty that Isabelle often sang went through her head on repeat, and she paced herself to its quick rhythm. *'Frosty weather, snowy weather, when the wind blows, we all go together!'*

The repetitive simplicity of it calmed her a little, and she managed to take a breath and steady herself. She went on in this manner for some time, her arms and back aching as she stepped over root and rock, around trees and thick clusters of rhododendron. When her arms finally gave out, she was deep enough in the woods that she thought she could afford to rest for a few minutes. In front of her, there was a fallen beech, old and crumbling and blanketed in moss. It would be wet to sit upon, but a damp backside was currently the least of her worries.

She sat, pulling Kolya tight to her body, hoping to keep him warm, though he tended to pump out heat like a small and compact radiator, even in cold weather.

It occurred to her now, that she'd only encountered Violet face-to-face the one time—that fateful morning in Paris. Still, the image of the woman's face rose clearly before her, the open staring eyes, dark in the faint light of the room. The look of surprise on her face, as if she truly had not seen death coming until his scythe was at her throat. And who had wielded that scythe, and was he—this very minute—following them down the hill?

Another woman had died so, with her throat cut, bleeding out into the bed she had shared with Jamie, or rather, someone called Yasha, who had lived in another world, inhabiting the body of a man who she felt had existed somewhere beyond the Jamie she knew and loved.

His voice was there in her head suddenly, something he'd said that night in Finola's cottage. "I have her watched to make certain she doesn't try to leave the country with him, and she knows that. But if something should happen to her, I don't want Kolya to become a ward of the state. I have her watched. Where was the man Jamie had set to watch Violet? She shuddered—was there another body somewhere on this hilltop? The thought brought her to her feet; she had to keep moving. Hefting Kolya once again, she began to move as quietly as possible down the hill. A stick cracked under her boot, echoing like a gunshot. She froze, heart hammering, listening for any movement near her.

It was then she heard the sound of a vehicle moving slowly along the road, down from Jamie's house. Coming down the hill, not up it. She could have sworn there was no other car up on the top of the hill, though. Had someone hidden it behind one of the outbuildings? She was frozen in place, clutching the unconscious Kolya to her chest. If the two of them were found, she had no doubt they'd both be killed and in a wood this thick, possibly never found.

"Pamela! Pamela—are ye near?"

She nearly fell to her knees in fervent relief.

"Pamela, can ye hear me?"

"Oh God, Casey," she sobbed, stumbling in her haste toward that voice calling her name.

"Pamela!"

"Here," she croaked, praying that the sound had reached him.

He came crashing through the underbrush then, uncaring of noise and she took as many steps as she could, her knees signalling that they were going to give out any second now.

She nearly fell straight into him, tripping over a rock and plunging forward, propelled by the weight of the small boy in her arms. Casey grabbed her, halting her velocity abruptly.

"Oh Jesus, Pamela. I went up to the house lookin' for ye, an' saw the car. I went in—the front door was standin' wide, an' I was afraid somethin' terrible had happened."

"Something has," she said, and Casey held her more tightly, causing Kolya to finally squirm a little.

"I know, darlin'. I went upstairs. That's when I truly began to panic. What the hell happened?"

"I-I don't know. She was l-like that when I f-found her. Wh-where are the ch-children?" she asked, teeth chattering.

"Pru is with them, do ye not remember?"

"Y-yes of course."

"Come on, woman, let's get you an' the lad into the warmth of the truck."

The truck was still running, standing in the open road like a promise of sanctuary provided by a lantern in the dark. Casey had taken Kolya from her, and the boy was awake now, apparently unperturbed to find himself in a near stranger's arms, being placed in a strange vehicle.

It was with profound relief that she closed the door on the truck, and felt it begin to move under them. She just wanted to go home, and somehow scrub tonight's images from her head.

"Why were you up here?" she asked.

"D'ye have a notion how late it is, woman?"

"No," she said, for time had felt both microscopic and like the distance between stars since she'd entered the house.

"'Tis near to ten o'clock."

"What?" She'd gone into the house just after eight. Nearly two hours has passed.

"Aye, how long were you and the wee man in the woods?"

"Not that long, I wouldn't have thought," she said faintly.

Kolya sat up between her and Casey, copper hair a lick of flame in the low light from the dash.

"Where's my daddy?" he asked, small voice as imperious as that of a Russian Cossack.

"He's away, sweetheart. You're going to come stay at our house for a bit," she said, flicking a glance at Casey. His face was grim, and his gaze was fixed on the road ahead, but he nodded in answer.

"Where's Mama?"

Bile rose in her throat, as the vision of Violet was there once again in the forefront of her mind's eye.

"He was mad at her," Kolya said, and his voice was a little tremulous.

"What?" Pamela blurted out, a ripple of cold fear waving over her from the top of her head to her toes. What if the killer had seen Kolya and now considered him a witness?

"They were yelling. I got up," Kolya said, his little face looking up at her, pale and afraid. "I saw him in the hall. He was mad and yelling, and so was Mama. I went back to bed," he finished. "I'm hungry, can I have something to eat at your house?"

"Yes, sweetheart, you can have whatever you'd like to eat. Can you tell me, Kolya," she paused for breath, her heart pounding madly, "did you know the man, had you seen him before?"

Kolya nodded, blue eyes deep pools of utter seriousness. "It was my daddy."

"It can't be, it's simply not possible," Pamela said for what might have been the hundredth time.

They had been home for over an hour. Kolya had been fed, and then put to bed with Isabelle, who'd woken momentarily to give him a smacking kiss and then simply curled up next to him, and fallen directly back to sleep. Casey had called the police and they had said they would dispatch someone immediately to Jamie's house. Someone would also be coming to see them to take a statement.

Pru had to be told, and while the girl had taken it in with her usual equanimity, Pamela could see that she was truly upset by the news. To her, of course, Violet was a known quantity, someone she had interacted with on a daily basis, while looking after Kolya. She went to bed shortly afterwards, having said little, her freckled face stark with worry. They had resumed their conversation in low voices once her door had shut behind her.

"She'll have to stay with us for now," Pamela said, "she can't go back to Jamie's house."

"Aye, she will," Casey said, "I'd not want the child near the place just now anyway."

They'd gone over the details more than once, the way one did in the wake of such a horrifying event that one could not make sense of just yet.

"It's not like we can pretend we weren't there," Casey said, when Pamela had voiced fear around calling the police. "That damn lemon of a car breakin' down there, shows that ye were Johnny-on-the-spot, so to speak. Ye say she was cold when ye touched her?"

"Yes, cold and flaccid." She shivered, her fingers still prickling from when she'd touched Violet.

"For what it's worth, Jewel, I agree, the boy must be mistaken. Maybe he heard yellin' an' dreamed that Jamie had come home. As much as I'd like to besmirch the man at times, I still don't believe Jamie would do such a thing."

"Neither do I. I think whoever did it was still there on the grounds. I saw a shadow when I was in Jamie's study."

"Why were ye in the man's study? That's rather deep in the house, no?"

"Because I knew that's where Kathleen's blanket was likely to be." She forbore to add that she'd been sitting down perusing the man's papers when the shadow had passed over her.

"Tea or whiskey?" Casey asked, holding up the kettle and the bottle of Connemara Mist which was always kept on the sideboard.

"Tea," she said, "with equal parts whiskey."

"Done. Go on with yer story while I get it ready."

"I left the study and went to the kitchen, on the off chance that Maggie might be there. Then I went upstairs. The whole house felt off, but I knew that I had to check. Thank God I did. I can't fathom if Kolya had woken up and found his way to his mother."

"Poor wee man. We'll keep him then until Jamie can be found?"

"Yes, we'll have to, I think. He hasn't really got anyone else. This is why Jamie had us sign those papers. Besides, even if Finola could take him, that would still leave him vulnerable in my opinion. She's getting older and her cottage is too isolated. I'll have to call her as soon as I can. God, Casey—what if something has happened to her as well? I didn't even think about her until now."

"What were ye meant to do? Go harin' down there with the wee lad, an' hope she was home? Ye might have been followed in that direction too, woman, an' then ye'd have been stranded an' entirely alone. Headin' down the mountain was the best thing to do. I tell ye, woman, I'm not happy that whoever was up there tonight, saw you."

"Nor me," she said, taking the whiskey-laced tea as he handed it to her. She felt it still—the touch of that shadow, slipping over her, sliding through her. It was oddly intimate, in a way that froze her blood. One thing of which she was certain though, was that she had, however briefly, looked into the eyes of a killer.

Neither she nor Casey slept much that night, both of them restless and worried and half-expecting the police to arrive at any moment. They took turns rising and checking on the children, and Casey went downstairs a few times to check that all was still secure. She drifted into an uneasy sleep around three o'clock, her dreams riddled with shadowy figures standing outside her window, staring in at her. By six she'd had enough and rose to go downstairs, leaving Casey asleep, though she thought he'd only just drifted off.

Downstairs, the kitchen was warm in the grey still light of morning, the Aga having done its work of keeping the bottom floor temperate. She stirred up the fire, and the few dormant coals still slumbering, grumbled into life with a glowering of red and a desultory lick of flame. She set kindling on it, waited until it was well caught and then added two bricks of peat. Conor would be up soon, and he would want breakfast. She decided to make pancakes, and was just finishing up the batter when Finbar, still curled up by the fire, rose and began to growl, his hackles up and his teeth bared.

Last night Casey had loaded their ancient pistol, and put it in the cupboard next to the hearth. She paused on her way to the door, and retrieved it.

A knock came then, and Finbar burst into a frenzied barking and walked stiff-legged to the door, like he was tracking prey. She stretched up on tiptoe and looked out the peephole. Noah had installed it for her, a month or so before he died. She looked and sighed, letting the gun fall to her side.

On her doorstep stood Detective Will Holroyd.

Chapter Forty-two

Born Under Mercury

EVERYTHING WAS A SPIRAL. Or everything *was* spiralling—the snow, the stairs, his mind. He couldn't quite remember how he'd gotten here, racing up, up, up on a stairway which seemingly had no end.

It was as though he had been cast in a silent movie where there were no lines, no sound except breath, and the film—backdropped by the entire universe of the night—was missing frames every few seconds, a void opening with each gap, and he knew he was missing vital information, contained in those hollow spaces. Was he the hero or the villain? He didn't know. The script was simply blank page after blank page, filled with falling snow and the sound of his breath as he flew up the stairs, a few of which were missing, like teeth knocked out after a vicious fight.

The script as originally written had been simple—dangerous, but simple in its outlines. Mordecai would set up the place where Dmitri could meet with the car of a British diplomat on his way to Finland for the weekend. It would take Dmitri—their Russian diplomat who had spied on their behalf for years—out of the USSR. Dmitri would strip down, and get into the boot of the car, where he'd be covered in a blanket that would trap his heat and scent in the hopes of fooling the dogs that were used at the border. He'd have water, food and a bottle to piss in, and with luck, by the time he needed most of those things, they'd be well clear of the Finnish border. It was simplicity of a convoluted order as such things always were in the spy world, for it also contained other things—months of planning, smuggling messages, other spies standing in the cold on Tuesday evenings for a full four months, holding a chocolate bar and a shopping bag, waiting for a brush contact, in this case a simple note passed from agent to agent, with no more than the words, *I'm ready*, inscribed upon it.

The possible problems were endless in number. The Soviet Union was, for all intents and purposes, a large prison, with guards at every entry and exit, and razor wire in between. Its citizens were watched constantly, and none more so than former KGB officers, or those suspected of any sort of contact with the outside world. Dmitri, as a former diplomat, fell into this category. Paranoia was rife within the country, and so neighbour watched neighbour, spy watched spy, husband watched wife, and wife watched husband. To extract a man under those conditions was next to impossible. Next to impossible, but not entirely impossible, which is what had brought Jamie here this night, and stranded him inside a country he'd thought to never see again.

The Soviet border had extensive electronic systems and patrols to prevent escapes. Their surveillance began a great distance from the actual border itself. In the train stations *militsiya* monitored any traffic they found suspicious. The border zone began seventy-five miles from the actual border. A special permit was required for entry, and the first line of control was electronic alarms. At the thirty-seven mile mark there was a raked sand strip to detect footprints, and a tripwire. At the twelve mile mark there was a ten-foot barbed wire fence, with a top that curved inward. The fence too, was equipped with an electronic alarm system. It was, however, as Jamie knew from previous experience, not protected underground.

Added to all these barriers between a man and freedom was the fact that Finland had a longstanding agreement with the Soviet Union to return any fugitives that fell into their hands. He was one of those fugitives now. He was also on the inside of all those barriers.

Scripts could be subject to re-writes on the spot, even as the film was shot. It was re-writes, however, which tended to burn a man. Dmitri had decided at the last moment to bring along his family, despite fears that his wife might be a KGB agent, and this was where the script had gone completely awry. Dmitri's wife wasn't willing to come, and instead of staying with her and the children, Dmitri, in some fit of madness, had taken the youngest child with him and fled. Jamie still had to keep the rendezvous, lest the man was actually crazy enough to show up there. Which, as it turned out, he was.

The plan had been smuggled to Dmitri on a small sheet of cellophane, hidden under the endpapers of a volume of Shakespeare, something a diplomat could easily explain away after all his years in England.

Jamie had changed all the place names to those of cities in France—Moscow was Paris; Leningrad was Lyons, and so forth. That way if the KGB should find it in a search of Dmitri's flat, a false trail would have been laid. It wouldn't buy them a great deal of time, but it would, perhaps, be enough. He only prayed that Dmitri's wife wasn't privy to the details of the plan.

Despite dragging a child in his wake, Dmitri had managed to get out of Moscow. He'd done exactly as Jamie had instructed him—gone through shops, changed buses, gotten on and off at a variety of Metro stations, in and out through a few apartment buildings, all while carrying a small blonde child, which no doubt made him look like your average harassed father on an outing with his daughter. Then it had been a series of trains, and a very long walk along a disused rail line, with which Jamie was very familiar.

So Jamie, having to change the plans, and needing to meet with Dmitri so that he would know the new meeting spot, and having no time in which to arrange any of this knowledge being transferred, had done the one thing he swore he'd never do again—gone inside Soviet territory, improvising as he went. It had been like juggling knives from the get-go, along with some trickster handiwork involving official-looking documents, and a blistering hailstorm of Russian aimed at the border guards by which he needed to pass. Fortunately, the abandoned village he'd chosen was near to a remote crossing, with young and inexperienced soldiers, who succumbed to a man who seemed to have all documentation in order and was, so his extremely official-looking papers said, a highly placed military officer from Estonia. If he hadn't been in the pre-supernova phase of his mania, he didn't think he could have pulled it off. But in that state, his thoughts were not yet disordered, but came at the speed of light, so that he could stay several steps ahead, and bamboozle his questioners with a rapid barrage of linguistic fireworks, and the utter certainty in himself and his story that he could so easily display during hypomania.

The abandoned village was just inside of the border zone, and dated from the height of the Stalinist era, when communes of select workers had been settled together in various locations, many of them remote, so that there were towns devoted to the space program, to diamond and coal mines and to forestry. The villages had been abandoned and left to rot, though they were not talked about, being that it gave the lie to the face the Soviets wanted to present to the world of prosperity and ingenuity. Old apartment buildings long deserted, seemed, while spooky, a good place to hide and wait. From there it was only a short distance to the spot where Dmitri and his daughter—and now Jamie as well—would meet with a circus caravan, and be ferried out of the country, a plan which involved bears, something that had given Jamie more than a few qualms. The circus company was a small one which had been given special permission to perform in Finland. The bear trainer was his contact, and was someone Yevgena knew from a long time ago, someone she swore could be trusted. The caravan would pass within a half mile of this place, stopping for a rest and ostensibly to tend to the animals, a fair cover story should they be questioned.

Dmitri had managed to get to the abandoned village, despite the land around being covered in snow and mired in a thick evergreen forest. He and his daughter had gone into the apartment building which looked least likely to fall in on their heads. Exhausted and worn down with stress, Dmitri had fallen to sleep, waking a few hours later to find his daughter gone. After that, everything had gone agley, to paraphrase the Scottish poet.

The little girl, waking and finding her father unconscious had, as little children were wont to do, gone exploring. She was only four, but Jamie thought, a rather precocious four, as she had made her way to the next building, climbed the rickety stairs, and gotten herself out across a rotting roof, large sections of which were missing. She had to have walked the girders, and sections of the roof which were just barely hanging on. She was so light, it was just possible. But now she'd stranded herself, for when she'd turned and seen what she'd crossed, she had become paralyzed with fear. Four was a bit young for trying to rationalize her out of her fright, and so it had been clear that one of them had to fetch her. Given that Dmitri was far heavier than Jamie, the choice had been obvious.

All of this had brought them here to this night, with Dmitri on the top of one building and him here on the other, with a little girl's life in the balance.

So here he was, still a half mile from where the caravan would meet them, losing time, his mind white-hot with impractical solutions and frantically searching for a way out. If they could just get to the meeting point on time, he felt certain he could still make this plan work. He knew, though, if they were late that the circus would not wait, they couldn't. Anything untoward would raise suspicions and bring down attention on their heads that no one wanted. Particularly not a vagabond group of performers. If they didn't make their appointed meeting spot, they would be trapped inside the Soviet Union. For him this was no less than a death warrant. He'd escaped the USSR once, he did not think the odds of doing it again were in his favour.

He'd seen the cars coming from one of the large gaps in the side of the apartment building as he flew up the stairs. Dark, somber cars, like a funeral cavalcade. KGB. Dmitri had been right to suspect his wife. Someone must have followed Dmitri's trail, after all.

There was no more planning, just desperation and improvisation. Using a script as metaphor had somehow helped him to keep his head clear. Metaphor was a way to keep control when your blood rushed in streams of fire, and your thoughts leapt out ahead of you, boundless and uncontrolled as an ocean wave in a storm. Metaphor: the airplane here—a meteor flashing through the sky; the trek through the Finnish wilderness to this border station—the tale of Kashchey the Immortal wherein a man was caught in that most Russian of paradigms, the nesting doll. Wherein also, said hero must find an island and on the island locate a tree, under that tree find a chest, inside that chest is a rabbit, in the rabbit is a duck, in the duck an egg and inside the egg the death of the trickster, which came in many shapes, not all recognizable at first sight. Only again, he didn't know, was he hero or trickster?

Yevgena always said he'd been born under Mercury—Mercury, the original trickster god, the one who let you fly, even while in the act of yanking the rug out from under your feet, giving you wings to soar and then melting the wax of them, so that you fell, fell, fell. Mercury, a quicksilver dealer of drugs, feeding you enough to addict with one hand, while killing you with the other. Mercury, making of mind an acrobat, but one with silver strings to yank it, and you, back at the worst moment.

Metaphor was refuge when the world was too much. As it was now, coming at him at one hundred miles per hour, sound becoming colour, colour becoming sound, vision the same as a cut along his bones, opening him, laying his heart wide to be contused, used up, burned in the fire of sensation. To be in this state now, to be without filter was dangerous. His view of the world was skewed, tip-tilted and shaken, so that everything was so gloriously dense, and also on the cusp of exploding outward into a great incandescence, a complete white-out of the senses. This always presaged a darkness akin to a primordial state, where the black was so complete that all movement was slowed to lizard-time, and fear subsumed all glory, all light, all hope.

Mercury, flying up the stairs, until suddenly the stairs were gone, and he was on the roof of the derelict building, where the little girl had run when her father had fallen asleep. The movie had flickered its way to a still shot, a child standing in the snow, a little girl—not his little girl, but the reason he was here all the same. Time stopped, the film in a long close-up, the small girl standing as still as a figurine in a snow globe, a tiny blonde angel who'd ventured beyond the bounds of the script. An angel—yes, he could see the wings sprouting from her back, an outline of gossamer and frost traced upon the air. This last bit was likely hallucination, meaning hypomania was behind him in the dust, and he was now in full-blown mania, which was mental quicksand at best. Sound came back then, cars stopping, men shouting, and the little girl so still, snow glittering like diamonds on her hair, on the woolen shoulders of her coat, on the tips of her wings.

The sound then of men pursuing, pounding up the stairs, clearly not having gotten the script memo that he was meant to be the hero; he was meant to live to the last page. One thing he did know was that the hero saved the child, no movie could end in the death of a child. He did then the only thing left to do—he ran, picking up speed as he went, the roof insubstantial beneath his feet, breathing in stars, exhaling clouds. He grabbed the child up, ignoring her cry of alarm, and with all the strength left to him, he threw her across the divide between the two buildings, watching as she arced out into space, the void waiting to clutch her fast to its crimson chest. He saw her land, saw the person on the other side grab her up, and run. For him, there was no time left;

he had to jump without the velocity to propel him across. No time. *Time, time, time*—that constant drumbeat in the human life.

There were men on the roof now, men with guns, picking their way across the girders. No time left. Here on the precipice it all streamed through him: old things, new things, love and loss; his children, both the living and the dead; the touch of the woman he loved. The night opened around him like a great bird unfolding its wings for one last flight. No more Mercury and his silver strings, no more black in the blood, no more falling, falling from a height guaranteed to smash. Well, one more fall, one more and then to weep no more, and to taste the peace of Heaven because the Earth was gone.

And so he jumped, knowing he couldn't make it. Mercury had cut the strings, had melted the wax, his wings were illusion, and he was falling—falling into that great incandescence, that white-out of the senses, the globe of the world bursting apart into a million shards of ice.

Chapter Forty-three

Where Justice Falls

A HARD RAIN was falling when Pamela finally found the church, ducking in out of the weather and collapsing her umbrella before breaching the threshold. Some superstitions held fast from childhood and never taking an open umbrella into a building was one of them, particularly not a church.

It was quiet, a fine and private place. She understood why Detective Holroyd had chosen a church, Catholic boy that he was, speaking to a Catholic girl. He sat near the front, immaculately combed hair a dull gleam in the gloom. The light of evening fell through the stained glass, and broke upon the altar like shattered blood. The altar was the traditional place of sacrifice and if nothing else, both of them understood the power of sacrifice, the entire Christian world, after all, was predicated upon that single notion. How well it had been executed in the world was another matter, but it was still the root upon which the foundation had grown.

This meeting had been arranged the last time she'd seen him. The time and place had been left on a note, tucked surreptitiously under the cup of tea she had given him. It was fortunate Casey hadn't found it. She had been of two minds whether to attend this summons, but had decided in the end that she couldn't afford to ignore it. The interview with him two days before had been simple enough, he'd merely taken down their statements and noted that they now had Lord Kirkpatrick's son with them. Still, it had made her uneasy, for she sensed that while something might appear simple on the surface with this man, what was below was infinitely complicated.

Jamie was not to be found, which wasn't entirely unusual, particularly when she considered their last conversation. It was expected that he be incommunicado just now, but it didn't lend itself to a portrait of innocence either. When he was off radar like this, he had told her to contact Yevgena in the case of an emergency, and so she had done just that. Yevgena had a network of contacts throughout the world that the head of the CIA might have envied. So far, however, she had been unable to get word to Jamie about Violet's murder. This worried Pamela a great deal, though she knew little about Jamie's life in the spy world, she did understand how terribly dangerous it was. Since Kathleen's birth, he'd never been out of contact for more than a few days. This time it was more than a week without so much as an indication of where he was and when he might return.

Casey expected her to be late tonight, and so it had been easy enough to keep this meeting without having to explain herself. She'd wanted to tell him, but knew there wasn't any way on God's green earth that he'd be all right with her meeting alone with the detective. Still, she'd felt it necessary to know what it was Detective Holroyd thought important enough to arrange a clandestine meeting. It had been easy to make her excuses as she'd had an appointment in the city with a young man to start on a series of sketches and to take down his story, then she'd had an appointment with a young couple to photograph their new baby. It was from this latter appointment that she'd come, still seeing the proud parents' in her mind's eye, and smelling the soft apple and talcum scent of the baby on her clothes.

Now, here she was at the appointed time and place. Detective Holroyd stood at her approach, tie perfectly aligned, hair neatly trimmed as though he was an advert for wholesomeness. He indicated the hard pew beside him. She wondered if he'd been praying, for his head had been bowed when she'd entered the church.

"I apologize for the informality of this meeting," he said, waiting until she sat before seating himself once again.

"I think, Detective Holroyd, that if you were doing this through the proper channels, we wouldn't be meeting in an empty church," she said, tone dry.

"Astute of you, but there are things I need to say to you which I'd rather not in an official capacity."

"Oh?" she said.

"Yes. If you'll bear with me for a few minutes, I'll explain. I've always liked puzzles, love them really. I tend to get a bit obsessed when there's one that needs solving. My puzzle began with a missing colleague, but I won't bore you with that because we've already talked about the constable. Of course, I did wonder why he'd been so determined to chase after you, why had he zeroed in on you with such zeal? That question had a couple of answers, I found, and it took me some time to find them, but in the meanwhile there were other things occupying my attention."

"Such as?" she asked.

"Well, it's come to my attention that your husband was missing for three years, during which time he was presumed dead. In fact, his return from the dead came shortly—very shortly—after Noah Murray's death."

"Yes?" she said lightly, though a cold trickle of ice water began to run through her veins.

"So, I went back to the workhouse, and poked around a bit more and found a shell casing. I've always thought that whoever did the shooting that night had to be up in that big oak outside the window, and also had to be one helluva shot. So I did a little asking around, and found out that your husband was considered sharpshooter material, had the reputation with the Provos for never missing what he took aim at."

Casey had been in a terrible rush that night, and wouldn't have given thought to whether he was leaving fingerprints on a shell casing. That something so small might be their undoing made her feel sick.

"Now, of course, there's the murder of Lord Kirkpatrick's wife, when he is conveniently absent from the country, but also a man with the sort of resources which would allow him to slip in and out, and over borders, unnoticed. It seems to me he had motive and means. A wife come back to him just when he'd moved on with his life, and had a child with the woman he truly does love—who also had means and motive. That murder was brutal—well, I hardly need to tell you that, do I? You saw the body after all. It was most definitely personal for whoever killed her, though, that much was clear. The man watching her was of course, collateral damage, the killer couldn't afford a witness."

This last bit of information wasn't news to her, he'd told her about the body found out beyond the paddock during his first visit. The man Jamie had set to watch Violet so that she wouldn't try to take Kolya out of the country during his absence. Whoever had done this, hadn't done it on the spur of the moment, that much was terribly clear.

"There's so much anger here, all the way around it would seem. Enough for several people. Anger is funny that way, it's a bit like a virus spreading outward and infecting everything it touches."

He paused, and she wondered if he was waiting for her to respond to his monologue. He wasn't telling her anything she didn't already know, however. That the person who had killed Violet was in a state of pure anger had been clear, but that didn't make the answer of just who that was any more obvious. As Jamie had stated, Violet had been an agent of the KGB, which made the array of possible enemies rather wide.

"Which brings me back around to the constable. I dug around and found a name connected to him, which appeared to also be connected to you. And so then, I went back a little further." He paused in his speech, letting the words sink in, and she understood why he'd waited to spring this upon her until the last. She simply sat silent, and waited. If he wanted his moment of drama, he would have to create it himself, she wasn't going to be part of it.

"Do you know what I'm talking about?" he asked.

She sighed. "No, but I suppose you'll tell me."

"You were raped one night on a train."

She held her silence. After all, what was there to say? What sort of confirmation was this man looking for? And why, she wondered, was a woman's body always in the public space, as though the very shape of it was owned by others, and any violence committed upon it was also fodder for public consumption.

It took him a minute to realize she didn't intend to respond.

"Constable Blackwood had a brother-in-law who went missing, he seemed to think it was connected to the event on the train."

"Event?" Pamela echoed. "That's an interesting term to use for rape."

"I didn't want to offend you," he said, and she thought the fool actually meant it.

"Offend me by calling it what it is?"

"Fine, we'll call it what it was then. The constable had a file on his brother-in-law, something off book, it was part log of what he'd done to try and find him, and part manual on vengeance should he ever figure out what had happened to the man."

"He must have been uncommonly fond of his brother-in-law to go to such lengths." Her voice was light, but inside she felt anything but. Rather than her normal panic, though, what she felt now was rage. Rage that she should still have this visited upon her all these years later. Rage that this man was trying to use it to manipulate her into telling him what he wanted to hear.

"Did he? I couldn't tell you, I don't know who the constable's brother-in-law is."

"Was," the detective corrected her. "He was never found."

"A pity, I'm sure," she said drily.

He didn't respond at once, but sat in the silence with her, as the light upon the altar grew ever more bloody. She sensed that he knew the facts of the night on the train; he wasn't merely guessing, he *knew*. She was tired of trying to cover things up, so tired, so bloody weary of lying to try to stave off the inevitable. That night was never truly going to go away, it would always trail behind her to a certain degree, making her remember when she least wanted to. And so, it was from that weariness that she spoke, her voice quiet and without rancor.

"Perhaps, whatever befell this man, he deserved it. Perhaps what he took, what he did, needed the sort of blood justice that was equal to what he meted out to others."

"Justice doesn't work in that way, you don't get to decide how to deal with a crime committed against you. You can't be judge, jury and executioner."

"Because the law deals so fairly with those who've been sinned against?"

"This is my way of giving you a choice, Mrs. Riordan. You get to decide where justice falls."

"I am not the law, and as you've so clearly stated, it's not for me to take it into my own hands," she said, quietly. "I am, after all, just human, not the law. But I ask you this, Detective—was the law not created to apply to humans, and to protect us from our worst impulses?"

"Are you trying to equate rape with murder?" he asked.

"Yes, perhaps I am. Have you been raped, Detective Holroyd?"

"No."

"Well, I have. By four men—four men who brutalized me. Do you have any notion what it is to have your bodily autonomy taken from you in such a way? To know that you have absolutely no control over what is done to you, to your body, to your spirit?"

"No, I don't. But that still doesn't justify murder."

"Doesn't it? What does justice have to do with any of this? Was there justice for me when those four men took away my sense of safety, violated my body, gave me nightmares and made it so that I believed I would never know security again?"

"You never took it to the police," the detective said, clearly entrenched in his stubborn belief that justice could actually be served in such a situation.

"No, because I knew what would happen. The man who initiated all the violence was, as you know, a policeman himself. Exactly what do you think might have happened to me, or to my husband if I had dared to report it?"

"But if you'd at least tried—" he began, but she just shook her head, and to his credit, he stopped and said nothing further. He was a bigger fool than she'd previously thought if he believed the police would have in any way helped her, or even sought those who'd raped her. At the time, Casey had been the man seen as the head of the newly rising Provisional wing of the IRA. She had made her choices knowing what the likely fallout from reporting would be. The damage had already been done to her and Patrick; they had sought to limit how much of it fell onto Casey and Jamie.

Detective Holroyd was looking at her now, as though he still sought an explanation, a story, something to explain why there had been so much blood. What he wanted could not be given. It was something a man could not understand. A woman's entire life experience revolved around blood. Women bled, bled to *be* a woman, bled to bring forth life, bled to death in back alleys, bled at the hands of men who were meant to love them. Likely even Eve had known—once the innocence of the garden was past—there would never be enough blood for the world, not even if every woman let her veins in sacrifice. There was certainly never enough for a particular kind of man, and she had known more than one of that sort.

She did not think the detective was that kind of man, but rather one blinded by his notions of justice. But there was no justice here, not for the men who'd died, and certainly not for her altered sense of self, which would be with her for the rest of her life. There was no story to give him, because he was not entitled to her tears or her pain; she would not empty the fury inside her for his consumption, just so that he might believe her. It did not matter how many times a woman spoke, nor in how many ways, she was still doubted, disbelieved and pilloried for the affront of admitting she'd been violated; that something sacred had been taken from her, which society in its impotence, could not give back to her and thus could never forgive. No, even Eve had known, there would never be enough blood, and the anger from that went to the root of the world.

"It seems to me, Mrs. Riordan, that almost everything that has happened since, is a result of that night in one way or another. Except, perhaps, the death of Violet Kirkpatrick. But, I suppose, it's possible that too is somehow linked to all of this."

"Or perhaps none of it is related," she said wearily, "perhaps life is just randomly cruel and hands out what it pleases. If you feel you know so much, why is it that we are here?"

"What I see here are all kinds of outcomes. But what I think is this—if I'm playing the odds, I figure I can make one crime stick. I understand how much power James Kirkpatrick holds in his fist, he has the ear of prime ministers and kings, it would seem. Your husband—well, I have the bullet casing, and the fact that all those people were killed after his mysterious return to the country. I think more damning to both men though is the death, one by one, of the men who raped you."

"You've laid out your plan, Detective Holroyd, but I still don't understand what it is you want from me."

"When I have all my pieces in place, and I understand the whole picture, I'll come to you. I'll let you choose."

"Choose what?" she asked, though she had a dreadful feeling that she knew.

"Who lives and who dies, so to speak. Who pays justice's price—James Kirkpatrick, your husband or you? I feel you're owed that much, to have a say, as you're the most sinned against. I have no wish to orphan your children by imprisoning both their parents, but I do feel the scales need balancing to some degree."

As his words pierced her, horror broke over her like a cold wave. The man was mad to propose such a thing. She also knew though, that if he had solid proof of all the crimes he'd just listed, he wouldn't be here talking to her and asking her to make such a terrible choice, he'd be arresting all three of them. So his guesses were good, and he was far too near the mark for comfort's sake, but he wasn't likely to have irrefutable proof that would convince his bosses or he would not be here playing games with her. He was hoping then to coerce a confession, one born out of panic and fear. His hope was in vain, however, because she would not be giving it to him.

"There's one other question I have for you," he said, "what happened to Noah Murray's body? Is he truly dead?"

"You can ask that? After what you saw in that workhouse? Of course he's dead." She closed her eyes and took a breath in to steady herself. "If you must know he died in my arms. I felt the life go from him. They took his body away after. I thought they'd likely taken him down to the basement of that horrible building. If he wasn't there when you searched, then perhaps you need to ask yourself who arrived on scene before you?"

"There was no one there when we arrived. We came right after Mr. Kirkpatrick called to report what had happened."

She shrugged. "Perhaps they weren't there when you arrived, detective, but that doesn't mean they didn't precede you there."

"Special Branch?" he asked.

Pamela shook her head. "That's for you to find out, you're the detective after all. What does it matter? He's dead, regardless of who took his body away."

He sat quietly for a moment more, as though digesting the words she'd just said. Finally, he stood. "I'll be in touch, Mrs. Riordan," he said, and then he paused, giving her a long look in which there was an odd sort of sympathy, before he turned and walked up the aisle and out the church doors, into the driving rain of the evening.

She sat for a time after he left, the church feeling better for his absence. Tiny flames wavered in the chill air—fire for remembrance, fire for hope. She'd lit candles any number of times for Casey when he'd been gone, praying for a miracle, or at the very least, for him to have peace. And now both had come to fruition, his return the miracle, and his coming home to the heart of his family, the peace. She would be damned if this policeman was going to take either of those things away from him.

Raised in the teachings of the Catholic Church, she had a deeply ingrained sense of justice within her. But justice wasn't a matter of words in a dusty old book, it was feeling that there was a fairness of sorts in the world. The detective wasn't wrong in his assessment of her, but it was only one piece of his precious puzzle. What he didn't understand was that in defense of those she loved, she had a blade at her core, one that could cut either way. If he came for her family, he'd find out just how sharp her steel was. She stood, gathering the thick sweater she wore more tightly around her shoulders. The small flames danced at her movement. Driven by need and tradition, she walked to the bank of flame, and borrowed from one candle to light another.

Long ago, she had been taught that one lit a candle before bringing a petition to God. And so she stood as the wick flared with blue before settling to a steady gold, and waited for the words to come. When they arrived, they were few in number but were the plea in the core of her heart.

Please grant us peace.

It was what she truly wished for—peace within which to raise her family, peace to allow her marriage to both heal and flourish, peace so deep and wide that it would settle in her bones, and give her a sense of security. Casey was right, they needed to leave.

She lit a candle for Jamie too, for his safe return, for his understanding that he might well be walking into a trap, if he hadn't already done so. For him too, she wanted peace.

The last candle she lit was for the man who had died in her arms, counting stars in a sky he could no longer see. Wherever he was she prayed that he too had found peace.

Yes, peace was what she prayed for, but if the detective was determined to make her choose, she would do it and have no regrets around it. She walked away from the tiny fires, feeling tired and wanting nothing more than to be home, with the comforting chaos of the bedtime routine—stories, cuddles, chats about everything from God to who was responsible for the newt in the bathtub, and whether badgers wore boots only on Sundays, or sometimes during the work week as well. And at the end of all that, there was Casey and a meandering chat by the fire, or the retreat to bed, where all was forgotten and subsumed in the joy of their physical joining.

She paused in the entry. This area had once been called the narthex, and had been the place where both penitents and catechumens were confined until their reconciliation with—or initiation into—the church, was completed. Sometimes she felt that, in the spiritual sense, she had been caught fast in this area for a long time, unable to move into the larger church but also unable to leave the building altogether. Too much had happened, too many things had felt beyond her control, and she had sometimes taken rash steps in order to keep those she loved safe. Both of the men she loved had paid for that rashness in a variety of ways. That all this stemmed back to a single evening on a train, after a day of fun, seemed impossible, and yet here she was. Events had spiralled after that night, and it seemed looking back that each thing was a bead on a very dark rosary, every addition adding weight and hurrying events along even further.

What had happened on that train had dragged both Jamie and Casey into a vortex of sorrow, fury and vengeance. And now, all that had spun forth from that, had come home to roost. The choice about how things played out from here was hers. Why it should be so, she didn't know, only that it was.

She glanced back once more before exiting the church. The blood light was still there, spilling now from altar to floor. The cold evening dim made it appear like it was flowing down the aisle toward her, and for a second she could almost feel it, the viscous, slick chill of it, rising like a tide, threatening to flood her life.

Chapter Forty-four

Time to Go

IN THE DAYS following her meeting with the detective, Pamela had put out a few feelers to her old contacts within the police force. From her time photographing various crime scenes she knew several officers, most of whom were decent human beings doing a very difficult job in a very difficult country. While she appreciated that, she also knew to tread carefully within that world. One wrong move, one wrong word and she'd be making a target of herself, particularly if they thought she was trying to get damning information on a fellow officer.

However, it turned out that her contacts knew enough to tell her just why Detective Holroyd had been banished here to the provinces. He'd had an informant who was killed while working undercover for him. This was, the policeman who'd told her had said, strictly rumour, but the further scuttlebutt was that he'd also been in a sexual relationship with said informant. It made the situation she now found herself in somewhat more explicable. However, if the detective thought she would lie down and let him use her family as a means to rocket himself back to London, he had another think coming. There was a journalist or two with whom she was acquainted who might find this information very interesting. If the man continued to threaten her she might have to use that particular weapon.

It was this matter she was mulling over when Casey approached her a few nights after her meeting in the church. He came and sat down across from her, taking a deep breath before speaking. A spike of fear opened in her, like a flower emerging while there was still frost in the air.

"Pamela, I've a notion about somethin' that I need to share with ye, an' I'm not so sure ye're goin' to like it, but I need to say it anyway."

"What is it?"

"Ye know how we talked about leavin'? I think we need to do it now."

"Now?" she repeated, feeling a bit like a stunned owl.

"Aye, now. I think it would be best to go while we're still allowed to. I've spoken to Pat an' Tomas about this, an' they both agree, now is the time."

"What do you mean by 'while we're still allowed'?"

"Woman, we were both in Jamie's house the night Violet was killed. If the police want to make a case for it bein' either one of us, they could likely do so. Ye know how this country works. They could order us to stay in the North, should we fall under suspicion."

"Yes, I do know how this country works. But we have nowhere to go *to*, or do we?" she asked, narrowing her eyes at her husband, who was looking a little like a man sitting on a lit stick of dynamite. "You haven't gone and bought another place without me, have you?"

"No, I'll not do somethin' that mad again. There *is* a farm out in Kerry though, that I want ye to see."

"Was that what the fight was about?" she asked. "You wanted the money for this?"

"Aye, the money gives us a down payment on the land if we should choose to buy it."

"Kerry?" she said, feeling a frisson of dismay. When he'd mentioned leaving, she had thought maybe Wicklow or Wexford, somewhere along the same coast at least.

"Aye, it's a distance I realize, but I think we'd be safer there for now. The old man who owned the land passed away, an' the family is eager to sell. They're willin' to let us stay on there for a bit before we make up our minds about buyin' or not. They want a caretaker for what animals are left there, an' this seemed a good solution for both them an' us."

"How many animals exactly?"

"A cow or two, an' an old ewe, maybe a cat or three as well."

"That sounds like utter madness," she said, visions of hordes of animals running through her future. "In case it has escaped your notice, we currently have four children, a sheep, a dog, a cat and a horse already. I'm not even sure about the legality of taking Kolya out of the country before Jamie returns."

"Aye, but that's what you an' I do, isn't it—utter madness?" He smiled, and she saw that for him, he'd found somewhere he truly felt could be their home, and was afraid she would reject it. The next words out of his mouth only confirmed her thoughts.

"I just need ye to see it, Pamela before ye turn away the idea of it. I think it could be our home."

"You're my home, man, wherever you are, that's home."

"Aye, an' you mine, but come next winter ye'll want a roof over your head—ye tend to be fussy that way. This land is where I'd like to build that house."

"There's not a house on the property?"

"There's a wee tumbledown cottage, but it's not fit to live in. We can stay in the Flyin' Tortoise for now, I thought, while I fix the cottage so it's useable. Until then, if we need the extra room, we can put up a tent beside the caravan."

"*If* we need the room? Do I need to list our dependents again?"

"No, ye don't. Just wait until ye see the place, Jewel, I know ye're goin' to fall in love, just as I have. An' in truth, I'd like some distance between us an' Belfast. Until we know who killed Violet, we're vulnerable."

He was right, though she had a few misgivings around the notion of moving Kathleen that far from Jamie. Particularly when he wasn't present to object. Still, if they could hold off a little on making a permanent decision, the idea did have its appeals, not the least of which was the shadowy figure outside of Jamie's windows that night. Whoever it was had gotten a good look at her face, and would know her on sight. It was possible, of course, that it was some-one who already knew her, which made her situation even more worrisome.

"So, what do ye think, Jewel, will we go?"

In her mind's eye hovered the blood light of the altar, and the determi-nation in Detective Holroyd's eyes to serve out justice to at least one of them. Standing there beyond him, in the shadows, was the figure outside the win-dows threatening all she held dear.

"Yes, let's go."

Part Six

A Home at the End of the World

Chapter Forty-five

A Good Morning for Beginnings

THE FIRST MORNING Pamela stepped down from the Flying Tortoise, she gasped at the sight before her. It had been twilight when they'd arrived the night before, and between getting the children sorted, feeding them and then collapsing into bed, she'd had neither time nor opportunity to have a look at the land upon which they now lived.

The farm sat in the still light of morning, like a painting from another time, mist glazing over it in a diaphanous bolt of silk, and frost limning the trees and grass with sparkling bits of diamond. Overgrown fields sloped down from the foothills of a distant mountain, unrolling emerald and umber under the morning sun. Above the fields, rising on a south-facing slope, was a thick forest of oak and beech, yew and a scatter of Scots Pine. Beyond was the silver scent of the sea, filling her senses completely. Her very blood began to thrum just at the knowledge that it was there, and that should this become their new home she would live near enough to the sea to hear it and see it every day.

Casey—always one to rise early—was already up and had lit the fire, where the kettle was now boiling steadily, and the scent of sausages cooking filled the air, making her stomach rumble. She walked over to him, kissed him and then departed for her morning ablutions, a routine bound to be more complicated than usual, given the lack of running water, electricity and warmth.

There was an outhouse near the tumbledown byre, the latter of which was the residence of the ewe and two cows which were now under their stewardship. Disturbed by Pamela's presence from her morning feed, the ewe blatted in her direction, fixing her with a baleful eye. The sheep's name, Casey had informed her the night before, was Matilda. Miss Matilda had already made it abundantly clear that she was not best pleased by the addition of a ram to her universe. Paudeen, like any male with a healthy ego, appeared completely unaware of this cold reception, and had happily settled into his new stall in the decrepit byre. The cows, being cows, were unperturbed by the new humans in their midst and placidly accepted their feed from the new faces in their lives.

It was, she thought, emerging from the outhouse some moments later, going to be a hard decision to know which building to attend to first—the ramshackle cottage where they might gain a bit of room for their brood, or the byre before it fell in on the head of the malcontent ewe, the *je ne sais quois* cows, the temperamental horse and the spoiled ram. The thought of sharing the tight quarters of the Tortoise with four children, two of them extremely active little boys, might come down on the side of the cottage however. Still, she looked about, feeling a tingling all over her body. It was an absolutely breathtaking spot, and she understood why Casey had fallen for it so swiftly.

Taking their leave of the house had been difficult, knowing as she did that it might never truly be home again. They had asked Pru to come with them, though in all honesty, Pamela had no notion where they would have put the girl had she said yes. Pru had thanked them but said for now she was going to live with Finola, as she was taking courses at the university for a few hours a week and needed to be near to the city. Pamela knew that while the courses mattered to Pru, the proximity to Ambrose mattered more, and had expected that she would want to stay. Still, she would miss her being with them each day, for Pru had become family to her and she worried about the girl even when she did see her regularly.

She joined Casey at the fire a few minutes later, hands freezing from their wash in an icy barrel of water, and her gums stinging from the brushing she'd given them with equally cold water.

Casey handed her a mug of coffee, and a plate with sausage, eggs and wholemeal toast on it. She was very hungry this morning, and tucked in with a good appetite. He sat across from her, spreading honey on his own toast, his coffee cup nearly empty. He'd likely been up for a while; she knew he was worried that someone may have followed them yesterday, despite the drive here on narrow back roads, which the Flying Tortoise, like the waddling hippopotamus it resembled, had just barely managed to squeeze down.

The food tasted divine, and she was chewing on her last bite of sausage when she realized that Casey was regarding her with a rather intense look.

"What is it?" she asked, putting her plate down, slightly alarmed by the seriousness of his expression.

"Will ye walk up to the waterfall with me? There's somethin' I'd show ye. We'll still be able to see the Tortoise from there, an' of course, there's other eyes watchin' over the children." His eyes flicked toward the edge of the forest, where a man named Jonno had his caravan parked in a ring of oak. The caravan wasn't visible from the land below, but the location gave Jonno a sweeping perspective out over the area. When she'd asked Casey about him, he'd merely given her an inscrutable look and said, "An extra set of eyes, an' a man with good aim seems a wise notion just now."

He had gone on to explain that Jonno was a man from his past, from the time when he'd fought in his teens. Jonno had seen him on the night he'd fought the giant, and they had renewed their acquaintance.

She put her hand to her hair, which she knew was in its usual mad disorder this morning, as it always was before she had the time to pick her way carefully through it and untangle all the knots.

Casey smiled. "Don't worry, darlin', ye're beautiful just as ye are. I'd like to show ye this somethin' before the children wake up, an' the day begins."

He stood and walked over to her, then held out his hand. She took it, mystified and wishing she had something on other than the ratty old jersey she'd worn to bed, along with her flannel bottoms, holey sweater and woolen socks which, due to the wintry temperature, she'd been wearing round the clock.

As they set off she noticed Casey nod toward the caravan in the oaks, and saw the man Jonno emerge, nod in return and begin to walk down to where he'd be closer to the Tortoise and the children.

The waterfall was near to the edge of the wood, a cascade of rock, moss and saplings, the water more of a burble than a roar. She knew keeping the children away from it would be a challenge. Kathleen had already shown a penchant for water, which was no small reminder of Jamie. She was clearly his daughter in more than just looks.

There were stones placed in a rough ascending order up one side of the falls, serving as stairs. She followed Casey, stepping carefully, for the stones were slippery with a fine glazing of ice this morning. Partway up he paused, scooping up a handful of water and drinking it straight from his palm. He bent again, filling his hand once more.

"Here, drink," he said and held out his cupped palm, the lines of his life magnified by the water. She tucked her hair behind her ears and drank, the water cold and tasting of the small pieces of grit and plant life which lived in it.

At the top of the waterfall, he led her to a vantage point which looked out over the entire sweep of land. She gasped at the sight of it. From here the sea beyond the trees was visible, and the great expanse of it, rising silver and blue in the morning light, made her feel as though her heart might burst with joy.

"I wanted ye to have the sea near enough to hear, an' to run to it when ye feel the need," he said simply, and yet she understood the depth of feeling behind his words. Casey was no great lover of the sea, and so she knew what it meant to him to find a place where she too would be at home.

"See that wee rise there, backed by that stand of oak? That's where I should like to build us a house. I want it to be somethin' that fits with the feel of the land here—a wee bit wild an' untamed. I've a notion of it in my head, that I'd like to show ye once I get it down on paper. An' there," he pointed to a level stretch some distance from the proposed house site, "would be a grand place for a paddock an' a new byre. We could even paint it red like yer one at home."

As he warmed to his subject, he walked toward the edge of the waterfall, pointing and gesturing, his face alight with his vision of what a future here could look like. There was a longing in his face that she knew all too well. It put a stitch in her heart to see it, to understand what it was he longed for, what he needed down to the very marrow of his bones.

She watched him as the morning sun gilded him in a frosty light, battered about his edges, but still standing tall and strong, unbowed by the hand fate had dealt him and here looking with joy and yearning at the fields below him. It still felt like she would never be able to look at him long enough to fill the void of those three lost years.

"Casey," she said softly.

He turned and met her eyes, his expression soft. "Aye?"

"I love you."

"I love ye too, Jewel." He came and stood beside her and took her hand in his, lifted it to his mouth and kissed it. "Well, darlin', what do ye think of the place?"

In truth, she couldn't imagine a location more suited to their family. Conor would go mad with joy at having this much room to roam, and it would more than accommodate the few animals they had as well. She could already see Khamsin running full tilt over these brilliant green fields. The horse had been left behind in a neighbour's pasture until Casey could get a trailer to bring him down here.

Just now, the trees were whispering in the morning wind, of secrets only trees knew but which she had always sensed might be told to those willing to hear. And beyond that, the sea, a great sigh this morning, that of the world waking and drawing in its first tidal breath of the day. When she answered she simply said what she felt.

"I think it's the loveliest place I've ever seen."

"Pamela." She turned, startled at the serious note in his voice, and was surprised to find him down on his bad knee.

"What are you doing?"

"I should think that's fairly obvious, woman. Will ye marry me, Pamela Riordan?" he asked.

"The last time I checked we were already married," she said.

"Aye, but I think with all that has happened in these last years, it would be right to renew our vows an' put a stamp on this new beginnin' of ours."

He reached into the pocket of his coat, and brought out an object which glinted gold in the morning sun. It was a beautiful ring, just as he'd promised it would be, long ago.

"Oh, Casey," she breathed out, vision blurred with the tears which had flooded her eyes. "Of course I'll marry you again."

She held her hand out and he slid the ring on—it was a band of gold, set with pearls, opalescent in the early morning light.

"D'ye like it?" he asked, and she looked down, surprised by the question.

"I love it, Casey. It's beautiful."

"It's only that pearls are a wee bit non-traditional when it comes to rings. The shop owner told me that the ancient Japanese believed pearls were the tears of mermaids an' angels. He mentioned they were symbolic of new beginnins' as well. I liked the notion of both, an' this ring just looked like it belonged on yer hand."

"Any ring that you give me belongs on my hand. You could tie a cigar band around my finger, and I'd treasure it."

Casey got to his feet, and then gathered her close, lending her his warmth. "I thought we could get married again here on this land. It had a death not too long ago; I think it should have a marriage now—reconsecrate it, so to speak."

"I'd love that," she said. "I will say though, man, that I cannot believe you proposed to me when I'm wearing wellies and pyjamas."

He smiled, leaning down to kiss her, his lips cold from the spring water, yet still tasting of the honey he'd had on his morning bread.

"I suppose," he said, leaning back and taking in her outfit, "it's a bit of an eccentric get up, but I don't notice so much, bein' that ye're naked to me most of the time."

"What?" she asked, pulling her ratty sweater a little more closely around her.

"Aye, I mean I see yer clothes, but I can just as clearly see," he tapped his forehead, "what's under them as well, an' to be honest that's what's topmost in my mind when I look at ye."

"Even when we're discussing feed bills and split hooves?" she asked, as ever slightly mystified by the thinking of men, not to mention how they ever managed to get a day's work done with the state of their minds.

"Oh, aye, I can think two thoughts at once, woman, an' while I might be considerin' how to build a lazy bed on a north-facin' slope, I'm also seein' ye naked, an' rememberin' what we were doin' in the bed the previous night.

Though, sometimes, I'll admit, I'm thinkin' about what we're *goin'* to do the comin' night instead."

She laughed. "It's a miracle you get anything done."

"I'll not take all the blame, woman. It's the way you look at me that gives me half the thoughts," he said, his grin driving his dimple deep into his morning whiskers.

She considered him for a moment, the long lines of him, the mischief in his smile, the dark eyes which always saw too much and yet just enough. Oh, aye, she flushed and his grin broadened a little, she did the same with him, part of her mind always occupied with their bed, with his body, with what he did to her and she to him. It was a sort of glorious madness, and she wondered if it would ever desert them.

"I'm not going to take responsibility for how you look. What was it your daddy used to say, 'a sugar bowl to a bunch of hormone-addled flies'?"

"Oh aye, well ye're the only one I'm interested in attractin' these days. Though, I suppose," he looked down the hill where the Flying Tortoise reposed, a bit of smoke puffing from its chimney like wee clouds of grey wool, "I've fixed it so we'll not be doin' much of anythin' in our bed other than sleepin' for the next while."

"No, I don't suppose we will," she said, thinking of Jonno's watchful eye hovering over them all. She sighed. Having just gotten Casey back into her bed not all that long ago, she wasn't keen on the notion of enforced celibacy just now.

Below, the red door of the Tortoise opened, and Conor stepped out, hair a mad corona of sleep tousled curls, small face tilted into the morning light as though he was scenting the wind. He likely was, she thought, no doubt the smell of the sausages cooking had wakened him.

"He'll be hungry," she said.

"I left him a plate. He'll scent it out, wee food hound that he is."

He put his arms around her from behind. She relaxed into his chest, savoring his warmth. They could spare another moment before heading down to start the daily routine with the children.

"So, Jewel, what do ye think?"

"It's utterly glorious," she said, "I can't believe this is what I'll look at every day."

"I love yer optimism, but it pisses rain plenty here, woman, so maybe manage yer hopes a little."

"What about you, man, what do you think?"

"I think," he said softly, "that it's a good mornin' for beginnings."

"It is that," she replied, looking up at him.

He kissed her and then stood away from her, offering his hand. "Let's go down an' begin then, shall we?"

Chapter Forty-six

Written on Air

SHOULD ANYONE EVER chance to ask the rather unlikely question of whether or not bears made for good roommates, James Kirkpatrick would be able to answer with a rather painful expertise, that indeed, bears were not terribly congenial in an up close and personal situation.

That he should fly off a building with the KGB in hot pursuit, and yet wake to find himself not only alive, but minimally damaged, and now tucked in a fur-lined cavity, with the sound of a bear snorting on the other side of a thin plywood divide, seemed beyond the realms of the ridiculous and more on the order of a strange fever dream. At first, when he'd woken he'd thought he was in purgatory—a small, dark space with minimal air, and the sound of a demon snuffling ferociously a few inches away. And then the pain had come, his damnable collarbone was broken yet again, and he'd thought the punishments of purgatory seemed rather minimalistic in scope, though still, indeed, rather hellish.

He'd been more than a little confused, but resigned. He had, after all, half-expected to go straight to hell, without the consideration of the anteroom of purgatory. But then movement had ceased and human voices—in the rough tones of Russians—had pierced the narrow confines of purgatory. This presented a few questions for him, all of them worrisome. His box had been briefly opened, and a swarthy face, brilliant with gold teeth, inserted itself into his crate. It was Yevgena's bear trainer—a narrow, wiry man, with muscles that looked like they'd been baked in a hot oven. He was a man of few words, though he'd conveyed the information Jamie needed. Enough, at least, for him to understand that he had survived his fall, because he'd actually made the insane flight between the two buildings, though he'd crashed through the roof of the building opposite and landed on the top floor. From there, they'd extracted him, though they had at first thought him dead. He should have been; he knew this and wondered for what it was that he'd been spared.

When he'd asked about the KGB agents on the roof behind him, he had been greeted with a puzzled silence. There had been no cavalcade of cars, only a busted up Lada and an irate bear trainer along with an aerialist, who, while impressed with his ability to leap through the air was less impressed with his brain, being that he'd seen no reason for the suicidal jump. This bit of information had given him great pause. He'd hallucinated a time or two before during mania, but never to the extent of creating actual people and a funeral line of cars. The bipolar was getting worse, something his doctors had long warned him about—that as he aged, the dark side of the disease could gain in virulence, and the manias would become less seductive and far more destructive. That the lithium would become more and more necessary in order to practice any sort of equilibrium. He had never adjusted well to the lithium, for while it gave him some stability, it also made his mind feel damp, as though there was mold growing in the corners of an unstable house, deteriorating it ever further. The only other treatment which had been recommended was electroshock therapy, and that had been when he was younger. His grandfather, who had been in charge of those decisions around his mental well-being at the time, had said no in vehement terms. Even as an adult—and at times, desperate for anything which might calm the fire in his head—he'd not been able to come to terms with the idea of shocking his brain with electricity.

While just now he still felt the jolts of mania, he knew he was hovering on the dark edge of the sucking whirlpool which was the low jester to mania's king, and prayed he would find shelter before it came.

He alternately soothed and entertained himself by composing letters in his mind to Pamela. It was habit this, to write upon the air, and say the words within him, as a way of sorting things in his mind, particularly now when everything rushed this way and that, his faulty synapses still lit up like a Roman candle. He'd done it even as a child—this writing upon air, a thing so vivid for him at times, that he would see the scrollwork forming and then dissipating in front of him. Always spendthrift with his talents, he'd written entire stories in that way, letting the wind take them away when he was done spinning them into the atmosphere, like the delicate parachutes of dandelion seeds, floating away on a summer breeze.

Just now, though, he had no desire to write in story, or to frame his thoughts as a fairy tale, he merely wanted to talk to his dearest friend in the world, the way he had so many times before. Like her, he had once believed their conversation would continue until such time as one of them left the planet. While that was not to be, he had yet to break the habit of their discourse, even if it was only written on air.

Dear Pamela,

(In which I run away with the Soviet Circus and become the Russian embodiment of le bon follastre. I know this will make you smile, because you've thought it before, maybe even mentioned it a time or two.)

I begin with humour, though I know you won't find it funny, but I'm in one of my strange states of being where what is appropriate and what isn't has neither bearing nor reason on my erratic mind.

So let me merely be blunt. If I do not make it home this time, I want to apologize in advance, here from this box in a bear's travelling den, where my words will be written on air, but which I still must believe will—in the sense of them—reach you one day.

So begin with love, which is where every journey ought to begin. For what is life but the journey between two breaths—the first one and the last. We have only two purposes in this life—to live in harmony with all other creatures and to learn how to love. That is all there is, and it is, in the end, more than enough. And yet, oh and yet, each of us always longs for more—more time, more love, more of those moments that make all the rest of life bearable. We are flame-lit creatures, both terribly dark and terribly bright, and the true tragedy of it is that we burn ourselves, for stardust is prone to fire.

Remember when we read Henry Beston's book that summer in Maine, and you exclaimed over that one line—'For a moment of night we have a glimpse of ourselves and of our world islanded in a stream of stars—pilgrims of mortality, voyaging between horizons across eternal seas of space and time.'

I stopped reading, and when I looked up, your face was rapt, eyes shining with tears. I thought at the time that you'd gotten a glimpse, something you needed in order to know that the pain you carried with you would perhaps, one day, become easier to bear. That you could live and love again, and I was, as it turned out, right. You did just that.

For in our separate journeys, if we are very fortunate, sometimes in that great vast illimitable, we reach out and touch another star in the night. For me, my sweetheart, this is what you have been and always will be, until the last breath is taken. A light in the darkness, a star I touched and held for a brief moment in that great and eternal sea.

And so then, regret—know that I have none. Because of Kathleen it is not possible to regret, but even if we'd never had our beautiful girl, I still would not regret anything. Because– because, love, of course. Love is never a waste, and if given with a full heart, never a mistake. Thank you for allowing me to hold you for a time. It has been my bittersweet privilege to love you.

Drifting then, hard not to with the lack of oxygen in the box. Afloat on one of the fairy tale rivers of milk in the deep heart of Russia, where forest maidens slept waiting for someone to wake them. But if a man should chance to stray into their territory, he'd be turned to a moth, and imprisoned by his longing for light. River turned to sea then, a great green cold, and he was flowing down on a sea of stars and memory.

He woke when the truck ground to a halt, coming up slowly from the depths, like a man long drowned. The bear was grumbling with annoyance. Hard Russian voices, wanting to search the caravan, the stomp of boots and the sound of riled Alsatians. This was where everything was poised on the head of a pin, like an angel with a clutch of dynamite in its hands.

The door opened to the bear's den, and the bear, annoyed at the intrusion of light and cold, roared with the indignity of it all. Jamie held his breath, knowing the fuse of the dynamite had been lit, and the explosion might well be imminent. He could hear, as though through a muffler, the sound of great claws upon cage bars and another roar. The roar of an animal that belonged to forest and mountain, but instead was doomed to always look out through bars and fetters of another creature's making. Immured in his fur-lined box, he couldn't hear everything, but it seemed the bear's agitation decided the soldiers, because the door shut and the sound of the Alsatians faded from his hearing.

It felt like hours passed in his narrow purgatory, but eventually the wheels began to turn again. He tried to count off the miles, to keep an idea of distance so that he would know when they cleared the border zone. While he was still in danger if caught, each mile under the wheels lessened the probability of that.

Sleep came again, drawing him down to those caverns of memory once more, and he dreamed in story then—a story of two gulls who lived out over the sea, and never again saw land, a story told one night in a beautiful house in Paris, created only for the one listener and then never told again. And then he dreamt in the language of fairy tale and myth: phoenixes rising in fire; bears wearing crowns; Baba Yaga come cackling in her mortar, brandishing a pestle with teeth and claws; Kashchey the Immortal wearing a cloak within which nestled tiny skulls, and slavering wolves.

When next he woke, there was no movement, but there was sound. The bear was snoring in great stertorous rolling breaths, which were the breaths of cave and forest, of cold and death. Human voices too, but no longer the voices of fairy tales, no more Baba Yaga, no more Kashchey the Immortal. But rather British voices—those of tea and toast, queens and mad kings. Upper class, and recognized by him, despite the silver streamings of his Mercury-mad brain. Oh, yes, he knew one voice in particular. And for a moment, just before the lid came off the box, he thought it might have been better, for any number of reasons, had he died in Russia.

Chapter Forty-seven

The Queen of the Fairies

"ACHOO!" PAMELA SNEEZED for the third time in as many minutes.

Casey looked over at her, from his position by the stove. "Are ye still glad ye decided to come live out here in the wilds?"

Pamela eyed him back over the folds of a large white handkerchief. Another thing, she thought to herself, that she'd have to wash. Though there hardly seemed any point in trying to keep anyone or anything clean when they were living in the midst of so much bloody mud. Literally this morning, for something had been slaughtered during the night and left on their doorstep.

"While the weather hasn't been ideal, and admittedly four small children in this space when it's raining cats, dogs and a few badgers, isn't as romantic as one might think—yes, I am glad. I don't want to live apart from you ever again, Casey. So if this is where you're living, so are we."

"All right, but you're stayin' put today. Did ye take the fire cider yet?"

"Um, well not quite," she said. She didn't want to hurt his feelings over the devil's brew he swore by for colds, flus, and other assorted ailments, but just the scent of the stuff made her eyes water. It contained, amongst other things, apple cider vinegar, horseradish, garlic, onions, ginger and Casey's own addition of a bit of whiskey. To say it was potent was the understatement of the year.

"My daddy dosed us with it every time we had so much as a tickle in our throats, an' we were always hale as horses."

"*ACHOO!*"

"Sneeze one more time woman, an' I'm rubbin' ye down with that foul eucalyptus grease ye put on me that one time. Now, yer tea is made, there's a bit of last night's soup tucked away for yer lunch, an' I'm away with the children for the day. It's the only way ye'll rest. If ye do so much as wipe the counter down, or feed the cat today, I'll put ye over my knee when I get back home."

"You're always threatening that, and yet you never follow through." She tried winking at him, but it dissolved in yet another flurry of sneezing.

"Come on, get into bed, woman. I'll put yer tea on the wee shelf beside ye, an' none of yer tryin' to seduce me with yer loose talk of corporal punishment."

He kissed her, and then gave her a stern look. "Try to behave yerself for a few hours."

"I will," she said and then promptly punctuated her promise with another set of sneezes.

She slept for a little while after Casey and the children departed, though it was the murky sort of half-sleep that always came with colds. When she woke it was midday, and she thought she might just lie there, and finish her tea before getting up to tend to the fire.

She thought back to that night they'd spent in the trailer after Casey's fight. It was the last time they'd had total privacy, and she often thought of it with longing when she looked at the bed. Their love life was rather stifled at present, living with children in such immediate proximity to their every move and noise. As if in response to her thoughts, a scratch on her hip started to itch violently. She'd gotten more than one scratch, the night they'd snuck away from the trailer to make love in the woods which skirted the edge of their small campsite. Close enough to hear the children should one wake, but not so close as to run the risk of waking them. It hadn't been quite the experience she'd been hoping for, due to roots, rocks, and the general mayhem of a wood at night, with noises designed to make one want the security of four walls and a locked door. They'd given up on the forest floor, and Casey had taken her—with swift expediency—up against the broad trunk of an oak tree. She had just reached climax when the sky opened over them, a hard and cold rain drenching them immediately. It had the swift effect of cooling their ardor, and they had run back to the trailer, clutching their wet garments to their bodies. The result of which was a few rather painful bark scratches on her back, and of course, the cold she now had, which had smothered whatever had been left of her libido.

The next day Casey had casually mentioned that perhaps they could stop using any form of birth control. The suggestion had taken her by surprise.

"You want to talk about having another child now?" She had gestured at the space around them, where Kathleen's small clothes were hanging wet and limp on a makeshift line which ran from one end of the ceiling above the bed to the other. Lying underneath was a damp and rather claustrophobic experience and one ran the risk of waking up to asphyxiation by terry romper.

"Aye," he said, "I'm not plannin' to get ye pregnant this minute or anythin'. I'm only sayin' maybe we should let nature take her course, an' see if she sees fit to give us another child. Just give it some thought, Jewel, there's nothin' we need to decide this minute."

The thought of another baby was, at present, more than a tad overwhelming. Living as they did right now, it wasn't just overwhelming but utterly impractical and gave her a feeling of panic just contemplating it.

Right now, there were dishes in a tin bath outside, waiting for the infernal and unceasing rain to stop, so she could wash them, and everything she touched was damp. She fully expected to see webbing between her toes any day now. She took another sip of her tea, thinking she ought to get up and warm it. The taste was slightly bitter, and she realized it was rosehip tea. Casey was apparently determined to get vitamins into her however he might.

Something made a slight crinkling noise as she put the cup down, and she saw that there was a note tucked under the saucer. She picked it up and unfolded it, smiling at Casey's bold scrawl across the scrap of paper.

I love you.
Get some rest today.
Did I mention that I love you?

Tears stung at the top of her nose. It was small things like this which caught her off guard at times, how naturally they'd slid back into their family life with all its complexities and troubles, and the small everyday joys which she had almost forgotten during his time away. Small things like having him make her a cup of tea or feeling his hand reach out for hers in the night. Little moments of watching him with the children and seeing how gentle and genuinely interested he was with each one, regardless of whether they were spinning tops on rocks, discussing how long a toad could survive outside of its pond, or drawing up plans for a rather elaborate treehouse.

Reflecting on their conversation from a few nights ago, she stretched, running her hand down over her belly, and feeling a warm glow just at the thought of her husband. Her libido clearly wasn't *entirely* squashed, cold notwithstanding. *Did* she want another child, apart from Casey wanting one? In truth, she had believed Kathleen would be her last child, and had not given thought to another baby. But now there was the miracle of Casey's return, and the resumption of their marriage. She understood why he wanted another child, and knew that he had given it careful thought before broaching the subject with her.

Four children seemed like madness, but then with Casey she thought it would be a beautiful sort of madness. There were other things to consider, of course, not the least of which were the two miscarriages she'd had rather late in her pregnancies. There would always be a sore place in her heart where their first two daughters existed. She understood that he wanted another child for a variety of reasons, and those reasons were complicated, but she felt many of them herself.

In actuality, if Jamie didn't return home soon, they'd have five children. Just the thought made her head swim. Two days before, she'd made the trek into the local village and gone to one of the pubs, put a fiver on the counter and used the phone in the back to call Yevgena. There was still no word about Jamie though, and she was beginning to feel a thrum of fear that perhaps he'd asked them to raise Kolya because he had known he wouldn't be back to do it himself.

Living out here in the wilds of the countryside, it was hard to get news of any sort. Casey would call Patrick any time he was near a phone, and was today meeting his brother halfway between Belfast and the farm to visit for part of the day. She had given Casey a list of things she wanted him to ask Pat, and Casey had nodded, tucking it into his pocket along with the list of groceries and other necessaries they were woefully short on.

Just then a knock at the door of the Flying Tortoise startled her out of her ruminations. She climbed down from the bed, wishing she had a minute to get dressed and do something with her hair. She glanced in the tiny mirror on the closet door, and sighed. She looked like an absolute madwoman, hair sticking out at all angles. A vain attempt at smoothing it down proved fruitless, and so she wrapped a shawl around her shoulders and opened the door.

Outside, stood an old woman. She was tall and rawboned, with long floating grey hair covered with a floppy hat. She wore a long leather coat, like something straight out of a western movie, and carried three skinned rabbits in one hand, and a knife in the other. Around her waist was strung a mug and a spoon and a pouch which was stained green.

"I were wonderin' if yer man were round about?" she asked, her voice hoarse.

"No, I'm afraid he's not," she said, wondering how the woman knew Casey.

"Would ye maybe tell him that Aine was by?"

"I will," Pamela said, "do you have a message for him?"

"Not a message, no. I brought him some rabbits."

The woman thrust the three pink, shiny bodies at her and Pamela swallowed and took them. For her, rabbits belonged more to the realm of the pages of nursery tales and hutches where they waxed and grew fat as pets, and died of old age, rather than something which belonged in a stew.

"Thank you," she said and stepped back into the trailer to deposit the rabbits on the counter. "Would you like to come in? I could make you something hot to drink."

"No, just wanted to bring the rabbits. I don't like owin' a debt, an' so the rabbits are a payment against all he's done for me."

"Done for you?" Pamela asked, wondering if she was still asleep and dreaming this odd figure.

"Oh, he's done a deal for me. Fixed up my wee house for me a few weeks back. One of the poles had split, 'tweren't well-seasoned enough I 'spose, an' I were worried the roof was goin' to fall in on my head. I'm not as strong as I used to be, an' I wasn't sure I were up to the task of fixin' it."

"Are you just down the road?" Pamela asked, remembering something Casey had said about an old woman who lived down the lane, who she might keep an eye out for. The details of his story had been drowned in Kathleen's howls at the time, however, and she'd missed most of it.

The old woman gave her a shrewd look. "Ah no, not so much down the road, as in the woods. He'll not have mentioned me?"

"I think he did, but I'm afraid I missed much of what he told me, as the baby was crying at the time."

"Oh, aye, the wee redhead. She's fairy folk, that one."

"She is, indeed," Pamela said wondering when this woman had met Kathleen. "Please do stay and have tea with me," she said, moved by some impulse she couldn't quite define.

"Aye, might be as a cup of tea would go down well. Would ye mind if we sat outside though, the rain's stopped now an' I can't breathe with too many walls around me."

"Of course. Just give me a minute to tidy myself a bit and then I'll make the tea and join you outside." She felt a little dubious about the proposition as everything within sight was doused and dripping with water.

The woman smiled at her, clearly having read her expression. "I'll make a fire, an' it'll not be so bad."

Pamela dressed hastily, yanking on a pair of jeans which felt decidedly damp and a sweater which wasn't in much better fettle. She pulled her hair into a ponytail, knowing she'd likely break the brush were she to attempt to drag it through her mass of curls right now. She set the kettle to boil, and then put her feet into her old pair of Wellies—also damp—and then hastily assembled the tea things: mugs, brown betty, and several spoonfuls of Lyons in the pot.

True to her word, the woman had a fire blazing away in the pit and was now sitting on one of the stumps which encircled the fire, the tails of her cowboy duster spread out around her as though they were the finest of Victorian silks.

"So, how is it that you know Casey?" she asked, pouring the tea out into the speckled mug the woman detached from her belt and held out toward her.

"Yer husband come across me in the wood one day, asked me what I was about, but he weren't cross soundin' about it, just askin'. I thought mebbe I should just tell him, like, be honest. So I says I'm squattin' on yer land, an' figured he'd give me the heave-ho. But to my surprise he says, 'I see, well do ye need help haulin' that pole back to yer wee house? 'Twere as if he weren't throwed in the least by my confession."

"He probably wasn't," Pamela said wryly, sitting down across from the woman, after laying a bit of canvas over a wet stump. "He is used to shocks of a rather bigger nature."

"So he brought the pole back for me an' fixed the roof. Then he set about fixin' every other thing he saw were wrong with the place. I fought him on it, but he said he were well used to stubborn women an' then he just set to work."

"He would," Pamela said, "and he *is* well used to stubborn women."

"He smiled when he said it, seems he doesn't mind yer stubbornness."

"No, he doesn't," she said. "Or at least he doesn't mind most of the time," she added, thinking about how he'd feel if he knew about her meeting with Detective Holroyd.

"Will yez stay then, do ye think?"

"Oh yes, we're going to stay," she said, the information startling her a little for she and Casey hadn't come to a firm decision. Yet, she supposed, they had, for there was no talk of going back to their house in the North, but they'd spent plenty of their time establishing a better foothold here, and talking about their plans for the future.

"Did you know the man who lived here before?" she asked, for she always liked to have the history of a place if at all possible.

"Oh yes, I knew him for a very long time. He was kind too, like your husband. I didn't know a lot of kindness before I came here, an' when he found me on his land, I expected cruelty, but he said he didn't mind if I stayed. He kept the place tickin' over well enough until the last few years. He was gettin' old an' had the rheumatism. He'd have liked the thought of a family livin' here, hearin' wee ones runnin' about laughin' an' playin'. He'd have liked that a great deal. It's a good place, an' it will show love to you an' yours."

The woman leaned forward suddenly, grey eyes a cold silver and her tone gone from amiable to harsh in the space between two words. "It's neither here nor there, is it girl? You belong here, an' ye know that. The sea has called you back, for you are its own. There's an old poem, one about a woman who has dwelt here long an' long—you put me in mind of it. *Time was the sea brought kings as slaves to me.* Aye, the sea has been waitin' for you, girl, for she'll have her due before the salt stitches itself to your lips, an' the crabs crawl through your blood."

Overhead a gull screeched, and Pamela jumped slightly, slopping tea onto her damp jeans. The woman stood abruptly, as though the gulls had been some sort of alarm reminding her of other appointments she needed to keep. She jammed her hat back upon her head and fixed Pamela once again with the penetrating grey eyes.

"The hag lives here in these hills, if ye see her of a night, turn an' walk the other way, an' get ye safe inside yer walls."

Pamela nodded, throat a little dry. She'd thought that herself since coming to the land—for there was a presence both ancient and female here, which felt in no way benevolent. She rather hoped that the walls the woman mentioned were more of the metaphysical sort, for the walls of the Flying Tortoise didn't seem the sort to deter an ancient hag who'd taken the trouble to come down from the hills.

"I'll be on my way now. Ye cook up them hares with some herbs, an' a few veg, an' ye'll find they make a right good stew." The strange silver light had gone from the woman's eyes, and she merely seemed an eccentric soul once again.

"I'll do that, and thank you again," Pamela said, thinking that if there was any hare cooking to be done, it would be Casey doing it.

"Ye come see me when ye've decided about me livin' upon the land. Ye'll need to speak it over with yer man. It's one thing for him to give permission, but it's another altogether for the woman of the house. I'll bide by your word, whatever ye decide."

"I promise I'll come soon," Pamela said, feeling a little winded by the woman's visit.

Aine began to walk away with long sure strides, but turned back at the edge of their clearing. "Ye mind what I said about the hag, lass. She'll slip inside yer bones if ye give her the space to do so."

Pamela nodded, squelching the urge to cross herself, as the woman disappeared into the woods.

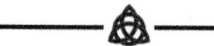

"Oh, aye, the Queen of the Fairies," Casey said in response to her relating the odd woman's visit to him.

"The Queen of the Fairies?" she asked, wiping down his back with a beautifully dry towel. While visiting his brother, Casey had the foresight to drop off all their laundry with a service, and had picked it up before his return home. On their bed sat toppling piles of towels, wash cloths, jeans, socks, sweaters, pyjamas, rompers and underwear. It would, Pamela knew, be damp and dirty all too soon, but for now it was clean and dry, and sometimes that was enough to make a woman feel all was right with the universe.

"Her name is Aine—it means Queen of the Fairies. Mind you, in the older tales she's either the wife or daughter of Manannán mac Lir."

Manannán mac Lir was the old Irish god of the sea; she shivered a little at that, remembering what the woman had said about the sea wanting her back. The visit had disturbed her more than she cared to admit, and she had been greatly relieved when Casey arrived home with the children, and she'd been swept up in getting everyone ready for bed. Now, the boys were tucked up in their tent for the night, with Finbar watching over them, and Isabelle and Kathleen were sleeping snug on their trundle bed, dark hair and bright glimmering in the firelit interior of the Tortoise.

"She wanted to know if we're going to stay," Pamela said. Casey went very still.

"Oh, did she? Well, what did ye tell her?"

"I said yes, of course we're staying. And don't even try to pretend that you didn't have the papers drawn up for the mortgage already."

"I like to be prepared," he said, and then turned toward her. The lantern light flickered on his face, and shoulders, leaving small gold lights scattered in his hair. "Are ye certain this is what ye want, woman?"

"I am," she said.

"Then I think there's somethin' I ought to tell ye."

"What is it?" she asked, alarmed by the shift in his tone.

"Well, I know ye've been worried about what Jamie would feel about all this, us takin' wee Kathleen this distance from him."

She nodded, wondering where he was headed with this particular topic.

"But the man an' myself had a talk about just this a few months back."

"You did?" she asked, surprised. While Casey and Jamie had always been civil with one another for her sake, and now for Kathleen's, she found herself somewhat disconcerted by the notion of the two of them sitting down for a chat.

"Aye, we did. Both he and I have reason to understand how uncertain things can be in this life, an' so we felt it was best to have things settled. He said to me that if we decided to move, he would understand. Ireland is a small island for a man such as himself, so he appreciated the notion of still bein' able to see Kathleen as much as he'd like, but not havin' to worry about her in quite the same fashion as he would, did we stay where we were."

"Oh," she said, not certain how she felt about this. She had been dreading telling Jamie, and yet, had known it was her responsibility to do so. It would have been her moment to really assess how he felt about it, and to make decisions together based on Kathleen's care going forward. Instead it appeared the two men had arranged things rather tidily without consulting her. It wasn't a mark of character in her favour, she thought, that she felt as she did about them meeting without her.

Casey was looking down at her with a bemused expression on his face.

"Well, I see it makes ye uncomfortable, but as we both father this wee girl," he nodded down at the slumbering Kathleen, "it seems wise to have the occasional chat about it. An' bein' that I know ye're fine with that angle of it, I have to ask what is botherin' ye?"

"It would be nice, occasionally," she said, "if you weren't quite so attuned to my facial expressions."

"Ye've a lovely face, Jewel, but it's not always built for hidin' things."

"You won't remember this, but I tried to keep my life with you separate from my friendship with Jamie for the most part. I suppose it feels odd and maybe a little dangerous to have the two crossing over now."

"I'm sure I had an appreciation of that in the past, but Kathleen makes that a wee bit harder to orchestrate now. It's best for her if her da an' myself are on the same page, no? An' forgive me for sayin' so, but there are things ye may not have thought about where fatherhood is concerned. I want to be certain I know what values Jamie has for her, how he sees her life unfoldin', what his dreams are for her. All that weighs into how we raise her, an' how I do my bit of the fatherin'."

"You're a wonderful father to all of them," she said, meaning every word. That he should take Kathleen as part of his brood and yet still respect the fact that Jamie was her father was a gift she was grateful for every day.

Casey shrugged. "Ye know I love the wee mite, Pamela but in truth it's more than that. The man did it for me, he loved my children enough to father them the three years I was gone. He did a fine job too, bein' that it's clear to me how much they love him in return. I won't do less for his children. An' Kathleen is yours too, which makes her ours."

"You're being very reasonable about the whole thing," she said, though she was touched by his words.

"Well, I think the least I can do is exercise a bit of magnanimity toward the man, beyond gratitude for his care of my children."

"Oh," she said, wondering just what he meant, "why is that?"

Casey looked at her, dark eyes fathomless in the dim of the trailer. "Because," he said, and she heard the fierce note low in his voice, "when given the choice, ye chose me."

"I did," she said, and held his eyes with the gaze of hers, giving him the gift of knowing how deep that choice went.

They spoke then of all the information he and Pat had exchanged. There was no further news to be had on Jamie, though this he had relayed immediately knowing it was a primary source of worry for her. The police had made no headway as far as Pat knew on discovering just who was responsible for the death of Violet, and so the investigation was stalled. Jamie's absence, of course, wasn't making him look innocent in the eyes of the police, and Pamela knew if he was in a place where he'd heard of it, he would have been home weeks ago. There was other news as well, Lily was saying da, or so Pat claimed, Casey said.

"Frankly, it sounded a deal like a wee sheep bleatin' at me, but I thought it best to let him have his moment."

Owen and Gert checked on their house, regularly, and Gert had sent a large tin of her *vanillekipferl* biscuits along with Patrick. Pamela knew it was a sign of how missed they were, for Gert usually made these cookies for Christmas, and Christmas alone.

There were plenty more tidbits of news to be heard: Pat and Kate were considering having another baby, Gert's sister was visiting from Germany, and even the ever patient Owen was at his wit's end with the squabbling between the two sisters. Tomas had been heard whistling around the office and had taken to getting his hair trimmed regularly, which had led Pat to believe he'd a romance on the go, as unlikely as the prospect seemed. At this bit of news, Pamela had hastily put her tea mug to her lips in the hopes of hiding her face, for she thought she had a good notion why Tomas was whistling, and knew Casey wasn't likely to be best pleased by the news.

After all the news and gossip had been digested along with the biscuits, they'd made the trip into the chilly darkness to visit the outhouse, to check the boys, and to bring back water for the morning's tea and *toilette*. Then, Casey, yawning widely, had followed her up into their nest of quilts and pillows and, having brought her a full and comprehensive report of the doings back home as well as clean laundry, groceries and *plätzchen*, fell swiftly to sleep.

Now, she lay on her side, and watched over her family. The fire in the wee stove glowed through the glass of the door, and pooled in a sift of gold on the floor. The girls were lit unevenly, so that she could only see pieces of them—the tilt of Isabelle's nose and the fan of her thick lashes against flushed cheeks, the round of Kathleen's soft baby cheek, and the spray of her curls, like a spangle of gold flame on her pillow. She would need a hair cut soon—her first. The thought of it caused a pang in Pamela. How was her wee baby old enough to need things like haircuts, proper shoes, and her very own drinking cup? In the tent outside, Conor was fast asleep with one arm flung over Finbar, and Kolya was upside down on his makeshift bed, feet tucked tidily under his pillow. Kolya brought Jamie to mind once again, though she pushed her fears for him down, knowing there was little she could do about it. Until Yevgena heard from him—or did not—there wasn't any reason to think some great harm had befallen him. And so, she would simply believe that he would come home, and that Kolya and Kathleen would have their father again.

Beside her, Casey was deeply asleep, worn out from his day of adventuring with the children. There was sawdust in his hair though, for he'd gone up to the cottage and done a bit of work after he'd returned. She reached out to remove it, but then thought better of it. She didn't want to disturb him, and she was well used to wood particles in the bed at this point. A missed bit of vanilla sugar sparkled in his beard—he'd polished off four of the *vanillekipferl* along with his night time cup of tea.

There had been one bit of news which had been unwelcome and it was that Detective Holroyd had been around to Egan and Riordan more than once, inquiring as to where she and Casey now lived. Pat had refused to tell him, and Tomas had reached out to his contacts in the RUC, only to find out that Detective Holroyd wasn't assigned to Violet's murder at all.

"Not sure why he'd still be nosin' around, but it appears he'll get his hands slapped sharpish if his bosses find out. Pat asked if there was reason that information should be leaked?" Casey gave her a rather pointed look as he said this, but she merely shook her head, as though to say the detective was of little concern to her.

"No, none that I know of," she said, fearing that goading Will Holroyd in any way would force his hand. There might well come a day when that was necessary, but it was not today.

Casey moved a little in his sleep, and then reached out and took her hand in his, without fluttering so much as an eyelid. She had forgotten what it was like, to have the man you loved there in your bed each night. She'd forgotten the security of it, how just his presence allowed her to sleep more deeply, and wake with a sense of anticipation each morning. What it was to laugh with someone who understood your jokes, even the truly lame ones. What it was to have him hold her, simply because she needed it and so did he.

Once, returning from a trip to Hong Kong, Jamie had brought her the gift of flowering tea. Knowing how she loved jasmine tea, the one he'd given her had held white jasmine at its core, surrounded by strips of tightly sewn green tea leaves. Even then, she had thought—watching the beautiful flower bloom under the influence of hot water—it was an apt metaphor for her life. How tightly sewn down her core was, for fear that if she let it go even a little, the cold of the world would damage what was left in her heart. Jamie's love had opened it partway, and Casey's return had given it the shock it needed to unfurl completely. She smiled a little to herself, knowing what Casey thought of being compared to water, earth-bound man that he was.

It occurred to her now, with some surprise, that she was no longer afraid to be vulnerable. Love, after all, left you with little choice. And so, still holding her husband's hand, she drifted off into a deep and dreamless sleep.

Chapter Forty-eight

Fleur

IT WAS A FULL week before Pamela was able to go visit Aine. She owed the woman an answer and had set out this day to give it to her.

The woods were familiar to her already, for she and the children had walked in them many times. She thought she knew where the house was located for Casey had told her it was near to the spring, where the ground rose up into a bank out of which hung the great roots of an ancient oak. Their land was filled with rolling hills and banks and drop offs but there was only one spring. It shouldn't be that hard to find it.

As it turned out though, the house was so well hidden that she could have passed it any number of times and never noticed it there deep in the small copse, tucked away as it was into the hillside. It was like a mushroom, grown in leaf-shadow, touched here and there by the light, but not enough to ever fully reveal it. She knew if she was to return to the same spot tomorrow, the tiny building might well be invisible to her.

The house was partially dug into the hillside, the trees above overhanging it and the thick shrubbery covering it rendering it next to invisible. Ivy grew up and around the windows, for there *were* windows, one rectangular and one round as a full moon, fronting the thick walls. A thick length of canvas covered the doorway. The front half of the house was round, built with sturdy poles, and a material which both looked and smelled distinctly organic in nature. The roof blended in with the flora round about, for it was shingled with moss and ferns. It was a proper sort of dwelling for a woman named after the Queen of the Fairies.

Movement caught her eye then, and she jumped as though she'd been shot—which was rather appropriate given that the figure who emerged from behind the small lean-to next to the house, was holding an ancient rifle.

"Jesus Murphy and the little green men," she said, taking a shaky breath while her heart hammered madly. It was the woman she'd come seeking.

"I'm sorry, but a woman can't be too careful about just who is lurkin' about her home."

"I understand," she said, for she did. She had answered her own door more than once with either pistol or rifle in hand. Just why the old woman might feel the need of such defense though, was a mystery she'd love to know the answer to. It was, however, far too soon in their acquaintanceship to ask such a question.

If she didn't know better, she would have sworn Aine had somehow materialized here out of the roots and soil. Despite her height and light-coloured eyes, she seemed a direct descendant of the dark people who had roamed the forests and shores of Ireland before recorded time. She had clearly long lived close to the earth, and carried its colours and scents with her. There was something entirely wild about her, as if she might well turn into a mountain hare when the moon was full.

Near to the little house was a rowan tree, abundantly green just now with spring growth. A witch tree, Casey had told her once, and sacred to the druids. A fitting tree for this woman to have beside her entrance.

"Ye should always have a rowan near the house," Aine said, "it's a deterrent to the devil."

"And is the devil a worry hereabouts?" she asked.

She'd meant the words in jest, but the woman gave her a sharp look. "Oh aye, there's mighty old gods what live in the forest, an' ye can be sure there's more than a few that are dark of purpose."

"What did you use to build your house?" Pamela asked, thinking—for the sake of her spine, which was far too attuned to both ghostly presences and dark gods—it would be wise to get the conversation onto a more practical footing.

"Clay an' horse manure, with a bit of straw to bind it. Took me a bit to get the mixture right, mind, but it's strong an' it keeps the wind an' the rain out." The woman was clearly proud of her little house.

"Come in, then," Aine said, pushing aside the canvas and entering into the gloom beyond. Pamela ducked low and followed, remembering a story about how the ancients believed that the forest held doorways, from one realm into another. If that was so, she was certain she was stepping through one right now.

Inside, she was able to stand upright, with the ceiling a few feet above her head. The roof sloped upward as naturally as a mushroom cap, braced with poles that were roughly five inches around. The crown of the wee home was a pentagram, formed from the same poles, these slightly smaller in diameter.

The walls were rough and rounded to the shape of the landscape and whitewashed so that the inside of the tiny home was far brighter than Pamela had expected. Suspended from the ceiling was a small drying rack, festooned at present with a variety of damp sweaters, scarves and well-worn trousers.

Opposite of where she stood was a small hearth, which appeared to be the remains of an old cast iron stove, inserted into a surround of stone and plaster. There were a couple of copper pots off to one side, and an ancient black kettle sitting on the hob.

The floor, planked in rough wood, was piled thick with layered rugs—old oriental ones, in an explosion of jeweled colours. She sat down cross-legged on one, and within minutes was accepting a mug of tea from the woman's rough hands.

Aine took her own mug of tea and sat down across from Pamela. She recognized the mug, as well as the one she held, as two of a group she had made at a pottery class some years back. They had gone missing shortly after their arrival here on the farm, and she had suspected Casey of slowly 'disappearing' them, being that every single project she had made in the class had been less than aesthetically pleasing. Now she knew where—or rather who—the mugs had gone to. For while they were as ugly as sin, they were also sound as a drum.

"So you've lived here a long time?" Pamela asked, uncertain as to how one began a conversation with one's squatter, so chose to simply dive in and tackle the subject.

"I grew up hereabouts, an' then I were gone for many years. When I returned, I'd nowhere to live, nor money enough to buy me a house. I were drinkin' a great deal back then, an' needed to cut myself off from the world. As I told ye at our last meetin' the old man who lived here before ye, didn't mind me bein' on the land, as he'd known me when I were young. But then he died, an' I was afraid of what the new owners would think. I couldn't move for I've nowhere to go. I understand if ye want me gone, though, an' ye only have to say so. Only I'll need a bit of time to find myself a new location."

"No, I don't want you gone," Pamela said, meeting the woman's eyes. "You'll be part of this land in a way we aren't yet, and it of you. I'm not one to part a person from their home. There's room enough for us all."

The woman nodded, her relief at Pamela's words was visible in both her face and the line of her body. "Yer man said ye would not mind, an' I can see he spoke rightly about ye. Ye're well matched, though he's of the earth an' ye're of the sea. He told me he got lucky an' caught himself a selkie maid one moonlit night."

"Did he, then? Well, he does wax fanciful at times," she said, though she felt slightly odd at the woman's words. As if, like an old dream she'd had since childhood, she would one day be expected to return to the sea from whence she'd come.

The tea was good, and tasted of the forest, that note of something wild, gathered when its oils were high. Pamela welcomed the warmth of it, for the day was cool.

"I came here all those years ago, because there's a wee graveyard not so far from here. Someone very dear is buried in it, an' I wanted to be near to her."

There was only one graveyard that was relatively nearby, and it was at-tached—or at least it had been—to the home for unwed mothers. Suddenly she thought she understood, and the woman's next words only confirmed it.

"Will ye know of the home the Sisters of Mercy had here for unwed mothers?"

"Yes," Pamela said. She had driven by the site where the home had been many times. It was a big old grey building on a barren hillside. A bleak and brooding sort of place, it always raised the hairs on the back of her neck. There had been a fire years ago, and the order had moved elsewhere, and the build-ing had been left abandoned ever since.

"I lived there for a long time, far longer than any should for it was an evil place. I'm sure ye've heard the whispers, though that's all they are is whispers, for people are still too afraid to speak out about the place. I had a wee girl out of wedlock. I named her Fleur, which the nuns said were a ridiculous name, but I liked it. An' it's what she were—a tiny flower, wid a face on her like pet-als openin' to the sun. Like yer wee one—skin so clear an' fine, it were near to translucent. I were only allowed to see her for an hour each day but I lived for that hour, it were everythin' to me."

"What happened to her?" Pamela asked, afraid she knew the answer already.

"I'll get to that bit quick enough," Aine said, reaching over to the pile of wood and adding another two pieces to the fire. "First though, I'll tell ye how I wound up there. I come from a big family, I was the oldest though, an' ex-pected to help me mam with everythin'. Me mam never took to me for some reason, an' so I was treated to the sharp side of her tongue from the time I was wee. Me dad was softer but he left us to go find work in Liverpool, an' he wasn't there to temper my ma. When I turned thirteen, she told me I was to go out to work. I was sent to a big house that belonged to a wealthy couple. He was a barrister, an' his wife thought herself quite somethin' in what society ex-isted in that wee town. It seemed like it might be a good thing at first, though I never saw so much as a ha'penny for myself; the money was given directly to my mother an' she never worried about me receivin' any benefit from it. The master an' his lady weren't unkind, but they were blind when it come to their son. Durin' the year he was away at a fine boardin' school, but he come home for the summer, an' I knew almost immediately that he was trouble.

"The house was in a right kerfuffle gettin' ready for him to arrive. The cook was makin' all sorts of treats for the young master, as she called him, an' everythin' had to be scrubbed an' dusted an' made bright an' shiny. I'd never seen anyone make such a fuss over their child comin' home.

"I admit I was a wee bit dazzled when he arrived, for he was a handsome young man, though I was wary too, for he seemed to think very well of himself, but then with everyone makin' such a fuss over him, why wouldn't he? I soon come to understand though, that his looks were no more than a coat of paint over a rotten buildin'.

"To be sure, it didn't take long for the paint to start peelin' off, an' I soon knew who I was dealin' with. He'd show up wherever I was several times a day. He'd rub up against me when I was tryin' to make the beds, or pinch my breast when he walked past, or put a hand up my skirts an' pull at my undergarments. I got in trouble with the cook, because she felt I was doin' somethin' to keep him about. She accused me of bein' a girl of loose morals. I knew then my goose was cooked—if I told them they'd not believe me an' I'd be cast out because I knew me mam wouldn't take me back in, not even as her slave.

"He come in to my room one night about two weeks into the summer. I was asleep an' only woke when he got on top of me. He pushed my nightgown up above my breasts, an' then stuffed the end of it into my mouth, so I couldn't scream. An' then he just shoved himself inside me. I didn't even know what was happenin', only that it hurt horribly an' that I was terrified. He told me no one would ever believe me, an' that if they did, they'd think I'd seduced him, an' that I was no better than a whore.

"I knew what he said was true, an' that I must simply endure it. He came every night after that, an' forced me to do things I'd no notion of before. I think he enjoyed humiliatin' me—I believe that was half the pleasure for him. Of course by the time he returned to school in the autumn, I was pregnant. It took me some time to understand, but I'd seen my mam fall pregnant often enough to know what was happening. Come October I was gettin' sick every mornin', an' my uniform was uncomfortably tight. I hid it for as long as I could. An' once I couldn't his mother fired me, an' banished me from the house after callin' me every filthy name she could think of. I went home—even though I knew my mother would be furious—because I'd nowhere else to go.

"She didn't react as I thought she would, an' I suppose that ought to have warned me. She simply said we'd figure things out, an' to keep my mouth shut in the meantime. I had a few days with my wee sisters an' brother though, an' it were lovely sleepin' in amongst them an' feelin' safe for the first time in so long.

"The priest came three days later, when I was peggin' out the wash. He'd another man with him, an' they forced me into the car they'd come in, an' drove away with me. I never saw my family again. They brought me to the home here, and left me under the care of the Sisters of Mercy. I thought I'd known cruelty before, but I'd been very wrong."

Aine paused to take a drink of her tea. The tension of the story was such that Pamela thought she could almost see it in the air around them, singing like wires strung so tightly that they vibrated with the memory of pain and loss.

"The first thing they did was take away my identity—shaved my head to the bone, took away my clothes and replaced them with horrible rags, and then gave me a new name—Enda for me, a man's name and one I hated.

"We were no more than slaves, an' there was no sympathy for sickness or exhaustion. We scrubbed floors an' walls, an' took in laundry—endless mounds of it, endless mountains of other people's filth.

"When my time come they strapped me to one of those cold iron beds, wrists an' ankles, so that I could not move about at all. The pain was tremendous, like nothing I'd ever even imagined could exist. It felt like a big red monster had taken me over an' was rippin' me apart with its teeth. I was certain that I'd die, but I thought that would be a relief—no more pain, no more laundry, no more nuns strappin' me for imagined sins. Maybe the baby would die too, an' we'd be together on the other side, somewhere better, not so much like heaven but more of a summer place, where there'd be flowers an' fields an' a wee hut for the two of us to live in.

"But we lived—the both of us. I was allowed an hour with her each day, an' I lived for that hour.

"I hadn't loved her father, for he had been little more than a leerin' face in the dark, an' someone who'd caused me great pain an' humiliation. There was nothing of him about her; she was completely herself from the first moment. I loved her so. I know most mothers love their babies, but she was the only person other than my sisters, an' my wee brother Davey, that I had ever loved. I just poured that love out on her, in that scant hour a day, kissin' that wee face an' brushin' her pretty hair, doin' anythin' to make her laugh an' smile. We had eighteen months like that.

"An' then one day I went to spend my hour, an' she was gone. The nun on duty told me she'd had a fever the night before, an' died very sudden-like in the morning. It made little sense to me for she'd not been sick the day before, she'd been fine, an' had been laughin' an' playin' with me. I said I wanted to see her, I needed to see her an' they said no, she'd already been buried. This seemed mad to me—already buried? So quickly, an' without tellin' me of it? I got hysterical, or so they said after, I just remember bein' cold with purpose—that somehow or other I must make them take me to her. I'd dig her up if I needed to, in order to say goodbye. Finally they took me out an' showed me a wee little grave, heaped up with fresh dirt. I got down on my hands an' knees an' started to dig with my fingers, for I was goin' to see her, an' say goodbye. They dragged me off, an' beat me about the face an' head with their fists, an' then finally someone jabbed me with somethin' cold, an' I passed out.

"When I came to I was locked up in the infirmary, where they left me for six months. I think all the life left me then, I just lay there drugged an' catatonic. Eventually they put me back in the laundry, where I stayed for another year. When I asked about visitin' her grave, I was told they'd moved her, an' wouldn't tell me to where, because of my 'mental instability'. About six weeks after that, I ran away. I managed to get out in a big container of sheets, an' was put into the lorry without anyone noticin'. I slipped out when the driver made his first stop, for it was still dark an' none could see me.

"I lived on the streets of Dublin for a bit, an' then found work lookin' after an elderly couple who'd no children to do for them as they aged. I stayed with them until they both died, an' it turned out they'd left me a bit of money in their wills. After that, I came back here an' lived in a tent in the woods on this land. The farmer an' I had an understandin' for years, an' I'd do a bit for him now an' again when he needed help. He was the sort kept himself to himself, an' so he never told anyone about me. I suppose ye might call him a hermit. Then he died, an' the family didn't want the farm any longer. I did think I'd have to leave, an' then I met up with yer husband, an' could see he was a good sort. I knew it would be you that would decide, though. Once we had our chat the other day, I saw ye were of like mind to him, an' that if I told ye my story, ye'd be able to understand, an' not think me a terrible person."

"How could I? None of that was your fault."

"Ah, but that's not how the world views women, is it? An' Lord knows we're expected to understand our business from the time we're wee. The world blames us for bein' the victim of its sorrow. Ye'll know the truth of that yerself. Ye'll know what it is to have things taken from ye that ye cannot ever get back."

She did know in part, for it had happened to her and she understood what it did to a woman to have something taken from her by force, which before had only been given in love. But that was the difference she supposed, prior to the rape on the train, her body had been loved, had been cherished and had succumbed to a passion larger than herself. This woman had been a child at the time, one who'd never known love or kindness.

"You've lost children too." The woman said it as a statement of fact, and Pamela nodded.

"Two of them," she said quietly, the delicate face of their first daughter rising there before her eyes, a water creature with the sheen of pearls upon her skin. A being not meant for this world. Their second child she had never seen, and so there was no tiny face to remember. There had been another child before that, one she'd had aborted, for that pregnancy had been the result of violence and hatred at the hands of brutal men. But after, as she'd made her way through the wilderness of what rape did to a woman's psyche and sense of safety, she'd had Casey, and his love had helped her heal in no small measure.

"I knew that ye understood what it was to lose a child, for I could see the knowledge of it there in yer face. I could not have told ye about my wee girl otherwise."

They chatted freely after that, as though with the telling of Aine's story they had cleared some sort of hurdle, and could now be easy with one another. Aine told her the news of the place, which was mostly about the lay of the land, the animals which came through during the nights, and which months were most fierce for storms, and how often the farm saw snow. It made her think of an old poem, one scribbled down by a 9th century Irish monk in the margins of his manuscript. *I have news for you: the stag bells, winter snows, summer has gone...Wind high and cold, the sun low, short its course, the sea running high. Deep red the bracken; its shape is lost; the wild goose has raised its accustomed cry, cold has seized the bird's wings; season of ice, this is my news.*

Aine knew the land and all its vagaries, and Pamela listened, fascinated, for while she knew some of it, she was still getting acquainted with the place and was happy to absorb the long knowledge of one who had seen it through many seasons. To her surprise the sun was well into its decline toward evening when she finally put down her mug, and stood to go.

"Thank you for the visit. It was lovely being here in your home with you."

Aine smiled, and she could see she'd pleased the woman with the comment. She'd meant it though, the old woman's home was the sort every woman dreamed of in some secret corner of her soul—a quiet place away from the world and all its demands. The sort of place one retreated to as a crone, with a goat or two, a spinning wheel and a kettle.

"I keep to myself mostly, but if ye've need of anythin' come by an' see me. If I'm not about, leave a note. I will warn ye I get strange moods that come upon me from time to time, an' I'm neither kith nor kin durin' those times, an' 'tis best to avoid me for a few days."

"How will I know to avoid you?" she asked, half in jest, half serious. She liked Aine, but she also felt she wasn't someone she'd care to cross.

"Oh, ye'll know, I've a foot in both worlds durin' such times. Bein' that ye're such yerself, ye'll see it clear."

Aine watched her walk down and away from her hermit's hut, and Pamela looked back once where the path bent down towards the farm, and saw the woman still standing, long grey hair dappled in green shadow. Aine raised a hand in farewell and then ducked back into her solitary home, and Pamela continued down the hill toward her own home, feeling the woman's loss in the very core of her.

She took in the land as she walked, the idea of the monk's poem tickling at the edge of her mind, even as she was thinking of what she could cobble together for dinner from three straggly carrots, four potatoes, two turnips, a leg of chicken and a half loaf of bread, providing Conor hadn't raided the ice chest in her absence.

She could see it in her mind—a monk's pages, illuminated flora and fauna and verse beside it. She could do a more modern version, a sort of breviary of nature and life here in her little corner of the world. A book of hours based upon the sweep of light, the sound of the sea, the quick glimpse of a fox, the movement of shadow through the leaves of a tree; an old woman standing at the crossroads of both sorrow and loss. Her publishers had made it clear they were open to more ideas, something new beyond *The Children of the Troubles* series. She thought she might like that, a work of this land, grounded in this new life they had begun.

I have news. There are baby badgers on the hill behind the house. The spring is stirring, the winds taste sharp and fresh, the sun is high, its course long. The bracken is green and the wild goose has returned home, sun upon its wings. A house is rising upon a hill. Children are growing in health and happiness. Life renews once again.

Chapter Forty-nine

Written on Skin

THE BUCKET OF ICE WATER took him full in the face, pulling James Kirk-patrick out of the unconsciousness in which he'd been happily immersed for some time now. There were no windows in the room where he was currently locked away, so he had no sense of whether it was night or day, or how long he'd been here. He'd been manhandled into this room by three brutes, who'd kicked and pummeled him, and it appeared, taken his shirt. The room was made of stone, and was perishingly cold. There were no amenities, and so he was lying now upon the freezing stone, wondering if he'd have to pry himself off, as he appeared to be stuck to it.

"Come." The voice was Russian. Please God that he'd made it across the border, and not been returned while unconscious. "She wants to see you now."

She? And then he remembered who *she* was, remembered the voices outside the bear caravan, remembered that he'd wanted oblivion again, and had gotten it through a series of blows that had been inflicted with a sort of methodical meticulousness that told him the men who'd done it had been hired for their expertise. It was these same men who'd just efficiently woken him with the application of ice water.

They dragged him up and out of his prison. He tried to find his feet, to get them properly under him but his legs weren't cooperating—cold or the beating, or maybe both.

Through a door then, this room warm at least, enough so that he thought he might collapse. The woman waited, seated by a roaring fire, legs crossed and the light in the room such that she looked many years younger than she was.

She had always been beautiful, and that had ripened to a sort of glorious opulence over time, but by this he was entirely unmoved. He was aware that she had been waiting a very long time for this moment, and like a spider who has known long hunger between feeds, wanted to play a little with its prey before disposing of it.

Normally he knew not to underestimate the power of hatred, especially when it had years to grow and build upon itself. Especially, perhaps, when it had been born of love. For this woman, with the eyes burning dark, had once loved him. There was no leverage to be had from that today, though. That he'd been so blind to just what route that might take was what bothered him.

"Diane," he said calmly to the mother of his oldest son, as though he weren't standing dripping, bruised, bleeding, half-naked, and in need of a wall to prop himself up.

"James. It has been a long time."

"Not long enough, I'm thinking," Jamie said, though he knew quips of any sort were suicidally stupid just now.

"Certainly you won't feel so by day's end," she said, smiling, something so cold in her tone that he felt the prickle of it like frost on a blade.

"No doubt you're right," he replied, wanting nothing more than to lie down beside the fire and pass out. "Perhaps while we're here, you'll tell me why it never occurred to you to let me know that I had a son."

She took the question in calmly, for she had surely expected it. But he saw from her eyes that he'd hit the emotional mark. "You had made it clear you were done with me. He's my son, not yours. I couldn't afford to have Neil know. I wanted some kind of a father for Julian, after all."

She had a point there. Still, he wished she'd seen fit to tell him. Some of the damage done might have been averted, and Julian might have become a different man in the end. It was too late now, however. It was too damn late for so many things.

"Diane," he said, and his voice was not unkind, "why am I here?"

"You do not know, my pretty peacock? No? You will find out soon enough." Her face was a mask, for she'd learned well to hide what she was feeling, but her eyes were dark with an anger which had simmered for years and was just now come to the boil.

The men returned and tied him to a chair. The restraints almost seemed a fair trade for the ability to sit down. He'd managed to break one's nose before they tied him, though. This had earned him a good thump for his trouble. Still, he no longer had to stand.

Now, there was a strange stillness to the air, with only the crackle of the fire to break it. And then he understood why, as another voice entered the room.

"We want to know why Mordecai met with you in Marrakech." The voice was one he'd recognized from his box—stiff upper lip, duty to Queen and country, and a traitor to everything he'd pretended to believe in. Felix Plum, walking out from the shadows in which he'd stood since Jamie had entered the room.

"Mordecai?"

"Yes, don't play stupid with us, James. What did Mordecai tell you?"

"He told me he was going into Russia. It was a goodbye visit of sorts." It had been too. The old man had not expected to return from that trip.

"What else did he say to you that day?"

The question seemed purposefully vague to him, which told him they were afraid to be specific. He knew why, and it was for that reason they were likely to kill him here today.

"What would you like to know—what we ate, what we drank? It was, as I recall a very good red wine from a little vineyard in Sicily. Or there was the balm I recommended for his rheumatism. As I remember it, he and the cook exchanged recipes that night—with adequate torture I might be able to remember his grandmother's recipe for kugel, or Farad's for fattoush. I also told him how the coffee was made, though Farad puts in a little too much cardamom for my taste. Good help with a hand for the coffee is such a rare thing to find."

"Quit being a bastard," Felix said through thin lips.

Jamie did not look up at him, but kept his gaze fixed upon the woman opposite.

"We spoke of everything and nothing, so I'm afraid you'll have to be specific about what it is you'd like me to say here."

"Don't be trivial, James," she said, "it's the refuge of a fool."

He shrugged as well as the restraints allowed, forgetting his collarbone for an instant. "Beyond that there is nothing to tell you."

"What you mean to say is beyond that there is nothing you are willing to tell us."

"Perhaps that too."

When Diane spoke again her voice was soft, but carried like iron held within a velvet glove. "Then you will die here today, and who will be left to mourn you? Your American tart, the child you have with her? She's gone back to her husband and they have a very cozy little family life, do they not?"

"I have friends in places other than my personal life," he said, though this wasn't strictly true. Whatever might be true, he did not want Pamela dragged further into this mess.

"An Irish spy who plays both sides of the game? You're inconvenient to them at best. You disappear into the snows of Russia—what could be more fitting for a Soviet agent?"

He was tired of games, and so he asked the one question which mattered here today. "What is it that you want, Diane?"

"What I want you can no longer give me, but today I will settle for you on your knees begging me to release you from this life."

One last silver pulse of mania, leading him to speak unwisely. "As I recall you've had me there before," Jamie said, "but you seemed much happier about it then." Felix slapped him at that point, which he supposed he probably deserved. It also confirmed that Diane had taken this man into her bed, in order to more effectively manipulate him. The next blow returned him to the edge of darkness.

When consciousness returned, it was to find Felix hunkered down on the floor in front of him. He had never liked this man, and certainly never trusted him and this opinion certainly wasn't changed by his current predicament. Felix spoke now in his clipped, nasally accent, each word bitten off with anger.

"I think you're a double agent; I think you were turned during your time in Russia. I could just throw you back to the Soviets; they know how to dispose of traitors."

"Go ahead," Jamie said, blearily. "If you plan to dispose of me anyway, what difference does it make who does it?"

Diane rose then, and Jamie closed one eye to limit her image to just one personage, rather than the three both eyes afforded him.

"Felix, give me a moment alone with him."

"No, that's not a good idea."

"Felix," voice like flint now, "go."

"Be a good boy Felix and do as she says," he said, earning himself a hit to the stomach.

The door clicked behind Felix, and it was then just him and Diane, a situation he had not foreseen ever occurring again. She walked over to him, and her scent arrived before her. A dry, crisp scent and not one he'd ever particularly cared for, even when he'd been her lover.

He put his head down then, attempting to regain his breath, and saw in his mind's eye his children from the last time Pamela had brought Kathleen to him, and stayed to visit for a little. They'd been in the paddock, and Kolya had been riding, while Kathleen had been on Danu with him. Pamela had her camera in hand, as she so often did, and had taken pictures of them all. The sun had been shining and the day filled with peace and warmth. If he could just distill the darkness in which he was sinking, he would be able to put himself there—feel it, smell the warm chamomile of Kathleen's shampoo, the solidity of his daughter's tiny body, leaning against him for protection. To look over at Kolya and smile at how the very set of his shoulders and the imperious way he had with horses, was a direct echo of Andrei. It would be a good picture to go out upon. Diane hit him then, pulling his head up by the hair and giving vent to her fury with a blow to his left cheek.

The picture in his head fractured into small fragments, before it too slipped away. Life was always a process of letting go, and at the end, simply letting go of breathing, of hoping, of believing in another day. Why he had such trouble with this last thing, he couldn't have said, only that he did, despite wanting it desperately at times.

"I want to know where Mordecai is. If you don't tell me then we'll send Dmitri and his child back over the border and let the Russians have him. Is that what you want?"

He did not answer because there was nothing to say. He could not save Dmitri if this woman was bent on keeping her secrets. Seeing his refusal to answer, she took another tack, one designed to hit closer to home.

"Your wife was a double agent, but both sides of her were allied against you. She's dead now—did you know?" This last was said in a casual tone, though every syllable was calculated to penetrate the place where he'd retreated.

"Your little lover found her. Found her with her throat almost slashed to the bone. Could be that Pamela did it herself, she had the motivation after all. The police certainly seem to believe it could be her."

Christ. Once again Pamela had been dragged into a mess of his own making. Please God, that she and her family be safe, that their daughter be safe.

"You used to be much better with your instincts, James. Your wits seem dulled these days."

"I knew Violet worked for both sides," he said, though he wasn't sure if he spoke out loud or merely inside his head. Apparently it had been aloud, for she responded with a question.

"You knew and you kept her that close to you?"

"It wasn't her fault that I didn't love her anymore," he said, placing his arrow dead centre. "I must say she took the news a lot better than you."

Another slap, and he felt the repressed fury in the blow. If it was left up to her, he thought he really might well die here today. If they were smart they would kill him and be done with it. He knew she was intelligent enough to realize that, Felix he wasn't so sure about. Diane was the one calling the shots though, of that he had no doubt.

"Your instincts were faulty with Julian as well, you didn't take any measures to protect yourself against him."

He had taken measures, but they were on behalf of those he loved, not for himself. Good Catholic boy that he was, he'd felt he needed to pay in some measure for his sins, but he would not inflict the measure of his guilt on others.

"Whatever you may think of me, Diane, he is my son and I wanted to love him if at all possible."

"But you couldn't, could you? Yet, you love the daughter you sired with your American whore. Your humanity has always been your biggest weakness, James. You let Julian in, you kept Violet close, and both were vipers in your nest."

She leaned down, touched his face, her scent in his nose, like something burning. "You're so near to breaking. You forget I have seen you so before. I know your other weakness has always been the foe that lives inside your own head."

She was accurate in her assessment. His current state rendered things transparent, as though all his sorrows were made visible, a rising tide of dark scrollwork inscribed on him—his life written upon skin. He had given very few people the gift of his vulnerability in this life, but he had given it in some degree to the woman standing in front of him. That was why, he thought, she now looked at him with such hatred. He wished it mattered, but found it did not. The dark side of mania always rendered him thus—flattened out, a black hole of nothingness centred somewhere inside him, a feeling that his mind was as slippery as soap, and might escape his tenuous grasp at any moment.

"Did you ever love me, James? Even a little?" Her voice had changed, the coldness gone now, something of desperation replacing it. He almost felt sorry for her.

"I did," he said, "once."

After that, it seemed, she had all she wanted from him for she let the men back in. None of them were inclined toward mercy.

Even now, when he knew it was impossible, he sought sanctuary, tried to pull himself back into that picture where his children were safe, and Pamela was laughing over something he'd said. But he couldn't find it, couldn't retrieve the picture, and so he turned to the refuge of every Catholic child—prayer. Prayer to the mother, because God help him, he wanted his mother right now. Bright-haired, light-spilling eyes, following her into the field, flowers all around, the edge of the pond, rocks in her pockets...*no, no, no.*

Oh Mary,
Most Great of women,
Queen of the Angels...

Prayer came in pieces, between the blows, random snatches interspersed with the memory of incense, with the chant of the litany—step, pause, recite, response, the heat of the candle he carried, one small flame in the great and encompassing darkness. *Gate of heaven, Golden casket, Temple of the Divinity… Star of the Sea…*

A particularly hard blow sent the chair over and he blacked out temporarily, the pain from his collarbone tearing into him like jagged fire, flashing cold metal around its edges.

Take hold of the thread…*words, words, words*—the bolthole his mind chose in these moments. *Mistress of the Tribes, Fountain of the Parterres, mother of the orphans*…pain fading, touching the edge of something that felt like redemption…*Crimson Rose of the Land of Jacob*… losing the thread again, the darkness threatening to overtake and obliterate.

…*Blooming like the Olive Tree…olive tree…olive tree…*words echoing in that great darkness, seeming to be a far distance from where he sat in the stink of his own blood and fear…*Light of Nazareth…Crimson Rose…*no, he'd already done that bit, thread slipping from his hand, a glint of gold beyond his reach.

Queen of Life…life…Ladder, ladder, ladder of Heaven—the words, he was losing the words, reaching into the dark for the filament of connection, and finding prayer of another sort, one which cut to the last of his quick.

…*I have fitted up some chambers there, looking towards the golden Eastern air…and level with the living winds, which flow like waves above the living waves below…*

Slipping, slipping below those waves, blessed merciful water…stars in the water and a woman waiting there, dark hair billowing like ink upon the unfurling parchment of the sea. She opened her mouth to speak.

"I'm not done with him," she said, and Jamie was brought back from that sea of stars to see the woman who had hated him for such a very long time now. And he realized that it was still possible to feel fear, that there were many things worse than a quick death, and that his tongue had always gotten him into trouble. It no longer mattered, though, because he understood how this day ended. And so he spoke.

"Are you wondering if he told me that you were both double agents for the Soviets? He did, but I had long since figured that out for myself. It is what the guilty do, after all—accuse others of their own sins." It was reckless and ill-advised, though in truth, he didn't think they'd let him live if he feigned ignorance either.

With pain, he'd found, after a certain level had been reached, one tended to detach, to drift away to seek another place in which to shelter until the storm was done. And so he drifted without purchase—holding his mother's hand, the sun upon water, snow in the streets of Paris, the scent of his child's hair, the voice of the woman he was fated to love, always. *But you are my soul, Jamie.*

...I have sent books and music there...in thoughts and joys which sleep, but cannot die...our simple life wants little...soul within my soul...

One last blow, he wondered that he could still feel it, so deep below the sea. And then the golden thread snapped, and the darkness came to bear him down to its fullest depths. On the black side of the moon now, without a star in sight by which a man might find his way home.

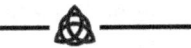

"Jamie, sweetheart, come with me."

His mother. His mother with her strawberry hair and light spilling eyes. He didn't think of her unless he had to, but it felt natural that she should be here now. Didn't all men want their mother at the end, no matter how old they were? For a long time now, he'd kept her safely behind a door, much like one in a fairy tale, where behind a padlocked entry lay a fairyland entire, where bad things didn't happen, and mothers who had never been free in life, were unfettered, were happy, were young and had no pain.

He followed her, recognizing the land around immediately, for it was home, both the large of it and the small—his country, and the corner of it which had belonged to his family as much as land might truly belong to a man.

She was headed toward the pond, for he knew the path well. The pond lay in a depression on the side of the mountain where his grandmother lived. A small body of water, deceptively placid, asleep in its bower of willow and lily pads and forget-me-nots. Wild roses and ivy wrapped the trees near its banks, and the sound of frogs and birds filled the air all around with their music.

In the manner of dreams, they were now on the bank quite suddenly, the ground giving up the scents of where water and earth mingled in its own particular perfume. Overhead was a liquid dusk, like blue pearls melting and covering the sky, wrapping like smoke through the dark lace of the pine trees. When he looked down, he saw tiny fires burning deep below the surface of the pond, and he thought of his grandfather's tales of the merrow men with their hearths on the floor of the sea.

"Here darling, just a few stones in your pockets. You love collecting stones, and these are especially pretty." She tucked them in his pockets, and the weight of them felt like both comfort and extravagance.

"The fires down there are beautifully warm, we can make toasted bread and cheese, and tell long tales all the night through. Come with me, Jamie, my beautiful boy, my darling boy."

He followed her, thinking they would have to swim at least part of the way, and wondering how the little fires continued to burn so merrily when they were encompassed by water. He was hungry and bread and cheese sounded lovely. His mother often read to him by the fire, though she hadn't done it so much of late. Often, come the dark, she was asleep, because she only trusted the hinges of the day—dawn and dusk, viewing all other hours as dangerous times in which to be vulnerable. And sleep was vulnerability writ large.

"Just take a breath, my beautiful boy, take a breath and let go."

And so he did, pulling in a great lungful of the dusk, tasting the world in it—pine sap, dark water, forget-me-nots, moss, stones and a soft curl of butter and tea upon his tongue from his last meal. The water took him in so easily, as warm and as lovely as a blanket, one he could curl up beneath and go to sleep, and so he kept moving, deeper with every step. Soon he could lie down beside those fires and rest.

But someone had seized his other hand in an iron grip, was pulling him up, pulling him back to the raw light of the living, and he was gasping into lungs which felt like he'd swallowed a bushel of nettles.

"Jamie, my darling boy, not today, not today." He looked up, dazzled by the brilliance of the sun, and saw there the face of safety, of security, of life—his grandfather.

"Jemmy, my darling boy, wake up."

Not his grandfather, not a pond with fires burning deep, but the woman who had always kept him safe whenever it could be managed. Yevgena.

"You came just in time," he said, though he wasn't certain what he meant. In time to save him? He who still wanted to sit by those fires with his mother, and listen to her speak to him once again, as she never would in life.

"I managed with more than a little help from this man," she said, and stood aside, revealing Richard behind her. His old handler. He tried to sit up, and failed.

Richard held up a hand. "Don't, Jamie, you're still very weak."

"Considering that I expected to be dead, weak is an improvement on my situation. You cut it rather fine, Richard."

"I know, my apologies, we lost Felix near the Finnish border and weren't certain where they'd taken you at first."

"Did he get away?" He had some dim memory of silence, as though the building was deserted for a time, during his period of unconsciousness.

"We have him, and thanks to you his life will be very uncomfortable for a long time. If he'd been wise, he would have fled into Russia while he had the chance."

"It's Mordecai you need to thank, he's the one who saw so clearly what they were. And Diane?" he asked, uncertain what answer he wanted in reply.

"She was gone before we arrived. We found you in that bloody awful stone room, half frozen to the floor. We couldn't find your pulse at first."

Gone, to where? There weren't many places she would be able to hide anymore, a double agent for the Soviets and the British. While she was free though, those he loved were in peril.

They spoke for a time after that, but he only half heard them and he replied in like fashion. His mind had trouble retaining detail once the mania was gone. And it was, most assuredly, gone. Yevgena with her sharp eyes, saw this and gently pushed Richard from the room, saying that Jamie must sleep.

She came back briefly, kissed him on the forehead, smoothing his hair away from his face. There were questions he needed to ask, but found the words would not stay within his grasp, and so he let them go. Yevgena would understand; she always had. Sleep came then, like a dark drowning, blotting out all his senses, and pulling him down to the bottom of the sea.

He woke some time later, and found the sun flooding the room he was in. It was spare as a monk's cell, but it was warm and he had enough of his faculties left to appreciate that. On a chair next to the bed there was a tidy pile of clothes for him, and on a plain wooden stand there was a basin and a jug of water.

Exhaustion nagged at his every cell, but he knew he needed to rise, to get dressed, to go home, so that he might deal with what still remained to be dealt with. He stayed where he was for a few more moments though, trying to tidy his thoughts. Yet again, he had been saved and for that there was relief of a sort and yet, and yet he still longed for that place deep below the water, where fires burned so brightly. He would not return there today, and perhaps not even tomorrow, but some day, with luck, he would find that place and know its peace again. But for now there were still things to which he must attend, and so he rose and began to dress.

Chapter Fifty

A Home at the End of the World

THE SUMMER WAS warm and stretched deep into the horizon like a great golden lion arching its spine. They lived it out-of-doors, from necessity, and were grateful for the blessing of such weather. It was a summer to be drunk in like blue wine, something rare and perfect in its flavour.

Their home in the hollow had been out of the way, but it had been in an area built up with tidy farms and neat roadways, and village shops. This land though was wild still, out here at the very end of the world, and something in Pamela's soul responded to it, something which was almost frightening in its intensity.

Here they became a world unto themselves. Her, Casey, the children, the animals and the land. The timelessness of the place seemed to gather up around them, sheltering and exposing all at once. The land dreamed, and they were caught in the warp and weft of her sleep, the undulations and sighs of her body, as though the earth had imagined them all into being.

Out here the old hag of legend was easily discerned; her hills and vales, cracks and crevices. Her old bones; her long ropes of thick grey hair; the rivers of her body, opening and gorging, rising and falling, up mountains and down into the sea.

They lived apart, so separate from the world that it seemed even the moon must be their own—poured golden as a cup of pollen, peeking in through the windows at night, or high overhead when they went about their land in the dark, sometimes merely standing in the night watching the sky whirl and dance overhead, lit with a streaming of stars so thick that it took the breath from a body.

Conor and Isabelle ran wild from the moment they awoke until she and Casey dragged them in at night for food, sleep and the occasional wash. Had she allowed it they would have happily hauled Kathleen along on their adventures—and had attempted to do so one morning, placing her in a little red wagon to cart her along—for she was as much a part of their rhythms as the beat of their hearts. Kolya had gone home with Jamie upon the latter's return, and though she'd had misgivings after seeing Jamie's lightless eyes, dense with a darkness she knew she could never truly understand, still she knew Kolya was not hers to keep. There were guard rails in place though, for Yevgena was staying with Jamie, and Pru had returned to the big house as well. If something went awry, they knew to contact her.

Jamie had been questioned by the police upon his return about the murder of Violet, but as he could prove to their satisfaction that he'd been out of the country at the time of the killing, they had largely let him alone after that. Though Pamela was aware he was still likely under suspicion. Violet's body had been returned to him, and he'd had a small private service for her, which Pamela, Vanya, and Pru had attended. It had put a sad coda to the life of a woman she had not known, but felt for all the same.

After, she had returned home to Kerry, putting her worries carefully aside in a compartment she kept just for this very thing—fears for Jamie. And then she gave herself over to their first summer on this land, for they'd bought the farm and sold the old place to Gert and Owen, who'd offered to buy it the moment they realized Casey and Pamela would not be returning. It gave her comfort to know their first home would be loved and cared for by people they knew.

Jonno had left once Casey relaxed his vigilance a little, and then it was just their wee family, with a house slowly rising beside the stand of oaks, and a sweet cascade of time which was not counted upon the clock.

Their days were a dance, from the waking to a sun rising over the land, to breakfast and sleep-tousled heads, and cuddling and stories amid eating bacon and toast and wandering through brambles picking sloe-dark berries so that their tongues and lips were perpetually blue. And then the unrolling of the day itself, bright as a guinea, spent roaming the land or down by the sea.

They had lunch on the strand on fine days; the stretch of it was theirs it seemed, for no other ever came to share it with them. They all turned golden in the sun, and even wee Kathleen had a smattering of freckles on her tiny porcelain nose.

May swept past, June dawdled a little, and July was a glorious span, bringing long hours brimming with simple joys: a wild apple tree loaded with fruit; a pair of kits who travelled, tumble-drunk with new life, in the wake of their mother; a patch of wild strawberries, sun-warmed and sweet, and the utter happiness of watching the children flourish in the deep, summer light. And so the lion of summer meandered on, down old pathways and new, scratched its back on blackberry bramble, wore sea pinks and blood fuchsia in its ruff, licked its paw in a spray of ember drops, and caught its green-gold reflection in the mirror of a long abandoned lake.

And the sea—every day, right there—the blue feather waves and the round of the hills running down toward it. Oh the sea—blue feather, emerald leaf and white-foam flower—the intoxication of it, always there, even when one knew of the open-jawed leviathans that drifted through its womb. And so each day she answered the call of it, whether to wade with the children, hunt flotsam and jetsam along the strand, or to simply stand watching and breathe it in, late at night when all her loves were asleep in the Flying Tortoise and the small canvas tent beside it.

The nights were spent by the fire, that gateway to the old mind, where meals were eaten, and stories were told, and where the children often fell to sleep and had to be carried to their beds. And then it was just her and Casey, and their quiet chat, and a slow rediscovery of each other—mind, spirit and body. They learned again old routes of communication, the recounting of the day, the bits of pleasure to be had in telling of silly things the children had done and said, the small milestones along the road of daily married life. And in the midst of it all, there was this—the hours when it was just the two of them, and they spoke then in their most instinctive language, and learned over and over of what gave pleasure and what caused madness of the body, of what lay at the root of intimacy, that wordless and consuming thing which lived between them in the bed, or up beyond the waterfall, where they went now and again when the moon was full bright. Some nights it was a sweet crazed rush, and some nights a slow lingering, because there was time, and their bodies were beginning to understand that once again.

And all of it—all the days and weeks, the nights and the land they lived upon and the endless sea beyond, sang in the ancient tongue of fur and salt wave, of green budding and gold flowering, and they listened all that long lion summer to that old, old song.

The return of the world was inevitable, but for a time they held the summer in the palms of their hands like stardust, as the great tawny stretch of the season ambled on, and in it they discovered they had gone to ground. They had found home.

Part Seven

The Smoke of a Thousand Autumns

Chapter Fifty-one

The Hag's Tale

"...AND THEN FLEDGE SET *out to sea, with the great horizon ahead of him and those he loved behind him, with only the compass of his heart, and the stars overhead to guide his way to the lands beyond the country of dragons."* Pamela read these last words quietly as Kathleen had drifted off just minutes before. Isabelle had fallen to sleep directly after supper, but she knew if she stopped reading too soon, Kathleen would open her eyes, and she'd have to start from the beginning of the story again.

"Is that not a dark tale for such a wee bit of stardust?" Casey asked, looking over the top of the book he was reading.

"A little, I suppose. It's not my fault though, Conor read it to her one afternoon and now it's what she wants all the time. I've edited out the worst bits."

"That boy is far too precocious for anyone's good," Casey said, though there was a note of pride in his voice.

"I believe your own father used to say something similar about you, no?"

"Aye, Conor's a more reasoned lad than I was. Still, I suspect there's a bit of karmic justice at play here."

She closed the book, laying it to the side. The story was a retelling of one she had loved in her childhood, an old Greek tale of a fisherman who noticed that some of the fish he brought to shore each day would disappear from a particular patch of herbs. Finally, one day he saw the fish he had placed there eating the herb and then leaping back into the sea. The tale had become an obsession for her the summer she was nine, and she had believed if she could just find the herb, she too could live in the sea. She had told the story to Conor the summer they'd been in Maine, and he, being her son and a child of the sea as well, had asked her if they could go on a hunt for the herb. Once she'd convinced him there was no such herb to be found on the shores of Maine, but still fascinated by the notion, he'd convinced Jamie to write the story down, and her to provide a few illustrations. This version was the one she'd been reading to Kathleen. It was one of several contained in this volume, which was bound in lavender cloth, for Jamie had told stories all that summer through.

"That longin' for the sea—that's you, no?" Casey asked, his tone casual as he continued to look at his book. "Conor did say Jamie had written that story down for him."

"No, not really, it's just an old Greek tale that Jamie put a bit of a modern spin on to make it meet the standards of a little boy."

"It's all right, Pamela. I know how much a part of yer life the man is, an' of the children's too. It's only that ye're somewhere in all of those stories; he's written ye into the fabric of each one."

"I don't think…" she began but then trailed off at the look on Casey's face.

"This honesty pact of ours hasn't been the easiest thing at times, has it?" he said.

"No, it hasn't, but it's still the right thing."

She rose from the tangle of blankets, taking care not to disturb either of the girls, and then climbed up onto the bed beside him.

"Here's a bit of honesty for you, man. I am profoundly grateful that you've brought us here to live, near to the sea. I do know after all that water is not your favourite element, and yet you know how I love it, and that mattered to you. It's one of the best gifts, outside of yourself and the children, that you could have given me."

"Aye," he turned to look at her. "I wanted ye to hear it when ye wake, an' have it soothe ye to sleep. I will say though, livin' near the sea has turned ye into a wild thing altogether, woman. I'm a wee bit worried that I've done a mad thing bringin' ye to live so close to the water. I'm worried I'll lose ye to a merrow one fine night."

He uttered the words in jest, but she knew she had, indeed, gone a bit wild here, not that—it had to be said—the man seemed to mind a great deal. It was only that on this land she often felt like there was no separation between her and the world, as if she could see with the eyes of an ancient, from a time when people believed and so they saw. It both exhilarated and frightened her, and she spent as much time out-of-doors as weather and her own motherly duties allowed.

Tonight though, it was entirely tempting to stay in the trailer and not venture out into the evening, for it was cozy with the fire glowing cheerily through the door of the wee stove, and both Isabelle and Kathleen asleep, and Casey stretched out beside her on their bed, glasses perched on the end of his nose, as he continued to read from his book. This book, large and crumbling, bore the rather illustrious title of *The Compleat Farmer, A Treatise of Animal Husbandry* by Doctor Phineas George.

She sighed. It would be lovely to just stay here next to him and let him read to her until she fell asleep, but she had to round up the small hooligan that was her son, and then she needed to do the final touches on a few sketches which had to go in tomorrow's post. For that she needed a bracing dose of fresh air or she'd be asleep before she located her pencils and sketch pad.

She didn't find herself getting up and moving, however, but rather indulging in a few minutes of peaceful observation of her husband. Casey was such a being of motion that it was rare to catch him in repose unless he was asleep.

The desire to touch him was always there, and there were times when she felt she had no control over herself, never mind her reaction to having him in such constant close proximity, and not being able to do much about said desires. Still, he was just laying there, engrossed in his book, a frown on his face that said he was likely trying to work out some knotty problem concerning the raising of a byre roof using no more than two ropes and a set of pulleys.

She glanced out the window to look for Conor. He was still working on his treehouse, a place he was determined to have built before his father finished the house. With Casey's guidance he had proved to have his father's talent with structure and form, and she thought if all else failed they might be able to use the tree house as an extra bedroom come the winter. Right now, she thought, looking at her husband, just a door with a lock on it would be welcome.

She touched the line of his jaw, her fingers welcoming the plush feel of his end-of-day whiskers. He gave her a sideways glance, raising one eyebrow, though his mind was now clearly only half employed in his reading.

She leaned over and kissed his neck, breathing in his scent and making a small hum of satisfaction. She ran her hand up under his shirt, and he made a low sound in his throat which sounded very much like a man who knows the frustration of living in extremely cramped quarters with three children, a dog, a cat and a family of crows, the latter of which had taken up residence in the tree nearest to their caravan. The crows awoke with raucous cries as soon as the dawn broke each morning, causing Casey to make several colourful promises as to the manner in which he was planning their long and painful demise.

"What are ye doin', woman? Ye know Conor is goin' to come through that door any second now. Ye'd best behave yerself," he gave her a stern look over the top of his glasses, "or there will be consequences. There's an entire chapter in here on the proper care an' discipline of a wife for me to consult."

"In a book about farm animals?" Pamela said, raising an eyebrow at him.

"Aye, chattel an' all that, I suppose. Here's a bit of advice he gives on the proper punishment for a misbehavin' wife. *'Spare not the woman, that which you would dole out to the ass. If she defy you more than the once, and you have given good warning as to her transgression, apply the rod with vigor until she has turned the red of violets. Do not however draw blood, lest she be asked by the other good wives, of the wound's origin. If the woman still persist in her wilful shrewishness, then ye must apply the rod with renewed vigor, until the woman does cry out for mercy.'* Hmm," Casey said, his eyebrows rising up, "I am beginnin' to wonder which sort of rod the good doctor was actually plannin' to apply."

"What on earth is that book—some sort of agricultural erotica?" she asked, trying to peer over his arm.

"It was the only book on farmin' in the wee van that passes for a library. I was lookin' for some sort of reference for breedin' an unwillin' cow."

"I suspect there might be a whole chapter in there on that very subject," she said, laughing. "It's a unique combination to be sure, a guide on sex and farming all in the same go."

"Farmers are busy men, 'tis best to kill two birds with one stone when a man can. An' I daresay there were as many lonely farmers then as now. Behave yerself, woman, or I'll be forced to apply that rod the good doctor mentioned."

"Just be certain to apply it with the recommended vigor," she said with a flutter of her lashes in his direction.

"Come here, an' I'll give ye a demonstration of vigor ye won't soon forget," he retorted, tossing the book aside, and pulling her back down to him. He had just begun his demonstration, and rather effectively too she thought, feeling instantly breathless, when the door to the trailer opened and Conor tumbled in with Finbar, filling the small space with the scents of a wet dog and a small, grubby boy.

"Daddy, we need to get started on the window frame," Conor said, oblivious to his parents' activity, "the light's startin' to go."

Casey sighed. "Aye, I'll be there momentarily, boyo. Go for yer walk, woman. We men will manage on our own, with luck I'll even have him to bed an' sleepin' before ye return."

This last bit she doubted, knowing that once her two men were absorbed in a project, however small, they lost their ability to judge time and light.

"Mind what I said about wanderin' up on that cliff, woman," Casey said, as she hopped down off the bed.

She merely rolled her eyes. The 'cliff' Casey was referring to was a small promontory out over the sea, where the view was splendid but the danger minimal. There was a small cluster of standing stones up there, one huge one and three smaller ones clustered near it. Set against the backdrop of the sea it had a dramatic and pagan feel to it. Some nights it was a place she avoided, for there was no denying it had an energy that could be very dark when the conditions were right. Casey seemed of the firm opinion that she was going to find a way to tumble off it to her doom.

"Just bear in mind that I've explicit instructions on how to keep a defiant woman in line," he said with a grin, and she thought it was possible he *would* be motivated to get Conor to bed before she returned, after all.

Outside, she headed toward the promontory, knowing Casey would already be lost in the precise and exacting work the framing required of him. The wind came in from the west, heady with salt and the iodine of sea wrack. The scent inveigled her blood, slipping in to spark in her cells, thrumming hard against the walls of her skin, so that her sleepiness fled and she itched to feel the wind beat against her skin and taste the salt upon her lips.

The climb was a fairly steep one, and she was flushed with exertion by the time she stood on the top. If she'd had any breath left to give, the scene before her would have taken it.

The night was clear, and the stars had begun to prick out through the deepening twilight. The stones reared up dark and foreboding against the backdrop of sea and sky. It was a scene set for a pagan sacrifice, a place where old rituals had been performed and old dances, meant to raise the fertility of the land, had been danced.

History lived in layers here, and if you stopped for a minute and really listened to the land, you could hear it, see it, feel it. The country of old, which had been utterly remote from the warm Mediterranean heart of Europe, had been thickly wooded, with wolves roaming in the forests, and the cities hardly more than overgrown villages. And then had come the European discovery of the Americas and the concerns of the globe had shifted dramatically to the shores of the North Atlantic, and Ireland had lost much due to her geography and been subjected to colonial occupation, loss of language, and a culture set adrift by a foreign power who saw the rain-swept island on the rim of civilization, as a mere stepping stone for the New World.

And yet, oh and yet, this land had always kept her soul—battered, defiant, proud, bloody and yet the hag of old still lived—the Cailleach roamed these hills, as wild and willful as she had ever been. Here in the west, her presence was felt in a way Pamela had not known in the east.

Long ago, Casey had shared something his father had once said—that it was arrogant to think that the people of old hadn't had their fair share of the world's wisdom. Once, people had looked at the world through a lens of faith—faith in the gods, faith in nature, faith in what they saw with their own eyes. It was as she had thought before—they believed and so they saw.

Movement caught her eye, and she turned, startled. There was a woman half hidden by the biggest of the stones, and like those stones, she stood as though neither time nor tide might touch her, a woman with flooding grey hair, roped like the reefs of a sail, her bones long and straight, and her face as fissured as the rocks upon which she stood. Aine. The line of poetry she'd spoken to Pamela at their first meeting, came back to her now, each word sliding through her like a cold drop of mercury.

'*Time was when the sea brought kings as slaves to me…*'

She made to turn aside, thinking she would simply go as she had come, and not disturb the woman.

"Girl, don't leave," the woman said. Pamela halted, though she now wished she'd stayed tucked up beside Casey, reading bits of agricultural erotica. Aine crossed the promontory, her long ropes of hair afloat on the wind, and for a moment it was as though the Cailleach of legend had formed and risen from the rock, and walked now in the guise of a mortal woman.

"What have ye come here to seek?" Aine asked as she drew near. Pamela could see that there was a mood upon her, just as the woman had warned her, for there was something in her eyes, a wild sort of light, which spoke of another time, something that lived beyond the edge places of this world. Clearly, she did not intend to dabble whatsoever in small talk.

"Lost cities, lost ships, lost lives," she quipped, feeling oddly nervous.

Aine fixed her with a sea-cold eye and said, "Don't seek those things, what is lost is meant to stay so."

"And what of yourself, what is it you're seeking here tonight?" She tried to keep her tone light, but didn't quite manage it.

"I come up here sometimes to seek the hag. I saw her once, but then never again. The night I saw her was a thin one, but thick with mist an' spirits. Like you, she came from the sea."

Pamela wanted to protest that she had not come from the sea, but rather by the very prosaic means of the Flying Tortoise, but she did not think such things mattered to Aine in her current mood.

"The night I met her, I too was seeking somethin'—I wanted an end to things, somethin' to take pain and loss an' drown it, like a draught of hemlock, only swifter an' more absolute."

A bit of wind puffed in from the sea, and grabbed the old woman's clothes, so that they flapped out around her, like the feathers of a broken-winged seabird.

"I thought maybe I'd just go to the top of the cliff, an' let the wind take me. There was nothin' left to live for, an' my heart had been dead ever since they took my child from my arms. The first night I saw ye, ye were walkin' up from the sea, with yer dark hair streamin' in the wind, an' yer babby in your arms. I did think ye were the hag who'd promised to bring me back my child one day."

"The hag?" Pamela asked, thinking it wasn't a terribly flattering comparison.

"Aye," Aine said, without apology, "for the first face she showed me was that of a young an' beautiful maid. 'Twasn't her real face, that she only shows ye when she speaks, but the maid is there to lure ye, the hag to tell the truth.

"It was one of those evenins' when the fog has rolled in early, an' everythin' is drenched in mist. It was a good evenin' for what I had planned though, for none would be out an' about but myself.

"I climbed the hill to the plateau, an' it was a bit clearer up here with the wind from the sea an' all. It seemed to me there was somethin' not right though, for I knew this land an' all the bits of it. At first I did not see her, for she was standin' next to the tallest of the stones an' she seemed merely part of it, as though a smaller stone had suddenly appeared beside the big one, come up out of the bedrock. An' yet I sensed somethin' other, human an' yet not. And I saw that it was a woman standin' there, watchin' me. I felt the prickle of her eyes over my skin—ye know that prickle what turns yer bowels to water."

Pamela nodded, for it was a feeling with which she was all too familiar.

"Her face was veiled, an' I could not see her features, only a sense of them. She seemed to me a beautiful young woman, no more than a maid, but one haunted by something from long ago."

Aine shivered, a fine tremor which seemed to transfer to Pamela, as though there were roots in the ground, ancient and knowing, which transferred the knowledge from one to the other.

"But then I moved closer, an' I saw that youth an' beauty were merely a trick of the light, for she was old, an' not like me but old like the hills, or a rock worn down by the sea. Old like the stone she stood beside, an' not human. I knew her at once for who she was—the Cailleach, the great hag. I hadn't been so scared since the day I'd been left to the nuns.

"It occurred to me though, that maybe she could tell me what had happened to my wee flower of a girl, an' so I walked up to her, so close I could see the chin whiskers of her wavin' in the breeze. Close to I could see just how ancient she was, an' with a look so hard I knew she could birth boulders an' turn not a hair over it.

" 'I had a little girl.' I blurted it out, thinkin' that small talk seemed of neither point nor matter when one was face-to-face with a hag of the rocks.

"She didn't speak, for I'd swear I never saw her mouth move, an' yet I heard her all the same. She spoke as the wind did, an' the bones of the mountains, with a great calm an' a weariness as old as the time before the world. She knew her of course, my girl, my Fleur—knew the softness of her and very bend of her bones.

"She had her, that old hag had taken my child, though she assured me she was well looked after, an' that the bog men held my child an' sang her to sleep of nights, locked in their leather arms. She said to me that my child had gone under the ground, an' was safe there, an' so I should stop lookin' for her above the earth."

Pamela shuddered involuntarily at the woman's words, thinking of her own lost babies clasped eternally in the arms of the earth. The picture of it came up vividly, as though it hung before her in the air—the long soil-soaked limbs, and streaming hair, and the small fair babies, as delicate as floating petals, taken by those limbs, shrouded by that hair. She shuddered at the vision, and Aine nodded at her, grey eyes narrowed.

"You see them, don't ye? Me—I smell them sometimes, the smell of the bog men an' their love for tiny children, brought down to warm their bones an' then kept with them to push away their long loneliness. An' I wonder why my loneliness never mattered, why is the pain of women of no account?" The question was uttered with so little emotion, that it seemed the woman was giving it no more mind than she might have a comment about the weather.

"The hag did tell me that one day I'd find my Fleur again, only I'd have to be canny to recognize her when she came. It was the last thing she said to me, though she kept lookin' at me, holdin' me in her gaze like a wee insect that's got itself caught in a bit of sap on its way to becomin' amber. I could hardly blink, an' I felt as if a great time was passin' as I was held tight in that ancient gaze. Then suddenly the air moved, an' three great crows came out of the mist an' sat upon her shoulders, two on one side an' one upon the other. And then I saw that she was stone again, so that the hag seemed an illusion, an' the stone always there.

"'Twas then I fled back down the hill, half certain I'd imagined the whole thing. Behind me there was a noise like a foot steppin' upon a brittle stick—*crack*—an' so I whirled about—not thinkin' how there'd been naught but stone an' moss on the hill, with not a stick for miles—to see what were there. There was no one, just a great shadow upon the fog, which set my heart to hammerin', for it loomed over me like a terrible giant. But then I realized it was me—just the outline of my shabby coat an' the flyin' bit of my hair, reflectin' within the fog, an' not that strange loomin' presence from before which had been, in part, what pulled me up the hillside. I could still see the crows though, sittin' still as the fog on the top of the stones."

Pamela fought with the desire to turn about, certain that the stone woman was standing behind her, two crows upon one shoulder and one upon the other.

"You believe she was real, not just a vivid dream?"

Aine fixed her with one of those looks, the ones that saw through to a person's backbone. "Ye know she's real, ye've seen her yerself. She's cruel an' kind betimes, givin' an' takin'. The hag is this damned country; she always demands blood, and the hag always gets her due. She took my child long ago," and then with that strange look still fixed upon her face, she added, "be certain that ye never give her a chance to take yers." Then she turned abruptly and without another word was gone into the stone and silence.

Pamela picked her way down the hill, unable to shed the feeling of someone watching her from the summit of the promontory, though she knew no mortal stood there.

Two days later, she had cause to remember Aine's words.

Patrick showed up unexpectedly, and the delight she felt upon seeing him for the first time in several weeks, swiftly dissipated once she caught a glimpse of his face upon his emergence from his car.

"What is it?" she asked, watching him as he walked toward her, his normally cheerful countenance set in grim lines.

Casey walked up behind her, put his hands upon her shoulders, and then simply said his brother's name.

"Patrick?"

"It's Ambrose an' Finian. Finian is in jail, an' Ambrose shot a soldier last night an' then went on the run."

"What?" Pamela said, a ripple of horror running through her.

"Christ," Casey said, so softly that she hardly heard him and yet she knew the force of emotion behind the brief utterance. "They'll go hard on him for shootin' a soldier."

"I wish it were only that," Pat said, dark eyes opaque in the still morning light. "The soldier died in the wee hours. Ambrose is wanted for murder, and," he added grimly. "Pru has disappeared."

Chapter Fifty-two

Turning Point
September 1980

EVER SINCE THE night near the apple orchard, Ambrose had been extremely wary about any and all checkpoints. Living in the North they were unavoidable, for the roads and the border bristled like a hedgehog with blockades, concrete barriers, metal spikes and craters. Bridges were blown up to make crossing via minor roads impossible. Annoyed locals would often remove said barriers, and then the Army would return to replace them. It was a bit like a deadly game of whack-a-mole, where both placement and removal required putting one's head above the parapet long enough to either have it solidly smacked, or lopped off altogether.

Before he'd dated Pru, he'd been less aware of how abnormal life was here in Northern Ireland. The inconveniences, the border patrols, the soldiers in the street were so normal to him that he'd stopped paying attention to a certain extent, until that night when they'd been stopped and nearly killed. Now, he found every time he came near a checkpoint he was filled with dread, and a terrible anxiety. Well aware of his state of mind, Pru had talked more with him about moving to the States and starting a life together there. It was a world, she assured him, filled with opportunity and if he was married to her it would smooth his path to citizenship. He had to admit the idea held great appeal. He thought he could possibly go to law school there, learn American law, and practice in the American system. Surely he could do good there too, just as well as here. It was, as Tomas had said to him, something to give thought to, and they had time, for they were young and there was room to make decisions though he often had the sense of late that they needed to hurry—to go before the choice was taken away from them.

He'd done the surveillance work which Cormac had assigned him. It had turned out to be tedious more than anything. At that point, he'd not seen a way out of doing as he'd been commanded, even though he'd not been comfortable with it, for he understood it might well result in more than the destruction of a building. It was likely to kill a few men also. Men who had families, lives and were merely going about their business. Well, most anyway. Ambrose had lived his whole life in the North and would always have a healthy cynicism about the security forces. He knew well enough they weren't his friends, though not all were foes.

Right now, he and Finian were approaching one of those border crossings with said security forces in command, and he could feel his nerves begin to twitch and a fine sweat break out under his collar. Finian was driving a car Ambrose had never seen before. It struck him as a little odd, but Finian seemed to always be cadging lifts, or borrowing cars to run errands of late. He was also being terribly circumspect about just what those errands were, which made Ambrose suspicious of what sort of irons his friend had in the fire. He wished just now that they'd left earlier in the day, for it was nearly dark and the soldiers tended to get more nervous as night approached. They couldn't see what was coming at them out of these isolated fields, and were therefore that much more jumpy. A jumpy soldier was more likely to panic.

They were on the Monaghan-Armagh border. Finian had agreed to bring Ambrose back from the wee town where he'd driven with his grandfather three days back to visit an old friend. He'd left the vehicle with his granddad, and returned with Finian. Finian had been a bit vague about just why he was in Monaghan, but Ambrose, distracted with thoughts of seeing Pru for the first time in several days, hadn't pressed him on it.

Finian had taken a few narrow backroads in order to go through one of the smaller checkpoints, one where there was only likely to be a few soldiers. There were four today, that Ambrose could see, one off to the side having a cigarette, the rest young and nervous looking.

The soldier who stuck his head in through the driver's side window, might be young but he wore the expression of a dour and much older man. His eyes scanned the interior of the car with great suspicion and Ambrose got the prickly feeling over his skin that he often did when the energy of a situation was off. Something felt very wrong here, beyond the ordinary frustration and fear that accompanied any crossing of the border in this country.

"Pull over, we're going to need to look through the vehicle." The soldier stepped back, automatic rifle leveled at them.

Finian pulled the car over, turned it off and then spoke, voice low and tight. "If they try to search the boot, get away from the car, as far as you can. Run into the fields. Just go as fast as you can."

Ambrose went cold all over at the words, a hard understanding coming to his mind almost immediately. "Finian, what the hell is in the boot?"

"Just somethin' Cormac asked me to bring back, now shut up an' play it cool."

"What the fock, Finian?" Ambrose said, horror rippling through his body, and threatening to lift him right out of the car. If it was Cormac, it had to be weapons. It wouldn't be anything innocuous, that was for certain.

"I'll explain later."

Ambrose couldn't believe his ears. He wanted to kill Finian, just grab him by the throat and throttle him to death here and now. *Stupid bloody eejit!* The soldiers would likely do the job of murdering Finian for him, once they saw what was in the boot. He was going to die too though, so the thought wasn't as comforting as it might have otherwise been.

He opened the passenger door, trying to present the soldier with a calm, stoic face. Inside though, his guts were roiling, and utter panic was causing his vision to pull in so that all he could see was the soldier's face, so vivid that he noted a tiny scar on the man's left eyebrow, and a narrow drop of gold within the hazel of his eyes, as though it had been placed there by a painter with a whisper-fine brush.

"Move off to the side," the soldier's voice was clipped, and had that superior toff sound to it of the upwardly mobile—or hoping to be—middle class. It was an accent Ambrose normally found irritating, but today it just escalated his fear.

The week before there had been an incident where two soldiers had accidentally driven into the cortege of a republican funeral. They'd tried to back out, but in their panic they'd hit an old woman, knocking her to the ground, and then backing up over her. She'd suffered minimal injuries, all things considered, and was currently convalescing in the Royal Victoria. No matter that, though, for the crowd had thought her killed and had dragged the soldiers from the car, stripped them, beat them and then taken them away in a black taxi. Their bodies had later been found in a tract of wasteland, unrecognizable at first, though everyone had known the identity of the dumped bodies.

These soldiers might well be looking for revenge, it was part of the cycle here—*murder one of ours and we'll murder one of yours. Commit a terrible atrocity against ours, and we'll double down and bring you your worst nightmare, right to your front door if need be.* They certainly wouldn't need much in the way of provocation, and guns in the boot would be more than sufficient cause for the soldiers to turn on them. Prison would be the best he might hope for.

As they watched the soldiers walk around the car, checking the undercarriage, looking in the windows, opening the doors, his anxiety built to a pitch that had him feeling like he was floating somewhere above his body, just watching and waiting for fate to drive down like an iron fist. Beside him, Finian seemed very cool for someone who was also going to prison, or eminently about to die. Ambrose wanted to pray but couldn't find words in the slipstream of adrenaline coursing through him.

The young soldier who'd ordered them off the road, moved toward the boot, the keys to open it in his hand and Finian's breath caught, a small wave of sound that broke on the shores of understanding for Ambrose, and he opened his mouth to yell, just as the boot lid cracked and Finian shoved him hard into the ditch behind them. The universe tore itself to pieces, bright spiralling tears in the day, throwing them all outward into darkness.

The darkness held for what seemed a long time, neither sound nor sight pierced it, and then he was aware that he was moving, Finian yelling in his ear. *"Run, run, run!"*

Finian had dragged him out of the ditch, into the field. Ambrose was half running, half staggering, unable to see beyond the bright flash which had scorched his eyes.

He tried to grasp at what had happened, why he was running, where he was even but he couldn't quite manage it. It felt as though someone had hit the fast forward button on a tape, and the music was playing in that horrible herky-jerky fashion, which made madness from melody. Having little choice he just kept moving.

He fell, but began to drag himself, only knowing in the way of animal instinct that to quit moving was to die. The strange and terrible light began to recede, and vision came back in pieces—thick stubble in the field, a green as pale as milk, a stick, a cluster of stones—the names of these things coming to him a few seconds after seeing them. Someone was shouting behind him and he realized it was one of the soldiers, fury and fear pitching his voice high enough to be heard through the pealing bells in Ambrose's ears.

With vision came the return of other senses—feeling for one, he'd taken a blow to his right hip, or maybe he'd been shot, or caught shrapnel from the explosion. Not that it mattered, the pain didn't care about the exact cause, it was simply a force unto itself, which made him temporarily black out as he attempted to turn over, so that he might see what was happening behind him. He didn't want to be shot in the back either; he would go facing death, not blind to it.

One of the soldiers was still alive—maybe even two or three, but certainly not four. The one who'd opened the boot would have died instantly. He knew one still lived because he was standing over Finian, with a gun held to Finian's head.

He cast about on the ground around him looking for something, anything he could use to protect himself and Finian. There was a gun, just beyond the reach of his hand. He had no idea where it had come from, though it looked like a military weapon. It might not be loaded, but he'd have to chance it or Finian would die, followed shortly by himself. He pulled his body toward it, feeling a bright, hot spill of blood pour from his hip as he moved.

The soldier had the gun up to his shoulder, still aimed at Finian's head. His eyes, even at this distance, were hot with hatred and fear. Ambrose couldn't really blame him, but nor could he allow the boy to kill Finian. There was no time to think, so he simply raised the gun and pulled the trigger.

After that everything moved in a strange slow motion—the soldier falling, the sky wheeling overhead, the flames on the roadway still flickering, and the time it took for Ambrose to pull himself to his feet. He could feel hot blood running down his leg, and the strange distance still clung to his vision, as though he was viewing events from the inside of a thick glass bottle.

He limped his way over to Finian, his ears buzzing with the aftershock of the gun.

"Are ye all right?" he asked, for Finian was pale, his hair and face splattered with gore.

"I-I don't know," Finian said. Ambrose stuck his hand out and pulled Finian up, checking him for injuries. His friend looked dazed, the blue eyes blank with shock, his normally mobile jester's face completely without expression.

"What do we do now?" Finian asked, his words sounding like that of a confused child who doesn't understand the events unspooling around it.

"We run, what other option do we have?" Desperation turned to fury and Ambrose grabbed Finian and shook him by the shoulders.

"What the fuck did you think was going to happen, you knew what was in that boot. Ye knew what ye were riskin' for both of us. Now, we're both marked men; we've got two outcomes here, death or prison."

Finian nodded, but it was like the movement of a marionette being controlled by an erratic puppeteer.

"I'm not goin' to wait here for someone to come an' kill me. We need to separate," Ambrose said, trying not to think about the blood streaming out of him, or the pain in his hip that made it feel like the bone was broken. We'll be harder to catch that way. You go that way," he pointed to the west, "an' I'll go this way." He was going to head north and then east, and hope he could get to the cottage before he collapsed.

Finian caught him in a hug, tight and breathless and then his friend was gone into the twilight, heading west across the fields. Ambrose turned south, the pain in his hip flaring so bright for a second that he thought he might pass out.

Running hurt too much, and he knew he was better off keeping to the shadows and moving at as steady a pace as he could manage. With the blood loss, he knew his stamina was going to fade quickly, and he had to be holed up and hidden by the time dawn broke. He was fortunate that it was farm country, fields neatly divided by low rock walls, and thick hedges which held the dark like a cloak within the tangle of vegetation. By his reckoning he managed three miles cross country in this fashion, until he came to a high wall which banded an old demesne area which had been deserted years ago and left to grow wild. If he could cross it without being spotted, it would put him within a half mile of the swan woman's cottage and sanctuary.

He stopped and leaned on the wall, fearing he was leaving a trail of blood with every step. He needed to catch his breath, and he wanted to check his hip to make sure it was still in one piece—logic dictated that it must be or he wouldn't be able to move—but was afraid to touch it for fear of feeling bone sticking out through his flesh.

The wall would have to be scaled, for he couldn't at present remember where the opening was, but was certain it was a long way off and in the opposite direction from where he was headed. Finding toeholds to hoist himself up and over seemed to take forever, and his leg was getting weaker. He managed to get to the top, though he was streaming sweat at that point, and so exhausted that he thought he might just lie there and have a rest for a few minutes, before attempting his descent down the other side. Just a breath or two was all he needed; he put his forehead to the dirty stone, and closed his eyes. His eyelids felt hot, and stars burst behind the lids. He so wanted to go to sleep, and wake up to find that he'd drifted off beside Pru, had a terrible dream, and now would need to madly scramble in order to get her back home in time. He could see her, and thought if he reached out he would be able to touch the shining gilt length of her hair.

It was then he heard the sound of a helicopter and knew it was there for him, thundering through the skies looking for *him*. He knew that it would have a searchlight on it, and men inside with guns and night scopes. Panic surged through him and he simply dropped down the other side of the wall, momentarily blacking out as he hit the ground. When he came to, the helicopter was close enough that he felt the circular *thunk* of it in his blood, beating in tune with his heart, and stirring the roots of his hair so that his whole body prickled with it. He'd fallen through an old hedge, half-rotted, but still with plenty of bramble holding parts of it up. He'd cut himself on the fall, but he'd have to ignore the additional injuries for now. He huddled down as small as he could manage near the roots of the hedge. When he was a small boy he used to make believe he was a hedgehog and could burrow tight for the winter, curled beneath the roots of trees, stirring only in the spring when the sun warmed his feet and fur. He devoutly wished he *was* a hedgehog now, and not a tall boy whose limbs seemed to stick out and glow like a beacon shouting—*Here I am, come and get me!* Any moment, he thought, that light was going to sweep over him, cut him in half, and deliver him up to men who might well kill him rather than wasting time taking him into custody. He could feel his grip on consciousness fading in and out, despite the high hot rush of adrenaline coursing through his body.

It was a small eternity later that the helicopter finally moved off to the south. He lapsed into unconsciousness then for a time.

It was near dawn when he crawled out of the shelter of the hedgerow. The bleeding had stopped, but his leg had gone disturbingly numb. He was afraid as he dragged himself up, that it would not bear his weight. It did, though he could feel that it wouldn't take him very much further. If his bearings were right, he could make it to the cottage before full light, he thought—though just.

It was fortunate—if such a term could be applied to his current situation—that he knew the land around here so well that he could traverse it in the dark. It was imperative that he be gone to ground by the time the sun rose, because he knew the country would be swarming with soldiers and police, all looking for him. He dimly noted the physical remainders of the old demesne—the fields where the potatoes had once grown, the ancient garden which held only weeds and wild roses now, and the crumbling remains of an old abbey which had abutted the deer park at the estate's edge.

His leg was dragging now, and he thought he might not make it much further. He thought briefly about holing up in the abbey ruins and just letting the day go by there, and hope that he lived to nightfall in order to finish his journey to the cottage.

It's just a little further. They'll search the abbey, you great eejit, you know they will, you can't stop yet.

He pulled up his will because it was the only thing he had left in reserve at this point, and kept walking, thinking he might have to crawl soon, because his leg had made it clear it was done with his nonsense and was going to give out. And just when he was certain the last of his reserves were gone, not to mention a good deal of his blood, the cottage was there, dimly outlined in the blue morning light and he stumbled toward it, grateful that he could now collapse.

Inside it was chilly, but there were blankets and for now, that was enough. He wrapped one around his shoulders, cold through to his bones, and collapsed onto the bit of foam he and Pru called a bed. And then, with one last prayer which was thought and not word, that Finian had somehow made it to safety, the last spark of his consciousness blinked out and all was dark.

Chapter Fifty-three

Swans Drowning

HE WAS DREAMING of the drowned swan, gazing down at her through the deep pond, down to where she swayed with the waterweed, her head wreathed in water lilies when suddenly she reared back, long white neck stretching out like that of a cobra, and bit him hard in the hip. He awoke gasping, to dark and to pain. Feeling had returned to his leg, and it now seemed to him that numbness was infinitely preferable. Someone was speaking to him from what seemed a great distance. A frantic voice—a girl's voice. His girl.

"Pru?" he said, though the word felt like it was little more than a whisper, a bit of dust in a maelstrom, and her on the far side of that great storm.

"Yes, it's me. Oh thank God you're awake! You've been shot, for heaven's sake. I thought you were dead for a bit, left in a ditch somewhere to bleed to death."

"How do ye know I've been shot?" Ambrose asked. He thought he might be dreaming, because he was warm and the touch of Pru's hands felt like little more than air passing over his skin.

"I checked you over, there was blood all over your clothes."

"Ye shouldn't be here, Pru, it's dangerous. Surely ye know the countryside is rife with soldiers lookin' for me."

"I came as soon as we heard about Finian."

"Heard what about Finian?" He tried to sit up but found he was too weak, and the mere effort made him so dizzy he thought he might throw up.

"He was caught near the border by the police. They say it was lucky the police found him, for if he'd been caught by soldiers he might not have survived. Still he's in jail now. Pat and Tomas were allowed in to see him, they say he's a little banged up and afraid, but other than that he's all right. They've charged him with murder for the soldier and also for the bomb. Ambrose, what the hell happened?"

Ambrose felt as though someone had sunk an anchor into his stomach, and he was about to drown in that dream pond, as the weight of all that had happened descended upon him. Finian in jail, Finian charged with murder and acts of terror. All because of his damn reckless notion that they could do something to strike back against the beating in the field. For that event was what had propelled them both into the situation they now found themselves in—Finian in jail, and Ambrose on the run.

It occurred to him suddenly that there was a fire, there was light, and Pru's face was swimming into focus—blue eyes, rose-gilt hair, and a look of both fury and fear.

"The fire—someone will see the smoke, or smell it."

"It's dark," she said practically, "and you need the heat. This cottage is so buried in the woods, I don't think anyone could smell the smoke, and they certainly can't see it in the dark."

"Ye shouldn't have come," he repeated, and yet at the same time he felt utterly grateful for her presence.

"I'm going to have to clean up your injuries, and dress them. It's not going to be a pleasant experience. Tell me exactly what happened, while I get everything ready."

He told her then, even while swallowing down his fear over the pain to come. About the bomb in the boot, about Finian having been a part of a plan, even if he was ignorant of a few of the details. And then he told her about his own role, and that he'd shot a man dead. This she already knew, and she simply looked at him as he told her, and then nodded.

"You did what you had to do," she said, and then having stripped him out of his clothing, washed down his wounds with dilute alcohol. He passed out briefly, though enough consciousness remained to hear her muttering as she laid out her tools. She washed her hands in the basin where she'd poured a kettle full of hot water and then faced him with a smile meant, he thought, to reassure him. "You needn't turn green, Ambrose Turner, I can manage this," she said with a confidence he thought she might actually feel. Her courage never failed to impress him.

"You have a bullet hole in your hip. I'm going to clean it up and then I need to make certain there aren't any bullet fragments in your wound. It will hurt quite a bit, but it has to be done," she said, with the fierce calm she always seemed to display in moments of crisis. "Finola walked me through this, so I know what to look for."

"Finola knows?"

"Ambrose, everyone knows. I needed her help with putting together a medical kit. I ran to her place the minute I heard. I left Kolya with Maggie. It was fortunate Jamie wasn't home at the time, or he would have known exactly where I was going, and likely done everything in his power to stop me. Here, painkillers first, so they're working by the time I'm done. Penicillin too."

He obligingly swallowed, the water tasting metallic to his tongue and then collapsed back onto the bit of sponge, trying to gird up his courage for her examination. It took precisely ten seconds of her poking at him to cause him to swoon like a Victorian maiden aunt, for which he was really quite grateful.

"Ambrose, can you hear me? Are you all right?"

"Aye, though that's a relative term. Have ye much more to do, because I'd just as soon have ye hit me over the head with a bit of firewood, an' then wake me up when you're done, providin' I'm still alive."

"You've been out twenty minutes, I'm all done now."

He was afraid to ask her what the damage looked like, but being Pru she simply told him without preamble.

"It looks as though the bone was chipped but there's no trace of either bullet or fragment, you've got an exit hole at the top of your buttock. I'm mostly worried about infection setting in, though with luck the penicillin will take care of that."

Because he loved her, he heard the fear in her voice, and understood she was nowhere near as calm about this situation as she was trying to make out.

"I'm sorry, Pru. I'm more sorry than ye'll ever know."

She shook her head. "Don't you dare say you're sorry. This wasn't your fault. You had no choice, it was either that or let him kill Finian and yourself."

"Life turns on these things, Pru. One thing happens and everythin' is changed. It won't matter to them that I was caught up in circumstances. I killed a man, an' that's the end of it."

"But if you explain to them that you shot in self-defense, that you didn't intend to kill the man…" she trailed off, clearly halted by the look in his eyes.

"Oh, but I did mean to kill him, Pru, that's the crux of it, it wasn't an accident of any sort."

The painkillers were beginning to take hold, and Pru's image was blurring, yet he could still see that he'd said too much, even if it was merely the truth. And so he gave her the small reassurance that he could.

"It will be all right; we'll figure it out." But he knew even as he said it, that he'd just lied to the girl he loved for the first time.

Once Ambrose was asleep, Pru moved about the room tidying, knowing that she needed to keep busy to still the shaking in her body. Her hands had held steady through cleaning and dressing his wounds, through holding the mug of sugar water steady as he drank and swallowed his pills, through adjusting the blankets and smoothing the hair back from his face, and holding his hand in comfort until he drifted off on the wave of oblivion the painkillers provided.

"You are perfectly practical in every way," Pamela had once said to her in jest, inverting the words from *Mary Poppins,* and Pru had laughed, because she was, indeed, a practical girl. She always had been the sort to weigh and measure, and to see the outcome which would serve all parties best in any given situation. From the time she was able to make up her own mind about anything, she always knew what she wanted in flavours of ice cream—strawberry or pistachio, how she liked her tea—with a squeeze of lemon thank you very much, cotton sheets for summer, flannels put on the bed the day after Halloween. It was this clarity of mind and purpose which had, in part, caused Jamie Kirkpatrick to hire her to look after his children. All of whom she loved with a ferocity which made them family to her. This included the adults: Jamie, Pamela, Casey, and their wider circle of Pat and Kate, Tomas, Gert and Owen. Her most fierce and protective love was reserved for Pamela and the children, though, for she had lived with them before Casey's return and had seen, first hand, how fragile Pamela had been. She had also been there to witness what Casey's return had done for her, and had begun to see the transformative power which love held.

She had always been an unromantic sort of girl, and had thought that if she married, it would be some plain and perfectly practical Maine fisherman, with whom she would build a home and have children. She hadn't expected to ever fall deeply, madly in love. And if someone had told her it would be with a young man whose ears stuck out, who needed glasses as thick as the bottom of Coca-Cola bottle, and who always appeared in need of a good feeding, she would have dismissed the notion with a wave of her hand.

Her parents had expected her to be well behaved, God-fearing, and to take up practical work until such time as that fisherman or farmer came along. But then Jamie had called her with an offer to come and be a nanny for Kolya and she had not even had to think about it for a moment, she'd simply said yes.

Despite the fact that Pamela and Jamie didn't live under the same roof, still she had seen that it was a relationship filled with love and respect. Both their homes were filled with books and laughter, and talks of fanciful things as well as the serious and the day-to-day. And Pamela's home in particular held a surfeit of love, one which Pru had witnessed each day between Pamela and her children, and now that Casey had returned, between a father and his children, and a husband and wife. It was a living entity—something which shifted and grew and took on a variety of forms, living, breathing and moving as it did so. She had drunk it in, seeing how beautiful and fulfilling a family life could be.

It was what she wanted for herself one day, and she had known shortly into her relationship with Ambrose that he was the one with whom she wanted to build that life.

Ambrose sputtered a little in his sleep and she went over to the makeshift bed, fear pulsing through her. His forehead was wrinkled a little, as though his fear and worry had chased him down a long tunnel into sleep.

The last thing Finola had given her—after cobbling together a medical kit for her—was a pistol, and a box of bullets. She had a rudimentary knowledge of shooting, as her father had taught her how to aim and load, and to hit a target. It would have to be enough, should anyone come looking for Ambrose. It was sitting on the broken-legged table so that she could reach for it at the slightest noise.

She took a few long breaths, steadying herself. Since the news had reached her about Ambrose, she had neither slept nor eaten. Finola had forced a cup of tea down her, and then driven her here on a variety of narrow back roads, which Pru knew she'd never remember should she need to trace her way back to Jamie's land on said roads.

She sat down then, all the exhaustion and fear hitting her at once. The chair was near to the fire, and the warmth of it was very welcome. It would have to be doused in a little while, for it would soon be morning and people would be up and about and they couldn't afford the smoke giving them away. Ambrose needed the warmth, but it was too much of a risk.

Practicality was of limited use when it came to trying to get her thoughts around what had occurred, sorted in her head. All avenues ended in a sort of dark panic, which didn't allow her to see an outcome which didn't end in tragedy or a life of crime. So she let her mind drift a little, finding this less frightening than trying to come to solutions around their situation.

A bit of reflected firelight caught in the mermaid glass, turning her head toward it. The flame wavered in the glass, trembling like water and in one of those strange quirks of memory, a picture emerged from it, of a spring day in Maine—a cold one, bright blue tinged with the pale green of the season.

She had woken that long ago morning with a thrum in her spine, a strange crackle to the air around her. It turned out she was not alone, for the feeling was there in all the residents, running through the community like a tremor of quicksilver, flashing against nerve and hope, pulling them from their beds before any of them even understood exactly why. And then it broke like a whisper, gradually gaining in decibel, a mackerel run was in, blown into the cove by a brisk north wind.

Some men had gone out in the boats, taking one end of the long nets piled deep on the sand, while others stayed on the shore, holding the other end of each net as it fed out into the cold water and thus creating a long loop which would close when the boats came back toward the land. This would effectively corral the fish in a large circle, from which it was difficult to escape.

It was a huge haul of fish, and the first she had seen in this manner—fighting to live. She had only been eight at the time and it had frightened her—all those leaping, straining fish, in the pure panic of a creature facing imminent death, pulling, flailing, jumping back toward the sanctuary of the open water, a swarm of steel grey panic in the merciless green sea. Some had managed it, though the mass of them had not. Those were piled high in baskets, still struggling to leap, to live.

And after, the death—so much death. The beach was filled with them—all the fish deemed too small, not big enough for the eating, not even worthy of being bait. The scream of the gulls overhead, waiting to feast, made her wish she could stop up her ears, and close her eyes to all the carnage on the sand. She had tried to save them, running to the water, fish slipping through her fingers, dying just short of the life-saving sea. There were too many, and she could not run fast enough. Some of the men laughed at her, others stared at her father as though they expected him to stop this unseemly behaviour in his child. He let her do it though, until her little legs could not run any longer and she had been near collapse. She had cried then, silent tears for the great, churning wheel of death and life, grinding away at every living thing.

"We'll eat this winter, no use in being squeamish about it," her mother had said, turning from her tears, clearly uncomfortable with her daughter's emotion over a bunch of fish. She had never cried again in front of her mother, and she hadn't eaten a single bite of the mackerel that year either, despite going to bed hungry more than one night as a result.

Her father had stepped up beside her on that beach, and while he was not a man given to many words, those he did speak were put to good use. "They are like us," he said, "prisoners to the tides of fortune and fate."

Unlike her father and herself, Ambrose was not terribly practical for he had a poet's heart, and that was never bound toward practicality. She wondered sometimes, if he wasn't the luckier of the two of them. She went to him now, and lay down beside him, suddenly very tired, and put a hand to his forehead, certain that he felt a little warm.

A great rush of tenderness washed over her, just at the sight of that face with the nose slightly canted to one side, the long, thick lashes shuttered over his eyes and the line of his mouth, as soft and innocent as a child's in sleep. No, she reflected, he was not very sensible at all, but he was hers in a way no other person had ever been, nor would be ever again, and that was all that really mattered. There was, of course, no practical way out of this. It didn't matter how well ordered her mind was, or how carefully things were planned, there was no exit point that didn't end in prison, death or having to run for the rest of their lives. It didn't matter though, because impractical or completely mad as she suspected it to be, she would not leave him, and if he chose to run, she would run with him, and damn the tides of fate and fortune.

Chapter Fifty-four

The Smoke of a Thousand Autumns

AUTUMN WAS AFTER all, Prudence thought, the best of the seasons. The light at midday, coming out of a deep blue sky, was like a prism of tourmaline, golden and thick, and faceted in its beauty. She had just crested a small rise, where there was a cluster of old beeches, and the honeyed light fell through the shimmering green-gold of the leaves. There was an old stile, a leftover from a long-vanished farm, which sat at the top of the rise, nearly invisible in its cloak of bramble and ivy. She liked to stand in this spot and let her mind wander, re-peopling the land in her imagination. It was never hard to summon those spirits for there was something old in this land, these woods, something that stretched back to the cave. There were ghosts in every stone, other lives long eclipsed, drifting through the trees of a night. Out here, hidden, there was no time, there was only being.

She had spent the morning gathering hazelnuts, and had found to her delight that at some point in the few days since last she'd roved about for-aging for food, mushrooms had sprung up. Fortunately, Finola had taught her what was edible, and so she knew that the small brown jewels she tucked into her basket weren't going to poison them. Which was, after all, the main thing. Three days before she had gone to the spot where she used to leave messages for Ambrose, only to find a burlap sack filled with potatoes, carrots and turnips. There had been a basket too, with two loaves of bread, a jar of blackberry jam, a cloth-wrapped round of cheese, a square little bag of salt, and a few bundles of herbs—all the necessaries as Finola would say, and so she knew then that Pamela had spoken with Finola, and was aware of their situation. Last, there was an envelope. This was from Jamie, and contained a brief note, money and her passport. There was a map as well, and she studied it, not understanding at first, but then realizing with a jolt that he was offering her a route out of the country. She need only say the word, and all would be arranged. Pamela too had left a note, pinned to the cloth the cheese was wrapped in which simply said, *'If you need anything, Pru, anything at all, just leave a note here for me or Jamie. Please don't do anything desperate.'*

She had laughed a little over that last line, for surely holing up in a tumbledown cottage with a boyfriend who was on the run from the law qualified as a desperate act.

Her basket was full now, one side with blackberries dripping with juice, and the other side with the clutch of brown-gilled mushrooms. Heaped on top were hazelnuts, still in their furry green wrappings. The nuts were just barely ripe, but she wanted to get a good haul of them before the squirrels and birds stripped the trees bare.

The wood was quiet in its midday fugue, and the sunshine felt so good on her shoulders that she sat down on the mossy hummock of an old stump, savouring the warmth. It was the sort of day to stretch out in a wood and just let thoughts run along where they wanted, like a slow-moving stream which meandered through hills and valleys before finding its way to the sea. Instead, she found herself taking mental inventory of their small larder, which she added to and subtracted from according to their daily intake and outgoing. Gathering and meals—she felt like her mind revolved around that for at least a third of each day. She listed it to herself, finding comfort in the itemizing of the contents of their small larder. There was still a full loaf of bread left, and half of the cheese. When she'd brought the food back that day, they'd toasted the better part of an entire loaf over the fire, and eaten it with cheese half-melted. It had been, they both agreed, one of the best meals of their lives.

Finola had taught her that if you looked hard enough, there was always something to forage, and therefore something to eat. Even in the middle of winter as long as the freeze didn't set in, there would be cleavers, dandelion and cow parsley, all chock-full of vitamins. Pru was well aware they'd need far more than that to survive the cold, but she'd cross that hurdle if and when they came to it.

There was a box filled to the brim with apples, for they'd gone to the abandoned orchard one night earlier in the week, when the moon was still full enough to light the fields around them. It had been the last warm night they'd had, and they had taken full advantage of it. The orchard had been utterly quiet, and she had felt like they crossed from one realm to another as they entered into the old rows of trees, hung thick with fruit, and scented with honey, on the still silver night. They'd picked all they could carry, relaxing as they made their way into the centre of the orchard. It wasn't easy going, for the land had been long abandoned and the undergrowth was thick with bramble and nettles. But in the very centre there was a space, where two old trees had grown into each other, their branches like the hands of an ancient couple who had been so long married that it wasn't clear where one began and the other ended.

"When I was little my grandda would tell me these were the trees which had grown over the graves of Bailie and Aillin," Ambrose had told her.

"Maybe they are," she'd responded, for the entire orchard felt strange, as if it were the portal to some strange golden world, where the Tuatha still lived in their shining halls, eternally young.

"I suppose it's as likely a place as any other," Ambrose said. "It's a funny place to be sure, for there's a mound at the far end where it's said the fairies would meet to elect their king, an' no one would dare walk abroad at night durin' those times. My grandda said it was so even when he was a young man. Ye had to leave the pub early for ye didn't dare risk getting caught out when the fairies were out an' about on official business."

"It feels like a sacred place," she said, and did not need to add that she did not mean in the sense of a church, but rather that of Nature and the places the wild had consecrated unto itself.

"It feels a bit like Eden must have," Ambrose said, and then turned to her, his long body warm and fitted to hers in that way which spoke of both urgency and a timelessness that said what was now would always be between them. There had been no need to speak, they had simply fallen into one another, and all about them had risen the sharp green scents of night, and the musk of overripe apples. There was an edge and a taste to the night, to the joining of their bodies, like that of wild apple cider, golden and sharp, something so beautiful that it could never be again. It frightened her even as it carried her beyond herself, so that she felt as much part of the night and the old apple trees, and the stars breaking rough over the shoals of summer's last night, as she did the boy who moved with her.

After, they had stayed there for a time, watching the stars drift overhead, their limbs entwined in an echo of the trees above them. It had been a perfect night, caught there in the silver light and she knew it would be a memory she would hold sacred until the day she took her last breath.

"'Tisn't a good idea to sit about wool-gatherin' in the woods when half the country is out lookin' for ye," said a gruff voice only a few feet off from her. She jumped, berries, nuts and mushrooms spilling from her neatly-arranged basket. She wished fervently that she had a weapon to hand—even a thick walking stick would do. But then she saw that it was Ambrose's grandfather who stood looking down at her, his face grim in the afternoon light.

She scrabbled to her feet, panic and relief making her clumsy.

"How—how did you know?" she asked, watching in dismay as blackberries, mushrooms and hazelnuts tumbled off down the slope of the hummock, disappearing into mossy crevices and hollow roots.

"Because I know my grandson. I thought he might go to ground in the cottage. Lad's always been a bit of a romantic, when bein' practical would have served him better. I did take you for a practical girl, though, an' thought ye'd have better sense than him."

"I love him," she said, stating the truth plainly. It was, after all, the reason she was here and the reason she had willingly put herself in the position of aiding and abetting a wanted man.

"That right there has made fools of even the wisest," his grandfather said. "Is he injured? The bulletins about it made it sound as though he might have been shot. I wanted to check on him, but I fear I'm bein' watched. I was out lookin' for an escaped sheep today, otherwise I'd not have run across ye."

"He got grazed by a bullet," she said, making light of his wound in an effort to appease the fear she saw in the old man's eyes. "But he's fine now, and it's healing up nicely. I know what to do for infection," she finished stoutly, hoping that he would believe her. And then because she had to know, she simply blurted it out. "Will you turn me in?"

The old man shook his head. "You—for what? Ye've not done anythin'. If ye know anythin' about this part of the country, lass an' about our family, ye'll know we don't turn on our own. If there's an opportunity to get clear of this country, though, I suggest ye take it with both hands."

She knew then that Jamie had spoken to this man, and that as far as anyone who actually had knowledge of their whereabouts, they were safe.

"Come on, lass, let's pick up yer berries an' such, I imagine ye'll need every bit of it."

They worked side by side, and soon most of the berries, nuts and mushrooms were tucked back in the basket. Ambrose's grandfather worked in silence, and did not speak again until they were done.

"On a clear day ye can see the smoke come up out of this wood."

"We only burn a fire at night," she said.

"Ye'll have to burn it durin' the day too, come winter. Ye'll both perish of pneumonia otherwise."

"I know. We'll have to hope that the weather covers us." She hoped they would be gone by then, but knew that too would be filled with risk. It seemed no matter which way she turned it was like trying to keep an over-brimming wine casket from spilling, and then being made to throw a rock in it and hope it didn't bleed all over the table.

"I've a wee propane stove, I'll leave it here for ye tomorrow. Come near the dim of the day. That way ye can at least cook yer food an' have a cup of tea without havin' to wait for nightfall. I'll leave a note lettin' ye know the next time I'm goin' to drop somethin' off."

He gave her a long look, and she was disconcerted, for his eyes were a great deal like Ambrose's and the look that he gave her was one of pity.

"Ye'll maybe not realize this child, but this country is good at destroyin' her own. If ye get clear of all this, ye ought to go home."

She shook her head. "I won't leave him."

The old man nodded. "Still an' all, ye'll need to make a decision before winter. Ye're on borrowed time as it is. It'll get frightful cold in that wreck of a cottage come November."

She nodded, not from agreement but simply because she knew the man was right. When winter came, they would have to be gone. The thought put a chill right into the middle of her, like an ice-tipped flint had passed through her.

"Ye do need to ask yerself if he's the sort who can run his whole life, or if he's the sort who always ends up facin' his demons, because that's simply who he is."

"I know who he is," she said quietly, though she was aware of a spreading darkness within, a fear that this world they were living in was make believe, and could not last.

"Ye tell him that if he needs anythin' he's to come to me. I'll do whatever he asks. That goes for you as well, girl. If somethin' happens an' ye find ye need help, ye come direct to me, don't hesitate."

"I will," she said.

"We'd best both be off, we've stood here a long time as it is. Mind that you hide that hair when next ye're out."

He was gone then, a flicker of brown tweed and bent stick, and then he simply melded with the woods and disappeared from her sight.

By the time she made it back to the cottage, the weather had turned and the golden day was gone. A heavy rain had begun to fall, and the cottage, huddled in a tangle of dark dripping vine, looked hollow and cold. She was chilled through, and thought longingly of hot drinks and the warmth of the Aga at Pamela's house. What she wouldn't give for one of Maggie's ambrosial meals right now. She musn't let any of that longing show in her face, however, and so she straightened her spine, despite the rain drops sliding down it and walked through the cottage door.

Ambrose was huddled in their tangle of blankets, and barely looked up as she came in. The dark feeling inside her spread a little further, like some terrible plant with hooks that attached themselves to her very marrow, and sent out vines to wrap around her heart.

"Ambrose?" she said, putting her basket to the side and walking over to the bit of sponge braced on two ancient pallets that constituted their bed.

He sat up, clearly wobbly and looked at her with eyes that were glazed and slightly unfocussed. He wasn't wearing his glasses, but she thought it was more than that.

"It's only a bit of fever, I think," he said, though his voice sounded hoarse. "I was fine this mornin', I'll likely be fine again tomorrow. Crawl in with me, an' then we'll both be warm."

"I will. First though I'm going to get you some water and some aspirin. Another dose of penicillin as well won't hurt. As soon as the sun goes down, I'm lighting a fire too. It's far too damp in here."

Ambrose took the aspirin and the penicillin and drank a few swallows of water before collapsing back into the blankets.

She shed her clothes, wanting to be skin to skin with him, so that he might take what he needed of her warmth. He was shivering and yet hot to the touch. A thrill of fear went through her. It was all too easy to imagine him getting so sick that he could die out here, or she'd be forced to get him to a hospital.

"I can hear ye worryin," Ambrose said. "Once the penicillin kicks in I'll be right as rain, ye'll see."

"I saw your grandfather today. I'm sorry, I wasn't being as careful as I ought to have been."

"It doesn't matter, I thought he would likely know or figure it out when I disappeared. Don't worry, he'll not betray us."

"He said you could go to him for help, any time of the night or day. He said I could come to him as well."

"Should somethin' happen, Pru, ye will go, won't ye? Go to Pamela or Jamie, ye know they'll help ye."

She nodded, knowing that he needed that reassurance, but wishing he wouldn't speak so plainly of it. Normally she was the one to want her truth unvarnished, but with their current situation she wanted to stick her head in the proverbial sand, until she was forced to take it out. It was this she expressed with her next words.

"I want to fade from the world, and just be here with you where the smoke of a thousand autumns might pass over our gate, and no one and nothing of the world could touch us."

"I'd need to become a better hunter," Ambrose said wryly.

"We could raise chickens, and grow a garden. I could put up preserves every fall, and you could bring in the wood and the occasional rabbit. I know how to fish too. We wouldn't need anything more than that."

"Well maybe soap an' gloves, an' a proper bed, an' a roof that doesn't leak," Ambrose said with a laugh, though he sent an owlish look toward the guilty bit of the ceiling which had allowed them to get thoroughly wet the night before.

"I'd add chocolate, maybe a propane lamp, and a tub for bathing. In winter you'd carve things and I would knit socks and scarves, and in the summer we'd keep bees and butterflies, so that there would always be bright bumbly bits floating about on the air, and 'winged things white and boundless as stars in a snowstorm,' to quote Jack Stuart."

"Sounds lovely," he said, hugging her more tightly to him. Huddling together in the scant shelter the blankets and their mutual body heat offered was their only way of getting through chilly afternoons such as this one. There was a hollow note in his voice though, one which sent frost all along her nerve endings, in a way the frigid air had not.

"What would we grow in our garden?" she asked, wanting to keep to the playful feel of their conversation.

"Rosemary and radishes, tea leaves and thyme, lavender and love," Ambrose answered, voice light, though she sensed his mind was still elsewhere.

"You'd write poetry, and I could roam the fields and hedgerows for apples and nuts, and bring home tales from the squirrels and the foxes."

"I'd write ye a poem, one just for you, every year on the anniversary of the day we met."

"I wish it all was real," she said wistfully.

Ambrose held her, and gradually she felt his skin begin to cool. The aspirin had helped; the antibiotics would do the rest.

"What if, my love, none of it's real?"

"What do you mean?" she asked, curious and yet almost dreading the answer. A fine stipple of goosebumps rose on her skin and she had an odd sense that they were on some stranded island, one that didn't exist in the world beyond.

"What if it's all some sort of strange phantasm? What if we're merely burnin' an' just seein' the spectres of our own smoke?"

"Don't talk so," she said, the cold chill at her core spreading out through her blood and bone, "it makes me feel like we're ghosts, caught on some sort of island of time."

"We are in a sense. Sweetheart, we're playin' house an' ye know it. I hate that ye're involved in this. Ye could end up goin' to jail too, an' the best ye could hope for at that point is gettin' deported back to America. This is not real life, Pru. We're just bidin' time before the inevitable takes over." His voice was adrift, though it held a core of stark realization that made her want to cry. Ambrose must have felt the tension in her body, for he stroked her back.

"I'm sorry, I'll quit goin' on. It was just a strange day, an' ye know how fever thoughts are—dark an' disturbin'."

"No, just tell me. You know sometimes it helps to talk about it, it makes it smaller and banishes the dark," she said softly, though she could feel the vines of that dark plant squeeze her heart a little more. "We promised, after all, to tell all our truths."

He was quiet for several long moments, and she had the sense he was weighing his words, against how much he thought they might upset her.

"Just strange thoughts driftin' through my head when I was awake. I kept thinkin' about somethin' I read last year, where this philosopher was sayin' that he thought it was possible that some of us see bits from the future, that if somethin' huge happens to us before the end of our life, then that event will send back miniature reflections of itself—like the visual echo in a hall of mirrors, an' we'll carry the sense of it with us always. Whether it's meant as a warnin' or simply an echo, he couldn't say, only that he felt all times exist at once an' occasionally the fractal waves of those times interfere with one another, an' the ripple of that becomes the echo that we hear."

"Ambrose," she said softly, "you're scaring me. What is it that you think you're seeing or hearing?"

"'Tis just brain fever, pay no mind to me. I've been ramblin' about in my head all day, an' now I'm spillin' it all out on you." He kissed her forehead, and then yawned widely. "I'm still tired, I think I'll sleep for a bit."

"I'll make something to eat, that way it will be ready when you wake."

He fell to sleep within minutes, and once she was certain it wouldn't wake him, she rose and shrugged on her clothes, and then pulled the canvas across the windows. She lit the fire then, building it with dry wood Ambrose had collected a few evenings before. Once it was flaring high and hot, she crouched down near it, holding her hands out to the blaze.

The fire settled to a steady burn, and she let the heat and dance of the flames take her over, looking into them, listening to see if she could hear an echo, or see what was reflected in that illusory hall of mirrors. But look as she might all she could see was herself—pale, freckled and frightened. And the only echo she could hear was that of Ambrose's grandfather's voice, telling her words she hadn't wanted to hear, and yet knew for truth as soon as they were spoken.

"Ye do need to ask yerself if he's the sort who can run his whole life, or if he's the sort that always ends up facin' his demons, because that's simply who he is."

Chapter Fifty-five

In Dreams You are Still with Me

PRU WOKE ALONE, and sat up immediately. The silence had a quality to it that it had not held these last two weeks; it was so complete that it felt like the space between snowflakes, when the snow absorbed all noise, even that of birds and the call of a fox on a cold night.

Her heart began to hammer immediately, panic coursing through her in a swift running current. Ambrose was gone. He had left while she slept, and he was not returning, that much she felt in her heart before she even spied the paper which held her name, sitting stark and white on the rickety table. He would go to the nearest police station and turn himself in, though she hoped with every fibre of her being that he'd gone to Pat and Tomas. It was tantamount to jumping off a bridge and hoping to survive to go straight to the police.

Still, she went outside, hoping against hope that he was merely taking in the morning light, something he'd done a few times this last week. And suddenly she realized that the plan had been there for at least this past several days, and that he'd been taking his last look at the things which would no longer be a part of his world—sunrise and starlit nights, and her face.

She went to the gate—the weathered, half-rotten gate, held together by moss and tiny white flowers. Held between two old willows, it guarded the pathway down to the pond. It no longer seemed a thing of romance, but rather just an old gate over which the autumns might flow, but which still led only to the past, and not to a future.

Once she was inside again, she looked around the cottage. It appeared dismal, when only last night it had seemed a place of enchantment. Vision changed in the wake of absence though, and so now the small blue jar was just a faded and cracked bit of glass, and not the hearth of a mermaid, the candles were grubby bits of wax, and the blankets were rife with holes eating away at the threads. Edward and Maeve's letters were tattered bits of paper, worn thin with reading, and yet in the end the words had mattered so little that someone had simply dropped them in a battered tin, and left them in a secondhand shop. She knew now that Edward had never come home, and that Maeve had likely just gone on with life as best as she could manage, though she probably never breathed deeply again, nor loved with her whole self and heart. No, she would have learned caution and self-preservation from allowing such a love to burn in her only to have it turn her heart to ashes.

Pru crossed the room, and tore the letters from the wall, blinded by tears, blood thumping so hard against the walls of her skin that she thought she might collapse from the force of it.

Edward and Maeve had seemed to exist in some lovely golden bubble, hung high in the airs of the past. They'd created a whole world around them, with their violets and poetry, their kisses and promises, and they'd foolishly thought that they too could live inside that golden bubble, and be safe to love for the next fifty years and more. They had been wrong.

She built a fire in the hearth, for it no longer mattered if anyone saw the smoke and came running to investigate. They would only find her, a girl in tears with messy hair and filthy clothes. A girl who'd lost the only boy she would ever truly love.

The fire was not for warmth, for she didn't care anymore if she was warm or cold. She fed the letters one by one into the flames, submitting it all to destruction. Love was a lie, and it couldn't keep you safe from pain that hovered all around you like a tidal wave—subsuming and total.

For a very long time, she sat simply holding the final letter in her hand, and feeling nothing, thinking nothing, believing nothing. Outside the window the day passed in showers and sunshine, the fields all around gold and brown with the last of the season's harvest. Twilight had begun its encroach in amethysts and apple pinks when she placed the final letter on the fire. The flames took it, the edges glowing crimson and just before it was completely consumed, one line flared bright gold from the burning page.

In dreams you are still with me.

And then that golden line—hung high in the airs of the past—turned to ash, and she knew it was time to leave, for there was nothing left here for her.

My love,

My grandfather told me once about the time he saw Halley's Comet—and though he was only a little boy of five at the time, he never forgot the awe and beauty of something so rare that it couldn't be seen in many people's lifetimes. Its incandescence had burned itself into his mind, and he said he would picture it far out in the dark reaches of space, turning at the limits of its elliptic and heading toward home. He said it inspired awe in him, but also a bit of terror—for it was around thoughts of this hurtling comet that the knowledge came to him of the brevity of a human life.

He said to me, "Most of us get eighty or so years if we're lucky, and that's so little time, son, but that's not somethin' ye can see or feel at yer age. Youth is immortal after all."

I think he was wrong about not being able to see or feel it when you're young though, because it's with me now, how short this life is, how fragile, how some lives get so little time that they are no more than an invisible sigh in the weave of the world.

My time is running down, we both know it, it's been hovering in the air from the minute you walked through the door two weeks ago. I have to turn myself in, there's really no choice about it.

Part of your love for me is because you perceived me to be a good person, someone with a moral code, someone maybe a little old-fashioned, who still believed in honour. Pru, we both know that there isn't anything honorable about hiding in a forest, pretending that I don't have to face the music at some point. And so my love, I am going. I have to go because if I stayed and never faced up to what I've done, I wouldn't be the Ambrose that you fell in love with. I would diminish with the burden of guilt. I would become less both to myself, and what would be more painful to me—to you.

We stepped out of time here in this cottage, and for a little it felt like we could do it—run off somewhere and live under new names, and make new lives. But you know as well as I do that eventually, it would destroy us.

Remember Casey's story about his night stranded in the snow? What we are, what we have been to each other exists always in that liminal space, for where there is love, time is no time at all. Love can fold time in half, and take us back to that one moment and let us live there for a spell. We live everything twice over—once in the event, and the second time through memory. We are there always and also never again. It is the pain at the core of the human experience. But I would not change a thing between us, because all the moments with you is where I would live over and over if there was a choice.

Somewhere, I think, in that alternate world of ours, there are chickens and maybe two rosy pigs, that we'd never have the heart to sacrifice to our table, and a garden filled with rosemary and radishes, with beans and bees, and a snowstorm of butterflies. And we walk in the light of us—of love and a life lived quietly side by side. I think that world hangs beside this one, and we only have to step to the side and know the magical password to have the door open to us.

It's in this world, however, that you'll need to forgive me. I don't imagine it will come easy to you, my stubborn girl, but for your own sake, you'll need to find your way there one day.

I'm writing this while leaning on the gate, and I can almost see it there hovering in the air before me—that magical password which would allow us to step through this crumbling gate, and have that other life. It's here all around me, I can taste it like pure blue gulps of sky, I can smell it—honeycomb and frying eggs, grain and earth and the scent of wool drying by the fire. And I see it in the face of a little girl, cheeks pink with cold, running to me with a gap-toothed grin, hair a rose-gold tumble just like yours. And I see you. Now and always, I see you.

I look upward. The sky above is adrift with stars, cold and clean. I'm going in to get you, so we can watch the night sky together. A scent fills me, and I feel my heart both rise and break. I know this smell, for it is the scent of that other world, it is the smoke of the thousand autumns which—there in that other world—passed over our gate.

Ambrose

Part Eight

Points of Fracture

Chapter Fifty-six

Blackbird's Tongue

"MAMA, IT'S PRU!" Conor shouted and ran toward the figure sitting demurely on top of her suitcase, beside the Flying Tortoise. Pamela, returning with the children from a seaside amble, felt a rush of both panic and relief. She picked Kathleen up—who gave a small shriek of fury at having her perambulations cut short—so that they might move more quickly toward that still figure.

It had been five days since Pat had called to tell them the news of Ambrose's surrender. After, Pamela had made the trip up North, and gone directly to the cottage in the woods, knowing the girl needed those who cared for her around her. All she had found though was an empty cottage, cold and damp inside, with a scatter of blankets, two mugs and an empty plate upon a makeshift table. She had packed everything up, including a tattered book of Rilke's poetry. Pru didn't want it now, but eventually she might change her mind, and wish she had the things which held the memories of her time in this cottage with the boy she loved. She had called Jamie from the nearest village, only to find he was out looking for the girl too.

And now, here she was. It was, indeed, Pru, but she was not the same girl she had been before. Even at a distance, Pamela recognized that. She rose from her suitcase, her hands clasped so tightly together that it looked as though her knuckles might break through the skin at any moment. Her pretty blue coat was buttoned up askew, and the beautiful rose-gilt hair looked as though it hadn't been brushed in days.

"Oh, Pru," she said, her heart hurting just at the sight of the girl. Her pain was palpable even at a distance. There was no point in polite greetings, they were all far past that now. She took the girl in her arms and held her, stroking the tousled hair and saying nothing, for there wasn't anything which could comfort her in the place where she now stood.

She drew back from the girl, and looked into the sea-bright eyes.

"We've all been mad with worry. I went to the cottage to find you, but you'd left already."

"I went to stay with Ambrose's grandfather for a few days. I thought if he—he ch-changed his mind, he might come there. But he didn't."

"No, he turned himself in, Pru. He went to Pat and Tomas, and told them his wishes, and they took him in."

She nodded. "I had hoped he might go to them. I was afraid of what might happen if he just walked into a police station."

"Tomas and Pat made sure everything was by the book, and they are going to represent him too."

It was small comfort, she knew, for this girl who had just lost her love and had to know the odds of him ever getting out of prison were extremely low. Pat had been brutally honest when he'd told them about what lay ahead for Ambrose. There had been no comfort in the telling for any of them.

"I'm going to make you something to eat, and a hot cup of tea. Sit down, I'll only be a minute."

She motioned to Conor to set up the canvas chairs they used around the fire in the evenings, and then went to fix Pru a sandwich and a cup of tea. Perhaps the tea and bread would steady her, and then they could talk.

Through the caravan window she could see the children watching Pru, for they all loved her, and would understand that something was wrong with their normally cheerful nanny. Even Isabelle, never one to hold back, was keeping a bit of a distance, dark eyes wide with concern. But then Pru opened her arms to Isabelle, and she ran straight to Pru and flung her arms around the girl's middle.

She saw something then in Pru's face, a sort of inner knowing, something secret and yet as old as the world. Her heart sank a little, but she picked up the tray loaded with teapot, cups and sandwiches, determined to show Pru nothing but compassion and confidence.

Pamela paused for a moment on the steps, and looked out at the sea, which rolled and glittered like silver foil in the late afternoon light. The hills beyond were the colour of wild honey in the sinking sun. So much beauty, so much tragedy. A land that demanded the sort of love which was always washed in blood. The ghost of an old song drifted through her, with words sung low about a woman who roamed the tall cliffs, clad all in black for the loss of her lover, and about how that woman stayed in the spot where she'd last seen her lover before he went to sea, and grew old there, waiting for his return, her black dress in tatters and her hair gone white as the foam on the sea. Until, a long time later, she too became a ghost, with only the threads of the black dress left in the long grass where she'd once lay with a young man. There were some loves that did that to a person, turned them to a ghost, one who walked and talked and drifted through the world, but a ghost, nevertheless. She knew what it was to love like that, and she thought, perhaps, Pru too had such a love and it frightened her for the girl.

The last two lines were the ones drifting about her now—

The woman's skirt held sorrow, sorrow
And she spoke in a blackbird's tongue.

Long ago, someone had told her that to speak in a blackbird's tongue was the gift of someone who had the sight, who saw things before their time, and knew of the grief to come.

She shivered a little then, and it seemed as though a dark cloud passed over the wild honey hills, and slipped into her bloodstream—a sinuous and dark note, reverberating through blood and marrow. *"Whisht, child, come back from yer fool's fancy."* The voice was from the land of childhood, where her old nanny Rose still dwelt with her sayings and superstitions. The matter-of-fact voice shook her from her dark thoughts. She went down the stairs, determined to let in the light, with whatever truth could salvage of it.

"There's something more, isn't there, Pru?" she asked, setting the tray with tea, juice and biscuits on the plastic table by her chair.

"Yes, there is," Pru said miserably, her face flushed and every freckle standing out in relief against the pink tone. "I'm pregnant."

Casey arrived home from his current project—renovating the cottage of an elderly woman in the nearest village—just as she was starting supper in the cast iron pot over the fire. It was too muggy to cook inside the trailer and she found the fresh air steadying to her nerves.

After dropping her news like a small bomb, Pru had pulled herself up, realizing that Conor and Isabelle were within hearing distance. They had spoken after that in the strange code adults used when small people were in the vicinity. The gist of it was that Pru did not want to leave Ireland and was hoping to find a home—even if only temporarily—with Pamela and Casey.

"Miss Prudence," he said, "It will be a grand thing to see that ye're all right. This one here," he nodded toward Pamela, "has been goin' a wee bit mad with the worryin' over ye."

Pru nodded, but remained at a wary distance. Normally she and Casey were friendly, though Pamela knew her loyalty still lay with Jamie in many regards. Right now though the girl was giving her the room to tell Casey and to allow him to give an honest response to what she was about to say. She thought perhaps she ought to feed him first, as she had learned long ago not to spring bad news on a man with an empty stomach. However, he had already seen the state of Pru, and raised a questioning brow at Pamela, just before giving her a kiss.

"She's come seeking asylum," Pamela said.

"Ye mean she needs a place to stay, no?"

"Yes, that's what I mean."

"Ye know I don't mind that, so what else is it ye need to tell me?" Casey asked, the cynical eyebrow rising a little higher.

"Well, she's also pregnant."

"Ah, I see."

"She says she can't go home, she's certain her parents will disown her, though clearly she has to tell them at some point."

Casey folded his arms over his chest, and gave her a look with which she was all too familiar. "I think I just caught a glimpse of the road this is headed down."

Pru came up then, hands once again knotted together.

"I'll earn my keep," she said, face dead-white and her freckles standing out sharply in contrast. "I'll cook, I'll clean, I'll look after the children. All I ask is to have a roof over my head. I can't go home, and I–I've come to think of you, Pamela and the children as family."

Casey gave her a long look. "That's all well an' fine, Miss Prudence, but in case it's escaped yer notice, I don't have a roof to place over yer head at present. But if ye don't mind sleepin' rough for a bit, I think we can manage. Nor do I expect ye to be some sort of indentured servant to us. I'm not such an ogre that I'd make a wee girl who finds herself in a fix, slave away just so she has a place to put her head at night."

"Th-thank you, Casey," she said, a flush fine as the petals of a poppy rising in her cheeks. "But I will help. I miss the children, and it does look like Pamela has her hands full here."

Casey smiled. "Perhaps with you around to help out, I'll be able to get that roof built now, so we're not all sleepin' under the stars come winter. I'll ask ye now—does Ambrose know ye're expectin' his child?"

"No, not yet. I wasn't certain and so I never told him, and now hardly seems the best time."

"Tell him, he's the right to know, lass an' it could make a difference to how he deals with what's ahead of him. We can ask Patrick if there's any way to get ye in for a visit, or if ye'll need to send a message."

"Thank you," she said, and Pamela saw that the girl was exhausted and needed more than anything to lie down and sleep for a bit.

"Go on up into the trailer and have a lie down, Pru," Pamela said, "I'll call you when dinner's ready."

Pru nodded and went, still clutching her blue coat around her. The children scattered to play, but remained well within parental line of sight.

Casey turned to her then. "Now that's all settled, do ye think I might have my supper?"

"Yes, you can have supper and anything else you might like," she said, feeling both relief and gratitude at his acquiescence to Pru joining their small tribe once again.

He sat down in a chair by the fire and sighed. "Woman, if ye move any more children, beasts or elderly vagabonds into our life, I'll never be havin' anythin' else I might like, an' nor, might I add, will you. Ye do know we'll have to put the girl up in the wee cottage, primitive as it is. It will need a decent wee fireplace too, an' I'll have to put new thatch on it before winter, not to mention the windows which need replacin', an'—"

She put a halt to his list by the simple expedient of taking him by the ears and planting a kiss on his mouth.

"It will all be fine, you'll see," she said, as he pulled her down into his lap.

"What am I to do with ye, woman?" Casey said, half in exasperation and half in jest.

"Do you mind taking her in, then?" she asked.

"No, I don't mind, though I will say that ye do have this strange power of attractin' every lost soul within fifty miles of yer person. I could move ye to the top of a mountain in Peru, an' ye'd find a cause to take up, or an orphan that needed shelter within the first week. Ye care for the hurt ones of the world, Jewel, an' I can't fault that. Ye'll allow me to worry about where that care takes ye though, no?"

"Of course. I'd be lost without your worry, man."

"Good, keep that in mind next time ye've some mad notion to take in more strays, would ye?"

"I will." She loftily chose to ignore the eye roll he gave her. "Will there be time, do you think, for everything that needs doing before winter?" she asked, looking out toward the hills where the dark was fast rolling in from the sea, and bringing with it that silver-sharp scent which heralded the coming season.

"Oh, aye, I'll have shelter for us all come the cold, an' then I'll put a plaque over the door that reads, *Riordan Home for Foundlings and Widows, established 1981*. I'm aware, of course, that it will only be the first of several buildins' ye'll demand I construct, so that ye might take in the riffraff from all about the countryside. An', yes, before ye ask, there will be time for all the other things too," he finished softly, and then kissed her for a very long time, as if to illustrate his point.

Later, once the children were asleep and Pru was made comfortable in the cottage, Pamela felt the chill presence of that dark cloud again, touching delicate along her spine, like the fingers of a phantom, feeling the future, and finding it uncertain. If she closed her eyes the woman in the song was still there, with dark fields and moon-slurried seas gathered up in the long night of her skirts. That skirt—that darkness—billowed out around all of them now, and there were none who would escape the sorrows held there.

Chapter Fifty-seven

Red Flower, Clay Urn, Broken Angel

CASEY ALWAYS FELT a bit melancholy at the end of a long project. It was particularly sharp when it had been a job he'd loved. Restoring Tomas' house had been just that for him—a job he'd loved. Since their move to Kerry he'd come up every few weeks to work on Tomas' house for a day or two at a time, and slowly the projects had come to completion. He would miss the house, and he would miss the man who owned it. They had formed a relationship of mutual respect and understanding, something which surprised Casey, and he would miss their chats over meals and cups of tea. He was, however, impatient to get on with the finishing of his own home, before his wife left him for a man with proper plumbing and a completed roof.

He was just doing one last walk through before he packed up his tools and left for good when he heard Tomas come in through the kitchen.

"Ye're home early," Casey said, looking at his watch. It was only one in the afternoon.

"Aye, I have a meeting here at the house in a little while, an' I thought I'd come home a bit early so I'd the chance to speak with you before ye left, bein' that this is your last day an' all."

"Oh?" Casey said, wondering if the man had complaints about any of the work he'd done. He wasn't best pleased himself with a few of the shortcuts he'd been forced to take due to substandard materials. Substandard in his view, leastwise—large Elizabethan oaken beams being somewhat hard to source.

"This is for you." Tomas handed him a scrap of paper, which Casey realized was a cheque once he unfolded it. He took one look at the amount written across the paper in Tomas' precise legal script and then looked at the man, fixing him with a narrowed eye.

"What the hell is this for? That's far more than ye owe me, an' ye know it."

"God help me, but ye're even more stubborn than yer damn brother, an' that's sayin' something."

"I'm not some sort of charity. Pay me what ye owe, but no more. I'll not take this money from ye."

"I don't consider ye a charity, though I will say ye can be a prickly bastard. Here's what I want to say. I thought ye very capable from the get-go or I wouldn't have hired ye, but watchin' ye slowly bring this place back to somethin' of beauty, I realize ye're an artist in yer own right, lad. If ye ever take a notion to revive that buildin' company of yers, then that money is to stake ye until ye're able to get back on yer feet."

"Well, thank you," Casey said, feeling entirely nonplussed by the man's praise. "I'm still not takin' the money, though."

Dark eyes glared at blue and received the glare back in full measure. Neither man blinked, but then Tomas sighed, taking the cheque back with some reluctance.

"I'll write ye one for the proper amount, but just know, the money's here whenever ye need it. I'd consider it an honour to help ye get yer company back on a solid foundation. Now if ye insist on refusin' my money, the least ye can do is stay to lunch."

"Ah, thanks for the offer but I promised Pamela I'd be home by supper time. I'll need to leave soon to keep that promise."

"Will ye have time for a cup of tea at least? There's somethin' more I'd like to speak with ye about."

That sense of trepidation he'd had earlier, returned.

"Aye, I can spare a little more time," he said.

He followed Tomas into the kitchen, only to find the tea was already made, and there was a plate of biscuits on the table. He noted that the table was inordinately clean and wondered which of the women in Tomas' life had seen fit to give everything a good scrub down.

He sat, and took a biscuit, the scent of ginger making his stomach rumble. Tomas filled both their cups, and then sat across from him, appearing rather twitchy. Casey wondered what was ailing the man.

Tomas filled him in on the legal doings with Ambrose, the gist of which was that the boy had been given medical attention while held in the Crumlin Jail, and was faring about as well as might be expected.

"The trial was what I've come to expect in these cases—a half hour in front of a judge an' then banged into prison. It's a joke an' no more than a kangaroo court, but they get away with it, an' there's little to be done but try to find legal inroads after the fact. He's bein' transferred to the Kesh any time now. If he'd only wounded the soldier, an' not killed him outright, there might be more hope that we could get him a bit of leniency, but as things stand it's goin' to be an uphill battle all the way."

It was what Casey had expected. The circumstances of the shooting would not be taken into account. Unfortunately, having ties to well-known PIRA commanders, wasn't going to help Ambrose's situation either. Pru hadn't spoken much of it, and hadn't told the boy yet that he was going to be a father. Casey didn't want to push her, but felt the sooner the better in this matter.

He took another biscuit and bit into it. "Did Kate make these? They're very good." He could hear Pamela's voice in his head telling him not to spoil his dinner, but he was hungry enough that the biscuits would barely see him home.

"Ah, no, yer mother made those."

"My mother makes biscuits for ye?" Casey asked, feeling slightly discomfited by the news.

"Well, in truth I think she makes them when she knows ye're here workin', but aye, she drops food by now an' again."

"Hmmphmm," Casey said, and took a swallow of tea so that he might have a second to digest this news along with the biscuits.

"Ye seem to be gettin' along well with the woman," Tomas said, though Casey had a sense there was a question somewhere within the man's simple statement.

"Aye, strangely enough losin' my memory has made it easier to have a relationship with her."

It was true, for Deirdre had come down to the farm several times now, spending the day with the children and Pamela, and often staying after he arrived home to visit for a while. An ease had established itself between them, and he found it was rather nice to have his mother back in his life. It was like having a bit of his father returned to him as well.

"I know she is grateful for that."

"For the loss of my memory?" Casey asked, only half in jest.

"Well, I imagine she meant the relationship part of it," Tomas said drily.

"What was the other thing ye wished to speak of?" Casey asked, wanting to get to it; if he didn't get on the road soon, he'd be late getting home.

"Well, we are speakin' of it, as it happens." The man looked terribly nervous suddenly, which alarmed Casey, being that he'd never seen Tomas truly ruffled. "Ye must miss him, yer father, that is," Tomas continued in what seemed a bit of a *non sequitur* to Casey. He picked up the teapot, and topped up Casey's mug, though it was still two-thirds full.

"Aye, I do," Casey said.

"He sounds the sort of man who might be hard to forget," Tomas continued. Casey leaned back, understanding coming to him along with a tiny jolt of shock.

"Aye, I suppose ye might say that. He was my father though, so I'm not likely to think otherwise."

"Well, I meant he might be such to a woman."

"Ah, are we talkin' about my mother here?" Casey asked, innocently, deciding to enjoy himself and maybe get a little of his own back after all the lecturing he'd received over his own romantic arrangements. Tomas flushed, and Casey felt a bit of alarm—was this man serious about his mother?

"Aye, I suppose I am. Only I have the sense at times, that she's never gotten over yer daddy, an' that she always felt they'd unfinished business between them. Did ye have that sense with yer da? That he felt the same?"

"I don't know, my daddy didn't talk about her a great deal after she left. I think it was too painful for him. If we asked about her, he'd answer, but he never offered up a lot of information otherwise. If ye want to truly know what the man was like, look to Patrick, he's very like our daddy, both in appearance an' temperament."

Tomas nodded. "That's what I was afraid of. Patrick is the sort of man women adore. You, they want to take to bed, but they want to look after your brother."

"I think maybe there was an insult in there," Casey said, taking another swallow of his tea in an attempt to regain his composure.

"It's not meant as one, lad, merely an observation. I suspect women have been at ye like flies to the sugar bowl much of yer life."

"I suppose in that respect, I do take after my father. My Aunt Sophie once said my da was like catnip to women. I do remember that much about the man—the women liked him a great deal."

Tomas nodded, looking a touch dismayed by this description of Brian.

Casey decided it was time to show a wee bit of mercy. "If ye're askin' me about datin' my mother, I have no advice for ye. She's been independent for a long time now. If she's cookin' an' cleanin' for ye though, I think that says all ye need to know."

"Well, as it happens, it's yer opinion I want. Do ye have any objection to my courtin' Deirdre?"

Casey almost choked on a biscuit crumb, and hastily drank some tea to wash it down.

"Christ on a cracker," he sputtered, clapping a napkin to his face.

"Ah," Tomas said, "ye'll not be delighted by the notion, I see."

"It's not that, man, but I thought ye were just considerin' seein' her, not marryin' the woman. I'll assume that's what ye mean by courtin'?"

"Aye, that's what I mean," Tomas said. "Yer mother is not the sort of woman to be taken lightly, an' so yes, I've serious intentions with her. I want to know if you object to that."

Casey had a moment where he wondered if he'd wandered into some strange and alternate dimension where Tomas became his stepfather.

"Does Patrick know about this?"

"Aye, I spoke to him a few days ago. I was waitin' on seein' you face-to-face before I spoke of it, because I feel I owe both of you boys the respect of that."

"An' what is it that Patrick had to say?"

"Well, not a great deal other than to mention he did wonder when I'd get around to talkin' to him. Kate had sussed things some time back."

Women, Casey thought, they always sniffed out romance even when it was just a thought in a man's mind. Which led him to wonder just how long *his* wife had known, but had somehow managed to refrain from mentioning it.

"As I said, she's grown, an' long used to makin' her own decisions. Ye don't need my approval, but if ye want it, then aye, ye have it. I'm not one to deny anyone a bit of joy in their lives."

"I thank you for that," Tomas said as formally as though he was accepting a blessing from a bishop. Casey decided it was past time to nip the conversation in the bud, but was saved from the necessity of doing so, by the ringing of the doorbell.

He stood and nodded to Tomas. "I'll leave ye to get the door then. I'll just finish packin' up an' be on my way."

Tomas stood as well, and put out a hand to shake his. "Give my love to Pamela an' the children, an' don't forget what I said about the money, it's yers for the askin' any time ye might need it for yer business."

"Thank you, Tomas, an' I'll think on it."

He returned to the library, where the last of his tools sat waiting for him to pack them up and take them home. It had been the biggest job he'd ever taken on as far as restoration went. He would miss the house, but for now there wasn't anything left to do on it, and there were other projects needing his attention, not the least of which was finishing his own home.

The afternoon sun lit the room gold, as though it was the centre of a beehive, rich with a thin veneer of honey. For a moment, he stood, letting the warmth and beauty of it all soak into him, and feeling the satisfaction of a job done to the best of his abilities.

Tomas' guest must have moved into the sitting room with him, for Casey could hear their voices rising and falling in conversation, snatches of it making it to his ears. It sounded as if they were speaking of a legal matter, and the guest sounded rather like Jamie to his ears, but the accent was wrong. Posh and English, whereas Jamie was posh and Irish.

He was bending down to lock up his toolbox, when the pain took him in the head like an anvil. It was so sharp that he thought he'd been hit at first, and looked around wildly, only to find he was alone, but had dropped to one knee. His peripheral vision had gone black and in order to see anything he had to look at it directly; he feared he was going to be sick. He needed to get outside and get some air.

The back garden was damp and chilly, and he went and sat on the edge of the fountain, dizzy now and the agony in his head steadily worsening. He couldn't remember the last time he'd had pain this severe. One of Doctor Alice's methods for calming himself was to list things he saw around him, things which stayed in place—*red flower, clay urn, beech tree, broken garden angel, sequoia*—no that last one wasn't right, Tomas didn't have a sequoia, that was the old place. He looked down at his hands, big hands, looked just like his father's, and trembling now. Small arrows of panic were shooting through him like electric darts.

He needed to re-orient himself—*red flower, clay urn, broken angel.* He said the words under his breath, like a mantra, a prayer so that he might still his blood, douse the fire in his head, know where he was located on the map of his world. But when he looked up, the garden was gone, and his vision seemed to run through a dark tunnel, at the end of which was a strange lens that both magnified and miniaturized at the same time. He saw the hawthorn tree on their old property in County Down, and him stopping that fateful morning to leave a bouquet for the woman he'd long ago found in a patch of boggy ground. He'd just started back toward the house that morning, half his mind thinking upon his tasks for the day, and half of it musing on the night before, when he and Pamela had danced in the kitchen with Isabelle between them. He'd been distracted, and so the first blow had taken him unawares.

The blow to the head turned everything dark, great black explosions of pain shooting through his skull, blinding him to the land around him. He was confused—had a branch fallen on him, something heavy? No, there were men, more than one. Focused entirely on beating him. He was held down, couldn't see, his face pressed into the dirt so that he couldn't get air, and the black in his eyes was shot with stars. He needed to breathe, needed to get up, get away. There were too many of them, though, and it was near to impossible to think between the blows that were coming thick and fast now, no break between them.

Voices, voices, voices—he knew one, someone he'd thought a friend, but who clearly was not. Betrayal like a blade running through the valley of his soul. Another one: posh, British, superior, and clearly wanting him dead. That voice too was one he knew, he'd heard it somewhere before but couldn't think, he just needed to breathe now and pray he'd survive. He couldn't see them, but he could hear.

"Make fucking certain he's dead. I don't care what you do with the body, just hide it well. Bury it where no one will ever find his bones."

He was going to die. Die here on his own land, unable to get up, to move, to at least fight before the end came for him. His fingers curled into the soil, and he smelled the land—the loam, the bitter scent of hawthorn, the decay of leaves, and like a tiny whisper so far away he could only grasp the echo of it, the smell of Isabelle's talc, from when he'd held her, fresh from her bath that morning. His baby, his son, Pamela. He would never see them again. In that moment of pain, desperation and understanding, he felt his heart break, as though it was made of glass, hit by a fist and shattered into a million tiny pieces. And then he was gone.

He came back to himself with a jolt, feeling as though he was scattered into bits all over the ground, a man with neither form nor understanding. His hand was reaching out for something, but he didn't know what. He swallowed, pulling the hand back. *Red flower, clay urn, broken angel.*

"Breathe, man," he said to himself, the sound of his own voice odd and spooky in the empty garden. Taking his own advice, he drew in a few breaths, letting each one out slowly, steadying himself until he felt he could rise from his seat on the fountain rim. He stood, his pants damp, and his legs shaking. Still, he thought they'd bear him to the truck.

He crossed the garden and then stopped, legs still shaking. He put one hand to the wall of the house. He knew the voice, knew that the man who had wanted him dead was sitting in Tomas' house right now. That voice was the voice he'd heard that day. Telling the men to kill him, delighting in his pain, gloating over what he believed was about to happen. That man sitting inside, had nearly cost him his very life. God knew the cost had been high enough as it was. Three years lost because of this man. Three years when his marriage might have crumbled entirely, and his children found him a stranger they no longer cared for. Three fucking years of wandering in the wilderness, while Pamela grieved herself into sickness, and nearly married another man.

Casey needed to see him, he needed to clap eyes upon this man and know, finally, who had wanted him dead. He might be gone by now, but Tomas would be able to tell him who it was. The back door which led past the buttery and into the kitchen was open. He went through the rooms, silent, his ears pricked to a high pitch of sensitivity.

As he neared the sitting room door, a board squeaked beneath his foot, sounding to his ears like the rending of nails from steel. That damnable bit of floor, try as he might he'd never been able to get the squeak out of it. He held his breath, poised for flight but the conversation continued in the sitting room. Tomas' voice was slightly raised in some sort of disagreement. Whomever it was, it was clear Tomas wasn't keen on him. Casey took a few more steps forward, breath held.

The door to the sitting room was ajar, and the afternoon light flooded the space, making it hard to see at first. Everything was limned in that sun, thick-gold as freshly forged copper—the couch, the low walnut table arrayed with tea pot and cups, and the man who sat with his back to him, opposite Tomas. The man turned just then as though he sensed someone watching him, and the light—copper-gold on lips and nose and chin—caught him in profile. Casey shrank back into the shadows, heart pounding madly in his chest, his breath tight, and fury pulsing right to the tips of his fingers. He realized he'd clenched his fists, and it took everything in him not to go in the room and simply grab the man by the throat.

Jamie. No, not Jamie. For a second, as the sun gilded the man, he'd thought he *was* looking at Jamie, for the light had glinted gold upon the man's hair, and the profile—the profile was so exact. But then he realized his mistake, for this man was younger, his hair darker, his eyes the wrong colour. Still, he understood just whom he was looking at. Jamie's son, the one he hadn't known about until the boy showed up in his life at the age of twenty. Julian. Jamie's son had wanted Casey dead. Now he knew the who, but he still didn't know the why.

Jamie's son who looked so very like the man himself. The words Kolya had spoken in his truck that terrible night so many months ago came back to Casey now. *It was my daddy.* No, not his daddy, but someone who looked so like him that a small child, befuddled with sleep and terrified, might well make the mistake.

The long windows of the sitting room looked out over the garden, and while Tomas' back was to said windows, Julian's was not. Odds were better than even he'd seen Casey stumble out to the fountain. And if he'd witnessed his odd behaviour, he might well know that Casey had recognized his voice, had remembered that voice from another time.

He needed to get home because now that he knew who this man was, he knew they were all in danger, every single one of them who had a connection to Jamie, though none more so than Kathleen and Pamela.

He crept out of the house like a thief, avoiding all the spots that squeaked, leaving his canvas bag in the kitchen. The trip to the truck seemed to take an age, he'd have to come back for the rest of his tools, as he wasn't willing to risk the man catching sight of him in the house. He'd just tell Tomas he'd taken sick, and had to leave abruptly, which was not far off the truth of the matter. While Julian would have long been aware he was alive, still Casey thought he'd rather not face him. There would be no way to hide the knowledge he'd just come to in these last moments. It might well be too late anyway, if the man had, indeed, witnessed him in the garden.

Downshifting the truck into neutral, and using the natural incline of Tomas' drive, he left as silently as he could. He didn't want Julian to know he'd been there, know that he'd overheard him, maybe recognized him. If the man believed in his continued ignorance, then that was all to the better. It was a layer of protection, albeit a very flimsy one, even though it was likely the man had seen him, he knew. He didn't start the truck until he was near to the road, and the engine could no longer be heard from the house.

There were only two things beating in his mind as he travelled the road home—how in the name of God he was meant to tell Jamie Kirkpatrick that his son was a murderer, and the fact that there had been another voice there that day, one he'd known for a very long time.

Chapter Fifty-eight

Long Time Coming

PAMELA WALKED TOWARD the half-finished house, watching the road below which led up the hill to where their home stood upon its foundations. The valley below was filled with shadows, and where she walked dusk pooled around her feet, while a low and glowering sun, the colour of a guttering lantern in a coal cellar, began to sink into the sea. A queer prickling tension had surrounded her all day, pulling at her nerves and making her less than patient with the children. Nevertheless, she'd kept them close and under her eye. Right now, they were with Pru in the cottage, playing a game of slapjack; she could hear their voices raised in excitement. Isabelle had a habit of slapping any card with a face on it, not just the jacks, annoying Conor and encouraging Kathleen to do the same.

Casey was late in coming home. He'd said he only had a few details to attend to and then needed to pack up his tools, and so she'd expected him home earlier in the afternoon. Restlessness had driven her up to the house, where a swirl of beech leaves, loosened by the wind, fluttered down, one landing clammily on her neck, while the others drifted damply around her feet. She plucked the one from her neck, though the feeling of it remained, like a cold hand had touched her in warning.

She walked into the house, the sight of it calming her a little. The windows still needed to be set into their frames upstairs, and the cupboards and shelving were still without hardware and stain, and the beautifully curving staircase which led to the top floor had only a roughed-in railing. A copper backsplash gleamed where the Aga would be inset, and a patch of blue tile glowed in the space above where the sink had recently been installed. Casey's many drawings and words filled in much of what was missing, so that she could see it as she moved into the kitchen to look out through the biggest windows, which sat next to the hearth.

"An' up there with its head amongst the trees, will be a wee studio for you to do yer drawin' an' paintin' in. The light will come in just right for a good part of the day, but particularly in the evenins'. I did think a room of yer own ought to face the sea. An' here down a small hallway off the kitchen, will be the room for Pru an' her baby. I thought I'd make a small sittin' room off the bedroom, so she has a bit of privacy for company. There's a hearth for our bedroom, an' of course one for the kitchen. I've got an eye on some river stone for that. I've a bit of that bog oak left, an' I thought it would make for lovely shelves in the kitchen, an' there'll be plenty of windowsills for all yer greenery."

She stood now in that kitchen, a grue firmly fixed in her spine, as she looked toward the great sea of trees, swaying gently, whispering its secrets one to another through leaf and vine and the pulsing core of growing, living, dying, decaying wood. One could hear them—those old gods—telling their ancient tales of the time before man, and of a world restless with gleaming tooth and glittering claw. She half expected the Morrigan to appear from behind a twisted old oak, a crow on either shoulder, and witchery on her mind.

It had rained heavily the night before, and as a result the waterfall was a roaring cataract, drowning out any possibility of hearing a truck in the distance. So she kept her eyes on the road, waiting to see the familiar outlines of Casey's truck, wending its way toward home.

The sun had sunk even further though, and she was picking her way down toward the Flying Tortoise, to start making supper when finally a vehicle appeared over the rise, before dropping down toward the valley. She sighed in relief, though the prickling tension still quivered through her skin.

But it wasn't Casey, it was Jonno. She recognized the rattletrap little Ford Anglia, with its distinctive green door, and rust-red body. Her heart rose into her throat, as she wasn't expecting him, but knew that he and Casey kept close contact. If something had happened, Jonno would know it.

She was partway down the hill by the time he stopped, parking beside her own car, a relatively new Citroën—this one red—which she had bought from a dealer in Newry after the old one had given up the ghost on that terrible night when she'd found Violet dead.

Jonno stepped from his car, and she saw that the look on his good-natured face was one of worry, but not, she thought, tragedy.

"What is it?" she asked, trying to keep the panic from her voice. Something *had* happened, that much was clear.

"Casey called me, he wants ye to pack up—just the necessaries—an' be ready to go. He'll explain when he gets here. I don't know anythin' beyond that, only that somethin' must have happened to make him want yez out of here, quick-like."

"I have to feed my children first," she said, firmly. She wasn't moving an inch until Casey came home and she knew why he'd sent Jonno to watch over them.

Jonno narrowed his eyes at her, but nodded. "I'll be up by the house, keepin' an eye out. Call out if ye see anything out of place."

By the time she and Pru had the children fed, and had packed up the necessaries, as Jonno had called them, a task made more difficult by knowing neither where nor why they were going, Casey's truck appeared in the distance. She was taking the last of the day's laundry from the line strung up between two trees, when he got out of the truck, clearly whole and sound in body, if not easy in mind. The relief in her was so strong that she thought she might collapse in a heap right there by the Tortoise, a clutch of sheets in her arms. She wanted to run to him, but found she couldn't move. Pru, standing next to her, gently removed the sheets from her arms, no doubt fearing she'd drop them in the dirt, and they'd have to wash the linens all over again, a chore not undertaken lightly nor with a glad heart.

The children, not constrained by fear, ran straight to him and he scooped Isabelle up on one arm, Kathleen on the other. Conor, however, stood by her side, and she could feel him looking up at her, seeking to understand what he clearly felt in the air between his parents. Casey kissed each of the girls, and then deposited them on the ground. "Miss Prudence, will ye take the girls for a moment?"

Pru, calm and collected as always, put the sheets in a basket, nodded and took Kathleen's hand in hers, then turned to Isabelle. "Bella, come on, let's go have one of your mama's strawberry scones."

Casey hunkered down in front of Conor, fixing his son with a serious look. "I have to speak with yer mammy, make certain yer sisters an' Pru are all ready to go, all right, laddie?"

"Aye, Daddy," Conor said, responding to the seriousness he heard in his father's tone. Like Casey, Conor always felt better if he had a task with a purpose, and Casey, knowing this, had given his son the right measure of comfort.

"Walk up to the house with me, Jewel. Pru an' Jonno will keep an eye on the children."

He took her hand, and led her up the hill toward the house, the structure silhouetted in the strange flame and coal light of the evening.

"Someone came to Tomas' house this afternoon, an' I happened to hear his voice. It brought back the day I was beaten and left for dead. The day I disappeared. It was the voice of the man who tried to kill me."

She merely nodded, eyes fixed to his face, barely able to comprehend what he was saying. And then he told her about seeing the man who had wanted him dead, who had done all in his power to kill him. How he'd at first thought it was Jamie, and was confused, but then realized it was not Jamie, but his son. Julian. Julian, who Casey also believed was likely responsible for Violet's murder. It made a horrible sort of sense, and she could feel the hand on the back of her neck again, a foretelling of the news that had been coming toward her all afternoon.

"I stopped to call Jonno, as I knew he could get here ahead of me. Then I called Jamie because he needs to be warned. It's him, I know it is, Pamela. And he likely knows that I've remembered him. What he'll do now is anyone's guess, but I'll not be surprised if he comes for me, or for Jamie. I need you an' the children out of the way, I'll be vulnerable if ye're here because I don't know who he might send, or how. I can't have you or the children in harm's way."

"Where is it we're going?" she asked, panic and anger coursing through her in equal measure.

"Ye'll know when ye get there, just follow Jonno. There's someone on that end waitin' for ye. Jamie chose the location. Ye need to know that this is a plan Jamie an' I put in place should it ever become necessary, an' it'll only be for a few days until I feel it's safe for ye to come back. Ye'll have Pru an' the children with ye, an' Jonno's men watchin' over all of yez."

"And where will you be?" she asked, the fear like a tympanic beat in her ears.

"I have business to attend to, an' so will Jamie. Once it's done, I'll come for you, but until then, ye're to stay in place. I mean it, Pamela."

"Casey, if anything happens to you…" she trailed off for it had all been said, and yet it would make no difference to the determination she saw in his face.

"I know, darlin'," he said. "I'll come for you; I promise you that."

Within minutes the children and Pru were sorted into the two vehicles, and she was standing by the open car door, her husband telling her goodbye. He kissed her, a hard kiss that tasted like cold silver on her tongue and then he nodded at Jonno, who jumped into the driver's seat of the Anglia.

"It's time to go, Jewel."

She got in the car, still cold with shock, and Casey shut the door behind her. Jonno took off ahead of her, at speed, and she shifted the Citroën into gear, feeling a wrench at the thought of driving away from the man standing next to the car, giving her a smile of reassurance which looked rather grim and did absolutely nothing to bolster her confidence.

Isabelle had been insistent on going in Jonno's car, and so Pru had gone with her. Kathleen was in the back seat of the Citroën, and Conor, always and ever her steady little man, had insisted on coming with her. He looked over at her now, his small face pensive.

"Will Daddy be all right here, alone? Maybe I could stay with him. I could run to Aine for help if he needed it."

"No, sweetheart, Daddy is best on his own right now. He'll be fine."

She wondered at Conor's faith in an elderly woman as a resource in the case of violence, and then remembered the woman's rifle and her ability to hit a target from a great distance. Perhaps Conor was right as to the woman's abilities. She wished she believed her own words of reassurance to her son, and that her husband would, indeed, be fine.

When they arrived at the bottom of the valley, she looked back. Casey stood at the top of the hill, outlined in dusk, as though liquid smoke purled all around him, and she saw that he was looking into the distance, as though waiting for something he had long known was coming.

Chapter Fifty-nine

Cauterization

THE PUB WAS empty when Casey entered it, other than the man behind the bar, who merely nodded at him and then melted into the backroom without a word. It was small and bare bones as to décor—a few tables, a television suspended over the bar, worn planks for the floor. It was a workingman's pub, tucked away at the end of a tiny village on the coast of County Down. He knew the man who owned it, and he knew the men who frequented it. It was the sort of place where people kept their eyes, ears and tongues bent upon their own business. Today though, he'd arranged to have a meeting here and had asked to have the place to himself and his company.

The table he sat down at had been prepared for him just as he'd asked. A bottle of the eighteen-year Connemara Mist and two glasses. It had been aged for those years in bourbon casks and then finished off for an additional six months in sherry butts, port pipes and madeira barrels. It gave the whiskey an exceptionally golden flavour, as if the distillery had managed to bottle autumn in all its splendour. When a drink was meant to be a man's last, he thought, it ought to be a bloody good one.

The man he waited for came in the door just then, wary as a caged cat and well he might be, and yet, he'd come. Knowing, Casey thought, that there was no choice about it. He regretted that it had come to this, but he could not afford to be a fool, and while a man might want a fresh start, he knew that wasn't possible until all his loose ends had been tied off, even if it meant some ends were tied with a cauterizing iron. A man might want peace, but sometimes peace was forged through blood. It was why he was here today, sitting in this out of the way pub in an out of the way village—to cauterize one last loose end.

"Dacy, it'll be good to see ye."

Dacy nodded, sitting stiffly and not returning his cordial greeting.

Casey poured two fingers of the golden whiskey into each glass. "As I remember it, the last time we met, ye seemed a wee bit offended that I wouldn't drink with ye. So I thought I'd remedy that today."

He pushed one of the glasses across the table toward the man, noting the uneasiness which had settled over his face, like that of a half-starved dog being offered a steak, but fearing it's poisoned. He looked at the glass of whiskey as though it was exactly that—poison. Well he might, Casey thought. It was likely he'd wish it was a bottle of hemlock before this day was out.

"Are ye not goin' to drink? By yer own admission that's ill-mannered."

"I'm thinkin' this is no friendly drink," Dacy said, skin gone the colour of old greasy parchment.

"That'll be perceptive of ye," Casey said, and took a swallow of his own drink, the dark amber of it settling like a slow, soft burn in his belly. "But as we're here together anyway, let me tell ye a wee bit of a tale. It's been a long time in the makin', an' it's only recently I've understood enough of it to be able to tell it to ye now."

He took another swallow of the whiskey before continuing. "I'll begin with this—my Granny Riordan wasn't given much to the superstition, so when she did say a thing we listened. She knew things, things other people didn't. She never liked ye, even when we were lads. She told me once to be careful with ye, as she had a dark feelin' when ye crossed her threshold. My wife tends to be the same way, knows what she feels about people. Long ago, she told me that she didn't trust ye. So I took that into account, an' stored it away in the back of my mind, my wife's instincts bein' what they are. There were other things as well, little things, but ye know how little things eventually add up to a full accounting. In truth, my memory bein' what it is, I needed a little assistance to get there, but I found a few gentlemen willin' to help me fill in the gaps. An' then of course there was our discussion, where ye tried to point me in the direction of James Kirkpatrick. That tickled at the back of my mind, wonderin' why ye'd wanted me to suspect him? My wife actually filled in a blank or two for me as well, because she said that when Noah Murray was dyin' he told her he thought someone inside the organization had been turned, an' was workin' for Special Branch an' that I'd come across that information. Only Noah thought 'twas his scent I'd caught, an' that he'd put my death in train once he told his handler that I was on to him. It wasn't him I'd stumbled across though, was it?"

He paused to pull an item from his pocket, and saw the man's face bead with sweat as he recognized it.

"For a long time, there's been rumours that someone highly placed must be workin' for Special Branch or the British, because it was clear someone knew far too much. Someone in the Nutting Squad, specifically, with the ability to root out anyone who suspected him. How many men died because of that? How many did you torture, an' put a bullet in, Dacy, because ye feared if ye didn't someone might finally suspect *you*?"

"Ye have no proof other than yer suspicions, man. Ye're not trusted within the IRA anymore, I made certain of that." It was said with a confidence the man clearly did not feel, and Casey almost felt a twinge of pity for him.

Casey smiled and took another sip of his drink. It really was a very fine whiskey. "I suppose ye could be forgiven for thinkin' me entirely a fool, but I'm not so reckless as to come here without insurance. I've changed over the years, but not so much that I'd meet with ye without makin' sure my own back was covered. I've been careful in gatherin' my information, but as it turns out there's more than one man with a grudge against you within the ranks, an' it wasn't so hard to find people willin' to talk."

"Has yer memory come back then?"

"Aye, I suppose ye could say it has. I had an encounter some days back which opened my ears as it were. I met the son of a friend, an' found that his voice triggered the entire day I disappeared. Well, up until the bit where ye beat me until ye thought me dead. After that, things are still a wee bit fuzzy."

"Ye need to give me a chance to get clear of here, let me get to England." Dacy was clutching the glass of whiskey, and his trembling caused tiny amber wavelets in the drink, fairy lights glinting in its depths. To the ancient Celts water was magical in the way that it could capture light, and lakes and rivers were thought to be the abode of otherworldly beings. *Uisce beatha*—whiskey, the water of life, the wellspring of more than one magical being, but today this man would need more than the spirit of this golden liquid to save him.

"That chance has come an' gone. As long as ye're alive anywhere, my family won't be safe, so *sin sin*."

"Ye're no better than me, ye have no more mercy than I had that day. At least I made certain ye had a chance at life, I made certain ye got on that boat."

It was, Casey saw, a last stab at hoping he hadn't remembered every bit of that day. He swallowed the last of the whiskey in his glass, before replying.

"I do remember enough to know that wasn't you. My nan said, once a man's been a ghost an' then returned from the grave, some bit of him always stays a ghost. An' ghosts can see through things—walls, people, lies." He put the item he held onto the table, gently, so that it stood upright, the lettering clear and bold, engraved into the brass casing. And then he stood, and he no longer smiled. "Ye made yer bed long ago, an' now ye're about to lie in it."

"My blood will be on you, man," Dacy said, the fear in his voice filling the room.

Casey shook his head. "No, this blood is not on my hands. I'll not lose sleep over it. I'll leave ye with what my grandfather used to say—better yer own than the British."

He walked away then, nodding to the men who entered the door as he exited it, and did not look back.

Chapter Sixty

Without Leave to Go

THE CONVENT OF THE Benedictine Sisters of Medical Mercy was a place out of time. Hidden away in the countryside of County Mayo, it was set near to the edge of a commercial conifer forest, which had been planted on a rise of ground in an old upland bog.

All around the convent were the remnants of both Stone and Bronze Age farms—bits of old rock walls, rings of stone thickly covered on their north faces with bright green mosses, and drifts of grey lichens. The entire area sat upon a complex of these ancient farms, most traces of which had been long ago swallowed by the bog. Here and there though, a granite boulder stood, half-drowned in long grasses, a reminder of another world which had once existed, in a time when the stone gods ruled from their lofty perches.

It seemed a particularly pagan sort of site for a convent, but the good sisters hardly seemed like the stereotype of what one might expect of a religious order. They performed the same services as most orders in that they were involved in the community, offering spiritual, medical and educational support to the surrounding area, but also making trips overseas where they maintained and staffed clinics, and assisted doctors on the frontlines in some of the world's poorest countries. They also counselled women about birth control, advised them on the health of their bodies, and made sure women had all the relevant information needed to make decisions about having children, or even the possibility of choosing not to. The entire atmosphere was one of camaraderie, good will, hard work and cheerfulness in the face of all setbacks. It was, Pamela felt, a place she would have thoroughly liked under less stressful circumstances.

It was here to this place of industry, sanctuary and peace that Colleen Kirkpatrick had retreated after the death of her and Jamie's third son, and never truly re-emerged. And it was here, currently digging up potatoes, that Pamela found herself waiting for word of her two men. Colleen was in the row beside her, fair hair tied up in a kerchief, wearing old trousers and an ancient fisherman's sweater, which might be rather undignified attire for a nun, but was wonderfully practical for harvesting the last of the potatoes.

Colleen had met them at the gates when they'd arrived two nights previous, and Pamela had known just who the woman was, who came and clasped her hands and smiling warmly said, "It's past time the two of us met, though I certainly wish it had been under different circumstances."

For the two days since then she had spent time looking after her children, who had been sticking close to her and Pru, sensing no doubt the worry and fear in their mother. Knowing busyness was always a good antidote to useless fretting, she'd asked Colleen to put her to work at whatever task might seem best. To that end, she'd spent the days in the kitchen garden, amongst the cold-blanched herbs, cutting back stalks and stems and covering the more delicate plants with a good layer of straw for their winter sleep.

Bundled up in sweaters and scarves, the children alternately helped and hindered the process, though having Pru nearby allowed Pamela a great deal less in the way of distraction. Conor, who had his father's affinity for the soil and all that grew in it, had worked steadily beside them in the potato patch, and filled three burlap bags with the potatoes he'd dug up.

"That child is a godsend," Colleen said, looking toward Pru now, who was helping Isabelle negotiate the lower branches of a tree which Kolya, blue eyes bright and cheeks flushed, was currently scaling. Kolya had already been in residence when Pamela arrived, as he too was here to hide until matters were settled between his father, and Pamela thought with a grimace, the man who was technically his brother. The children were delighted to see each other, settling swiftly into their normal patterns with one another, as her children treated Kolya as a sibling who lived with them sporadically.

"She is, indeed," Pamela replied. Pru was another of the things on the list of worries Pamela had compiled in her head, but there was little she could do for her other than offer her a shoulder to cry on should she need it. This list of worries also included the children missing several days of school in a row. Pamela inwardly cringed at the thought of having to explain this absence to Sister Mary Eugenia, who, at four foot eleven, had the bearing and aura of a long-seasoned military general. Her particular field of battle just so happened to be the Catholic school which Conor and Isabelle attended in the town nearest to their farm.

Other and sundry items on the aforementioned list included, but were not limited to: the roof of the house and whether Casey would insist on finishing it alone, and possibly fall off the ladder, thus breaking his stubborn neck; whether a handful of berries, an egg, three bites of chicken, two of porridge and a mouthful of potatoes was adequate nutrition for a five-year-old over a twenty-four hour span; whether the rash on the back of Kathleen's neck was mere irritation or some obscure malady which required a doctor's immediate attention; the whereabouts of the frog which she'd seen her son carrying into the kitchen yesterday; if it was feasible to get a few more sketches done for her book within the next week, and last, but certainly not least, when the last time she'd had her period was. With a pregnant young woman on her hands, Pamela thought yet another baby in their lives, might be pushing the bounds of sanity a wee bit too far. At the top of this list, and the worry which would render all others moot should it come to pass, was whether her husband and Jamie had survived the last few days.

"There's the last of them," Colleen said, rising and rubbing ruefully at the small of her back, "if there's any left in the ground, they will have to stay for the fairies." Conor looked up at her with interest. "You can't harvest after Samhain," she continued by way of explanation, "for that food isn't for humans to eat anymore. So we leave it for the Gentry."

Pamela tied off the bags she had filled, her artist's eye on a trio of barnacle geese flying in the distance, miniature ink sketches in smoke-grey and black, and her mother's eye on Kathleen who was toddling past, shoving a fistful of twig-laden rosehips into her mouth. Pamela set off after her, and Kathleen ran as fast as her wee legs would carry her, intent on keeping her bitter treasure for herself. She ran straight to Colleen for sanctuary and lifted her arms up to the woman. Colleen picked her up, fixed her upon her hip and neatly removed the macerated rose hips and twigs from Kathleen's protesting mouth. Colleen presented her with the replacement of a biscuit from her pocket, and after an abbreviated howl of outrage, Kathleen settled to chewing happily upon that.

Pamela had noted the familiarity between her child and Jamie's first wife from the moment they'd arrived. But now curiosity caused her to ask about it.

"Jamie has brought her to visit you?"

"He comes now and again when he has her with him. It's been lovely for the both of us."

"I'm glad for that."

Colleen had been a bit of a surprise, for she had seen pictures of her in Jamie's house but those had been of a very young woman, who seemed always to be shrinking back from the camera. The woman standing beside her just now, brushing the last of the twigs from Kathleen's green jumper, appeared far more substantial. Lovely still, but nothing shy nor retreating about her.

Kathleen clambered down, toddling over to where Conor was putting the last of his potatoes into a sack, and Colleen smiled, still watching the children. When she spoke, her voice was quiet, so that the words wouldn't carry any further than Pamela. "You've been good for Jamie, I hope you realize that. You brought him out of a very long winter of the soul, that those of us who love him thought he might well never emerge from."

"I've brought him a great deal of heartache too," she said, for it was the truth of the matter.

"Perhaps some, but Jamie's greatest gift in this life is caring for those he loves. It's what makes life worth living for him, and you have let him care for you, and have given him a child who will always need his love and guidance. She looks more like Jamie every time I see her."

It was true, Pamela thought, for Kathleen resembled her father a great deal, both in feature and temperament. There was something a little otherworldly about her baby, something which even at this very tender age, seemed to flit betwixt this world and the invisible one which always hovered near. It worried her at times, that it might be an indication of an inheritance of the Kirkpatrick curse—as Jamie was wont to call his manic depression—for it stretched back in a long line along the family tree. Having dwelt in the abyss with the monster, Jamie's fear of passing this on to his child was of a magnitude she knew she could never truly understand.

A soft silver peal echoed through the air just then, and Conor lifted his head, looking hopefully toward the kitchen entryway.

"There's the dinner bell. I do hope you're all hungry, because I've heard Sister Carina has made us a special meal tonight."

Pru gathered all the children together and went toward the dining room, which was just off the kitchen area, Isabelle's hand tucked firmly in her left hand and Kolya's in her right, while looking over her shoulder to make certain Kathleen was following. Kathleen scampered behind like a leaf borne lightly on the wind, the low light of the October sun caught—copper and fire—in the delicate whorls of her curls. Pamela smiled at Pru who, even while pregnant, managed everything with a calm competency, which Pamela was certain covered over the pain the girl must always feel, for the father of the child she carried.

Conor, despite being clearly hungry, lingered behind, dark eyes fixed to her face as she gazed down the road toward the gates. The dark came in early on these nights and already the sun was low upon the horizon. A cold wind blew up the convent drive, and the words of an old song came to her along with the chill prickle of the stirring air.

'To feel the wind of longing blow
From out the dark of night…'

Where was Casey? Where was Jamie? Were they safe? Would she know if something had happened to either of them?

Outside the gates, hidden in various spots in the surrounding forest were small caravans, some the old brightly coloured wagons pulled by beautiful Gypsy Cobs, and others small aluminum trailers, pulled by a different sort of horsepower. All here to see to the safety of her and the children. Jonno checked in with her each evening, and it seemed he was well assured of Casey's safety. She had asked the man just why it was he was so willing to hang about and protect them on what had become a disturbingly regular basis.

"He'll tell ye the story if he's a mind to, but I will say this much—he saved my life for me once." And that was all the man deigned to say upon the subject. She stored the information away for future questioning of her husband.

"Do you think Daddy's safe?" Conor asked, and it was the sober question of a boy who understood that they'd fled here not for adventure, but because of danger.

"Daddy is pretty good at looking after himself, Conor." He was too, as was Jamie, but she still worried for the both of them.

"I just don't want him to disappear again," Conor said, and she saw the ripple in his throat and knew he was attempting to swallow back tears.

"He won't," she said, and put her arm around her son, pulling him into her side. Her beautiful boy would be eight in the spring, and he'd grown so much since his last birthday that his head fit comfortably under her shoulder now.

"You go into supper, make certain to wash your hands and say thank you for the food. I'll be along in a minute."

She stood a moment longer, a still watching settling over her. The sun flared gold then red, before it died, sinking rapidly behind the whispering pines. The lights of the convent pricked out, creating shifting pools on the ground. Her stomach rumbled a little and she knew she needed to go in and eat, and make certain Isabelle consumed more than a bit of bread and air for her dinner. Still, she lingered and watched, until the dark became an entity, and the quiet waiting within her unfurled into something more, a black certainty which caused the wings of panic to flutter a warning in her chest. There were things she did not know the substance of, but felt all the same, and the first of these things was that there was something crucial which Casey hadn't told her, something which had come to him along with his knowledge that Julian had been the one who wanted him dead.

The second thing had come the first night at the convent, in the form of a flash, a thing which might have been merely imagination, but which she knew from past experience was something more. She had woken in the wee hours, panic coursing through her blood, and had gone outside to stand under the sky, needing the cold air. It was then the flash had visited her and what had come to her senses was this; a house in Paris with a small winding stair, lines of poetry carved over the mantelpiece, and the scent of roses adrift upon the air. A room edged in moonlit gilt, and within it a man, filled with a despair so absolute that it begged for an ending. This house she knew, for Kathleen had been conceived in it. Like an open channel receiving a signal stronger than her own consciousness, she understood his mind as she did her own, and she had bowed her head before the pain of it. All she could manage to send back was the one word which repeated over and over—*No, no, no!*

How long she had stood there in the dark of that October night trying to will a man to live, she did not know, only that morning had broken by the time she had come out of the strange fugue. Even now, the feeling lingered around her, as though her spirit was once again back there in that house, shrouded in despair.

Sound suddenly penetrated the shroud, returning her to the here and now; the bark of a distant dog, the sound of a cup breaking in the kitchen behind her—please let it not be Isabelle who'd broken it—and the laughter of one of the older nuns, a stout woman whose mirth sounded like that of joyous whooping crane. She must go in and attend to her children, but first she turned back toward the evening, and spoke to the greater darkness, which felt now like heavy folds of fabric, weighty and suffocating.

"Please, Jamie," she said. "Please, hold on."

The bridge was a tiny structure, providing a span over a pond which was little more than a large puddle. Tonight, the pond held the reflection of a waning half-moon, a gauzy silhouette held in dark water.

Pamela stood in a small grove of boulders just beyond the bridge, the rocks lit eerily by the faint moonlight, small wisps of fog threaded through and around them, giving her the impression of walking on a cloud of mist. Here and there a ribbon of quartz glittered in the greater granite whole.

The land within the grove had sunk a little over the millennia, and more of the ancient farms that ringed the area were visible in the form of the boulders as well as small sections of the ancient stone walls which had once partitioned the land. There was a sense of no time here, and she could feel what had once been, could see it, as if there were a great hollow somewhere beneath her feet, well under the bog, and in that hollow was an entire village of people who had tilled the fields, built small homes that weren't markedly different than the cottages which dotted the same landscape today, fell in love, had babies, grew old, grew sick and lived their lives out until death inevitably paid its call. It felt oddly as though it might have been yesterday, when in truth the settlement here would have been ankle-deep in peat by the time the pyramids were built, and waist-deep when classical Greece reached its zenith.

The area was within the walled grounds of the convent, and she had come here earlier in the day with the children to let them play amongst the ancient structures. Tonight, unable to sleep, she had decided to return, in the hopes that she might find a little peace and that a dose of fresh air might induce an hour or two of sleep.

There was a sense of being watched in this small grove of stone and wood, and she turned, thinking it was perhaps a fox in the undergrowth, or a bird peeking over the rim of its nest wondering why this ill-mannered human was disturbing its slumber. Instead she saw the face of a woman encased within the trunk of a large oak. It startled her at first, though her vision adjusted quickly so that she realized she was looking at a statue, one carved of some fine stone, the age of the figure testified to by the growth of the tree around it. Part of the statue's body had been subsumed into the wood, and the parts left showing were a hand, a glimpse of a dark face, and the coils of a serpent wrapped around her feet. Something very old and very powerful hovered around the spot, that same energy and sense of standing in the presence of a being which filled her with both dread and awe.

The face was forbidding and yet she found herself drawn forward to the figure, and she reached out a hand, ran her fingertips over the bark skin of the torso, and felt something stir deep within her own body, something with an understanding even more ancient than the tree and the woman it held within it.

A light step sounded behind her and she turned to find Colleen entering the grove.

"Trouble sleeping?" she asked.

"Yes," Pamela said, "you as well, I see?"

"Yes. I would imagine for much the same reason. I see you have found the Lady." She nodded toward the statue.

"Who is she?" Pamela asked. "She looks a little pagan for a convent, though I saw a Black Madonna some years ago that looked a bit like her."

"No one knows. She was here when the convent was founded, and she will be here when it has long crumbled to dust, along with all the women who have worked and lived here. I would think she's one face of the Goddess. After all, that's what Mary is, the Goddess made human and saint; she who held the serpent of knowledge within her grasp, which is the root of life itself. She's had many names, and been worshipped the world over, here as Brigid and Mary, and as the hag who is both benevolent and a fury who destroys lives. In other places she's had other names, but they all mean the same thing—the Great Mother, the Goddess. Women always know her, even when they deny her presence. She is there when we are born, when we make love, when we give birth and when we die."

"I have long felt her presence, I guess I'm just surprised that a nun would see her so as well."

"Such things are only symbolic, of course, and symbols are a way of lighting the deepest aspects of our humanity, and all the things we carry within us which defy language. It's to give form to a knowledge we have but cannot remember in a way that lends itself to words. I think, perhaps, what name we give it does not matter so much. Where do you feel her most strongly?"

"When I'm in the sea, or near to it."

"I thought that might be the case. She comes where it is natural for you to find her. For you, like James, are a child of the ocean. It is, after all, the most primitive of the faces the Great Mother wears, so that connection is clear."

"Does that make Jamie and me primitive life forms?" she said, laughing.

Colleen laughed in return. "No, only perhaps two very old souls who have journeyed a long way together, recognizing one another in each successive life."

A fine shiver rose like an arc of silver wire along her spine. Jamie had told her a story once, about two gulls, returning to one another, life after life.

"I want to thank you, for giving him a living child. I know it means a great deal to him, to have a child born of such love."

"It means a great deal to me too, particularly now with all that's taken place." She meant Julian, of course and Colleen responded in kind to the unspoken words.

"You've met him—Julian?"

"Yes, both with and without Jamie. I can't say I enjoyed any of the encounters with him, though. It's as though you're seeing Jamie, but a darker, twisted version. His mother raised him to hate Jamie, just as she did, and now so many have paid the cost of that."

"You think he's responsible for Violet's death?"

"Yes, it's the only thing that makes sense of what Kolya said the night his mother was killed."

She told her then, of that dreadful night and what had followed, taking care to leave out her interactions with Detective Holroyd.

"Did he love her?" Colleen asked. "He's never said anything to me, so I admit to curiosity around her."

"I believe he did, though Vanya always told me it was camp love. Love that you feel when your options are limited and your circumstances dire. But it's Jamie, so I think there must have been a bit more to it than that. He's never really spoken of her with me."

"Nor me. He has spoken of you often over the years, though. There is no doubt in his love for you."

She looked at the woman, wondering at her frankness on this matter, and yet not minding, for there was room for truth here between two women who loved Jamie and had borne him children. And so, she could speak another truth, which was the thing which had driven her from her bed in the guest cottage to this primitive grove under a cold moon.

"I am afraid of what he might give, in order to stop Julian from hurting others."

"He will give everything. He must be reminded that there are greater purposes in life than that of sacrifice. His son needs him, as does his daughter."

"I am afraid for him."

"I know, I am too. When he dropped Kolya off he stayed only a few moments, but it was long enough for me to see that he is not well."

"I think he has not been for some time now," Pamela said quietly. "His manic episodes are coming closer together. I think he's off his lithium too. I don't know what to do about it, though."

"Pray to the god of the crossroads," Colleen said, "for that's where Jamie stands. One road is life, and the other is a broken bridge with only an abyss beneath."

"I fear he is already on that bridge, entangled by a single thread. What frightens me most is that it's his hand which holds the razor to cut that thread."

"May I be blunt with you?"

"Of course."

"It is within your power to pull him back. You must do it."

"By what means do you bind a man to his life, who no longer wants to be bound?"

The grey eyes were frank, and the words came without compromise.

"By two means alone—love and promise. He has given you the first, and now you must find the means to extract the second from him. You have the knife; you must find it within yourself to use it. Now, I think I must go to my bed for what remains of the night. I suggest you do the same."

"I will," Pamela said, wanting to linger a moment longer.

Before departing, Colleen touched her shoulder, and Pamela turned toward her. The woman's face was serene as she spoke. "The Lady is also there when a woman realizes she is carrying life within her; that is why you felt her presence so strongly tonight."

Pamela returned to her contemplation of the statue in the tree, as Colleen crossed the bridge, leaving her alone in the small grove. She looked again to the face of the Goddess, and found that the presence was gone, but knew, nevertheless, that she was not alone.

Prayer, Pamela had always believed, was intended for the comfort of the one praying, rather than any real possibility that God would promptly attend to one's petition. For she tended to adhere to the old adage that *'Man proposes and God disposes'* as He sees fit. Still, she had prayed every day and night during the time Casey had been gone, and that petition had been granted. However, a woman might wish she didn't have to pray quite so often nor so fervently, as *she* did for the two men whom she loved.

There had been many times when she had wondered if it was wrong, if it was sin to love them both as she did. She no longer felt that way, not since that night long ago, when she'd spoken with Brother Gilles by the fire.

'Perhaps the love of both men was a pattern laid down in your being before you were even born. The Creator might occasionally make monsters, but he does not make mistakes.' She felt there was a great truth in those words, that she had been meant to love them both, and they to love her, for love was a blessing, even when it occasionally felt like a curse.

She had come to the convent chapel to pray, to petition on behalf of both men, to ask that they be kept safe and whole. The night was hushed, and the only sound that of the burning of the sanctuary candle, flickering redly through its glass. The chapel was small, with three pointed-arch windows down each side, and a rose window above the altar; a long ago gift from some nearby landowner, most likely, making a gift to appeal to God, or to assuage guilt over something the landowner had done. There were four pews to a side, for this had always been a small order of nuns, and more space had never been necessary. In sconces set beneath each of the windows burned thick white candles, meant to last the night through.

Her prayer tonight was formless, just the deepest worries of her soul put forth into the night beyond the stone walls and windows. That her men might be safe. That she might be allowed to continue to love each of them. That they might live to raise and see their children grow into the fullness of adulthood.

She watched then the flame of the sanctuary candle, the presence of Christ in a sin-darkened world. Caught in the movement of the steady burning, she allowed it to carry her down into that place inside, where she held a pool of dark water, shimmering at its surface with the flame of adoration. Down, down, down, to a place of sanctuary and peace. It came sometimes in this way—peace—in the midst of worry and fear, as though some larger presence had put its arms around her and soothed her with words which need not be spoken aloud. The silence was so absolute that she could hear the movement of the night air around the chapel stones and the thud of her own pulse. How much time passed in this fashion, she couldn't have said, for it was time without the boundaries of minute and hour, when suddenly someone above her spoke.

"Is this seat taken?" The voice was one she knew and she looked up, feeling a flood of joy at the sight of the man she'd just been praying over.

"Jamie!" She jumped up and threw her arms around him, breathing in the scent of the cold on his clothes. "Thank God, you're safe."

For a brief few seconds, she held to him tightly, and in that space, she felt the exhaustion in him and feared that she knew what had happened. She drew back, looking into his face, but he avoided her eyes.

"Casey is safe," he said, beginning where he knew her greatest worry lay. "He'll be here when you and the children wake in the morning."

She sat with a thump, relief loosing both muscle and joint. Jamie followed suit more gracefully, sighing a little as he took off his coat. Watching as he settled, she took in the dark crescents imprinted beneath his eyes, the lines cut by his mouth and the hard crease between his brows. Always slim, he'd lost weight, and looked as though he'd been shorn down to his very essence.

"You've been hurt," she said, "your hands are burned."

Jamie shook his head. "It doesn't signify; they will heal."

There was a white bandage peeking above the collar of his shirt, and she found herself suddenly afraid to ask what had happened. Jamie, however, answered the question she could not manage to speak.

"No, I did not find him."

It had always, of course, been one of the possibilities, and the one in her estimation which might cost them least.

"Do you think his mother is helping him hide?" she asked. "Or maybe he fled the minute he saw Casey at Tomas' house?"

"It seems likely. Something very odd is afoot, that's for certain. A man as high up in the service as Felix was, turning out to be a Soviet asset should be huge news and yet there hasn't been a whisper of it in the press. Diane is in the wind, and I don't have the sense anyone is looking for her with any particular devotion."

"Could she have escaped *into* Russia, do you think?"

Jamie shook his head. "I can't see her living out her years in Moscow, she's not a creature of discomfort and poverty. Nor was she ever particularly enamored of Russian culture. I suppose it's possible that they planted her to expose Felix, and she used that opportunity to take her vengeance on me, with Felix only too willing to help her. It is immaterial whether she is helping Julian or not; he's clever enough to hide all on his own."

"I'm relieved that you didn't find him," she said.

"Relieved?"

"Yes, I don't want you forced to a choice with him, Jamie. I fear you'd let him kill you in that situation. Nor do I want the blood of your own son on your hands."

"It has occurred to me that perhaps it would be easier for him, if I was no longer in this world. Perhaps that would give him peace, and he could make something of his life. Maybe even find joy in it."

"No, Jamie. Your absence will not fix his life. If he had the ability to do that, he would have by now. You have given him every chance required."

"It is my fault, though, he has my dark blood in him, the roll of the genetic dice fell true. When that blood comes across your vision, it renders everything black. That is what I have given him, and nothing more. What if I have given it to Kathleen as well?"

"You haven't," she said, "she is only herself, Jamie, without shadow or portent. If that changes, we will deal with it then. Until that day, though, we must love her without the shadow of fear."

"I am so sorry, Pamela, for what Julian has wrought in your life." His voice was that of defeat, and something darker which she knew must be brought out into the light.

"Don't, Jamie. Do not take his sins upon your shoulders. You don't deserve that."

"If not me, then who? I am, after all, the father he never had."

They sat quietly then, for Jamie would accept no counterpoint to his statement she knew, and so she would not waste breath in speaking further on this matter. It was still, except for the small breathings of the world around them—a dawn breeze, rustling in last year's leavings in the trees, whispering its way through the long blush-stained windows of morning, and an owl, finishing its hunt, crying out three times.

Through the quiet though, she knew they were both marshalling their forces for what was coming. It was for her to speak first and fire the opening salvo.

"I think it's time, Jamie for you to let go of that side of your life, the side that puts you continually in harm's way."

He did not require specifics in order to understand; he never had. He had been expecting this conversation, after all.

"It's just a game, Pamela, no more than chess with live pieces played out on a very large board, but still just a game."

"It's a game that will get you killed, and you know it."

"I didn't intend to die," he said, though his words were less than convincing.

"Didn't you?" she asked, tartly. "Because I could have sworn you did."

"I sometimes forget about your inconvenient senses," he said, and while the words were light, the tone was not.

It had not been the first time she'd felt his despair even from half a world away. When he'd gone to Russia, she'd been wakened one night from a sound sleep, heart in her throat and a feeling of thick darkness coating all her senses. Keeping watch through the night, the darkness had settled deep in her bones and she had feared each minute ticking by as the one which would bring her the news she dreaded most. It had not come. Still she had felt as if the psychic skin between her and the universe had been flayed from both body and soul. The weight had only lifted near dawn.

"By my reckoning it would have been about three in the morning for you, it was midnight for me."

"I was in Finland, so two in the morning," he said.

She faced him, tears pooling in her eyes. "James Kirkpatrick, do not try to make light of this. It's not in any way funny. I won't have you fall in some godforsaken corner of a foreign land, with no one there to bury nor mourn you."

"And why is that, Pamela?" he asked, voice soft now and tired.

"Because I love you and so does your daughter. There are, in fact, several of us who love you. We take it personally when you do utterly mad things which could end in your death. That feeling I spoke of, it came again two nights ago."

"It might have been Casey you sensed, it need not be me."

"Casey carries his own brand of darkness; this was not his."

Jamie took a long breath, his hands spread on his thighs and even in the dim light she could see they were white with tension.

"That feeling I had, that sense of grave danger. I think it's because—despite what you've just told me—you did find Julian, and you offered him your life in exchange for ours."

He started a little, and she knew then that she was right. It had been a guess, based on an intuited moment that had contained only this man and his despair.

"Jamie?"

"Why would you think that?"

"Because it's what you would do; you think that's the price he demands for your lack in his life. Because," she choked a little then, "it's what you want, isn't it?"

The silence stretched so long this time that she felt as though an age passed over them, a time in which they both moved toward an understanding neither of them cared for. When at last he spoke, his voice was winnowed down to its core, beaten, exhausted.

"For now, will you trust me when I say he is no longer a threat? Someday, if you need, I will tell you why and how. As to what I want, let me say this—it is only that sometimes things are more difficult than they once were."

It was the answer she had feared, but had armed herself to face.

"I know you are tired, Jamie. And so, when you need my hand, you must take it." She reached over and slid her hand into his carefully, in illustration of her words. "Ask for help. I'll always do whatever I can, you only need to say the word. I can't live in this world without my dearest friend, do you understand? I simply cannot. 'To bear life,'" she said, quoting from a dusty text, "'is the duty of the living.'"

"And if it requires a strength past bearing, which I am in no way certain that I have?"

Once he had told her she held a knife, a locked razor poised between the two of them. *It would perhaps be only kind if you wielded it less often.* It made her feel sick, but she would have to wield it, twist it if need be in order to hold him fast to life—to the living, beating, bleeding, breathing pain of it. She hesitated over it, knowing what hurt him, what cut him, what made him bleed, would also do the same to her.

"Then you must bear it in whatever way you can, for my sake if not for your own."

He nodded, and took an abbreviated breath, the sort which the knife wielder hears, in the climbing scales of pain.

"In this house I have long inhabited, there are only so many doors. I have but two left. In order not to exit through the one you have barred to me, I am going to have to step through the other. I am going to have electroshock therapy done," he said, his tone flat, as if commenting that the weather had recently been uncommonly grey.

"Oh, Jamie," a ripple of shock passed through her. "You've always said you'd never do that."

"What are my options, Pamela? To drink the syrup of poppies and roses from the skull of a ram what *has not meddled with a ewe*?"

She recognized the recipe for she'd read the book from which it came, long ago, one which sat upon the shelf in his study—*Anatomy of Melancholy*—though she believed it was the brains of the ram one was meant to eat, not merely drink from its skull. This seemed rather beside the point, so she didn't mention it.

"An old-fashioned cure, but even that is surely preferable to shock therapy—it's barbaric."

"Not as old-fashioned, perhaps, as the traditional method out of one's troubles. It is the final freedom a man has, that his life should be at his own disposal." He said it with something akin to longing in his voice, the green eyes shuttered by golden lashes. "I am, to paraphrase the poet, *'playing against a sickness, past my cure.'*"

Extract a promise, and bind a man to life through so doing.

"I won't allow that, Jamie. Even if I do not have a claim upon you, Kathleen and Kolya do."

Again the intake of breath, a higher point on pain's scale. "You do have a claim, you always will; this you know." It was no more than a bald statement of fact, but it was what she needed in order to press the knife home.

She raised one hand and touched his face, forcing him to look at her. His golden hair was lit by the candle flames that fluttered around them, and exhaustion was carved into every line of him. "Then let me say this to you, Jamie,

I hold you by what you've said here this night. I stake that claim, and tell you that you do not have leave to go. I need you to promise me you will not seize that final freedom, even if it is your right."

Never a coward, he looked long into her eyes, and she saw there, somewhere beneath the dark abyss, the distillation of grace which he had always carried with him through the world.

"Pamela, I am so tired," he said, and she felt the tears in her eyes gather, and spill down her face. His exhaustion was palpable, she could feel it to her very marrow. The razor was hers, and it was the only weapon she had, so she must cut him where it would be most effective.

"If you do this, Jamie, I will never know another day's joy in this life. I will take you to therapy and even hold your hand through it, if that's what you choose to do, but you must promise not to leave me or Kathleen, because I could not bear it. If you bring yourself to do this, it will break me. Promise me, Jamie."

By two means alone—love and promise. She had leveraged the first, to extract the second, and now she must wait. Time strung out on its silver thread, while they both waited by the gate which would take him over, take him away. A gate, through which, despite her threats, she could not follow.

"I promise," he said so faintly that she could hardly hear him, but it was enough, it was the choice of life, even if that meant—to quote that poet once again—he was his own hell just now.

She held him then because he was tired and so was she. Later, she knew, he might well be angry with her, but he was now bound by the promises he'd made. He might want his chains broken, but this was something she could not do. She would fetter him however she might, as long as it kept him here in this world.

Chapter Sixty-one

A Good Man

CASEY SAT QUIET, as the gloaming spread over the land, slipping in over the gates and turnstile, the rock walls and shorn fields. In the distance a gull wheeled, screeching, over the sea, and nearer to a blackbird—like an arc of smoke—skimmed the fields, looking for the last of the seed from the gathered hay. There wouldn't be much left, he thought, for there had been an entire flock of the birds earlier in the day, and they'd likely gleaned every bit of grain they could see. There wasn't another soul about, and he might have been the only man alive in the world. It reminded him of the first year after his return to Ireland. He'd spent that year close to the land, getting the soul of it back into him and in the process finding himself—his name, his home and his story, the one single thread in an entire tapestry of stories. But his, and that was what mattered in the end.

The sun was low now, barely above the edge of the horizon, creating one of those edge places his wife was so fond of. Here and there the bones of the earth showed through, limestone, grey and worn through eons, here long before man, and he expected, here long after.

This place was *scim*—that Irish word which meant so many things, but one definition that occurred to him now was that of it describing a fairy film which covered the land, or a sleep which allowed you to succumb to the world of the fae. That was what this land brought to mind—a fairy land shimmering in and out of his view, right there in his periphery, but when he turned to face it front on it disappeared and simply became their farm and all the bits and pieces that made a whole of it. He felt such an affinity with the place, that at times it seemed as though he'd called it up into being merely through longing for it, as if his thoughts about wanting a bit of land for his family, had crystallized from an amorphous need to a reality.

From the first time he'd stumbled upon it he had known Pamela would love it too, for she belonged in a place where one could feel that there was only a sort of covering between this world and that, a glamour that was as fragile as a scattering of dust. He'd been right, for she'd settled in here as though she'd been born to the life of a rural farm in Ireland, when in truth she'd been born in a different sort of world entirely.

As though his thoughts had summoned her, he saw her then, walking towards him across the field, twilight touching her with its blue hand, limning her slender form, and laying dusk upon her hair. Behind her, Khamsin trailed, stopping now and again to grab a mouthful of grass, and then breaking into a trot when he saw Pamela getting too far ahead. If Pamela was outside, the horse was never far from her.

One of those swift, sweeping rains of emotion passed over him, and he remembered Doctor Alice's words of wisdom, shortly after he'd begun treatment with her, about accepting that emotion would always be harder to control than it had once been for him, and yet he found he did not mind it so much. There were many things in a man's life which were worthy of a few tears.

He realized to his own surprise that he was praying, and had been since he'd sat to watch the dark gather upon the land. He halted in his thoughts, startled by it. But he thought of all that had happened, all the small things which had brought him back to his marriage, to his children—to home, and thought that a man would have to be a fool not to believe in some force greater than himself when he'd known such miracles. He thought too of the innate understanding his wife had shown him from the day of his return, and which she still gave him at every turn. That alone was a miracle and worthy of prayer, which to his mind consisted of both profound gratitude and love. His heart, of late, was filled with both. Gratitude that they were all whole and well, that he had his family again under one roof.

During the time Pamela and the children had sheltered at the convent, he'd kept watch from a point above the waterfall, each night, waiting, waiting for someone to come, a car to crest the rise, drop down into the valley, for men—hired men, for he had no illusions that Julian would come himself—to disgorge from it, arriving with guns, with knives, with fists. Jonno had summoned a few of his men, men from his family who were hidden in the trees, waiting, watching. Still, Casey had stayed awake through all the dizzying hours of the clock, afraid to close his eyes, lest he sleep and wake again to a world he could not understand. There were other arrangements he'd needed to make, requests to be made and he'd had to wait for word to come back to him, as to whether those requests would be accepted or denied.

Sometime during the third night, he'd felt a presence behind him, and had swung about, ready for violence, for pain, for blood. But it was Aine, her rifle in the crook of her elbow, a tin pail held in the opposite hand.

"I've come to watch with ye, an' to bring ye a bite to eat."

There was stew in the bucket, and she'd brought two tin mugs with her as well, and it was into these she ladled the meal. It was good stew, though the meat was of a flavour he wasn't entirely familiar with. He had a small qualm wondering if it was squirrel, and then shrugged it off. He'd crossed a continent with Eddy Two Feet Walking, and they had eaten what came to hand, during long stretches away from any sort of civilization.

"You go sleep, man. I'll watch this night, an' fetch ye if I see anythin' amiss—if I don't shoot it first that is, an' in that case ye'll hear the shot an' be warned in that way."

Casey thought briefly about the tubby little priest who'd visited them a time too often, clearly bent on returning them to regular church attendance, and eating them out of house and home during the visits. Then he dismissed it as unlikely that he'd come by in the wee hours, and rising, thanked Aine. He'd slept rolled up in a blanket some small distance away from the woman, tucked under a clump of rhododendron shrubs. The sleep had been profound, and he'd not woken until morning was well advanced. Aine had been sitting where he'd left her, though he'd sensed her up and about during the night at various times. She was gazing out over the land, storm-cold eyes calm with purpose.

"I know what it is to fear what might come in the dark, an' figured ye needed a bit of rest if ye were to keep on here. I do think though, that what ye're waitin' on is not comin'. I think ye know ye must go out to meet it. After that, it will be safe to go fetch yer selkie maid, an' yer wee ones."

The look on his face must have been slightly dubious, for she fixed him with her gaze and added, "Sometimes a knowin' steals across me, comes to me from the land, just as yer lovely wife speaks kin to kin with the sea. An' this land will protect ye, it won't allow any upon it that means ye harm. So go deal with yer enemy what was once yer friend, an' then bring your family back, they will be safe."

As ridiculous as it seemed, Casey believed the woman. The word he'd been waiting upon had come that morning via Jonno's brother, and so he had gone to Belfast that very day, and made his arrangements to deal with his enemy. Then two days after that, he had fetched his selkie wife home, along with all their babies. They were as safe as a man might hope for in this world of chance and mischance. There were still pieces of his story he did not recall, and he worried a little that, like a long forgotten bomb buried in a field, one of those pieces might one day emerge and blow up. He still did not know who it was that had saved his life and had paid for him to be on that boat. He supposed though that a man who'd paid to save him, wasn't likely to be a threat to either him or his family. For now, that bit of the past must remain buried.

He looked toward his wife now, as she raised a hand in greeting, and he felt it, the pull of her, just as he always had, just as he always would.

He rose, and went down the hill toward her.

They stopped near the byre, and Pamela was perched on the paddock fence, while Khamsin nudged in her pockets for apple slices. The children were inside with Pru, and safe for the moment, and there was just now no rush about anything.

Casey stood between her knees, and she could tell by the look on his face that he was making a mental list of what needed doing for the next day, and no doubt the next week, month and season. Such was a farmer's mind. Therefore when he spoke, she was more than a little surprised by what he said.

"I was thinkin', Jewel, that maybe we should set aside a wee parcel of land, an' then sell it to Aine for a dollar. Make things official, so she's not worried lest somethin' were to happen to us."

"You're a good man, Casey Riordan," she said, wrapping her arms around him and drawing him close.

He put his forehead to hers and closed his eyes. "Am I? I've more than a few things to make up for in this life. This is only a small thing, an' it'll give her a bit of security, somethin' which has clearly been lackin' in her life thus far."

"Yes, you *are* a good man. Even if you weren't, I'd still love you more than the breath in my body. You know that, don't you?"

He opened his eyes and pulled back a little so he could look into her face. "Aye, I know it. I love ye too, Jewel, ye're as necessary to me as the blood in my veins."

"Speaking of your blood," she said softly, "we're going to have a baby in the summer."

"I did wonder when ye might tell me," he said. There was no rebuke in his tone, but there was, she thought, a question.

"I wanted to be certain first," she said. "I'm a little scared. We were lucky with Conor and Isabelle, and I was lucky with Kathleen. What if all the luck is used up?"

"It's not, darlin'. I believe we're meant to have this baby. Ye're happy about it? Only I thought ye weren't quite certain about us addin' to the madness around here. I'm aware that we've a full life already, after all."

"I am happy about it. I want another child with you. I was just really enjoying *us*, even if I was already sharing you with three children, a dog, a cat, two sheep, a horse and two cows," she said wryly. "Since we've moved here, it's been like a bit of a honeymoon in some ways. I think I felt like adding any more responsibility to our lives might end that."

"I don't think that will ever really end between us, Jewel. Do ye not know that this—us—is somethin' rare?"

"Oh yes, I do know that," she said, leaning forward and kissing him.

She had spoken the truth; this man was the very breath in her body and there was, in the way in which they fit one another in all aspects of their lives, a completion both physically and emotionally which satiated something cell deep in her.

"There's another matter I should like to speak of with ye," he said, and she noted the particular tension which outlined his words.

"What is it?" she asked, suddenly nervous. They'd only been home a few days, and had barely settled back into their routine and she did not think she could, at present, manage anymore upset.

"I think, darlin' that we should ask Jamie to stay here for a bit once his treatments are done. We'll be completely moved into the house by then, an' he can have the cottage. I'll finish fixin' it up for the man. He'll need peace, an' I think this is a good place to find it. That way he'll have Kathleen near to him as well, but not be entirely responsible for her care. He needs to be with the people who love him, an' I suppose that's us."

"Oh, Casey, are you certain?"

He sighed. "About as certain as I ever am when I have one of my mad ideas."

"Thank you, man. I've been so worried about him being alone at home, even though I know his grandmother would keep an eye on him."

"I know ye have," he said, "an' that's why I think it's best to persuade him to come here, providin' the children don't drive him mad within the first week."

"I do love you so, Casey Riordan," she said, dabbing at her eyes with the cuff of her sweater. Her worry over Jamie both doing the treatment and having to deal with it alone afterwards, had taken up a large part of her mind these last few days. Clearly, Casey had been fully aware of that.

"Don't cry," he said drily, "because I've no doubt I'm goin' to regret extendin' this invitation sooner rather than later."

He looked up toward the house then, where light flickered in the kitchen windows. He'd installed the Aga while she'd been at the convent, and had promised the plumbing would be finished early the next week. Once that was done, they could bring their things from the old house and settle in properly for the winter.

"How is she, d'ye think?" he asked, watching as Pru passed one of the windows, lamplit for a moment, the small mound of her pregnancy now visible.

"It's Pru, so it's a little hard to tell sometimes, but I think she's about as broken-hearted as a woman can be and still manage to get up and face each day."

"I worry for the lass. What's comin' is likely to be dark."

A hunger strike had begun in October in the Long Kesh prison, where Ambrose was now in residence. It had gone on for more than thirty days. The strike was led by Brendan 'the Dark' Hughes, and involved an additional six republicans. The strike was the culmination of five years of protest over the withdrawal of their Special Category Status, wherein the British government had seen fit to deem them merely criminals and not political in any way. It had begun with the blanket protest, where prisoners refused to wear the prison uniform, and then had progressed to a 'dirty protest', which consisted of the men refusing to leave their cells to wash, and spreading their excrement onto the walls of their cells. Now the protest had evolved to that last great stand of the Irish—the refusal of food unto the death.

"If this doesn't get them what they want, there will likely be another. It seems like the sort of terrible sacrifice that Ambrose might be willin' to make. There's a dark fire in that boy, an' he's facin' a life in prison."

"Maybe the demands will be met," Pamela said, though it was more a question than any kind of statement of fact.

Casey shook his head. "I have a feelin' they won't, or the Brits will play fast an' loose with them, an' then there will be a great anger. If the lad will listen to her, I'd advise Miss Prudence to give him every reason not to radicalize."

"I'll talk to her," she said, knowing even as she said it that it would do little good. Ambrose had, thus far, refused to see Pru at all, and her letters were returned to her stamped with 'Refused' across the envelope. "It might be better if Pat speaks to him."

"He's still refusin' to take her letters?"

"Yes."

"Damn," he said softly. "I'd hoped the lad was smarter than that."

"As I recall you were every bit as stubborn and stupid when you were on the prison ship," she said.

"Aye, that's why I know what an eejit the boy is bein'. I'll ask Pat to speak to him, then. I suppose we ought to go in, those wee mongrels will want feedin' soon."

"I've fed them, and your supper is in the Aga keeping warm."

"Good, I'm starvin'."

"Do you think your stomach can wait a little? We have a stall with fresh hay in it and no animal," she said, "and all our children are presently fed and occupied."

Casey's face went blank for a moment, as though she had just informed him of a miracle which had, only moments before, seemed entirely impossible.

Due to the fact that they'd all been sleeping clustered around the hearth in the room Casey insisted on calling 'the parlour', there had been no renewal of marital congress since before she and the children had fled. A grin slowly spread into his whiskers, as he realized the implication of her words.

"Aye, I think I can manage a few minutes, or maybe even a little more," he said.

"Why, Mr. Riordan, you're making me blush."

"I intend to do a lot more than that," he said, lifting her from the fence, with the clear intention of taking her into the byre.

The byre was warm and dark, other than the lantern Casey had hung for the evening milking. He laid her down in the fresh hay of the empty stall, and then joined her, his shirt half off already and hers tossed in a corner.

"By the way, ye'll be sharin' me with a bull too."

"What?" She half sat up. "So *that's* why there's fresh hay in this stall."

"Oh, aye, I did a trade with old man Gerrity for a bit of work I did for him. The bull will be arrivin' on Tuesday. Though it occurs to me," he said taking in the look on her face, "that I probably should have told ye that *after* ye ravaged me, rather than before."

"Yes, you should have, but d'you know," she smiled up at him, falling back once more into the sweet-smelling hay, "I think I'll ravage you all the same."

"I'm a lucky man," he said and rolled over top of her.

"Yes, you are," she said, taking him in hand, and causing him to gasp. "Now if you can't think of a better use for your tongue, can you at least have the good grace to keep it silent?"

Part Nine

Hunger

ON THE FIRST day of March in the year 1981 an ordinary young man by the name of Robert Sands, a prisoner in the infamous 'H' blocks of Long Kesh prison, began a hunger strike to protest the criminalization of Irish political prisoners. He would be followed by nine of his fellow inmates. Their demands were simple and numbered only five. They were as follows: the right not to wear a prison uniform; the right of free association with other prisoners; the right to organize their own educational and recreational facilities; the right to one visit, one letter and one parcel per week.

None of these men were convicted after trial in due process of law. They were tried by single judge courts without any juries. As they were not tried under the ordinary processes of the law, these men were asking for special category status. Historically Britain had acknowledged the special status of Irish republican prisoners convicted of political crimes. In 1975, despite the continued presence of British soldiers on Irish soil, the British government decided to revoke this special status for republican prisoners.

When these men began their fast, they were invoking an ancient Irish weapon called *Cealachan*—achieving justice by starvation—which had its roots in the *Senchus Mor*, the civil code of medieval Ireland.

On March 1st, 1981 the world began a death-watch, both horrified and fascinated by the spectacle of ten men willing their own deaths in the face of an indifferent government and seemingly implacable odds.

Ordinary men in extraordinary circumstances.

From the Journals of Ambrose Turner

Long Kesh Prison
November 1980

Last night I dreamed I was a blackbird, rising from a branch into a cloud of gold shimmering light. It was spring and I could feel the warmth of the sun on my wings, and my body was light as air.

When I woke it was to a mattress skimmed with snow, and flakes of snow caught in my hair and beard. It wasn't warm enough to melt the snow from my face, and so I woke as though in a shroud, and for a moment I panicked, unable to see, my breath cold as ice in my throat.

Three weeks I've been in this cage. It's November and brutally cold. One of the men I talked to along the heating pipes said it was minus 17 last night. It's a miracle that none of us have frozen to death yet. I still have a few seconds each morning when I forget and expect to wake in my warm bed at home, with my books arrayed on the shelf above my head and a picture of my girl on the wee table next to me.

My trial was a farce, even though Pat and Tomas did their best for me. My fate was decided before I ever stepped before a judge, though, and I think they both knew it but they gave it a valiant effort, nonetheless. Within the space of forty-five minutes, I was tried, convicted and banged into a cell. Patrick was so angry that I thought he might commit murder right there in the court room.

A guard came into my cell early one morning, three weeks ago, kicked my bunk and told me they were moving me out to the Kesh. And so I went.

Even in the small space between the cell and the van, which was all I would have of outside, I could smell the autumn. I took it in, as I was hustled along. It's the coldest fall we've seen in a while, and the ground was hard as iron. I breathed as deeply as I could, and the air was like a bitter-clear wine, causing the throat to ache with its taste.

Whenever the panic rose, I did what Casey taught me to do and put my mind elsewhere, far away. He told me once that when he was in prison, he'd think of the stars, and imagine all their properties in detail, and then list them to himself as if he were taking a test, and how it had helped him keep his mind away from what was happening to his body. For me it's all the hours I've spent watching spiders spin their webs, from the first fragile thread strung between vine and leaf, to the final thread which finishes the grand design of their web. In my head, I made myself that spider, and felt each quicksilver thread spinning out as I built my home. Even as I was taken into the van, along with six other prisoners—most of them Loyalists—inside my head I was climbing rungs of air upon slipstreams of gossamer. I was letting the autumn wind take me to a warmer and kinder place.

The van stopped at the reception area at the Kesh, and offloaded the lot of us. I was put in a cubicle alone and told to put on a uniform. There was no way I was going to wear the uniform because it would be as good as admitting I'd committed a crime and that I wasn't entitled to Special Category status, despite the illegal presence of the British Army in Ireland. I stood there for a moment, hesitating, wanting to clutch my clothes to me like the only skin with which I was familiar, and knowing there was no way on God's green earth that they would let me keep them.

I stepped out of the cubicle, completely naked and freezing cold, to be faced with eight guards, all burly specimens ready to beat me. One of them yelled at me to put 'the fucking uniform on' and I said no. He slapped me full across the face, so hard that my ears were still ringing several hours later. And then they proceeded to beat me with glee. They'd been waiting to do it, and I think even had I put the uniform on they would have had a go at me anyway. Somehow the beating itself was less frightening than the anticipation of it. Afterwards, they led me to my cell, naked, bruised and bleeding, parading me in front of the other prisoners and assorted screws. It was the worst bit of the day and maintaining a distance was very hard, though I knew it to be necessary.

The cell contains a filthy mattress, a broken window, and a cell mate named Noel. We spoke a little, exchanging our vitals—name, crime, time.

For my day's food I got a sandwich and a cold cup of tea.

I had a couple of bad moments today, mostly when I think of my Pru, and knowing how she cannot understand all this. I hate that I left her with only a note as my farewell, but I was too much a coward to face her and tell her what needed to be said.

I know she would wish me to put on the uniform, if only to spare myself the beatings and thousand small humiliations which come with this one defiance to their order. But I cannot. If I could tell her I would, but it's near to impossible to put into words what I feel and what this means to me in my stronger moments. It's an obedience to that higher thing, that thing outside and beyond a person, which involves a change of self, no matter how painful. No matter the loss it incurs.

Yeats put words to it in ways I cannot.

> *'... know that when all words are said*
> *And a man is fighting mad,*
> *Something drops from eyes long blind.'*

My eyes are no longer blind, I see things exactly as they are.

Oiche Mhaithe

December 1980

I am slowly adjusting to life here. There is a raw ferality to it that still abrades my nerves, as though someone grates my skin off on a daily basis, and I have to start anew to build what small defense I have. Our living conditions are like nothing I could have imagined were I not experiencing it firsthand. The mattress I lie on at night is soaked with piss, and rife with maggots due to us not being slopped out properly. We often have to slop out under the doors, and inevitably some runs back. The food is disgusting for the most part, and we pick our way through it, taking the edible bits, and drinking the cold tea. The rest gets thrown in the corner.

My cell mate is in for setting fire to a Shorland tank. Which would take, in my estimation, a fair bit of raw nerve. It's unfortunate for him that there was a soldier in the tank when he did it, though the man escaped with only minor burns and less his eyebrows. We get along fine, which is good as we're locked in together round the clock, without the privileges of exercise or bathing.

The hunger strike ended, and the Brits have left us high and dry. It seemed that an agreement was coming down the pike, and so The Dark (as Brendan Hughes is called) had to make a decision before all the information was in, due to the fact that Sean McKenna (one of the strikers) was in a critical state and had been taken off to the Victoria, with doctors and priests giving out declarations that he'd hours left to live and if The Dark was to save him, he'd have to make a split second decision without any guarantee from the British. The priest was on his way from the airport with the papers containing the new offer, but he couldn't get there quickly enough. The Dark had the life and death of a young man, holding by a rapidly fraying thread, and he had to call the strike off before the offer could be read. There was a deal of hope when Bobby came back from his meeting with the priest, and men calling out—Cad é an scéal? What is the news? It was soon sussed by the set of his shoulders though, that the news wasn't good. The offer was—as Bobby said—as full of holes as a sieve. It left everything wide open for the British to drive through it in their usual fashion—a wide road, where duplicity is the norm, and reneging on even the vaguest promises is to be expected. And with the British, treachery is always expected.

December 31ˢᵗ, 1980

There was no celebration on the final night of the year. Holidays only seem to increase the darkness some of us feel inside, to the point where you can't ignore it, and so you draw into yourself, hunker down and attempt to just get through it emotionally intact. That was my plan for this long, dark night, just put my head down, run through books I love in my head, and hopefully go to sleep early, and wake to just another day. Alas, it was not to be.

The day was a quiet one, and the mood somber as night fell. It was to be expected, as we all miss our loved ones with an especial poignancy on such nights. After our miserable dinner was served, we could hear the SOs on the wing. One of the screws—Higgins by name—was stopping in at every cell asking the men how they were. It was clear he'd drink taken, for his speech was filled with false jollity and was not a little slurred. I prayed he'd stop before he got to our cell. The man hates me, and I fear him—for good reason as it turns out. Why he hates me is a mystery, but I suppose me being one of those, 'filthy fucking Fenians' is enough for him.

We held our breath, the two of us, hoping he'd continue down the wing and give us a miss. No such luck was on offer, though. In he came, blue eyes veined with fine threads of red, and the smell of sour scotch rolling in along with him. Higgins is no amateur drinker.

He got in Noel's face real tight, right away. "Howya doin'?" he asked, just as he had all along the block. No one had answered him, as the mind boggled a little over how he could ask such a question, considering our circumstances.

Noel simply looked down at the floor, as if it was the most interesting thing in the world. I could see he was hoping Higgins would get bored and go hassle someone else. Again, our luck was not in, for he hauled off and popped Noel right in the face. Noel staggered back and blood sprayed out of his nose, some hitting me, and some running down the back wall. It seemed Higgins realized what he'd done, for he said to Noel, "Ye hit yer face on the pipe, didn't ya? Ye hit yer face on the pipe."

He turned to me then. "He hit his face on the pipe, didn't he?"

I merely shook my head, even though I felt a little paralyzed, like a lamped rabbit.

"He hit his fucking face on the fucking pipe—just say it!" He was screaming now and so close that I felt the spray of his spittle all over my face. A tense quiet had settled over the rest of the wing.

"No, I'll not say that," I said and backed away a little. His face was red as a pomegranate with fury, but I wasn't going to stand down when Noel was hunched over bleeding in the corner.

"Ye'll say it, ye fucking Fenian piece of trash!"

I shook my head, resolute, despite the pure icy terror I was feeling inside. He grabbed me by the arm and pulled me from the cell, and then he got one of his fists into my hair and used it to drag me down the wing. I lost my blanket of course, and so was dragged naked for all to see. I was truly afraid then, for he'd a look in his eyes that told me he'd not stop short of killing me unless someone else stepped in.

He ran me all the way down the wing into the canteen and then shoved me hard through the door. I fell and then scrabbled to my feet as quickly as I could. Then he grabbed me by my hair again and bent me backwards over a table, so hard that my feet came up and I fell back onto it. The next thing I knew he was on top of me, face swollen with rage, so that he looked like a poisonous toad. His hands were on my throat and he was choking me. It came to me then—this was how I was going to die.

All that was inside me was a great crimson terror, and nothing more. I couldn't breathe and enormous black stars kept exploding across my vision. I managed to get my hands up at his face, but I couldn't see at that point, so I was just blindly hitting at him, trying to gouge at his eyes, in the hope it would be enough to get him off me. Finally, I managed to get a leg up and knee him hard enough that he fell off me, taking me with him so that I tumbled to the floor, still choking, my chest on fire from lack of oxygen. He started kicking me then, those hard boots of his striking at my bones, so that I was afraid he'd break my arms, or maybe my ribs. And then very suddenly it was over, another screw had run in and pulled him away from me. Higgins was still punching out at me, face raw with belligerent fury. I know, if the opportunity arises again, he'll kill me.

Two screws escorted me back to my cell. Screws who'd stood by and done nothing to stop a madman from choking me to death. They didn't speak a word, and nor did I.

I went back to my cell. Noel was still dabbing at his nose, his blanket red with blood.

"Are ye all right, man?" he asked.

"I'll do," I said shortly. I crawled onto my filthy mattress and turned my back to the room. There was nothing to say. A man had tried to kill me, my throat was still throbbing, and I could feel every print of his fingers burned into my skin. It is possible that he'll try again, and there's nothing I can do to stop him.

All the things I thought I'd have to barricade my spirit—those things we use like a ring of sacred salt in the world outside, don't work in here. It's as though I have no skin, no proper defense against the violence and the darkness.

I lay there with my eyes closed, wishing with every fibre of my being that I could simply go to sleep and wake up to find this is all a nightmare and that I'm in my bed with my girl beside me. I could hear the last bit of advice Casey had given me before I went inside.

"Keep the things that are precious to ye close—ye don't want the screws to find out what matters to ye, or they'll use it. They're goin' to find out anyway, don't make it easy for them."

And so I keep Pru tight in my heart, as though she is a rose before blooming, petals wrapped so tightly, so that the flower can only be recognized when the necessary sunlight and temperature is applied. But oh, how badly I want her, to simply hear her voice in the dark, and smell her scent—that warm scent that makes me think in poetry, as though the most beautiful lines are written there beneath her skin, and I can almost read them, but in the end, they always elude me.

Oiche Mhaithe. Tomorrow is a new year.

January 1981

Word came today that Big Seamus wanted to talk with me. This, to use one of Pamela's sayings, curdled my wame just the wee bit. Big Seamus is legendary in the republican world. He's in here for the bombing of a furniture store, doing fourteen years, minus time from remission, if remission is ever restored. He's got a wife and two children on the outside, children he hasn't seen in three years. He's the reputation of being a straight shooter, but also that of a man for whom very little is sacred. He lives in the cell next to us, so I've heard him talking, and he will often shout out any bits of the scéal he's come into, but he's never asked for a meeting.

Because we refuse to wear the prison uniform, we aren't allowed either exercise or free association with other prisoners. So the meeting was conducted at our windows. As his cell is next to ours, it allows us to keep our voices just the bit lower. Noel pretended not to hear, as he picked at threads from his blanket in order to make a wee rope by which we can move things from cell to cell—tobacco, comms, and occasionally fire.

"About yer man Higgins," Big Seamus said, "He's been filled in, laddie."

"Filled in?"

"We let him know he's on our watch now, he understands what that means. He'll be checkin' the undercarriage of his car extra careful now, an' he'll not want to be drinkin' at his local either."

"Thank you," I said, uncertain as to why he'd done this for me. This must have been clear in my voice for he said, "I grew up with Casey. He's a friend, an' *he sent in word about ye. Said ye were good people an' that he considered ye family. His word is enough for me. Besides, wee Ambrose, we're all in here together. This is the only family ye've got right now."*

I put my head down then, pressing it against the grill over the window, not wanting Noel to see the tears which had rushed to my eyes at Big Seamus' words. It hit me suddenly what I had lost in a mad moment of choice, and yet if I'd not made the choice, I'd be dead right now. Still, it touched me sharp to the quick to know that Casey said I was family. I know that's not a light thing coming from him.

"Thanks," I repeated, not knowing what else to say.

His words came back through the night between us. "Ye're safe now, or as safe as a man can be in this fockin' place."

January 1981

"Bears on the air, bears on the air!" The shout woke me, though I'd only just fallen asleep minutes before, or so it felt to me. I looked across at Noel, who was still sleeping, the shout not having reached him yet.

"Get up, ye lazy sod, screws are about, it's shift change."

Noel scrambled up, panicked, and we stood, braced, wrapped in our threadbare towels, knowing what's coming and that there's no way to truly prepare yourself for it.

They come in a storm of black, truncheons at the ready. They grab us and drag us out into the assault of light in the corridor.

"Bears on the air, bears on the air!" Voices rising in panic now as we're dragged, bumped, kicked and punched to the top of the wing.

"Wing shift!" Shift changes are always bad news for us.

Over-excited, smelling blood, a screw I haven't seen before kicked me hard, and I thought I'd pass out from the pain, but managed to stay conscious, more's the pity. Surrounded now by black-suited demons, pumped up on their own fear, their hatred and prejudices.

"Right then, drop that towel, turn around and bend over."

I'm starting to think some of them are right arse-bandits, with the amount of time they spend prodding my arsehole. I wasn't quick enough though, so then I was thrown over the table at the top of the wing, like a slab of meat, pulled apart by arms and legs, hit, hair pulled back while some pervert probes at my arse. Thrown to the floor then, kicked a few more times for good measure, my meagre towel thrown over my face, all while they laugh—what great fun this must be for them, sick bastards.

Dragged back to a random cell, alone, bruised, battered, bleeding and violated and I haven't even seen breakfast yet. When it comes it's the usual disappointment—freezing cold tea, so weak it's not even the colour of piss, cold lump of porridge and two slices of moldy bread. I ate what I could, mouth sore, and a tooth loose.

Voices from other cells, "What's the scéal?" There is always some scéal—good news, bad news, all of it hoarded like a squirrel taking in nuts for a particularly harsh winter.

I walked then, freezing, pacing my little space over and over and over to get my blood flowing. Back to my own cell later, dragged there again in my little towel, grateful to be back in our filthy grotto where there's a blanket to be had. Noel, black and blue in the face with a fat lip, nothing new here to see.

And so the day proceeds, lunch, walking, staring out the window, talking to the crow that comes to visit outside the window—he's a mad good listener—longing for a book, a proper pen, a sheaf of paper to write on. Wishing for a hot cup of tea with one of my mam's scones. Trying not to wish, not to think about the world out there, because I am no longer part of it. This in here is where I live now.

Late morning—"Slop out on the wing, slop out on the wing!" We get ready, buckets held, we'll only have a minute and we'll have to be fast, and there's always the fear they'll grab you while you're out there, give you a good kicking, while you lie writhing in your own filth. At least we're slopping out and not just trying to pour it under the door today.

We slop out, pouring out buckets into the middle of the corridor. We retreat into the cell and the door clangs shut. Feeling lucky, and knowing it's insane that this is what luck has been reduced to, not being beaten while pouring out piss and shit onto the corridor floor. Other lads are not so lucky, we hear screaming, banging further up the line. A high-pitched howl—someone being beaten, heads being smashed into walls, pipes, floors.

Then the wee man with the big industrial squeegee, pushing the urine back into the cells, brushing it under the doors, where it soaks into our mattresses, and slimes every corner of the cell. We spend the next hour trying to squeeze the piss out of our mattresses and then set them up against the pipes to hopefully dry a little.

And the day moves on. Lunch—cold tea, shouts of 'Tea on the air, cups off the air' delineating the day into its depressing increments. Then after dinner—"Bears on the air, heavy gear!"

"Ah, fuck," Noel said. We know what this means, they're going to disinfect the cells. We grabbed our mattresses, putting them against the far wall, stashing our blankets behind them, wrapping ourselves in the wee towels. We could already hear the liquid being blasted at the cell doors opposite. The coughing and gagging began almost immediately. It's why the windows on this side are all broken out; the cleaner is industrial strength and acts like tear gas on the eyes, nose and lungs. I could hear men vomiting, and couldn't see anything as I stumbled to the window, trying to gasp in any bit of fresh air, Noel gagging beside me. Then

the water came in under the door, to dilute the cleaning solution, but I knew it would be several minutes before the effects wore away. We stayed there at the window, eyes streaming, throats raw, lungs seared, for as long as it took for the cold air to revive us.

Once we could manage it, we began the long task of pushing the water out under the narrow crack of our door. There was at least an inch of it sitting still and foul in the cell. We were exhausted and sweating by the time we were done, despite the cold of the cell.

"All right, Big Seamus?" I yelled to our neighbour.

"Fuck no, ye wee mad eejit. I'm wrecked in here." He was still coughing, his lungs sounding like tin foil being scrumpled up in a ball. "Youse over there?"

"We're grand," I said and laughed.

"Mad bastard," he called back, but he laughed too, even though it set off another fit of coughing.

It was going to take hours before the floor was dry, if it dried at all. We'd have to put our mattresses down on the wet floor tonight, or have no rest. There was no help for it. For now, I continue to pace to the window and back, trying to walk down my anger, keep it from taking over, for fear that that is all I will become—just rage, just fury, just madness.

It comes then—the depression. It's like a black swamp that suddenly engulfs me, and I feel like I am drowning in it. It is the worst and most dangerous thing in here, to let it get its hooks in you, to feel it beat your will from you. In these moments, as its claws sink deep into my spirit, I know I won't make it, I can't do a life in here. There is simply no point.

And then a voice calls out. "Will we have a sing-song then?"

We need it, anything just now to stir our sinking morale. It starts with a loud and not terribly tuneful rendition of The Foggy Dew. I almost can't bear the words tonight. Music cracks me open at the best of times, in here it's like a knife that never stops going into a man.

Next song up is The Rising of the Moon, and it buoys my spirit a little.

And then, "Ambrose, it's yer round."

I sing The Men Behind the Wire, because that's who we are. That's who we've always been, though I pray to God it's not who we will be in the future. Please God let our daughters and sons be free. Despite the melancholy of the words, I feel the strength of it stiffen my backbone a wee bit.

After, Big Seamus calls over to me. "Put yer hand out, Ambrose."

I put my hand out the window, knowing he's sending something over. After he swung it a few times, I managed to catch the potato he'd used to weight the line. I pulled it in and found two hand-rolleds attached. We'd have a wee bit of a smoke now, and maybe that would cheer Noel up enough to get him off the mattress before sleep. An improvised wick comes next, and this is harder to catch, and there's always the fear it will go out in the effort. But I catch it at last, and light the cigarette, taking in a lungful of smoke with gratitude before I light Noel's off it and hand it to him. He rouses himself enough to sit up and smoke it.

Further down the line someone begins the nightly prayers, it's Tuesday so it's the Sorrowful Mysteries for us tonight. After the prayers are done, Seamus calls over.

"I'm for bed. Going to try to warm up under this wealth of blankets," he says, and then gets swept up in another paroxysm of coughing. "Oiche Mhaithe, wee Ambrose."

"Maith thú, Seamus. Oiche Mhaithe."

It's quiet then. Noel finishes his cigarette and lies down on his mattress, huddled under his blankets like a small boy. My heart hurts just looking at him. If he can't find a way to bear up, prison is going to break him into tiny pieces, and he'll never find them once he's outside again.

I stay at the window. It's snowing again, and it's strangely peaceful despite the day behind us. The snow sparkles like a million diamonds, and my breath makes small clouds of fog on the air. Overhead, lost somewhere in the snow, a curlew cries. I lean my head back, and feel the touch of snow upon my skin.

"Oiche Mhaithe," I whisper, though I don't know who it is I'm saying it to.

January 1981

There's going to be another hunger strike. The strikers will be staggered this time, so that their position is strengthened rather than having too many men hovering on death's doorstep all at the same time.

Big Seamus tells me that hunger strikes are always a chancy thing.

"It's a risk, that's what. It could be the graveyard of the entire republican movement if it ends prematurely again. We're only as strong as our weakest link, an' none can blame a man if he finds hesitation in the face of death."

But a risk worth taking? There's not much left to us other than something that is extreme enough to wake people up and make them pay attention. Risk or otherwise, Big Seamus has put his name forward for it.

February 1981

I am back from three days on the punishment block. I am surprised to still be alive and whole, though that last is a relative term, and a mixed thing in terms of blessings.

They grabbed me when I was slopping out three mornings ago, without a word, without warning, just grabbed me, bending my arms behind my back, kicking at my ankles with those industrial boots of theirs. They tore the blanket from me, so that I was naked and completely vulnerable to their brutality. It is hard to adequately describe the fear which seizes a body in those moments. The pain is there, but it's secondary to the fear of the pain that is still to come, to the fear that this is the beating you won't survive.

In the moment, I can't take in the entirety of it, so it came at me in pieces—the pain in my head as they dragged me by the hair across the hard rubble, tearing open my knees and shins, until dropping me so that they could ring the bell for admittance to the punishment blocks. I lay there dazed, confused, as they kicked at me—face, arms, back, legs, blood in my eyes so that I could not see anything but a thick red haze. I faked unconsciousness, though it wasn't a big stretch to do so, but then they picked me up by hands and feet, slamming my head into the corrugated iron that covers the punishment block gates. My head exploded with pain and everything went a brilliant white and then black. I passed out with the second impact to my head, and woke up on the freezing concrete of one of the punishment cells, the blazing white light making me believe at first that they'd blinded me with the blows to my head. I knew I had to get up or risk catching pneumonia from the cold. As it was, I vomited the little that was in my stomach due to the pain in my head, which was still blazing like a pulsar.

Some time later they sent in a screw in a white coat, which I guess they think makes him a medical authority. He poked and prodded at me, and said I was fit to be bathed, because a doctor couldn't see me until I had been cleaned up.

I fought. I wasn't going easy, but I had little hope against six screws. They lifted me and carried me to the tub and dropped me from well above it, so that I slammed my head into the porcelain and went under. The water was freezing, and it could well be what saved me, as the shock of it brought me upright gasping, attempting to drag air into my lungs. The water was reeking with nasty chemical disinfectant, and burned my skin, razoring into the cuts and contusions which peppered my entire body. They scrubbed me with a broom, one of those big industrial ones, with the straws like wire, abrading my body further, making me want to scream. I nearly bit my tongue off keeping it in. Bucket after bucket of ice-cold water was poured over me, along with the lye-like soap they use.

They lifted me from the tub, though I was nearly unconscious at this point, and one of the screws lifted my testicles so they could scrub them with the brush, while they laughed all around me. That is the last thing I remember, until I woke up in the infirmary, eight stitches in my head, one eye swollen shut, and my entire body a mass of throbbing pain.

They took me from the infirmary and put me back in the punishment cell. I had a board for my bed, a concrete block for a table, another block for a chair. It was freezing, so I wrapped myself up in the blanket on the bed, which reeked of stale smoke and piss.

Later they dragged me in front of the prison governor, to stand trial in this farce which passes for justice. I was accused of not submitting to the commands of the screws—I'd fought the anal search when they dragged me from the cell, this apparently was my crime. I stood there in front of them—naked, humiliated, wrecked with pain and was sentenced for my 'crime' to three days in the punishment block. I was isolated, alone, freezing, unable to sleep and given even less to eat than is the usual. The daily breakfast on the punishment block is a scummy, cold cup of tea with two slices of bread, a watery bowl of soup for lunch, and for tea, the same scummy cold drink and two more slices of bread.

They wouldn't allow me to slop out my bucket unless I agreed to wear prison clothes. This I would not do, so they let it overflow, and so I had to walk the floor, feet wet with cold urine. If I didn't walk—oh the endless fucking walking one does in here—I'd die from the cold, and so I walked, back and forth, back and forth. Sometimes I think this is what hell might be—eternally trudging in the same small circle, in an effort not to freeze to death or lose my mind. I was half unconscious when they dragged me back here this morning to my own cell. I am tired, in pain, and I can't hear very well out of one of my ears, where one of the screws hit me particularly hard. Still, it's good to hear the other men stirring, talking, the Irish spoken in the evenings, the cries of 'Bear on the air! Tea on the air!'

Big Seamus called out to me after tea—cold tea, cold potato, a bite or two of fish, because the fucking screws ate most of mine, and twenty or so freezing cold peas—"Ye're back, wee Ambrose?"

"I am that," I replied.

"Are ye all right?" he asked. Big Seamus has been on the punishment blocks countless times, so he knows how it is.

"I'm still breathing," I replied.

"Maith thú, wee Ambrose," he said.

February 1981

I've named the lame crow that haunts my windowsill. It looks as though his wing was broken in the past and it has healed poorly, so that he can only fly short distances and low to the ground at that. A dangerous situation for any creature. I call him Ben.

I toss bits of food out the window to him, enough it seems to keep him alive. So he returns each day, expectant of his meals. I watch him for hours sometimes, and he watches me in return. It has become a sort of meditation between the two of us. All those hours of communing with the crow have allowed me to think hard on what I want, and what I feel is the right path for my life going forward. Accordingly, I sent my statement in a comm to the Army, relaying my intention to go on hunger strike, and got the expected denial in return. It's merely form, though, on both sides, and everyone knows it. I am a good fit for a few reasons: I'm facing a very long sentence, I killed but it was done in self-defence, and I was born in Armagh and lived my childhood there, so I count as being from that county. They want a representative from each of the areas. Big Seamus has been chosen as the man from Tyrone.

It's mad to give your life for five demands, they say. And perhaps it is. But it's a very Irish sort of madness. While the demands matter a great deal there are so many other things which come into play in a decision like this. For this is not only about those of us here within these prison walls, it is not just about the five simple demands, it is about all those other things—the losses, the sacrifice, the perseverance. We are just the latest bead upon a long string, stretching back to ancient days: Cú Chulain, Saint Patrick, Tone, Pearse, Emmett. Sacrifice has been the one recurrent theme in Ireland—sacrifice and perseverance. Through loss of language, loss of land, loss of life, we have persevered. Left our country, left those we love. Lived on the fringes of land stolen from us, forced to eke out an existence and pay landlords for that which had once been ours. Oppressed by a Protestant ascendancy, murdered by the English Crown. Setting sail upon a strange and terrifying ocean, dying along the way, thrown into watery graves, into ditches, sacrificed on battlefields, forgotten, never returning to the land we loved, the one which was home in the very marrow of our souls. It is the small children, arriving in that distant place, alone, afraid, and yet making a stand, finding a way to survive, never again seeing their kin and becoming strangers to who they'd once been. It is about all of us Irish, every bead on that long, long string, that broken string which threw us across the face of the earth, killing so many of us in the scattering.

And so we sacrifice, for in this way we have always found our resurrection as a country, as a people.

March 1981

Bobby Sands started his hunger strike two days ago. Francis Hughes will go after him, then Raymond McCreesh and Patsy O'Hara will go on at the same time. Big Seamus will follow a week or two later, and then it will be me that is next unto the breach.

Father Jim has been in to talk with me, hoping to dissuade me from my chosen course.

"Is this suicide by another name, Ambrose?" he asked me.

"No, suicide has no meaning outside of an escape from pain."

"What meaning does willing yourself to death have?"

"You know what meaning it has, you've read the history books. It's about eight hundred years of occupation by a foreign power, and then to be treated as though that circumstance doesn't exist."

He sighed, a great outpouring of breath, which sounded a bit like defeat. "Ambrose, it's a sin to take your own life, this you know."

"Is it? What is the Church's view on the matter?"

Father Jim looked at me for a long time and there was a weariness in his face which this country has given him. He knows the Church's view is rather complicated, particularly here in Ireland with the renegade priests and bishops who pepper our history.

"As far as the church is concerned there are two bodies of thought. One holds that it's suicide regardless, even when it's a matter of the hunger striker experiencing injustice at the hands of his captors. The other holds that it is not intentional when it's a simple refusal to cooperate with the injustice being perpetrated. Death then is seen as not so much chosen, but rather a means to an end, not intended, even though it could be foreseen. The Church does not require Catholics to bow rigidly to Church teaching. So, if a Catholic, for reasons that seem good and sufficient to himself, finds he is at odds with the Church's position on a given matter, the Church does not condemn his actions as sinful. It gives the benefit of the doubt to the conscience of the person involved."

"Ah, the good old Mother Church, washing both hands of us while turning one face to us and another to the world. And what of you, Father Jim? What is it that you believe?"

He shook his head, and I saw that he had tears in his eyes.

"Oh, Ambrose this world is so small, and at times so mean to its citizens. I know you're smart enough to see that. I know you love the Greek philosophers, so I'll quote one of them at you—

'Having seen a small part of life, swift to die,

Men rise and fly away like smoke, persuaded only by what each has met with. Who then claims to find the whole?'"

"None of us, Father, none of us can claim to have found the whole, but if we're fortunate we find our own piece of it. This is mine."

"You're willing to throw your life away for five demands?"

"It's about so much more than that, Father and you know it." There were things I could say about the British yanking the Special Category Status away, criminalizing us all while they continued their occupation of our country, but he knows it. He knows what I know, that this is a stand to say, 'We are fully human, acknowledge it, see us as men in charge of our own destiny, a country with the right to shape its own rules, lay down its own laws, fulfill the promises made by the Irish for the Irish.' It is not about the five demands at all, and yet it is completely about them as well. Irish destiny is always a complex and tricky thing, and it is also as simple as the right to breathe free, and to die, if you so choose, in a way that has meaning.

April 1981

It snowed today. Woke up to a fine coating of it on my beard and face. I had fallen asleep with my head angled towards the window, watching the moon for the scant hour the narrow opening allows. The snow seemed fitting, a fresh start, or the beginning of the end of winter. It would seem that my season of indecision is over as well. I've gone on hunger strike as of this morning. I chose today out of respect for Dr. Martin Luther King who was killed this day thirteen years ago.

Francis Hughes went on strike on the 15th of March, Raymond McCreesh and Patsy O'Hara on March 22nd. Big Seamus followed the next week. And now, in this first week of April, it's me.

This journal is not meant to be a political manifesto, only my own musings and thoughts. Still, I feel I should lay out my reasons for doing this (with the unromantic and impractical aid of bog roll and leaky pen). First of all I am not an idealist, revolutionaries rarely are. There is only so much blood and pain and senseless death a man can witness before the idealism in him dies. I believe that things have come to a point where the British government has left us no choice. The hunger strike is the only door open and we either walk through it or crawl back on our knees to them. We will not crawl.

I believe this is about the Irish people, not merely a show of our intractable will in the face of endless British oppression. If we believe strongly enough to give our lives, then maybe the Irish people will believe in themselves again. The struggle within the prison is, and always has been, a microcosm of the larger Irish struggle for freedom. I once heard Bobby say that if they aren't able to destroy the desire for freedom, they won't break you. I know where my freedom lies and they will never be able to destroy that desire.

The crow was here today. I worry that when I am moved he will be unable to find me. It was maybe wrong of me to allow him to become so dependent upon the food I provide. What could I do though? He cannot fly and I know the pain of that well enough.

The screws have come and taken my tea away and asked, all sneering concern, will I be feeling up to a bite and sup tomorrow? Silly bastards, they can't see the forest for staring at a tree all their lives.

Oiche Mhaithe.

April 1981

Feeling a little weak today. Things are taking more effort and I must be careful what I expend my precious store of energy on. The hunger pangs have disappeared and, for some reason my food, which comes like clockwork, has increased in portion and quality. Christ, there is some small-mindedness within these walls the likes of which I've not seen before.

Father Jim has laid things out for me bluntly. God bless him, but I know what to expect physically from this. I know it will be neither pretty nor comfortable. First the body uses up the glucose reserves that are essential for the functioning of the brain, then it will go after the protein reserves in the muscles. It will try to compensate by lowering metabolic rates, slowing the pulse, dropping the blood pressure. Father Jim says I will begin to feel constant cold in my extremities within the next two weeks. Cold I can live with. Once the potassium and sodium are gone, the vital organs have difficulty functioning properly. Most affected is the heart, which will begin to skip beats. The list goes on—brain lesions, loss of muscle control in the eyes, vomiting, anemia, loss of hearing, difficulty speaking, possible blindness, inability to walk, confusion, and the top of the heap—death. Pretty list, isn't it?

I'm depressing myself and know it is a deadly trap to fall into. I must go and conserve some of that energy I spoke of and get some sleep. The elections are tomorrow, and we've all got our fingers crossed for Bobby.

April 9, 1981

Today, Robert Sands was elected as a Member of Parliament. There was great joy on the blocks, howling and shouting that we'd show the bastards now. One poor fellow actually had the naïveté to ask, 'Haven't we won? How could they allow a member of the British Parliament to starve himself to death?' They will allow it. They will stand by and watch it and not care nor give an inch. Upon hearing of Bobby's win, Miz Thatcher said, "A crime is a crime is a crime. It is not political. It is a crime." Who can fight against that sort of logic? Though, if I were her, I'd fire my speech writer.

Ben has taken to sitting all the hours of the evening on my windowsill, turning his back on the crows who sit on the acres of barbed wire—fencing that imprisons the prison within. He cannot make the short flight to sit beside his comrades and I am beginning to feel much the same way. The strike causes a distance between those who are on it and those who are not. I know the inevitability of death showing in my face is uncomfortable for some. So we keep company, this maimed, black-winged bird and I. We keep faith.

April 1981

I have news. It came to me by way of a smuggled bit of paper, brought in by the visitor of another prisoner. It was so tightly folded that I knew it was only mine, and that no other eyes had seen the wee letter. I had to wait until after lunch to unfold it. Noel was sleeping, back turned to me. The screws were off the wing, in their office where the television blares all blessed day, and so the risk of being caught with a contraband note was low. I was safe for a few minutes. Safe to read the tiny words on the bit of paper.

After I read it, I sat there for a long time, not even hearing the sounds of the block around me. I was all turned inward, seeing a vision of something I'd tried not to imagine, not to know, but of course, there are things in a life that a body cannot put in a tidy compartment. I could feel tears gather behind my eyes and blinked them away. I can't let it begin, for if it does, I might never be able to stop.

Noel wakes then, and the day moves on. I keep the note hidden at my waist in the fold of my towel. I haven't been able to tear it up and throw it away as I know I must. I want to share the news contained therein, but I have to wait. Because this is news I can't share with just anyone. It needs to be told properly and to the right set of ears. So I have to wait all day because he's late turning up. Even though I've thrown out an entire crust of old bread which Noel had kept by, to lure him in. I start to panic, fearing something has happened to him, and if he's gone, if he's been killed, then I will cease to exist as well—snuffed out of existence just like that. I know this isn't logical, but logic stopped mattering too much for me some time back. Finally, near evening there he is, floating in like a lopsided plane, one wing tilted down, and landing with a series of hops meant to stabilize him on the ground. He begins to peck at the bread, but I need his proper attention for this sort of news, so I call to him. I have to repeat the call several times, as he's entirely intent on his meal.

Finally, I have him though, and he eyes me with his beak to one side, eyes bright as shiny new buttons. Now that I properly have his attention, I tell him. "Here is my news. I have a daughter, Ben. Seven pounds, seven ounces, rose-gilt hair, brown eyes, and pray God, not my ears. Her name is Abigail. Abigail Rose Turner."

I stand there for a long time, watching as the sun sets, watching as the light fades. Before I turn from the window, I whisper it again, one last time for my own ears.

"I have a daughter."

April 1981

Visiting day. This month it's meant to be Jamie. My mam won't visit, though my sisters came last month. Visiting day means bad clothes, picked I'm sure for their utter hideousness—mustard golf shirts, checkered pants, clod-hopper shoes—anything to humiliate us no matter how small-spirited it is.

The walk across the courtyard, with the screw looming behind me, took all my energy, and yet it was grand—the air and light, breathing as much in as I can because it will likely be my last. The yelling from the lads perched on the pipes overlooking the courtyard started then.

It's the usual bit of craic, and about all there is to be had outside of the odd cigarette, and it makes the men feel lighthearted for a minute or two. Shouting out the usual stuff—'Look at the state of that one there!' The screws always fall for it and join in thinking they are part of it, when they are only the butt of the joke. 'Not him, youze—is he takin' ye for a walk, ye wee dog?'

I snapped my fingers at the screw, as if summoning a cur, and kept walking. He has the misfortune of looking like a small Pekingese. I have no doubt I'll pay for my snapping fingers, but it doesn't matter to me if it gives the lads a bit of fun, a feeling of laughing in the face of the fuckers for a second or two.

Through the compound doors. Through more doors, more locks, more barriers between me and the world. Thinking already of what Jamie might say. He's *been good about not having a go at me over my decision. I was looking forward to seeing him, having a decent conversation, a bit of humanity and erudition to carry with me for the next few weeks. Thirty minutes that will have to last me.*

Then I walked into the room and felt as if someone had sucker punched me hard. For instead of my usual visit with Jamie or Father Jim, it was Pru, holding our daughter in her arms.

Despite all the other visitors in the room—the women, the children, the parents and siblings, I suddenly felt as though the world had narrowed to the three of us. Pru, looking uncomfortable and flushed, holding a tiny, quiet bundle, which is all that remains of that boy and girl who loved one another so hard for a short space.

"I told you not to come here," I said, sitting down at the table across from her.

"I know, but I did think you should see your daughter at least once."

I shook my head, but she merely looked at me with those uncompromising blue eyes of hers, something very angry in the depths of them. I cannot blame her, and yet it hurt still to see the anger and pain that I have caused.

We spoke in halting phrases, while underneath I had an entirely different conversation taking place. I wanted to say mad things like 'Wait for me, marry me, forgive me'.

She wanted me to hold Abby, but I knew I couldn't. If I know the feel of her, the scent, then it will become a crack through which vulnerability will creep and then grow. I could not help but see her, though. And that is enough of a knife in my gut. She was perfect, despite having my ears. So soft, like a little pearl, and her hair that wondrous rose colour just like Pru's. Fortunately, one day that hair will hide her ears.

"She has your eyes," Pru said, and I could see that she was trying to hide the tears in her own.

It's true, she does, though they were closed most of the time during the visit. Which was best, I thought, because I don't want this to be her memory of her father—even if she's too young for memories to form and take hold, still some trace of the ugliness might remain somewhere inside her, and she would one day associate it with me.

The visit went on forever it seemed, and yet it was over within seconds as well. Pru kissed me before she left, and I let her, because I cannot help it. I will always need her touch, will long for it until the minute I die. Between us the baby wriggled, and I thought I might break there, start crying and knew I must not. It's not something I can afford in here. The screws would see it and use it, even if it was only to make fun of me. I don't want them to have any sort of leverage when it comes to those I love.

"Pru, please don't come here again," I said. "You don't belong here, and neither does Abby."

She didn't reply, her mouth set in a stubborn line, the baby clutched fast to her chest. I had to go then, with that my last picture of them.

Walking back to my filthy cell, in the ill-fitting ridiculous clothes, I felt it again—all that has been lost and can never be regained.

During the walk, I managed to palm the wee package she'd dropped in my pocket, into my mouth. Later in the evening, I dug it out from where I'd hidden it in my mattress, unwrapping the wee bit of paper and tobacco she'd done up so tightly that it took an age to open it.

The letter wasn't long, just a few lines to beg me to reconsider, and to tell me she will always love me. I know she means it; her character is such that she loves with a depth and commitment that will last for always. The tobacco is to share out, and that I will do.

I read the letter over until I knew every word, until each one was emblazoned on my mind's eye, so that later I will be able to close my eyes and see it there, hovering in the air in front of me. Then I tear the paper into tiny shreds and go to stand at the window. It's cold tonight, and one of those freak spring storms is passing through—snow and rain dancing in the vortex of wind. And so, I open my hands and let her words go, watch them fly into the night like a flock of swans, like a tornado of butterflies—'winged things white and boundless as stars in a snowstorm.'

April 1981

Several winters back, my mam made me a coat. A sturdy brown thing, meant to last a few winters. I loved that coat, and always had all sorts of things squirreled away in the pockets: bits of stone and feather, shells, coins, plaster broken from buildings, half a button from an army coat I found one day. Crow things, as my mam said, for I loved anything shiny, though I loved the broken things more.

A few winters ago, I gave the coat away to an old man in the streets who was clearly cold and needed the warmth more than I did. But I still miss that coat. Perhaps that's why I dreamed about it last night.

In the dream there was an old woman. She didn't smile, but I felt no fear of her. She came to me and laid that old brown coat over me, and it was made of autumn things—earth, dry leaves, fallen bark, cold rain, decay, and then I could feel myself become part of the earth too, layered in with it, slowly turning into dirt along with the leaves and the bark and the rain. I was fused with the earth. And then suddenly in that strange way of dreams, I was walking in the streets of Belfast, toward the gate of my old home, wearing my coat, thinking about playing a game of football with Finian and the boys later that night. I reached into the pockets for my keys and found they were filled with earth, soaking with cold rain. And then I was in the earth again, so deep that I could feel the movement of it. I woke in a panic trying to clear leaves from my eyes and dirt from my nose and mouth, feeling as though I was suffocating.

The dream lingered all day; I know what it is, I know what it's telling me.
'The grave's a fine and private place but none do there I think embrace.'

May 5th, 1981

Bobby Sands died this morning at 1:17 am, on the sixty-sixth day of his hunger strike. He was twenty-seven years old. It has been a day of strange emotions, anger and despair at Bobby's death, that the British government has been so intransigent as to allow this death to happen. There is a small thread of hope in that he has finally been accorded the political recognition he sought. All the U.S. daily newspapers carried the news of his death. For most, Father Terry tells me, it was their front- page story. The New York Times stated in an editorial that, 'By willing his own death, Bobby Sands has earned a place on Ireland's long roll of martyrs and bested an implacable British Prime Minister.' But has he? She will live to see another day. Bobby will not. Eventually this will fade into the annals of history and she will be forgiven and remembered for other things.

Over 110,000 dock workers boycotted the entrance of British ships into U.S. ports. That one made Father Jim smile. "My fellow countrymen," he said to me, "know how to honour a man's memory." Around the world, there were silences observed, statements made, sympathies rendered and people paying homage to one slim boy from Belfast who had the nerve to go the distance. I wish I could ask him—was it worth it in the end?

The news that made me cry though was that the women of West Belfast, upon hearing of Bobby's death, took to the streets, banging dustbin lids on the pavement, letting the wind carry their grief and broadcast it to the entire city. Father Jim, who was out walking at the time, said it sounded like the wail of a cloud of banshees howling out their pain. It is the women who mourn, always, and the women who must continue on regardless of wars or politics. How will my own two survive this?

I look through the window to see a small star, newly hatched from the nebula it seems, and wonder if Bobby has joined the galaxy of patriot ghosts that whirl within the republican universe.

Oiche Mhaithe, Bobby.

May 1981

We have become Other. I see it in the faces of the men—those who aren't on strike, as though we have moved into a different realm and no longer move amongst them. This will shortly be true in my case, as they are going to move me to the hospital wing, where I can be more closely monitored. Even Noel looks at me funny, and so it's best if they take me away where I am not a daily discomfort for him. I think the other prisoners both resent and admire us. At times I think they are also relieved not to be one of us.

I have Ben though, and he visits daily. I have to feed him from Noel's food, of course, or they'll claim I'm eating mine and cheating. If so much as a bean goes missing it will be headline news. Noel doesn't mind though, and says he'll continue to feed him once I'm moved. I've asked Father Jim to make certain Ben is cared for later on, and he's assured me if he can make it happen, he'll get him out of here, and make sure he has a life any crow would envy. It is the little things about which I worry and fret now, it seems. But it is my story, and I do not regret the writing of it.

When this is over the men of learning will come and they will talk of our little lives, making them mean and small in scope, picking over our bones for their philosophies, for the justifications of their own lives, their studies. But we, each of us, from the day we are born, are a world complete. We each have a story, we are story—for what is Ireland if not a grand tale told from the beginning of time?

May 12th, 1981

Francis Hughes died today. He lasted fifty-nine days. There are three more between myself and Death. There are times at night, when I cannot sleep, that I see Death's face. Sometimes it is frightening, and sometimes Death merely looks like an old friend, whose visit will be welcomed when he arrives.

A journalist came to interview me a few days back. I gave him the usual jabberwocky beginning with, 'I was born in Armagh in the month of June…', the whys and wherefores of the strike, how I came to be in prison, my trial, etc. The man stopped me cold by asking what I believed in. I think I replied, 'Freedom for all mankind, education, food, a roof over one's head…' and so forth. But here I will write down my own personal articles of faith.

I believe that faith can be maintained even in the face of the greatest pain and the greatest losses.

I believe that given the choice, more often than not, humans will choose to do that which is right.

I believe that time is relative, and that twenty years with meaning is better than a hundred without.

I believe that the time of my death is near at hand and, like all dead men, I will be forgotten, except by those who have loved me.

I believe that mankind is capable of visions and ideas, which will endure long after we have all faded to dust.

I believe that one man, with conviction and belief, can make a difference.

I believe, when I look at the stars, that we are, as the poet said, children of light. Death is small.

May 1981

Father Jim came to conduct mass for those of us in the infirmary. It was held in the television room, and it was just a few of us. There was what appeared to be a bundle of rags in a wheelchair when I first entered, and then the bundle of rags emitted a deep, rasping cough and I realized it was Big Seamus, so diminished now that I would not have known him had Father Jim not said his name. I knew such a sadness then—it engulfed me, as the cost of all this was once again borne home.

When it was my turn to take communion, Father Jim knelt in front of me with a face filled with so much sorrow it seemed one man could not contain it, and perhaps he cannot. There was a great hush in the room, the candles flickering into long shadows on the walls, as each of us took the wafer, the silence punctuated only by Big Seamus' coughing.

I have never been a particularly religious sort of person, but I have always believed in something greater than myself. I've never felt the need to call it God or anything else really, only to pause now and again to acknowledge it.

During the prayer, I listened and yet my soul roamed free for those moments. I was in the apple orchard of my youth, wandering, the way I did as a little boy, safe in the knowledge that my granddad walked behind me. I could smell the scent of the apples, dusty and warm, the sharp cider of the ones on the ground, the bees a-buzz on their nectar. I could feel the rough bark as I swung up into one of the trees, and looked out through its branches, feeling like a pirate sailing a wooden ship, laden with booty. I looked down expecting to see my granddad, and instead saw a little girl, big brown eyes, rose-gilt hair, tiny hand reaching up to clutch at my own. Abby. My baby girl. I reached back and felt her small, soft hand settle into mine with such trust.

"Ambrose? Ambrose?" It was Father Jim, bringing me back from that far place and for a moment I hated him for it. I wanted to stay in that place where I once might have lived. I realized I had reached out in that moment, when I thought I was touching Abby's hand.

"Are you all right, do you need me to call for the orderly?"

"No, Father, I'm fine," I said, but I didn't mean it, and I could see by his face that he knew it. I know every time he looks at me, he wonders if this will be the last time he sees me. I wonder too.

May 1981

Death creeps cold along the corridors now, like a low-lying fog which traps us all in its sinuous net. I can smell it on my own skin, a strange scent, for my body understands what my mind cannot—I have condemned it to a lingering death. I think about it a lot—death, that is. It's impossible not to. The nights here in the hospital are so quiet, and I only sleep a few hours here and there, and often find myself staring at the ceiling in the wee hours and pondering what's to come.

I wonder about what is after, or if there's nothing—just a blank where my form and energy used to be. It's the energy that's the sticking point for me—for energy simply is, it can be neither created nor destroyed, and just transmutes itself into something new.

That dream I had the first few weeks I was in prison keeps coming back to me. The one with the blackbird flying up in a cloud of gold. I think maybe the bird is me, and I'll simply rise up and leave my body when the time comes. I'm praying it will be that simple because Big Seamus is near the end, and he is not going gentle into that good night. He's in a terrible lot of pain, and I hear him scream out several times an hour, though mostly he just moans. It's an inhuman sound, long and low and very deep—the noise of an injured animal caught in a trap and gone beyond hope. I don't want to die like that, though I realize I'll have no choice about it.

One of the last things Big Seamus said to me, before he could no longer speak, was that he wasn't afraid, only committed and very, very tired. I haven't found that place yet, that place beyond this one, which seems like a state of transcendency one must earn, where one need not be afraid. Because, in truth, I am terrified.

If I could have the universe hear but one plea, it would be this—Please God, let me fly at the end.

Part Ten

The Blood-Dimmed Tide

From the Journals of James Kirkpatrick

March 1981

When Casey showed up, waiting to drive me home after my final treatment, I said to him, 'I thought **I** was meant to be the mental patient.' I truly did wonder if the man had parted entirely with his good sense, but he just shrugged and said, 'I think it would be good if ye were near family just now, an' we're yer family, like it or not.'

To my surprise I found myself agreeing, and in this way became an occupant of a very small cottage, occasionally sharing my abode with an angry ewe, five children—though wee Abby cannot get here under her own power—a raggedy cat and a dog who is nearly always muddy. The ewe clearly feels I have invaded her territory, and shows her discontent by knocking at my door with her front hooves each morning.

The electroshock therapy appears to be working, though I have gaps in my memory both before and after the treatments. I feel quiet now, which is a vast relief, and that feeling is perhaps worth the loss of a few memories.

This land has some sort of magic in it. The rhythm of it gets into your blood within the first few days and as you walk it, work with it (there is always something which needs doing here), it pulls the thorns from your soul, steadies you, enchants you and makes you long for your bed by about eight o'clock each night.

Sometimes in the evenings, Pamela comes to sit with me, knitting in hand, usually with Kathleen, though sometimes not. Sometimes it is Casey, and he whittles and we talk. I've been helping him with finishing the house, and it has been as satisfying as any work I've ever done in my life, seeing the dream of a *home come to fruition. Pru comes often with Abby, and for the most part we don't talk, mostly because I think she doesn't have words for what's happening with Ambrose. Nor do I, come to that.*

There is a strange peace within me, and a larger one within the microcosm of the farm. But beyond, back home, there is no peace. The Hunger Strike crawls onward, and the entire country is held in a sort of agonized stasis. We are all, of course, grieving the course Ambrose has chosen. Father Jim is the only one who has been able to get in to see him, and says he is committed fully to his decision, and there seems to be no way to sway him.

What have we done that our young are willing to self-immolate?

April 1981

This house Casey has built is a love letter. I see that clearly in every detail, in the placement of each window, the flow of the stairs, the incorporation of natural elements, making the house fit perfectly into its background, as if it might have grown just so over many seasons to fit the land and the sound of the sea beyond. He is a master at this—bringing the outdoors in and yet leaving the space cozy and feeling like a real home with comfort and happiness built into its core. Pamela has a studio at the top of the house, looking out toward the sea. The light in there is of the sort every artist dreams about.

The house holds all the nooks and crannies a child could imagine, and deep windowsills where one can bask like a cat while reading or dreaming. There are trunks from fallen trees fashioned into a bower for little girls to sleep in and traipse off into woodland dreams. There are built-in bookshelves chock-a-block with much loved books. Open shelves for the china are set into the walls and yet appear to be floating, setting the kitchen alight with the cheery glow of blue and brown pottery and the more delicate filaments of pearl and oystershell china. There's the long shimmering length of the bog oak table Casey made long ago, which is often cluttered with the detritus of family life: snacks; homework; dog-eared books; hair ribbons; half-drunk mugs of tea; the scattered puzzle pieces of the model of a tea clipper; a bit of toast still with a sweet trace of bramble jelly clinging to it from the morning's breakfast, blueprints (Casey is working on the plans for a community centre in a neighbouring village) and wee, fanciful sketches that Pamela jots away at during the quieter moments of her day. But the thing which really sets the house alight, and gives it that feeling of enchantment is the love within its walls.

I have always thought a house is the outward expression of the lives lived within it. This house will be a happy one, it has all the ingredients necessary. It will be a wonderful place for the children to grow and thrive.

Pamela has been at work on her 'Book of Country Hours' and has enlisted me to write the words once she gives me the general gist of what each drawing is meant to represent. It is good work to have just now, and I find I look forward to my evenings by the fire, cat in lap, Kathleen asleep on the bed behind me. Kolya sleeps in the main house, because he hates to be parted from Conor and Isabelle. So it is quiet here, and words troop to my pen, as the land all around seems to breathe in and wait for me to tell its tale. I can write again, in a way I think I haven't since my days at Oxford, when I felt on fire with the need to twist and weave words to my purpose. It is a lovely and yet peace-filled intoxication.

April 1981

I have finally been able to visit with Ambrose. I find though, that I don't have words for those brief minutes I spent with him. Some things truly are beyond the power of description, and what those visits make me feel, what that young man is enduring, is one of them.

The British, as was expected, have delineated themselves as the peacemaker, the honest broker just trying to bring two warring factions together. It rejects out of hand the history of the country—the partitioning, the inaction and ignorance of all that has taken place since partition to the extent that parliament disallowed the issue of Northern Ireland to be mentioned at all, thus turning their face from the entrenchment of Unionism in all the institutions of this country, both locally and at the national level. They refuse to look at their actions since the civil rights movement took off, and prefer to pretend a lofty innocence, as though they are unaware of their interference, the killing done both by them and also with their implicit blessing. They want to believe in the myth of their benevolence, and turn a blind eye to what they have truly wrought and how filthy their part has been in this very dirty war of ours.

April 1981

I have met Aine now. She came down with the rising moon last evening, to bring Pamela a clutch of pheasants. A gift for which Pamela will show appreciation, though I know she will hand them directly to Casey for him to deal with. When it comes to the dressing of fowl or fur, she is not a natural farmer.

I was walking down from the house, Kathleen asleep in my arms, when I encountered Aine.

"Ye'll be her father?" she asked, without any polite preamble to our discourse.

"I am," I said, feeling instinctively that this was not a woman given to any sort of gossip, and so I was safe to speak truth to her.

"Aye, she looks a deal like you. Ye've fairy blood too, just like her. So does her mam, though."

"Indeed, she does."

She didn't inquire any further into the matter, leaving me to wonder how much she knows and muse a bit on how odd our situation must seem to outsiders who don't know the whole story.

I took Kathleen into the cottage and put her down on the bed. When I returned outside, Aine was sitting next to the firepit, with the clear intent of staying for a visit.

"Would you like something to drink?" I asked.

"Aye, a bite of somethin' wouldn't come amiss either," she said.

It was clear she didn't want to come inside, so I built a fire in the sunken pit, and then I brought out the toast fork, and I toasted bits of bread, while Aine produced a bottle of blackberry cordial from under her coat.

"Will ye look at that?" Aine said just as I was handing her a slice of toast. She pointed off to a slight hummock of earth to the north of the cottage and I looked to find two badgers bathing in the moonlight, trundling about slowly as though waiting for the tea to steep whilst readying their spider eggs and worms for the eating.

"Do you know they sometimes keep the same home for centuries?" she asked.

*"That **is** something I know," I said, "we've had generations of badgers on my land, and my family kept records of them. They've belonged to the land longer than we have."*

"The ones on this land live up beyond the bramble hedge, it's rare for them to come down this far. They tend toward shyness, after all."

We were quiet after that, watching while the badgers ate and occasionally gazed up at the moon, as though pondering the state of the universe. We enjoyed our buttery toast and got slightly tipsy on the blackberry cordial. As we sat, a story rose in front of me, a whimsical thing following the seasons, about a family of badgers who had for their friends, rabbits and deer, and mice and birds. One story for each season, in which there are winter balls, autumn foraging, spring picnics, summer weddings and all sorts of lovely things to eat: butter flavoured with rosemary, wild strawberries, bottles of dark ale bobbing on strings in cool streams, warm bramble jelly, and syllabub whipped with apple cider. Something I could dedicate to Kathleen, that she could have as a memory of this time together on the land where she'll grow up. I was caught by the fancy of the idea while we watched the two badgers, and shared the thought with Aine.

She took her leave abruptly, and I thought perhaps I had waxed a little too fanciful for her comfort—but what is one to do under the influence of the moon and badgers and blackberry cordial? Before she reached the edge of the field though, she came back, striding with great purpose. She fixed me with that straightforward look and said, "I like you. Come for tea before you leave." She then went back into the night, without waiting for a response. I will, of course, have to go, as I feel I've been summoned by royalty, and mustn't risk refusal.

April 1981

Accordingly, a few days later I went for tea, Pamela having given me directions which contained a lot of vague instructions like—'turn left at the oak with the arthritic knee– you'll understand when you see it. And then right at the clump of rhododendrons.' As the land has about two hundred of these clumps, this was less than elucidating. And then she followed that with—'Go around the hummocky sort of thing, and skirt the bog, and look for a hillside that appears to have a large mushroom growing out of it.'

As it turns out, though, the directions were perfect, and there's not a chance in hell I would have found it without them. The mushroom was, of course, the house.

I stood there for a moment, merely taking it in, half-expecting a mystical creature to emerge, curse me and my line for a hundred generations and then pop back into the burrow—house, that is. But then Aine emerged from the shimmering woods, hands stained green with foraging.

"Greens for the pot," she said, gesturing with her handful of dripping plants. "I've made us a meal."

And so she had. We settled in on the rugs in her fairy abode, after she put her greens into the pot—without washing them—but what's a little grit to a man invited for fairy tea?

"It's as well ye've come today, for ye'll be gone soon; there's a man coming for you with a summons in his pocket," she said, handing me a steaming bowl of soup.

"Is there?"

"Aye, he'll be dressed as a blackbird, an' ye'll not be happy to see him."

This sounded rather ominous and so I changed the subject and asked her about the land, the village, the things she foraged for after winter's long drought.

We chatted then more generally, and she told me how she's made enough to scrape by all these years by helping locally during the lambing season in the spring and the haying in the fall. She helps too with planting hereabouts in the spring, though says the machinery which does it now has taken a great deal of that sort of work away. We talked then of what it is to live so close to the world, to feel its roots and rhythms, to depend upon it for food and fuel when one plants and harvests these things and doesn't rely upon the market. Her nearest neighbours have been the beings of feather and fur, and she knows them all well—their migrations, their births and deaths, their comings and goings, whether local or international in scope. She knows every tree in her vicinity—the plants, the rocks, where the best patches of mushrooms grow, and where the healing plants are. I think she and Finola would get along grandly.

During this conversation, I ate two bowls of her greens soup, which tasted just as soup made by the Queen of the Fairies ought to—wild, earthy and slightly foreign to the tongue.

After, as I was taking my leave, she fixed me with that slightly eerie gaze of hers, and said, "Casey," like the name alone was both statement and challenge.

"Yes?" I said in acknowledgement, if not understanding.

"Ye consider him a friend?"

"I consider him family," I replied.

"He is a good man," she said, her eyes fixed in the distance. I understood then what she was trying to say.

"I don't intend to hurt them," I said.

"You won't mean to," she said and then did one of her about-faces and marched back into her house, closing the door firmly in my face.

The words left a chill in my spine, especially considering that the next day, one of her predictions came true, for Father Jim came calling.

When I saw his tin heap of a car coming down the road, I knew the world was about to return. I was right. Father Jim has been working with the ICJP—Irish Commission for Justice and Peace—a group of well-meaning people from various walks of life, who are trying, in vain, I fear, to somehow mediate between the British and the hunger strikers.

He is always plain-spoken, and this visit was no exception. He made clear just why he'd come to see me.

"We should like you to visit the PM," he said, giving me that direct look of his which must often cow parishioners into doing his bidding.

"You want me to go visit Thatcher?" I asked, feeling incredulous at the very thought.

"Yes. Just ask her to soften her stance a little, to maybe give on one or two of the demands, things that won't make her appear weak, being that that seems to be her biggest worry."

"What on earth makes you think she will give me an audience, much less listen to anything I say?" I asked.

"Am I wrong, Jamie? Only I thought you were the man they called the Blue Angel, the one who was the conduit between the IRA and the British government."

This silenced me, as I suppose it was intended to. I thought it was a futile effort, but I reached out to my contacts, via the village telephone. My conversation will certainly give Mrs. Gillivray some good gossip for the forthcoming week, as she polished the wood molding in the hall—a treatment it hasn't seen in many a year judging from the usual state of it—for the entirety of my conversation.

My contact got back to me within a day. I have a meeting with the Iron Lady. I can't say I'm looking forward to it. Pamela has convinced me to leave Kolya behind for the time being, and as that seems the wisest decision, I will be leaving him here where I know he's safe and loved.

The world, alas, has indeed returned.

Chapter Sixty-two

The Irish Question

10 DOWNING STREET glowered in the evening mist like a grande dame, who was up past her well-regulated bedtime, and felt rather resentful about it.

Jamie was expected and so was ushered quickly through the famous black door, and up the stairs to the White Drawing Room. A fire burned cheerily in the white marble hearth, and drinks were laid out on the low table between the comfortable chairs.

She was waiting for him, and offered him a drink while he seated himself. "I only have scotch," she said, "rather remiss of me, I suppose, considering your trade."

He looked around as she poured the scotch, taking in the atmosphere of an eighteenth-century drawing room, with all its beautiful touches. Here was wealth and power—an inestimable amount. Turner paintings on the walls, elegant furniture and pale draperies over the long windows, which looked out into the garden, invisible in the rainy twilight.

She was a busy woman, and wasted no time getting directly to the point. "I understand you've come to talk about the hunger strikers?"

"I have," he said, and then waited.

"I have said most of what needs to be said on the matter. You aren't likely to change my mind as to the fate of a bunch of violent criminals." Her tone was strident, as it had been through this entire matter, at least publicly. It was as it always had been—Ireland, the mad cousin, the thorn in the empire's side, who could never behave for long.

"No one is denying the acts they've committed, only that were the British not in occupation the acts would never have occurred."

It was probably not the best opening he could have chosen, but it had the virtue of truth. She leaned back in her chair, scotch held lightly, as she met his gaze with her famously direct one.

"The damnable Irish question, the thing that has plagued every prime minister since there's been one sitting in Westminster."

"Perhaps if that question had ever been answered properly, neither of us would need to be here right now."

"Somehow," she said, "I doubt there is an answer to that, which would satisfy all concerned."

She placed her drink on the table, and fixed him with the steely glare for which she was known. He did not blink.

"Will someone please tell me why they are on hunger strike? I've asked so many people. Is it to prove their virility?"

The feckless ignorance of the remark caught Jamie off guard. And so, after placing his own drink upon the table, he told her, explaining it both in terms of geography and history. England had long claimed this section of Ireland as its own, but it had never truly understood the history and he thought it possible she was stereotypical in this particular sort of blindness. Perhaps all empires came to this—a belief in their innate superiority, an arrogance that blinded them to their own weaknesses, and a lack of understanding for the world outside their rules and borders.

He told, with patience, the things which had happened, and what it had done, and how it had affected the very soul of the country. He explained that the border was artificial, how it cut through the most ancient territories of Ireland and across parish boundaries, so that some priests administered to their flocks in two countries. He spoke of households that had a kitchen in one country and a bedroom in another. How there was no true name for the country that could even be settled upon; Ulster, a name favoured by the Protestants, had originally contained nine counties, not six and Northern Ireland was a misnomer because it wasn't the most northerly area of Ireland. North of Ireland was awkward but came the closest to the truth for Catholics and Nationalists.

Stepping out onto what he knew to be thinner ice, he went on to speak of the illegality of England's presence in Ireland, the laws which had taken away Irish language, Irish culture, the Celtic aspects of the Catholic Church, all justified by the English opinion that the Irish were in some way inferior. He spoke too of the country's greatest wound, the Famine, and how it had been—rather than a true lack of food—a genocide, and how no king, queen or politician had ever apologized for it. And last, he touched on the reneging of the agreement between the two countries of the Special Category statute, rendering all that had been political now criminal, despite the continued presence of the British Army in Northern Ireland.

"Your nation has fractured mine into pieces because you feel it does not matter, because you feel we have no rights to our own land, our own history, our culture and language."

"Thank you for the history lesson," she said drily, "still I hold to the facts, and the facts show that the acts of these men are all merely criminal, not political, James."

It was one of her favourite talking points, and he saw that she was unwilling to abandon it even here in a private conversation.

"How is it not political when a country has been occupied by a foreign force for eight hundred years?" Jamie said, wishing he hadn't taken any of the scotch, for the taste of it was bitter as aloes in his mouth.

"Eight hundred years of occupation?" She laughed, a dry humorless chuckle. "You certainly have the Irish flair for drama, James."

"A dose of truth is drama?"

"The present situation is not of the government's choosing. It is the men of violence trying to play what will be their last card. They are manipulative, playing on the most basic of emotions—pity—to create tension and stoke the fires of bitterness and hatred. While you may see it as a tragedy, I say it is a tragedy of their own making."

"You speak as though all this happens in a vacuum, when it doesn't. England sowed the seeds and continues to water them with blood, and yet claims an innocence it has never had. You continue to use force, though according to your own laws force is no way in which to solve a dispute between neighbours, particularly force used by the stronger upon the weaker."

"We use our strength to limit the damage to a nation which cannot seem to adequately govern itself, and is insistent upon murdering its own."

"You set up that situation hundreds of years ago, if it keeps bearing fruit you will have to keep harvesting it," he said, knowing his temper was beginning to break through his words.

"The mistakes of the past don't justify the violence of the present."

"Except the mistakes aren't past, are they? The war in Northern Ireland is an extremely dirty one, and British fingers aren't clean by any stretch. Don't bother denying it, regardless of whether it makes its way into the history books, you know the truth, as do I."

"Why can't the Irish be friendly?" she asked, voice slightly strident, "we've fought against the French, we fought against the Germans, and they are friends, why must the Irish always be the exception?"

"Perhaps it is because you are no longer occupying the Ruhr," he said and rose, understanding that anything further wasn't going to help and might possibly hurt. She was clearly so entrenched in her position that there was no turning her. There were polite noises of farewell, but they were no more than noise. He had achieved nothing by coming here. There was a time he'd thought she practiced her flinty exterior because being a female leader she had to be twice as tough as her male counterparts, but now he saw she actually believed in the union between Ulster and England. And that she did not understand the country across the sea, and had no desire to either. Ireland was merely an annoying sideshow to her, of little consequence on the international stage.

He had reached the door, before she spoke again. "I will never understand those people," she said, and Jamie turned, his nerves shot through with rage.

"No, you won't. You didn't yesterday, you don't today, and you won't tomorrow. The shame of it is, you've never truly tried. Of course, you won't feel the shame—any of it—because you don't have the grace for it. In the end that will be your downfall, and quite possibly, that of your country."

He left then, knowing that there was little hope for the men dying in the prison, knowing that he'd failed Ambrose, and let his anger get the best of him. The fragile peace that had been woven from the treatments and his time on the farm, was gone—an ephemeral cloud which had been shredded by the reality of his country.

Chapter Sixty-three

The Blood-Dimmed Tide
June 1981

BELFAST WAS A city cloaked in black. Black flags fluttered eerily from the lamp posts and the entire city felt as though it both mourned and held its breath at the same time. The city was on death watch, waiting for the next hunger striker to die, waiting for the British to say, 'No, enough, let us stop this immolation of young men.' Yet, of course, the British did no such thing.

The breath now held was personal for the Riordans. Because that next young man, sacrificing himself for the pyre of country, was their own. It was why Pamela was here in Belfast with Pru, despite being in an advanced state of pregnancy which was becoming increasingly uncomfortable.

Once Ambrose had been moved to the infirmary, he'd allowed Pru to come see him on a regular basis. So today, knowing the end was drawing near and not wanting the girl to face that alone, Pamela had accompanied her. They'd left Abby and Kathleen with Gert, who was always happy to spend time with the children, and who had taken Abby to her heart just as she had Pamela's brood.

Jamie was with Ambrose when they arrived, reading out loud to him. He looked up and smiled as they entered the room. Pru went directly to Ambrose, her face alight with love. She never let her fear or pain show, and yet Pamela knew Ambrose saw it all the same. It was what love did—made plain things which would otherwise remain hidden.

Her eyes met Jamie's then, and for the space of a breath he wore no mask, had no shield and she saw there something so raw and vulnerable that it cleaved like a hatchet through her heart. A breath, no more, and the expression was gone, the pain and vulnerability hidden like a ripple upon water, fading long before it finds the shore. What this was costing him she could well imagine.

"I was just leaving," Jamie said. As he'd been turning a page in the book as they'd entered, she knew it was more that he wanted to absent himself so that Pru and Ambrose might have their time alone.

"Do you have a minute to spare?" she asked.

He nodded. "I'll wait in the corridor for you."

She turned back to the bed then, as always fighting not to let her expression show her dismay. It was hard just to look at Ambrose. He had always been thin, but he'd also had a clear strength to him which showed in his every movement. This emaciated figure laid out on the sheepskin-covered bed was so insubstantial that she felt like he might simply dissolve were any of them to make the mistake of touching him. The beautiful brown eyes were the same though, despite looking out from a skeletal visage. There was even a little of the profound curiosity left there, deep within his gaze. A small chill chased through her, cold as frost; there was something of him that was already gone, as though some essence which made him Ambrose had crossed into that far land where the rest of him would soon join it.

She kissed his forehead. He felt hot to her, but she knew her perceptions were directly linked to the knowledge of imminent death. If he had a fever it no longer mattered. It was day sixty of his strike and at most it was likely he might have a few days, or if his will could hold fast, a week. It was hard to know what to pray for—that he should hold on and perhaps the British would cave, or that he should go sooner and be spared the additional days of suffering. What would be best for Prudence? While she prayed several times a day that the British would find it in their hearts to come to a settlement which would be acceptable to the strikers, she knew that it wasn't likely to happen; Jamie's face had told her that much.

"I'm going to go out and talk to Jamie for a bit," she said. She did, indeed, want to catch Jamie before he left but she also always made certain to give Pru and Ambrose what privacy she could despite doctors, orderlies and the ever-present guards. There were always assorted other people coming and going from the strikers' rooms as well, as the last-ditch attempts to save their lives swirled all about them.

There was a small alcove with two chairs where visitors could sit a moment, if needed, and it was here she had known that Jamie would wait for her. She sat down beside him and took a good look at him. He seemed outlined by the ink of tension, as though the tragedy unfolding around them, like a poisonous lotus, had clarified him and brought his edges into sharp relief. There was a bright glitter about him, which set an alarm pulsing through her blood. It was a look she knew in him, and it told a very dark tale.

Had it been another time, she might not have asked the question she did. "Jamie, are you taking your meds?" It was a loaded question at best, and an overstepping of their mutual boundaries at worst.

"Are you attempting to diagnose me?"

"No, I'm only worried. I think I have the right to that, no?"

"Yes, you do," he said, "though at times it's difficult to allow you it."

"Jamie," she began, but he held up a hand to forestall her.

"I'm fine, Pamela, only a little tired and unable to keep up my morale around you."

"You don't need to—surely you know that by now," she said. It was another overstep, but she thought it did not matter perhaps, just now.

"I do."

"Pat said the meeting with Thatcher didn't go well."

"It was a mission of futility. I won't be going again," he said, and there was both finality and defeat in his voice.

"I'm sorry, Jamie," she said, knowing how difficult these last months had been for him.

"The Foreign Office has done an end run around the Commission; at this point the Commission is about as useful as a screen door on a submarine. The Foreign Office is talking directly to external members of the IRA. So far, no one is budging, and I don't see—given my meetings these last three days—that changing in time to save Ambrose, or any of the men who follow."

There was a hollow space beneath her heart which opened a little further. It was one thing to know it, but to have it acknowledged by someone who knew the players and had spoken to both sides, was yet another level of confirmation that this would not—could not—end well. The damage it would leave in its wake—the bitterness, the pain of an entire nation, the personal losses drowned in the wave of Shakespearean drama—was just now, more than she could fathom.

"The costs will come due regardless, both sides will declare victory, when in the end it will be no more than a stalemate, and the price of that intransigence, the lives of all these young men. London will have learned nothing and conceded nothing, and this will be little more than a blip for them. The British will likely lose the day as far as the world stage goes, but they know there are more days to come. Here, the strikers will enter the halls of patriot martyrdom, but eventually this wound too will heal over; there will be a damn big scar to remember it by, but it will heal. And the loss will be for the families—the mothers and fathers and brothers and sisters and wives and children who won't forget and who won't find the remembrance of it each year a comfort at all."

She felt suddenly lightheaded, and knew she would have to eat soon. There was a lunch in the car for her and Pru, but neither of them was likely to have much appetite. It was always hard to eat without feeling like you might choke on a bite of whatever you were putting in your mouth. It was survivor's guilt, present in advance of death, before there was anyone to survive.

"It's not about the same things, though, is it? For the British it's so little, for us here, it's everything."

"Of course it's about so much more, you know it and so do I. And certainly Ambrose understands it, but the British don't and they have no desire to learn. We're the problem that they fervently wish would simply go away, but yes, we're a small problem for all that."

"So no compromise?"

"None that will matter. I've spoken to people other than Thatcher, and while she may not know it, negotiations are ongoing. It looks like eventually they'll extend the right to their own clothing to all prisoners in the North, that way it doesn't look they are admitting to any sort of special status. The strikers will get what they want on visits and parcels too, but London isn't going to bend one iota on work, restoration of lost remission or association. To even get those first two they must end the strike, which means they'd have to trust the British."

"Which isn't going to happen," Pamela said. "And so then there is no hope?"

Jamie shook his head, and she felt something crumble inside her at the affirmation of what she already knew to be true. Because if Jamie had said there was even a glimmer of possibility that the British might change their minds, might relent, she knew she would cling to that hope like a life raft on stormy seas. He would, she knew, keep going, keep trying because it was not in his nature to do otherwise.

"I'd like," he said, "to come get Kathleen for a few days, if that's all right."

"Of course it is," she said softly. "Abby and Kathleen are with Gert and Owen today. Pru and I came up last night. These visits are getting harder and harder for her."

"I sometimes think I did that child a great wrong when I brought her here to look after the children. She would be happy in Maine, and living a good life and not facing the imminent death of someone she loves."

"I think if you asked her, you'd find that she doesn't regret anything, and can't imagine a world in which she never met and loved that boy in there."

"Logic dictates that she wouldn't have known any better, had she never come here."

Pamela shook her head. "No, I don't think so, Jamie. I remember a discussion we had in our philosophy class in university, where we started talking about choice, and how each choice was a fork in the road, and how the road of your life would endlessly fork, even by a decision so simple as which bus you'd taken or whether or not you'd gone to a party. There was this small girl who sat in the back of the lecture hall, quiet as a mouse, and no one hardly paid her any mind all semester. Suddenly though she pipes up and says that we all live the life we're meant to and that if we'd chosen other paths this life would be the one we'd long for. It started quite the debate, but she stood her ground and convinced most of us that she believed it, even if we didn't."

She touched one of Jamie's hands and the long, tensile fingers slowly relaxed. "I've thought about what she said many times over the years, and I think she was right. We live the life we're meant to."

He looked at her for a long time, the green eyes lightless and dense with the flickering shadows of sorrow. In the merciless light of the small alcove, he was pale and strung so tight with both nerves and fury that she could feel him vibrating like a plucked wire.

"We can't move backward, only on into the future. Isn't that what you once told me, Jamie?"

He laughed, but it was a pithy sound without humour. "Must you always have such flawless recall when it comes to my prattle?"

"You've tolerated all my nonsense for years, the least I can do is listen when you attempt to set me straight."

"The greater question might be why you've put up with *my* nonsense all these years?"

His words hung there between them, the greater import of them not lost on either of them. It would be wisest to lie, to make light and yet here only feet from a dying boy, she found she could not give tongue to anything but truth. Truth mattered, even when it was only of the accord between two souls.

"It's just love, Jamie," she said, "forgiving of all sorts of nonsense, and," she added, "infinite while it lasts."

When she returned to the room, it was to find Prudence with tear tracks marking the fine grain of her skin, the normal rosy glow of her cheeks whiter than freshly fallen snow.

"What is it?" she asked, panic coursing in a great billowing tide through her body. Last week the man next to Ambrose had died very suddenly. Father Jim had been visiting with him, and the man had been lucid, sitting up and asking Father Jim if he'd mind getting a packet of cigarettes off the orderly. Father Jim had accordingly gone to do just that and returned to find the man had died in the five minutes he'd been gone. It turned out he'd had a massive coronary which had killed him instantly. Still, it had been a shock for Father Jim returning to finish his conversation. The man had been a Catholic, but there had been no time for last rites or a final recounting of sins, for the purpose of absolution.

Pru shook her head, tears stark in her eyes. "He keeps raving on about blood coming into the shore."

He wasn't raving, Pamela thought, he was remembering. It would be poetry, of course, at the end, for it was a natural language for Ambrose, and so would dwell in memory when all else had been burned away.

'The blood-dimmed tide is loosed and everywhere the ceremony of innocence is drowned.' Yeats, of course, that most Irish of poets, for a most Irish death.

She took a breath. She must not cry in front of Pru, the child would lose all hope if she did. "He's probably having strange dreams, the doctor said that would happen."

"His eyes weren't closed, Pamela; he's hallucinating. You know as well as I do what that means."

There were no real words of comfort to give her. That boy in there was going to die, and even if Margaret Thatcher decided to relax the iron rod in her back, it would be too late for those already gone, and for those standing at the gate, with death's hand already upon the latch. Ambrose had understood that from the day he put his name in for the strike, and the men who'd decided who would go on strike had chosen only those they felt could and would go the distance, even with the certain knowledge that the journey ended in death.

"I do know. I think I just wanted to spare you this for a little longer."

Pru shook her head and gave Pamela's hand a squeeze.

"You don't have to lie to me. I know the truth of what's happening. But I would ask a favour of you."

"Anything, Pru, you know that."

The girl looked at her and drew in a deep breath, smiling despite her tears.

"I need a dress."

Chapter Sixty-four

To Love While We May

"ARE YOU READY?" Pamela surveyed the girl in front of her, blinking back tears at the sight of her. It had been a challenge to find just the right dress, and then it had to be taken in in a few spots and let out in a few others. Fortunately, Ciara's nan was a dab hand with a needle, and had done the alterations within two days. The dress was a delicate pink, and brought out the apple blossom tint in Pru's cheeks. Pru was currently flushed with nerves, and kept plucking at the pins Pamela was fastening into her hair.

"As ready as I can be," she replied and then suddenly turned and threw her arms around Pamela's neck, shaking so hard that Pamela could feel it vibrating through her. "Oh, Pamela, I'm so scared. I'm scared to go in there. After today, I'll have to let go. I'm going to have to admit he's dying."

Pamela simply held her. There were no words she could say to comfort Pru because the girl was right. Ambrose was going to die soon, and this young woman in front of her would be a widow.

It had been a whirlwind few days since Prudence had announced her intention to marry Ambrose before he died. Pamela had her reservations about it, worrying about the emotional cost of it to Pru in the aftermath of Ambrose's death. When she'd taken her worries to Casey though, he'd merely said, "Let the lass love while she can, it may be it will bring her comfort, an' it will legitimize wee Abby, an' that's no small consideration."

It had taken a bit of arranging to get the prison to allow a wedding during a time of such stress and tragedy. Father Jim had taken up their case though, and finally the prison warden had agreed. Which had brought them here, to the young woman shaking in her arms.

Casey popped his head in then, taking in the shaking girl and the look on his wife's face. "It's time, Prudence, he's lucid right now, an' the doctor thinks we've a window of a half hour or so."

He gave Prudence his arm, and Pamela flashed him a watery smile of gratitude. They were this girl's family now, and would see her through this day, and the ones to come beyond today, when her groom departed this life. Casey bent down and said something in the girl's ear, and she turned to him and flashed him a smile. He'd been both a support and a guide for Pru through all this, and Pamela had been utterly grateful for his measured dealing with the situation. There was an understanding he had, which she could not possibly hope to share; it was this he'd shown and given to Pru over the last few days.

The ceremony was as brief and yet as beautiful as Father Jim could manage with a groom who was barely keeping his hold on consciousness, and a bride who was as pale as the sheets on the bed. And yet, in the midst of so much despair, here in this prison room, with the scent of impending death all around, there was love. Something so utter and replete that there were no words necessary beyond those simple ones of 'I do' and 'I love you'.

Pru was steady as a rock, her vows given in a full voice with a sincerity that could not be doubted. Ambrose's voice shook a little and his eyes were bright with tears.

Pamela felt as though her heart was held in a vice, which was being slowly turned with every word uttered, and every glance exchanged between this young couple. She saw it suddenly, how horribly fragile it all was—love and life, and time, oh yes, that greatest of all tricksters—Time. Jamie's voice echoed within her—*The horologist steals whether we will it or not, Pamela. There is no earthly way, despite what we wish, to make time stop.*"

No, no one could make time stop, for it was something that ran and fell and passed through a person's hands like smoke, leaving so little behind. Leaving so little for a girl who would need threads to grasp come the long winter that was grief.

Ambrose had to struggle to do it, but he brought Pru's hand to his mouth and kissed it, his eyes shining as he looked at her with enough love visible there, to know that it would have, indeed, lasted a lifetime for him. And then it was done, this young couple without a future were married, and Pru leaned down to hug her new groom, touching the fragile shell of him with such reverence, that Pamela turned her face into Casey's shoulder, unable to bear watching the two anymore.

She heard Ambrose murmur, and Pru reply, a catch in her voice which spoke of the tears she'd held back all day, and on that small sound Pamela felt her heart fracture, for the both of them, and for all the promise this day should hold, but did not.

"Will they let them be?" she asked, fearful that they wouldn't be given time.

"They'll let her stay now until the end. Father Jim an' Jamie saw to that. An' now, darlin', it's time for us to go," Casey said softly, and turned her, blind with tears, toward the door.

Outside the prison, it was mid-afternoon, and the air was raw and chill. She shivered, exhaustion washing over her, and she stumbled slightly, causing Casey to reach out and grab her by the elbow.

He stopped and looked down at her, face sympathetic, yet stern.

"I'm goin' to take ye home, feed ye and put ye to bed. Ye're all done in, an' ye need to rest. I can't think any of this has been good for you or the baby. There isn't anythin' more ye can do for the two of them, Jewel, surely ye see that."

"I know, I just hate leaving her here alone."

"It's the last bit of time she'll have with him, she'll need the memory of it later."

"I know that, Casey. It's just not what it should be. I think back on the days after our wedding, and I wish she could have the gift of a time such as we had."

"That's not her story. Ye have to let her write what she will. Come on, woman, let's away home now."

She took his hand and followed in his wake, grateful for his strength. He was right, she was exhausted, and worried about the baby. The thought of a meal, their warm bed and a fire sounded like a portion of heaven right now.

But she looked back once more, to the long low compound of buildings, and felt the fracture in her heart crack a little further. Heavy cloud was moving in and was lit a strange umber on the underside; it would rain hard tonight. Two lines from a long-ago letter written by another patriot who had died at the hands of a British firing squad the day after marrying his sweetheart, echoed through her heart.

'Darling, darling child I wish we were together. Love me always as I love you. For the rest everything you do will always please me.'

The subject of that letter—Grace Gifford—had never married again, and had at times lived in abject penury. Life, for the one left behind, was never the stuff of romance and poetry. She feared this would be Pru's lot as well, for the girl knew her own heart, and knew there would never be another love like Ambrose for her. Pamela understood how certain such knowledge could be for a woman.

'I was never meant to be so happy . . . I love you, love you, love you altogether, body, soul and spirit.'

The words of that long-ago patriot were full of a youthful passion and zeal, perhaps easier to feel when one's death was imminent. Words were cold comfort, however, when the man you loved was forever lost to you.

Her own man was looking at her now, the sorrow in his face a mirror of hers. "Come on, Jewel, let's get home before the storm breaks."

It was dark by the time they reached home, and Pamela sighed with relief to see the lights of the house gleaming warmly across the valley. Rain had begun to spatter the windshield and the wind was tossing the tops of the trees to and fro as they exited the car.

The house was quiet, other than Finbar padding over from his place beside the Aga, wagging his tail and yawning widely. Pat and Kate had come down two days before and taken Conor and Isabelle away with them. Jamie had Kathleen, and Abby was with Ambrose's mother.

Despite the quiet, the house enfolded them, the Aga humming warmly and the fire in the kitchen hearth casting a warm amber light over the oak floors and counters. The table was set with the everyday china, and the scent of something savoury wafted through the warm air.

"That'll be Kate's cookin'," Casey said, sniffing the air as his stomach growled audibly. "Aine must have come down an' set somethin' to warm for us, an' lit the fire too. I'll have to remember to thank her."

"I'll go and see her tomorrow. I'll take her some food too; she never seems to eat enough."

"No, woman, I'll do it. Ye're goin' to sit by the fire with yer feet up for a day, an' do nothin' more strenuous than drink yer tea an' read a book. I'll go fetch the children home in the mornin'."

"That sounds lovely, I just might take you up on it, man."

"Ye're not goin' to have a choice in it, woman. Now let's sit an' eat before one of us takes a faint."

Like all of Kate's cooking, the food was delicious—split pea soup with chunks of ham in it, as well as warm spices and herbs, and corn muffins—this last something Kate had added to her repertoire when she learned how much Pamela loved them. For dessert there was apple crumble with cream, and Casey nodded in approval as she ate a full bowl of this on top of her meal.

After, she rose intending to clean up the dishes. Running back and forth to Belfast and the prison had left her far behind on her usual daily tasks and she was determined to get a few things done before collapsing into the bed. Casey waved one hand at her. "I'll clear this lot away, you go sit yerself by the fire," he said and stood, stacking the bowls, plates and cutlery in his usual efficient manner.

Sheer exhaustion demanded that she do as bid, and she went and collapsed into a chair by the fire. To her bleary eyes the flames seemed a living thing, a cat perhaps, twisting this way and that, uncurling and arching its back and occasionally opening its mouth to bare its fangs and let out a long hiss.

She stretched with relief as the warmth began to penetrate her chilled skin. Casey came and sat down across from her, taking her feet in his lap and rubbing them. She smiled, relaxing into the sure touch of his hands, and squeaking a little as he hit a particularly tender spot in the arch of one foot.

"Ye feel sad, darlin'," Casey said, his fingers pressing in around her ankle, which had an ache in it that had started in the morning. That ache was always persistent and sharp when the weather was damp.

"Of course I feel sad," she said, wondering why he was making such an obvious statement.

"What I mean is yer body feels sad in the touch of it."

"How so?" she asked, though she thought she understood what he meant.

He shrugged. "My hands can feel it, for ye carry it within yer body in a way that speaks more loudly than words."

"I just wish I could make it stop for her, give her back Ambrose whole and filled with life. I wish I could do it for his sake as well, and even for my own. Selfish, I suppose," she said, and pulled her shawl a little tighter around her shoulders, as if she could feel the chill of the H-Block and the cold prescience of impending death once again. "She needs to believe his death—this whole hunger strike—has meaning. To believe anything else right now—well, that way lies madness."

"I know she does," Casey said. "What it will mean though, in the long run, remains to be seen, Jewel. I hope it changes things, I hope it cuts a path through the woods so that we can see a way forward to a different future, but I don't know that it will. I don't trust the British not to twist it somehow to their own advantage."

"No, nor do I," she said, smoothing her hands over the round of her belly. The baby was quiet just now, but tended to be active once she lay down at night.

Casey's eyes followed the movement of her hands, and he smiled, though the worry was clear in his expression.

"After it's over," she said, her voice breaking a little on the last word, "I think I'd like to illustrate a children's book, or some more fairy stories like I did for Jamie."

"Aye, I think that would be a good idea—creatin' somethin' beautiful."

"I'll probably want to do a book on the hunger strike too—eventually."

"Aye, I know ye will," Casey said, a note of resignation in his tone.

"It won't be right away," she said.

The fact that he didn't argue with her over this, spoke of the understanding that had grown between them these last two and a half years, and how the parameters of their relationship were fluid enough to allow others in, but also at the centre of it all, remained the core of the two of them.

"Darlin', I just want ye to be happy."

"I know, it's what I want for you too."

"I have that, woman. You and the children give that to me every day."

"Will that always be enough, though?" she asked, well understanding his restless nature.

"Aye. I have my work, an' I get great satisfaction from that—makin' somethin' which will provide shelter and warmth for a family, or a buildin' where community can gather an' form. Beyond that, I've a bit of land to myself, an' I come home to you an' the children each night. It's more than enough, darlin'. For those three years I was gone, it was you an' our family I longed for, an' who I'd been with you, not the man I was before I met ye."

She reached across the space between them and took one of his hands. "I love you so, Casey."

"I love ye too, darlin'." He smiled, a flash of white and dimple, and in that moment, she saw the boy fresh from prison whom she'd met while posing half-naked for his brother. The husband who'd had to forgive so many things, the lover who'd made her body feel his lack to the point and place of illness. The son of a good father, who now was a wonderful father too. One day he would be gone, or she would, and this—what they'd built together—would end. She wanted to grasp the *now* of it fast in her hands, but she could no more hold it than she could hold smoke or starlight. Oh, time—bittersweet in passing, and yet caught here between them like a perfect round of crystal—beautiful, fragile and gone even as it happened.

He was looking at her oddly, as if she was something both precious and puzzling to him.

"What is it, Casey?"

"Ye remember on the day that we married, what Father Terry said about cherishin' one another?"

"Of course I do," she said softly.

He held out one hand to her. "Come to bed with me, an' allow me to do a bit of that cherishin' right now."

She might have said no, that it could wait until later when she'd finished the twenty things which still needed doing before she could go to sleep, but in truth she needed him more than she needed to wash clothes, make bread or mend Conor's good Sunday trousers—which he'd taken the knees out of yet again. And so she took his hand, and followed him up the stairs, feeling as weightless as a ghost, and yet heavy with the toll of the day.

He led her to the bed, his hand warm and reassuring in its strength. She sat, all the starch gone from her body quite suddenly, and the drifting sensation of exhaustion taking her over. Outside the rain still poured down, the sound of it muffled against the bulk of the walls.

Casey lit the bedroom fire, which had been left ready with kindling and paper. It caught at once, and lent a soft glow to the room. He moved up behind her, and she shivered in anticipation of his touch. Her blouse was unbuttoned, and he slid it down her arms, where it puddled on the bed in a fine heap of linen. She unsnapped her bra and let it fall as well, relieved to be rid of it for the day. His hands came around and cupped her breasts, and she sighed with relief at his touch. Her entire body was extra sensitive with all the heightened sensations of pregnancy, and Casey's hands were the balm she needed.

"Ye glow in the firelight, Jewel, like something made from ivory."

He kissed her shoulder, his lips so light that she shivered at the touch. Then he kissed his way up the side of her neck, his fingers gathering up her hair so that her neck and shoulders were bare to him. The day began to melt from her, as sensation heated both flesh and blood, following the path of Casey's hands and lips.

The sheets were warm as he laid her down, his eyes keeping faith with hers, as he followed her into the bed.

"I need you now," she said, and she knew he understood the sense of her words for he moved over her, his mouth touching hers, softly and yet with need of his own. Her exhaustion began to melt away as he moved inside her with a sigh of relief.

Time suspended itself for a brief space, for there was only this—the connection of their two bodies into one flesh, the heat and life of him as he moved against her, and she met him, body rising to his touch and scent and need, and the sense of that deep and fathomless knowing, which was neither thought nor feeling, but rather something beyond, which held neither border nor limit.

After, she held him tightly, not letting him go, feeling fiercely grateful for the strength and heat of him, the thud of his pulse and warmth of his breath. For the aliveness of him between her two hands. And for a moment she felt guilty that she was here, safe and warm in Casey's arms, with the sound of the fire snapping in the grate and the wind howling around the eaves. In a prison room in Belfast, Pru was alone in her marriage bed, and Ambrose was dying in his.

Casey turned onto his back and put out one arm. She snuggled into his side, and he wrapped the arm around her. It was peaceful, the world outside kept at bay by the thick walls and the sanctuary of their bed. She felt Casey fall into sleep, though his arm still held her close, protecting her from the vagaries of the world beyond these walls. Sleep took a little time in coming, despite the weariness which had left her feeling oddly weightless and like she might drift off the bed and float out the window.

Seen through a haze of exhaustion, the entire room was edged in mist. The fire reflected in the window looked like a candle, flickering inside a lantern, held aloft by a wayfarer in the night. She found herself mesmerized by the flame's reflection, even as her eyes grew heavy and she started the slow sinking down into the mattress which presaged unconsciousness.

In one of those floating dreams that came just before sleep, she saw the wayfarer—one from a tale told long ago, in a house by the sea, walking the country lanes in the night, shoes full of holes and with years of wandering imprinted upon his face. Around his lantern, fluttered a dozen moths, translucent as powdered pearl. And buoyed in that sea of floating dream, she felt the roots of the wayfarer, deep in the land, and the ancient sunsets and storms which still lived in his memory. She knew his long walking and felt the restlessness which had tried all paths, known all horrors, felt all betrayals. Still in that drifting of consciousness she wondered if this was the reaper, and he had come seeking for one of his flock, or to acknowledge that one had been taken. And just before sleep claimed her for its own, she looked into the wayfarer's eyes, which were as green as the spring sea, and the little light, still surrounded by wraith-pale moths, flickered once, twice and then went out, leaving only a wisp of smoke behind.

Chapter Sixty-five

The Ghost of Future Present

AMBROSE DIED THREE DAYS after the wedding. Three days—such a narrow sliver of time and yet it was the divide between life and death, between hope and a sorrow that was never truly going to leave the hearts of those who had loved him. The strike would grind on, with every death generating less in the way of headlines, and causing less sorrow, less pain except for those who loved each young man who went into that dark breach. Even if the British acceded to any of the demands, it was too late. For Pru and Abby, it was too late. For every person who had loved that tender boy with his poet's heart, it was too late. For a country whose heart was entirely broken, it was too late.

For such a pyrrhic sacrifice to end so quietly, was in the words of Father Jim, quoting Eliot in his despair at the terrible waste of these young lives—'*This is the way the world ends, not with a bang but with a whimper.*'

The British government, of course, did not care and remained smug and self-righteous in the wake of each death. In their refusal to look at their own history, their meddling in Ireland, the brute force often used and the murders committed in their name, or by their hand, they remained in their ivory tower of assurance in their own nobility and their belief in the justness with which they had dealt with those difficult ruffians over the sea. They simply didn't understand, but then they never had. They had conceded nothing, and they had learned nothing, and did not yet see that even victory, when hollow, has a terribly high cost.

For the strikers it had been and was about something far more than the clothing they wore, or the privileges they were allowed. It was about eight hundred years of frustration and anger, of heartbreak and bloodshed, of trying in the most extreme way to make the other understand what they had done, the injustice which was graven on the hearts of the Irish in the North of Ireland—a country which was both theirs and not theirs at all.

Life in the North of Ireland, inexorable and merciless, went on, caring little for the broken hearts and lives in her wake.

They had all gone up to Belfast for the funeral. Ambrose's mother had him laid out in her parlour for the wake, his thin sensitive face given colour by the undertaker's brush. The effect was garish, and Pamela had wished it a sight that could be unseen. She did not want to remember him this way, and the strange look of him had almost put Pru on her knees.

Pru had come home with them directly after the funeral, and retreated with her baby and her grief to her bedroom. She emerged for meals, pale, red-eyed and speaking very few words. Two weeks had passed since then.

Pamela worried about her, but also knew that Pru had the one thing she needed to keep her grounded, and that was wee Abby. Still, worry for the girl often kept her awake into the wee hours. Casey sometimes was awake with her, and they would talk into the dawn about Ambrose and Pru, and also about other things—the children, the garden, the stitches Conor's knee had required after he fell out of a tree, and the other more transitory things about the day and week, which would be forgotten come morning.

This night, however, Casey was deeply asleep, and she wanted to leave him that way, for he'd had a long day of working on the community centre he was building, and he had fallen asleep shortly after dinner. So, she slid out from the blankets and made her way downstairs, thinking that a cup of cat-mint tea and maybe a few pages of a book would make her drowsy enough to salvage a couple of hours of the night in rest. The baby, due within the next week, was restless as well, kicking and turning like a prize circus performer.

When she entered the kitchen though, it was to find Pru standing, still as a ghost, looking out the windows into the dark. It was the deep of night but there was a waning moon hovering amongst the branches of the beech tree which guarded the right half of the house, like a candle burned down and guttering a little.

A feeling of utter helplessness swept over her, a feeling she had experienced often in these last few months—a helplessness in the face of events in progress that couldn't be stopped or staved off. Pru was going to have to grieve and other than a warm pair of arms to hold her while she cried, or someone for the girl to talk to should she come to it, there wasn't a bloody thing she could do for her.

She went to stand beside the girl, wishing she could pour comfort into her like it was no more than a cup of tea or a tincture made expressly for profound grief.

"Do you need anything?" she asked.

"Just my daughter's father," Pru said, and Pamela saw that her face was streaked silver with tears.

There was nothing she could say to this; she wished it too, that somehow the clock could be turned back and Ambrose would never have encountered that roadblock, nor been put into a situation where his choice was kill or be killed. She wished that they could all undo the damage done by the vicious vagaries of life in the North, and that this girl was in school now becoming whatever it was she was meant to become before the blood cycle of Ulster had swept her up in its unforgiving tide.

"Ciara's moving to London. She told me at the funeral. She asked me if Abby and I want to come with her."

"Are you thinking about going?" Pamela asked, feeling a sharp pang of loss just at the thought of this girl leaving, and taking that wee mite with Ambrose's ears into the stews of London. One day, of course, Pru would leave but she had hoped it wouldn't be this soon.

"No, I—I'd like to stay here with you and Casey and the children, if you don't mind too much. I feel safe here, and able to manage with Abby."

"Mind? We love you Pru, we love Abby too. You can stay for the rest of your lives if you want to. You know Casey's putting an extension on the cottage for the two of you, in case you find you want a bit more privacy in the coming months. You'll miss Ciara, though."

"Yes, I will, but things have changed so much, Pamela. She's a smart girl, she'll get on with her life and leave all this—these last few years—behind. She's not like me, a great fool for love."

"You're not a fool, Pru. He loved you too."

"That's the thing though, isn't it? He loved me, past tense. I love him, and it's always going to be present tense. Oh, Pamela," she said voice suddenly fierce, "I feel like I'm burning from the inside out. I'm so mad at him. And yet, there are things you know in your bones, certain truths that go so deep you can't even give words to them. This is what I know; I'll never love anyone again the way I love Ambrose. This is it for me, Pamela. I'm twenty-one, I'm a mother and the love of my life has just starved himself to death for reasons I can't fathom. Abby will never know her father, because in the end her father loved an idea more than his own flesh and blood."

"Oh Pru, I'm so sorry," she said, knowing how ineffectual the words were, and yet having to say them all the same. It was only a tiny light in the maelstrom, but it was light all the same. "I know how small those words sound, and how tired you must be of hearing them."

"I don't mind when you say it. You understand," Pru said, turning from the window. "You did lose the love of your life for three whole years, and you'd no reason to think him alive. You were a bit like a ghost, Pamela."

Pru was right, she had been like a ghost, for she'd felt only half alive, and as though she had been transparent most days, and there had been nothing—neither barrier nor boundary—to keep the pain of the world at bay. She remembered only too well what it was to feel like you existed in parts, but never in full. There were moments though, like three bittersweet days in Paris, when she had felt whole—a different kind of whole than she'd had with Casey, but still, whole. But she couldn't talk of Jamie to this girl, who loved both men, and was fiercely loyal to each.

"It won't ever go away, Pru. I won't lie to you and say that it will, but one day you'll realize you're breathing without having to think about it, and you'll remember the love and not just the darkness."

"Right now," Pru said, and her voice was low and fierce, "right now I hate him."

Pamela did not reply, for she understood all too well how Pru felt and knew there were no words to use as anodyne. And so she simply held the girl, knowing how helpless they both were against the blood tide which rose and rose again to take the young in this country.

One day, there might be another man, but it wasn't something she could say to the girl right now, in part because it would be sacrilege to do so and in part because she suspected Pru was right, there would never be another whom she loved as she did Ambrose. Love another man—someday yes, but it would be a pale flame compared to what she'd experienced, and the man would be likely to know it.

"You're chilled to the bone," Pamela said at last, letting the girl go and fetching a shawl from the chair by the hearth. She wrapped it around Pru and then held out a handkerchief. Pru gave her a watery smile and accepted the handkerchief, mopping her face with the starchy white linen.

"Now, we either tuck you back into bed with a hot gin jar, or I'll make you a cup of tea and we can sit up for a bit."

"I'll take a cup of tea. I don't want to go back to bed just yet."

"Sit down, then. I'll get the tea made and maybe you could eat a bite?"

"I—yes, I am hungry actually," Pru said in a slightly shocked tone, as if she'd never thought she would regain her appetite.

"So am I," Pamela said, setting the tea to steep and then getting the eggs from the larder.

It felt absurdly normal to be up cooking eggs, sausage and wholemeal toast in the wee hours of the night. It was the first few moments which had felt normal since Ambrose had gone on the strike. And yet, it wasn't normal, certainly not for Pru, and in many ways for them as well. The Hunger Strike had changed the entire country in ways both too large and too small to understand just yet. Ambrose's death had changed their family too, for a sorrow had touched them from which she did not think they would ever entirely recover. For Pru the touch of this sorrow went far deeper, and she mourned that too—for the girl Pru once was and the woman she would never quite become because of losing Ambrose.

She took the food and tea to the table, and sat, shifting her legs to accommodate her belly. The baby was quiet now, and must be asleep, for which she was grateful.

She poured out the tea, and then looked up to see that Pru's fist was so tight around her mug, that Pamela half-expected it to shatter in the girl's palm. The blue eyes looked fixedly at the table-top, and Pamela knew it was because she found it hard to look anyone in the eyes and keep her composure just yet.

"Do you understand why he did it?" she asked, her voice so low it was hardly more than a whisper. Pamela slid the plate of food she'd made for her, across the table, but she felt certain Pru's appetite had once again left her.

She looked at the food on her own plate, feeling a sudden rush of nausea. She shook her head. "In theory maybe I can understand a little, but in practice, no, I can't. That may be my own lack though, and not reflect on the soundness of what they've done."

"I want to understand," Pru said. "I don't want to feel so angry with him but I just can't get to that place where any of it makes sense. Maybe I can't understand it because I'm from away, just as you are."

"There's something to that, certainly, but in truth we're all bound by our own mythology," Pamela said softly. "You and I are bound by the America that exists only in our hearts, which isn't truly reflective of what America is in reality—it can't be because every person's experience is so different, and what is a country if not its people and their stories? Just as we're bound by those stories, so are our men by their mythology."

"And what myth is grand enough," Pru asked, "to make it worth the dying?"

Pamela knew it was a real question and she wanted to give it a real answer, yet she knew anything she could say at this point would be inadequate.

"Every country has a mythology which seems worth dying for, only we decide how much we believe in that story. Some stories are worth dying for, and some are not. Each person makes that choice in their heart."

"Then tell me what story Ambrose told himself to make it worth never seeing the face of his child again? Tell me that, Pamela," she said, blue eyes dense with feeling, and once again filled with tears.

"It's one we can never truly understand because it's not made of things which can be touched, other than maybe the land itself. Myths are always strange things because they aren't ever told the same way twice. They are complicated too; you'd have to live in another man's skin to truly understand what his country's myths means to him. I understand Casey's a little because I've been with him a long time."

"And what is his?"

"Blood—that of his family, and a belief that a person must be able to control his own destiny, that's it's an inherent right as a human. I think for him it's about the world he wants to leave behind for his children, and it's the land itself. He's connected to the earth in ways most people simply aren't, so his love of this particular island goes right to the core of who he is. And in a larger sense he grew up in a community which had that mythology at its very core—that of patriot ghosts and the idea that if violence didn't achieve the aims of that core group, the shedding of one's own blood just might. It's the twice-born god myth—that the sacrifice of one might save the many. In religion, of course, what's reborn is faith; when it's a country, what's reborn is its own identity and that of its people. Their roots are revived and they enter some sort of ideal society, which for most people here just means getting on with an ordinary sort of existence."

"Don't we women get to have a mythology or some sort of heroic destiny?" Pru asked. "I mean, do you have one? What story would you give your very breath for?"

"Yes, I have one. It's the story I created with Casey, and with Jamie too. It's the people I share my life and love with. My children, my husband, my family and friends—that's the only story I know worth dying for."

Pru nodded, the gilt of her tears still shimmering over the round of her cheeks.

"Not to mention, we women have to be more realistic, don't we? We have children to raise after all."

As though in response to this statement, Abby let out a cry, which would soon, they both knew, become a howl. Responding to the most primal pull of all, Pru left the table and disappeared into the glowing rectangle of light spilling from her bedroom door.

Pamela sat for a little time, the quiet of the house folding around her, only the soft murmur of Pru talking to Abby and the warm rumble of the Aga disturbing the great still of the night.

What she had told Pru was the truth, that myth played its part in this blood cycle that Northern Ireland washed itself in repeatedly, but there was also something about the Irish spirit which lent itself to the grand romance of an impossible cause. The men who had given everything to that cause had understood better than any the impossibility of what they were attempting to achieve. Those men had known, and yet had felt it worth the sacrifice, to say something larger than even the cost of the beats of their hearts and the breath in their lungs.

There were things that she understood about the impossibilities. To give in to the strikers' demands would require something Britain simply wasn't capable of—to admit that it was—through imperial arrogance and a deeply ingrained belief in its own innate superiority—partly responsible for the bloodshed and violence which had spanned hundreds of years. To support the aims of the strike, the Republic would have to come to terms with its own apathy regarding the wee troubled corner of the island, and admit they'd both abandoned and failed their own people. Northern Ireland itself would need to let go of its old myths—the one of blood sacrifice providing the alchemical magic which would set free a country, and its entrenched belief in its own victimhood, one that made it a country apart, and special, even if only to its people. It wasn't going to happen right away, and in fact, she suspected, was likely to take years.

It might even mean letting go the Ireland of legend, the Ireland that never was but lived only in men's hearts. The country that bred heroes to last the ages, and music and poetry to break the world's heart. The country with freedom as part of its very fibre so that nothing less could ever satisfy the appetite for it.

It was time to go back to bed and see if she couldn't get a little more sleep before her household was up and at their energetic lives. She wanted Casey's warmth and just the feel of him next to her, reassuring her that life could roll forward on a continuum that was something like normal. Before she joined him, though, she checked on the children. She never could return to her bed without doing so. There was always the mother's fear that something might have happened in the hours since the children had gone to sleep, that something might have crept in under doorsills and over window casements to steal away that which was most precious.

Isabelle and Kathleen faced each other in their shared bed, both deeply, profoundly asleep. Isabelle's hair was a mad cloud about her face, spilling across the pillow in curly abandonment. Kathleen a lick of flame and flower, her skin opalescent where the moon touched it, and her hair a living coruscation of fire. Her beautiful babies, growing so quickly, changing, it seemed, even as she looked at them now. *The horologist steals whether we will it or no.*

Conor's room was across the hall. He was asleep on his stomach, legs asprawl—long legs, he was going to be at least as tall as his father—and Finbar was curled up alongside him, his great brown eyes shining through the dark as he watched her. She touched Conor's head lightly, the silk of his curls warm beneath her hand. His hair felt a little gritty; she ought to have made him bathe this evening, but the routines of normal life had been upset these last weeks, and Conor—who saw bathing as a waste of good play time—was wont to take any chance of skipping out on the whole procedure. Time enough for it tomorrow, she supposed, and leaned down to kiss his cheek. It hurt sometimes to look at him, to see how quickly time was moving and how her tiny son was now an unruly, sensitive and whip-smart boy, who before too long, would be a young man. To love a child was to know the pain of that particular emotion, the pain of being fully alive because part of yourself was now away from you, with that space only growing as the years passed.

In her own room, she put another chunk of peat on the fire and then slid into the bed beside Casey. For a time, she simply lay, listening to the sound of his breathing, and the comforting hiss of the fire. She rested one hand over the round of her belly, and felt the occupant roll over, the strange rippling that shifted a woman's entire body, and was sometimes a tad uncomfortable, and yet as inexorable and wondrous as life always was.

This wee being, who would soon join them, was the next chapter in their book, a few more lines in the blood and gold ink of life, an addition to this long and winding tale of love and existence. And for a moment it was as though an actual book hung before her eyes, bound in dark and light, telling of a long unfolding of years. It seemed that she might read all of it—if she so chose—in that moment, and know the joy and the sorrow which must come. For this fact alone, she closed the book in her mind, losing sight of it with small regret, certain in the knowledge that—given the choice—she didn't want to know the story before its time.

Chapter Sixty-six

Ranunculus and Ruthlessness
August 1981

TOMAS, AWAITING HIS final appointment of the day, and wondering why Miss Mundy had yet to show the man in, went out to reception to see if said appointment had been cancelled, only to find his client perched on the edge of Miss Mundy's desk. Miss Mundy, neat as a pin and formidable in a periwinkle twinset and pearls, was fussily arranging a bouquet of pink and white tulips, starred with a drift of frowsy-headed ranunculus. Miss Mundy was also flushed and flustered, something which only ever occurred with this particular client. Tomas rolled his eyes, and the man grinned in response.

"Do come in, James. If it's not too much trouble, Miss Mundy, some tea please."

"No, it's no trouble at all," she said, all but dimpling at Jamie, who gave her one of his loveliest smiles, before hopping off the edge of her desk, and following Tomas into his office.

"I wasn't aware the woman could blush," Tomas said. "She gets utterly twitterpated any time ye grace us with yer presence, though. I'll not get any decent work out of her for the rest of the day."

"As it's nearly five o'clock," Jamie said drily, "I think you'll survive the loss."

He sat down, unbuttoning the coat he wore. Despite the advanced hour of the day his shirt was crisp, his trousers uncreased and his shoes polished to a dark gleam. There were times, Tomas thought, attempting to surreptitiously straighten his own tie, when the man's sartorial elegance was a tad annoying.

"I thought you were going out west this week?"

"I am. I'm heading out there tomorrow to pick up the children and take them to Cork for a few days. Kolya has been with the Riordans for the last week. When school goes back in, he's in for a rude shock being that he won't be able to live part-time with them any longer."

Tomas sometimes itched to ask him just what the parameters of their shared family life was—the three of them and their various children. Casey and Pamela were, however, just as circumspect as Jamie, and so he had no idea what feelings might simmer beneath the surface of their seemingly genial arrangement.

They chatted of light things—the weather, they were having an un-precedented streak of fine days; the opera Tomas had taken Deirdre to see in London the week before; the new Aga cooker that Casey was currently fitting in Tomas' house—until Miss Mundy brought in the tea tray and set it down on Tomas' desk. Cynically, Tomas noted that the tray was loaded with homemade goodies, something she only bothered to do for her favourite cli-ent—which was to say, James Kirkpatrick.

"Take a cup, man an' tell me what I've done to deserve this visit."

Jamie took his tea, squeezed a bit of lemon into it and leaned back, cup in hand.

"I have papers I'd like to leave with you. They detail where Julian is, at present. I have him watched so that I'm aware of his movements, but I think it's wise to have someone else know too." Jamie pushed a heavy envelope across the desk to Tomas. "Put it in your safe and leave it there, until it's needed."

"An' how will I know when it's needed?"

"If Julian returns, then you will know I failed. Should that day arrive, the necessary measures which will need to be taken, are outlined in the papers I've given you."

"Ye've not said what happened, but as Casey an' yerself allowed Pamela and the children to return home, I figured you must have dealt with the prob-lem in a way you felt adequate to the danger posed by Julian."

"Adequate? The only thing adequate to the danger would have been to kill him. As it turns out I was too weak to do that."

"It would have damaged you beyond repair, James, so be glad you couldn't bring yourself to do it."

"The only measures I have managed to take are somewhat inadequate. If he steps foot in this country, or the Republic, Intelligence will alert me. Still, he has resources, and I think is disturbed enough to possibly try it one day."

"Ye see no other recourse?"

"Unfortunately, no. It is my word against that of a young man whose father is the right hand of Thatcher's cabinet secretary. His father has been tapped as the rising star of the Tory Party, and may well be the next PM after Thatcher finishes her reign. If he can keep his wife's double agent status quiet, that is."

"So no police?"

Jamie shook his head. "No fingerprints, no traces of Julian left behind, no record of him traveling to and from Belfast that night. All I have is a confession without a recording. The police did their due diligence on this, I'll give them that, though I'm certain I'd be in the frame if I wasn't able to prove I was nowhere near the country that night. Julian is now in a place that has no extradition treaty with Britain. Also, an investigation and trial would be likely to open other worm cans, things which would be costly to Casey and Pamela and possibly myself as well. Not the least of which is that I harboured a double agent inside my own home. Do you see the quandary? It was kill him or nothing."

"That night—did he say why—why Casey, why Violet?"

Jamie paused, something like grief rippling over his face, and Tomas got a glimpse of what that meeting with Julian must have been like. He wondered if anyone outside of Jamie and Julian would ever truly know what had happened between them. He thought, perhaps, Casey knew more than most, but he didn't speak of it either.

"The why won't ever make sense to you or me, Tomas. But it appears he thought he was removing obstacles to my happiness. With Casey, at least that seemed to be the thinking. Violet, he said, was an accident. They got into an argument and things escalated. I'm not sure how much I believe of that, being that her throat was cut nearly to the bone. He asked me that night in Paris, why I wasn't grateful to him because if it wasn't for him, I would not have Kathleen."

There was, Tomas reflected, a dark truth to that statement, and for a mind such as that which Julian possessed, it made a horrible sort of sense.

Jamie placed his teacup back on the tray, and took another of the shortbread biscuits. "I have a second matter to put before you. We've discussed Detective Holroyd before. Things have come to a place where I felt he and the threat he poses, need to be addressed. What I want from you is simply to tell Pamela that the threat to her is gone. Don't bring me into it, however. Just tell her he's been sent back to London, and is no longer a worry. It's as much as she needs to know."

"Dare I ask the reason ye can't tell her this yerself?"

Jamie smiled. "It would be, shall we say, less fraught, if you were to tell her you'd dealt with the threat."

"Ah, I see," Tomas said, helping himself to a dollop of cream and a scone. "By which you mean you don't want her knowin' in what manner the threat was removed, nor, clearly, by whom."

"No, I don't. We both know, Tomas, that she's finally settled and happy. I don't want anything ruffling the waters for her, but I should like to take away this last worry."

"I agree. Now how do ye propose we go about makin' that happen?"

"Tell her it's been dealt with, that she needn't fear him anymore. It came to my attention recently, that some time back he gave her a choice, about just which one of us he would throw on the whimsical mercy of justice in this country."

"And being Pamela, she chose herself."

"Indeed, she did."

"Have you offered yourself in replacement?" Tomas asked.

"Not as such, no. Suffice it to say I've sent him sniffing down another pathway."

"What if one day he comes for you?"

Jamie shrugged. "I suppose it will be no more than I deserve. If it keeps Pamela from throwing herself on the fire, then it's worth whatever may happen. There's a man as well—a bit of a loose end—someone Noah hired to occasionally do his wet work for him. He's an ex-soldier, and you'll find his name in those papers too. He's a mercenary and so his morals are questionable at best. Holroyd did manage to track him down at one point, but he moved on before the good detective arrived on his doorstep. I think I've managed to persuade him that financial reward is more likely with me than with a man on police wages."

"James, I don't mind tellin' ye, I don't like this at all. It sounds a bit too self-sacrificial. I think we've all had enough of that of late, no? I will say, though, it's very Catholic of ye to choose this route."

Jamie merely raised one gull-winged eyebrow at him. "Will you tell her or not?"

Tomas sighed. "Yes, of course I'll do it. She's likely to put up less of a fuss if she thinks I interfered, rather than her realizin' it's a case of you puttin' yer neck under the guillotine blade."

"It's not inevitable that I'll get my head chopped off. I still have friends in Intelligence, and I think if we can get the detective rerouted and back onto his career path, this may simply die a natural death. He will be more than happy to leave this country behind. His refusal to understand how justice works here, would have proved his undoing eventually. He's more likely to live a long and fruitful life if we send him back to London. That point will be pressed home to him in no small degree."

Tomas, who had lived in Belfast most of his life, understood the deeper meaning of Jamie's words. In a city of ruthless men, this man had honed the edge of that particular knife in a way Tomas had only encountered a time or two in his life. He was extremely fond of Jamie, but had often thought he wouldn't care to fall on his bad side.

It was how he thought of Jamie—as a damascene blade, one wrought in silver and gold, brilliant and blinding, though at other times dark and dulled with blood. Often, though perhaps less often of late, it felt as though the man had an electric current running along that edge, a sort of wild vibrancy and enchantment that ordinary mortals rarely, if ever, experienced. He both envied and pitied him that very quality. For, in this particular case, the blade was always more likely to cut the bearer.

"And Julian—how will you manage that threat? As ye say he has resources and the help of a woman who hates you."

Even as he asked the question, the incongruity of it all struck him, for here they sat amidst the detritus of tea time; delicate bone china, biscuit crumbs, the remnants of clotted cream and the scent of an oolong brew Jamie had gifted Miss Mundy, after his last trip to Hong Kong. Incongruous, because they spoke of blood and violence, and men who also drank tea, ate biscuits, made chat and plotted pain for others whilst doing so. It was, in part, the way of the world, and had been for a very long time. This, of course, was of little comfort.

"I live my life, and some small part of me waits. I know it is possible that one day he will come for me again. He will either kill me, or I will have to kill him. I've failed at it once; that will be his weapon now. In the meantime, I intend to raise my children and keep them safe. I will not have it touch Pamela and her family."

"I fear for ye, James. Ye've left yerself vulnerable here, an' ye know it."

"That is my fault and therefore my responsibility. If I falter in the latter, those papers are in part a fail-safe. There are names in there, men who will complete the work if I am unable to finish it myself. You understand?"

"Aye, I understand," Tomas sighed. "I understand, but I don't like it one little bit."

"I don't require you to like it," Jamie said smoothly, "only to carry out the instructions therein, should it become necessary. Now, you old curmudgeon, let me buy you dinner. I know Deirdre's visiting Casey and Pamela, so you haven't a reason to say no."

"Oh, aye, I'll not pass on a free meal. Just let me tidy things away here, an' I'll join ye out front. I'm sure Miss Mundy will want to say goodbye to ye, after all."

Jamie rose, brushing down the front of his shirt, though there was nary a crumb to be seen on the crisp poplin, and then, placing his coat over his forearm, exited down the hall.

Tomas looked in the tiny mirror behind his office door, readjusting his tie yet again, and brushing down the shoulders of his coat. He could hear Jamie chatting with Miss Mundy and, heaven forfend, inviting the woman to dinner with them.

Ruthless this man might be but still it worried him—this situation with Julian, because while Jamie tended to look after those he loved with great commitment, he exercised very little care when it came to himself. Julian had, figuratively speaking, tasted Jamie's blood now, and Tomas thought it likely once the boy realized how much he liked the flavour, he'd be back for more. Please God, that when and if that time came, Jamie could do what must be done. Otherwise, it was going to be down to an old reformed alcoholic barrister. Still, this mad bunch was his family now, and he would do what was necessary to protect the lot of them; he just prayed the necessity of it would not arise.

After dinner, Jamie and Tomas parted ways, Tomas to go home, and Jamie to the house which had been violated in such a way over these last few years, that he wondered if it would ever again feel truly like his home. He stopped halfway up the hill, near a set of old gates that led to a winding track, at the end of which was the old gamekeeper's cottage.

As a child, he'd played in and around the cottage a great deal, and sometimes he and his grandfather would go there when the weather was warm and camp out for the night. Sometimes, his father had joined them too. It was still a place he liked to go on fine nights, simply to think and sometimes to camp with his children.

Tonight, under a half-moon, the old place looked haunted by times long gone, and people who'd once lived under its thatched roof. Moss furred the stones here and there, and the chimney rose aslant in the light of the late summer moon—the Moon of Dispute, the Celts had called it.

There was a low wall in front of the cottage, and sitting on it gave him a view down through a tumble of oak and beech, where a stream glinted silver as a knife through the tangle of trunk and bough.

The night was warm, but there was a thread in it which spoke of chilly days, smoking leaf fires, warm sweaters, and long nights when folk hunkered down, told stories, made drawings and dreams, conjured birds from wood, and wolves from stone.

School would resume in a couple of weeks. Kolya would be in year three at his primary school. It would only be another year before Kathleen went off as well, and while the local Catholic school her brother and sister attended would suffice for now, he knew eventually he and Pamela would have to decide just where and how she would be educated. That his tiny daughter would begin that next phase of her life so soon, saddened him a little. Life rolled on, even when young men starved to death on the king's threshold, and young girls were widowed in the bloom of their youth.

He did not think he would ever forgive himself for bringing Pru here, and all that had resulted from that. And yet, it was utter hubris—which the gods always delighted in punishing—that made a man think he could keep others safe, and yet it had to be tried, even if it was a fool's game. Tomas' statement from their conversation earlier in the day came back to him now.

"Ye've not said what happened, but as Casey an' yerself allowed Pamela and the children to return home, I figured you must have dealt with the problem in a way you felt adequate to the danger posed by Julian."

He had replied honestly, in the full knowledge that the only thing that would truly end the situation was Julian's death. Nothing else would ever satisfy him, and the hunger he carried was always going to hurt others, if not outright take their lives. It was why Jamie had offered his own life in exchange that night, thinking that might be enough, might fill the gaping hole the boy carried with him.

Parts of that night were still a blur, and there had been a hope, just a narrow one, that the electroshock therapy might take it away entirely. He was not so fortunate, however.

Casey's call that day had found him at the distillery, and he had left for home directly, fearing for both Maggie and his grandmother. Kolya's safety he had ascertained immediately, and had directed the woman caring for him to take him to the convent where Colleen would be expecting him. Casey would look after Pamela and the children, and so he needn't fear for them. They had arranged this between them months before, knowing a threat hung over both their heads, a sword which might fall at any time.

His house was empty when he arrived, and apparently undisturbed. Or so he had thought before he entered his study. There it became clear that Julian had been and was now gone. The fire still glowed in the hearth, the smoldering coals consuming the last of what had been thrown upon it, so that he could still make out the last two words on the cover—*of Heartbreak*. Pamela's gift to him, which had been in the safe. Within the ashes were the remains; seed pearls, twists of wire, ribbon, and stone; the head of a white deer; the crumbled remains of a tower, which stirred on the air, as he approached, and collapsed into ash.

There were books all over the floor, some with pages ripped out, and his grandfather's chair had been cut open, shredded with a knife, revealing a hate that knew no boundaries. It had been his favourite chair, and he wondered how it was Julian had known that. A lamp had been smashed upon the floor, and tiny crystals shone like diamond amongst the wreckage of paper and ink.

"Oh, Julian," he said to the air around him. The boy was no longer here, and so he would have to follow. The map had been left for him, though, clearly marked. For sitting on his desk, with the lamp shining directly onto it, had been the miniature of Montmartre, torn from the pages of the book, but strangely not destroyed as the rest of it had been. He had understood then, just where it was Julian waited. It had made a horrible sort of sense too—to defile yet another of the places Jamie loved best. And so, later that night, after he had ascertained the safety of Maggie and his grandmother, he had gone to Paris, where his murderous son waited for him.

The streets of Montmartre were quiet, for the hour was late. The house too was quiet. Madame Felice was currently on a retreat at a convent in Italy, for which he was very grateful. Otherwise, he feared, she might well be dead right now.

He entered, and stood for a moment—listening, assessing. A dim light filtered through the stained glass window over the chair beside the hearth. The window had been commissioned by his grandfather and showed a scene of a snow-capped mountain with a single tree atop it. It was just the sort of minimalistic art his grandfather had often loved, though he'd always suspected this particular piece had a significance to it which had to do with Yevgena.

Upstairs then, for there was no movement from the kitchen—though it was there he found a broken window, explaining the boy's entry—then the pantry and the halls. The spiral of the stairs, and then the long narrow passage, a line of light there under one door—his bedroom, of course, for the boy had blighted every room which was sacred, where repose or love had been sought and found.

Jamie took a breath, and put his hand to the door knob, turned it and went in. The only light was a fire in the hearth, casting a dim glow over objects: the old high bed with its curtains drawn, the marquetry wardrobe with faded-paint roses on its doors, the antique lamps with their crystals catching and reflecting the low-burning fire.

On the bed was a girl—dark-haired, skin as white as a petal—this flower bruised on arms and legs, with a delicate stippling of blue under one brown eye. He wondered briefly if green-eyed prostitutes were thin on the streets of Paris this night, for he understood why this one had been chosen. Her bruises were old, and so not ones Julian had given her. Still, she looked afraid.

Beside her, his son. The one he had failed from the start, by a complete ignorance of his very existence. A long body, lean, well-made, chestnut hair with a gleam of red in it, and sapphire eyes, resting now upon Jamie's face, with a sort of petulant satisfaction. He looked again to the girl. She must go, it was imperative she not be used as a weapon.

Julian spoke then. "She's a prostitute, the dirtiest one I could find. This is the bed where you brought your whore, no?"

"I suggest you get your clothes, and go," Jamie said to the girl, who as well as being clearly frightened, looked frightfully young. There was no point in dignifying Julian's words with a response. His words could not touch Pamela, and were only meant to antagonize.

The girl scrambled from the bed, sheet clutched to her chest, and Jamie left the room. When she emerged, clothed, he escorted her downstairs, tucked a fold of francs into her pocket and told her to go as quickly as she could. Then he simply said, "I'm sorry, this has nothing to do with you, but the hurt has, unfortunately, fallen upon you as well."

Up the stairs again, his legs leaden with exhaustion—when had he last slept more than a few minutes? He was too tired for this, his mind in that ashy state where nothing connected to nothing, and so things did not make sense, action did not lead to consequence, words did not have meaning. And yet, there was no choosing of the time, and perhaps it was best this way, it might well be easier in the end.

Julian was sitting up now and had pants on. He gestured to the bed behind him—the rumpled coil of Kirpatrick linens, the dent in the pillow where the girl's head had lain, the dark blue quilt thrown back and sliding to the floor.

"You had your whore here, and I had mine."

Jamie merely looked at him. For while the sheets were soiled, and the air permeated with the scent of a loveless coupling, it would not do what Julian had hoped. He didn't understand that what had been created here during those three days could not be destroyed by something so simple as a different woman in the bed, because what had happened here had existed beyond the bounds of both time and space. It would always be a place inviolate, because it had been made of the truth between two people. None of which were things this young man would ever understand.

"Does that bother you?" Julian asked.

When he spoke his voice was flat with exhaustion. "Not particularly. I think we are far past the time of games, Julian. Tell me what you want. Tell me what I can give you that will make you stop hurting those I love. For the love of Christ, tell me and let's be done with this madness."

For what felt like a long time, the boy merely looked at him, and Jamie took him in: the finely grained skin, still with the clear and glowing density of youth; the eyes so deeply blue they appeared black in this low, stuttering light. Beautiful hands, his grandfather's hands, his own as well. Genetics was such a strange and deep well. Julian's hands were spread on his thighs but strung tight with tension.

Pamela had long ago told Jamie that his own hands were a tell, that she watched his hands and not his face to understand his emotional state. And so it was with his son. Afraid, furious, and filled with despair of a sort that Jamie understood all too well. And yet, still, a young man with gifts, who might have had all he wanted of the world.

"Can you turn back the hourglass? Do you have that power? No? Then you cannot give me what I want."

"I did not know about you until it was far too late, Julian. The harm had long been done before the Reverend brought you to my attention. This you know."

Julian's reply was quiet, but spoken with a ferocity of tone which made clear his anger. "My mother loved you, and then she hated you and then she hated me for looking too much like you, and yet she loved me too. It was a dark love and it could never forgive me for not being like you—not gifted, not a young god, not a spendthrift poet, not a man who took hearts as though he were tearing them from the chest of an enemy, and then threw them back half-eaten. For years, I thought you were merely a bedtime story, even though she always said Neil was not my father. I thought you were a tale—young Lochinvar come from the west to destroy her; that's how she described you once."

A spurned and furious woman, seeking revenge through the medium of her son. There was no hate like that which had once been love. Long ago his grandfather had warned him about this.

"You have a talent for love, James, both the giving of it and the receiving. Be careful how you spend it, people are fragile creatures and easily hurt, you will always need to remember that."

He had tried to remember, to take care, but at times he had been profligate with those things, those gifts. He had poured it out, taken it in, and then one day, had simply stopped. It was clear to him now that he had not understood the woman to whom he had given those gifts; he had not understood her at all. Some love burned like a clear, steady flame—it warmed, it sustained, it gave life. Others were made of less pure ingredients—desire disguised as something more, an intoxication which came with a terrible hangover. His affair with Diane had been the latter. For her it had clearly been something else entirely and it was to his everlasting shame that he had not recognized it at the time.

"I gave you what you wanted most—Pamela. And if the men I hired had been better at their job, you would have had her for good. I made your daughter possible. I did that for you."

It was, he thought, more damage than a parent, even one filled with resentment and hurt, might have done. It was that deep and glittering well of genetics, which so often hid demons in its depths. He too must take his share of what this young man both was and would never be.

"You love her freely, your child with Pamela, I was not so blessed."

"And yet, you might have allowed me a chance to love you, to show you another world much kinder and brighter than the one your mother showed you. But you did not. There was choice, Julian, even if only for a moment."

Julian shook his head, and the glow of red upon chestnut in his hair brought to mind his lost son, Stuart, and his living daughter, Kathleen, whose hair was like sun and fire. He saw, for Julian, built as he was, there had not been a choice. There was little use in trying to convince him otherwise.

"And Violet?" he asked.

"She was a mistake. I did not mean to kill her, but I did not regret it later, lest you think I have a touch of humanity within to appeal to—let me assure you, I do not. I had come to see you, and she argued with me, tried to make me leave the house. I think she was afraid I would harm her child. I struck her and she fell and hit her head."

"You cut her throat open, Julian. She didn't merely hit her head. That was no accident."

"She was suffering, she kept moaning and there was so much blood. She couldn't have lived. It was like putting an animal out of its misery."

A flash of fury broke through the thick dark in his head. He wanted to hit the boy, hit him hard, until his head rang with it, until his ears bled. Violet had been a human, a woman rendered helpless by the child she had sought to protect. And he had, after all, loved her once.

"You did not touch Kolya—why?"

"He is not your child. He was the woman's. He is not significant in this game of ours."

Before returning to the upstairs, Jamie had made a side trip into the kitchen to retrieve what he now held out to his son. "I am sorry, but I cannot turn back the clock. I can only offer what it is you seem to need." He stepped forward. "Here is the knife, and here is my throat. If it will set you free, you may cut it, and let me bleed to death here in this room." He opened his collar and bared his neck to the boy. This strange, angry boy who looked so like he had at the same age. This boy who carried such darkness within him. It was the only offer which might satisfy Julian, and so it must be made or this would never be finished.

The offer had startled Julian, it was clear, though he must have known this was one of the possibilities of the night. It was the shortcut out of their difficulties, but it still ended with them in the same place. The knife lay, balanced in his palm, a blood offering to a hungry young god.

"If you cannot find it in yourself to do it, the offer will not be made again."

He stood, knife in palm, feeling strangely vapourous, as though he was sat upon a boundary, and on either side was a country, neither of which he belonged to. Behind him, were his dead. Those who, if not for his presence, would still be alive: a friend with a mind of fire, who had danced near the same deep well he always had; a woman who had loved him in a cold land where one took warmth when it was offered; a gangster who'd been his blood brother; two men who had killed some part of that bright spirit he'd met one fated summer beside the sea; his sons, luminous with the water world of the womb, not fated to live aboveground.

"I see doubt in you," Julian said, "perhaps you don't want to die tonight, after all."

His grandfather's voice in his head now. Seeking comfort after his mother's death, he had asked him about what came beyond death, afraid as he had been that his mother was simply in the cold ground, with worms about to feed upon her. His beautiful light-filled mother, gone dark and silent. Gone. He had been afraid that she had just disappeared into utter darkness; even as an adult she had a nightlight on in her bedroom, and lights all down the halls, like fairy torches to guide one's way at night. The dark had terrified her.

"What if she's just lost in all that darkness?" he'd asked, sitting beside his grandfather, his fear for his mother overwhelming him. His grandfather had put his arm around him, and drawn him into the shelter of his strength.

"Oh, my beautiful boy, our eyes adjust to the dark. And beyond, out there—my God, boy, think of the stars—so much light, light you cannot even conceive of, so much you can swim in it, a great vast sea of stars."

The words were with him now, as he stood before a young man who had not known such love or shelter. If he took the offer, it would deliver Jamie to that sea of stars, which would not be so terrible, and surely must be a place of peace.

Julian spoke. "You coward, is this what you offer me? Your death? Perhaps you should kill me, if you can find the courage. One of us must go, you know it."

"No," he said wearily, "I do not know that, and I cannot give you what you ask."

Julian stood and crossed the floor. He took Jamie's outstretched hand and folded his fingers over the knife. "Is this not why you came here? To finish what I have started? You can offer up your throat, but I cannot? I have inherited your propensity for darkness, father, here I am. Look in the mirror—do you like what you see? Are you not afraid that if you do not kill me here and now when you have the chance, that I will wreak more havoc upon your life? If you don't take your chance here tonight, you will live to regret it."

There was truth in it—the reflection was there, all his darkest impulses, all his sins made flesh, brought here on this night to punish him or to bring him justice.

The blade was there in his hand, but it was here that cold logic failed him, that side of him which had embraced the knife more than once in his life, that side which had saved his skin. He could not, however, kill his son, and he knew it was likely Julian would find a way to make him regret that weakness.

He let the knife go, heard the thunk as it hit the carpet, and then Julian was on him, and they fell to the floor. He knew the full fury of his son then—the slippery and fluid muscle of youth and weight. Grappling and pushing—the instinct to survive was there, that primal call which lived in a man's core, that life *was worth any cost. Except, of course, the life of one's child. He fought because there was no other option, because it was what Julian wanted. Twisting, writhing, grappling with sinew and bone, muscles burning, hands sliding, slick with sweat, hitting out blindly, connecting with flesh which he had never been allowed to cradle, to cherish, to love.*

Body to body, the only intimacy they had ever known that of violence. Time slowed to the rhythm of blood and pain, and yet everything was a flash caught from the corner of the eye—a foot kicking the fire, coals smoldering on the rug, broken glass from a candle shade, the blue counterpane like a shimmering sea, lapping at their edges.

Julian had the knife, had pushed it into Jamie's hand, and then pulled with relentless force, inch by muscle spasming inch, until he had forced the blade against his own throat, with Jamie's hand as the lever.

He goaded him then. "This is your moment to save your daughter, the one you love so easily. Your perfect daughter gotten upon a woman you managed to love, rather than one you used and threw away."

Kill one child to save another? A question straight out of Greek tragedy, or perhaps only a very Irish one. His hand hurt as though the bones were breaking and he knew in the effort to keep the blade out of his son's flesh, he might well plunge it into his own. Their strength was equal, and so the knife stayed here, poised like the fulcrum of death that it was.

Julian's face was pressed to his now, tight as that of a lover. "Kill me, kill me, I'm begging you, kill me." It was a cry from the depths of a hell Jamie knew too intimately. It was the ill-spirit leaching every cell, the scarlet blood pulse of pain. His hand was cramping around the knife, slick with blood. His or Julian's? Perhaps it no longer mattered. The boy had brought him here tonight for death, Jamie had only been mistaken about whose death it was meant to be.

Julian raised his head and sapphire eyes looked deep into green, as night looked into the dawn. Here it was, Hopkins 'cliffs of fall,' and they, the two of them teetering there out over the void, the cliff edge crumbling. Below the deep dark well with its demons, gnashing their teeth and waiting for the tumble. The blade was turned, red blade touching his own throat now, and he felt it—the hot rush of blood. He closed his eyes on it, floating again in that vapourous place. He thought of Pamela, Kathleen and Kolya, and heard the cry of a gull in the distance. And then suddenly, the knife was gone, the weight removed, though he could still feel the blood trickling down his neck. And Julian stood, head hanging, as though deeply ashamed.

"I cannot kill you. I am my father's son, a coward to the bone."

The knife was on the floor now, bright with blood, harmless unless held. Jamie pulled himself up so he sat, back braced against the wall, his breath rasping his lungs where the boy's weight had pressed. Julian picked up the fire shovel from where it sat, and shoved it into the glowing coals, filling the scoop. He flung the coals—streaming gold and crimson sparks—across Jamie and onto the bed. The hangings caught immediately, the fire winding through the airy material, strangely beautiful even as the heat shrunk his skin in toward his bones.

He looked up, noting in a distant way, the shimmering lake of rose on the ceiling. Below him was a blossoming of blood, running from his veins, pooling in the hollow of his throat, and then slipping in a stream to the carpet. It would be so easy, so beautifully simple to let go now.

And then in all that lake of fire, a cry in the night.

'No, no, no!' An echo down a long hall in a house he had believed abandoned. A cry meant to pull him back from the edge, claw him back if necessary.

Julian stepped forward, and despite the summons from that house, that place of life and promise, Jamie knew he was too tired to rise, to fight anymore. Youth always had its advantages, and he was so very, very tired. The flat of the shovel, still warm, came down, and the roses on the ceiling exploded in blood and iron anvils of pain. Consciousness was lost, though he thought he felt a hand touch his in passing before the blackness was absolute.

When he awoke the fire was out, the windows open, and his son was gone. He moved then, sluggish, senses dulled by smoke and exhaustion, knowing he needed fresh air. Outside, the sky was like a bolt of violet damask, unrolling over chimney tops, gables, slate roofs, and dotted with casements of gold. A pre-dawn breeze ruffled his damp hair. He breathed in, and then succumbed to a fit of coughing as his lungs expelled the smoke.

He turned back to the room then. There were puddles all over the floor, and what was left of the bed curtains dripped with dirty water. Julian had put the fire out before he left. Jamie could not quite make sense of that.

He staggered down the hall, filled the bath, dunked his head in the ice-cold water until the worst of the confusion had passed. He patched himself up—the cut on his neck, still leaking bright blood, the burns on his hands, blistering now.

The fire had never grown bright enough to attract attention, for the street beyond the garden walls was quiet. The damage to the room could be repaired; the damage to his soul was likely to be another matter entirely.

Downstairs, the sitting room was chilly, but he was too tired to light a fire, though he shivered incessantly. He sat in the chair nearest the hearth. His eyes were seared with smoke and heat, his spirit as cold as the snow pictured in the stained glass window above his head.

How long he sat there, he did not know, but he thought it was just past dawn when the words engraved over the hearth, seemingly detached from the wall, unwinding like a skein of dark thread before his eyes. Exhaustion? Hallucination? There was little difference between the two at this point.

'The sunlight clasps the earth and the moonbeams kiss the sea...'

The words floated past him, ribbons and streams, bright as a penny, dull as coal. He grabbed at them, thinking to tuck them in his pocket, put them away for another day. But he had no pocket and the words dissolved in his hand, like quicksilver turned dark and contrary.

'What is all this sweet work worth, if thou kiss not me?'

What indeed? No answer came and for a moment he wished his son had had more courage.

Time passed, and still he sat, unable, it seemed, to move, to get up and decide what came next. It was full day, and the street was stirring to life when he saw more words floating in the air, coiling like smoke, round clouds of it, as though the Cheshire Cat had drawn a puff off his hookah and breathed the words out, and yet it was his grandfather's voice which spoke them at the end of that long-ago conversation. "A sea of stars is a tempting thing, and wonderful in its time, and yet, Jamie, I should like you to stay. This life is a hard thing, but it's beautiful too. Yours will have more than most, both the difficult and the beautiful parts. It would be a terrible thing to miss out on any of it."

Jamie sighed and stood up from the wall—the very wall where he'd sat with his grandfather so many times—his immaculate tailoring damp and moss-strewn. There had been one thing missing from the wreckage in his study that night, one thing which had caused him more alarm than the rest of the destruction. He had not realized it until his return home, and by then, of course, it was too late.

A tiny mermaid with a shock of red silk hair, resting on a shore of translucent shell.

Chapter Sixty-seven

Written in Water

"I HAVE COME TO banish your ghost," Yevgena said, walking with aplomb through the door of Jamie's study.

"I have a ghost?" Jamie asked, rising from his chair to greet her.

"You know you do, and it's past time to get rid of her."

"Where exactly is this ghost?" he asked, looking pointedly toward the floor, where Kathleen was playing with a motley grouping of teddy bears, dolls and what appeared to Yevgena to be sticks wrapped together with rags.

"Do not worry about her, she can see ghosts more readily than you. As to where your ghost is, you already know. She's in your bedroom."

"There is no ghost in my bedroom," Jamie said, tone swiftly becoming exasperated.

"Do you sleep in there?"

Jamie sighed. "No, I don't."

"And why is that?"

"I'm not comfortable in it, as it happens."

"I rest my case, the ghost needs banishing."

"Be my guest," Jamie said, shortly. "I'll take Kathleen outside. Come on, sweetheart," he held out a hand to his daughter, "let's go see Kolya out in the paddock."

"Can we ride Danu?" she asked, bolting up at the mention of horses.

"Yes, we can," Jamie replied, shooting Yevgena a look that clearly stated she'd best be done with whatever ritual she planned to perform in his home by the time they returned from the stable.

"It is best if I am alone," she said, though she did not think the child would be disturbed by what she was going to do. Little ones lived closer to the spirit world, and understood what was worth fearing and what was not. Still, it was likely best not to have anyone in the house to which the spirit might attempt to cling.

After the door closed behind them, she walked through the house, opening doors and windows, for the spirit must be provided with an exit. She pulled in her focus—for a Russian ghost, you said Russian prayers, you spoke Russian words, you banished with Russian spells. The language was sometimes rusty with her and she would need to speak carefully, though she found herself now in old age, thinking once again in Russian, the throaty vowels and consonants with their hard-bitten edges, bringing comfort and warmth. Today, however, she must speak it out loud, which required greater concentration, so that the woman might understand it was far past time to depart.

Sometimes, spirits were caught fast through longing, through an inability to understand that they were no longer part of the life they'd inhabited, and so they lingered. But murder was something else, it left terror behind, a dark energy which could get stuck in place, and linger for years. So one must banish the evil along with the spirit.

She watched through the long windows of the sitting room, as Jamie walked down to the stable, Kathleen at his side. Then she went to the kitchen and boiled water upon the stove in a cast iron kettle which had accompanied her on her travels for many years now. She had brought it with her today, for this very purpose. Once the water boiled, she reached into the leather pouch she kept in her pocket, and added three pinches of valerian root, three pinches of astragalus root, and three pinches of powdered thistle to the water. Over the steam of the roiling kettle, she spoke the necessary words. "I unite these three herbs; I unite them against evil and wickedness."

It was fortunate that Maggie was not here today, having gone to visit with her sister for a few days. Yevgena got along well with Maggie, but knew she would consider such things black magic, and not a simple purification of space. She had timed her visit for Maggie's absence, not wanting to violate the sanctity of the woman's kitchen.

When the water had cooled enough to move the kettle, she washed each threshold in the house, beginning with the room furthest from the kitchen, and over each threshold she spoke the same words.

"With this charm, I call you, with this boiling water, I command you! Be gone from this threshold, all evil spirits, all dark and wicked forces! Do not hide in the corners, do not flee into the other rooms, but go directly to the exit!"

She washed the threshold of Jamie's bedroom last, and here she poured out some of the water, unwilling to take a chance of missing any part of it. Then she entered the room, and sat upon the edge of the bed. The room was very cold, and it was a cold that was more than just the air coming in at the open window. The woman was here.

Yevgena folded her hands in her lap, bowed her head and opened the channel of her mind. Softly, the presence came to her, and she felt a great sadness overwhelm her. The woman had loved Jamie, but had come to realize that she was not loved in return. She did not belong here, and had known it from the first, and yet she had clung on, just as her spirit did now. Yevgena felt a sorrow for her, and yet also a need to make the energy leave. For some people there was no end to the unravelling which pain caused, no end to the longing for something which had never been meant for them.

"I am sorry," she said, feeling the spirit deserved this much acknowledgement of its pain, "but you must move on, it is time. You are free to go now. Leave him to his life."

A small sigh, which might have been no more than air moving through the chimney, ruffled the ashes in the grate. Yevgena waited, for spirits could be tricky, hiding in corners and up chimneys and biding their time. A half hour passed in this fashion, and slowly the room lightened, and she knew the spirit had gone, the woman passed on to that place of great mystery. Yevgena hoped that the peace which had not been hers in this house, would be waiting there for her.

She was tired by the time she descended the stairs, and found Jamie once again in the study, on the floor with Kathleen and Kolya, the three of them colouring on large sheets of paper, their faces still flushed from their time out-of-doors.

It was a joy to see him thus, with his children, lost in something so simple and the happiness in his eyes in no way tainted. On the sheet of paper, the colour yellow predominated, as Kathleen had drawn several sunflowers with glorious abandon, Jamie adding stalks and stems and definition to the petals. Kolya had, in typical boy fashion, drawn train tracks and a train to run about the edges of the paper.

Memory ascended through the waters of time, and brought with it a moment, an afternoon, an eternity in which she had stood in a field of sunflowers with her children. They had seen the glow from a distance down the road, and had known enchantment lay ahead. Her husband, Mihai, had stopped the horses, and she and the children had dropped down from the wagon, overwhelmed by the glowing field which surrounded them on both sides of the narrow track. She'd walked into the field with her babies, barefoot and relishing the heat of the sun and the warmth of the soil.

They had gathered petals, handfuls of gold, eating the occasional one, the children making faces over the slightly bitter taste. For her, it had felt like eating sunlight, storing a bit of the beautiful day in her body.

The children had brought the petals to her like offerings—some plucked, some from where they had fallen to the ground, filling her hands with them—with gold, with life, even as the wind came and took them, set them to dance upon the air, and then let them shower down around all of them. A tiny moment of life, caught like light within a drop of dew, and yet here now all these many, many years later, for her to hold and then, once again, let go.

She wanted to tell Jamie, speak to him what she saw in her memory, what she felt in her heart to be truth—that time would run like the petals of a sunflower through his hands, that it would never be enough, no matter the pain that came with it. But he knew this and did not require to be reminded of it, and so she did not speak the words.

The evening was lovely. She had made a red lentil stew with winter spices, cardamom and paprika, and a dusting of cinnamon, the sort to warm the blood when one lived out-of-doors. Warmth surrounded them. It was made of parts—Kathleen and Kolya's lovely chatter, and Jamie's responses, as he took delight in his children. Kathleen was a child of both worlds, inevitably, for both her parents were such as well. After dinner there came the rituals of the childrens' bedtime. Pyjamas and stories, and kisses and questions, and requests for water and yet more questions and small ponderings on the universe, which ranged from ducklings to stars to God. She savoured every moment.

Once the children had fallen to sleep, Yevgena and Jamie retired again to the study, and sat with drinks in hand, comfortably silent, with the dark long fallen through the boughs of the oaks outside, the windows reflecting the pools of light within the study and the unfurling rose of the fire in the hearth. Yevgena knew she must depart soon, and make the chilly walk down to where her vardo was parked. Still, she lingered, nursing her whiskey drop by drop, reluctant to go and leave the day behind.

"Perhaps you can banish one other ghost for me," Jamie said, eyeing her in a direct manner which made her fear the question that was coming.

"Perhaps. What is it that you want to know, Jemmy?"

"When I was little, did my grandfather pull my mother and me out of the pond?"

Yevgena returned his gaze with a very long one of her own. In that space she weighed how much truth he needed with her answer.

"I need the truth, Yevgenka," he said.

"You want it, but perhaps don't need it. Be careful my darling boy, there is a difference between those two things."

"Yevgena, I'm well into middle age; I believe you can trust me to deal with the truth of my past."

"When I look at you, I still see the boy I met so long ago. You are still very young to me, and I feel the need now and again to protect you if I can. Occasionally, you might indulge an old woman in her wants."

"You are timeless, Yevgenka. You might let me look after you, as well. It is what my grandfather would want, you know that."

"You do look after me, in the ways I allow."

Jamie laughed. "I suppose that is true enough. I'm not to be distracted from my question, though."

"Yes, Jemmy, that happened. But you were not so little, and your mother was not with you."

"What?"

"You were fifteen at the time. Your grandfather was worried about you, as he'd been seeing signs of the family malady—as he referred to it—in you and so when you left the house that afternoon, he followed you. You'd always roamed a great deal, so he wasn't worried about that but rather what he said he'd seen in your face that morning. When he found you, you were halfway into the pond, your pockets filled with rocks. He pulled you out just in the nick of time. You don't remember any of it?"

Jamie shook his head, face troubled, and she wished for a moment she had not given into his need for honesty. Still, it was his right to understand his history, and he was certainly old enough to be given the truth of it.

She stood then. "I will say goodnight now, Jemmy."

She walked over to where he sat, and looked down at him, brushing the beautiful golden hair which he'd inherited from his grandfather, back from his face.

"You look well, my darling boy," she said, for he did. There was a certain peacefulness about him, which had been lacking for a very long time. There was light in his eyes too, a clear light like that of spring.

He rose, reaching for the sweater he'd thrown over the back of his chair—his grandfather's chair, recently reupholstered—earlier in the day.

"Are you sure you wouldn't rather stay up here tonight?"

"Jemmy, you worry too much. I am fine. A walk in the night air is good for my constitution. Besides you cannot leave the children alone in the house. You need to consider getting a new nanny if Prudence isn't coming back."

He hugged her then, ignoring her meddling. He walked with her outside, where the stars hung like smoke in the air above. At the treeline, she put a hand on his arm and said, "Go back to the house, I am fine. I could walk this path blindfolded."

Jamie stood there at the edge of the light, watching her as she followed the path down to her vardo. The moon tonight was a golden crescent and it provided enough illumination to see her the rest of the way.

She turned back one last time, and Jamie's hand rose in a wave. The older he got the more he resembled his grandfather, something she found rather painful at times. Like his grandfather, he was a fine and beautiful spirit, pierced through with both the pain and the joy life invariably handed out. Such souls were rare, and so one took care for such a thing, and one did what was necessary to neutralize threats to it. For of all people, she understood how evil began with a single stem and so easily became a field of poison flowers.

It had not been as difficult as she had feared to find the woman. Fear made people act in predictable patterns. And there was no fear more potent than a mother's for her child.

She had found the woman in Damascus, a city with which Yevgena had long been familiar. Long ago, she'd had reason to spend some weeks in the ancient city, and from that time she knew a locksmith equipped with wondrous skills. The man could move in and out of places like a ghost. The three locks on the woman's door were almost an insult to his talents. Still, he had owed her a favour, and had been happy to do the work for her. She might have done it herself, once, but her hands weren't as steady as they had been in her younger years.

Once inside, she had dismissed the locksmith and simply sat, waiting, for the woman to return. She had been gratifyingly frightened to find an old Gypsy woman sitting in her parlour when she came in some hours later.

Diane recognized her almost immediately. They had met once long ago, and Yevgena had issued a warning to her at the time. She was here to do the same today, though the content of the warning differed slightly from the original one.

"What do you want?" the woman asked, eyeing a cabinet near to her right leg.

"Is this what you're looking for?" Yevgena asked, holding up the pistol she'd removed from the cabinet shortly after arriving in the apartment.

The woman merely shook her head, and then repeated her question. "What is it that you want?"

"I have come to offer you a few words of advice, or if you prefer, we can just call it what it is, a plain statement of the facts."

"I do not need your advice, old woman."

"I do not care for what you want or need. All this fuss and bother for years and years, destroying your own child over a simple affair."

"It was more than a simple affair," the woman said.

"Perhaps for you, but I think not for Jamie. I have seen his face when he looks at the woman he loves. He never did look at you that way, and you have never forgiven him for it."

"You will have to fire your barbs better than that, old woman." The bravado was false, for Diane had flinched at the words.

Yevgena waved her hand in the air, as though dismissing all that had come before. "Sit down, would you? Your legs are shaking."

Diane sat, clasping her hands together, attempting a show of being calmly collected. "Speak your piece, you Gypsy bitch, and then get out of my home."

"Here is what I have come to say," Yevgena said, the steel in her voice as sharp as a knife fresh from the whetstone, "make no mistake, I will have you killed if you go near him again. There will be nowhere for you to hide, because my people will find you no matter where you go, and no matter who you think can save you. Hear me, girl, when I tell you there is no protection. I am an old woman, and I have nothing left to lose. If not you, then your son, do you understand me? You come for mine, I will kill yours."

"I am not without allies and resources, and you are, as you say, an old woman."

"You think you worry me? I have lived through the Nazis, girl, you hold no terrors for me."

"I could kill you here today, and who would know you were gone?"

Yevgena nodded. "I suppose you could, but I think Jimmy would not care for that." She nodded toward the shadows, and a man emerged, knife in hand. "Here is a bit of Gypsy wisdom for you—never go alone into a den of treachery." She stood. "I will be going soon, for I only have one thing left to say."

She had named it then, an old city in an ancient country, the sort about which many legends had been written. It was here that Julian was hidden. The woman's face had gone pale, and Yevgena saw that she understood then that the threat was real.

It was best to leave when the enemy's fear was still sharp and hot, and so with a nod to Jimmy, she had done just that.

The lanterns burned warmly to either side of the vardo's door. Dear boy that he was, Jamie had sent someone down to light them and no doubt the fire would be crackling in the small cast iron stove as well. She relished the thought of it, for she felt the cold much more keenly these days.

She paused for a moment, letting the chill wind stir her hair. The very earth smelled of spring: dull roots stirring, water moving, renewal, growth and new beginnings. This land was both joy and heartbreak to her, for it was impossible not to think of James when here, impossible not to long for him as though he'd only departed from her yesterday. There was a porousness which had come with old age, making her feel like a cracked vessel, without guard against nostalgia or beauty, against pain and memory.

Inside, the caravan glowed with warmth. Her bed, heaped with brightly coloured quilts, beckoned in invitation. She wasn't quite ready for sleep just yet, though. There was one last thing to do. But first she put the kettle on for tea, and then while the tea steeped, she fetched a basket from under the bed. From the basket she took a deck of cards, a very old deck, the first she'd acquired after leaving the concentration camp. They had been a gift from James, these cards, and she had read for people one magic summer as they travelled about the countryside, pretending to a life they could never really have.

Once the tea was properly steeped, she poured out a cup, added a little brandy and then sat down, the cards stacked neatly in front of her. She took a few swallows of tea, letting the brandy do its work of warming her and muffling the pain in her joints, before picking up the cards.

She shuffled them slowly, the cards slipping one over the next in a rhythm she found comforting. For a time she sat contemplating the deck, her sight shifting as it did in these times, so that a long corridor opened before her, a rift into time and space. Then she pulled a card and turned it over slowly. It was the Wheel—the Wheel of Fortune and Fate. The four Hebrew letters for the name of God were inscribed on the wheel's face, as well as the letters for Law. It was a card which had many meanings, many possible outcomes.

She placed the tip of one finger on the middle wheel with its alchemical symbols for mercury, sulphur, water and salt, the building blocks of life. On the left the Egyptian god of evil descending, on the right and in the ascension, Anubis, god of the dead who welcomed souls to the underworld. It was a card of great power, of life renewed and life ending. There were times when the cards were simply that—cards which could be interpreted in whichever way seemed best for the person sitting across the table, wanting to hear only good things. And there were times, like the night long ago when she had seen that Casey was both dead and alive, and tonight as she glimpsed a corner of the future—when a card told a larger tale, one which she often wished she had not seen, for knowledge was not always a virtue.

Outside, the wind had picked up and branches tapped against the windows of her vardo. The card seemed to vibrate beneath her hand, and so she turned it face down because she did not want to see any more than she already had.

The wheel always turned, and the one constant of life was change. It would come in all its forms—joy, grief, love, hate, birth and death.

Fate was not done with her children, but Fate was a thing written in water, and did not—just now—worry her overmuch, for there was a space of peace and happiness, and she knew well enough to leave that be. Sometimes the price of knowledge was too high, this she had understood for a very long time.

Chapter Sixty-eight

Where Butterflies Dream of the Life to Come

I WAKE TO DROWNING, *I am deep under the pond, the dark blanket of it cold, the lily pads beneath my head neither cradle nor comfort. So I rise out of the depths, slowly, slowly making my way, feeling the brush of weeds, soft as silk, against my skin. Feeling the touch of a woman, rising too, a woman who drowned long ago, but rises now with me.*

We walk from the pond together, this drowned woman and I.

I ask her a question, though I can't hear the words and am uncertain what it is I want to know. She does not answer, merely touches my face, an understanding in her eyes as old as the world. Light blooms within her, and I can see through her to something else—a land of legend and mist, a land of blood and betrayal. But mine, I know. Worth dying for, or so I believed.

When I look back to the woman, it is to find she has become a swan and is rising into the morning sun, until the swan breaks into pieces and a cloud of butterflies emerges, white and translucent, becoming light, becoming air. I want to rise with her, become light and air too, but something holds me here, and I understand I am not ready.

I know where I am now, for this is my map, my land, my country.

Maps are not merely geography, for they tell a bigger tale for each of us. Places we went as a child, days by the sea, the spot where we learned to swim, the hillside where we first fell in love, the trees we climbed and the perfect apple we ate in an orchard on a moonlit night. The spot on the road where we knew betrayal, or the way the moon looked through a particular screen of pine on the night we knew we'd never be all the things we'd once believed we would. It is that spot where we looked back one last time, knowing we were about to break someone's heart irrevocably and forever.

This is my map, and each of us carries one—our very own—within.

There is the garden, and the moon tip-tilt on a golden chain. There is the cottage, surrounded by the crumbling stone walls, and the roof made of reeds. In the garden, there is a woman, a woman who waits for me, or perhaps it is I who is waiting for her. I walk toward her and the woman sees me then, and smiles, holding out her hands, and I see that beside her is a little girl. I cannot touch her, for I am merely yearning, no more than air and light and molecules of longing.

Before me is the gate, both geography and so much more, weathered and grey, a thing held together with moss and tiny white flowers. I put my hand to the latch, open it, and walk through.

July 1982

CASEY AND JAMIE had gathered wood all afternoon for the fire, with the four children helping them, though Pamela suspected that the only real help had come from Conor and Kolya. Kathleen and Isabelle had returned damp with bits of moss and twig tangled in their hair, carrying all sorts of treasures from the day in the woods, including what turned out to be a mouse corpse.

Inside, the kitchen buzzed with the sounds of children laughing and crying, and women cooking, comforting, rocking and chatting. She looked down and smiled. In her arms, blissfully slumbering, was the newest member of the Riordan clan. Daniel Ambrose Riordan was currently a year old, and was the great love of his older siblings, all of whom doted over him. Born very suddenly in the middle of a warm July night, Daniel had been attended into the world by his severely harassed father, who felt women might occasionally give birth in hospitals as the good Lord had intended them to, and where a father could have some peace. Nevertheless, when the doctor had arrived two hours after the birth, he found all in good health and good cheer.

Today was a celebration of many things, but mostly of the people she and Casey loved and had simply wanted to gather with in the light and warmth of the summer, and Daniel's birthday had provided the perfect excuse to do just that. It was also a celebration of other things, for Casey and Pamela had renewed their vows in a simple ceremony two weeks ago, with Father Terry once more doing the honours, and with Pat and Kate and all the children in attendance.

She looked around the kitchen, where Gert was stirring something in the big cast iron pot that she referred to as Pamela's witch's cauldron, Aine was cleaning a salmon, which they'd later roast in the fire, Deirdre was peeling potatoes and keeping an eye on both the chowder she had cooking on the Aga, and on Lily who was in the flour bin, insistent on helping her grandmother with the cooking. Kate was whipping up some lovely summer dish called flummery with Isabelle—sugar dusting her mad curls and the stain of strawberries on her lips and nose—helping her. Kate, who was voluminously pregnant with her and Pat's second child, was flushed and laughing at something Isabelle had said. It was good to see Kate so happy. Two months ago, on a beautifully clear May day she had accompanied Kate, along with the box containing Noah's ashes, to the top of Slieve Gullion and there they had scattered him where he might view the counties of his country spread out below him.

She turned her attention now to Kathleen who was seated on Yevgena's lap helping her to wind a long skein of crimson wool into a ball, which the new orange kitten (found in the reeds by the pond, with no sign of a mother or siblings about) had unwound only moments before.

Pamela felt a pang as she looked at Yevgena, for she had suddenly grown old since their last visit. There was a stoop to her shoulders, and a tiredness which emanated from her, which had not been visible before. She knew Jamie wished Yevgena would allow him to take care of her, but so far Yevgena was proving rather resistant to the idea. One day—and she feared it would not be too far ahead—Yevgena would have to accept that she required help.

Pamela's eye moved on to Pru, who was crossing the floor with Abby, holding both her hands, as the little girl took several steps, squealing with delight at her accomplishment, and lighting her mother's face with pride. While Pru still grieved, she had gotten on with her life, as Pamela had thought she would, her tough New England spirit standing her in good stead, like a ballast in a storm. She'd returned to school, and was working towards a degree in nursing, a profession at which Pamela thought she was likely to excel.

A crow cawed loudly just then, breaking into her thoughts, and reminding her that she'd not set out his peanuts that morning. Ben, the crow which had been Ambrose's companion in prison, had been brought here by Father Jim, after Ambrose's death. Ben had taken one look at Aine when she came down to visit the afternoon of his arrival, and had decided upon his new life companion. He came down each day, though, for his peanuts, and then returned to Aine's home, where he'd built a nest in the low branches of the rowan near her door.

Dinner was a lovely affair, with everyone seated at the long bog oak table, with a smaller table Casey had built just for the children set alongside. The food was ambrosial, the talk both entertaining and enlightening, and the general feeling was one of a warm and encompassing happiness, something worked for and now to be taken in with gratitude.

Pamela looked around the table, and felt tears gather behind her eyes. Each person here was someone she loved. Tomas sat next to Deirdre, looking over at her every so often with a tenderness in his expression that warmed Pamela's heart just to witness it. Deirdre too was lit from within, and it was this which had softened Casey toward the whole notion of Tomas and his mother's romance. It was a good thing too because Tomas had proposed to Deirdre the previous winter and she had accepted. Gert was holding Daniel and speaking German endearments to him, while Owen said little but beamed a gnomic happiness around the table. To Jamie's left sat Vanya, with his partner Darin on his other side. To Jamie's right was Aine, the two of them engaged in animated conversation. They'd formed their own friendship when Jamie had come to stay after his treatments, and Jamie sent the woman occasional parcels now, filled with useful things for one who lived mainly outdoors, which she knew Aine greatly appreciated. Father Jim sat next to Pru. He too had aged, due more to the toll the hunger strikes and their aftermath had taken on his spirit than to any advancement of years.

She saw too those who were not there anymore. Their old neighbour Lewis had passed away during the spring, finally succumbing to the shooting he'd been subjected to some years before, and what it had exacted upon his body. And there were others, not present, and yet through the memory of love, always part of them. Sylvie, Lawrence, Ambrose, and Finian, who though alive, would spend much of his adult life behind bars. Casey and Pat's father, her own as well, Jamie's grandfather and all the others who had been loved and lost along the way.

She exchanged a smile with Pat, realizing he too was sitting back and taking in the tableaux before him, and seeing how far they'd all come over these last few years. And then she looked to the head of the table, where Casey sat, chatting with Tomas, as Isabelle ate his dinner. Feeling her gaze, he looked up and smiled, dark eyes warm. She returned the smile, and knew he understood what it encompassed—the house, the children, the people surrounding them this day, and at the core of it, the two of them, which was the bedrock of all that had sprung forth in their life together.

After dinner, they rose as a company and went out to where Casey had the fire burning high and hot, long threads of gold and violet leaping into the summer night. They seated themselves around the fire, and continued with the laughter and conversation which had started at the dinner table. The talk was animated, roving from one topic to another, as the wine and whiskey were passed about, along with juice or chocolate milk for the children. Lulls came and went as the fire worked its magic, and everyone relaxed into their chairs and the beautiful night around them. It was into the last of these lulls that Pru spoke, looking steadily at Jamie.

"Before he died," she began, voice small, "Ambrose said to me that you'd told him a story, one that soothed his fever and made the blood dreams go away. Will you tell it now?"

Jamie returned the girl's look, his gaze clear, but one who knew him saw that there was also a great sadness there. "I don't think it's an easy tale to hear, Pru, and it was only one I told him when I knew there was no way he'd turn back."

"Please, Jamie," Pru said, and there was something in her tone, something so torn, that Pamela felt physical pain in her heart for the hurt Pru now carried with her, and would for the remainder of her life.

Pamela's eyes met Jamie's and she understood the question in his, and answered with her own. He gave a small nod, and then took a deep breath, and she saw there, the turning inward he did when readying himself to tell a tale. She knew this tale held a cost for the teller though, for it was made of the pain both they and the country were still feeling.

"*Fad ó, fad ó,*" he began, which was the Irish storyteller's equivalent of *long time ago,* "or perhaps it was only yesterday, for on my way here, I stopped by the roadside at an old orchard I know, where the apples grow especially sweet. I walked for a time, and came upon a tree, far more ancient than the others, with gnarled branches and very few leaves left upon it, though the other trees shimmered with life and green. Upon this tree, hung a single apple, the hue of a just opening rose, with glints of pale green glimmering deep within the skin. And on the skin of this apple was a single dewdrop, trembling in the morning breeze, but clear as the purest crystal. As I looked down, I saw within this single dewdrop, a kingdom by the sea. And in this kingdom lived a prince, who was of noble heart and brave beyond measure. This prince had a horse, a beautiful beast, with a coat as silver as the first moon of winter. Within one eye, this stallion had a strange mark, a crescent like the blade of a scimitar, and it too was silver. Within that crescent blade, was yet another kingdom, this one a land of green rolling hills and soft sweeping rains, and of a long and terrible war which no one was able to win, and thus bring an end to it."

A piece of wood dropped in the fire then, sending up a spray of living sparks into the air, where they floated like a thousand fireflies, before extinguishing into the night. It seemed a portal, through which they would now follow the incantatory lead of Jamie's voice.

"And in *that* kingdom, once upon a time, there lived a boy, a boy who loved books, and ideas and having his tea on time. He was known for being absent-minded and always having a half-eaten teacake in his pocket, which led to dogs following him about the countryside, in the hope of a bite. He had a shambling sort of walk, and his shoes were always out at the toes, and he would often walk into trees, or find himself in a stream, knee-deep, before he realized where he was. More often than not there were leaves in his hair, and twigs in his ears, where he'd used one to scratch during a particularly troublesome thought. He was, in short, a dreamer.

"And then one day, when he was on one of his rambles in the woods, he saw a butterfly, not the most beautiful butterfly, just a small, dun-coloured thing, which might not have caught his attention but for the fact that it lit upon his shoulder, and stayed there for an entire afternoon. Just before it flew away, it had whispered in his ear, just the one word, and that word was *courage*.

"This troubled him greatly, for he felt his courage was of the small sort, which might readily collapse at the first challenge. But how could he find the knowledge he wanted above all others—that knowledge of what life was, what was its meaning, why could his land never find peace—if he didn't have the courage to follow the butterfly wherever it might lead. It wasn't an easy decision, because out on the road he knew, there would be no teatime other than ones of his own making, there would be no mother and grandfather, and bossy but loving sisters to make certain he changed his shirt when it was necessary, or took his shoes to the cobbler when they went out at the toes. Still, though his heart sank a little with the thought of all he'd leave behind, he knew he must follow where the butterfly led.

"When those who loved him heard of the journey he intended, they thought perhaps he'd gone a wee bit mad, for he was so absentminded, forever forgetting teaspoons behind his ears and such, that he was sure to get lost on the first day of his journey. In truth, though, he wasn't so much absentminded as that he liked to think about things the way a pearl diver catches pearls, by diving deeply into the dark and coming up only when the treasure was grasped. And so, loaded up with bread and cheese, and small glass bottles of ale, as well as dire predictions from his family about losing his glasses, losing his way, his senses, and his marbles, he set off onto the road.

"The road was as the road always is—long, winding and filled with both joys and sorrows, with adventures and bleak days where hope was in short supply. His family had been both right and wrong, for he lost his way more than once, lost his glasses a week into the journey, felt like he lost every speck of sense he'd ever had, including every marble in his possession, but he always found something to replace those things—well, other than his eyeglasses that is—for he was given wisdom, patience, and understanding along the way, as well as the stories of others who had travelled the same path before him. Teatime was had with strangers, who told of far lands and exotic people, and the tea was brewed over fires built in ditches and fields, near crossroads and old wayside inns. He travelled far and wide, and tasted the tea of many lands, talked to shamans and wise women, learned the paths of the stars and the moon, fell in love once, and was wise enough to know it to be the only love he would ever have. Still, even love could not hold him fast, and so he kept walking, looking for those elusive answers to life's great questions.

"Until one day he looked down to find he'd walked his boots right off his feet, and that somewhere along the way those feet had become crooked and crabbed, so that he hobbled now and felt the ache of age throughout his every bone. He stopped then for a bit, to make tea and eat a bit of bread with cheese. After his meal, he found he could no longer rise, and he realized then that he'd grown old, not just in the ways of the body, but also those of the soul, and was so tired with wandering that some days, beyond pain, he felt like he was little more than dust, ready to scatter to the four winds at the slightest touch. So, exhausted with the wandering, he managed to hobble to a place where he could lay down near the sea, where the water rolled in eternally from lands far away. There he stayed and let time and the tide roll over him, both sleeping and not sleeping, watching the sun rise and fall, and the stars as they flowed in the river of the sky each night.

"And then one day he no longer slept, but neither did he wake. Time and the elements did their work, and slowly he scattered to the winds as he'd once wished he might, leaving only his bones, bleached clean by the sun and rain, behind.

"A long time later, there came a cloud of butterflies, in all the breathing colours of the world—roan and verdigris, cobalt and crimson, silk grey and saffron, amethyst and topaz. And when he found his end, and came to see the truth of his tale, it was then he realized his soul had flown and left his body behind. He had become light and air, and he was, after so much struggle, free. And it was then that the dun-coloured butterfly—now turned the purest white—returned to see him on this final journey, and he asked it about the last secret, the one he had always sought, but never found. For every land he'd travelled through, there had been war, and none had ever been able to tell him how to end it. He knew from travellers he'd encountered along the way that the war in his own land still raged on all these years later, and he'd never found words of wisdom to carry back to his people so that the bloodshed might be ended.

"There is no secret," the butterfly said, "just love, for that is the answer to every question and the key to all journeys. And then the boy understood at last, and went with the butterfly, into the light which was just love by another name."

There were tears on the faces around the fire, for many of them had loved Ambrose, and would feel his loss all their lives. Pamela swallowed over the pain in her own throat and smiled across the fire at Jamie, for she saw in the telling of the story of Ambrose and the butterfly, Jamie had also told their story—all of them, the story of a family, a people, a country. And he was right in all the parts—for all of them, the only truth was love.

The evening moved on after the tale, with talk and laughter, tea and coffee, cake and cream, and then some began to depart with the echo of a beautiful day filled with love, tears and laughter in their wake.

Casey and Pamela stood together, bidding their guests farewell. Tomas and Deirdre were going to a small hotel in the nearest village and Aine simply took her lantern and set off into the wood beyond the house, the crow riding on her shoulder. Then it was a matter of arranging where to put the guests who were staying. Jamie would sleep in the cottage, and Kathleen would stay with him. Conor and Kolya had opted to sleep in the tree house which would free up Conor's room for Gert and Owen. Vanya and Darin had set up a tent, earlier in the day, in the circle of oaks. Yevgena had brought her vardo along, and it was parked beside the Flying Tortoise, where Pat and Kate would spend the night. Lily was bunked in with Isabelle, and Pru had already taken Abby to her rooms off the kitchen, the small form limp in her arms. Pamela had hugged Pru before she went, feeling that Jamie's tale had—through that strange alchemy which story possessed—given the girl a measure of healing.

She stood outside in the yard, half-listening for the baby, even though he slept soundly through the night and had since his third month of life. Part of her ear was listening to the land all around, the burble of the waterfall in the distance, the soft soughing of the stars caught in the branches of the trees, and the voices of her loved ones abroad in the night. Light glowed in the various windows, the lanterns of Yevgena's vardo flickering in the night breeze, light spilling too from the open windows of the Tortoise, from which she could hear snatches of Pat and Kate chatting as they readied themselves for sleep.

Some months back Tomas had come to her with the information that Detective Holroyd had been returned to London, and that he was no longer someone she need fear. When she had queried how he'd known about the detective, Tomas had merely said, "Pamela, when ye need help, ye need to learn to ask for it. In this case, I managed to get out ahead of the problem, an' nip it in the bud. I'll not say he won't sit on the information he has like a broody hen with a favourite egg, but he'll think long an' hard about it before he dares to do anything with it."

"How did you know?" she'd asked again, pressing him on it. She suspected Jamie's hand in this but knew she'd never get Tomas to admit it if Jamie had asked him not to.

Tomas shook his head, before saying, "I told ye long ago, ye're the daughter I never had. I meant it, an' now the lot of yez are my family. I protect those I love, just as you do. Information comes to me in my profession, an' someone inside the police department gave me a warnin' about Will Holroyd. It would be good, girl, if ye—to quote yer husband—gave up yer mad antics an' occasionally behaved yerself."

"I'll try," she'd said, and then leaned over to kiss the man's cheek.

Tomas had sighed. "No ye won't, but ye could at least give the appearance of it for the sake of those that love ye."

Tomas' words had released her from the last threat which hung over her head and now even months later, it felt like a wondrous gift to have no present worries other than those which were normal to this time in life—children and their growth, their schooling, their happiness, whether Casey was working too hard; if the twin lambs the irascible Matilda had birthed back in April were gaining weight rapidly enough; whether Aine was remembering the heart medication the doctor had prescribed for her the last time Pamela had taken her into town for an appointment, and if the cocoon she'd found on the outside of one of the kitchen window ledges, had survived the last wind. Included in this list was, and always would be, Jamie and his happiness. He was much more settled since the shock therapy, and over the last year the two of them had collaborated on the first of four planned books for children about a family of badgers and their life through the course of one year. Much to her delight, the first one was selling briskly, particularly in the United States, and they'd embarked upon the creation of the second.

She had work, she had love, her children were as safe as children were in this life, and so she stood in the night, under a sky crowded thick with summer stars, and felt herself a woman blessed.

Kathleen slipped up then, her wee fairy child with her spill of red curls and her infectious laughter. She took her mother's hand and Pamela felt it again, the knowledge of the fleetness of time. Pamela looked down at her little girl, overcome with love for her, filled with gratitude for all that had brought her into being.

"Mama, look up! It's goin-a fall into the sea!"

She looked up, and saw blazing bright across the sky, a falling star, and she thought of the story Jamie had told, and of a boy filled with light, set upon the next step in his journey. Her father's words from such a very long time ago, echoed in her head. *Just think of all the stars that have fallen, the sea is full of them. Such a fall from grace, from the heavens to the deeps in seconds.*

"The sea is filled with stars, sweetheart," she said, watching the tiny face tilted up toward the night, filled with wonder and awe.

Casey and Jamie had walked down with Conor and Kolya to get them settled in the tree house for the night, making sure they had adequate comfort in the way of blankets and a torch, and water should they wake and want it. She could hear the two men talking now as they walked up the hill toward the house, where it sat glowing with warmth and light.

Kathleen's hand slipped from hers, and she ran down the hill, shouting, "Daddy!" and Jamie caught her up in his arms, her tiny nightgown glowing white against the greater darkness. She said something then, in her high-pitched warble, and both Casey and Jamie laughed, their laughter floating up to Pamela in the night air, and in it she heard real joy.

She smiled and moved down the hill toward them.

Dawn rose in the east, and light moved in across the land bringing with it the colours of morning, spreading from the shadows, glazing the fence posts with early morning gold, lapped with edges of crimson.

A soft wind came in from the sea and met the light, the growth in the fields rippling as it touched them, and as it moved it brushed the cocoon which Pamela had so recently discovered. Life stirred within, and the caterpillar stretched, finding its home suddenly too small.

During the caterpillar's long struggle, the farm went about its day, oblivious to the new life emerging from its chrysalis. There was the laughter of children, the blatting of sheep, the bark of a dog getting old, and of a new pup that chased at his heels. There was the sound of a woman calling to her children and to her husband, whose voices echoed back to her in answer.

The people had long disappeared from view, and the sun was sinking down toward the sea when the butterfly tested its wings for the first time. They were wet and crumpled, and so it pumped blood through its veins in small vibrations, and let the air do its work. The wings slowly opened, celadon touched with a drift of twilight blue. The butterfly waited a little, barely understanding that it was now, indeed, a butterfly, and no longer a caterpillar. It yearned toward the air, nearly tipping off the window ledge, and then it waited—a pulse, a beat, a lifetime. Once, twice, three times it flapped its wings, and then made its way—trembling—into the air.

We are all dreamers upon this earth, held for a time in the cocoon of this life. And one day when the burden is too great and the pain too long, we leave the cocoon, we spread our wings, still wet with the struggle of a long birthing, and then, oh and then, we fly.

For we are all just blood and love, borne aloft on butterfly wings.

Afterword

When you write about recent history, as I do, it's important to pay your respects to those who actually lived that history. Below is a list of the 1981 Hunger Strikers. I chose the month of April for Ambrose to begin his strike because there wasn't a real hunger striker who began his strike in that month. I wanted to respect that fact and leave their dates alone. I've only included the names of those who died on strike, though there were more men who participated but went off their strikes early for a variety of reasons. Big Seamus and Ambrose are both fictional creations but their experiences were drawn from the words of the real hunger strikers.

Bits of Jamie's conversation with Margaret Thatcher were taken verbatim from an actual meeting between Thatcher and Cardinal O'Faich during the time of the Hunger Strike.

One last note—the massacre in chapter 38 was based on the real Lough-inisland Massacre. However, I've placed the massacre in October of 1979 so that it might fit within the time parameters of the story. The real massacre took place in June of 1994.

Names of Hunger Strikers (1981)

Those who died:

Bobby Sands (26)
Irish Republican Army (IRA) and Member of Parliament (MP) began hunger strike on 1 March 1981 and died on 5 May 1981 after 66 days without food

Francis Hughes (25)

Irish Republican Army (IRA) joined hunger strike on 15 March 1981 and died on 12 May 1981 after 59 days without food

Raymond McCreesh (24)

Irish Republican Army (IRA) joined hunger strike on 22 March 1981 and died on 21 May 1981 after 61 days without food

Patsy O'Hara (23)

Irish National Liberation Army (INLA) joined hunger strike on 22 March 1981 and died on 21 May 1981 after 61 days without food

Joe McDonnell (30)

Irish Republican Army (IRA) joined hunger strike on 8 May 1981 and died on 8 July 1981 after 61 days without food

Martin Hurson (29)

Irish Republican Army (IRA) joined hunger strike on 28 May 1981 and died on 13 July 1981 after 46 days without food

Kevin Lynch (25)

Irish National Liberation Army (INLA) joined hunger strike on 23 May 1981 and died on 1 August 1981 after 71 days without food

Kieran Doherty (25)

Irish Republican Army (IRA) and Teachta Dáil (TD; member of the Irish Parliament) joined hunger strike on 22 May 1981 and died on 2 August 1981 after 73 days without food

Thomas McElwee (23)

Irish Republican Army (IRA) joined hunger strike on 8 June 1981 and died on 8 August 1981 after 62 days without food

Michael Devine (27)

Irish National Liberation Army (INLA) joined hunger strike on 22 June 1981 and died on 20 August 1981 after 60 days without food

www.ingramcontent.com/pod-product-compliance
Lightning Source LLC
Chambersburg PA
CBHW050118030726
47505CB00007B/1921